CUT
DECK

CUT DECK

No more traitors, no more snakes.

JULIA ROSEMARY TURK

Cut Deck
Copyright © 2024 Julia Rosemary Turk

Library of Congress Control Number: 2024909541

ISBN 978-1-962876-05-6 (paperback)
ISBN 978-1-962876-04-9 (ebook)

This book is a work of fiction. Names, characters, places, and incidents either are the product of the author's imagination or are used fictitiously. Any resemblance to actual events, businesses, companies, locales or persons, living or dead, is entirely coincidental.

Cover design by MAD Book Covers
Select interior illustrations by Gonzalo Mansilla

Lost Island Press LLC
Oro Valley, AZ
lostislandpress.com

CUT PLAYLIST

CURATED BY THE AUTHOR

♪ I HOPE I BECOME A GHOST - THE DEADLY SYNDROME ♪

♪ DROWN - THE SMASHING PUMPKINS ♪

♪ SECRETS - THE WOODEN BIRDS ♪

♪ HEAVEN UP THERE - PALACE ♪

♪ SNAKE SONG - MARK LANEGAN ♪

♪ WHEN I GROW UP - FIRST AID KIT ♪

♪ UP IN SMOKE - TIGERCUB ♪

♪ GASOLINE - DEAD SONS ♪

♪ FEATHERY - MILKY CHANCE ♪

♪ IN LIKE THE ROSE - BLACK REBEL MOTORCYCLE CLUB ♪

♪ YOU WOULD HAVE TO LOSE YOUR MIND
- THE BARR BROTHERS ♪

♪ GASOLINE - THE NEW YEAR ♪

♪ SEARCH AND DESTROY - SANDERS BOHLKE ♪

♪ RIGHT HAND - ALL THEM WITCHES ♪

♪ CRAWL BACK IN - HALF MOON RUN ♪

♪ THEM SHOES - PATRICK SWEANY ♪

♪ SPLENDOR AND CONCEALMENT - HUMAN BELL ♪

♪ WHISTLEBLOWER (ACOUSTIC) - ARKELLS ♪

♪ EVERYBODY KNOWS - THE EVENS ♪

♪ THE CLOCKWISE WITNESS - DEVOTCHKA ♪

♪ HUSH, I'M ON TV - ALL THEM WITCHES ♪

♪ BURNING EFFIGIES - TIGERCUB ♪

♪ YOURS TO STEAL - GREYHOUNDS ♪

♪ CARNIVAL - KEVIN DEVINE ♪

♪ HOW LOW - JOSÉ GONZÁLEZ ♪

♪ WHISTLEBLOWER - ARKELLS ♪

♪ STRAY - YELLOW HOUSE ♪

♪ AM I GOING UP? - ALL THEM WITCHES ♪

♪ HEADACHE - FRANK BLACK ♪

♪ DON'T YOU FIND - JAMIE T ♪

♪ BLACK RIVER KILLER - BLITZEN TRAPPER ♪

♪ HONEST - BAND OF SKULLS ♪

♪ MAUERBAUERTRAURIGKEIT - CLOSURE IN MOSCOW ♪

♪ CHAMELEON SKIN - THE FLATLINERS ♪

♪ I KNOW NO PARDON - VETIVER ♪

♪ THE CHASE - BROKEN BELLS ♪

♪ THE EXECUTION - ABSYNTHE MINDED ♪

♪ BROTHER'S BLOOD - KEVIN DEVINE ♪

♪ IN CIRCLES - SUNNY DAY REAL ESTATE ♪

♪ KINGFISHER - WOLF PEOPLE ♪

♪ MORBID FASCINATION - BLOOD RED SHOES ♪

♪ MISS EVENING - MAÑANA ♪

♪ PERFECT SPEED - 13 & GOD ♪

♪ BLEEDING MUDDY WATER - MARK LANEGAN ♪

♪ ALMOST WAS GOOD ENOUGH - SONGS: OHIA ♪

For Grandpa.
Love you always.

"Had fun. Good cookin'."

PROLOGUE

Monday, July 31

The vase shatters when it hits the floor.

It's blue and ugly. The vase, not the bird—although the bird is blue too.

The vase isn't really much of anything anymore. Which is good, because I've spent my whole life hating it. I just never had the guts to throw it out.

But I'm too busy chasing the bird around my kitchen with a broom to thank it for breaking the ugly thing.

The bird rebounds like the collision never happened—a flurry of flapping wings and stray feathers that blanket the floor. Beads of sweat glide down my back as I swat at the creature, careful not to actually hit it. The bird chirps in alarm, but instead of flying toward the open sliding glass door, it circles the ceiling fan again, bumping into cabinets with every frantic zig-zag. It's like it can't even see the way out.

But that's impossible. The door is open. The windows are open.

There is every way out, and the bird chooses to stay trapped.

Its next victim is an expensive-looking oil painting of a white rabbit. A picture frame. A wooden cutting board, which clatters so loudly it scares the bird into increased hysteria. But above all else, what really makes my teeth grind is the cereal box it knocks over next.

The box flies off the island and lands on the floor, adding cornflakes to the sea of feathers. I curse under my breath. *I was going to eat that.*

With a sigh, I use the back of my hand to wipe the sweat from my forehead. I've been at this for half an hour, and nothing seems to work. *Maybe it'll go away if I ignore it.* I lean against my broom and glance up at the fan, which spins but hardly addresses the heat drifting in from outside. *When it's gone, I can close the windows.* I scan the ceiling for the bird—but it's nowhere to be seen.

Before I can celebrate, something blue catches my eye.

The bird stands in the pile of spilled cornflakes, pecking at the cereal like it's lived here as long as I have.

I frown. *Those can't be good for him.*

As I crouch by the mess and watch the bird eat, it either doesn't notice me, or doesn't care that I'm there. I swat at it with my hand. It doesn't budge. I point my broom at it instead. "Go."

The bird ignores my demand.

I glare. "There's gotta be cornflakes somewhere else. Now *get.*"

Before I can make another threat, someone knocks on the door.

Slowly, I rise to my feet and glance over my shoulder to study the foyer. *I didn't order anything, did I?*

Three more knocks cut through the silence, neatly spaced and perfectly timed. *So it's not a package.* I turn around and point at the bird. "We'll discuss this later."

With my jaw clenched and broom in hand, I walk toward the foyer. *Who would want anything to do with me on a Monday morning?*

I open the door, saying, "Were my instructions unclear last week? I thought I already told you *exactly* where to install those solar panels, and believe me, they won't get any sun where they're going..."

A young woman with long black hair stands on my porch holding a duffel bag. She wears a pair of deeply tinted shades—and a suit as dark as night.

Every drop of blood in my veins ices over. My shoulders stiffen, and I blink a dozen times to ensure I'm seeing straight. Shades. Suit. A holster on her belt, carrying something that looks awfully similar to a black Night-jade gun.

Only one occupation requires a uniform like that.

But the panic subsides when my gaze settles on the cobalt ribbon pinned to the back of her hair.

"Jade Silva?" I can't suppress a smirk when I lean against the doorframe. I look her up and down with a chuckle. "How long has it been? Three years? Four?"

"Agent J. Sparrow," she corrects. She holds up a dark blue poker chip before shoving it back in her pocket. Her brows crease as she takes in my disheveled hair, the feather-covered broom, and my current state of shirtlessness. "I'm here on business."

"So formal." I toss the broom aside and cross my arms. "To what do I owe the pleasure?"

Jade hesitates, then slowly removes her sunglasses. I miss the chance to be alarmed by the look in her eyes before the words come out. "Your brother is dead."

I blink.

Somewhere beyond her, beyond me, a car drives by. A gust of wind bends a pine branch. A robin plucks a worm from my lawn before flying away.

"Well don't just stand there. Come on in." I turn around and head inside, leaving the door open. "You know your way around. Make yourself at home."

Jade closes the door, following close behind as I cut through the foyer and into the kitchen. I pause in front of the espresso machine on the counter. "How do you take your coffee again?"

"Mal—"

"Cinnamon." I snap my fingers. "You always put cinnamon in your coffee."

"Mal, I don't think this is a good time—"

"It's always a good time for coffee." I preheat the machine and start measuring the grounds, spilling a few.

From the corner of my eye, I can see Jade part her lips, then close them. She takes a seat at one of the barstools lining the island and sets the duffel bag on the counter. She folds her hands together over the marble, observing the mess on the floor. She doesn't mention it. I tamp the grounds and get the machine going after a few fumbles. My hands shake.

I find the broom again and busy myself by sweeping up the cornflakes while we wait. I don't see the bird anywhere. *Maybe it finally left.*

"Is that your grandmother's old vase?" Jade's question splinters the silence.

My throat tightens. I glance at her, then at the shards of blue and white ceramic on the ground. I nod.

She shakes her head. "You're lucky your dad isn't here to see that mess. He'd kill you."

I nod again, flex my fingers into fists, then relax them. "Yup."

She asks no further questions as I clean the broken vase.

Eventually, I prepare our coffee, remembering to add cinnamon to Jade's —and extra honey for good measure. I slide her a mug and down half my drink in one gulp. "God, that's good stuff."

Jade doesn't touch her coffee. "Mal..."

"So glad I went ahead and splurged." I slap the espresso machine and turn around to study it. I take another sip. "I'm thoroughly convinced that I wouldn't survive without this thing."

"*Mallory.*" I freeze. Jade lowers her voice. "Did you hear what I said?"

I glance over my shoulder at her, then turn back around. "I heard you just fine."

I can't look at her, so I drink the rest of my coffee and bring my mug to the sink.

"I don't think you're understanding the severity of your situation right now. Your brother was..." She bites her lip.

A knot forms in my throat, and I swallow through it. "I know what he was."

"And that's exactly the problem." She stands up and walks over to where I stand, hugging her abdomen. "Without your father's position, you'd be in a refrigerated truck halfway to New Mexico by now."

It's quiet. Through the still-open sliding glass door and windows, a bird chirps cheerfully. My voice lowers. "Is that where Randy is?"

"No."

I start washing my mug. "Why not?"

She stares at her shoes, then at me. "I made arrangements for you."

The mug is clean now, so I scrub a pan instead, knuckles clenched. "You didn't have to do that."

"Of course I did." She almost sounds hurt. "Undergrounder or not, Randy deserves a funeral."

The pan is crusted with burnt eggs. No matter how thoroughly I scrape it, or how much soap I slather it in, nothing changes. *I should've let it soak overnight.*

"Is that what you arranged?" I scrub the pan harder. "His funeral?"

"Well... not exactly."

I pause. "And what do you mean by that?"

Jade sighs, unzips the duffel bag, and pulls out an urn.

Carefully, she sets it on the counter. It's blue and white, just like the shattered vase I thought I was finally rid of. My breath catches in my lungs.

"Please don't be mad at me," she says, her voice nearly a whisper.

My legs tremble. "How did he..."

"He was finally caught. Got mixed up in some Underground operation that went south." She stares at her hands. "They exterminated him at a training facility a few hours south of here."

I nod.

"Randy doesn't belong in the Tombs, Mal." She stares at the urn, eyes glossy. "I couldn't let them send his body there."

I swallow. "Thank you."

"But... there are other arrangements in place too."

I return to the pan, clutching the handle with white knuckles.

"You knew Randy better than anyone," Jade says. "Even after he... disappeared... I think deep down, you knew what he was up to."

I hold back a nod. All I can do is stare at the pan.

"This is what the Agency thinks too. Especially my father."

I scoff. "How is Agent Canary doing, anyway? Still pressed about the last time he caught me climbing out of your window?"

Jade glares. "I'm being serious here."

My fingers are already wrinkling from the water, but I keep it running. "Go on."

"Traitors don't usually get nice funerals, Mal." She sighs. "But your father wasn't usual, and by default, neither are his sons."

"I'm aware."

"As Head of House, Agent Canary has agreed to make an exception to the rules, given who your father was, and... what you were. To me."

I scrub the pan hard enough for the sponge to finally cut through the crust. "So no refrigerated trucks for Randy."

She pauses. "You can have a nice ceremony for him. I can help, if you'd like."

"But there's a catch."

Jade sighs. "If you were anybody else, even with your Immunity, you'd be exterminated for your brother's associations. In the eyes of the law, you're just as much of a traitor as he was." Her voice is stern. "You realize this, right?"

My neck twitches. I keep my eyes fixed to my task. "Yup."

"It took some... convincing, but Agent Canary is willing to offer you a pardon. Under one condition."

"And what would that be?"

Jade hesitates. "There are shoes for you to fill."

I drop the pan. It rings so loudly against the sink's steel that Jade nearly jumps back. "No."

"Mal, listen to me—"

I get back to scrubbing. "Not happening."

"Just think about it for a second, okay?"

"There's not a chance in hell, Jade. I've said it before and I'll say it again."

"But—"

"They've been sending me letters and knocking on my door for years, and there's a reason why they never hear back." I shake my head. "It's *not happening*."

"You need to be realistic here," she says between clenched teeth. "Your brother ran off to join the Underground. Randy was a traitor, so they killed him for it. It doesn't matter that you stayed put or inherited your father's

Immunity, alright? Policy will earn you that exact same fate if you don't agree to this deal. The only reason you're still breathing is because I'm the one who begged my father to make an exception. Your dad was one of the greatest Agents this region has ever seen, and Canary *still* needed convincing."

"If they want me to join so bad, then why did he need convincing in the first place?"

"My father has his... motivations. But you know how the Corps feels about legacies and success rates. He has higher-ups who are eager to see if the son of Agent Finch will bring them the same results his father did."

"So it's political."

"It doesn't matter."

My hands feel like they might fall off, but I keep scrubbing. "I'm not joining."

"You're being ridiculous."

"Am I?"

"They'll kill you if you don't agree to this, Mal!"

"You of all people should know how I feel about putting on a suit."

"How you feel about it doesn't exactly matter here, alright? This is your only option."

I grind my teeth. I don't realize my fingers are stinging until I see pink skin and blood under my nails. "It's not the only one."

Jade scoffs. "Do you even hear yourself right now?"

I abandon the pan and shut off the faucet, finally turning to face her. "You said it yourself, Jade. If enlisting is filling in *his* shoes, the alternative is looking pretty damn friendly."

She looks at me like I've just plunged a knife through her ribcage. "You don't mean that."

"And what if I do?"

Her eyes widen, and a twinge of guilt twists in my gut. I grip the sink with both hands, let my head hang low, then bring it back up to study her. The quivering of her jaw. The gloss over her gaze.

God. I hate it when she looks at me like that. I close my eyes and take a deep, shaking breath. *She could get me to do anything, couldn't she?*

When I open them again, she's still staring at me.

"You need this pardon. *I* need this pardon. And if you can't bring yourself to do it for me"—her voice cracks, and she softens it—"do it for Randy."

She stares at the urn, and I do too. Tangled within the florals glazed over its surface, I notice a bluebird with its wings outstretched, carrying an olive branch in its beak.

"It's what he would have wanted," she says.

My throat burns. It feels like my heart is lodged inside it, pounding in my ears and mouth. I nail my eyes to that painted bird to keep the room from spinning.

"Agents have privileges, you know. Resources." She looks at me. "You could get answers."

I glance down at her, then back at the bird.

"Don't you want to know where Randy disappeared to?" She hesitates. "Or what happened to him in the end?"

I want to tell her no—that I have the urn and places I think my brother would like to be as a dead person, and that I don't need answers. That would be the reasonable reality, wouldn't it? Pretending I already have the closure I've been starving for, no matter how unbearable the hunger pains may be?

But in spite of the shoes, in spite of myself—there is a deeply rooted part of me that wants to know. Something tells me this is my only chance to get answers.

Am I really ready to die without knowing what happened?

"Just... think about it, okay?" Jade grabs her bag and walks toward the door. "The collection of drunk voicemails in my inbox tells me you still have my number. Use it by the end of the week."

She pauses, giving me one last look before putting her shades back on. "Thanks for the coffee."

I stare at the mug as she lets herself out. It's still untouched.

I'm not sure how long I stand here with my palms pressed against the countertop, staring at the veins in the marble, trying to notice a pattern I can't find. When that becomes too much, I look at the bird on the urn again.

I'm not surprised about the way things turned out for Randy; I've been waiting for this day ever since he ran off. He knew what he was signing up for, and I knew it too. I thought I'd broken into the acceptance stage by now—that it would be soft and easy to wear, like a well-used pair of shoes.

I grip the edge of the counter so tightly it burns. *Then why does it feel like I'm still getting blisters?*

My foot taps. I stare at the marble again. The urn. The remaining feathers and cereal on the floor. The chipped paint on the wall, previously hidden by a painting. Jade's cold mug of coffee. I can see my reflection within it, with cinnamon where my freckles should be.

I swipe my arm across the counter, and the mug goes flying.

It hits the floor and shatters. Dark liquid spreads over the black and white checkered tile I'm sure my dad paid a fortune for. I wonder if it'll stain.

I pull away from the island and run my hands through my hair. I pace back and forth. I kick a cabinet and stub my toe. I cuss out the cabinet and pull at my hair again. I squeeze my eyes shut. My pacing quickens. Every heartbeat feels like someone's punching my throat. I walk past one of the fallen paintings, and I kick my foot through it. My vision blurs and my ears ring and my lungs feel like they're shrinking, and the ceiling is caving in, and it grows closer, and closer, and I can't take a single full breath, and everything is shrinking, and *I'm* shrinking, and—

My fist cracks into the wall.

I freeze, palms planted against it, shoulders hunched up to my ears. Even as my breathing slows, my hands won't stop shaking.

A chirp emits from the corner of the kitchen by the sliding glass door.

Slowly, I walk over to investigate—and my heart rises into my throat.

Sprawled out on the floor and drenched in sunlight, a bluebird rests on its back with crooked, outstretched wings. It faces the open door, studying the grass outside and the sky overhead. It's a nice day for Seattle. There isn't a tile closer to freedom in the entire kitchen.

What a beautiful place to twitch, and twitch, and stop.

I stand there for a long time, unsure if I should blame the bird or the cage that killed it, watching the light shift with a passing cloud. A breeze enters through the open windows and tangles my hair. Somewhere out there, a lawnmower starts, and another bird sings. I want to cry. I *should* cry. But I don't.

There was every way out.

A feather falls onto my head. I look up again, and I have my answer for Jade.

My nails carve into the flesh of my palms. I watch the ceiling fan spin, dropping feathers with every rotation. Morning light seeps through the windows. The urn's glaze catches it with a glint.

I'm going to find the person who put my brother in there.

And when I do, there will be no way out.

PART ONE
DEAD
LOW

EDDIE

Monday, April 1
64 Beds Made

I have no shortage of uncertainties, but there's one thing I know for a fact: the Vermillion Keep is definitely haunted.

I wake before sunrise. There is no light when I blink my world into place. Even while I stretch and pat my face to make sure I'm still here, I can't see a single inch of my own skin.

The air in my room tastes like it's spent decades in a canning jar. A deep, strained breath of it helps soothe the dull ache in my head, but only a little. It never really goes away.

I drag myself out of bed and check the window. There is only more darkness when I part the drapes. *Good*, I note. *No one will see me leave.* I close the curtains and walk back over to my bed to begin wrangling the comforter back into place.

I never believed in making beds before End Harbor. What I once saw as wasted time is now a habit I execute without thinking, like breathing. It's easier to make beds than count the days that pass me by.

I make my bed for the sixty-fourth time.

I grab my knife, lace up my boots, and tiptoe across the room, relying on touch alone to reach my closet. I slip inside a brown wool sweater, my rust-orange puffer jacket, and the only pair of jeans I own before clipping my sheathed blade to one of the belt loops. The jeans are two sizes too big and faded with age, but I can't bring myself to care. This whole town feels like a second-hand outfit anyway.

There isn't much furniture in my room, making it easier to navigate in the dark. Either way, I've been here long enough to have its layout memorized. A closet next to the entry door. A quilted bed whose headboard sticks to the right wall. A bathroom with a clawfoot tub that's chipped in five places. An old wood nightstand, and a matching dresser across from the bed. A salt-stained window overlooking the sea.

That's what my world has been reduced to.

I make my way to my nightstand and instinctively reach out to grab the jackalope and cow carvings I keep there, but my hand pauses two inches away, suspended in midair. Guilt twists my stomach. *Remember what Aaron said about sneaking around?*

I frown. *Screw that.*

I grab the carvings and shove them deep into the pockets of my jeans, flinching when my hand brushes against something cold. Something metal. A shudder runs through me.

I never go anywhere without Aaron's carvings, but carrying Carmody's lighter with me is a different kind of need. A reminder that I can't bring myself to get rid of, no matter how many times I've tried. *A toll.*

I pull out the lighter and walk toward the door as quietly as I can.

I twist the knob and open the door, wincing when a chime rings through the corridor. I squeeze my eyes shut, and open them when the sound fades. I wait for someone to stir. To my luck, I am the only one here.

In the dark I can make out enough of my surroundings to notice a familiar brass bell hanging from the top of my door frame—one that I *definitely* remember disabling yesterday. I grit my teeth. *I'm going to kill him.*

I stand on my toes to reach up and remove it, but it's screwed in place. With a glare, I close my door and move forward, mindful of the bell.

The floor is soft beneath my shoes as I tiptoe down the hall. It's a stretch of lush emerald carpet that's been here since the Yesterdays, like most of the Vermillion. Or all of town. I assume it was in much better condition before the Wandering drove every End Harbor resident elsewhere. Today, the carpet is rough and faded, distorted by layers and layers of old footsteps. Ruined by those who are now nothing but ghosts.

I rub my eyes as I walk, unsure of how much sleep I really got last night. True rest is fleeting these days. Though I have no alarm here at End Harbor, I have unintentionally formed an internal clock, one that always pulls me from slumber long before the first tendrils of light seep through my curtains. I occupy hours of solitude, rising and falling before and after everyone else.

This is how I know the Vermillion Keep is haunted. When you stay up late and wake up early with little rest in between, your eyes are open while others' are shut. You come to understand certain things that most don't have the chance to realize.

You see ghosts.

They say the hotel has always been compromised by spirits, even in the Yesterdays. That the once-seafaring souls who called this abandoned port town home now wander the halls at night, creaking floorboards and ringing bells and whispering old names. But I'm not sure it's haunted in the way everyone seems to think.

I can't tell if it is my ghosts or theirs that follow my footsteps. There is an echo after every sound that I mistake for company, a melody in certain winds I mistake for lost voices. Every shadow I stumble across never fails to perfectly match the shape of one of the gaping holes in my core.

But when I reach out to touch them—when I turn around to see what is following me, or try to catch the voices in the breeze—it all dissolves into nothing.

It's easier to believe in their ghosts than mine.

I count my steps to the stairwell, staying close to the walls on my way down, carefully tracing the crimson paneling to make sure I don't stray too far to the side and tumble over the railing.

I know I've reached the lobby when I smell mildew and cinnamon. The walls morph from crimson to faded teal, and red floral carpet appears beneath my feet. I walk farther, refusing to meet my gaze as I pass a dirty bronze mirror. It hangs above a set of plum armchairs to my left that sit centered around a chipped black coffee table. I avoid the mirror at all costs.

I walk over to the door and study the antique brass bell installed above it. Unlike the ones Aaron likes to surprise me with, this one is a permanent resident of the Vermillion and older than I am. I've gotten pretty good at disabling it—which means someone else has become even better at fixing it.

I drag a coffee table to the door and use it as a stool. Sure enough, a new clapper has been reattached, made of wood instead of brass. There is only one person in all of End Harbor who is that skilled at carving.

I take my knife and fidget with the clapper, but it's hard to see. Although my eyes have adjusted to the dark, there is still a blur I cannot shake.

My sight would have been back to normal by now if it weren't for what happened that day on the beach. Thanks to Carmody, my left eye never had the chance to properly heal from being debugged. Now it feels like half of everything I see is beyond a layer of frosted glass.

Aaron still likes to remind me that I'm one of the lucky ones. In emergencies, when debugging must happen quickly, and the debugger lacks the skills to extract the microchip without permanent eye damage, it's common to remove the organ completely. A small cost paid by the debugged to free their bloodstream—free *themself*—and become Unseen.

Fortunately, Aaron is a skilled surgeon. I didn't lose my eye, and it wasn't mutilated and scarred by a rushed or inexperienced operation either. My eye is not clouded and white like Aaron's, and I don't have a jagged pink scar like his that cuts through the left side of my face.

But Carmody and his sand ruined what should have been a perfect recovery. While my eye has improved over the months, healing has plateaued. I'm still not used to the imperfections in my vision.

I can't even think about my other scars.

I work with what I have, squinting through the blurriness. When I look closer, I see a small, engraved message on the side of the clapper and roll my eyes. The familiar two-word phrase is a staple in Aaron's vocabulary.

I use my knife to silence the bell before shoving the clapper into my pocket, returning the coffee table, and taking my exit.

I slip outside quietly. Even with my sweater and jacket, I shiver. The air is cold and crisp, and I down it in sweet, desperate gulps. I ignore the haunting stench of salt and sand and stare up at the sky. *I wonder where the rain went*, I think to myself. It always rains in End Harbor.

The journey to the lighthouse is habitual and instinctive—something felt, not planned. I'm not sure how much time has passed when I reach it, still under the cover of darkness.

I stand in front of the lighthouse with my hands in my pockets, letting the wind whip my already tangled hair into knots. Even from the height of the cliff I stand on, mist pricks the skin of my face as waves crash upon the rocks below.

The salt smell is harder to ignore now that I'm so close to the water. Sometimes, when I breathe in the scent of seaweed or hear a gull calling overhead, I remember the blindness I felt that day in the sand. I remember the burning in my arm. The white sea foam that turned pink when it washed over Carmody's lifeless body.

And I remember the moment after. The arms that held me together when I felt like I was falling apart.

Don't go there.

I shove my hands deeper into my jacket pockets, wrap it tightly around my torso, and step forward.

Aaron says the lighthouse is over a century old. It stands tall against a charcoal horizon, its white stone walls grayed and smudged by age. It's topped by a metal cupola the shade of dried blood, infected with the rust of a steadfast enduring.

Damp gravel crunches beneath my feet as I walk closer. Wild rye hisses and bends in the wind, carrying the stench of wet stone. What was once a parking lot is now overgrown and untamed. With every passing year and every new patch of weeds, the lighthouse deteriorates a bit more. I wonder how long it will be until it is no longer here at all. Until it too is forgotten.

I reach the door, then stop dead in my tracks when I see the padlock. I press my lips into a thin, tired line, nostrils flaring. *This is new.*

I pull out my knife and pick the lock with ease, surprised that Aaron assumed his little trick would keep me out. He's the one who taught me how to pick locks in the first place.

Dust lifts from the floor as I enter, curling around my boots with every step. Despite the dim lighting, I'm familiar enough with my surroundings to see everything clearly in my head. I know there are cobwebs spread across every surface, infecting the rotten wood shelves and the little trinkets that decorate them. I walk past stacks of folded maps and photography books from the Yesterdays, taking in the sharp scent of old paper.

I walk upstairs. The first floor was once a souvenir shop for tourists, but the second story was once someone's home. It's small but comfortable enough for two to live happily within its walls. An antique kitchenette decorates one edge of the room. An oak table with two chairs resides on the other. There's an old quilted twin bed in one corner, a closet in another that's always been padlocked, and a blue and white striped rug spread across the center of the floor. Everything is coated with dust.

I reach the outer balcony circling the lantern room. A soft breeze bites at my cheeks as I find the last door, which guards a small staircase. I'm not paying attention as I climb the last steps and open the trapdoor.

The hairs on the back of my neck stand on end. *I am not alone.*

I close the trapdoor behind me.

Someone is waiting in the lantern room.

EDDIE

Monday, April 1
64 Beds Made

♪ DROWN - THE SMASHING PUMPKINS ♪

I expect to see the barrel of a Nightjade gun, but instead, I find a young man leaning against the beacon with his arms crossed, glaring like I've done something unspeakable. "You're a liar."

The relief subsides, and I narrow my eyes. "Some greeting, asshole."

Aaron wears a black knit sweater and faded jeans, with a familiar leather satchel strung over his shoulder. His dark brown hair is long enough now to be tucked behind his ears, and while it's usually unkempt, it seems neater this morning. Combed, to my surprise—which tells me he's been up for much longer than I have.

"You're not supposed to be up here."

His face is characteristically displeased, and his usual round glasses rest on his nose. Now that he's no longer sneaking around in Chip territory on smuggling missions, he has no reason to hide his scarred left eye behind shades. We are all Unseen at End Harbor.

I walk to where he stands and shove the disabled padlock into his chest.

"Then use a better lock next time."

He takes the lock and puts it in his satchel with a sigh, then slides his hands into his pockets. "Don't know why I even try anymore."

"You clearly expected me to get past it if you're up here waiting for me," I say. "And how did you get inside after locking the door?"

"First-floor window."

"Committed to the bit, I see." I lean against the beacon and hand him the bell clapper too. "And would you quit it with the bells already? You're not fooling anyone and it's getting annoying."

"Maybe annoyance is the point."

We stare through the lantern room's dust-coated glass walls, studying rolling waves and distant pines that loom beyond End Harbor's wall.

"You know it makes me nervous when you come up here by yourself," he mutters.

I press my lips together, trying not to think about what he's referring to. "So are you going to tell me why I'm such a liar, or is that just my latest nickname?"

He faces me, his expression softening. "Why didn't you say anything about your birthday?"

I avert my gaze as guilt churns my stomach. I hate when he looks at me like that. "It's not my birthday."

"And there it is again."

I ignore the fact that lies no longer taste bitter on my tongue and hug my abdomen tighter. "Did Milo tell you?"

"You don't remember the day we met?" Aaron pouts with a hand over his chest. "I'm hurt."

"I said nothing about my birthday when we met."

"When you met Cedar, sure. But what about the cabin?"

I roll my eyes at his ridiculous alias—and our reunion outside the Cut. "Of course I remember meeting *Aaron*. He tried to kill me." I jab a finger into his chest. "You and Cedar both, actually."

"I did not try to *kill* you. I was being cautious."

"By threatening me with a knife? On multiple occasions?"

"One, a threat is not a murder attempt. Two, I do not *attempt*—I achieve.

And three, I thought you were an imposter."

"Believe me, I remember."

"Then you should also remember that I asked you questions about your identity. Like your birthday, for example."

My face warms. *I completely forgot about that.*

I don't remember things the way I used to. Now, it feels like a mist has settled over everything I know. Lines blur. Everything feels warped, like someone has taken a lighter to the edges of a picture. The faces fade with every passing day. Sometimes it feels like I can barely recall the night I lost everything—or the day I lost it all again. There are only sounds and shapes, colors and hazy recollections.

The fog never lifts.

But with Aaron's reminder, the memory floods back. I can picture the scene perfectly: the Unseen rebel caging me against the wall with a knife to my throat, making sure I wasn't an undercover Chaser. I did tell him my birthday.

"How do you know I wasn't lying back then?" I ask.

"Oh, I know everything, Voclain." He tilts his head. "Surely you've learned that by now."

I roll my eyes and stare outside again. I can't lie my way out of this one.

Aaron studies the scenery with a sigh. "I'm glad you were born, Voclain." He pauses. "I may not act like it sometimes, but it's the truth."

I avert my gaze and wait for him to begin one of his lectures. To explain why it's important for us to be honest with each other. But he doesn't, and for some reason that feels worse.

He slouches his shoulders. "If you ever want to visit the lighthouse... I don't care what time it is. I'll take you, okay? We don't even have to talk." He shrugs. "We could even stay here instead of the Vermillion, if you want. I could fix it up easily."

I shake my head.

"Please, just don't go alone anymore." He glances down at me, then looks away. "I'd rather lose sleep than wake up and find you gone again."

A knot forms in my throat and I stare at my boots. "Fine."

"Thank you."

We're perfectly still for a while, until he reaches into his bag and pulls out a small rectangular object wrapped in old Yesterday newspaper. "Here."

"You didn't have to get me anything."

"Lie. Liar."

I shake my head and remove the yellowed wrapping paper. It's a dark wooden box, engraved with intricate floral designs I trace with my finger. *Lavender.* I suppress a grin and remove the lid.

The inside is lined with dark blue velvet. Resting on top are three black throwing knives made of polished steel. I trace the edges in awe. "Where did you get these?"

"I have my secrets."

I flatten my eyelids. "You stole them?"

"I'm an honest man now, alright? I traded for these, fair and square." He shrugs. "I redid some Harbor man's kitchen cabinets."

"Aaron." More guilt tugs at my stomach as I imagine the care that must have gone into making the box, or the work it took to get the knives. *He's been planning this for a while, hasn't he?*

"Don't worry about it, alright? The job was too easy."

I close the box and try my best to smile at him. "Thank you."

He grins, and for a moment, I forget about the fog.

The peace is quickly overshadowed by guilt and falls through my fingers. *I don't deserve peace.*

I close my eyes, trying not to think about the absences that grow heavier with each passing day. About the people-shaped gaps in my world that are so empty it aches. Aaron looks at me like he understands what I'm thinking. I brace myself for what he'll say next.

But I know Ren isn't gone.

There is no acceptance. There is no moving on—not when there's still a chance that he's out there somewhere, breathing although I cannot hear him, heart beating although I cannot feel him. There are some things you know to be true, even if you never have an explanation. Even if every piece of solid evidence disproves it.

Everyone else is wrong about Ren. *I know it.*

I wait for the words, but Aaron doesn't say them. Instead, we watch the world turn a little less gray.

The sun rises, painting the lantern room in streaks of desaturated light. If we were anywhere else, it would be ethereal—a pearly slice of heaven flooding through the gaps in the clouds. But this is the farthest away from heaven I've been.

My head feels heavy and I let it fall against Aaron's shoulder.

"You really think he's out there somewhere?" he asks, so softly I almost miss it. I nod. There's a pause, and he nods back. "Then I think so too."

Static interrupts the silence.

Aaron, do you read me?

I immediately recognize the voice as Lori's. Aaron retrieves the walkie-talkie from his belt, mumbling something under his breath as he brings it to his face. "What do you want?"

Where the hell are you?

"Lighthouse."

Why?

"Doesn't matter."

The line goes silent for a moment.

And Eddie's with you?

"Yeah, she's here."

Both of you need to get back to the Vermillion. Now.

Aaron's brows furrow. "Is everything okay?"

Asa is here. Noriko too.

Aaron and I exchange confused glances. That could only mean...
"She's awake?" we exclaim at once. Aaron's lips curl into a relieved grin.

They're not the only ones here.

Aaron gives me a puzzled look. "Okay, who else?"
Silence.
"Who else, Lori?"
Lori lets out a strained sigh.

Everyone.

"What do you mean?" More silence. Aaron's voice diminishes. "Lor?"
For a moment, there is only quiet. I wonder if we've lost connection. Maybe the device stopped working. Maybe we'll never hear a reply.
But when Lori finally speaks, every word sounds off-balance—and I feel the same.

There's been an evacuation. They found the Cut.

EDDIE

Monday, April 1
64 Beds Made

Aaron and I follow the path downhill from the lighthouse, sprinting through grassy cliffsides until we reach pavement. At first, I can barely hear more than my own breath. The pounding in my head. The echoes of our shoes against asphalt. But the slope evens out, and when we reach Main Street, the sound arrives.

Hundreds of voices and sobs melt together, growing louder and louder until we are close enough to see the Vermillion through the morning fog creeping in from the harbor. Aaron runs a hand through his now-tousled hair, his breathing shaky as we stumble to a halt at the edge of the mob. "*Shit.*"

The air is thick with iron, dirt, and pine. A crowd of Cut residents and End Harbor onlookers gather in front of the Vermillion Keep, tangled into one writhing knot of flesh and bone. Dozens of blankets and makeshift cloth stretchers are scattered across the pavement, each one holding someone worse off than the last. Every incapacitated body is painted with bruises and grime. Some groan in pain, their foreheads glistening with sweat. There are arms in slings, crutches made of sticks, stretchers too few to go around. Too many people who can no longer keep themselves upright.

Aaron carves through the crowd. I clutch his satchel to stay close. I can barely see my own feet as I struggle to keep up, dodging an angry sea of confused Harborers demanding answers.

A group of people huddle close in the center of the cacophony. I spot Noriko first, her long black hair billowing in the wind as she whispers to three other figures. Seeing her awake soothes something in me, but the feeling vanishes when I notice her uneasiness. Asa stands out like a sore thumb, his lean, towering frame and graying hair a familiar comfort against the uproar. I can't fight the relief that the sight of him brings, but even from afar, I can tell his eyes are hollow. He doesn't say a word.

Cecil stands next to them with his arms crossed, mustache twitching and face pinched in anger, arguing with an older man in a clean suit. *Mayor Wagner.*

We approach the heart of the commotion. The noise makes my ears ring and my throat tighten. Lori hurries past us carrying fresh blankets and water canteens. Her black hair whips in the wind as she looks over her shoulder at Aaron. "Mom's fine. Dad's looking for you."

Aaron nods, and she disappears into the crowd to help the wounded. I spot Viv, Milo, Hugo, and Beau doing the same, and I'm not surprised when my brother pretends he doesn't notice me.

We keep walking. Aaron cranes his neck, trying to pinpoint his father in the crowd, but we pause when someone calls his name.

A woman sits on the ground with a child in her lap. Strands of chestnut hair stick to the sides of her clammy face, and dark circles rest beneath her eyes.

The child can't be older than four. Her brown curls are laced with dirt, and a brutal gash runs along her outer arm. As we get closer, I can see that the wound is already scabbed over. *This couldn't have happened recently.*

Aaron crouches in front of the child. "Hi there, Abigail."

The girl leaps to her feet and wraps her arms around his neck. "I missed you."

Aaron chuckles as she pulls away. "I missed you too."

The child sits down and points at me. "What's her name?"

"This is Eddie," Aaron says.

I crouch by his side. "It's very nice to meet you, Abigail. How old are you?" She holds up three fingers and I gasp. "Three?"

She nods proudly. "And a half."

"So, Abbie," Aaron says gently. "Can you tell me what happened to your arm?"

She glances at her mother, who gives her a nod.

"We were trying to get away and a mean man took me away from my mom. And there was a loud noise, and when the man fell, she took me right back. But I scratched my arm on a tree when she picked me up. And then we ran."

"You must have been so brave." Aaron smiles at her, then retrieves rubbing alcohol packets and a roll of bandages from his bag. He glances at the girl's mother, lowering his voice. "You did what you had to do."

The woman nods, swallowing nervously. I realize what he means and a shiver snakes down my spine.

"You're Lavender, right?" she asks.

I nod. She reaches out to shake my hand, and I flinch before accepting it. Gently, she squeezes. Like she knows something I don't. "I'm Henrietta, but most people call me Henry."

I pull my hand away and slide it into my pocket. "And most people call me Eddie."

She gives me something resembling a smile.

"Hey Abbie, wanna hear something exciting?" Aaron asks. He tears open a packet of rubbing alcohol. "You have a little cut, but we'll fix it up real nice and turn it into a *battle scar*. Isn't that cool?"

Abigail's face lights up. "Whoa."

"I have one too, you know." Aaron raises a playful brow. "Wanna see?"

She nods excitedly.

Aaron pulls up his right sleeve. A thin scar I've never seen before carves his arm like a river. Unlike the still-red marks on my own arm, his scar is paled by years of healing. *Why has he kept it hidden?*

He notices me staring and averts his gaze, yanking the sleeve back down. He clears his throat and shifts his attention back to Abigail with an uneasy chuckle. "That's what happens when you run with knives."

Henry stares at her shoes.

"That's so cool!" Abigail giggles. "Will mine look like that?"

"Yes, but only with the help of this super special magic potion." Aaron gently takes her arm in his. "It might sting a little. Is that alright?"

Abigail nods. Aaron uses a pad of rubbing alcohol to wipe away the dirt surrounding her cut, then another one to clean the wound itself. Abigail squeezes her eyes shut and turns to bury her head in her mother's neck.

I watch him work, taken aback by his gentleness. Something about this unfamiliar patience brings me a bit of warmth, but beneath his calm composure, something doesn't seem right—like a framed painting hiding a crack in the wall. His hands won't stop shaking.

Aaron finishes cleaning the wound and bandages it neatly before giving Abigail a soft pat on the back. "Now all we have to do is wait for the scar."

Henry nudges her daughter. "What do you say?"

Abigail wraps her arms around Aaron's neck for a second time. "Thank you."

She pulls away and returns to her mother's lap.

"How are you feeling?" Aaron asks, turning to Henry. "Is there anything I can get you? Water? Tea? Something to eat?"

"I'm not sure I have much of an appetite, but tea would be lovely. Thank you."

"I have lavender with a bit of honey and valerian root. Brewed it this morning." Aaron pulls a thermos from his satchel and pours a steaming amber liquid into the lid. He hands it to her, and she nods in thanks. "This should help you relax. And maybe even get some sleep, if you're lucky."

She sips the tea and hands the lid back to him. "Thank you, Aaron."

He bags the thermos and nods toward Abigail. "Make sure to keep an eye on her wound. Once you two get situated I'll be swinging by to change the dressing every now and then." He lowers his voice so Abigail can't hear. "We don't want it getting infected."

We say our goodbyes and weave back into the crowd. Aaron walks so fast I struggle to catch up, and when I do, I notice his hands are curled into fists. They haven't stopped shaking.

"Are you okay?" I ask, trying to match his pace. He nods unconvincingly. I don't have the chance to press further until he stops walking. I do the same.

Aaron stares at an older man about Asa's age, with dark brown curls that move with the breeze. He stands with one hand in his pocket while the other clutches a wooden cane.

"Dad," Aaron mutters, voice trembling. "What the hell happened?"

So this is Simon.

"Good to see you too, kid," the man grumbles, emphasizing the resemblance I now notice.

"What do you want, a kiss?"

"A simple *glad you're not dead in a ditch somewhere* would suffice." Simon kneels on a blanket spread across the pavement, pulling first aid supplies and herbal tinctures from a familiar satchel to arrange them in piles. "I'm taking inventory. There wasn't enough time to grab everything, so we'll need to work with what we have."

"You didn't answer my question."

"Noriko will fill everyone in later."

"If I wanted an answer *later* I wouldn't have asked *now*."

Simon keeps his eyes glued to the supplies before him. "We had a run-in with a few Chasers. That's all you need to know right now."

"What did they do?"

Silence.

"Did they take any prisoners? Try to gather information or evidence?" When Simon doesn't respond, I watch something leave Aaron's eyes. "They just attacked?"

Simon sighs, unable to meet either of our stares. His voice softens. "They slaughtered."

The world feels like a knife to the stomach. My arms press against it, lips parting. I blink rapidly, unable to settle on one place to look as my knees begin to tremble. Everything around me spins.

Slaughtered.

"They were willing to wipe out an entire settlement of people," Aaron says. His shoulders stiffen. His jaw twitches. "We have *children* with us."

Simon changes the subject. "We need more supplies. Splints. Clean cloths. Surgical tools. As much water as you can manage. Whatever else you can find that could be useful. We'll have our work cut out for us these next few weeks."

"I'm not running errands, alright? Not when there are..." He swallows the rest of the sentence and shakes his head. "I'll help you. Shouldn't there be wounds to tend? Stitches to sew?"

"I told you what I need. Now go."

"Dad—"

"This is exactly why I didn't want to say anything. Because I need your help, and you get like this."

"I can help."

"Yes, by getting supplies." Simon sighs. "You can't save anyone in anger."

Aaron raises his voice. "How else am I supposed to react? What else am I supposed to do?"

"Learn to control your emotions," Simon mutters plainly.

"*God*, Dad." Aaron's hands fly to his head and he pulls at his hair. "How can you be so—"

"Because our people need me," Simon seethes, rising to his feet. He lowers his voice. "And they need you too."

Aaron's arms fall to his sides in defeat. His voice is soft now, cracking as he speaks. "How many, Dad?"

Simon's gaze glosses over, and he averts it. "Twenty-three."

The world spins. My pulse stutters, lungs pinching shut.

Twenty-three.

I look up at Aaron. Every part of him trembles. His eyes are red and glistening. His lips press together like he's trying to keep his breathing steady, but I stand close enough to feel that every rise and fall of his chest is strained. Slow, but shaking, like something is rattling to get out. I look down at his hands. They're curled so tightly that beads of red form around his nails.

"Aaron," I mutter, unsure that he can hear me.

He's gone before I get an answer, storming off into a crowd that swallows him whole.

I turn to face Simon, who doesn't look up from his task. "He'll come back around. He always does."

I glance over my shoulder. "I've never seen him like this."

"He's more sensitive than you think." Simon arranges a row of surgical tools on the blanket. "It's his best and worst trait."

"What do you mean?"

He sighs. "My son will bear any burden he can get his hands on. And when he stumbles across something he can't fix—people he can't help—he gets frustrated."

"And why do you think that is?"

Simon stares up at me, almost perplexed. He observes me for a moment before looking away and clearing his throat. "I wish I knew."

Something tells me there is more to be said, but I'm too fixated on Aaron to dwell on it. I look into the crowd again and bite my lip. "I should go find him."

Simon nods, and I turn to walk away.

"Oh, and Lavender?"

I pause and glance over my shoulder.

He waves. "It's nice to finally meet the girl I've heard so much about."

If it were any other day, I'm sure my face would warm. But it's cold, and there is so much gray. I wave goodbye and walk away.

I retrace Aaron's steps, moving past the Vermillion until I break through the edge of the crowd. I jog down the street with towering brick shops to my right and the sea to my left. I slow to a stop once I'm far enough from the commotion and scan the empty street for any sign of Aaron. I turn to my right—and spot him.

There is an abandoned parking lot filled with rusted cars, tucked between two brick buildings, so narrow I almost mistake it for an alleyway. The back wall is covered in vines, and the wall to my right displays a faded, whitewashed mural of a galleon at sea. The painting is barely visible and cracked in several places, a testament to End Harbor's age.

Aaron occupies the far-right corner, nearly hidden by a corroded white van without doors or windows. He presses his arms against the painted wall, leaning forward with his head bowed. His shoulders are stiff and hunched up to his ears, and his whole body convulses in silence.

I jog around the van and stumble to a stop when I see his right hand, balled into a bloody fist. His knuckles are completely torn, and there are places where the mural is stained red.

I walk to his side, reaching into his satchel to retrieve the same supplies he used to help Abigail. He doesn't protest when I take his hand in mine. Remembering his process, I clean the blood away and carefully bandage his broken skin. He winces when I touch his swollen, crooked index finger.

I observe it gently. "It's broken."

He nods. I find medical tape in his satchel and wrap the broken finger with his middle to stabilize it, then return the supplies to his bag. He uses his now-free right hand to wipe his nose with a sniffle. His other arm is still propped against the wall, his head still lowered like he can't bring himself to look at me. "Thank you."

I lean against the wall and stare at the sky. I close my eyes and take a deep, shaky breath. "Do you think…"

I can't finish the sentence.

Aaron lifts his head up with another sniffle. His eyes are red. "What are you saying, Voclain?"

I roll my head over to look at him. "Did I draw them in?"

Aaron straightens his posture, turning to face me. "Of course not."

"All of this happened three months after I showed up." A lump forms in my throat, and my vision suddenly seems foggier than usual. "That can't be a coincidence, Aaron."

He hesitates. "It's not your fault."

"Then whose is it?"

He folds his arms across his chest. "We both know the answer to that question."

We stand like that for a long time, letting the moments drip past like slow-falling honey. I'm not sure when the tears begin inching down my cheek, or how many minutes have passed until my eyes have no more left to give. Wind toys with my hair, but I can hardly feel it.

I look at Aaron, trying to locate him in his own gaze, but he is elsewhere. There is something cold and hollow behind his stare—something so empty I can barely find a single recognizable piece within it. He pulls a flask from his bag and takes a deep swig.

"If we ever run into another Chaser..." He walks away without sparing me a glance. "Hold me back."

EDDIE

Monday, April 1
64 Beds Made

There is something eerie about being in a church again.

When Aaron and I step inside, it takes me a while to remember that I am here in End Harbor. For a moment I see hundreds of documents pinned to dark blue walls. Beau's pool table in the corner, stained glass, and walnut wood pews. The round table where I once sat with Ren—the corner where he tried to convince me that I was angry with him. I shudder when I think of his touch, how close he was when he wrapped his arms around me.

But his arms are not here anymore, and my memories of the Cut drip away like candle wax.

Now we are in a neater place. Brighter, though the evening is melting into night. Cream-colored walls and vertical paneling give the illusion that the ceiling is much higher than it is, lengthening walls in a way that makes me feel smaller than usual. The pews and podium are light oak, and the floor is a lush, outdated green carpet. The air is thick with the stench of dried blood and sweat, though I try my best to ignore it.

These meetings happen quite often in End Harbor, though I've never actually been to one. I can't say I blame them for their lack of invitation. But I doubt this particular meeting will be anything like its predecessors.

Now, the building is crammed with Cut exiles and Harbor citizens, waiting for the answers we've been promised. Every pew is filled. Frantic chatter and hushed whispers flood the room. It's so crowded that Aaron and I have to sit on empty folding chairs in the back. Anyone who doesn't find a chair in time stands. There is simply no room for everyone.

I glance at Aaron, who has been quiet all day. After he stormed off, we gathered supplies for his father from the general store and the town's rundown hospital, where the Cut escapees with the most pressing of injuries are stationed. Everyone else has been assigned a room at the Vermillion or with a Harbor resident generous enough to share their space. I wasn't surprised when Aaron gave up his own room to a family who needed it.

We spent the rest of the day helping as much as we could manage. But aside from a few grunted wound-stitching demonstrations here and there, he's barely said a word since our conversation in the parking lot.

Sitting next to me, ignoring his broken finger, he shaves ribbons of wood from his latest carving project, which looks like a spoon. He clenches his knife so tightly I worry the scabs beneath his bandages will crack. The pain doesn't seem to faze him.

My attention is pulled away from him when all conversation comes to an immediate halt. Mayor Wagner has taken the stand.

Earnest Wagner is a rigid, unsmiling man with perfectly combed gray hair and suspiciously pearly teeth. He stands before the microphone in a neatly pressed gray suit with a navy blue tie—which he wasn't wearing this morning when I saw him arguing with Cecil. *He dressed up for this.*

"Good evening, citizens of End Harbor." He pauses. "And good evening, my dearest Cut folk."

It's quiet for a moment, like he expects some sort of applause. He clears his throat. "I'm sure you are all wondering what's going on—and that is exactly why I called this gathering tonight. You deserve answers. I know we have all heard more than our fair share of horrendous rumors, but by the end of this evening, I hope we will all have an adequate understanding of what happened to these people we have let inside the island's walls, inside our town, inside our homes.

"This is why I have invited a special guest to the stand tonight. Someone who is much better equipped to provide a decent explanation than I am." Wagner steps away from the microphone, gesturing with his hands. "I would like to introduce you all to Noriko Teshima—the commander of the Cut."

Wagner nods his head before taking his exit, making way for Noriko.

She walks up to the podium, adjusting the microphone to her height. She opens her mouth to say something, then stops herself. She closes her eyes, takes a deep breath, and speaks. "I know none of you want to be here."

The room stirs as the audience exchanges confused glances.

"I know you would rather be with your families at home, holding them a bit closer now that you've heard the rumors. You want answers, and you want facts. And I am here to deliver the truth—so we can try to find a way to move forward, to the best of our ability."

Noriko sighs, lowering her head ever so slightly. She stares at the worn grain of the wood podium. "Three days ago, the Corps launched an attack against the Cut."

The audience erupts in a fury of frustration and confusion. A few Harborers even rise to their feet, cupping their mouths to shout.

"So you came here and put us all in jeopardy?"

"We'll be next, thanks to you!"

"You really think we have enough resources to go around?"

My entire body trembles. I want to stand up and say something, to put a stop to this madness. But I know my own voice will do nothing. I bring my knees up to my chest and hug them tightly.

"This isn't our problem! We have enough to worry about as is."

"First you bring the Voclain girl, and now this?"

Aaron rises to his feet so quickly that his chair falls back and clatters behind him. The sound echoes throughout the chapel, ceasing the discord in an instant.

Everyone has turned to stare at him, unblinking, all eyes glued to the knife in his hands and the scar running through his eye.

I fix the chair and tug at his arm, yanking him back down in his seat.

"I know you are all feeling a lot of things right now. And trust me, I am too," Noriko continues. "But we can't waste our valuable time and energy being angry right now, nor can we change what has already happened. That energy needs to be spent elsewhere."

The audience stills.

"Now here is what we know." She crosses her arms. "We know that my home—my people—were attacked by Officers and Agents of the Chaser Corps. We know that most of us managed to escape to a very generous End Harbor as a last resort. We know that…"

Noriko's voice cracks. Her eyelids flutter closed, and I hear her unsteady breaths through the microphone. Her mouth opens and closes, like she's trying to muster up the courage to finish her train of thought. Cecil brings her a cup of water, but she doesn't drink from it.

"We know that twenty-three of our own were lost during the attack."

The room is dead silent. No one dares to speak, not even those who were shouting only moments ago.

I watch Noriko wear her shield so well. I know she is trying to remain an example of resilience, but I see her cracks beneath the surface. She swallows the pain and continues. "And before all of this, they took my son from me." Noriko's voice is almost a whisper, even with the microphone. "The system has taken both of my children from me."

It feels like someone has ripped my lungs out. My entire body grows cold, like a candle being snuffed out.

Noriko believes that Ren is gone.

I always thought she would be on my side. Before her return, I found comfort in the thought that Ren's parents were still out there, believing the same thing I was. That if everyone here didn't believe me, there were others who knew that he is out there somewhere—anywhere. *That he's alive.*

Her head hangs low as we soak in what feels like an endless silence.

"We know how little we are wanted in your town, but I ask of you. I beg of you. Do not assume we have sacrificed nothing. Because some of us have sacrificed everything, if it wasn't already lost long ago. The Corps has taken so much from all of us. Do you really think we can afford another divide?"

When she opens her mouth to continue, my legs move against my own command, and before I know it, I am standing.

Aaron's hand returns to my shoulder, but I swat it away, keeping my stare fixed straight ahead.

And the words tumble out cracked. "Ren isn't dead."

My voice rings throughout the hall. Every eye is glued to me, and I can feel each one burn.

The moment I realize what I've done, I want to cover my mouth with my hands. I want to curl up into a ball and hide somewhere dark and sleep everything away. But I am perfectly still.

"He's not," I add softly. My shoulders sink, and I look down at my filthy boots with flushed cheeks.

I feel Noriko staring at me from behind the podium, and I glance up. I can barely make out her face behind the fog in my vision, but I can tell that tears are forming in her eyes.

"We all saw the gunshot, Eddie." Her words soften to a whisper. "We all saw him fall."

I want to close my eyes and shut everything out and let someone else bring me back down to my seat, or out of this church, or out of this entire town. There is nowhere I want to be less than here—and I am so horribly tired. A part of me wants to cry right where I stand.

But the greater part of me succumbs to the rage, which tastes much sweeter than the grief, and numbs a little less.

My face feels hot, and I can't bear to look at a single person in this room anymore. I weave between the chairs until I'm no longer in the church but beneath a sky far too cloudy for me to believe it has a single star.

I hear the echoes of Noriko's words as I walk outside. "My apologies for her behavior. She and my son were... quite close."

I storm across the lawn with my hands in my pockets until I find a secluded corner of the building. I press my back against the wall, slide down, and bury my head in my hands.

I hear footsteps crunching against the grass, but I don't look up. I can barely move. "Not now, Aaron."

"Relax, alright? Your boyfriend's not here. Just me."

My head snaps up at the sound of Milo's voice. He stands by my side, leaning against the wall.

"He's—"

"*He's not your boyfriend*, yeah yeah, whatever." He swats at the air with a scoff, and folds his arms across his chest.

I clench my jaw, propping my head up with my fist. It's been days since we last spoke, and it feels strange to hear his voice again—especially at a time like this. If we were the people we used to be, I wouldn't have expected any less from my brother. Now, he's the last person I would have expected to follow me out here.

I know he blames me for what happened. I can't even bring myself to be upset about it, because I do too. Behind every fire he's had to walk through, I have been standing there holding the match.

I can understand the distance he's put between us since our arrival at End Harbor, but I can't say it doesn't affect me. There isn't a day that goes by where I don't wish things were different—that I don't plead for the chance to get my brother back.

But I lost him the moment he saved me from that Chaser.

Milo pulls something out of his pocket and places a cigarette between his teeth.

"When did you start smoking?" I seethe. I reach up to swipe it from his mouth before he has the chance to pull out a lighter.

He snatches it back. "When did you start caring?"

"And when did you stop?"

Milo shakes his head. I wait for him to light the white stick, but instead, he tosses it up and down, watching it perform little cartwheels in the air. *He's just fidgeting*, I realize. He chuckles bitterly when I roll my eyes. *And tormenting me.*

"I use most of my ration slips on these." Milo's tone is empty as he holds the cigarette out in his palm to study it. "They're the best currency. You wouldn't believe what people are willing to trade for their vices."

"What could you possibly want that you can't get with ration slips?"

"Information. Anything else people are willing to give up."

"You're cruel."

"You call it cruel." He tosses the cigarette in the air again, catching it just as swiftly. "I call it clever."

I shake my head and stare at the distant harbor. The waves seem still from afar, but I know that if we were any closer, I would see them rolling against the docks, tossing and turning, restless without slumber.

I stare up at Milo again, who either doesn't notice or doesn't bother to look. He keeps his eyes fixed ahead, twisting the white stick back and forth between his fingers.

Something about him seems different. Not in the way his dark curls have grown past his ears, or the way his face has hardened with the slightest bit of age. He feels painfully unfamiliar, and I can't understand how.

Milo glances at me before staring at the night sky. "He's gone, you know."

My nails dig into my palm, and I try to center my breathing. *He's just acting out*, I tell myself. *He's trying to get on your nerves.*

"Let me guess—if you had a dollar for every time someone said that, you'd be so rich you could buy your *other* boyfriend back from the Corps."

I whip my head around to glare at him, then soften my expression. I'm too tired to fuel the fire he's clearly trying to start. I avert my gaze. "It wasn't like that with Ren."

"So Aaron *didn't* walk in on your passionate kiss back at the Blurt?"

I scowl at the grass, trying to ignore the guilt churning my gut or the tightness in my chest. My throat constricts and I swallow painfully. Although I still don't know what to make of that moment in the control room, I can't deny that I think about it more than I ought to. A small part of me longs to be caught in that moment again. But a greater part of me wonders if that is simply because I miss him.

"Since when were you and Aaron so close?" I say quietly, changing the subject. I have a hard time imagining the two of them talking about anything that isn't Yesterday music or a joke.

Milo ignores my question and gives me a look. "You're not denying that it happened."

I pluck a blade of grass and wrap it around my finger.

"Eddie."

The blade snaps.

Milo sighs. He stares at me like I'm something faulty he wants to fix, but he isn't sure how to dissect the parts. It feels more pitiful than kind. "Look. I have no reason to care whether you did or didn't, alright? I'm just... trying to get a sense of the situation. That's all."

I stare at the broken blade of grass between my fingers. I carry a version of me within myself that would love to give my brother a piece of my mind, but she is shrouded in fog, and I cannot seem to find her.

Then, something settles. "You said *buy him back.*"

"What?"

"About Ren." My brows meld together, separating again when the realization hits. "You think he's..."

"Gone doesn't mean dead." Milo slouches against the wall with crossed arms. "But that doesn't mean he's coming back either."

My jaw tightens. "You don't know what you're saying."

"The Corps is brutal, Ed. We both know that," he snaps, then lowers his voice. "He has a connection to the Unseen. Do you really think they'd dispose of somebody so valuable—a puppet they can string up and use against you? Against all of us?"

I let the broken piece of grass fall, watching it disappear amidst a sea of green.

"Whether he's alive or not... do you really think he'd be the same Ren from that control room?" He hesitates. "Do you really think he'd be Ren at all?"

My nails carve slivers into the flesh of my palms, chin trembling as I try not to succumb to the tightness in my throat. *He doesn't know what he's talking about.*

"Look, Ed. I'm saying this as your brother, alright?" Milo lets out a long sigh. It's so cold I can see his breath unfurl beneath the lamplight, curling upward in a translucent, moth-like flurry. He shoves his hands in his pockets. "Ren's not coming back. The sooner you accept that, the better off you'll be."

I rise to my feet, blood running hot. "What the hell is wrong with you?"

"I should be asking you the same question." He peels himself away from the wall. "For months you've been hiding away in your room, or in that lighthouse, never setting foot outside unless you have to. You don't sleep.

You barely eat. You're rotting away for a guy who tried to *kill you*. Are you forgetting about that part?"

"I swear to God, Milo. Stop. Talking."

"He's a *Chaser*, Ed. A Chaser." He laughs cynically. "Did you forget about that too?"

"Of course not."

"But you love him, don't you?"

Everything stops. My arms feel heavy and I let them fall loosely at my sides, blinking slowly, holding my breath mid-inhale.

I don't know.

"If you had the opportunity..." Milo's tone softens. "Would you go after him?"

I look at my brother, eyes glassy as I try to keep myself from unraveling. Even with our recent distance, Milo knows me better than I know myself. He looks at me like he already knows what I'm going to say.

In my mind, the answer arrives quickly, because there is never a single moment that I am not asking myself the same thing, dreaming of a way to leave this cursed town behind and find my way back to him. There is nothing in this world that I want more. And yet, no matter how thoroughly I brainstorm or how intensely I desire it, I can't find a single solution that doesn't involve skills I don't have, knowledge I don't possess, or endangering everyone around me. But if there were a way...

"I wouldn't even have to think about it."

"That's stupid, Ed."

"I don't care."

Milo goes quiet. He nods, but he doesn't look me in the eye. "He tried to kill you."

"That's not true."

He was following orders, I reassure myself, hands shaking. *He was playing pretend to keep me safe from Carmody.*

He didn't want to hurt me.

"You can tell yourself whatever you want, but the only part of him that's pretend is the part that tried to come back." Milo gives me a brief side glance. "He's shown who he really is, and I think you should believe him."

"If that were true then he wouldn't have..." I can't finish the sentence.

He sacrificed himself for me. He jumped in front of that bullet so I could live, whether I deserved it or not.

"He felt *guilty*, Ed. Can't you see? He saved you for himself. It's his conscience he was protecting. Not you." Milo laughs again, every note bitter until it dies down. "He wouldn't have a reason to feel guilty unless part of him wanted to follow those orders, and you know it."

Every part of me goes cold. I can't tell if I want to scream or cry or break something—maybe all three. But I can't manage to get a single word out.

"I'm just trying to look out for you, Ed." Milo's volume lowers, but his tone doesn't soften as he meets my gaze, holding it for a moment too long before turning his head away. "Some people can't be saved."

A twig snaps.

I turn to see Aaron approaching, hands in his pockets. Far behind him, the crowd streams out of the church and into the street.

"Everything okay?" he says.

"Everything's just dandy." Milo shoves his way past Aaron and around the corner, disappearing into the night.

Aaron slows to a halt a few feet away. "What was that all about?"

I wipe my nose. "Nothing."

"Didn't seem like nothing." He stares at me for a while, waiting for a response I can't bring myself to give. He clears his throat. "Meeting's over. You're wanted back inside."

I can't bring myself to wonder what I could possibly be needed for. All I can do is stare at the lawn beneath my feet.

"Hey." Aaron's voice lowers. "Are you sure you're okay?"

I hug my abdomen.

"You can talk to me, Voclain." He hesitates. "About anything."

"I'm fine."

We both know I'm lying but he doesn't push it, nodding instead. "We should head over now. It's starting soon."

I lift my head up. "What is?"

"We have a strategy meeting to attend." He turns back around to walk away. "Apparently there's something we need to hear."

EDDIE

Monday, April 1
64 Beds Made

I don't want to be here.

The church feels smaller now that it's empty, save for a handful of familiar faces. Noriko and Cecil stand in front of the podium, arms folded somberly. Viv, Hugo, and Beau occupy the front pew, and Aaron and I slide into the one behind them. Asa sits in the very back of the chapel.

Wagner stands off to the side, watching closely with a young girl around Milo's age who I don't recognize. She leans against the far-right wall with one leg crossed over the other, hands shoved in her pockets. Blonde hair falls to her elbows, and the bridge of her nose is dotted with freckles. Unlike the overdressed man standing next to her, she wears a dark blue hoodie with a baggy pair of torn gray jeans.

I lean over to whisper in Aaron's ear. "Who's that?"

"Alice Wagner," he whispers back. "His daughter."

The front doors swing open and closed. I turn around to see Lori walking inside, my brother following close behind. She slides into our pew next to Aaron, and Milo takes a seat next to Asa. Alice sees Milo and nods in his direction.

I wrinkle my nose at Alice's gesture, giving Aaron a puzzled glance. "Do they know each other?"

"He and Lori hang out at the nursery sometimes." Aaron shrugs, pulling out his knife and current carving. "Alice runs it. Used to be her grandmother's place."

I nod, unfazed by how much he knows. Gathering knowledge is one of the few things that brings Aaron something resembling peace of mind. When he isn't holed up in End Harbor's old library or hospital, scouring Yesterday books and learning as much as he can, he's implementing what he absorbed. I wouldn't be surprised if he told me he ran a full investigation on every citizen in End Harbor.

But what does get to me is the fact that I no longer know my brother as I thought I did. *Even Aaron knows more about what he's up to than I do.* An ache spreads through my chest as I try not to think about our conversation outside.

Wagner clears his throat. "Let's begin, shall we?"

Viv scoffs, and Aaron slides his knife along the wooden spoon a little louder than usual. Beau mutters something under his breath and Hugo elbows him in the ribs.

Noriko steps forward. Cecil places a hand on her shoulder, letting her know he'll be there right behind her. She nods. The room stills.

"It's nice to see you all." Her voice is quiet, and she stares at an empty pew. "Though I'm sure we all wish it were under... different circumstances."

I stare at my boots. Aaron pauses his carving.

"As my most trusted personnel, I owe you guys an honest explanation. No sugarcoating." Noriko exhales shakily, closing her eyes. "The Cut is gone."

Cecil sees her struggling and leans forward like he wants to step in, but she raises a hand to stop him.

"On the night of Friday, March 29th, exactly one hundred Officers and Agents of the Chaser Corps infiltrated the Cut, armed to the teeth and ready to destroy everything in sight. They were given only one order." Noriko swallows slowly, every part of her trembling. "Exterminate."

A chill settles over the room, prickling my skin. Every hair on the back of my neck stands on end. Aaron resumes carving.

"It's a miracle they didn't fulfill that command to its full extent," Noriko continues. "As a primarily civilian group of people, we were outgunned; there was simply no way of fighting back. Those who did fight were only doing so to give those who couldn't a head start.

"We only had so much time to prepare. We had barely enough room and resources to bus our survivors toward End Harbor as far as we could before running out of gas. The rest of the trek was made on foot, and now…" She sighs painfully. "Here we are."

"Bus?" Hugo questions, adjusting his glasses. "I wasn't aware we even had buses back home."

"We didn't," Cecil says, giving Noriko a hesitant side glance.

"And you mentioned time to prepare," Viv adds. "We don't have any active Doubles in the field, do we?"

Doubles. The word replays in my head, reminding me of the deal I made with Ren so long ago. How he wanted to support the Unseen from the inside, just like Lori did before becoming Unseen herself. *He didn't even get the chance.*

I dig my thumbnail into the side of my index finger and try to think of anything else.

"Not exactly," Cecil answers.

Noriko's face turns grim. "But we were given a warning."

"A warning?" Hugo raises a brow.

Noriko exchanges an unsure glance with Cecil, who nods before pulling a crinkled sheet of travel-sized notebook paper from his pocket. He holds it up for everyone to see.

"It came in the form of a note," Noriko says. "I found it on my nightstand the morning of the attack."

"We believe whoever sent it must be involved with the Corps, in one way or another," Cecil says.

My heart stops, like someone has reached inside my chest and caught it in their fist. When it starts to pump again, it feels like it'll burst beneath the pressure.

"Can I see it?" I call out without meaning to. All eyes lock on me, and they are noticeably wary.

Cecil nods, stepping closer and reaching over the front pew to hand me the paper.

I take it carefully and quickly, afraid of crinkling it any further but too eager for patience. I unfold the paper and read the message inside.

> *Extermination order. They know where you are.*
> *Leave while you still can.*

My lips press together. It's dishearteningly vague, and when I squint to analyze the handwriting, my heart sinks. *It's not Ren's.*

I don't realize I'm shaking until Aaron places a hand on my shoulder, snapping me out of it. I clear my throat and hand the paper back to Cecil without a word. He gives me a saddened, knowing look before returning to Noriko's side.

"So let me get this straight." Hugo leans forward in his seat, folding his hands together beneath his chin. "You think there's a local Chaser in the Corps—not planted there by us—who's sympathetic to the Unseen?'

Cecil sighs. "I think we have a rat problem."

Everyone goes quiet.

"Now, we don't know that for sure," Noriko reasons, about to say more when Wagner interrupts.

"A mole?"

Cecil nods.

Wagner's face pales. "You have a traitor among you?"

"We have no theory to suggest otherwise," Cecil explains. "This person not only knew the Cut's location, but also knew to leave the note in Noriko's room, of all places. Only an insider would know which room is hers and where to find it."

"And that she's in charge," Viv points out. "That's not exactly public knowledge either."

"I can't believe it." Wagner swears under his breath, rubbing his temples with a sigh. He folds his arms across his chest, glaring in Cecil's direction. "I was generous enough to let you within our walls when you came pounding at our doorstep three months ago with a wanted criminal in your party."

Aaron stops carving again.

"I had no idea that nearly *two hundred* Cut exiles would then seek refuge here, but I allowed it, so generously opening our walls once again. But a traitor I cannot allow. I *will* not allow it."

"Earnest—"

"We are an extremely fragile ecosystem here at End Harbor," Wagner continues. "For generations we have worked tirelessly to rebuild what the Wandering abandoned. For decades we have transformed this old port town into one of the Pacific coast's most secure places of hiding for Unseen civilians—who want no part of this foolish notion of rebellion you and your people seem to uphold. A traitor feeding information to the Corps puts all of them at an unimaginable risk. Do you think the Corps will care that End Harbor chooses not to fight? That we only wish to live in hiding?"

"Let's be decent here, Earnest," Cecil grumbles.

Wagner raises his voice, face turning red. "If they follow you here, they will slaughter needlessly. All thanks to this reckless evacuation and your traitor and—and that foolish girl too."

He points in my direction, and my face heats up.

If things were different, maybe I would have the energy to fight back. But I can't even bring myself to disagree. By hiding in End Harbor, I've put everyone at risk. The alliance it shares with the Cut doesn't matter if the Corps is looking for the girl from the broadcast.

And I'm just so tired.

"You know that's unfair, Earnest," Noriko says, voice grim. "We had no other option."

Cecil scoffs. "We're just as pissed about this as you are, Wagner, if not more so. Betrayal isn't exactly something we allow either."

Wagner clenches his jaw. Alice picks at her nails, unfazed.

"Like I said before, I trust each and every one of you. I have no reason to believe there is a traitor in this room," Noriko says. "But I ask you all to be vigilant. Pay attention to things you wouldn't normally notice. Keep a watchful eye out for anything out of the ordinary. And please... this stays between us, alright?"

We all nod.

"However, this is not the main reason I called you here tonight," Noriko continues. "As I said, our priority was escaping with our lives, not fighting back. I believe our losses would have been much greater without the warning we received, but unfortunately, it was still not enough time.

"When we evacuated, we were barely able to grab anything more than the clothes on our backs. Our maps, our documents, our tech, our tools, our weapons, our Nightjade research—everything we've worked so hard to gather and build is still exactly where we left it."

"This means more than just a loss of resources on our part," Cecil adds.

"The Corps now has access to everything." Noriko exhales heavily. "Every secret we once guarded so well is now within their grasp."

"This includes the alliances we've formed with other Unseen bases over the years," Cecil says. "There were a few small camps up and down the coast that we often shared resources with—and a handful of larger establishments like End Harbor. Unless we do something about it, all of these populations are at risk of meeting a similar fate."

"So what do you suggest we do about it?" Viv asks.

"We assigned a few scouts equipped with burner phones to walk the trek here instead of riding with us in the buses," Noriko explains. "Their job was to clean our tracks and create as many red herrings as possible to throw the Corps off our trail, but they've also been reporting back to me. As far as they know, the Corps hasn't made any attempts to send organized troops after our survivors."

"Which could be the result of a job well-done by our scouts," Cecil adds, "but there's also a likely chance that the Corps is focusing the bulk of their efforts on investigation. Agents will be treating the compound as an active crime scene—analyzing as much as they possibly can while it's still fresh, and before we get the chance to do anything about it. This means that if we're going to act, we need to do so soon."

Noriko nods. "We need to go back to the Cut."

"And do what?" Beau asks.

"Take back whatever we can... and destroy whatever we can't."

"They won't expect a retaliation—at least not this quickly," Cecil says. "We can use a couple of the vehicles available here at End Harbor to bus a small, specialized group back to the Cut to carry out this mission. We'll be in and out like that." He snaps for effect.

"This gives us an opportunity to not only restore some of our losses and protect vital information," Noriko says, "but also to make a dent in our efforts against the Corps... and while they least suspect it. We can manage to make this a setback for them in one way or another."

I look at Aaron, who's back to working on his spoon. He keeps his eyes glued to the knife, leg shaking.

Noriko continues before I have the chance to question Aaron. "Is this something you all would be on board with?"

"I'm in," Viv and Beau say in unison.

Hugo and Lori nod in silence.

Noriko skips over my gaze and looks at Aaron. "You've been awfully quiet this evening."

Aaron's leg stops shaking. He uses his knife to make a long, whispering sweep against the wood in his hands. "I'm in."

I nod too.

Noriko is about to continue when a burst of laughter echoes throughout the chapel. I turn my head to see that it's coming from Wagner.

"This is absolutely ridiculous." The laughter fades. "You can't possibly believe this is going to work."

"I'm aware of the risk, Mayor. Do you really think I'd take it if I didn't think it was worth the reward?" Noriko argues. "This is for our own good. The wellbeing of every Unseen individual in our region could be at risk."

"You've already put them at that risk by being discovered," the mayor seethes. "Going back to the Cut? Multiplying that risk tenfold?"

Cecil steps forward, but Noriko holds out an arm.

"If you are not careful—if they find any one of you—the Corps will not be merciful enough to exterminate you on sight. The system runs on efficiency; they'd harvest as much information from you as possible before ending your life. And do you really think any one of you would be able to withstand their captivity? How much would you be willing to go through before you'd crack and give us all away?"

Metal scrapes against wood.

I hold my stomach, unable to keep myself from bending forward. It feels like the ground is quaking beneath me, and the chapel walls won't stop spinning. *Don't think about him, Eddie. Don't you do it.*

But I can't heed my own warning. No matter how I plead, I can't stop picturing Ren, wandering through every unthinkable possibility as I do nightly. In my mind I have seen the worst unfold, and even that must only be scratching the surface. I don't think any one human has the ability to imagine the worst of what the Corps is capable of.

But I've come pretty close.

Aaron notices my discomfort, and this time, it is my leg that shakes. I can feel his eyes scouring over me as he realizes what must be on my mind. He pockets his carving blade, scowling at the mayor.

"I don't think we really have much of a choice here," Cecil says. "We aren't saying it's not a gamble... but it's one we have to take."

"Willingly making yourself prey for the Corps puts the entire Unseen network at risk." Wagner glares in my direction. "And you already have a walking target amongst you."

"Alright, dipshit, that's enough." Aaron surges upright, folding his arms across his chest—spoon still in hand.

Noriko's face grows stern. "Aaron."

"No, I'm sick of this." He laughs cynically, pinning the mayor against the wall with his glare. "You're acting like we've brought this on ourselves. Like End Harbor is somehow superior for the bout of good luck you think you've had. But you wanna know the real reason why you haven't been discovered yet? I'll give you a hint—luck has nothing to do with it."

Aaron takes a few steps closer to Wagner.

"You've been hiding for decades on a secluded little island so small the Corps hasn't yet detected its location—putting you at the perfect advantage for taking action. Or for helping others seek refuge, at the very least. And what have you done?" Aaron stands in front of Wagner now. "Absolutely nothing."

"I think you should take your seat, young man."

"Do you know what the population of End Harbor was before the Wandering?"

Wagner stays silent.

"Superlative. The mayor's never stepped foot in his own library."

"*Aaron*," Noriko warns again.

"Ten thousand," he continues. "And what's your current population? Three hundred?"

Wagner presses his lips into a tight seam. "And seventeen."

"So you have the infrastructure to support forty-seven and a half *additional* influxes like this one, and you're throwing a tantrum?" Aaron scoffs. "You're pissed that we're here, so you clearly know your advantage. You're just too selfish to risk sharing it. Meanwhile, we've been operating for almost *twenty years* with a fraction of the resources you have, and never have we questioned helping anyone on our side. Because we are on the same side here, whether you like it or not. The only difference between us and you is the stick up your ass."

Wagner's face turns purple. "How *dare* you talk to me in such a—"

"We've gone through hell and back over these past few months. Because we're willing to risk our lives for the possibility of change. Because we choose to believe in something better. And I don't think there's anything wrong with that."

"You clearly have no idea what you've done. The consequences of *your* actions. The danger you've put us all in by *simply being here*." Wagner waves a hand in my direction. "And if they don't come for the Cut, they'll come after her. She's got a public bounty on her head for God's sake."

"You don't know the half of it, alright?" Aaron points the spoon in the man's face, so close it nearly touches his nose. "You have no idea what she's sacrificed. What she's given up for the good of *everyone*—including you. You should be thanking her."

Wagner scoffs. "*Thanking* her?"

"I mean, look at you! You've been sitting here on your ass, living a cushy Debugged life far away from the Pick, privileged and Unseen and completely oblivious to the absolute *horror* of the world she grew up in. And doing what? What have *you* sacrificed?" Aaron's fingers curl tighter around the spoon's handle. "At least at the Cut, we tried to make a difference. At least we're still trying to fight back."

"Fighting back?" Wagner chuckles. "Oh, please. The only *difference* you fools ever made was getting yourselves run out!"

"Aaron." I stand up, clenching my teeth. "Just drop it."

He ignores me. "How is that worse than isolating yourselves from the other Unseen? Forgetting all about our real enemy and villainizing the ones who don't? Abandoning the rest of the world like it means nothing to you?"

"*Aaron*," I hiss.

This time, he hears me. He lowers the wooden utensil, leaning closer to the mayor's face. "Say what you want about the Cut, but if you say another word about *her*..." He points in my direction. "I swear to God I'll hit you with this spoon."

Wagner's face pales, too stunned to say another word. No one protests when Aaron storms out of the church and lets the door slam shut.

Instinctively, I turn to run after him as I did before, but Lori grabs my arm, pulling me back down to my seat.

"Let him go, kid," Cecil says.

"But—"

"He gets like this sometimes," Lori says softly, placing a gentle hand on mine. "He'll be okay, I promise."

Noriko eyes Wagner warily from where she stands. "I apologize for his behavior. He's... been through a lot. You would understand his rage if you've seen what he's seen." She clears her throat. "But I can't say I disagree. I think there's been enough stagnancy. The best option for us all is to move forward with our plan."

Wagner's nostrils flare, and Alice elbows him in the side. He glares down at his daughter before sighing in defeat, rubbing his temples. "Fine. Do what you must. But leave End Harbor out of it."

"Thank you, Earnest." Noriko nods before turning to face the rest of us. "As for all of you, preparations must begin as soon as possible."

"How soon?" Lori asks.

"Tomorrow," Noriko says. "We leave on Thursday."

Aaron is waiting for me outside the church. He walks me to the Vermillion in silence, neither of us in the mood to articulate what's on our minds.

I enter my room, removing the carvings and Carmody's lighter from my pockets and placing them in my nightstand drawer. I look at Aaron as I hang up my jacket. He leans against the doorframe, hands in his pockets.

"You gave up your bed, right?" I ask, remembering that the room next to mine is now occupied by a Cut family instead of him.

He nods. "To Henry and Abigail.

"Where are you staying tonight?"

He shrugs. "Lighthouse."

"That's far." I look away to close the closet door. "You should just stay here."

"I'm not sharing a room with you, Voclain."

"Why not?"

He steps outside and grabs the doorknob, but he pauses before taking his exit. "You're a slob."

I survey my room. The nightstand is empty, and my bed is made. There is no mess.

He closes the door before I can tell him that.

EDDIE

Tuesday, April 2
65 Beds Made

The knife hits the tree with a thud, exactly where I intended it to.

The sound echoes throughout the trees, sending a handful of cawing crows in every direction. I wonder how many hide in the evergreen without my knowledge. I've been doing this for hours, and there always seems to be something to scare.

Save for my throwing and the occasional line of birdsong, the woods surrounding Ever Point have been silent all morning. I stand in the middle of a clearing tucked behind the lighthouse. I can see all of End Harbor from my elevation—a little island wrapped in a decaying stone wall, hidden in plain sight. I can see where the wall breaks like a crescent moon, leaving the western shore exposed to an endless, glittering gray sea. If I didn't know any better, I'd assume it was a ghost town.

I frown at the tree. I've been getting decent hits for a while now, but no matter how many times my knife nails the makeshift bullseye I carved into the trunk, it doesn't satisfy the itch that burns my hands. *It's still not good enough.*

I'm no expert, but it doesn't take expertise to know that my form is sloppy and my movements are slow. If I were in a situation that called for it, my lack of efficiency would get me killed. Or somebody else killed.

I'm still not good enough.

I pull out a second throwing knife and pinch its smooth black handle. I ready my stance, take a deep breath, close my eyes, and throw.

A twig snaps right as I move my arm, and the knife misses the bullseye by a centimeter.

Someone breathes against my neck. "You missed."

I spin around, fingers already clenching my third and final throwing knife. I point the blade toward my company—only to find myself standing face-to-face with Aaron.

His grin is crooked. "This feels awfully familiar, doesn't it?"

I lower the knife with a scowl, turning around to walk toward the tree.

"Ending the fun so soon?"

"I almost cut you." I yank the two knives from the target and sheath them. "And I would have made the throw if you hadn't shown up."

"If you say so."

I pocket my knives and give him a look. "I mean it."

He raises both palms in innocence. "She means it."

I wave out my sore wrist with a wince, massaging the joints as I squint in Aaron's direction. "Why's your hair wet?"

He shrugs, running a hand through it in a failed attempt to smooth out some of the stray strands. "I showered."

"It's after noon. You're usually up before sunrise."

"Yeah, well, I don't exactly have a shower of my own anymore, alright?" He frowns. "I went for a swim."

"There isn't one at the lighthouse?"

He hesitates. "Not one with running water."

I raise a brow. "The water runs, last time I checked."

"Yeah, well it doesn't right now." He reaches inside his satchel, pulling out a glass jar filled with something orange. He walks over to where I stand and holds out an empty hand. "Here."

Reluctantly, I reach my right arm out. He opens the jar and dips a finger inside before applying the strange substance to my wrist. It smells like hot cider. Almost instantly, a warm tingling sensation spreads through-out my skin, easing the soreness.

"What is that? Cinnamon?"

Aaron nods, applying some to his neck before putting it away. "It's a beeswax and olive oil salve. Infused with all kinds of good stuff. Camphor, cayenne, cassia bark, tea tree, clove, peppermint—the works."

We start walking back toward town. "And you made it?"

"You really think I'd trust anyone else to make my medicine for me?"

I roll my eyes. "Where do you even find all of that?"

We don't exactly have a greenhouse anymore—not like the one Aaron established back at the Cut, at least. Yesterday was the first time I've thought about healing in months.

"You see, Voclain, as per usual, I happen to be one step ahead of you." He takes a larger step forward to prove his point, spinning around to walk backward. "That's actually why I've come to fetch you. We're going to the nursery."

"End Harbor has a nursery?" I raise a brow. "Like for plants and stuff?"

"You bet. Hey—check this out." He pauses to pluck a flower from a nearby shrub, handing it to me.

I stop to inspect the flower, spinning it between my fingers. It reminds me of a strawberry blossom, white with silky leaves. It smells like one too.

"Thimbleberry." Aaron stares down at my hands, voice soft. "Every part of the plant is edible. Antiemetic too. Especially the leaves."

"They prevent nausea and vomiting?"

He suppresses a grin. "So you *do* pay attention when I talk to you."

"Your ego is gluttonous."

"You're the one feeding it, not me." He reaches out to trace the petals, so gently they barely bend, lowering his voice to a near-whisper. "The flowers are useful too."

I nod, observing as he points.

"The berries are good for anemia, though those aren't in season yet," he explains. "But if you're in a pinch, you can use the other parts of the plant to make a tea, if vomiting is the issue. Or the leaves to make a poultice, if you're treating a burn or some other wound."

"Should we collect some?" I look up at him. "For the trip?"

He grins. "I like the way you think, Voclain."

I hand him the clipping, and he slides it into his pocket. I use my usual knife to harvest bundles of stems, roots, leaves, and flowers, passing them all to Aaron. He stores them in his satchel.

"It's amazing, isn't it?" he says, shoving the last clipping into his bag. "What is?"

"That healing can be found in so many things." Aaron rises to his feet and helps me to my own. He walks backward again, holding his arms out. "There's medicine all around us, Voclain."

I start walking, Aaron still facing me. I flatten my eyelids in his direction. "So philosophical of you."

"What can I say? I'm a philosophical guy." He bumps into a tree.

"So wise. So aware." I step past him with a stifled grin.

"You have no idea, Voclain," he shouts behind me. I keep walking, but I can hear that he remains still. I turn my head around, and he's grinning.

I frown. "What's so funny?"

"Nothing." He shrugs, jogging to catch up. Soon, he's walking ahead of me again. "Nothing at all."

He slides his hands into his pocket. For a moment, I swear I almost smile.

But he still wears bandages, and I can't forget the reason why.

The nursery is tucked between a spread of trees on the edge of town, with rustic wooden framework and a gravel patio displaying more potted plants than I can count. There's a modest greenhouse on one side of the building, and although it's nothing compared to Aaron's, it's a comforting sight. A reminder of what we used to have—and what we still do.

A light breeze weaves between the pines, tickling glistening wind chimes and ruffling patches of wild grass. Today brings no rain, but it's cold nonetheless, and I hug my jacket closer to myself.

Aaron comes to a pause before we step onto the property, holding his breath. He stares at the greenhouse like he's seen a ghost, and I realize that maybe he has. The last time he set foot here, the Cut was still in one piece. His greenhouse included.

I open my mouth, but he steps forward before I get the chance to speak.

Gravel crunches beneath our feet as we walk down the aisles of plants. There must be hundreds of mismatching ceramic pots and containers, each one housing something different. The air is thick with the hum of bees and herbal notes of rosemary, rose, and mint.

When I breathe it all in, something warm ignites within my chest. It's been months since I've last seen so many plants at once; I'd forgotten the way they made me feel. The excitement, the curiosity, the wonder, the joy—

I stop my train of thought. *You don't deserve this anymore.*

You couldn't save them.

"You coming?"

Aaron holds the door open, brows pinched as he studies me from afar. I pretend that he doesn't know what I'm thinking and walk inside.

The interior of the nursery is a lot smaller than its front yard. Shelves overflowing with supplies line dark wood walls, and more run throughout the center to display an overgrown selection of herbs and vibrant flowers so aromatic I can practically taste them. Rows of seed packets cover an entire wall behind the counter where none other than Alice Wagner sits on a stool, waiting in a light gray hoodie and faded jeans, her long platinum hair tamed into a low knot. She frowns in Aaron's direction. "Took you long enough."

"Good to see you too," Aaron grumbles. "You said you had something for me?"

Alice nods, hopping off the stool to disappear into the back room. "My old man will kill me if he finds out I'm giving you some of our stock." She returns carrying a dusty wooden crate, filled with cobwebbed glass bottles and jars that clink together when she sets it on the counter. "He's throwing a pretty big tantrum about this trip of yours."

"Is that so?"

"Oh yeah. Won't shut up about *her* either." She nods in my direction, then meets my gaze. "Lavender, right?"

"I go by Eddie."

"And I go by Alice." She gives me a smirk. I can't help but mirror her expression.

She starts to pull out a few bottles of herbs and tinctures, each one a varying shade of yellow, amber, and green. She retrieves a tiny corked bottle filled with a viscous golden liquid and hands it to Aaron. "Castor oil. Just like I promised."

Aaron grabs the bottle, eyeing it like a prized gem before tucking it into his satchel. He grins. "I owe you, Wagner."

"Then don't call me Wagner."

"It's a deal." Aaron holds out a hand, and reluctantly, she shakes it. He slings his satchel over his shoulder and backs away from the counter. "Really, if there's anything you need—plant nerd to plant nerd—I'm your guy."

"Whatever." Alice begins putting the bottles back in their crate and then pauses, looking up at Aaron. "Is Lori going with you guys?"

Aaron stops walking, studying Alice for a moment. He shakes his head. "I talked her out of it."

Alice nods, and something like relief smooths out the edges in her expression as her shoulders relax. She puts the last bottle away, takes the crate, and disappears around the corner. "See you around."

The first half of the walk back to Vermillion is quiet. Aaron walks with his hands in his pockets, staring at his shoes.

"Did you really talk Lori out of going?" I ask quietly.

"I know she has training and everything, but... I just feel a lot better when she's safe." He shrugs. "And we can't exactly afford any irrational mistakes on this particular trip."

"If Milo tried to go, I'd talk him out of it too." My brows crease. "I'm surprised he hasn't, actually."

"He likes to do his own thing." Aaron gives me a brief glance, then averts his gaze with a shrug. "Maybe he could use some company."

I stop in my tracks, shooting him a glare. "I'm going."

"No one's stopping you." He pauses. "It's just... something to consider."

I pause, remembering what he said about mistakes. *He doesn't want me to go.*

I stare at the damp pavement beneath my feet. *Of course he doesn't.* As hurtful as it is, I can't find it in me to be angry. I trace my sleeve, feeling the texture of my scars beneath my sweater. *I'm bad luck.*

"I'm not helpless, okay?" I glare. "I'm the one who got you all into this mess in the first place. I think I owe it to the Cut to try and help."

"I don't think you're helpless."

"But you think I'm going to screw up."

"Not *you*, alright? You make me..." He lowers his voice with a sigh. "If anything were to happen to you out there..." He shakes his head, kicking a pebble before shoving his hands into his pockets. "I don't think I have that kind of forgiveness in me, Voclain."

My muscles relax, but my throat suddenly feels tight. "So then you understand why I can't stay behind."

Aaron meets my gaze, trying to find something to say or the means to say it. But someone calls his name before he gets the chance.

"Aaron."

We spin around to find Henry running up to us, eyes wide and face pale. She stumbles to a stop, out of breath. Aaron and I jog to her side, but he gets there first. "Is everything okay?"

Henry looks up at him, eyes glistening. "Something's wrong with Abigail."

EDDIE

Tuesday, April 2
65 Beds Made

Aaron is the first to burst through the door.

Henry and Abigail have settled into Aaron's old room at the Vermillion, the one left of mine. Everything from the layout to the furniture to the wallpaper is identical, save for a couch and a kitchenette in the corner, where Aaron and I usually made breakfast up until yesterday.

And the little girl who lies in bed, fast asleep.

Lori sits in a chair by the bedside, holding a damp washcloth to Abigail's forehead. Henry hurries to them. "How is she?"

Lori stands. "Still feverish. She threw up a couple times too."

Henry places a hand to her chest, nodding. "Thank you for watching her, Lori. It means a lot."

"Of course." Lori gives her a hug. "I came as soon as Aaron radioed me."

Aaron looks at his sister. "We can take it from here."

Lori nods. "Let me know if you guys need anything else." She walks toward the door.

"Oh, and Lor," Aaron says, pausing her. "Alice was asking about you."

Lori freezes, then quickly exits, her face turning red as she leaves.

I take a seat at the foot of the bed and watch Aaron pull up another chair. He opens his satchel as he sits, pulling out fresh bandages and alcohol packets before placing them on the bed. "How long has she been feverish?"

"Not long." Henry shakes her head. "She seemed a bit off earlier this morning, but given everything she's been through, I just—I didn't think anything of it until she started throwing up."

Aaron nods, removing the bandages from Abigail's wound he dressed just yesterday. He peels them back gingerly, expecting the worst—but the cut seems fine. Maybe even better than yesterday, from what I remember.

"I thought for sure it'd be infected," Aaron mutters. He cleans the healing scab before beginning to apply a fresh set of bandages.

"Is it just a stomach bug, then?" I ask. "Maybe bad water from the trip?"

"We can't rule either of those out, but..." Aaron creases his brow in thought. "We can't rule out infection yet either."

Aaron reaches out to give Abigail's bandaged arm one last once-over, then checks her other arm. Nothing. He takes her small hands in his, studying every finger, and still, nothing. Then, something flickers behind his eyes, like he's made a realization.

When Aaron removes Abigail's socks, Henry gasps. My eyes widen as I stare at her blistered skin, so red and inflamed that I almost mistake it for being burned. For a moment I'm brought back to that cow field with Ren —when he tried to hide the blood on his feet. This is what I always thought it looked like underneath.

Don't go there.

Aaron observes Abigail's feet, carefully holding them in his hands. "This is an infection, alright."

Henry's lip trembles. "But—I don't understand."

"I'm assuming she acquired a couple blisters on your trip here. From all that walking." Aaron sighs, taking a closer look. "The blisters themselves aren't too bad—only whatever got inside them."

"I had no idea she even had any. I've been so..." Henry shakes her head. "She never complained about her feet hurting. Not even once."

Aaron is still, unable to stare at anything but the blisters, like someone's held a remote to his head and put him on pause. He clears his throat and returns his attention to Henry. "Wounds get infected easily, especially when you're out there." He gestures at the window with his chin. "Don't beat yourself up about it."

"But—"

"People are better at hiding pain than we think they are. Especially kids." He gives her something resembling a smile, but it fades quickly. "They like to be strong for the people they love."

Henry stares at Abigail's feet for a moment, swallowing painfully and hugging herself tighter. Dark circles frame her eyes.

"You look tired," Aaron says. "You should get some rest."

"I don't think I can sleep."

"Then try to relax, at the very least." Aaron gestures to the couch. "Taking care of yourself is taking care of Abigail."

She nods and walks away to curl up on the couch.

Aaron shifts his attention to me. "I've got a mix of calendula, geranium, and green tea leaves right here." He reaches into his satchel and pulls out a glass jar, which is filled with the thimbleberry we harvested earlier, as well as a smaller tea jar filled with an assortment of dried herbs. He hands them to me without looking, then starts opening one of the alcohol pads strewn across the bed. "I'll clean her wounds."

I nod, running to the kitchenette in the corner of the room. I set the jars on the laminate countertops and rummage through the cabinets until I find a big pot, which I fill with tap water and set on the stove to boil. I pour a generous serving of the bottled herbs into the pot and toss a couple thimbleberry clippings into the mix. It bubbles quickly, and the air fills with the smell of steeping greenery and florals. I turn off the burner and stir with a wooden spoon. As soon as it's cool enough, I fix a mug for Abigail and set it on one of the nightstands.

"We'll give her some of that in a second," Aaron mutters, still removing dirt and debris from Abigail's wounds. He tosses the used alcohol pad to the side and pats around for another fresh one without any luck.

"Well, I'm officially out of rubbing alcohol. My stash is back at the Cut." He swears under his breath. "Remind me—I'll need to restock on a few things when we're there."

I nod.

"There's a jug of apple cider vinegar under the sink."

I hurry back to the kitchenette to retrieve it, then hand it to Aaron, who pours a small serving onto a cloth. "This should help kill a good amount of the bacteria. We don't exactly have oral antibiotics on hand or anything, so it's the best we've got."

"And the tea?" I grab the mug I prepared and hand it to him.

"Everything in here is anti-inflammatory, so it should make a dent, at the very least."

"And the thimbleberry will help with her nausea?"

He nods. "Which should help her keep some of the tea down. Hopefully lots of water too."

Aaron finishes cleaning and rises to his feet, gently scooping the still-sleeping Abigail into his arms to position her upright. I hurry over to help, taking a seat at the edge of the bed so he can set her into my lap. She clings to my neck and rests her head against my chest. He stands over us, one arm on my shoulder as the other holds the mug of tea.

"Hey, Abigail," he whispers. His voice is so soft and warm that I almost forget this is the same Aaron from yesterday—the one with bandages on his knuckles and emptiness behind his eyes.

Abigail's eyes flutter open and shut at the sound of his words, and he grins, though I'm not sure she can tell.

"I need you to drink some tea for me. Can you do that?"

She trembles in a way that looks like a nod. Carefully, Aaron helps her down a few slow sips. She swallows painfully before burying her head into my neck.

"You did such a good job," I whisper, forcing myself to bear a smile she can't see. Aaron sets the mug on the nightstand, his hand still on my shoulder. "We're going to put you back to bed now, alright?" I add.

Abigail holds my neck tighter, shaking her head.

"You need rest, Abigail. So you can have lots and lots of good dreams."

I'm surprised when she speaks up, her raspy voice barely audible. "I don't have good dreams."

Something in my chest sinks. Aaron studies her sadly, seeing something

I cannot. His lips part like he wants to say something, but he closes them quickly, swallowing a lump in his throat. He can't bring himself to reply.

We remain like that for what feels like ages—Aaron standing over me with his hand on my shoulder as I hold Abigail and wait for her to fall back asleep. I look up at him, but he is too busy pinning his gaze to her blistered feet to notice, staring at them like he can feel the wounds himself.

There it is again—the emptiness he has been so fluent in weaving in and out of since yesterday. *No*, I correct myself. Longer than that. *He's been half-hollow ever since we got here.*

I can't tell if he's angry or afraid.

Aaron snaps himself out of it soon enough. "She's fast asleep. I'm going to make a poultice."

I nod, standing as he takes Abigail into his arms and lays her back down at her pillow. I walk to the couch to check on Henry, and we watch as Aaron works, too focused and just far enough for our whispers to evade him.

"He's good, isn't he?" Henry asks as we observe. I glance at her briefly and nod. "He's known Abigail her whole life. She loves him like a big brother."

I suppress a small smile. "That's sweet."

"He's looked out for her ever since my..." Her breath catches. "Since her father disappeared."

My heart sinks, throat tightening. "How long has it been?"

"Three years."

My lungs pinch shut. A chill slithers down my spine, the hair on my neck and arms standing on end. I close my eyes and exhale shakily.

Three years.

Three years of not knowing. Three years of wondering what you could have done differently. Three years of missing someone so badly you can feel it in your bones—that deep, acidic ache that breaks down every part of you until you are nothing but withered.

Three years of hating yourself for not being able to do a single damn thing about it.

"He was a good man. You would have liked him, I think," Henry says. "Always had something to say about everything. He had quite the spark."

Was. Something twists violently in my stomach. *How long will it take until I start using that word too?*

"I'm sorry," I whisper.

"Thank you." She stares at her hands, twisting a ring I hadn't noticed before, with a gold band and what looks like jade, surrounded by tiny little diamonds. *I wonder if that was his.*

I stare at my hands too, trying to keep myself steady, but they won't stop shaking. "Can I ask you something?"

Henry nods, and I turn to face her. Her eyes look like they're coated in glass. In their reflection, mine look just the same.

"How did you know?" I ask.

She breaks away to look at Abigail. For a moment I worry I've crossed a boundary I shouldn't have, but then she whispers so quietly I can barely hear her. "I know it sounds crazy, but when you care deeply enough for a person... I think you gain a sixth sense, just for them."

"And what do you feel?"

Henry stares at me once again, eyes clouded. The growing lump in my throat burns, and I can feel it bubbling up. If I hold her gaze for another second, I'll start crying, and I don't know if I'll have the strength to stop.

She averts her eyes first. Her voice cracks when she finally says, "Nothing."

"What does static mean?"

She glances at me, then takes my hand in hers. This time, I don't flinch.

"White noise is still noise," she says. "Trust in what you know."

I nod and rise a little too quickly. "I'm gonna see if Aaron needs help."

Her words resonate as I walk away, stretching and echoing like piano keys played with a pedal. *Trust in what you know.*

I want to follow her advice more than anything. I want to trust this unidentifiable feeling in my gut that tells me Ren is still out there somewhere, wherever that may be. But how can I believe myself when I've been wrong about so many things? How can I trust my emotions when they only seem to lead me astray?

"Hey."

Aaron's voice snaps me out of it. I'm standing next to him, staring at a sleeping Abigail. He's sitting in his chair by the bed, paused in the middle of bandaging up the child's feet so he can look at me instead.

"You okay?"

"I'm fine."

He stares at me like we both know that's a lie, and suddenly I can't shake the feeling that he overheard more than I wanted him to. He decides against confrontation and shifts his focus back to the task at hand. "You can leave now. I'll finish up here."

"You sure?"

"Go back to your room and relax. You'll need as much rest as you can get before Thursday."

"So do you."

He gives me an impassive side glance. "I'm almost done."

Too tired to argue, I turn to leave—but I pause to look back at him. "How did you know?"

He raises a brow. "Know what?"

"About the infected blisters."

He hesitates. "There's always a root." He continues with the bandages. "See you later, Voclain."

I take my exit.

EDDIE

Tuesday, April 2
65 Beds Made

When I enter my room, I'm relieved to find that Aaron has yet to fix the bell he installed on my door. Too busy with preparations for the mission, I assume.

I remove my jacket and swap my sweater and jeans for a hand-me-down tee that's so large I'm practically swimming in it.

I go over Aaron's instructions in my head. Rest and relaxation before Thursday. How am I supposed to do that?

I think about what he said, and I can't disagree. I'm not sure I deserve relaxation, but I'm definitely sleep-deprived. Maybe I could use a nap.

I flip on my ancient space heater and try to find warmth beneath the covers of my bed, but the old quilts here at the Vermillion Keep are inefficient at best. I feel exactly the same—so worn down I've lost my color, my substance, my warmth. Held together by fragile threads that might snap at the slightest tug.

I stare at the ceiling until the sight of the floral patterns make me dizzy, squeezing my eyes shut when I can no longer stand it. But sleep is slow to arrive. Now that I have nothing else to focus on, every ache I've been carrying throughout the day is more noticeable than ever. The one in my chest especially. It's like something with talons is clawing at my insides, trying to break its way out. I curl up on my side to preserve what little comfort I have.

Moments like these are the ones occupied by Ren. All moments, really, but the thoughts tend to move more freely when I am drifting off to sleep with my barriers down, until they are so firmly nestled into every corner that I end up getting no rest at all.

There is no greater anguish than missing someone who is not here.

It's the thought of him that finally lulls me to a state of half-slumber. He was my safety net once—an anchor among riptides. I think back to what things were like before, when I found solace in his presence and warmth in his closeness. Back then, he was the only person I knew who understood what it was like to bear the burdens I bore—the secrets I kept, the lies I told, the risks I took behind closed doors. He knew what it was like to love Margot the way I loved her.

I needed him. *I still do.*

Barely conscious, my thoughts shift away from the Before, hurling straight into the After. Away from the river and the cow field and to that moment in the control room when I learned what it was like to feel his lips against mine.

The moment that complicated everything.

I crave that feeling because I want him near. Because he's Ren—*my* Ren—and I want him back. I want him safe. To feel his arms around me or his forehead pressed to mine would mean that he is here. But I can't tell if I want it for the reasons I should.

And there is nothing more corrosive than the guilt I feel because of it.

He took a bullet for me in that control room. He'd been taking bullets for me long before that, and I didn't even have a clue. All that time spent in the woods with Carmody—he was looking out for me, in his own confusing way. He saved me in the snow and he saved me in the sand and he saved me in the sea.

And in that river, when he fell by my side and we remembered what it was like to be children again, he saved me before I knew I needed saving.

So why don't I feel it?

In that control room, I was sure that I did. That when I looked into his eyes and felt his heartbeat close to mine, I was feeling what he was feeling. What I was *supposed* to be feeling.

But what if what I wanted wasn't him at all? What if all I wanted was to feel human one last time before standing in front of that camera? Something resembling comfort and safety while I still had the chance to receive it?

Maybe I was right back then. Maybe all we've ever done is survive. *Maybe I never deserved saving.*

I swallow the thoughts and roll onto my other side, picturing him until I really am sleeping, and the image shifts into a dream. Only this time, there are no bullet holes in his chest, and no blood either. His eyes simply go blank. He stands still in that white room, alive but empty. His heart beats, but something about him is missing, and I can't for the life of me figure out what it is. I reach out to touch him, but he doesn't flinch. His eyes don't meet mine. I try to say his name but I can't find my voice. My mouth doesn't move. All I can do is watch as he fades, growing more and more translucent until he is nothing but a ghost. Until he is gone.

I wake up and fold forward like the bed is made of hot coals.

Cold sweat glues my hair to my face. I run a hand through the curls, clutching it in fistfuls and squeezing my eyes shut as I try to steady my breathing. *It was only a dream.*

I roll out of bed and check the windows. It's dark now. A sea of fog has rolled in for the night, and a few street lamps still glow amber in the haze. They switch off automatically at midnight, so it can't be too late. I spot a few Harborers strolling along the sidewalk down below. *I must have been out for a few hours.*

I close the curtains and stare at my bed. As groggy as I feel, the thought of climbing back into it makes me more nauseous.

The routine plays out almost automatically. Knife. Jeans. Carvings. Lighter. Jacket. Before I know it I'm walking out of the Vermillion and down the street, hugging my puffer close around my torso as I hike the trek to Ever Point.

I need to clear my head. Aaron's right; I need sleep, and I'm not going to get any if I'm still sore about the conversation with Henry. *Or preoccupied by my guilt.*

And he's also right about us not being able to afford any irrational mistakes on our upcoming trip. The Cut will be swarming with Chasers, both Officers and Agents. I'll need to stay focused if I want to make it out of there alive—and make sure that everyone else does the same.

But deep down, I know the real reason why I want to go on this trip so badly. If I'm lucky, maybe I can find some sort of clue—some piece of information that could lead me to Ren. Maybe I'll overhear something valuable or stumble across something that confirms his survival.

And if I don't, I could extract intel through... other means. But even if I had the guts to intimidate a Chaser or the skill to isolate them from the rest of their group, the odds of one Officer or even an Agent knowing anything about Ren are slim. Letting them go afterward would also blow our cover, putting not only the strategists at risk, but maybe even the entire Unseen.

And I'm not silencing anyone—Chaser or not.

I sigh. Simple good luck will be my safest bet, and I don't exactly have much of that.

You're getting ahead of yourself, I think. *Clear your head. You'll get there when you get there.*

Damp, crumbling pavement crunches beneath my feet as I approach the lighthouse. When the road starts to curve up the side of the hill, I step off to the side and onto the dirt shortcut that leads me up to the top of the cliff, cutting through the woods and wild rye until I've reached the gravel parking lot. The night grows thicker around me, fog clinging to my stiff shoulders as I try to ignore the biting cold.

I freeze in my tracks.

Warm light seeps through the second-story windows, spreading out into the night.

End Harbor folk don't like the lighthouse; funnily enough, they're convinced it's haunted, just like the empty Vermillion Keep, whose only occupants are Cut strays.

I should see who's up there. My throwing blades are in my room, but my hunting knife is in my hands and tucked within my sleeve before I take another breath—and then I pause, sheathing it again just as quickly.

Aaron's staying in the lighthouse now.

I let out an exhausted sigh. I wanted to spend some time alone. *Maybe he'll let me sit in the lantern room for a while without pestering me.*

There's a padlock on the door that I recognize as Aaron's from before. The door's regular lock is rusted and broken in its age. It's his only way to keep unwanted visitors out, a precaution he'd definitely take now that this town has doubled in size and the Harborers are getting angry. I pick the lock without a second thought.

I walk through the dusty abandoned gift shop and make my way up the staircase. "Hello?"

I wait for a reply, but instead, I hear a pair of muffled, frantic whispers coming from the level above. I furrow my brows and march up the stairs at a quicker pace until I've reached the second floor.

Aaron and Milo sit at the table, Aaron's deck of playing cards spread out across the surface. He clears his throat uncomfortably, staring at his hand. Milo can't make eye contact with me either.

I squint to make out the details of the game. A messy pile of cards is dumped in the center. There is no draw stack. Some of the cards in their hands are backwards, and others are scattered on the floor. I may have grown up in a world where playing cards were illegal, but I've learned enough from Aaron during my time at End Harbor to know that this isn't a real game.

I glare. "What are you two doing up here?"

Aaron mirrors my expression. "I could ask you the same question."

"Answer mine first."

"Playing cards." Aaron pulls one from his hand and tosses it into the pile. He nods toward Milo. "Your turn."

Milo places a hand over his mouth like he's deep in thought. He takes two and discards one before handing the other to Aaron.

I cross my arms and nod toward the table. "What are you playing, then?"

Milo shrugs. "Poker."

"Go Fish," Aaron says at the same time, then clears his throat. "Poker."

"Cut the bullshit. I know you two are up to something."

And then I notice that the closet is open, just a crack.

The closet that is always closed, always locked, covered in so much dust I thought it hadn't been used in decades. I realize now that the glistening, good-as-new padlock doesn't match the rest of the room. It's unlocked, and it looks a lot like the one Aaron keeps on the front door of the lighthouse.

The faintest amount of light seeps through the closet, and I walk toward it. Aaron and Milo jump to their feet, abandoning their faux game. Aaron jogs to my side. "Voclain—wait."

I open the door before he can stop me.

It's a walk-in closet with a pull-chain pendant light and a built-in desk nestled in the back, which is occupied by a typewriter, an old Yesterday laptop, and a wooden model of something I don't recognize. Before I can study it closer, the walls pull my attention away.

Every inch is completely covered. Dozens—if not hundreds—of paper scraps and sticky notes are pinned to the walls, connected by spare bits of yarn and twine. From lists of information to spare thoughts and questions, everything is either scrawled in pen or typewritten. I even spot a few torn-out book pages that must have come from End Harbor's library.

It looks like the walls of the church back at the Cut.

I take a step closer to study one of the notes, which I recognize as Aaron's handwriting.

Seattle, WA
San Francisco, CA
Albuquerque, NM

"There are Agency headquarters in Seattle and San Francisco, aren't there?" I mutter, creasing my brows together. "The Tombs are in New Mexico."

I step farther into the closet and read another note. This one is a dated and typewritten list on a sheet of white paper. There are dozens and dozens of names, each one paired with a single word—and a cause of death.

"*Officer Troy Cannon: Dead. Cause of Death: Drowned,*" I read. I whip around to face Aaron, jaw twitching. "What the hell is this?"

Aaron swallows nervously.

My hands tremble as I turn back to continue reading. "*Officer Mattie Williams: Dead. Car accident. Officer Todd Hampton: Dead. Nightjade. Officer Sandra Wood: Dead. Head injury.*"

I scan down the list, and I'm about to move onto the next note when an underlined name snags my attention.

Officer Ren McLellan: Dead
Cause of Death: Classified

My heart plummets. The room starts to spin, every scrap of paper blurring together as I place a hand on the wall to steady myself. I take a deep breath that I can't seem to release.

Aaron takes a step closer. "Voclain—"

I hold out a palm, stopping him. "*Don't.*"

He freezes.

"He's not dead," I mutter, head pounding. The names on the list blur together. "He's not."

"Eddie, please. Let me explain—" Milo says, but I cut him off.

"That's not—no. That isn't right." I shake my head, breaths quickening.

"Voclain, I'm gonna need you to breathe, alright?"

"I don't know what you two have been up to lately or what's going on here, but whatever this list is—it's wrong."

"The list isn't wrong," Aaron says softly. "It's just—"

I spin to face Aaron again. "He's *not* dead, alright?"

"I know."

My breathing slows. "What do you mean, *you know?*"

"That's what we're trying to tell you." Aaron closes his eyes with an unsteady sigh. "We don't think that bullet killed Ren."

The spinning stops. Everything suddenly feels too quiet. I swear I can hear the wind scraping against the sand far beyond the cliff, and it sends a shiver crawling up my spine.

"That right there?" Aaron nods toward the paper on the wall. "It's a death count for all the Officers who died that day."

"How did you get it?" I whisper.

"Lori."

"She came to us the moment she and Hugo found it," Milo explains.

"And why not to me?"

They exchange glances, and Aaron continues. "She didn't know how to interpret the information. She didn't want to get your hopes up before understanding what this means."

She thinks he's gone. Nausea twists my gut into knots. "Who else knows?"

Aaron sighs. "Everyone."

I let my arms fall to my sides. *Everyone knew.*

The thought tastes bitter and my mouth goes dry.

They all think he's dead—and no one told me a thing.

My hands won't stop shaking. "Then what makes you so certain he really is alive after all?"

"Because the cause of death is undisclosed," Aaron says. "It's an untouchable case."

"What does that mean?"

"Agents are handling it."

"How do you know that?"

"Just trust me on this."

I scoff.

"He's right, Eddie," Milo says. "We thought it was strange, so we looked into it, and... some things about this whole case just don't line up."

"I mean, look at the date." Aaron walks to the list and points at the top. "The broadcast happened on January 26th. This is a death count for February 2nd."

"Why didn't Lori and Hugo think the date was unusual?" My throat is so dry that it burns to speak.

"They have a... different theory."

"They don't think the bullet killed him either," Milo explains. "They think he was... used for information. Which we can't rule out as a possibility."

Aaron shoots Milo a glare, which my brother returns.

I tune out their whispers and scan every note, every word, until the realization hits like shattered glass. "You're trying to find him. All on your own."

Neither of them say anything.

Without me.

"Lori was able to find something else too," Aaron says quietly, changing the subject. "The location of his alleged death."

"Aaron," Milo warns through gritted teeth.

"She deserves to know," Aaron snaps, then softens his voice. "The Corps database says he died at the Agency HQ in Seattle."

I bite my lip and shake my head, trying to hold myself together. What could this possibly mean? And why is this the first time I'm hearing about it?

"Now, that doesn't mean he's located there now," Milo says, shooting Aaron another glare. "If he's alive, he could be anywhere, really. But it's a starting point, at least."

"Ren's alleged death by Yesterday bullet was broadcasted everywhere," Aaron says. "If that's really what killed him, they wouldn't mark his cause of death as *classified* in their database. They would have just mentioned the bullet. And it would have been recorded on the actual day of the broadcast."

"But there's still no guarantee that he's... okay," Milo adds warily.

Aaron softens his voice. "We're just trying to figure everything out. That's all."

I stare at the grains in the wooden doorframe, my throat tight. "So what is your theory, exactly?"

"The world already believes he's dead," Aaron says. "I think the Corps is keeping him alive, for one reason or another. And they don't want anyone in their system without the right clearance to know about it. Identifying it as *classified* marks the case as Agent territory, and any suspecting lower-ranks won't question it."

"But none of this makes any sense."

"That's what *we're* saying," Milo mutters.

"But we know one thing for certain," Aaron says. "They're using him for something. I just hope for his sake that they're not done with him yet."

"*Aaron*," Milo hisses. "We talked about this."

"Look, you were the one who wanted to keep this all a secret, not me," Aaron seethes.

"And you still agreed." Milo lowers his volume. "She can't handle—"

"Hey," I snap. "I'm right here, asshole."

Milo presses his lips into a thin line, nostrils flaring. Aaron shoots him a look.

For weeks, I thought the distance between Milo and I was the result of everything I've done. That he was slowly realizing how much I lie and screw things up for people, and he no longer wanted anything to do with me. But all this time, he's been brewing lies of his own—all because he thinks I can't handle the truth.

And Aaron... I shake my head. *I never expected this from him.*

I clench my fingers into fists. "And you've been keeping this from me for how long?"

Aaron and Milo exchange another set of unsure glances.

I narrow my gaze. "How long?"

Aaron's eyes mellow. I can tell he wants to look away, but he holds contact. "February."

I'm going to be sick.

It feels like my head is filled with cotton. The glare of the pendant light feels sharper, each ray drilling a hole into my skull. I press my crossed arms closer to my chest, struggling to maintain my breathing as my heart pounds faster.

This is why Aaron didn't want me in the lighthouse. Why Milo was so adamant on convincing me to move on.

"February." The word falls out quietly, unsure, like it's still finding its place. When it settles, my whole body stiffens. My muscles quiver and everything feels like it's catching fire. "*February?*"

"I know, Voclain, we just—"

"You've known about this—this very real chance that Ren might be alive —since *February*? And you didn't think to tell me?"

"I—"

"Do you have *any idea* how exhausted I am?" My voice cracks. "How hard it's been to manage the guilt and the fear and the..." The words jumble together and I can't finish my sentence. I try to take a deep breath, but it feels like trying to force gravel through a sieve. "There is nothing I want more than to find him. But it's not exactly easy to believe he's still breathing. Not when it feels like every odd is stacked against that possibility."

"Voclain..."

"I've spent *every day* trying so damn hard to convince myself that he's alive. That he's out there somewhere and not *used* or—or *disposed of*." My throat burns as the words scrape against my throat, my voice growing raspy. A lump forms in my throat, and I can feel my eyes glossing over. "Every day of not knowing is another living nightmare. And you didn't tell me."

"I know. Please believe me when I say that."

"You couldn't."

"You're right, and maybe I never will understand. But I'm trying." Aaron swallows. "You think I haven't noticed how hard this has been for you?"

I grit my teeth together.

"Every single day, I see the toll it takes on you. How hard you try to keep yourself together. And I can't stand it."

"Well I'm sorry it's been so hard on you."

"*God*, Voclain. Can't you see? I'm just trying to..." He runs a hand through his hair, laughing bitterly before letting out a deep, trembling sigh. "You carry enough already, alright?"

The way he looks at me tugs at something in my chest. I avert my gaze, staring at the wall.

"We're just trying to protect you," Milo says.

"If I needed protecting, I would have said so."

"Everyone needs protecting, Eddie."

"I can handle myself."

"It's not about what you can handle, alright?" Aaron says. "It's about what you *should*."

"Neither of you have the right to make that decision for me." I chuckle. "You two lied to me for *weeks*, and now you have the audacity to say you did it for *my* sake?"

Milo glares. "It's the truth."

The truth. I don't even know what that is anymore. I inhale sharply and run my fingers through my hair, clutching fistfuls of it. My jaw trembles, and I'm trying so hard to keep from crying that it hurts. When I open my eyes again, they sting. "If you were doing it for my sake, you would have told me."

"Do you really think that knowing would've hurt less?" Milo laughs cynically.

I hone my glare, mouth glued shut.

"We have proof that Ren didn't die from that bullet. But knowing isn't exactly better, Ed. Because you know what this means? It means that the Corps weighed their options and decided that Ren is worth more alive than dead. Whether they've already gotten their use out of him or not, that's a worse fate than any Yesterday bullet. Don't you agree?"

"Milo," Aaron warns under his breath.

"If he hasn't already been interrogated for information or shipped off to the Tombs, then he'll be strung up as a puppet. Or worse," Milo mutters. "Either way, it would've been easier for you to stay blind."

"And let Ren suffer all on his own?" I shout.

"And let us take care of it," Aaron corrects, stepping between my brother and me. He lowers his voice. "Let *me* take care of it."

He looks at me like a wounded animal, and I can't stand it. "I'm not weak."

"Believe me, Voclain. I know," he whispers. "But I'm not strong enough to watch you try to prove it."

I want to break something. I want to shatter glass and pull out my hair and scream into the night until the sound carries over the sea and fades to nothing. But if I open my mouth or move another inch, I know I'll cry, and I can't let myself break down in front of them. Not when they already pity me enough.

"You should have told me."

That's all I can manage to say as I take my leave.

I don't make it halfway through the woods before slumping against a tree and sobbing into my hands.

EDDIE

Wednesday, April 3
66 Beds Made

The note isn't signed, but I don't need a signature to know who it's from.

I know the handwriting well. Thin, condensed letters with *Y*s and *G*s that curl into themselves—the habit of someone who switches back and forth between print and script to write things quickly.

Droplets of water cling to the yellow sticky note, smudging the ink. I stop walking to zip up my jacket and stare at the blanket of dark gray clouds that covers End Harbor. There hasn't been a downpour for days, but I can feel the sky getting restless. It wants to rain.

For now, it barely drizzles.

I furrow my brows and stare at the note in my hands again, scanning it for the dozenth time since I found it slipped under my door this morning. Every time I read it, I carve the crescent lines in my palms just a bit deeper.

Let's talk. Please.

I crumple the note into a ball, shove it into my pocket, and continue my trek to the square.

End Harbor's square is located downtown, surrounded by abandoned brick shops on three sides, with the western edge left open to view the harbor and the sea beyond. It's a sad excuse for a square, really—a large patch of grass, barely the size of an elementary school soccer field, with a few benches on the edges and a crumbling cherub fountain in the middle that's overgrown with thorny vines. Some sort of wild rose, by the looks of it, though it's too dead to bloom.

The grass is damp and slightly muddy beneath my feet as I approach the crowd of Cut folk, and the few End Harbor stragglers who are too curious not to watch but do so over their shoulders, as though they shouldn't. I spot Cecil standing in the middle, conversing with people I don't recognize and taking notes. Viv is there too, wearing a burnt orange sweater and brown cargo pants as she jots something down on a notepad.

"My wedding ring." A woman I don't recognize stands in front of Viv, fidgeting with her hair. "I left it on my nightstand."

Viv nods, her black curls breathing in the morning breeze. "Anything else?"

"In the drawer, there's a photo of my son as a little boy," the woman says. "Do you think you can bring it back to me?"

"Of course." Viv forces a sad smile. The woman nods in thanks before exiting the square.

I shove my hands into the pockets of my jacket and walk up to Viv, who's still writing things down on her notepad. "What's going on?"

"We're taking requests. It's a lot to keep track of, but..." Viv sighs, clicking her pen closed. "They've been through enough already. It's the least we can do."

A rush of guilt spreads through me. Sometimes it's easy to forget that the Cut was more of a home than a base. Some people have lived the majority of their lives knowing nothing else, including Aaron—and Viv.

"I'm... sorry," I manage to mutter. "About the Cut."

Viv studies me for a moment, then places a hand on my shoulder. "You have nothing to be sorry for."

I understand what she means, but I'm not sure I believe her.

I clear my throat and avert my gaze. "I wanted to see if you guys needed any help with anything."

"Cecil and I have this covered for now, and Noriko and Beau are handling equipment and supplies."

Of course. I nod, staring at my shoes.

Viv notices my change in expression and gives me a small smile. "But I think Asa could use some help."

I lift my head up a bit. "Where is he?"

Near the Gate, in a dirt clearing, a row of old white vans and rusting pickup trucks line the ivy-shrouded wall, surrounded by a few pines that shadow the makeshift parking lot in their canopy. Located on the far-east side of the island, the Gate is the wall's only entry and exit point, leading to the small strip of woods that connects End Harbor to the mainland. I spot Asa with his back pressed against a mechanic's creeper, his long legs sticking out beneath the newest-looking van. An open toolbox that I recognize from his old mechanic shop back in the city sits next to him. Seeing it tugs at something in my chest, but I shake the thought aside.

"The fuel line's a bit loose," Asa says from under the van when he hears me approach.

"Is that bad?"

"A tiny leak. Just gotta tighten a few things up a bit." He reaches an arm out. "Hand me that wrench, will you?"

I hand him the tool, then sit down in the dirt to watch him adjust the bolts and fittings. "Is this the van we'll be taking down there?"

Asa nods, still working. "You won't want any leaks while you're on your trip. Otherwise things could go south pretty fast."

"You're not coming?"

He shakes his head.

"Why not?"

He hesitates. "I don't think I can stomach seeing what the Chasers have done to the place."

I stare at my hands. *I'm not so sure I'll be able to either.*

It's quiet for a while as I try to listen past the cawing crows and rustling pines, honing in on the familiar clicks of a wrench. I close my eyes and inhale, pretending that I'm breathing in a sticky-sweet summer afternoon and not the intoxicating perfume of a dark evergreen spring. I think back to those younger days with Ren and Margot, when Asa would buy us ice cream and let us observe him as he repaired cars at his old shop. I almost laugh at how simple life was. How interesting everything used to be when we were all living beneath the veil of childhood ignorance. Now, nothing makes me more restless than sitting still and watching something be fixed.

"Why didn't you tell me about the list?"

Asa freezes, and I swear the crows stop cawing for a moment. So many seconds pass that I expect him to ignore me until he rolls out and speaks, blandly, as though nothing has changed since those summers at all. "Why didn't I tell Margot about her Immunity?"

The question catches me off-guard. After all this time, I've learned to understand why he did what he did—but I've never had the chance to ask him for an answer. "For her protection."

He barely nods and rolls back under the van.

I frown. "Everyone keeps saying that."

"Then it must be true."

"But I didn't ask for it. And protect me from what?"

"The truth."

"What does that even mean?"

"Sometimes it's necessary to keep secrets. For the sake of both parties."

I draw slow circles in the dirt. "It's like everyone here thinks I'm weak. Or a time bomb waiting to go off and do something stupid."

"No one thinks you're weak or stupid, Ed. There are people here who care for your well-being and want you to be safe."

"It's still unfair." My throat tightens. "I deserved to know."

"Well, now that you do... what's changed?"

I stare at my shoes, eyes cloudy. *Milo was right.* Knowing hasn't made the hurt go away; in fact, I think it hurts even worse than it did before. And it doesn't make this whole situation easier to understand either. Now I just have more questions than ever. "Nothing."

Asa continues working, and the air fills with the clinking of metal.

What does he think about the list? No matter how closely I watch Asa, I can't find a solid answer.

I stare at the circles I traced in the dirt, but they're hard to notice among the tiny rocks and decaying pine needles. It's almost like I never made a mark at all.

I'm tired of making no marks. I'm tired of waiting around, tired of withering away, tired of nothing changing. There is so much static and I don't think I can stand it anymore.

I pluck a brittle orange cluster of pine needles from within one of my circles, pinching it between my fingers, spinning it back and forth. With every little rotation, every small movement, a needle falls off until I'm left with nothing but a stem.

I can't stand to sit still any longer. I don't know how or when it will happen, but I'm going to find Ren. And I'm going to bring him back, one way or another.

I finish helping Asa ready the vehicle for the trip, then head to the woods behind the lighthouse for more target practice. I turn left on Main and begin the trek uphill. The town begins to fade into trees, with nothing but pine on my left, and a secluded strip of sand and an endless expanse of sea to my right. A light breeze toys with my hair, the droplets in the air making it frizzier than usual. It's still pretty early in the morning, and the sun hasn't made much of an appearance. Shivering, I pause to zip up my jacket—and that's when I notice something move.

In the corner of my eye, I see a figure standing in the water with only their upper torso visible as they dunk their head in. It takes them a moment to come back up, and I squint when they do, trying to make out the details of their shape over the distance. I spot a familiar satchel in the sand next to a pile of dark clothing.

Aaron slicks his hair back, then cups his palms to splash his face with water. I watch as he glides what looks like a bar of soap over his arms, then turns his head to get his shoulders.

He doesn't flinch when he notices me, but he freezes, studying me without any recognizable expression as I watch him right back. We stand like that for a long time until I remember the crumpled note in my pocket. I glare in his direction and continue walking.

When I'm far enough up the hill, I look over my shoulders, just to see if he's still there. He's looking too.

I don't look back for the remainder of my walk.

I reach my target tree and remove my jacket, setting it on a large rock before taking out my knives. My form has somehow gotten sloppier since yesterday. For the next half hour, no matter how many times I throw, I can't seem to focus enough to hit a decent bullseye. My throws are too jagged and forceful. Even when I close my eyes to drown everything else out—a comfort I've trained myself to rely on over these past few months—it still does nothing to drown out what races through my head.

My mind is like a hornet's nest. Among every worry and preoccupation, what burns most is the anger about that list.

In End Harbor, everyone I interact with is either pitiful or angry. The rest of the strategists underestimate me. Even my own brother thinks I'm fragile and irrational.

But I thought Aaron was different. Sure, he's been paranoid ever since that Harbor man tried to turn me in—but at least he didn't distance himself from me. He's barely left my side since the broadcast, and he treats me exactly the same as he always has. Or so I thought.

This time, the knife hits.

"Not bad."

Aaron leans against a tree, hands in his pockets. His hair is messy but partially slicked back, still wet from his swim. I ignore him and try to pretend he isn't watching when I throw a second blade at the target. It barely hits the outer edge of the ring with a thud.

"You didn't get my note."

I give him a brief side glance before readying my third knife. "I did."

I can feel his stare like pinpricks against my skin. This throw doesn't even hit the tree. I suppress an exhausted sigh as I retrieve my knives.

"We should talk."

"I'm not in the mood." I step back, positioning myself a few yards away from the tree so I can start another round. Squaring my shoulders to the target, I pull my elbow to my ear and throw. I watch the knife spin in the air—and bounce right off the tree.

"Don't flick your wrist like that. Keep it locked." Aaron walks up to me, stands by my side, and nods toward the tree. "Your natural momentum is what's gonna carry your knife to that target. Not a forceful throw."

"I thought I said I didn't wanna talk."

He shrugs. "You don't have to."

I hold back the urge to shoot him a dirty look and focus my attention on the task at hand. With his advice reluctantly in mind, I launch another throw. It spins less and hits the tree, a few inches away from the bullseye.

"Better."

I clench my jaw and ready my third blade, extending my arm to point it toward the bullseye. When I'm confident in my aim, I pull my arm back. But Aaron steps closer, removing one hand from his pocket to point at my feet. "Stance."

I glare at him before checking my footing. *There's nothing wrong with my stance*, I want to tell him. But I remember I'm giving him the silent treatment and hold my tongue.

"Your balance is all off. One foot in front of the other."

I grind my teeth and do as he says, lowering my arm and adjusting so my dominant foot is forward.

"Good." He steps closer. "And you're gonna wanna keep your shoulders square to the target the entire time, not just when you're aiming. You've been pivoting your hips a little."

Aaron walks around to my left, away from my throwing arm. He gives me a look as though asking for permission, and while there are about a thousand things I'd rather do than talk to him right now, I can't pretend that I don't need his advice. I keep my scowl but give him a small nod.

He drops his satchel and stands behind me, placing his hands on my upper arms to straighten my torso. He rests them on my shoulders. "You're too tense."

I wonder why, I think to myself, but I bite my tongue again.

"If you're too rigid, you won't have as much control over the knife's release. It'll lower your accuracy," he explains quietly. "Your throw should be one fluid motion. A seamless transfer of balance."

I soften my posture and try to adjust again, but I'm not sure it's even possible for me to be any more slack than this.

"You hold yourself like that too often. You'll get knots, if you don't have them already." He points to where the curve of my neck meets my shoulder. "Just try to relax."

Relax? I grit my teeth. Relaxing is the last thing I feel like doing right now—especially with him.

"Pretend I'm not even here. It's just you and that tree." I can feel his words against my neck. "Deep breaths."

I close my eyes, breathing in the sharpness of pine, the earthiness of the dirt, the salt of the sea below the hill. No—the salt is coming from his skin, his still-damp hair. The smell of cedarwood and sawdust tickles my nose when I inhale too deeply. I breathe in every piece of my surroundings until I too feel like a part of the whole, a fraction of something endless. My shoulders drop.

"Good. Now aim." Aaron's voice is almost a whisper. "Think beyond the target. Like you're throwing straight through that bullseye."

I open my eyes, extending my arm to aim one last time.

"Now ready your throw. Elbow to the ear."

I pull my arm back.

"Remember what I said about your throw. No flicks, no pivots." He brings his hands to my waist, his touch so light that I wonder if it's really there at all. "Just one fluid motion, that's all it is. Easy as breathing."

Drown it all out, I remind myself. When I close my eyes again, it's like the target is still there, painted to near perfection in my mind. There are no scars in my vision. No distractions. No cloudiness.

But the sounds sharpen and the scents grow stronger. No matter how hard I try to make the rest of the world melt away, the smell of wood dust remains. Wind rustles through the pines, and I swear I can hear Aaron's heartbeat within it.

A thud tells me when my knife hits the tree.

I open my eyes. A perfect bullseye. And all I can think about are the hands that linger on my waist and the breath that melts against my neck, and the minutes that pass like slow-dripping honey. For a moment I'm convinced that no time is passing at all. This is all there is.

"You were right, Eddie," Aaron finally says. "I should have told you everything."

My shoulders tense again. I still can't bring myself to say another word, but this time, I can't remember what point I was trying to prove.

It's not about forgiveness. As much as it pains me, I can understand why they did what they did. Because I've been there before. I'm all too familiar with hiding the truth to protect the people you love—and the gnawing guilt that comes with it. Although I can't shed all of the anger just yet, I know they wouldn't have subjected themselves to that kind of ache if they didn't have a good reason for it.

I'm the one I can't forgive.

Because while Ren is out there all alone, experiencing horrors I can't even bring myself to imagine, I am here, and I am safe. Privileged enough to succumb to the grief and lose myself in the decay of static.

I'm the reason why he's gone. So I should be the reason he's found again. Not them.

I swallow the growing lump in my throat, trying to ground myself, but my breathing is sporadic and shallow, my skin prickling with goosebumps. Aaron's hands are still there, his heartbeat still near. Time is still standing still. Every breath he takes seems to linger on my skin.

Why won't either of us move? I begin to wonder if we can't, like flies who don't know they're trapped in amber.

He sneezes.

It startles us both into separation, and he pulls away. I turn to face him, arms crossed. I can't meet his gaze. "Allergy season?"

"Forget spring. I think I'm allergic to you, Voclain." He sniffles, unable to meet mine either. "Don't let me get so close next time, or I might get hives."

I frown. "You reek of salt."

"Well, as much as I'd love to stay and continue this lovely chat of ours, I have shit to do." He grabs his satchel and slings it over his shoulder. "Are you packed?"

"I own nine things."

"Then keep practicing." He turns around to walk down the hill.

"We're still not speaking!" I shout.

"Whatever you say, Voclain."

I watch him disappear into the trees before removing my knives from the target. But no matter how long I stare at that bullseye, I can't bring myself to throw a single one.

It's dark by the time I get back to my room. I strip out of my clothes and step into my chipped clawfoot tub, turning on the showerhead to let the warm water rinse me clean. Steam rolls off my skin in curling droves, like the fog that creeps into town every morning. The heat unravels some of the knots in my shoulder; I've gotten so used to carrying them with me, I never noticed their presence before.

Relax, I tell myself. We leave tomorrow, and it'll do me no good to stay so worked up. *I'll have to sort out this whole thing with Aaron and Milo once we get back.*

For now, my best next step is to try to get a good night's rest—as hard as that may be now that I can't exactly visit the lighthouse anymore. Not without the same kind of solitude, at least.

I finish my shower and change into an old shirt and the only pair of sweats I own—a luxury in End Harbor, where our clothes are either stolen goods or handmade. If it weren't for the buzzing in my head and the nerves I try to swallow down, I'd almost be comfortable. I *should* be comfortable.

But I can't be when I know what tomorrow brings.

I climb into bed and try to sleep, but I can't stop thinking about Ren. Ever since I saw that closet, I've only had more questions. I want to believe he's alive somewhere. I *do* believe it. I'm just terrified of what truths I'll find when I start looking for them.

Tomorrow, I remind myself. Tomorrow we'll be heading back to the Cut, and I'll finally be in a place where I can start searching for answers. Anything that will lead me back to Ren.

I'm yanked from my thoughts when I hear a loud sneeze outside my door.

My eyes widen, heart pounding against my chest as I whip my hunting knife from beneath my pillow and unsheathe it just as quickly.

I slip out of bed and tiptoe toward the door, knife in hand. I flip on the light switch and open the door, whose bell still has yet to be fixed.

Aaron scrambles to a seated position, taking what looks like a pillow and tossing it down the hall a little too late for it to go unnoticed. He clears his throat and stares at me, shielding his eyes from the warm light flooding out of my room. "I tripped."

I sheath my knife and shove it into my pocket. "You. Get up."

He glares. "I thought we weren't speaking."

"We aren't." I reach down and grab the collar of his shirt, pulling him up. He yanks free once he's standing and leans against the wall, head turned in the other direction.

It's quiet for a moment as I fold my arms across my chest. "Do you do this every night?"

He mirrors the gesture, not saying a word—and then it hits me. His delay in fixing the alarm bell above my door should have given it away days ago. *The lighthouse is too far from where I sleep.*

I understand why he gave up his room for Henry and Abigail. But if he was never planning on leaving my side, the simple solution would have been to stay with me instead—not outside my door.

"I offered to let you stay," I say.

"I know."

I nod, still unable to look at him. "Why didn't you?"

"I did."

Silence.

"This must be killing your back."

"I've slept in worse places."

"And you still refuse to come inside."

He glances at me sideways, then averts his gaze. "Someone has to keep watch."

I stare at my shoes, then back up at him with a sigh. "That was a long time ago. It happened once. Nothing's happened since then."

He shakes his head and stares at his hands, swallowing. "It happens more often than you'd think."

My heart sinks. I notice his leg is shaking. He taps his fingers against his folded arms, like they're itching to do anything but remain still.

I stare at the patterns in the carpet as my mind brings me back to that night. We'd only been in End Harbor for a few days. I was bedridden with grief—wouldn't drink, wouldn't eat, yet somehow couldn't stop sobbing and throwing up either. I did nothing but weave in and out of slumber and bursts of nauseating tears.

That first week felt like an eternity. My memories are fuzzy and blend together, but the one thing I know for certain is that Aaron didn't leave my side. Not once. A few of the strategists came in and out to sit in silence that I can't recall or tell me stories I could barely hear, but all I remember is that Aaron was the one making sure that I was fed and hydrated. That I wasn't alone. He was there for me at my absolute worst. Even Milo couldn't stand the sight of it all enough to visit for long.

The night Aaron finally decided to allow himself to catch up on sleep in his own room, I received a visitor.

In his sleep-deprived state, Aaron had forgotten to lock the door on his way out. The Harbor man entered quietly with a kitchen knife. At the time, I was too out of it to realize that Aaron had made sure my own blade was tucked beneath my pillow. I was weaponless, weakened by malnutrition and days spent barely moving at all.

I woke to the kitchen knife pressed firmly against my neck. The Harborer said he'd kill me if he had to—the reward was less for my dead body, but still substantial enough that he wouldn't think twice before slitting my throat. That's how he got me to exit my room and walk down the hall toward the staircase without making a sound. Half of me thought I was dreaming. He was muttering something about being fed up with his life at End Harbor, about wanting to go back to the way things were before his arrival. About trading my life for his old one, because when it matters, this side is going to lose.

If he hadn't tripped over his own feet in the dark, I don't think I would've had the energy or the will to fight back. What finally woke Aaron was the series of thuds that traveled down the stairs, and the sound the man's neck made when he struck the bottom.

Aaron found me sitting on the top step, clinging to the railing that had saved my life. It took him a long time to pry my trembling fingers from the wood.

He installed the alarm bell the next day.

I blink away the memory and stare at the Aaron of this moment, who still seems to be stuck in that one. "Come inside. You need sleep."

More silence.

"Let me take the floor," I whisper. "Let me keep watch."

Aaron's gaze finally meets mine. "Allergies, Voclain. Remember?" He peels himself from the wall to retrieve his thrown pillow, then lies by the door again with his back facing me. "Now go before you give me hives."

I glare at him for a moment longer before turning off the light. I can't bring myself to close the door completely on my way back to bed.

EDDIE

Thursday, April 4
67 Beds Made

♪ HEAVEN UP THERE - PALACE ♪

My entire life fits in my pockets.

Carvings. Hunting knife. Throwing knives. Lighter. Margot's locket and my father's bracelet never leave my person, but I trace them both, just to be certain they're still there. It's a habit I practice more often than I should.

I slip into my baggy pair of jeans and a thin but warm black long sleeve shirt. I zip up my dark orange puffer and shove the rest of my clothes into the backpack that Aaron must have dropped off while I was still asleep, which is filled with a few days' worth of oats, a tiny jar of cinnamon, a thermos of water, and the final product of the wooden spoon he'd been carving, which has a message engraved in small letters across the handle.

Eat.

I flip it over.

We both know you'd forget without me.

I roll my eyes and shove it back into the bag. There's also a mint tin first aid kit with a handful of bandaids, a pair of tweezers, a needle, a roll of medical thread, and what looks like a tiny scalpel. *Of course.*

I sling the bag over my shoulder and head for the door, pausing with my hand wrapped around the knob to give my room one last glance. *I'll be back*, I reassure myself. I take my exit.

Although it's tainted by pale gray clouds, the sky is clear enough for me to see the sunset as I walk away from the Vermillion and head left, down Main Street. I still can't help but question the lack of rain, but the colors give me a little bit of warmth to hold onto. There is some noteworthy healing quality to the pale golds and honey ambers that streak the sky with just the slightest hint of blood orange, like a flickering hearth in the middle of a snowstorm.

The strategists agreed to meet by the Gate at nightfall, so I know I'm a little early. But I couldn't stand sitting around and waiting in my hotel room. Just as I'm about to head east, I spot a familiar figure to my right.

Aaron is swimming again, and I frown. *What is he doing?*

I almost keep going but I stop myself, looking back over my shoulder and then up at the sky, which is shifting by the minute. *We still have a little bit of time.*

I turn and cut across the pavement, pausing once I reach a wooden bench at the edge of the sidewalk. I don't even want to think about the last time I set foot in sand. I swallow, the lighter in my pocket suddenly heavier than the bag over my shoulder.

I take a seat, waiting for him to see me so we can get going. All of town is crammed inside the church for their weekly gathering, leaving the beach and the rest of End Harbor completely vacant, save for Aaron and me. At this hour, in this emptiness, I'd believe it if someone told me it was a ghost town.

The warmth in the sky has desaturated to a cool silver, with a few rays of pale gold extending through the breaks in the clouds, showering down on the dark waves like little flecks of precious metal floating upon the surface.

Everything glistens to the rhythm of the waves, shimmering in the light in a way that's almost blinding.

I watch Aaron's head sink beneath it all, swimming so far out there until he disappears. A rush of panic floods through me until I see his head reappear again. He swims back to shore and emerges in the waist-deep shallows, whipping his head back and running his hands through his hair. In the light, he almost looks ethereal, his body a silhouette against the nearly colorless sunset behind his back.

He sees me waiting on the bench and folds his arms, giving me a look I have to squint to read from my distance. I furrow my brows, and he rolls his eyes before nodding toward a pile of clothes on the sand. My face warms and I turn the other way.

I wait for him to get dressed, facing straight ahead once he takes a seat next to me.

"I didn't know you like swimming," I say.

"I don't."

"Says the guy who's out here every day."

Aaron flinches, giving me a brief side glance. "So you noticed."

I stare at the sea, watching the waves roll back and forth. Even with the setting sun—even as the sea drenches itself in a soft, almost citrine glow—everything is so blue. Deep, desaturated, melancholy blue.

I turn to face him, our gazes catching on each other. They simmer like that for a long time. "Why do you come out here?"

"Do you have any idea how beneficial cold swims are for your health? And in saltwater too? I'm telling you, Voclain. You should try it sometime. Strengthened immunity, better circulation, soothed anxiety, better lymphatic flow, leukocyte production, better sleep—"

"What the hell is a leukocyte?"

"Very funny." He gives me a look, and when I'm still just as clueless, he sharpens it into a glare. "Leukocytes? The white blood cells that keep you from, I don't know, *dying*?"

I shake my head.

"They fight off diseases and shit?"

"I didn't know that."

"You're killing me, Voclain."

I scowl. "I'm not gonna apologize for not knowing what a leukocyte is."

We go quiet for a moment. I know there must be more to his answer, but I don't question it.

He sighs, leaning back against the bench, staring at the sun as it sinks deeper below the horizon. "Doesn't it always seem to be breathing?"

"What?"

He pauses. "Everything."

I pull away my gaze to see what he's talking about. I watch tufts of wild grass sway in the breeze. Above me, an arrow of geese heads north. Sand crabs bubble beneath the surface of the wet sand closest to the edge of the water, and the waves roll back and forth in an endless lull. I see what he's talking about. I feel it.

I keep my eyes fixed straight ahead. There is something entrancing about the waves, but I don't like the way the feeling settles in my stomach. The dying sun gilds the tide in an eerie glow, like an illusion of heaven designed to draw you into its riptide and never let go. I trace the lighter's edge in my pocket, trying not to think about how much the sea has already taken. About what the waves can't give back.

"Sometimes I think, *If I just swim far enough—if I just keep going—I'll reach somewhere. Anywhere but here,*" Aaron mutters. "You know?"

I do, but I don't say anything.

"Some days I tell myself I'd give anything for things to be different." He stares at the sea, then at his hands. Like he's scared of what anything could mean.

"Do you ever think about leaving?" I ask.

"Don't you?"

I pause. "Why don't you? Leave?"

For a moment I'm convinced I know the answer. He has responsibilities to tend to here, and he's sacrificed the majority of his life to this cause; there would be no point in leaving it all behind now, as dreadful as End Harbor may be. I wonder if he even knows who he is without a role, or if the suit he's been told to wear has been sewn into the fibers of his skin, impossible to remove even if he wanted to. But he looks at me in a way that makes me question my line of thinking

Maybe he does want to leave, I realize. Just not alone.

I can feel puffs of breath against my cheek when I look at him again, even with the wind. He turns his head away, straightening his posture to stare at the fading sun instead.

"When you go out there in the water..." I reword my question and lower my voice to a whisper. "Why do you turn back around?"

He looks at me again. His eyes bore into mine, and for the rarest fraction of time, I swear I can read him clearly. "The tide."

I nod, staring back at the sea. "Must be some tide."

He nods too, but his stare doesn't shift. I can feel it burrowing into my skin like it never intends to leave. I can still feel it when he finally looks away. Even as the horizon darkens. Even as he answers like it's the surest thing he's ever said. "The strongest pull I know."

For the briefest of moments, I swear he gives me one last glance.

I clear my throat, standing up and slinging my bag over my shoulder. "We should head over."

Aaron doesn't move. "I'll meet you at the Gate. I just need a few more minutes."

I nod, turning around to walk away. When I look back over my shoulder, watching him hold onto the last sliver of dying light, I can't help but wonder if he sees ghosts too.

I'm the second-to-last person to arrive at the Gate.

The strategists involved in the mission crowd around it, broken into little discussion groups while they wait. I spot Lori chatting with Milo and Alice off to the side. Mayor Wagner watches it all unfold with his arms crossed, though he doesn't spare me a glance.

Cecil notices me approach and raises a brow. "Where's—"

"Moping on a bench."

"Ah. Of course." Cecil sighs. "Well, he better get here soon. We want time on our side."

I nod, understanding what he means. If we had nothing to worry about, the trip would only take us a few hours. But since we have to be careful about the breadcrumbs we're leaving and who we run into, we'll have to take winding back roads to get there. And we won't be driving logically either—we'll be going in different directions to leave as subtle of a trace as possible. In other words, it could take a whole day's worth of driving to reach the Cut.

Milo spots me, averting his gaze when I notice him looking. I almost expect him to keep ignoring me until he breaks away from his group, walking over to where I stand. "Hey."

"Hey."

He shoves his hands in his pockets, staring at his shoes. I wrap my arms around my stomach and look over my shoulder, pretending to watch for Aaron as a light breeze ruffles my hair. Milo uses his feet to fidget with a pebble in the dirt, rolling it back and forth.

"So the day's finally here, huh?" he says, still unable to meet my gaze.

I nod, clenching my jaw, trying to suppress the growing frustration festering in my gut. *You'll work everything out when you get back*, I remind myself. *Worry about it then, not now.* "It is."

Milo nods too, still kicking at the rock with his shoe. "You got everything you need?"

"I do."

He hesitates, lifting his chin up to stare at the Gate, and then finally at me. "Do you know how long you guys will be gone?"

I shrug. "It depends. A few days. A week, maybe. Could be longer."

We're quiet again for a while. I see Aaron approaching from the corner of my eye, and before I can say my pathetic goodbye, Milo steps forward and wraps his arms around me. I'm taken by surprise for a moment, eyes wide and brows creased. Then my shoulders relax, and I hug him back, finally remembering what it feels like to embrace the brother I've missed more than anything.

"Don't do anything stupid, okay?" he says. "That's my job, not yours."

I hold him tighter, closing my eyes and trying not to think about what will happen once I let go.

"Alright, guys. Time to hit the road," Cecil announces to everyone once Aaron arrives.

Milo pulls away, eyes glossy as he forces something resembling a grin. "You'll be okay."

I give him a small smile. "I'll see you around."

Every strategist is silent as we pile into the van. Hugo takes the back seat, the other half of the row folded down to make room for supplies. Viv and Beau slide into the second row first, and then Aaron, who lets me have the left window seat. Noriko takes shotgun, and once Cecil climbs into the driver's seat, we're off.

I stare out the rear windshield, watching the colossal set of wood doors swing shut behind us and lock once again. I realize this is my second time seeing the outer side of that Gate.

As it grows smaller and smaller, vanishing into nothing at all, all I can do is hope there will be a third.

EDDIE

Thursday, April 4
67 Beds Made

The first hour stretches on in a syrupy, suffocating kind of silence. No one wants to talk about the fact that the last time we were all in a vehicle, we were fleeing—even Noriko, who may not have escaped the Blurt with the rest of us, but sure as hell escaped something just as horrible. Maybe even worse. I shiver as I try to forget about the frigid floor of that milk truck, and the feeling of cold milk and blood running through my hair.

No one else can sleep either. It's hard to willingly close your eyes when there is no telling how much time you have left to keep them open. So we sit and marinate in the absence of conversation, listening to the sound of wheels churning against crumbling pavement, and the concentrated sweeps of metal against wood.

"You really shouldn't be playing with knives in a moving car, buddy," Cecil finally says, glancing at Aaron through the rear-view mirror. "I feel like we've had this conversation already."

"Says the man who gave him his first knife before he knew basic multiplication," Noriko points out from the front seat.

"Would you rather have him piss himself?" Beau asks, his uncut auburn hair bouncing as he flicks his chin in Aaron's direction. "*Buddy's* still afraid of cars. That knife's like his binky."

"Yeah C, would you rather have me piss myself?" Aaron keeps his eyes glued to his carving while he kicks Beau in the shin. Beau moves his leg like he's going to kick back, but Aaron gives him a side glance. "Bite me, Hackney. I dare you."

"I will and you know it."

"Well, everyone's afraid of something, I guess," Cecil says. "Even Aaron."

I hold back a smile, fondly remembering our smuggling jobs from last summer. Particularly the threat against my life in the event that I crashed the car with him in the passenger's seat.

"For the record, I'm not *afraid* of cars. I just don't trust them." Aaron sets the chunk of wood in his lap, crossing his arms and glaring at Cecil. "I won't be taking criticism from the guy who's scared of snakes."

"And you're not?"

"They're cute as hell."

Viv nods. "Aaron has a point, C."

"They're like worms," Beau adds.

Aaron points a thumb at Beau. "Yeah, what he said."

"Then what's your poison, kiddo?" Cecil says. "There's gotta be something worse than driving."

"Or snakes."

"You know," Noriko says, turning to face us. "There's a pretty good story behind his fear."

"*Worst* fear," Cecil corrects, shaking his head. "There's nothing like getting bitten by a rattlesnake."

Aaron's eyes widen. "I never knew you got bit."

"I'm surprised your dad never mentioned it. He's the one who saved me, after all."

"Yeah, well. You know how we are." Aaron resumes his carving. "We don't exactly talk about things like that."

I look up at Aaron, and if he notices he certainly doesn't show it.

"You mentioned a story and we're still waiting," Hugo says.

"Well, Simon and I were on some smuggling run in our earlier days.

I don't even remember what we were doing. All I can remember is that damn bite."

"They'd set up camp somewhere and Simon was off getting water," Noriko explains. "When he came back, he found Cecil trying to saw off his own foot with a pocket knife."

"I still have the scars to prove it," Cecil chuckles. "He got there just in time. It was swelling like crazy, but he was able to clean it and bandage me up. Luckily we had some antivenom back at the Cut. If he hadn't carried me back, I doubt I would have made it." Cecil turns to face Aaron. "How long's the shelf life for that stuff?"

"Three years when stored frozen."

"Would there be any left, you think?"

"He stocked up last year."

"We should definitely raid your dad's old lab, then." Cecil faces the road again. "Just in case."

"The key is keeping the bite below heart level," Aaron adds, sweeping his knife against the unrecognizable piece of wood in his hands. "Slows the spread of venom."

"That's what your dad said back then." Cecil lets out a descending whistle. "Man. That bite was the only injury that made me cry in years."

"What did it feel like?" Viv asks.

Cecil pauses. "Fire."

"And there's *my* poison," Hugo mutters.

"Oh really now?" Noriko turns to face him, raising the brow above her eyepatch. "You're afraid of fire?"

The lighter in my pocket suddenly feels heavier again.

"Who isn't?"

"Fire is much worse than cars," Aaron mutters. I glance at him, noticing the discomfort in his gaze. *He's a healer*, I think to myself. He's probably seen what it can do to people.

"Fire's great," Beau adds.

"Not when you come from California."

"You're from California?" I ask, turning around in my seat to face him. He nods. "Wildfires are no joke."

I nod, remembering everything I learned back in school. As global climates worsened before the Pick was put into place, California seemed to take the country's worst hit. They were the most populated and still had less water to go around than some of the smaller states—and there seemed to be a newsworthy fire every week. There are still fires occasionally, from what I've heard, but at least they have more than enough water now. I don't think I can stomach thinking about why that's the case.

"Then how'd you end up in Washington?"

"My parents heard about the Cut through a chipped man passing through town who'd done business with them in the past," Hugo explains. "We were already desperate to get out of California. It's like its own little world. Barely any room to breathe—or breathable air, for that matter. Not to mention the cost of living. My moms both had well-paying jobs and we still barely got by."

"I'm sorry. That sounds..."

"Awful?" Hugo chuckles. "It was."

"So why the fear of fires?" Noriko asks.

"They woke me up in the middle of the night saying something about a fire. They put me in the car and just... drove. Never even looked back. Though I was too young to remember much about what life was like before to miss a thing about it." He stares down at his hands. "I do remember the firestorm in the rear-view mirror, though."

"Even I never knew that," Noriko says quietly. "I'm so sorry, kid. That must have been terrifying."

He nods, staring out the window. "Even the rain is no match for a fire that size."

"Didn't Cecil mention a big Unseen base up in northern California?" I ask, trying to change the subject.

"My parents didn't exactly see eye-to-eye with their... overarching philosophy, if you will."

I nod, about to ask more questions until Hugo speaks first. He looks up at the front seat and nods at Noriko. "What about you?"

"My worst fear..." Noriko says, trailing off in thought. "Getting caught, probably."

All of us nod in unison.

Aaron's knife scrapes loudly against the wood in his hands. "No one wants to run into a Chaser."

I glance at his hands. He no longer wears bandages, but I can see the remaining scabs on his right knuckles and the slightly crooked finger that is still taped to another. I think back to what he said that day and wonder if he really meant it.

I can't shake the feeling that he did.

"And yet here we are, willingly walking into a whole den of them," Viv jokes.

"While we're on the subject of fear, I'll admit it. I don't think Viv is scared of anything," Hugo says.

"Viv is probably *my* worst fear," Beau adds in agreement.

"And you're mine," she snaps. "On like, a societal level."

Beau sticks out his tongue.

"But I'm scared, alright," Viv mutters, shaking her head. "You don't last long in this world without being afraid of something."

"Then what's your Achilles heel?" Noriko asks.

Viv pauses, placing a finger on her lips while she stares out the window in thought. "Spiders."

Cecil snorts. "I've seen you scare off a grizzly bear with a few pots and pans, and you're telling me you're afraid of *spiders*?"

"I've seen you do much worse things for a guy afraid of snakes."

"Spiders are pretty cute too," Aaron points out.

"They're like the puppies of bugs," Beau says. "I mean, have you even seen a jumping spider?"

"Actually, *domestic silk moths* are the puppies of insects," Aaron argues. "Give me one of those and I'll love you forever."

"It's a deal, babe."

Aaron chooses violence again, kicking Beau's shin without hesitation.

"Those don't even exist out in the wild," I note, remembering something I read in one of the McLellans' old encyclopedias and ignoring the sharp twinge in my chest that comes with it. "Out here, your best bet for a puppy moth is a Polyphemus."

"Fine. I'll take one of those, then."

"Hey Beau." Viv folds her arms, nodding in his direction with her lips curled. "Am I really your worst fear?"

"You're definitely far up on the list, but probably not."

"Then what is it?"

Beau hesitates. "Guns."

Viv scoffs. "No way."

"So you're telling me our weapons specialist is afraid of guns?" Cecil asks.

"Everyone should be afraid of guns," Beau says, taking me by surprise. It's not often that he says anything with substance. "That's why I was interested in them in the first place. Because I wanted to understand them."

Noriko nods. "I get that."

"When you understand the things you're afraid of, they're not as scary. And easier to defend against," he continues. "I mean, when I think about a gun as a collection of a bunch of different components that I do understand, then the whole itself... I don't know. I'm less afraid of it." Beau stares at his hands. "But... still afraid."

"Which is a good thing," Noriko says, giving Beau a smile.

"So, Aaron," Cecil says, glancing at him through the rear-view mirror. "Your worst fear can't be driving now, can it?"

"Oh, Cecil. You should know me better than this by now." Aaron smirks, chuckling as he scrapes a curling sliver of wood from the unidentifiable shape in his hands. "I wouldn't trust anyone with a secret like that."

Cecil gives Aaron a knowing look in the mirror, grinning as he shakes his head.

Trust, I realize. Is that what he fears?

"So that leaves us with you, Ed," Cecil says before I can dwell on the thought for any longer. "If you could pick a worst fear, what would it be?"

My throat tightens as I take a moment to think. "I... don't know yet."

Cecil raises a brow. "So you're not afraid of anything?"

I shake my head. *I'm afraid of too many things to choose.* "I'm just saving it."

I have a feeling I'll know when I find it.

Cecil drives for another hour or two until he can no longer keep his eyes open. We're still too far out into the woods for there to be any other cars on the road, especially at this hour, but we hide ourselves just in case. Cecil finds an abandoned rest stop from the Yesterdays and pulls the van over into the nearby woods.

We're all too tired to complain about the state of the place. Even Aaron doesn't say much as we step out to stretch our legs and wash up for the night in the old cabin-style bathroom that hasn't been touched in decades. Everything is laced in cobwebs and reeks of rot. I notice termite holes in the walls and shudder. There's a run-down gas station with a market too, though it's clearly been out of order for longer than I've been alive. The mirror above my sink is cracked in a mosaic of shards, a thousand eyes staring back at me when I look into it. I shudder, unable to hear my own heartbeat over the sound of flies buzzing somewhere in the background.

Viv washes her face in the sink next to me. "What is it they say about a broken mirror? Isn't it supposed to bring seven years of bad luck?"

"Something like that."

She turns off the faucet, pulling a clean cloth from her bag to pat her face dry. "I read somewhere that you can reverse it, though."

I raise a brow. "Oh really?"

She grins wryly. "You're supposed to cloud a piece of it with fire and bury it a year later. You still have bad luck for that one year, but it's better than seven, I guess."

I stare at the mirror again, unable to think of anything but the jewel-red compound eyes of a house fly rubbing its hands. Or a spider.

"All in the name of preserving your reflection or your soul or something."

"Makes sense." I turn my head to face Viv, suppressing a grin. "I didn't know you were superstitious."

"Didn't know you were either." Viv shrugs and slings her bag over her shoulder. "People will surprise you every now and then."

She gives me a wink and takes her leave.

After she's gone, I steal one more glance at the broken mirror. I take a shard, shove it into my pocket, and follow her outside.

"*Shit.*" Cecil winces when he checks how much gas we've blown through. "We must've been driving for longer than I thought."

While he and Noriko chat and fill up our vehicle, I roam around for a few minutes, scoping the area. Aaron leans against the side of a tool shed, carving in a silent concentration I'm almost afraid to break.

I head to the old market, curious about what's inside. The automated doors don't open when I stand in front of them, so I have to peel them open myself. Something squealing scurries away the moment I step inside. I set off a digital welcome bell and jump back at the sound, which is distorted and out of tune. Spider-like shivers crawl down my spine and the hair on the back of my neck stands on end.

I turn on a light, which emits a cool green that flickers and hums like it's swarming with flies. Broken glass crunches beneath my boots as I walk down aisles of rusty metal shelves stripped nearly barren of goods, save for a few rows of cleaning supplies, boxes of Yesterday candy, and cheap souvenirs that tell me we're somewhere near Olympic National Park. *End Harbor must be farther north than I thought.*

I stare at a sun-faded keychain, trying and failing to ignore the painful twist in my gut and the hitch in my breath. I'm so far from my home in northern Oregon, so far from the home I'd briefly made near its border at the Cut. I don't even know what to call home anymore. Maybe I don't even have one. *Maybe I never will.*

The door slides open, making a scraping sound as it shuts again. I hear footsteps too light to be Aaron's and turn to see Beau strutting inside with his hands in his pockets, observing the rows of Yesterday goods in child-like excitement.

"Holy shit." He chuckles, pulling out an old chocolate bar from one of the boxes on the shelves. "You think this is still good?"

"Absolutely not." I walk over there to take it from his hands, putting it back in the box. "What are you, four? Do I really need to be babysitting you right now?"

"Twenty-one," he corrects. "And to answer your question, probably."

I roll my eyes as we continue to browse the aisles, my curiosity too strong to ignore. I look over my shoulder and out the dusty sliding glass door behind us. I can see everyone except for Aaron exploring the truck stop. *Is he still over by the shed?*

"Hey." I turn to face Beau, who's churning one of those solar-powered hand crank flashlights they give to kids. This one is pink and shaped like a pig. "Do you know what's been up with Aaron recently?"

Beau stops rotating the handle. The mechanic whirring ceases, and the lights emitting from the pig's nostrils wane into nothing. He gives me a glance before shoving it in his pocket with a shrug. "I dunno. You'd know better than me."

"Is it the trip?" I ask, remembering the way he insisted on taking a few minutes at the bench. "Is he angry about what happened? Or scared to go back?"

Beau shrugs again, picking up another chocolate bar. This time I'm too preoccupied to stop him from peeling open the wrapper. The chocolate is powdery white now, grainy and muddled from the fat and sugar blooms swirling across its surface. "How old do you think this is?"

"Older than you." I swat it out of his hands before he can take a bite. "Now tell me."

"There's nothing to tell. He's just like that."

"Like what?"

"Angry. Closed off."

I stare at the shelf in thought. My eyes linger on a faded tin of sardines with a smiling cartoon fish on the label that looks a little too happy to be on the receiving end of a hook. Almost like it doesn't even realize it's been caught.

Aaron has been inherently cynical for as long as I've known him; I'm no stranger to his anger. *But why is he suddenly overflowing with so much of it?*

I don't blame him. Not even a little bit. I'm just trying to understand.

"Did something happen to him?" I ask.

"What do you mean?"

"Before I met him," I say. "What's making him so angry?"

Beau goes quiet for a moment. "He's just... the guy's seen some really dark shit, alright?" He sighs. "I mean, we all have our fair share of monsters to fear. But... he has more hiding under the bed than most of us."

"So he's... seen things." I swallow, my mouth suddenly dry. "Like, on smuggling jobs?"

I remember the gunshot in the parking garage, the man he had to silence.

Beau looks at me like he wants to say more, but he only nods. "Something like that."

I lean against the shelf, staring through the shop's front glass again. "I just wish he would talk to me, you know?"

Beau leans against the shelf across from me. He picks up a dusty box of collapsible metal roasting sticks, pulling one out and extending it like it's a fork-tongued sword. "Trying to get Aaron to open up is like poking a snake with a stick."

"What do you mean?"

"It doesn't matter how curious you are." He stares at the two-pronged blade, not meeting my gaze for a long time. "Keep at it for long enough and you'll only get bit."

I open my mouth to say more, but Beau shifts before I can say anything, and before I know it we're browsing the aisles again as though the conversation never happened.

"Do you think they have ice cream?" Beau says as we walk toward the freezer room in the back, whose glass door and windows have been painted with so much grime it's impossible to see through. More broken glass crunches against the bottom of my shoes like snow.

"Doubt that freezer's still working, Beau."

"We'll just have to see for ourselves, then." He slides open the door, stirring up a cloud of dust. It's so thick I can hardly see through it, and I swat it away with a cough, holding my elbow to my nose.

When the dust finally clears, the world goes quiet. My arms fall to my sides. The lights stop buzzing. My breathing stops.

I'm staring directly into the hollow sockets of a human skull.

EDDIE

Thursday, April 4
67 Beds Made

I'm not sure how many moments we stand there, frozen in a corrosive, blood-curdling silence, until we both scream at the same exact time.

"Shit shit shit *SHIT*." Beau's hands fly up to his head as he grabs desperate fistfuls of his hair, tugging at it like a lifeline. "Please tell me you're seeing this too."

I can't reply, because I stumble off to the side, keel over, and vomit on the tile.

Barely seconds after the screams, the front door flies open. Frantic footsteps grow louder and louder until Viv and Aaron are standing behind us. From the corner of my eye, I see Viv bring a trembling hand to her mouth, like she's trying to keep herself from doing exactly what I'm still finishing up.

I turn my head back to the skull. The sounds and sights around me flood back into focus as I realize the skull is attached to a spine, and a ribcage, and a pelvic bone and femurs and—

I swallow more vomit before it can escape.

There are four whole skeletons, asleep beneath a blanket of dust, crawling with a dozen screaming rats who scurry away like we're what should be feared and not them.

I shiver so violently it aches. I keep my eyes glued to the bones as Aaron helps me up, wiping dirt and broken glass from my knees. I still haven't blinked by the time he pulls away, stepping back to get a good look at the whole picture.

Viv points at a Nightjade syringe on the ground. "This was an extermination."

I can hear Beau swallow. He trembles. "They just left the bodies?"

"Maybe the Cleaners didn't want to make the trip out here," Viv says. "Too much of an inconvenience."

"Unless the Cleaners were never called."

We all stare at Aaron, who can't peel his gaze from the skulls. His eyes look just as hollow as theirs.

"Elaborate," Viv says.

"I used to see things like this all the time," Aaron says. "On smuggling trips."

"Like what?" Beau asks, unrecognizably quiet.

"Usually when you stumble across an extermination that was never properly Cleaned..." The muscles in his jaw convulse, like he's trying not to grind his teeth to dust. "It wasn't exactly authorized."

"And any potential civilian witness wouldn't be able to report an incident because a Chaser would be the one to report it to," Viv realizes. "They'd get exterminated for Slander."

"So they just get away with it?" Beau's voice wavers. "Even when they do a shit job of covering up their mistake?"

"They didn't even bother to hide their evidence," Viv mutters.

"Even a Chaser isn't fully Immune to murder charges," Aaron says. "Not an Officer, at least. An Agent, definitely. But a higher-up is more likely to turn the other way than crack down on an Officer who's doing their job and fulfilling quota... in one way or another."

He steps forward and crouches in front of the bones, studying them. Somber, but unfazed, like he's done so a thousand times. *He is a healer, after all*, I note. He's probably seen his fair share of human bones.

"What I'm having trouble understanding is the reasoning behind an unauthorized extermination." Viv shakes her head slowly. "Some sort of agenda? Something personal?"

"The reason?" Aaron chuckles, shaking his head. "More often than not, there isn't one at all."

I try to keep my last bit of food down.

"How is this even allowed to happen?" Viv's lip quivers. "Killing without reason... I don't understand it."

"They're Chasers." Aaron rises, rigid and stiff. "That's kind of the whole point, isn't it?"

We stand still for a long time until Viv turns to leave, shepherding a shaking Beau through the aisles and out the door. Aaron and I stay behind, neither of us able to say anything as we stare in unblinking silence. Eventually he places a hand on my shoulder, letting me know that he's still here. That *I'm* still here, frozen in time and space, even though I'm trying so hard to pull away. When I finally peel my eyes from the bones, I can still see them clearly in my head, like a photo that's been permanently seared into my vision. Another scar to blur my sight.

I'm still trembling when Aaron guides me out. Still trembling when I take one last look and notice something that I hadn't before.

Two of the skeletons are holding hands.

No one says a word as we set up camp next to the van, which is parked about a three-minute walk into the woods. It's still not far enough away from the gas station. Cecil gets some sleep inside the vehicle, along with Hugo and Noriko, but I haven't been able to bring myself to even try shutting my eyes. Beau and Viv seem to be having the same problem, and we sit outside on a few logs circled around a moth-buzzing lantern. Aaron leans against a boulder a few yards behind us, keeping watch. The rhythmic sound of his knife scraping against wood is familiar enough to provide a little comfort, but not much.

After a while, Cecil climbs out of the car, his broad shoulders wrapped in a red knit blanket. Because he'd been sleeping, his eyepatch is nowhere to be seen, leaving his scarred and empty left socket exposed. A fur trapper hat covers the sides of his head, and he pulls the blanket tighter around him as he takes a seat next to Beau and me, shivering with a thermos of coffee in his hands. "No campfire?"

"No campfire, no smoke," Aaron calls out from behind us. "Unless we want to get noticed."

"Whatever you say, buddy," Cecil shouts back, then lowers his voice, shaking his head. "That kid…"

"He has more paranoia than an eighty-year-old survivalist who hoards canned beans for Armageddon," Viv says, zipping up her windbreaker. "It's freezing."

"He has a good point," Cecil says. "Smoke is the best way to get yourself seen."

"I'm hungry, though," Beau says.

"Don't look at me. You have oats in your pack."

"Yeah, but cold oatmeal is gross."

"What do you want me to do about it?" Cecil frowns. "There's probably a stove somewhere back at the rest stop."

"I'm not going back in there," Beau says quietly, staring at his hands and fidgeting with his thumbs.

A light breeze laces through the pine branches above us before making its way through my hair. I bring a numb hand to my head, trying to wrangle the strands behind my ears.

"Here." Beau takes a seat next to me. He pulls a rubber band from his pocket and holds it in his mouth as he divides my hair into three strands. "Your hair's a mess."

Before I form a comeback, a memory floods through me, of Ren's voice and river clay, of muffled laughter and gold glints of light and dark green water—and falling. Sinking. Reaching.

The feeling passes through me like the breeze, and I'm left with an ache in my chest.

I shove the thoughts aside as Beau weaves my hair together. "Where did you learn how to braid?"

"I grew up with younger sisters," he says through the hair tie in his teeth. "I'm a pro at this."

"I don't think I've met them yet."

Viv and Cecil flinch. Beau pauses, then clears his throat. "They're not at the Cut. Or, weren't. Still aren't, I guess."

"God, that's getting real annoying," Viv says, changing the subject and looking over my shoulder at Aaron. "Can't he put that thing away for one second?"

"It's like I said before. A knife to Aaron is like a pacifier to a crying baby." Beau finishes the braid, ties it off, and gives me a pat on the shoulder. "That'll keep your hair out of your face."

I suppress a small grin. "Thank you."

Beau returns to his seat. "I'd rather deal with the carving than Aaron's version of *crying baby*."

"Alright you two, quit it," Cecil mumbles. "He's the one keeping watch so *you* can get some sleep."

"He's always keeping watch," Beau says.

"I just don't get why he has to *carve* while doing it." Viv rolls her eyes. "It's like nails on a chalkboard."

"He's gotta be carving something," Cecil says quietly, taking a sip of coffee from his thermos. "Just be thankful it's only wood."

"Oh, come on. Ease up a bit, will you?" Beau says. "Surely there's *something* about Aaron that drives you absolutely nuts."

"I could list ten things about *all* of you that I can't stand." Cecil shoots Beau a glare, then lowers his voice. "You both know he's been through a lot. Just cut him some slack, alright? These past few days have been torture for all of us."

Everything goes dead quiet.

"Well, I'm tired." Beau rubs his hands together as he stands.

"Me too," Viv says. They head inside the van to join Hugo and Noriko, leaving Cecil and I alone at our makeshift, smokeless campfire.

The silence drags on as I observe the lantern and its moths. Cecil extends the thermos to me. "Coffee?"

I nod and take a sip, savoring the warmth. No sugar, no milk. Just plain black coffee, exactly how I like it. I hand the thermos back to Cecil.

"How are you feeling, kid?"

I glance up at him, unable to tell which of the events swirling through my mind he could be referring to. "Fine."

"That doesn't sound too convincing." He takes another sip and sighs, leaning forward with his elbows on his knees as he nods toward the light. "Sad, aren't they?"

"What?"

"The moths."

I stare at the lantern. A moth helplessly circles it, imprisoned in a dance it looks desperate to escape. No matter how hard it tries, it can't evade instinct. The insect will satisfy its craving for light, even if it burns.

Cecil offers me another sip, and I take it. "Something's been eating at you. I can tell."

I turn to look at Aaron, who's still leaning against that boulder, scraping his blade against a shapeless piece of wood. His gaze briefly catches mine before returning to the knife.

I turn back to glance at Cecil, then at my hands. "I don't know. He's just been... off. And he won't talk to me about it."

"I've noticed."

"Beau says he... gets like this." I pause. "Do you know why?"

Cecil lets out a long, exhausted sigh. "I've known Aaron for... how many years now? He turned nineteen in November, right?"

I nod.

"Fourteen years, then." He leans back, folding his arms across his chest. "Fourteen years of cleaning up scraped knees, reading to him. Making sure he didn't eat anything weird or poisonous. We all raised him, really. His dad and Noriko and I. Asa too, when he was around." He shakes his head fondly, but with a sad undertone I can't place. "Aaron was the only child at the Cut for a long time."

"You taught him how to read?"

"Oh yeah." Cecil grins. "He'd struggled a lot in school, at least for the short time he attended one at Port Keys. Hated reading—until he met the library at the Cut. He'd never read a Yesterday book in his life and fell in love pretty quickly. It was one of the only things there *was* to do, really."

"I didn't know he struggled with reading."

"Simon was really supportive about it, of course. But he spent so much time trying to understand *why* it was happening that it frustrated Aaron. You know how they both are."

I nod.

"He just needed someone to read to him every now and then. Someone to hold his hand and guide him through it until he figured out how to guide himself. Someone to simply enjoy the story with." Cecil smiles to himself, staring at the lantern. "As challenging as it was at times for him to get through a sentence on his own, he learned to love it. Crave it, even. Never wanted to do anything but learn new things and explore the world around him."

I chuckle tiredly, thinking back to every excited botanical rant I've been subjected to over these past few months. To the light that ignites behind his eyes whenever he talks about something green. "Sounds like Aaron."

Cecil nods. "I knew that child well." Slowly, the grin fades. The lantern's moth sends shadows leaping across his face, flickering like a flame without heat. "Sometimes I wish I knew where he buried him. That I could help bring that part of him back up to the surface before it suffocates."

"And?" I mutter, throat tight.

Cecil shakes his head. "I think the only person who can wield that kind of shovel is Aaron."

I avert my gaze, picking at the skin beneath my thumbnail, pressing my lips in a thin line. "That still doesn't feel like much of an answer."

"He's like a son to me, and even I don't know the full extent of what's haunting him. I don't think any of us ever will. When it comes to opening up, we'll only get as much as he wants to give." Cecil sighs. "And I don't think we can do much about it in the meantime but love him anyway."

After a while, Cecil rises, leaving me with the blanket and thermos as he heads back inside the van to get more sleep.

Now, I feel like I'm left with more questions than I had to begin with. And I still can't shake the feeling that there's something people aren't telling me.

I turn my head around. Aaron lowers his gaze as soon as I catch him staring. *I wonder if he heard more than he's letting on.*

"It's cold. And late," I tell him from afar. "You haven't eaten either."

"Voclain, Voclain." He keeps his eyes fixed to the carving, but can't suppress his smirk. "Ever so sharp."

"Fine." Frowning, I stand. "Freeze. Starve."

He salutes without looking. "On it."

"I'm going to bed." I head toward the van, then pause. "You should too."

I leave my blanket on the log. The lantern and the moth catch my attention again as I'm about to step away.

The moth continues to dance until it lands on the glass, twitching violently, glad to be burning. Because even as it falls to the dirt, it can finally say it's held the light in its hands. The smallest curl of smoke unfurls into the night air, and it smells like burnt hair.

I shudder and turn off the lantern before heading to bed.

Friday, April 5
68 Beds Made

We drive again at sunrise. I managed to sleep for the first hour of our second stretch, but when I wake up from the nap, my neck and shoulders are stiff from sleeping upright, and my lower back is pinched and sore. I slept on my wrist weird too, so I keep rubbing it to try and soothe the ache.

I try my best to *make my bed*, folding up the red knit blanket that Cecil brought and placing it neatly on top of my lap. I thought I'd given it to Aaron last night. *He must have let me have it while I was sleeping.*

I look around and realize that everyone is still fast asleep but Aaron and me, and Cecil, who drives in silence. I turn to face Aaron. "Hey, do you have any more of that salve?"

"Hmm?" he says, turning his head to face me. His leg is shaking tirelessly, one arm folded across his chest while he chews on the nails of his other hand.

"The one with the cinnamon," I say.

He nods, reaching into his satchel to retrieve the jar. He hands it to me and continues biting his nails.

I apply the salve to my wrists and the back of my neck, too cramped to think about applying it to my back. I close the jar and hand it back to him.

I place a hand on his knee, lowering my voice to a whisper to let the others sleep. "Your leg is shaking."

The shaking stops.

"I don't think you ever told me why you hate driving so much."

"Why don't *you* hate driving?"

"Because I'm used to being in cars," I say. "Because I've driven myself."

"Then why aren't you *more* afraid of it?"

"I'm just trying to understand, okay?" I cross my arms and stare straight ahead. "And we *still* aren't speaking, by the way. In case you've forgotten."

"I haven't." He crosses his arms too. "And for the record, you're the one who started this conversation, not me."

Silence. His leg starts shaking again, and in spite of the quiet I'd like to keep, I can't help but whisper again. "Why aren't you carving? Doesn't that help?"

Aaron keeps his eyes pinned to the stretch of road outside our windshield. "Everyone's sleeping. Don't wanna annoy them into consciousness with my *nails on a chalkboard*."

My heart sinks a little. *Did he really hear our whole conversation?*

I open my mouth to respond, but just as I do, the van begins to sputter, then slows to a complete stall. The engine goes quiet.

I furrow my brow. "Why are we stopped?"

"I'm not sure." Cecil turns the key to start it up again, but nothing happens. He tries again and again, and the engine is still silent.

Aaron's face goes pale. "This isn't funny, C."

"Yeah, I know," Cecil snaps.

He steps out of the passenger's seat and onto the road, and I climb out of mine to join him. Aaron follows.

While Cecil pops open the hood, I remember what Asa said before we left about the fuel line and crawl under the van to check.

"Aaron, check Beau's pocket," I call out.

"What?"

"Just do it."

I hear Aaron open the van door and wait for him to find what I need. "What the hell is this?"

"Bring it to me."

"Are you crazy? I'm not going under there."

"Oh my *God*."

"Fine. *Fine*." Aaron swears under his breath as he crawls under, lying on his back by my side, fuming. "Here's your *pig*."

"Crank it."

He gives me a look I can only describe as *done* as he starts to crank the flashlight. Light floods through the pig's nostrils with a toyish whirring sound. "This is demeaning."

"Good." I squint to make out the shapes of the van's underbelly with the pig's faint glow.

"The things I do for you, Voclain," he mutters under his breath. "I deserve an award."

My stomach churns when I take a closer look and notice a gap where two sections of the fuel line should be securely connected. One of the fittings that Asa tightened is now loose again. I look to my side to see a sheen puddle that shimmers in the faint light—gasoline.

"Uh, C?" I call out. "I think we're out of gas."

"I filled up right before we left," he calls back. I hear him slam the hood shut. "Everything looks good up here."

Aaron shoves the flashlight into his pocket, and we crawl out. Cecil walks over to meet us as we stand in the middle of the vacant road, surrounded by nothing but oceans of pine on either side for miles. Somewhere, a distant bird of prey shrieks, its cry echoing throughout the trees.

We're literally in the middle of nowhere.

"I think it's the fuel line," I say, right as Noriko walks out to join us. "Asa tightened it before we left but some of the fittings must have loosened up again."

"She's right," Noriko says, pointing to the back of the vehicle. "Look."

Sure enough, a thin, iridescent trail of gasoline extends down the pavement as far as we can see, leading right up to the van.

Beau, Viv, and Hugo climb out to join us. Beau yawns. "What's going on?"

"Leaky fuel line," Noriko says before turning to Cecil. "Can you fix it?"

"Well yeah, but even if I had the right tools on me, there'd be no point if we don't have extra fuel on hand."

"So what you're saying is..."

Cecil sighs, rubbing his face with his hands. "We'll need to make the rest of the trip on foot."

Viv's jaw drops. "You've got to be joking."

"If it's been leaking this entire time, then haven't we led a trail straight to End Harbor?" Hugo asks.

"Not if we abandon it here," Noriko says.

"Should we torch it?" Beau says. "You know, for evidence or whatever?"

"With a fuel leak? That's just asking for an explosion." Cecil crosses his arms with a frown. "And a great way to meet a Nightjade syringe if any Whiteboots happen to see the smoke."

"Well he's right, we can't just leave it out here," Viv says. "If any Officer on patrol sees an abandoned van in the middle of the road, they'll find it suspicious enough to follow our trail back home."

"Can anyone here hot-wire a car?" Beau asks.

"Asa taught me once," I say.

"Then I suggest a joyride."

"If we steal a car, we'll draw attention to ourselves. Leave more bread-crumbs," Aaron says.

Beau frowns.

"Okay, here's what we're going to do," Noriko says. "The whole reason why we came out here in the first place was to get our stuff back. Our tech, our files, our weapons—as much of it as we possibly can. And destroy the rest."

"Right..." Hugo says.

"We need this van to do what we came here to do, and to get back home. No torching it. We're going to push it into the woods and hide it. I'm going to walk back to the gas station on foot and bring back some tools and fuel, and the rest of you are going to hike your way to the Cut. We're only a few miles away by now. But this entire job is extremely time sensitive; we can't afford to wait any longer than we have to. The longer we wait, the more they know, and the less we'll have to salvage."

Everyone nods, except Cecil. "I'll go."

"I know these woods better than anyone," Noriko says. "We need to be efficient here, C. Alright?"

He hesitates, then nods.

"Good," she says, then walks back around to remove her backpack from the passenger's seat, slinging it over her shoulder. "Now help me push this damn thing."

With the seven of us giving all we've got, the van easily rolls off the side of the road and down into the woods. We push it until it's far enough into the trees that none of us can see the road—and that the road won't be able to see it either.

We set up camp next to the van again, too exhausted from pushing it to start the trek now. Noriko hugs each one of us goodbye before turning to leave.

"Hey," Cecil calls after her. She pauses to look over her shoulder. "Stay Unseen, alright?"

Noriko smiles with a salute. "Unseeing, Unseen."

And with that, she takes her leave. Cecil can't take his eyes away until she disappears between the trees.

It's quiet for a long time after Noriko's departure. Every part of me feels sore and stiff. I yawn, rubbing the dark circles beneath my eyes. Sleep hasn't been any less forgiving now that we're away from End Harbor.

Cecil naps inside the van while Hugo leans against a log with a book spread open in his lap. Viv and Beau bicker about something somewhere, and I sit on a rock. Aaron has wandered off a few yards away from our camp, observing every shrub, flower, tree, and fallen log. I rise to my feet and walk over to join him.

"What are we looking for?"

"Anything we can find." Aaron shrugs. "I didn't prepare for this trip as much as I usually do. I have a pretty good antiseptic salve for emergencies.

That castor oil Alice was able to lend me. A little bit of thimbleberry and a few good teas." He sighs. " But... I should have been more focused."

"Was that *my* fault?" I ask quietly, thinking back to the lighthouse argument that still doesn't feel as resolved as I'd like it to be.

"Hey, don't take all the credit. The fault is all mine." He tries to force a smirk but it falls away quickly. "Anyway. We'll need to be extra careful until we can stock up at the Cut."

I nod, staring at my feet as we drift farther away from camp. The woods are peaceful today. Dark gray clouds loom overhead, shifting the light as they move. A few birds chirp in the distance. I take a deep breath of cold, clean air, inhaling the taste of pine needles and damp earth, of wet stone and moss and every bitter yet irresistible scent between. I notice a bluebird perched on a branch above us, but it flies away when we walk past, startled by the sound of snapping twigs.

I glance at Aaron, then look away so he doesn't notice. I'm not sure why a wave of guilt begins to churn within my gut, but wrapping my jacket tighter around myself doesn't do much to soothe it. I shiver as cold droplets poke my skin. There aren't enough of them to call it a drizzle, but it's cold, and I shove my hands into my pockets. I crinkle my brow when I feel a piece of paper inside them.

Aaron's note, I realize. I never took it out.

He sneezes, pulling me out of my thoughts.

"Bless you," I mutter out of habit.

"These allergies are killing me." He sniffles. "I blame you."

I roll my eyes, then face him again, this time letting my gaze linger a little bit longer. I trace the note in my pocket.

My heart still sinks every time I think about what he and Milo kept from me—of how badly it hurts, no matter how deeply I understand why they did it. But over these past few days, I'm beginning to realize that pushing away the one true friend I have left is a pain much worse to bear. I can't afford to isolate myself even further. I can't afford to lose even the smallest part of the Aaron I have.

"Aaron..." I say, trying to formulate the words in my mind. He stops walking to listen, and so do I. "I'm—"

"Wait. Do you hear that?"

I glare. "Hear—"

"Shh." He places a finger over my mouth. I frown, ready to protest—until I hear a faint buzzing sound, quieter than a whisper.

I glance upward, trying to locate the source of the noise, wondering if there could be a wasp nest nearby. Still looking up, I take a step back. The buzzing grows louder. I take another step.

Something sinks into my right ankle.

Two little knives dig their way through the denim of my jeans, through the wool of my socks, burying themselves into my flesh before retreating.

"*Shit.*" I stare at the ground. "Something just bit me."

Aaron's face pales. "What?"

I wince. "I think it was a spider or something." I spin in a circle, trying to locate the source of the sting.

All the color drains from my face when I realize what I'm staring at.

For a moment, I wonder why there would be a rope coiled into a figure eight inches away from my foot. For a moment, I see the criss-cross pattern of braided fiber—until I squint, and the image clarifies.

Those are scales.

And that's when the fire ignites.

EDDIE

Friday, April 5
68 Beds Made

The snake slithers away when I cry out. It doesn't get far before Aaron throws his knife. The rattling stops.

My knees buckle and I slump against the tree, tears already welling in my eyes. I clamp my teeth down on my tongue so hard I taste blood. It takes nothing away from the burning.

I grab my ankle with both hands. The fire pulses beneath my flesh. It only seems to get worse with every fractured breath I take, greedily tearing at every nerve from the ankle down like something ravenous is mauling it from the inside out.

Aaron crouches in front of me. He cups my face with his hands, trying to get a hold of my slipping attention. "Voclain. Look at me."

It feels like I'm underwater; I can barely make out his words. There is no part of me that doesn't shiver. Cold sweat already drenches my face.

"Tell me where it hurts, Eddie." Aaron swallows, trying to keep his own breathing steady. "Can you do that for me?"

"My ankle—" is all I manage to mutter before calling out again. My eyes squeeze shut so tightly I fear my head might burst as a sharp pain shoots through my leg.

When I open my eyes again, Aaron is retrieving his knife from the scaled carcass behind the tree. He's back in an instant, the wooden handle of his knife clenched between his teeth as he rolls up my jeans. He swears under his breath. "Shit, Voclain. It's already swelling."

He cuts a strip of denim from the bottom of my jeans, folding it up. He glides his thumb across my lip. "Open up for me, okay?" I do as he says and he tucks the denim inside. "Bite down on that. Your tongue is bleeding."

He unlaces my boot. I call out as he pulls the shoe off my foot, clenching the fabric with my teeth between sobs.

"Shh, I know. I know." He pulls off my sock and grimaces. I peel my eyes open. I'm dizzy, but when I force myself to look at my ankle, I can clearly see two tiny puncture wounds. The skin around it looks red and puffy, each toe slightly larger than I remember.

Aaron retrieves a canteen of water and a flask from his satchel. He unscrews the flask and pours a splash of alcohol onto a clean cloth, then brings his unoccupied wrist to my hand. "This is going to sting. Keep biting that fabric and squeeze my arm if you need to, alright?"

I nod and bite the denim harder. It's impossible not to whimper with every new fire shooting through my leg. I'm convinced someone's plunging a knife into my ankle, over and over and over again until it's all I can feel, all I can think about. All I can taste—metallic and salty as adrenaline sparks across my tongue.

The burning only intensifies when Aaron pats the alcohol-soaked cloth around the wound. I squeeze my eyes shut and clench the denim between my teeth. I dig my nails into his wrist so deeply his skin breaks, but he doesn't flinch.

"You're doing so good, Ed. I'm almost done."

He applies more alcohol to the wound and I squeeze his arm even tighter, struggling not to scream. But I've never felt a burning like this before. My vision blurs. Aaron rinses the wound with clean water.

My fingers are still curled around his left arm as he uses his free hand to rummage through his satchel. He fishes out a roll of fresh bandages, cutting a strip with his teeth as he wraps my ankle. My grip loosens and he uses both hands to tie it off.

"It burns, Aaron." I sob, too dizzy and weak to care about how pathetic I must sound. "It's burning and it hurts and I can't—"

"I know, Eddie. I know," he whispers. He tucks a strand of hair behind my ear. "We need to keep your heart rate steady. Can you take a deep breath?"

"No," I choke out. Every inhalation is jagged and cut too short.

He takes my hand in his, holding it to his chest. "Can you feel my pulse?"

The rhythm is steady. Grounding.

"Close your eyes and count for me, Eddie." His voice is slow and soft.

I do as he says, shutting my eyes, centering myself around every note until his heartbeat is the only thing I can feel. Until I take it and make it my own.

"Now breathe with me. In through the nose…" His chest moves beneath my palm. My fingers clutch the fabric of his shirt. Every knuckle is desperate as I try to inhale with him. "Out through the mouth."

I barely exhale. I can't stop trembling.

"In through the nose…" His chest moves again. Mine does too. "Out through the mouth."

I exhale again, sobbing more as he repeats himself. Until we breathe in rhythm. Until time slows, and my tears fade away with the rest of the world. For a moment there is no burning—only Aaron's heartbeat.

"We need to get you to the Cut," he says, shoving his supplies back into his bag, along with my boot and sock. He rises to his feet and helps me to mine. My knees buckle but he steadies me before I fall, looping his arms beneath my own. He holds me closer to keep me upright.

My teeth chatter. "It's so cold."

"You're pale, Ed." He presses the back of his hand against my cheek. "And clammy." He swears under his breath. "You're going into shock."

Twigs snap behind us. Cecil and Viv run up to my side.

"We heard screams," Viv pants.

The color drains from Cecil's face. "Don't tell me…"

"Rattlesnake," Aaron says. My knees tremble again, and he catches me once more. He takes my backpack off my shoulder and puts it on his own before scooping me into his arms. "I'm taking her to the Cut."

"Are you sure you can carry her the whole way? It's a three-mile hike south."

"I don't exactly have any other choice," Aaron says, his voice growing more muffled by the second as my head falls against his chest. My eyelids flutter. I try so hard to keep them open, but they feel like lead.

"I can walk," I protest. My words are whispers.

"She can't," Aaron says to Cecil. "She can barely hold onto me."

I try and fail to glare. Every muscle burns and I'm too numb to move. I think I'm crying, but my vision is darkening and I can't tell. "Screw you."

"Why don't you stay with her here?" Viv says. "We can run over there and bring the antivenom back from your dad's lab."

"We don't have time for that," Aaron argues. "If she doesn't get it soon, her body will shut down."

"Why don't you let me take her?"

"I'm the only one who knows where to find the antivenom. Or how to administer it."

"But—" Viv begins to say.

"I've got it," Aaron snaps, his voice firm. "I'm taking her." He readjusts me in his arms before turning to walk away.

"At least let us go with you."

"You'll slow me down." Aaron is already a few yards away. He doesn't even bother to look over his shoulder.

"We'll meet you there," Cecil shouts behind us. "Don't worry about coming back. We'll start the job when we get there."

"And don't try anything stupid until then!" Viv yells.

My eyes fall shut.

"I've got you, okay? I promise, you're gonna be just fine." Aaron's whispers are desperate enough to be a prayer. "You have to be."

The fire burns brighter in slumber.

I dream of its gnarled amber hands, twisting through the dark like branches of a tree, smoke curling higher and higher until the night is choked with gray.

I can feel it spreading through me as I drift between consciousness and numbness.

Beyond the muffled crunch of footsteps, I hear Aaron humming. He whispers broken words to himself about wrinkles in time, about space, about hearts and headaches and finding. Like he's singing his own lullaby.

Soon, there is no drifting, no weaving in and out. The humming fades. Cedarwood is the last thing I smell before everything is nothing at all.

Funny, how fire is the pinch that snuffs my candle out.

Everything is dark.

Saturday, April 6
69 Beds Made

The gray is blinding when I open my eyes.

It's light, I realize. Cold, gray, glaring light that cuts into my eyes and skin.

I hold a heavy hand up to shield my eyes, blinking rapidly until my surroundings fall into place, defining themselves as an unlit room with a rusty metal sink in the corner, a small round table, and a few old wood chairs. Aaron sits in one of them. I can hear his knife scraping against wood.

He glances at me, and the sweeping stops. He blinks for a moment like he can't trust what he's seeing. Before I can take another breath, he sets his carving down and kneels by my side, which is when I realize that I'm lying on the ground in a sleeping bag with Aaron's balled-up sweater as a pillow beneath my head. Even in my jacket, I shiver, and he wears only a thin black tee and jeans, leaving his arms exposed—and his scar.

He doesn't seem to notice or care that the scar he usually hides is left vulnerable; he's too busy pressing his hand to my forehead. "No fever is a good sign." His hand falls away. "How are you feeling?"

Only when he asks the question do I notice the deep, dull ache in the bottom half of my right leg, and the nauseating emptiness in my stomach. I clutch it when it growls. "Hungry."

Aaron returns to the table. He digs through his bag, pulling out a bowl, a canteen of water, and one of his own instant oatmeal rations. "Hope you don't mind cold oatmeal."

He pours the oats and some water into the bowl, then rummages through my backpack to retrieve the jar of cinnamon. He sprinkles some into the bowl and stirs with the wooden spoon he'd packed me.

He didn't pack any cinnamon for himself, I realize. I can't tell if it's guilt or hunger that tugs at my gut.

I sit upright, propping myself up with my elbows. "Where are we?"

"The cabin." He brings the bowl and spoon to me, then sits cross-legged by my side. "Not the good one."

"I can tell." I try to ignore the smell of rotting wood and dirt. "Why not?"

He stares at the bowl, still stirring. "I noticed smoke coming out of the chimney."

My heart plummets. *Chasers.*

The thought of them being so nearby—and in the cabin, of all places—makes my appetite melt away.

Our cabin. The place that Ren carried me to all those months ago, where he nursed me back to health after nearly freezing to death in the snow. The place I reunited with Aaron after wondering if I'd ever even see him again. The place that led me to exactly where I am at this very moment, and everything that happened to get me here.

Don't go there.

"Do you think my stuff is still there?" I ask, thinking of Ren's green sweatshirt and my old white running shoes. I force myself to ignore the pain that claws at my chest when I remember the way the fabric felt around me, the smell of the McLellan's herbal laundry soap still strong in my memory.

I would give just about anything to breathe it in again.

"Unless your stuff gained legs and conscious thought, then yes." Aaron prepares a spoonful of oatmeal and brings it to my mouth. "Here."

I frown. "You're not feeding me."

He mirrors my expression. "Can you even feed yourself right now?"

"Of course I can." Glaring, I reach out to take the spoon, but the back and sides of my neck and shoulders burn, as well as the soft spots under my arms and ears. I grimace, biting my lip and squeezing my eyes shut as I rub my neck.

"Your immune system's working overtime right now," Aaron explains. "If your lymph nodes are sore, they're doing their job."

I don't protest this time as he guides a spoonful of oatmeal into my mouth. I chew and swallow in disgust. Beau was definitely right about cold oatmeal, but the cinnamon makes it tolerable.

I let him feed me another bite. It's hard to hold my head up. My neck burns and my skull throbs, and I can feel every pounding heartbeat behind my eyes.

"Where is everyone?" I ask.

"Back at the van." He retrieves the jar of hot salve from his satchel and scoops the orange substance onto his finger. "Mind if I..."

I shake my head.

He sits behind me, gently massaging the salve into my neck and shoulders. "They're getting ready to move forward with the job. Beau will guard the van and wait for Noriko. The others will be here soon."

The salve burns immediately, but not like my snake bite. This warmth is soothing, like a hot bath. It smells like apple cider and I can't help but sigh in relief. "I love this."

Aaron's hands go still. "Hmm?"

"The salve," I say. "It smells like I should eat it by the spoonful."

Aaron clears his throat and continues. "Well, enjoy it while you can, then. This is the last of it."

I close my eyes, trying to breathe, soaking in the relief while I have it. Every muscle aches. My bite no longer burns, but my leg still feels sore and weak.

"What happened?" I try to turn and face Aaron but wince when my neck pinches. He works the salve into the spot I reach for and I lower my hand, letting him continue to massage it into my skin.

"I brought you back here. Ran to my dad's old place to get what I needed. Was able to administer the antivenom just in time." He pauses, then clears his throat again. "Didn't have time for a full raid. Chasers were swarming the place."

I nod—and then I realize what he means, and why we're here. This time, I do spin around, even with the pain. "You snuck back into the Cut *alone*?"

He glares. "It was my only option, alright? It was dark. No one saw me."

"Among every stupid thing you've done, this ranks pretty high on the list."

"What was I supposed to do? Let you die?"

I don't know what to say to that, so I frown at the bowl of oatmeal instead.

Aaron sighs, setting aside the empty jar. "I did what I had to do and that's it, alright?"

"Thank you," I mutter, still scowling.

"Don't thank me for doing my job." He picks at the scabs on his knuckles, and I notice that two of his fingers are still taped together. My heart sinks. *He carried me here with a broken finger.*

The memory of that day and the bloody wall seeps into my mind, along with his promise. I glance at Aaron. "Did you... do anything?"

"What?"

"At the Cut."

He pinches his brow and opens his mouth to say something, then pauses, clenching it shut when he realizes what I'm referring to. The muscles in his jaw twitch. "As much as I would have loved to, no. I did not *do anything* at the Cut."

"Don't be mad at me for asking." I glower as he feeds me another spoonful of oatmeal.

"I'm not stupid, Voclain." He gives me another bite, then sighs. "Look. Cecil said to wait to do anything until he and the others got here. I'm following orders. My job is to help you right now—not put you in danger."

It's quiet for a moment as he helps me finish my food. When the bowl is empty, he walks to the sink in the corner. I watch him wash the bowl clean, and my glare melts away. "Did you really mean what you said that day?"

That's all I have to ask for his shoulders to turn rigid. He stops scrubbing, staring at the sink. "I always keep my promises."

He keeps scrubbing, long after the bowl is clean.

Sometime after a lunch I couldn't bring myself to eat, exactly seven knocks crack against the door, staggered in a rhythm that Aaron taps back against the table. There's a pause as we both wait, until the doorknob turns.

In walks Cecil, Viv, and Hugo, each carrying light, unoccupied backpacks over their shoulders. Cecil tosses two to Aaron and one to me, leaving himself with two. Hugo and Viv each hold three.

I climb out of my sleeping bag, kneeling while I roll it up into a neat bundle. I set it aside. *Another bed made.* It does little to calm my nerves.

I sit cross-legged on the floor while the others find a seat at the table. Aaron leans against the sink with his arms crossed. He's wearing his black sweater again, scar covered.

"We've already lost enough time, so I'm not going to waste any more here. We need to go over the plan." Cecil retrieves a map from his bag and spreads it over the table. "Our primary goal is to salvage what we can and find a way to destroy the rest. The Corps will be treating the entire compound as a crime scene, and we need to make sure they haul back as little evidence as possible. We call ourselves the Unseen, after all—and I know we'd all like it to stay that way."

Cecil points to a location on the map that I have to crane my neck to see. I swallow the grimace that follows, resisting the urge to massage the back of my head and shoulders. The effects of Aaron's salve are already fading, but if I want to be involved in this job, I'll need to convince them I'm okay. There's no way they'll let me go if I show even the slightest sign of discomfort.

No mistakes. I reach inside my pocket, tracing the smooth surface of the glass shard I stole from the broken mirror. *No bad luck.*

"Eddie and Aaron, you two will be handling all things plants and medicine. I trust that you two know what we need in that department, so go with your intuition, but try to focus your efforts here and here." Cecil taps two locations on the map, then looks at Aaron. "The greenhouse and your dad's old lab are located at the northwest corner of the Cut. If you have to head a little farther north to grab anything from your house, by all means, go ahead. Just keep in mind that the greenhouse will likely be guarded, and probably occupied by at least an Officer or two who might be interested in what you and your dad were working on. Maybe even an Agent. That Catnap stash of yours will be like a gold mine to the Corps, so you'll need to be extremely careful."

Aaron nods, and Cecil turns to face me to make sure I heard. I nod too. He gives me a reassuring wink with his visible eye.

"Now, I'll be handling the armory, which is on the eastern side of the square," Cecil says. "I'll also be handling all home requests at the Block."

I think back to the tour Aaron gave me all those months ago, about the awe I felt at the fact that so many people could be living in one place, away from the Pick, away from Nightjade, away from every horrible thing I grew up familiar with. To think that all of those homes are now abandoned makes my stomach twist into knots.

"Viv and Hugo, you two will be handling our intelligence, which we stored in the church. Tech, files, maps—all of it. Be strategic about what you grab because we'll only be able to carry so much."

"Won't the church be the most heavily guarded?" Hugo asks, his leg shaking up and down. *He must be nervous*, I realize. Hugo's always been a thinker, not a fighter.

Cecil nods. "That's exactly why we'll be hitting everything in shifts. You all have radios, so make sure to listen for signals, because timing will be extremely important here. I've also packed you all a few smoke grenades, courtesy of Beau, to create diversions as needed—but only when I give the signal.

"I'll hit the armory first, and immediately after, Eddie and Aaron will hit the greenhouse and lab while I draw units away from the square and into the Block, where I'll be staggering home requests and smoke grenade diversions. They'll want to go after me the most if I've hit the armory, which leaves Hugo and Viv with a small window of time to raid the church."

Cecil turns to face them. "You two will be carrying the heaviest loads, so remember what I said about strategizing. Our goal is to retrieve as much as we can in as little time as possible."

They nod.

"I've given you each a loaded handgun in one of your bags. And if any of you find yourselves in a situation that calls for it, do whatever you need to do to get out of there alive. You got that?" Cecil looks each of us in the eye. "Whatever you need to do."

My gut churns. I stare at the rusty nails in the floorboards, tracing every crack and wood grain with my gaze to avoid thinking about what that could mean. I pull Carmody's lighter out of my pocket, flicking it open and shut as Cecil continues.

"After we've done enough damage, we'll exit separately to avoid drawing Chasers to the van, where we'll meet. By then, Noriko will be back with fuel and we'll be able to take our leave." Cecil's voice turns grim. "The van will leave at sunrise, no exceptions. If you miss it, you'll have to find your way back on your own."

We all nod in silence.

Cecil turns around to face me. "How are you feeling, kid?"

"Better," I lie, though there is some truth to it. The fire in my leg is gone, though the all over aches aren't much of an improvement, or the headache chiseling away at my skull.

"Are you sure you're feeling up to this?" Cecil asks. "You can say no, Ed. We'll still love you just the same. I know how brutal a bite can be."

All eyes fixate on me, waiting for an answer. But I don't have the chance to give it.

"She's staying behind."

Now, it's Aaron who has everyone's attention, but he looks at me.

I scoff. "Excuse me?"

"Can you even stand?"

I glare, grinding my teeth together. "I can stand just fine."

He nods his chin in my direction. "Show me."

Scowling, I use my arms to push myself up to my feet. In an instant, my vision turns black. My knees buckle. It feels like I'm standing on the roof of a moving car as Aaron hurries to my side to help me regain my balance. Putting weight on my ankle almost makes it feel sprained.

"I'm fine," I snap, pulling away from Aaron and placing my hand on the wall to steady myself. The dizziness fades a little, and my vision melts back into place. "I just stood up too fast."

Aaron hands me his canteen of water, unamused. I take it without hesitation but keep my glare pinned to him as I down desperate gulps, shoving it into his chest when I'm done.

He takes the canteen and faces Cecil. "She can't go. She needs rest, and we need to be as careful as possible if we want to make it out of here in one piece."

"I said I'm fine," I seethe.

"You clearly don't know the meaning of the word *fine*."

I hold back the urge to give him a good blow to the face, though I'm not sure I could even swing that kind of punch in my current condition anyway. "I'm not an idiot, Aaron."

"I agree."

"I came all this way to help, and that's exactly what I'm gonna do. I'm tired of sitting around and letting people treat me like a wounded animal because I'm not one. I swear to God, if one more person tells me how much I've been through or how little I should be doing, I'm going to scream, and I'm going to hurt someone, and it'll probably be you."

I shoot Aaron a cutting glare and he averts his gaze, jaw clenched.

Cecil lets out a deep, exhausted sigh, then faces Aaron. "I know you're just trying to keep her safe, kid. But at the end of the day, it's her decision to make. And we need all the help we can get."

"I'll take her bag. I'll get just as much as she'd be able to carry and she can stay here."

"Aaron," I warn, catching his gaze.

He inhales, his fingers curling into fists, nails digging into his palms. We stare each other down for a long stretch of silence until he finally looks Cecil in the eye again. "If she gets hurt out there, that's on you."

Cecil's face remains calm, and I think back to our conversation by the lantern as I continue to flick the lighter open and closed. *He's used to this.*

"Eddie can handle herself," Cecil says. "I think we'll be lucky to have her on our side."

I can't bring myself to smile. The scars on my arm itch, and I pocket the lighter to scratch them, staring at my socks. "Thank you."

Cecil nods, then rises to his feet, rolling up the map. "Any questions?"

"None at all," Aaron mutters. No one else says a word.

Cecil tucks the map into his bag. "Let's look out for each other out there, alright?"

We all nod. I can feel Aaron's stare digging into me.

"Good," Cecil says. "Now let's get our shit back."

It takes us an hour to reach the pine-crested hill that overlooks the compound from the south.

An hour for us to smell the smoke.

An hour for us to finally see what's left of the Cut for ourselves.

From up here, the compound looks like it could fit in the palm of my hand. Like I could reach out and hold it to study the bustling insects that scurry across its surface like ants.

But this is not an infestation I'd touch with a ten-foot pole.

Cecil was right. Everywhere we look from our perch is an Officer dressed from head to toe in shining white armor. I even spot a handful of Agents in their black suits and shades, and my throat tightens, lungs pinching shut as I try not to think of the first and last time I saw one up close.

I don't realize I'm shaking until Aaron's finger brushes against mine. When I look up to my right, he can't even bring himself to face me. But I can see it—the hollowness in his eyes. I realize that he's shaking too.

He starts to pull his hand away, but I curl my pinky finger around his before he gets the chance. I stare back at the sea of buildings and insects and swallow the lump in my throat.

"What are they burning down there?" Hugo mutters, his whole body stilled by the smell of smoke. He can't peel his eyes away from the glowing bonfire that flickers in a clearing west of the block.

"I don't know," Cecil mutters. "But we'll find out soon enough."

I'm not sure how long we stand in silence until Cecil, Viv, and Hugo begin to make their way downhill. Aaron and I don't move. I'm not sure we could if we wanted to.

A breeze tosses my undone hair, which has fallen out of its braid. The wind carries with it the taste of pine and dirt and something burning.

Aaron can't stop trembling. For a moment I forget about my frustration and all the things I want to say to him and curl my finger tighter around his, like an oath sworn in silence.

"They won't get away with this," I whisper.

"They won't."

"Is that a promise?"

He holds my finger as tightly as he can.

EDDIE

Saturday, April 6
69 Beds Made

♪ WHEN I GROW UP - FIRST AID KIT ♪

Aaron's house smells exactly like him.

It's an A-frame log cabin tucked away into the woods north of the compound, secluded enough for us to remain both hidden and watchful, perched upon a hill that's high enough for us to see the greenhouse and his father's lab.

The moment Aaron opens the door, I breathe in the scent of wood, evergreen, and herbal tea. He sneezes when he shuts it. "Dust." He looks over his shoulder. "Or you."

I roll my eyes as he flips on the light switch. Immediately, the entryway is flooded with a dim amber glow.

"Wow."

"What?"

I shrug. "Everything looks so... normal."

He scoffs. "What'd you expect?"

"More sharp things hanging on the walls."

He sets his bags down on the couch. "You have your radio on?" I nod. "Good. We'll just have to hide out here until Cecil's done hitting the armory, I guess."

The living room is off to the right side of the entryway, with a big ornate rug, a handmade and asymmetrical wooden coffee table that looks like a slice taken straight from a tree, and a brown leather sofa cracked with years of use. A Yesterday TV is mounted above the fireplace, with a set of speakers and a bookcase full of CDs and DVDs to match.

My jaw drops as I set my bags down and approach the bookcase. I've never seen this many Yesterday movies and albums in all my life. Every shelf is stocked full with more music and cinematic content than I knew existed.

The McLellans had Yesterday shows and movies, and Milo was always obsessed with old music. But Asa would only let us watch that kind of TV in half-hour intervals, and only once a week. He was too paranoid of the mics picking up on anything Slander-worthy. All I remember is bits and pieces of an animated show about pirates, with episodes that were short enough for us to squeeze into our allotted time, and easy to come back to later.

"I don't think I've ever seen a Yesterday movie before," I say. "At least not that I remember, anyway."

"And I don't think I've seen a Chipped movie either. Not that I'd remember."

"Then you've been spared a lot of sappy, lifeless romances about Chasers saving damsels in distress and action thrillers where every plot has something to do with slaughtering rebels."

"And *you've* been spared an ungodly amount of animated rodent films."

I crinkle my nose, just as a title catches my eyes. I crouch to grab it with a gasp while Aaron pockets a CD case from the music shelf. "They made a *Pride and Prejudice* movie?"

"Oh yeah. Multiple." Aaron takes the case from my hands, putting it back in its place. "I'd stay away from the romance shelf if I were you. My dad and Beau will literally kill you. They have them organized by trope; they spent an entire week one summer going through and taking inventory to sort them."

Aaron opens his mouth to say more, then pauses, remembering that it no longer matters how the shelves are organized. That this will be the last time he'll ever be inside this house.

He's leaving behind his entire life for a second time, I realize.

I know exactly what that feels like.

"Did Beau come around a lot?" I ask, changing the subject.

"Uh, yeah. He lived here."

My eyes widen. "I didn't know that."

"He didn't really have anywhere else to go," Aaron explains, tracing the movies on the shelf. "Asa brought Beau to the Cut when he was fourteen. Dad offered to take him in; didn't make sense for him to be assigned a portable all by himself."

I nod.

"He's only two years older than I am, so my dad was convinced he and I could try out the whole brother thing." Aaron shakes his head fondly, studying the organized shelf. "The most annoying roommate I've ever had."

"You two sure bicker like brothers."

Aaron grins. "We do, don't we?"

"He mentioned having sisters," I mutter carefully, unsure of where I may be treading.

"He had three."

My heart sinks. "Had?"

"One of them was Picked," Aaron answers softly, averting his gaze. "His family protested her death, but… you know how that goes." He sighs. "He and his old man managed to escape. His dad left him in the woods one day. Told him to stay put—that he'd be back with help, and they'd have a place to live again, and they'd sort everything out."

I swallow dryly. "He never came back, did he?"

Aaron shakes his head. "Asa found Beau starving in a cave a month later."

I nod with nothing else to say.

We move onto the kitchen, which has a butcher-block island and an expensive-looking navy blue stove. I walk over to trace the knobs. *It's from the Yesterdays.*

"Did your dad build this place?" I ask, wondering where they could have gotten appliances like this, or a big leather couch that even a smuggler wouldn't waste time stealing.

"It was already here when Noriko found the Cut," Aaron says. He grabs a handful of stovetop dinners from the pantry and shoves them into his satchel. "She offered it to my dad so he could move my mom and I out here. I was only one at the time." He closes the cabinet. "He spent years trying to convince my mom to come with him... but we both know how that turned out."

"Why was she so against it?"

"It's not like she didn't want to. She was just... scared."

"So let me get this straight." I lean against a cabinet, crossing my arms while Aaron rummages through the drawers, pocketing what I assume to be his favorite kitchen knives. "Noriko and your dad already knew each other?"

"I never told you?"

I shake my head.

"Oh, man." Aaron can't resist a smile. He leans against the pantry, crossing one leg over the other with his hands in his pockets. "They grew up together in Port Keys. Asa and my mom too."

My eyes widen. Asa barely told Ren and Margot anything about his life, let alone their mother's. It makes sense that this is the first time I'm hearing about this, but I'm still surprised. "I had no idea."

"They got into all kinds of trouble together. Especially my dad. It's hilarious. Asa always had the best stories whenever he was visiting." Aaron leads me out of the kitchen and up a wooden staircase. He looks over his shoulder. "You got it?"

I nod, using the banister to take some of the weight off my right leg as I make my way up, one step at a time. "I can't even imagine Asa getting into trouble."

I shake my head at the idea of it all. While I was growing up with the McLellans, Aaron was growing up with Asa too. The twins and I had no idea he was living this second life without them.

I understand why Asa couldn't tell Ren and Margot about it. Noriko's identity in relation to them was a secret; they'd all be killed if the Corps figured out their mother was a Runner. But it's still strange to think that even the people you think you know best hold secrets you don't even know about. Secrets you may *never* know about.

"Asa was the peacemaker, he liked to say. Or as my dad and Noriko like to call him, the *babysitter*. And other choice words." Aaron pauses, glancing to his left. I realize he's staring at the photos that have been pinned to the wall. Some of them look digital, but most of them look like they were taken with a polaroid, and a few with film. *Before and after he came here*, I note.

I recognize the one from Esmerelda's photo book, with young Aaron and Lori at the beach. They look so happy there, so young and innocent, untouched by the cruel hands of the world they hadn't yet realized they lived in. There are more of Aaron than Lori, who lived most of her life separately at Port Keys.

We stand there, frozen in time, as I watch Aaron grow up on the walls. Polaroids of a toothy preteen Aaron and Cecil holding a fish. One of Aaron and Simon laughing by a campfire. One of Aaron at no older than seventeen, kissing a bullfrog. Aaron and Beau hugging a baby goat. That's where the photos stop.

My gaze finds its way to a photograph of Aaron sketching in what looks like the greenhouse, surrounded by ferns and bushes of flowers. He can't be any older than ten, but the drawing on the page is beautiful and astonishingly accurate.

I trace the photo in its frame. It's small, like the pocket-sized kind you'd fit in your wallet. "You never told me you like to draw."

With that, Aaron snaps out of his trance. He keeps walking upstairs, moving past the photos without bothering to look back, almost like he's trying not to. "I stopped."

I don't ask why, and I have a feeling that I wouldn't get much of an answer even if I did.

When Aaron isn't looking, I remove the photo from its frame and shove it in my pocket.

We reach the top of the stairs, and Aaron helps me with the last step. "Anyway. That's how we got the house."

He leads me down a hallway, pointing to a bathroom and a primary bedroom, which belonged to his father. We walk past an open door, and I pause to peek my head in. "What's this?"

I step inside, and Aaron follows me in. I turn on the light and my jaw falls to the floor.

It's an art studio, with a messy wooden drawing desk and about a dozen easels in different shapes and sizes. Unfinished wood sculptures sit on a table surrounded by carving tools and wood shavings. Every surface—table, floor, or walls—is covered in botanical sketches in varying stages of completion, some of them no more than an ink doodle, others elaborately filled in with watercolor. I step inside, picking up what looks like a hand-bound leather book and flipping through the pages.

My heart stops beating.

I know these illustrations.

Every page is filled with elaborate depictions of plants in alphabetical order, complete with detailed statistics and paragraphs of notes I remember reading long ago. Some of the sentences match the photographs stored in my mind, word for word.

"Did you make these?" My heart has returned, and this time it races.

"Learned from my dad."

I close the book and set it back down on the desk. "Did you ever give any to the McLellans?"

Aaron shrugs. "I might've given a few to Asa. My dad too. Can't really remember. We've made a lot over the years."

I clear my throat, unable to take my eyes off the sketches on the walls. "Do you make copies of them?"

Aaron nods. "I'd mostly copy the ones my dad made. That's how I learned the majority of what he was trying to teach me about plants and medicine and stuff like that—by duplicating his old encyclopedias, replicating the paintings, binding them. I probably made a few edits here and there, though. I just made them to have something to do with my hands, really. It was repetitive and thoughtless. Like breathing. Or carving wood." He pauses. "I didn't pay much attention to the medicinal part of it all until later. It took... other methods to get me to truly appreciate healing, I guess."

I can't blink or think or even take a full breath. *This is where it all started,*

I realize. My interest in plants, my desire to heal—my *need* to read.

I think back to those summer evenings in elementary school, reading to Margot when she was too sick to do anything but drift in and out of consciousness in her bed. Ren lying on the floor nearby, head propped up by his elbows as he kicked his feet and read something about the stars.

I would give anything to go back to those days.

But when I try to think back and hold onto those moments, it feels like they're slipping away. As vivid as my recollection tends to be, even *I'm* not immune to forgetting.

I should have tried harder to memorize it all while I had it.

"You okay, Voclain? You look a little pale."

My eyes remain unblinking. "I'm fine."

My hands won't stop shaking as Aaron leads me into the next room. *His* room. A simple wooden bed, a patchwork quilt. Paintings on the walls, notes about medicine, random thoughts about everything and all things in between. It looks like the walls of the church that is no longer ours—the closet of information that Milo and Aaron kept hidden. The room of Ren.

"Voclain?"

I face him, throat tight, vision cloudier than I remember them being a second ago. "I can't remember what their laundry soap smells like."

He stands there for a moment, staring at me in silence. He doesn't have to ask to know what I'm talking about.

As he walks up to me, hands in his pockets, I stare at a painting of a bluebird taped to the wall. "I miss them," I mutter.

Without saying a word, he pulls me into a hug.

My shoulders slouch and my throat convulses and I realize that I'm crying into his chest. Everything I've been holding onto—every wound I try to hide, every night I've lost to a torturing state of consciousness, every breath I've been stifling, every ounce of anger I felt towards Milo and Aaron for hiding what they were trying to do for me. All of it releases into him as I press my palms to his chest, clutching the fabric of his sweater. "It feels like they're all fading away."

He pulls me closer, resting his chin on my head as one of his hands holds my hair.

I think back to the memories, trying to see the details of Margot's young face as I read those encyclopedias to her, trying to remember the sound of Ren turning pages next to me. Trying to remember the smells, the flavors, the warmth. My mother's laugh. My father's voice. But no matter how hard I try, the details are still fuzzy. I can't recall the sunlight I once tasted on my tongue as anything but gray.

"I don't want to forget them."

"I know." He says it like he knows what it's like. Like he knows about the aching I've felt every day since I started to make my bed. Like he's felt it himself. He holds me even tighter. "You won't. I'll make sure of it."

We stand like that for a long time until the radio in Aaron's back pocket goes off.

Aaron, do you copy?

Shouting in the background muffles Cecil's voice, and my pulse skips a beat. Aaron pulls away from me as I wipe my eyes, composing myself. He fishes out the walkie-talkie and speaks into it. "Yeah?"

Time to go, kid.

Cecil pants as the background shouting grows louder.

Be quick, you two. Stay safe.

The line goes quiet. Aaron looks at me, and I can tell he's trying as hard as I am to stay calm. "You ready?"

Barely able to take a full breath, I nod. But we both know I'm a liar.

EDDIE

Saturday, April 6
69 Beds Made

♪ UP IN SMOKE - TIGERCUB ♪

I try not to think about the last time I touched a Yesterday gun as I hold one in both hands.

The grip is ice cold in my grasp as we weave between shadows and trees, until we're standing on the slope that overlooks the back of the greenhouse.

Aaron's breath hitches at the sight, but he catches and quickly swallows it to regain focus. He leans over to whisper into my ear, pointing to tendrils of smoke in the distance that can't be coming from the bonfire we saw on our way in. "Cecil's drawing the Chasers away, but stay quiet. There could still be a few standing guard—anywhere, really."

"That's all from his smoke grenades?"

Aaron nods. "I'm carrying our supply in one of my bags. We only have three to use if we need them since Cecil took the bulk of Beau's stock. But only for emergencies or at Cecil's command. Where are your knives?"

I lift up my jacket to show him the leather belt holster Cecil had packed for each of us, where my throwing knives are sheathed.

"And your other one?"

I show him my boot.

"Good. And you remember how to shoot?"

Too well, I want to say, but I nod instead.

"Follow my lead and stay close." He glances at me briefly. "Absolutely wrathful?"

I hold back the faintest urge to smirk. "Absolutely."

The sun is already setting, painting the endless expanse of gray above our heads with streaks of gold. What little light cracks through the surface of the clouds casts drastic shadows, providing at least a little cover as we follow the slope down to the back wall of the greenhouse. I bite my lip to try to distract myself from the pain in my ankle and neck as I limp closely behind Aaron's silent footsteps.

He presses his back against the wall before peering around the corner, watching and listening for any sign of movement. "Coast is clear."

Mindful of our footsteps, we hurry across the grass and make our way to a side entrance. It's a chipped white door draped in a curtain of ivy that Aaron brushes aside before opening. He pulls me inside and shuts it.

My heart breaks at the sight of the greenhouse's main room. Everything is shadowed since we can't turn on the lights without getting noticed, but even in the darkness, I can see that what once was a lush green escape brimming with life is half dead and overgrown with weeds. The persimmon trees are barren. I don't spot a single butterfly either. The pool that was once glistening and perfectly clear is now clouded and thick with dark green algae.

"What happened to this place?" I spin slowly in a circle, neck craning as I try to make sense of what I'm seeing. If I remember correctly, Aaron said that the greenhouse was still thriving when Noriko stumbled across it. Overgrown, but alive, at least. But everything in here is the color of wheat, so brittle and dry it could snap with the smallest pinch.

"They must have messed with the controls. Or broken some of the sprinklers," Aaron mutters uneasily, then gives me a glance. "In and out."

It sounds more like a reminder for him.

"What exactly are we getting?" I ask, jogging to catch up to Aaron, who's already making his way toward the storage room that leads to the other section of the greenhouse. This time, he doesn't offer me a mask as we part the curtain. *I've been debugged for long enough,* I note. *The Catnap can't affect me if I don't have the trigger in my system.*

"Our priority is my dad's lab," Aaron answers as we walk into the back section. Rows of Catnap still grow in their planter boxes, but most of the old lab equipment has been cleared already, probably confiscated to be sent back to the Corps for closer investigation. "But I wanted to get a few clippings to bring back to End Harbor."

He kneels by one of the planter squares, and I do the same, pulling out my hunting knife as he retrieves his. "I'm giving us five minutes to get as many as we can fit inside your empty pack, since you should be carrying the lightest load. I'll carry whatever else we find later—you shouldn't be putting too much weight on that leg."

My right ankle throbs, so I don't protest.

I follow Aaron's lead, cutting leaves and shoving them in the plastic gallon bags he'd packed in his satchel. The minutes fly by in wordless silence.

"Our five minutes are up." Aaron rises to his feet. "These are hardy as hell and propagate easily. Think succulents. So we should be fine with what we have."

I close the last plastic bag and toss it into the backpack Cecil gave me, which is now stuffed to the brim with clippings. I stand up and sling it over one shoulder while my traveling pack hangs off the other.

"You got everything?"

I nod. "Let's get out of here."

We hurry through the curtain and back into the main room—and freeze when we both hear voices.

Aaron ducks behind a ceramic planter overgrown with dead boxwood, pulling me down with him. He presses a finger to his lips.

"Can't believe one of them came back." An unfamiliar male voice echoes throughout the room as the front door closes behind them. I hear two pairs of footsteps. Every click echoes between the walls like claps. *Those are boots.*

"Can't believe any of them got *away,* let alone the majority," another voice says, this one female.

"What, you think they got tipped off?"

"I'm not saying anything."

My pulse pounds against my ribcage so loudly it's nauseating. My lips tremble but the rest of me is frozen, rooted to the spot where we crouch. I feel my leg muscles tighten, ready to sprint, eyes darting across the room. *If we get caught...*

I can't think about what that would mean right now.

Aaron's Yesterday gun is still in his holster, but he holds the handle of his knife—the only weapon he really trusts—with pale knuckles. The tendons in his neck stand out, his shoulders tight.

The footsteps grow louder for a moment and then pause. I grab Aaron's arm, worried we've been seen. He nods to his right, and my grip loosens when I see a pair of Officers leaning casually against the wall. It's too dark for them to see us as we crawl to the other side of the pot so we can stare at them directly through the dead plant that hides our faces.

"Yeah, well, at least we snagged a couple on their way out," the man says. His blond hair is cropped short, and a beard covers the bottom half of his face.

"Twenty-three, to be exact." The other Chaser has light brown hair that falls barely behind her ears. She pulls out a cigarette from the compartment in her suit. I think of the lighter in my pocket, gut churning. "Smoke?"

"No." Her partner chuckles. "That stuff will kill you."

"It's no worse than what we're breathing in out there." She uses a mechanism in her suit to light the cigarette with a disgusted frown, wrinkling her nose with a shudder. "I know I complain about patrolling this place, but I'd hate to be on body-burning duty right now."

Aaron's eyes widen, whites showing, nostrils flaring. Every muscle and vein in his neck and arms strain against his skin, as though trying to tear their way out.

My body quivers. I blink rapidly as my stomach twists, trying to process what I've heard. I cover my mouth and nose with my hand. As if that will keep me from breathing in any more of this air than I already have.

I don't have time to think about it before Aaron jolts upward, knife at the ready. I yank him back down, locking my arms around both of his. "Are you *trying* to give us away?" I whisper fiercely.

He attempts to free himself, but I hold him down. I don't need to look into his eyes to know what is—or isn't—there.

"They're burning them, Ed. *That's* what we're smelling," he whispers, turning his head to seethe over his shoulder. "And they're—like it's nothing."

He can't even get the words out straight.

"We can't think about that right now, okay? We need to focus on getting to your dad's old lab, remember? That's all. Then we'll run back to the van, and when we're safe, you can let it all out. But right now, we have to do our job. We can't put everyone else in danger by being stupid."

He clamps his teeth shut, clawing the skin of his palms with his nails, broken finger and all. I'm not sure he even feels the pain.

"Remember what Cecil said?" he hisses. "About doing what we need to do?"

"What we *need* is to get out of here," I whisper. "Let's just do what we came here to do and think about it later."

"They're Chasers, Ed," he spits through woven teeth. "I'd rather hurt them than have one of them hurt us."

"They're still people," I snap, keeping my voice low. "Disabling their trackers will turn both of us into targets, and we still haven't hit the lab."

Aaron's stare is wide-eyed, and he carves me with it. "They're *Chasers*."

"So was he." I soften my glare. "So was your sister."

His muscles loosen, arms falling to his sides. He can't look at me anymore, so he stares at the Officers instead, gliding his thumb across the hilt of his knife. Like it's taking every ounce of strength in his body to fight the urge to use it.

"Let's go." I nod toward the row of barren fruit trees. Their planter boxes are overgrown with towering weeds—the perfect shielded pathway toward the side door.

Aaron hesitates, then nods. His glower fades. The hollowness behind his gaze is filled in, and he returns to his senses.

Before we get the chance to move, the radio in Aaron's pocket goes off.

Aaron, do you copy?

The Chasers freeze, exchanging confused glances. "Hello?"

They wait for a response.

The radio goes off again.

I hope you're finished out there because I need you to make some noise. Soon.

"Is someone there?"

The room goes dead quiet. Aaron freezes, unable to reach behind him and silence the radio without giving our position away.

We crouch lower as footsteps approach. My heart races and I ready my gun, hands trembling and clammy as I pray that I won't have to use it. I squeeze the gun so tightly my skin burns. The footsteps grow close. Closer. *Closer*—until they stop completely.

Aaron's knife moves before they get the chance to pull out their guns.

It hits the blond-haired Chaser in the neck. A shining wave of crimson blood cascades down his uniform. The other Chaser pulls out her white Nightjade gun, aiming it at Aaron, who runs to retrieve his knife.

I tackle her before she can pull the trigger.

The still-lit cigarette flies out of her hands as we roll to the ground, barely missing the wall of weeds behind us. Her fist cracks against my cheek— which only makes me angry as I struggle to make it out on top, so I swing, and miss. She kicks the Yesterday gun out of my hands. It glides across the cement, spinning in violent cartwheels until it's too far out of reach to even think about retrieving.

I throw another punch and hit her square in the jaw, then again. But when I swing a third time, she rolls out of the way and I cry out in pain as my knuckles crack against the ground instead. I don't have time to check my bloody fingers for damage before she's on top of me, pointing a Nightjade gun to my forehead. I'm not strong enough to overpower her, at least not in my current condition. I can't reach my hunting knife in my boot, and she's kneeling on my legs. My throwing blades are still sheathed but painfully dig into the skin of my right thigh against the weight of her knee.

She pins my injured right hand to the ground, her other arm busy with her gun. "You're dead, traitor."

I can taste the smoke from her abandoned cigarette. It curls into my nose and burns my throat. *Is this going to be the last thing I smell?*

I think of Carmody, of the forbidden habit he was able to buy with his Immunity that always lingered on his clothes. His breath.

Before she can pull the trigger, I reach the only thing I can access. I flick open Carmody's lighter—and I hold the flame to her eyes.

She shrieks in pain, clawing at her face with one hand—but the other still holds the gun. She can't see a thing, but I've made her angry. She shoots it aimlessly and I roll to the ground, dodging a dark purple capsule. I know the Nightjade won't kill me, but if it knocks me out, a Chaser certainly will.

Nightjade bullets bounce across the walls and floor. There is nowhere for me to go. I cover my ears and squeeze my eyes shut. *Maybe this is a fight I can't win.*

No.

I open my eyes. She's still shooting, but she can't see me. She can't see where she's going either, and she walks backward, right into the wall of weeds.

I crawl to the end of the planter box. Before she can pull herself up, I open the lighter.

The tinder ignites in an instant.

A Chaser's uniform is fireproof—but a human head is not.

Her skin is melting right off.

She's still screaming.

Aaron retrieves his knife from the dead Chaser and hurries to my side, pulling me up by the shoulders. "We gotta go, Voclain."

I can't peel my eyes away from her burning skin. I think back to the skeletons at the gas station. *Her bones are the same as mine.*

Beneath the flesh, she is just as human as I am.

"Hey, hey. Look at me." Aaron turns me around so I'm facing him. "Are you hurt?"

I shake my head frantically, out of breath. "You?"

"Thanks to you, no." He retrieves a bandage from his satchel and ties my right middle and ring finger together. I wince.

Something crashes behind us, and we spin around. The flames have spread quickly. They eat away at the brittle ivy growing up the wall, cracking and flooding the room with smoke and embers. Aaron's eyes reflect an amber glow as he watches the room burn.

"We need to go. Now." I tug at his arm, pulling him out of his trance. We run toward the exit as fast as we can.

I ignore the sharp pain in my leg and the aching in my muscles as we sprint across the grass outside the greenhouse, making our way west toward Simon's old lab, which is a brick building I can barely make out from our distance. We crest a small berm about a football field away and stumble to a stop, hands on our knees as we desperately try to wrangle our breath. We're still panting when we slowly turn to assess the damage we left behind.

In the growing shadow of twilight, our horizon clouds with smoke. Cecil sets off another diverting bomb in the distance, followed by an eruption of shouts. The bonfire of bones still burns.

And the dome of the greenhouse finally shatters, every shard falling like drops of glistening rain as the building is swallowed by flames.

EDDIE

Saturday, April 6
69 Beds Made

♪ GASOLINE - DEAD SONS ♪

On the outside, Simon's lab is an unassuming block of crumbling bricks, laced with English ivy and crawling with spiders. But the moment we burst through the front door, I realize how foolish the Chasers were to overlook what they must have mistaken for a tool shed.

The lab has only one room, but it holds more knowledge than I've seen in my life. Everywhere I turn there is a stack of books, a table sprawled with test tubes, an anatomical poster plastered to the wall. There isn't a single inch of free space in sight, and when I study the scrapbook walls, I suddenly understand where Aaron inherited his thinking process from.

"We don't have much time," Aaron says.

He pulls open a white cabinet, then starts dumping vials and tools into his bags with the generosity of a child robbing a candy store. He barely spends a second in thought before making the decision to throw something in. Clean syringes, bottles of dried herbs, fresh bandages—every item is a healer's dream. He raids a stash of almost two decades' worth of smuggled medical goods in seconds. I'm unsurprised to see him go for the surgical blades too.

"This is all we can carry," he says when both of his backpacks are stuffed. He pauses in front of a bookcase and stares at it for a moment too long before grabbing a book from the shelf and tucking it into his satchel. "Let's get out of here."

We sprint out of the lab and head into the northern woods to go around the burning greenhouse, which is probably already swarming with Officers and Agents. I tell myself to swallow every pain in my body as we run as fast as we can, breathlessly dodging trees, rocks, and roots to make our way east, hidden beneath the cover of pine trunks and falling night.

Nice going with the fire.

Cecil's voice breaks the silence, and we stop running, slumping against a large fallen log. When I turn my head around, through the gaps between trees, I can see the church in the distance. It's eerily quiet. *They must be sending most of their units to the greenhouse.*

Aaron's eyes are glued to the smoke in the distance.

I grab the radio from his hands and speak into it. "What should we do now?"

You hit the lab?

"Yeah."

I'm all out of smoke grenades. Viv and Hugo are still raiding the church; you two are gonna have to create a few diversions to keep their coast clear. I'm hiding in a portable to talk to you right now, but I'm gonna head back out soon and try to lead these Whiteboots south the old-fashioned way. Avoid the armory and greenhouse—most of the Agents stationed here will be investigating them. As far as I know, Officers are the ones addressing combat

right now. Stay away from those areas, and you should be fine.

"Where do you want us to drop the smoke?"

Where they don't expect it.

"What does that—"

Shit. I gotta go. Good luck, stay smart. And whatever you do, stick together.

The radio goes silent.

"If Cecil's heading south and the church is in the center of the compound, we should draw them east," Aaron says. "Past the armory."

"But didn't Cecil say—"

"Past. We'll run through the woods and go around it, drop a few smoke grenades over there, then run back to the van." Aaron goes quiet, studying me. "You can't run very fast right now, can you?"

"I can run just fine."

"Eddie."

I open my mouth to argue, then bite my lip, crossing my arms and averting my gaze.

"I think you should head back to the van."

I glare. "There's no way I'm leaving without you."

"Then go back to the cabin, at least. Not the occupied one. I'll meet you there."

"I can help, Aaron."

"Once a smoke grenade goes off, Chasers will be sent after us like that." He snaps his fingers, and the sound echoes throughout the trees. "We'll have to sprint to avoid being seen, and then drop another one somewhere else to throw them off our trail. Do you really think you can handle that?"

I stare at my shoes because I know he's right. I'll only slow him down. I shouldn't endanger the others either.

"I'm not asking because I think you're *weak*, Voclain," he says, losing his patience. "I'm asking because I know you better than you think I do. Because I know you're resilient enough to endure whatever pain you think you have to bear until you can't anymore. And I don't want it to get to that point. It *can't* get to that point."

"Aaron—"

"Eddie." He whispers my name like a plea. "For me."

When I meet his gaze, I realize this is no longer about me. This is no longer about my pride. If I go out there with Aaron, it'll hurt him more than it'll hurt me.

"Fine." I let my eyes fall again—until I have an idea. "What if we split up?"

Aaron's brows furrow. "What?"

"I set off one smoke grenade, then radio you, and you set off another immediately after. That'll give me enough time to drop another one somewhere else without sprinting. We'll be far enough apart for it to confuse them. We'll meet at the cabin after."

"But—"

I frown. "You suggested splitting up too, remember? What makes this any different?"

He lets out an exhausted sigh, rubbing his face with his hands. "You're killing me, Voclain."

I glare, ready to argue—but we're running out of time, and I'm tired as well. My expression softens. "You trust me, right?"

He flinches at the word, then freezes, his shoulders rigid. He studies me, analyzing every inch of my face, my eyes, until his muscles relax. His clenched fingers uncurl. "Of course I do."

"Is that a promise?"

His pinky twitches. He exhales softly. "Yeah."

"Then keep it. Trust me to look out for myself." I step forward. "Trust me to look out for you."

Reluctantly, he nods. "Okay."

To the east of the square, beyond the Agent-infested armory, is a neighborhood of portable rooms that once served as homes for the residents of the Cut. It's not as dense or populated with as many buildings as the Block, but that means the gaps between the houses are filled with more trees—and more places to hide.

I jog from the northern woods, breaking through a barrier of trees until I reach a narrow dirt road surrounded by towering pines that must be older than I am. A light breeze whispers through the branches, tossing my hair and pricking my skin with biting breaths of cold.

The sun has fully set now, shrouding me in deep blue shadows as I jog behind one of the portables, find a tree, and press my back against it. In this blanket of dark, I am perfectly hidden.

I stand still, listening carefully to the sounds the wind carries my way. Shouts echo across the compound, muffled by the distance as Chasers scramble to put out every literal and metaphorical fire. The armory, Cecil's smoke grenades, the greenhouse—every piece we've played has Officers and Agents spread thin while they try to balance investigation with pest control. There are too few of us; we slip out of their hands easily. We could be anywhere.

And the greenhouse still burns.

That's where most of the commotion is coming from, I realize. With all of that dead vegetation inside, the flames must be growing quickly. They need as many hands on deck as possible to contain that fire before it devours the entire Cut.

The wind continues to whisper, and I stare at the sky. *Or this entire forest.*

I'm pulled out of my thoughts when the walkie-talkie in my back pocket goes off.

Voclain, do you read me?

"Yeah."

I'm in position.

With the noise and interference from the wind, Aaron's voice sounds distorted. His words cut in and out.

I'm—the southern border.

"I'm having trouble hearing you."

You're—cutting out, Voclain.

I stare at the sky again, not a star in sight with all the clouds and smoke. The branches shake above me. A few pine needles rain down like snow, and a speck of dirt flies into my eye. I rub it out. "Must be the wind."

The breeze wavers for just a moment, barely leaving enough room for Aaron to speak.

Set off when you're ready. I'll pop mine the moment I see yours. When we're done, don't try and find me—go straight to the cabin, and I'll find you. Promise?

"I promise."

Think smart, Voclain.

The wind starts to pick up again, but I swear I hear the word *wrathful* before his line goes silent.

"Absolutely," I whisper, though he can't hear me.

I pocket the walkie-talkie, then reach into my clipping-filled backpack. I have two smoke grenades inside, and I pull out one.

It's a metal canister the size of a soda can, capped with a round pin. The breeze shakes the tree again and it drops a few more pine needles onto my head. I tilt my chin upward.

Seeing the branches above me makes time shift. I think back to summers in Ren and Margot's backyard, remembering the way we used to climb the Callery pear tree that Asa planted before the twins were born. I close my eyes, clearly picturing the white blossoms it would be covered with during this time of year, and the little acorn-sized fruits I would chuck at Ren's head from the highest branch.

I open my eyes.

If I can climb this tree, I'll have the advantage of height, concealment, and a good view of what's going on below. I'll be above the smoke, and I'll be able to throw the grenade far enough to negate the need for me to overexert myself by jogging from Point A to Point B. I can throw them both in either direction—and save my leg strength for my escape. No slowing anyone down.

I can't leave my bags by the base of the tree without giving away my position, but they're light enough that I keep them slung over my shoulder as I jump to grab the lowest branch.

Remember the pear tree.

I swing both legs until the bottom of my boots are planted on the trunk, walking up the bark with my fingers still gripping the branch. I bite my lip, trying to ignore the pain in my right hand, and bring my legs up to the branch. Blood rushes to my head as I hang upside down.

Remember the pear tree.

I close my eyes, take a deep breath, and swing my body upright.

I look down and realize I'm a lot closer to the ground than I thought. I stare up at the rest of the tree that towers above me. *I can do this.*

I have to.

I swallow the lump in my throat and try to keep my trembling under control as I hold onto the branch, pulling myself up until I'm standing. I place my foot on a small stubby branch and use it to propel myself upward.

"One fluid motion." I remember the words Aaron whispered to me during target practice. *"A seamless transfer of balance."*

I reach for a higher branch, relying on momentum to pull myself onto it without putting too much weight on my injured hand and ankle. *Don't look down*, I warn myself. *Don't you dare.*

I was never scared of heights as a kid. I must have climbed that pear tree a hundred times. Even as I stood on that bridge with Ren last summer, before we fell together in the leap of faith that started far more than I ever could have realized in the moment, the height didn't faze me.

But as I pull myself higher and higher—as I start to see beyond the rooftops, beyond the smoke, beyond the smaller trees beneath me—I realize that I am no longer fearless. *Where has the child within me gone?*

Why does it feel like I've lost her?

Part of me wonders if I'll ever get her back.

When I am as high up as I can be with a clear path back down, I rise to my feet, holding onto the branch above me for support. My knees buckle, and I force myself not to think about how far I'd have to fall to reach the ground as a pile of fractured bones.

I retrieve the smoke grenade. Up here, the wind is no longer a whisper, but a bellowing voice that beckons every branch to bend. I taste metal on my tongue as I nearly lose my footing. I swallow the adrenaline down, every part of me quivering.

I pull the pin with my teeth, aim north, and throw the grenade as far as I can.

The second I spend waiting passes like minutes.

And the grenade finally combusts.

I hold the branch above me with both hands now, steadying myself as a cloud of smoke erupts in the distance. Far away from my trees. I can already see a unit of Chasers in their white suits of armor running down the stone streets and dirt paths to try and locate the source. The traitor.

I pull out my radio. "Aaron, do you copy?"

I wait for a response. Nothing.

"Aaron, do you copy?" I repeat, louder this time.

There must be interference from the wind. I turn my head south to watch for his bomb to go off. We agreed that he'd pop his the moment after he saw mine, with or without radio communication. *Then what's taking him so long?*

I wait. One minute passes, then two. Aaron's smoke never appears.

After what must be the third minute, panic floods through me. Every muscle in my body tightens. My breaths turn rapid and shallow. I squeeze my eyes shut and pry them open again, as though that will make his smoke appear. As though that will pull me out of this tree and place me back down on the ground and I can forget about all of this and just go to sleep.

I'm still here.

There is still no smoke signal.

I'm about to pull out my walkie-talkie again when I see something move in the distance. I squint to make out the details of the Cut's chaos with my blurred vision and realize that I'm staring at the square. I can see the church, its towering steeple so small as I watch from such great heights.

My heart plummets when a stream of Chasers file inside the building. *Viv and Hugo are still in there.*

Without thinking, I crouch and drop to the branch beneath me. I ignore the darts of pain that nearly make me cry out with every sharp movement as I climb back down—and I slip on the last branch.

A patch of grass cushions my fall, but my left wrist is not spared from a sprain. I call out in pain as sparks fly through my arm. *This can't be happening right now.*

I stand, head spinning. There is no time to wrap my arm, no time to find Aaron. There is only me and my one good leg, and that has to be enough as I run to the square, no matter how desperately every bone and muscle in my body is begging me to stop.

I take the woods again to avoid the armory until I am up another slope, staring at the backside of the church. There's a stained glass window illuminated by a glow from within, but I can't see through it. I run as quietly as I can and press my back against its white walls, wait until the coast is clear, and sprint around to the front.

Now, I press my body against the front wall, and I peer my head inside.

For a moment, it feels like time is standing still. I am back inside these walls, watching Ren from across the room. But the moment fades the second I count five Nightjade guns. Five suits of armor. Five Chasers lined up in front of Viv and Hugo, unmoving.

"Requesting Agent backup." One of the Officers speaks into what I assume is a built-in communication device in his wrist. "We have two Undergrounders that should be questioned and exterminated."

While the Chaser is distracted, Viv's eyes meet mine. I place a finger over my lips as Hugo notices me too, and they avert their gazes quickly.

"What are you looking at?" one of the Officers barks.

I pull away from the door and keep my back pressed against the wall, heart slamming violently against my ribcage. I squeeze my eyes shut.

"Nothing," Hugo says a little too frantically, then clears his throat.

"Just a bird," Viv adds.

The Chaser pauses in silent disbelief. "Check the perimeter while we wait for backup. Just in case any more traitors are hiding nearby."

I hear a pair of footsteps crack against the floorboards, echoing throughout the church as they grow closer and closer. *Think, Eddie, think.*

My eyes widen. I take out my last smoke grenade, pull the pin, and throw it inside.

The Chasers call out in unison as the room explodes with smoke. I cover my mouth and pull away from the doors as white-gray clouds drift through them, reaching out and curling around the stagnant jackalope fountain in the square's center. I take another look inside and notice something glowing orange behind the screen of smoke. Something moving.

The paper lining the walls made the church a perfect tinderbox.

In an instant, Hugo and Viv bolt through the doors, almost running into me as the Chasers inside scramble in search of their missing prey.

"Where's Aaron?" Hugo asks.

"There's no time to explain," I say. "Run to the van. I'll find him. We'll meet you there."

They exchange worried glances, and Viv pulls me into a tight, brief hug before sprinting away with Hugo. They go north, disappearing into the woods before I can draw another breath.

I don't wait a second longer to run.

I move as quickly as I can with my bad leg, but it's still not as fast as I'd like. I exit the square and run in the dark through the nearly empty Block, heading south in the direction of the cabins.

When I'm far enough away from the flames and shouting, shielded by the cover of evening, I pause to catch my breath, grimacing at the pain in my ankle. *No,* I correct myself. My entire leg—my entire *body* feels like it's on fire again. Cold air and exhaustion sear the inside of my lungs. The three months I've spent sitting around haven't done me any favors.

I try to take in my surroundings, desperate for any sign of Aaron. All I see are trees and abandoned homes.

Wind tangles my hair, sending shivers that trace the rings of my spine with cold, prickling fingers. *Where is he?*

I pull out my radio again. "Aaron?"

Nothing.

Fear tightens my stomach into knots. I hug my abdomen with one arm, rubbing the fingernails of my free hand against my lips in trembling, dreadful sweeps. *Think.*

If his smoke grenade never went off, that can only mean one of two things. Either he was unlucky enough to have a faulty grenade, or he never got the chance to set his off.

Beau may be many things, but as hard as it is to believe, he's no idiot. I don't think I've ever met a person who loves explosives more than he does. The likelihood of a faulty grenade is much slimmer than something going awry in a place crawling with Chasers.

My body is weak, and I feel like throwing up, but there's no time for weakness. If Aaron is in trouble, I need to act. Now.

I look around again, biting my lips as the wind blows, carrying ash with every invisible current, spreading every ember I've left behind in my wake.

I think back to what Aaron said—about the promise we made to meet at the cabin, no matter what. That is our surest chance of reuniting. Maybe our only chance. Wherever he is, I can't go looking for him. Because if I'm not at that cabin when he gets there, something tells me that not even a promise could keep him from searching for me.

I stare at the sky, watching something orange follow the breeze. An ember falls to my feet, barely a grain of sand. A blade of grass catches fire and burns for only a moment until the wind snuffs it out. But a tendril of smoke curls into the sky, rising long after the flame dies.

I hug my abdomen with both arms and stare at the faraway flames. That's where most of the Officers are being sent—to put out the fires.

I pull Carmody's lighter out of my pocket, tracing the engraving of his initials, feeling its frigid metal surface as I stare at an empty portable to my right.

Smoke is the best way to get yourself seen.

If something really did happen to Aaron, he'll need all the diversions he can get. While I can't search for him, and I can't stay long enough to wait for him to find me, I sure as hell can light a few more fires on my way out.

Absolutely wrathful.

I think of the way Aaron held me in the home he left behind for good. I think of every home left behind, including my own. I think of my aching chest, of this gnawing rage—always tearing but never able to claw its way out. I think of bones.

I think of every single thing that has been taken from me as I open Carmody's lighter.

They will see me.

I cough up smoke as I sprint out of the last burning portable.

I run into the woods, and I don't look back.

Every inch of my body begs me to stop by the time I reach the cabin—the rotting one, where Aaron and I agreed to meet. It feels like there are no breaths left for me to give. As though all the strength I ever had has been sapped from me, like blood to a drawing syringe.

But I made it.

I fall to my knees and unroll the sleeping bag I'd left behind. *I'll just close my eyes until Aaron gets here—and then we'll go to the van.*

The door opens.

I scramble upright, eyes wide. A figure stands in the doorframe, leaning against it. I'm too exhausted to grab my knife from my boot before I realize there's a Nightjade gun in their hands, and I freeze.

"Lavender Voclain." A voice I don't recognize cuts through the dark, sending shivers crawling around my neck and down my spine as he closes the door. He takes a seat at the table like it's his own. "What a pleasure it is to finally meet you."

EDDIE

Saturday, April 6
69 Beds Made

♪ FEATHERY - MILKY CHANCE ♪

I'm not sure how long I stare at the stranger before scrambling backward, right into the wall.

He stands to yank the chain hanging from the ceiling. A flickering light floods the room as he sits down again, leaning back in his chair while he tosses a black Nightjade gun back and forth between his hands. Like it's a toy and not a lethal weapon that could knock me out for hours.

The image before me sinks in. He has warm olive skin and a wavy mess of golden-brown hair that curls behind his ears, almost the color of sand. His sharp nose looks like it's been broken before, and spread across its bridge is the smallest collection of freckles. He's older than me, but only by a few years. *He's too young.*

"I saw you sneak inside and thought I'd invite myself in." His thin lips creep into an amused grin when he sees me trembling. "What? Am I really so frightening?"

My hands clench into fists, so tightly my nails cut crescent moons into my flesh, save for the middle finger I'm sure I've broken. I itch to grab the knife from my boot, but I hold myself back. *Any sudden movements and I'll be shot unconscious.*

Which is as good as dead in the presence of an Agent.

Or at least, that's what I think he is. I've only seen one real Agent up close in my life, but I grew up hearing the stories, fearing the people in neatly pressed black suits with shades covering their eyes.

He fits the description perfectly.

The Agent uses one hand to remove the shades, folding them and letting them hang off his collar to reveal a set of soft brown eyes that look too human to belong to a creature like him. "That's much better, isn't it?"

It's worse. But I can't tell him that.

He resumes tossing the Nightjade gun back and forth, gesturing with his chin toward the chair in front of him. "You look uncomfortable. Have a seat."

I glare at him, unmoving.

"Go on." He smiles, revealing a set of pearly white teeth. "I don't bite."

Slowly, I stand and do as he says. *No one questions an Agent.*

That's the narrative they always spun in school, anyway. *Agents are the best soldiers the Chaser Corps has to offer*, they'd say. *Keep your head down. Don't make eye contact. And whatever you do, always follow their command.*

My teachers never had to explain the *otherwise* half of that train of thought. We always knew that even looking at an Agent the wrong way meant death. Most of the time, people pretend they don't even exist. *Because that's the best way to deal with what you fear, isn't it?*

I take a seat. Head down. No eye contact.

"You're Lavender Voclain, right?" The Agent crosses his arms, casually pointing the gun in my direction like it's a finger. "You seemed a lot more talkative on that broadcast. A lot less pale too. Or—green, I guess. Jesus, you're clammy."

My eyes snap up to meet his. "Why do you think?"

The room goes quiet, like a vacuum has sucked every last bit of oxygen straight from it.

Shit. My pulse thuds in my ears. *Shit shit shit.*

I broke the rule.

I expect him to put a Nightjade bullet in my forehead right then and there, but instead, he laughs. A real, almost sunny, belly laugh, human to match his eyes, youthful to confirm that he is in fact as fresh of a cadet as I thought. *And he's on a job as important as this?*

I swallow the lump in my throat, trying not to think about what that could mean—or what he's done to get here.

"What do you want?" I seethe, trying to keep my fear and anger contained. Both are either weaknesses he could easily exploit, or a way to test the narrative. Again.

"That's a very interesting question." He leans back again, acting like he's lost in thought. As if he couldn't already answer in a moment's notice. "Why don't I start by introducing myself?"

He extends one arm away from his chest. The other one still has a Nightjade gun tucked beneath it. "Agent M. Heron, at your service."

I keep my arms pressed against my abdomen.

"Oh, come on. A little manners wouldn't hurt now, would they?"

Manners? An Agent wants to talk to *me* about manners?

Crescent moons, crescent moons.

I shake his hand.

"Now that we're properly acquainted, I think I should make one thing clear." He leans forward, folding his hands on the table, gun still in his grasp. "I'm not interested in taking down the Unseen."

I blink.

"That's what you Undergrounders call yourselves, right? The Unseen?" He points at me again with his gun.

I clench my jaw, unsure of what this guy is playing at. "Then what do you want?"

I brace myself as his grin fades, knowing exactly what he's going to say. *It's me, isn't it?*

If he can't manage to swing the downfall of the Unseen, then at least he can turn me in to his higher-ups and enjoy the prizes that will surely follow. I think back to what Aaron said about rewards in that gas station market and shudder. *I'm currency.*

"Information," Heron says.

"Information?" My brows knit together. I blink a few times to make sure he really is nodding. "But you're an Agent."

"I know. Strange, isn't it?"

"You have access to… everything."

Anything he could possibly dream of lies at his fingertips, and he wants information from me?

"That is true, to an extent. But… not applicable in the context of what I'm looking for."

Crescent moons. "And what is that, exactly?"

"You guys had Chasers on the inside, right?" Heron chuckles. "Sorry, let me rephrase that." His dimples smooth out. "I know you've had Chasers on the inside. Ren McLellan is living proof of that, isn't he?"

The world stops spinning. My heart leaps into my throat, choking each unstable breath as I sit in silence, unable to inhale as much as an ounce of air. My lungs keep still for so long I can feel them start to ache. A searing, gut-churning pain that I try and fail to swallow down as I dissect Heron's words in my mind.

I go over them a dozen times, and there is one word stuck on repeat.

Living.

My muscles relax. I absorb the word, letting it settle into my skin like honey being stirred into hot tea. These are the words I've been waiting for, begging—praying to hear for so long.

But can I trust them?

My hands clench again, every muscle in my neck and jaw twitching as I hold back the urge to claw his eyes out. "Where is he?"

"We're getting ahead of ourselves here," Heron says, his voice smooth. "Being an Agent is only five percent skill. Ten percent connection. The other eighty-five is purely performance—and I certainly have quite the watchful audience."

He leans forward in his seat, so close that I can smell stale coffee on his breath. "You traitors know how to cross barriers that I cannot. You have both the means and the freedom to harvest whatever knowledge you could possibly desire without the same repercussions I'd have. You can find answers to questions that even an Agent like myself would get silenced over, just for asking. And you can do it all without being traced. Because that's what this whole thing's been about, right? Remaining unseen?"

I keep my teeth sewn together as I ask the question one more time. My crescent moons draw blood. "What do you want?"

All the humor and faux politeness the Agent has conjured up until this moment falls away, revealing a familiar kind of hollowness that's almost cutting to look at. "I want you to find the Chaser who killed my brother. Only then will we even *discuss* a trade."

My breath hitches, my guard crumbling as desperation wraps its hands around my throat, squeezing it so tightly that my next words slip out as a whisper. "For Ren?"

He doesn't nod, but he doesn't deny it either.

I can't breathe. My hands won't stop trembling. *If Ren is alive... if Heron knows where he is... that would make him a prisoner, wouldn't it?*

I don't know if I should feel relieved or sick.

"So you've seen him?" I manage to choke out. "And he's alive?"

"I've seen him, alright," Heron says. "I'd even say I know him."

My stomach churns. I scour his eyes with a glare, desperate for any scrap of information I can get. I commit them to memory, like the pages of a book, or a bullseye carved into tree bark. I memorize every grain in his iris —and I find nothing that tells me how he knows Ren, or what he could have possibly done to him.

Behind those eyes, there is nothing at all.

"Your brother," I whisper. "He was killed by a Chaser?"

Heron nods.

"Why do you think I'd know anything about that?" *He's closer to any Chaser than I am.*

"Because my brother was a traitor," he says quietly. "Just like you."

I clear my throat. "What was his name?"

Heron pulls out a black burner phone, the flippable and untraceable kind with a touch screen.

"Everything I thought I knew about him is on a document I've stored in here. Along with the most recent photo I took of him." Heron flips open the phone, pulling up the photo and turning the device to show me. "Have you seen this man before?"

The photo shows an unshaven man in his late twenties, with shoulder-length brown hair and smiling brown eyes to match his brother's. That's the only familiarity I can place—the eyes.

I shake my head. "Never seen him before."

He snaps the phone shut and sets it on the table.

"Was he a part of... my group?" I ask, choosing my words carefully.

"You would know better than I do." Heron leans back again with his arms crossed. "So what do you say, Lavender? Care to do me this one little favor?"

I clench my jaw. "I'm not doing shit until you tell me where Ren is."

He stares at a watch on his wrist, then at the door, like he has somewhere to be. Then back at me, his stare cold and corrosive, even as he grins. "I thought I made it clear that you'd be delivering on your end first."

A scream lurks in my throat, trying to claw its way out. I can't stop imagining every different way that I could end this man's life right in this very moment—Nightjade gun or not.

Instead of peeling his eyes out of his skull, I bite back the scream. I make crescent moons until drops of blood trickle down my palm in a stream of warm crimson.

Didn't I say I'd do anything to get Ren back?

Isn't this what I really came all the way out here for? To find some piece of information that could lead me back to him?

I wouldn't trust this Agent with as much as my middle name if he didn't already know it. And still, the opportunity he's presenting me with could be my only chance at saving Ren. *My Ren.*

"Can I ask you something?" I say, voice dry. He waits for me to continue. "Why me?"

"All I need is a half-decent traitor. Any one of you would have done, I suppose." He grins. "We just happened to be lucky enough to cross paths tonight."

I feel like I'm going to be sick.

"I'd suggest gathering your answer sooner than later. You know..."

Heron stands and adjusts the sleeves of his suit. "Before he's too far gone."

My eyes widen as he walks toward the door, all the boiling rage in my gut instantly replaced by something frigid, something petrifying. No part of me refuses to tremble. Even my voice wavers. "What are you saying?"

He stops, hand wrapped around the doorknob as he shines me a cruel, opalescent grin. "That's for you to figure out on your own, Detective."

I don't have the time or the breath to say a word as he chuckles. "And if you tell anyone about this little arrangement of ours..." His voice softens. "I just hope you two have already said your goodbyes."

With that, the Agent disappears, the glistening black burner phone on the table the only sure sign that he was ever here at all.

Before I have a chance to blink, something explodes.

My blood runs cold as a sound I know all too well echoes throughout the trees, sending an eruption of crows scattering between branches in curdling cries for help. The very sound that keeps me awake at night and still manages to corrupt my mind every time I fall asleep.

That was the thunder of a Yesterday gun.

It was too far away to have any relation to Heron—and Agents know the truth about trackers. If he really did have a Yesterday gun on him, wouldn't he have threatened me with that instead?

My heart drops to my stomach.

I don't spare a second to think as I grab Heron's phone and my bags. I don't even bother turning off the light or closing the door behind me as I sprint through the trees in the direction of the sound, following the fleeing crows and the echoes of their cries like the clearest map. Thin branches whip my cheeks as I break past, drawing slivers of blood. I nearly stumble over every root and rock that meets my path. My leg must be burning, but if it is, I don't feel it, because time has gone still, and I am imprisoned in its amber.

Before I realize it, I'm stumbling to a stop in front of the cabin—the real one with glowing windows and smoke curling out of its chimney that I'm supposed to be avoiding at all costs.

I spot the blood-stained suit of armor before I notice the still-eyed Chaser inside of it, whose throat has been sliced open. He rests in the dirt a few yards away from where I stand.

Only when I hear a sneeze do I slowly force my body to turn around.

Sprawled across the porch steps, soaking in a lake of his own blood, Aaron clutches the bullet wound in his right thigh with trembling hands, barely able to choke out his next words.

"Hey, Voclain."

REN

Monday, January 29

No matter how many times I count my fingers and toes, I cannot convince myself that I am not dead.

I'm not sure why hell is designed like heaven. It has sand-colored walls and oak floors, and a dresser with a vase of cream tulips at the end of a bed that engulfs me in white linen. There is a nightstand to my left and a brass lamp to my right. Through lace curtains floods enough light to drown in. Too much light.

From my place in bed, I blink the world into existence. Slowly, things begin to fall into place. The lines become crisp. The ringing in my ears fades to a low hum. My eyes adjust to enough of the morning glare to stare beyond the window, where wild rye and untamed tufts of grass stretch to the edge of a cliff. If I listen carefully enough—past the jarring thuds of my own pounding pulse—I can hear a whisper.

There is an ocean beyond the cliff with impossibly dark water.

I turn my head away from the window. The moment I do so, something sharp stabs at my gut, drawing my attention to a pain I hadn't yet realized

I'm suffocating in. I wince, angling my chin to study my abdomen. My entire chest is bare, save for the tightly wound bandages that keep me mummified. A blossom of red seeps through the milky cloth like paint. I reach out to touch it, but something stops me. My right arm is handcuffed to the bed.

It is at this moment that all of the world crumbles beneath me.

It is at this moment that I die all over again, because slowly, like the spread of blood through fabric, I remember everything.

Eddie.

How her lips felt pressed against mine as we stood in solitude, illuminated by the blinking cityscape of control panels.

The broadcast that was cut short before she could tell the world about their eyes.

The Agents that stormed in to end my world with a Nightjade bullet— and how my body moved to stop it.

That was when everything turned dark.

The fractions of what I can recall are hazy, but I remember pieces of being dragged back into consciousness, only to find the remaining Agent watching me in a strange room with white walls. No more darkness. Only light. So much of it I could barely breathe. So much of it I could barely make out the Agent's hand, gripped around the throat of a confiscated Yesterday pistol.

And then I wasn't breathing.

I stare at the bandages again, wincing when I move my head. *This isn't right.*

I'm no expert on the afterlife, but I doubt you take your wounds with you when you die. *Maybe the rules operate differently for Chasers.*

But no matter how hard I try to convince myself this is it—that I have really met my end—I cannot shake the feeling that something vital is out of place. The ache that devours every inch of my body is too real. The gray morning sunlight burning my skin is too intense. But there is one thing that gives it away before anything else does.

The afterlife would not have lace curtains, linen bedding, and cream tulips for someone like me.

Against all my odds and intentions, I am still here.

I want to shake my head, but a pulsing ache keeps it in place. *No.* This can't be happening. This *shouldn't* be happening. I died, didn't I? I took a Nightjade bullet for Eddie that didn't kill me, so the Agent gave me a lead one that would.

Every part of me trembles. My throat suddenly feels tight, my skin feverish and slick with sweat. *If they have me, then why am I still alive?*

Eddie.

I snap forward, sitting up in bed. The movement is so jarring I can see stars. I ignore the pain and swallow the urge to dry heave. I can't hear anything beyond the thudding of my own heartbeat. My eyes dart around the room, searching for her, desperate for some sort of sign that she is alive too. She has to be. *She has to be.*

But it is not Eddie that my gaze finally rests upon.

In the far-left corner of the room is a young man in a black suit who leans against the wall, one hand beneath an open book and the other in his pocket. A wavy mop of light brown hair falls to his chin, tucked behind his ears in a way that seems too casual for his attire. His face is unshaven and his nose is slightly crooked, likely from a previous break.

He doesn't notice me, I think. I haven't decided by the time he speaks.

"You're awake."

There's a long pause. He keeps his eyes glued to the book while he finishes his sentence, then snaps it shut. He tosses it to the ground and folds his arms across his chest.

"It's about damn time."

PART TWO
TIDAL
PULL

EDDIE

Saturday, April 6
69 Beds Made

Not another second goes by before I'm kneeling by Aaron's side, calling for help.

He covers my mouth with his hands, grimacing through the pain. "Are you *crazy*? They'll hear you."

"But you're—"

"I'm fine," he snaps. "But if you call for help, I can guarantee you won't be getting any from a Chaser." He gestures to the dead Officer. "They'll be looking for him soon."

His breathing is heavy as he tries to keep his eyes open. I glance at the corpse, then back at Aaron. Both of them are covered in so much blood. *And what is he doing all the way out here?*

"I thought we agreed not to go after any Chasers unless we had to," I say through gritted teeth, pulling my knife from my pocket to tear a crimson patch of fabric from his pant leg. My shoulders slump when I sit back on my knees. "*Shit*, Aaron."

It's worse than I thought.

"I didn't, alright?" He winces as he tries to get up, leaning back against his elbows when he realizes he can't. He opens his satchel and pulls out his flask. "You need to go. Now."

"What?"

"*Dammit*, Voclain." He speaks as quickly as he can, breathless. "They'll start to wonder where that Officer is, and when they can't find his little dot on the map, they won't play nicely once they find you here with the *guy who killed him*."

"I'm not going anywhere."

He ignores me and opens the flask to take a swig. Thanks to my sanitized snakebite, there's barely anything left inside. He downs the rest in one gulp.

"What are you doing?"

He pulls out a pair of surgical forceps. "Getting this bullet out of me. Now go."

"You're not performing your own surgery."

"I've done it before."

When? "I don't care."

"Leave."

"No."

I try to take the forceps from his hand, but he holds them higher, swallowing the pain that comes with it. He looks me dead in the eye. "I swear to God, Voclain, if you don't leave *right now*—"

"Why won't you let me help you?" Now I'm the one sending crows away. I remember where we are and lower my voice. "For the last time, I'm not going anywhere."

My throat constricts. He keeps glaring, but I can tell he doesn't have the energy to hold it for much longer. The furrow in his brow softens.

"You're losing a lot of blood." I pack the forceps back into his bag and reach over to investigate the wound. I hold back a gasp when he grabs my wrist, eyes wide. He squeezes it as tightly as he can. I can still barely feel the grip of his trembling hand.

"When they get here..." His voice cracks like he has to force the words out.

Like it's taking all the strength he has left to say them and it's still not enough. "I can't protect you."

"I know," I whisper. "But *I* can protect *you*."

I remove his belt and tie it a few inches above the wound site to get the bleeding under control. My eyes dart back and forth to observe our surroundings in the dark. Wind tangles my hair, obscuring my vision. There are no Chasers around yet, but I know Aaron's right. As soon as they notice the dead Officer's lost signal they'll know a traitor is at fault. They'll send more soldiers after him than I'd be able to handle on my own. I'm not sure I have the strength to fend off just one in my current condition.

Aaron needs medical attention, but I'd be killing us both by deciding to operate on him here. We need to get somewhere safe—and the van is too far to be an option.

The van. I pull out my radio. "Cecil, do you read me?" Silence. "Hello?"

I change the channel. "Viv?"

Nothing. "Hugo?"

The wind whistles.

"*Shit.*" I shove the device back in my pocket and turn to Aaron, whose eyes are fluttering closed. I crawl closer, patting the sides of his face. "Hey. Stay awake."

"I'm here, Voclain," he says, eyes barely open. "I'm here."

I glance around again, eyes snagging on what looks like an old sled propped up against the cabin walls next to a spider-infested pile of firewood. I scramble to my feet and grab the sled, trying to ignore my sprained wrist and the raging pain in my fractured finger. I still wince while I haul it over to Aaron and set it down on the ground next to him. *It's heavier than I thought.* Or maybe I'm too weak.

No. No matter how exhausted I am, no matter how my head pounds or my bones ache, I can't be weak. That's not an option. Aaron carried me with a broken finger. Surely I can do the same.

He squeezes his eyes shut, biting down on his lip as I help maneuver him onto the wood. I kneel by his side and pull off his sweater, tying one sleeve to the sled. "Can you hold on?"

He barely nods, but his fists clench the side of the wood as tightly as he can.

Holding onto the other sleeve of his sweater, I step forward and pull, dragging Aaron away from the cabin and into the woods. I don't have time to open Margot's locket to check my compass; all I know is that we're heading away from the Cut, not towards it.

Even from here, the air is thick with the smell of smoke. The wind whistles louder, carrying ashes on its back.

I bite my tongue and haul Aaron farther. Every part of my body screams for me to stop. The sprain in my wrist tingles and burns, and the ache in my leg worsens with every step. I try to hum a song to distract myself from the pain, to keep my eyes open, to make sure I don't collapse. But in spite of the memory I once trusted with my life, in spite of all the Yesterday music Milo tried to show me when we were younger, I can't remember enough of any one melody to form a full track in my head.

"*Way back,*" I whisper to myself, trying to remember what Aaron was humming to himself while I was half asleep in his arms. My throat burns. I try not to cry. "*Counting trees.*"

The wind sings with me. The hair on the back of my neck stands on end. I stop to stare at the sky as a roll of thunder cracks through the night, and with it finally falls the first rain of spring.

I find the cave tucked behind a curtain of ivy.

It's not much of a cave, really; there are no rock formations and it doesn't extend very far. It's barely any bigger than the bad cabin, an alcove carved into the side of what could be a hill, or a massive boulder. I can't tell in the storm.

Drops of rain slam against my head. The wind carries them sideways so they cut into my skin and eyes, making it impossible to see as I drag the sled through the mud and into the mouth of the cave that's not a cave, muttering my song that's not a song. My teeth chatter. My entire body shivers so violently it makes the muscles in my jaw sore. It's giving me a headache.

"*Headache,*" I sing, choking on my own breath, though it sounds more like a cry. *That was part of the song, right?*

It feels like I'm moving an inch a minute. I look behind me, unable to make out much of Aaron's face in the dark, but I can tell he's barely holding on. In fact, he isn't holding onto the sled anymore at all. His hands lay limply at his sides, fists unclenched, head lolled over. "*Shit.*"

I pull him all the way to the back wall of the cave. Aside from the few water drop echoes that keep us company, we're spared from the rainfall for now.

"*Something, something,*" I sing, desperately, throat tight as I kneel down in the cold damp dirt by Aaron's side. I grab Carmody's lighter from my pocket and flick it open.

It doesn't light.

I try again. And again. Not even a spark. *I must have used up all the fluid at the Cut.*

My chin quivers. I keep humming nonsense to myself, trying to keep my breathing steady. *Maybe Aaron has matches,* I wonder, rummaging through his satchel. *If they're not in here, then maybe he grabbed something useful at his dad's lab.*

My face pales. Aaron's backpacks are gone. Either he lost track of them before I found him, or I was too focused on getting away from that cabin to think about grabbing them.

I slump back against my knees, closing my eyes to take a deep, unsteady breath. I feel like I'm going to scream. Like at the drop of a hat, I'll start to tear out my own hair in fistfuls. *Focus, Eddie.*

My eyes fly open. Maybe...

I lean over Aaron, reaching inside the pocket of his jeans to retrieve a familiar plastic pig.

There's no time to laugh or sigh with relief. Using my left hand, I crank the flashlight over and over again until a faint white light floods from its nostrils. But the light dies out quickly; I have to keep on cranking it to see anything at all.

"Aaron." I pat the sides of his face. "Aaron, wake up."

His eyes flutter open, then closed. I crank the flashlight as fast as I can to shine the most amount of light possible in his face. The toy whirs obnoxiously and his eyes snap open.

"That's annoying as hell." He doesn't have the strength to bring a hand up to shield them, or even hold them open for very long, but he clenches his teeth as they close again. "I'm awake."

"Good. Stay that way."

Herbalism is one thing, but surgery is another. If Aaron goes unconscious, that's more than just a bad sign; there will be no one to guide me through the operation, or what to do after.

Still cranking the flashlight with my left hand, I remove his glasses and place them back into the case he stores within his satchel, then pull off my waterlogged boots to retrieve my sheathed knife. I writhe out of my jacket —*Aaron's* jacket—and place it under his leg like a cushion to keep it elevated.

His teeth chatter. His water-soaked shirt sticks to his skin, its fabric heavy and cold. I peel it off and give him my oversized sweater instead, which the jacket kept dry, leaving me in nothing but my undershirt as goosebumps crawl up and down my exposed arms. It's so cold I swear I can feel it in my bones, but I can't pay it any mind. I need to manage his temperature if I expect his body to heal.

I start by cleaning. I use his old shirt to wipe away the mud, saving the clean rags in his satchel for sterilization. He doesn't have any more alcohol left, so all I can use is water from his canteen, which I ration out carefully. The bleeding seems to be under control now, so I remove the tourniquet and toss the belt to the side. Keeping it on too long would lead to complications we can't afford. *No mistakes.*

I know enough about first aid to understand that a sterile environment is essential, and I try not to think back to Abigail's infection, or the one I had while I was on the run. But the ground is made of dirt. We're running out of clean fabric, and the supplies Aaron stocked up on from his dad's lab are gone. All I have to work with is a bit of antiseptic salve, which I'll need to ration like the clean water. It's too damp to start a fire with no lighter and no tinder. I won't be able to boil more.

I don't have any anesthetic either. *He'll be awake the entire time.*

"Scalpel," Aaron mumbles, eyes barely open.

I dig through his satchel to find a scalpel covered with a plastic cap, which I remove.

"Make an incision." His voice is barely audible over the crackling of the rain outside and the whirring flashlight. My left hand is already starting to get tired, and my sprained wrist aches.

"How big?" I whisper, trying to get my trembling under control.

"Big enough to extract the bullet without causing excessive tissue damage."

I swallow nervously and make the incision. Aaron shuts his eyes and inhales sharply through his nose, but otherwise doesn't flinch. He keeps his eyes closed. "Forceps."

I set the scalpel aside and retrieve the forceps from his satchel. With no further instructions, I know what I need to do. Slowly, I insert the forceps into the wound.

For a moment his eyes peel open in full consciousness, until he squeezes them shut so tightly that wrinkles form. He clamps his jaw closed and leans his head back as I locate the bullet. Almost instinctively, his hand grabs my knee. He doesn't dig his nails into my skin the way I did to his when I was in pain, but he still holds it. Like he needs to.

His breathing is heavy when he lifts his head up just enough to catch a brief glimpse of what I'm doing.

"Easy on the way out, Voclain." His eyes flutter closed once more. "Please."

I nod, biting my lip as I clamp the forceps onto the bullet and tug.

This is the first time I've heard Aaron call out in pain. My left arm feels like it's going to fall off, and my entire body shakes as I carefully pull the Yesterday bullet from deep within his thigh up toward the wound's opening, following the same path it took to enter his flesh. I move honey-slow to preserve my precision, trying my best to keep a steady grip with my compromised hand. He seethes in agony, still holding onto my knee—until his grip relaxes.

His eyes gloss over. His eyelids droop, skin pale and clammy. His head falls back.

This isn't about his pain tolerance, I realize as I take in the signs. He's lost too much blood.

"Aaron?"

I wait. Nothing.

"Aaron, wake up." My pulse escalates. I shine the light in his face, still cranking it. Not a single part of him moves, save for the faint rise and fall of his chest.

"Please."

The silence tells me I'm on my own.

Breathe, Eddie. I try remembering what his heartbeat felt like out in the woods. I try to hold onto its rhythm, its tempo, grounding myself in its memory.

I pull out the bullet.

I clean the wound again with fresh water, this time applying the last of his antiseptic salve. My left hand is so tired from powering the flashlight that I've slowed the pace to a series of bursts, working partially in the dark as the faint glow flickers like a firefly. I rummage through my own bag to retrieve the surgical thread and sewing needle Aaron had packed in my first aid kit.

He can't guide me through the stitches, but I close my eyes and think back to the books I've read, scouring over the hazy diagrams on their pages. My work is sloppy but I get the job done.

My hand shakes violently, long after I let the flashlight die out.

I use the one ounce of strength left within me to curl up by Aaron's side. In the rain, in the dark, in the empty, fireless cold, he is still warm. His heartbeat is what finally lulls me to sleep.

R. STELLER

Saturday, April 6

I can't see a thing through these windows.

The glass is tinted, almost to full opacity, shielding the sea of evergreens from my stare. Leaning my head against its cool surface does nothing; even with less than an inch of space between me and the outside world, I can't see through.

"You alright back there, Steller?"

From the corner of my eye, I see Kingfisher trying to meet my gaze through the rear-view mirror as he grips the steering wheel, which he turns every now and then to follow the bends in the road.

The question nearly makes me laugh. If I had the energy for it, maybe I would have. *What about any of this is alright?*

I peel my forehead from the glass to stare at my hand instead, spinning my ring around my right index finger. "Why wouldn't I be?"

Heron groans from the passenger's side, the bottom of his feet planted to his seat. He presses his forehead against his knees, wrinkling his already creased suit. "Easy on the curves, Fish." He covers his face with a paper bag.

At the next bend in the road, King makes a sharp turn.

Heron's head hits the side of the door. He swats at King's arm, face still buried in the bag. "Homicide."

King scoffs. "What?"

Heron pulls his head up, skin green. "Oh, I'm sorry. I thought you asked me what I'm thinking about right now." He lowers his face into the bag again. "You're lucky I don't vomit all over your car."

"Want me to hold your hair back?" King says, expressionless. "Feed you saltines and rub your shoulders too?"

"That would actually be quite nice."

King gives him a stern side glance. "Quit complaining."

Heron stares directly at King, and he vomits into the bag.

King swears under his breath and pulls over. He leans to open the passenger door for Heron, practically shoving him out of the vehicle. "Get out."

Heron gives him the finger as he tumbles out of the car, bag in hand. All I can see outside the open door is dirt until he slams it shut.

King turns around in his seat to face me. "Need to stretch your legs? We've been in here for a while. There's an old gas station up here too. Might find something interesting."

I shake my head.

He nods, unbuckling. "Well, I for one am feeling a bit cramped. I'll be back."

The sound of the car door slamming closed echoes through the pines, and I am left completely alone.

I stare at my hands, spinning the ring, rubbing my unshackled wrists. I could run, if I really wanted to. I could open the door and sprint as fast as I could into the woods and disappear into the pines, maybe for good. I am bound by no chains. I've felt worse blisters than the one's I'd get from running in dress shoes. I've had a tracker taken out of me before. Surely I could handle removing one a second time. I'm not even sure that King would pursue me if I were to bolt. Heron certainly wouldn't.

But I can't convince myself that a life spent rotting away in the woods wouldn't become another prison.

I glance through the window again, trying to make out my surroundings through the glass that cages me in. All I see is my own unclear reflection staring back. My freshly trimmed hair. My neatly pressed suit. I haven't yet earned my Eyes, but I try to picture what shades would look like on the face I recognize less and less with every passing day. My imagination fails me.

I squint to stare beyond the mirror, beyond the darkness of the glass. I can't make out the details, but I know there is only evergreen for as far as I can see.

My leg shakes. I stare at the door handle. *Go,* something tells me. *Who knows when you'll have another chance to escape?*

Why won't you leave?

Heron and Kingfisher are back in the car before I have an answer, bickering about something as they slam the doors shut.

"That's odd," Heron says.

King pauses, seatbelt half-drawn over his torso, brows furrowed. "What?"

Heron points to King's sleeve. "Is that a wrinkle in your suit?"

King frowns, smoothing out the fabric. He buckles his seatbelt with a click, and we drive away.

"I can't believe it. A *wrinkle* in his suit." Heron shakes his head, holding his hands up like he's detailing some elaborate vision. "I can see tomorrow's headline. *Breaking News: Agent I. Kingfisher Isn't So Perfect After All.*"

That earns him an elbow to the ribs.

The bickering continues, but their voices grow muffled as I tune them out. Like I'm sinking underwater and they're still above the surface.

I stare out the window that I can't see through, wondering if I'll regret choosing to stay behind it.

I stand in front of the jackalope fountain with my hands in my pockets, staring at the murky water inside.

My hair is not long enough to tangle, so the wind tousles it instead, undoing the efforts King made this morning when he combed through it with gel. I protested first, covering my nose and mouth, not wanting to breathe in the smell. But then my shoulders relaxed. I remembered I had no one to protect—no one in my circle to shield from the toxic fragrance and chemical throat burn but me.

I remember this fountain. It was clean once, frozen over and ridden with toothy icicles that sprouted from each branch of the rabbit's makeshift antlers.

Now, every inch of stone is coated in a thick, slimy blanket of algae. There is no one left who cares enough to keep it clean.

I lift my chin to study my surroundings, trying not to think back to what it was like to be here when everything was coated in snow, before spring melted it away and the runoff took everyone with it.

Instead, I remember a playground I used to visit with my sister as a child. There was a curved tube slide no grown adult could fit inside. Even my own long legs gave me trouble. But for the brief moment of time before I eventually outgrew it, that slide was my favorite. It was my sister who discovered that if you went down on your back, head first, you could pause at the very end with your feet sticking out the entrance, static prickling at your neck, and study the wheat-colored ceiling to read the message someone had written in fading black ink. I must have spent hours upside down in that slide, lost in thought, tracing the words of a stranger who didn't even know I existed.

If the world ended now and everyone was wiped out, no one would be left to care.

The fountain water is ridden with mosquitos.

Something slams. I turn to see Officers in shining white suits of armor carry plastic crates of evidence, loading them into the backs of unlabeled box trucks under the direction of Agents who whisper to themselves with fingers pressed to the sides of their shades. Nothing is left behind because there is something to extract from every book, every piece of clothing, every child's toy. There is no stillness; everything is a moving part as we dissect the compound like ants to a carcass.

Heron and King walk up to my side, gray light reflecting off their dark glasses and into my eyes. They're tinted like car windows. Heron struggles to keep his hair away from his face with the wind, but King's gel keeps his own dark brown strands perfectly in place.

"Canary's car just got here," he whispers into my ear. "I'm assuming he'll want to meet with you as soon as he's settled."

I nod, still staring at the fountain.

"Pig's got the nice room," Heron adds. "The portable with the king-sized bed and the really good shower. It's like a whole house. It's all the rage among Officer gossip. They're pissed about camping in tents with so many empty rooms available. They're not even allowed in the ones already cleared."

My pulse skips a beat. Of all the rooms he could have chosen, of course Canary had to pick the commander's suite. My hands clench into fists.

King shoots Heron a look that both of us can read, even with the sunglasses. He mutters under his breath through clenched teeth. "Eyes all around, Heron."

"My bad. The *very nice* pig."

"I mean it."

Heron shrugs. "He's heard worse things from my mouth."

King ignores Heron and leans in closer. "He's expecting a tour of—what did they call this place? The Cut?"

My eyes are still glued to the water and the writhing larvae inside.

"Anyway, I'd suggest preparing something good to say," King mutters, then lowers his volume to a near whisper. "Think carefully about what you want to—"

He doesn't have the chance to finish his sentence.

A loud blast echoes throughout the square. I drop to my knees, hands over my ears as shouts ensue, followed by the slamming of boots against dirt. I open my eyes as Heron and King do the same, dragging myself up until I'm standing.

Smoke curls through the windows of the building. *No*—I realize. The smoke is coming from outside, and it doesn't look like the kind of dark, debris-filled clouds that follow an explosion. These tendrils are lighter, almost white.

"Smoke grenade," I say.

Heron and King exchange glances. Another one sets off, this time somewhere in the middle of the Block, amidst the rows and rows of trees and empty portables that offer plenty of spaces to hide.

I don't have any more time to speculate until an Officer runs up to us with a brief salute. "Agent I. Kingfisher."

He nods.

"Agent Canary is asking for you," she says, her breathing quick. "Someone's just robbed the armory."

The wind blows. No one says a word until Heron laughs, shoving his hands into his pockets. "What do you mean, someone's just robbed the armory?"

"I mean exactly what I said, sir."

Heron's grin fades. He crosses his arms. "Who?"

"That's what we're trying to figure out, sir," the Chaser says, her patience declining.

"Robbed. While this place is swarming with Chasers." Heron chuckles in disbelief. "Now who in their right mind would do that?"

"We don't know, sir. Witnesses keep referring to an eyepatch. Canary's convinced the man's an Undergrounder, probably one who survived the initial attack."

All at once, every vessel in my body stops pumping blood. The wind whistles right through me, shivers crawling down my back like spiders.

"And then came back?" King asks. The Officer nods.

"And you're sure he's working alone?" I ask.

The Officer looks surprised to hear me speak. "As far as we know, yes."

A pair of Officers runs up to retrieve the one in front of us. "More traitors. Two just hit the greenhouse and we need backup."

"Backup?"

One of the new Officers nods. "We've got a fire to put out."

There are no more questions asked. They run off before I can blink, following the pull of shouts and commands as more white smoke begins to rise above the Block behind us.

But amidst the noise, everything suddenly feels so quiet, like I'm underwater again. The only sign that I'm still breathing at all is the thud of my own pulse cracking in my ears as my head spins.

The greenhouse?

My legs move on their own accord, and before I realize it, I'm sprinting. I run away from the square, away from Heron and Kingfisher, away from everyone and everything. She is all I think about as I speed past every tree and alleyway in my path until I'm running toward that hill. I see the greenhouse in the distance. I can barely hear King calling after me, his words far and unclear.

In the middle of an alleyway, Heron tackles me to the ground.

I swing a punch without thinking. My fist cracks against his cheek as he tries to pin me down.

"You little shit!" He swings one in return, hitting my stomach so hard it knocks the wind out of me. He throws another one, this time hitting me in the face. I spit in the dirt and manage to roll over, trying to rise to my feet, but he drags me back down, pinning my wrists to the ground. "Get a hold of yourself, man!"

"Get the hell off me!"

"You're being an idiot, Steller."

"Let me go or I swear to God *I'll kill you.*" I break one of my wrists free and try to throw another punch, but he catches it in the air. I kick, and although I have the advantage of height, Heron is stronger and overpowers me.

I couldn't give a damn about fighting back. This isn't about Heron. I don't have anything to prove. I just need to get free. *I need to reach her before it's too late.*

Something clicks as a new voice appears. "Both of you are being idiots."

Heron glances over his shoulder, then leaps to his feet. "What the hell, Fish?"

"Keep that up and you'll both make a scene." King stands at the mouth of the alleyway with his Nightjade gun pointed straight at us. I scramble upright, joining Heron as we hold our palms in the air. "Don't think I won't pull the trigger."

"Fish, this is petty. Just put the gun down."

"Against the wall. Both of you." King gestures the gun toward the side of one of the brick buildings we stand between. "*Now.*"

We do as he says.

"What the hell are you doing, running off like that? Are you trying to get us killed?" King walks up to me and holds the Nightjade gun to my chest. "People are watching you. Closely, might I add. Trust is a thin layer of ice to walk across, and if you lose your footing, you can't expect it to hold up beneath you. Especially in the Corps." He lowers his voice to a gritting whisper. "You're smarter than this, McLellan."

The name stirs something within me. It's like I'm walking into a room and kicking up dust.

I clench my jaw. *That's not my name anymore.*

"I don't think I am," I reply.

King furrows his brows, but they relax once he understands, eyes wide. His expression hardens again and he leans in, digging the gun into my skin. "Don't even *think* about running after her."

"If I don't find her, they will first," I seethe, every breath slow and heavy.

"She's run from a Chaser before. She can do it again."

"She *can't*—"

"Steller, you run to her, and you'll lead them right to her." He points the gun toward my left eye. "Or have you already forgotten about this?"

My face twitches reflexively, but I keep my mouth sewn shut.

"Don't give the Corps a reason to question your loyalty. Show any emotional attachment to the Unseen and you're dead. We'll be cast as traitors too. And how do you think she'd react if she saw what you've become?" His glare softens. "Do you really think she'd understand?"

My chest tightens. Every muscle in my body grows rigid. If she saw me like this—if she knew the things I've done to wear this suit that I have yet to properly earn—she would never look at me again.

And even if I did somehow reach her, the Corps wouldn't hesitate to exterminate me for conspiracy if they knew I was in contact with a traitor.

"*That's* what this is about?" Heron scoffs, peeling himself from the wall. He stands next to King and places both palms against the brick, caging me in. "You really think Lavender Voclain—"

King elbows Heron in the ribs, straight-faced. "Eyes all around."

Heron shoots him a dirty look, then returns his attention to me. "Everybody in the whole damn country would kill to get their hands on that bounty. Do you really think she'd be stupid enough to return to the very place she's running from? For a few Yesterday guns and some flowers?"

There has to be more to it than that, I tell myself. But I don't have time to think about why she's here. I just know that she is.

"I do," I answer.

Heron pulls away. "Traitors are everywhere, Sparks. Anyone could have robbed that greenhouse."

"Look. We all agreed to help each other out, alright?" King says. "If you don't learn to compartmentalize... if you let your emotions get the best of you and do something stupid... your life isn't the only one that'll be put on the line. You'll take us down with you, and then no one can help her. And you best believe they'll put you through Extraction before you get the injection. Do you really think you can go through that? Do you *really* think you wouldn't give her away?"

I clench my teeth together so tightly my jaw trembles.

"The path you're on is your best shot at keeping her safe. From the rebels, from the Corps—from all of it. From behind the scenes, you can make sure nothing bad happens to her. But you have to be willing to make the right sacrifices." King sighs. "If you really want what's best for her, you'll stay away."

His words feel like another punch to the gut. No matter how badly I want to argue, I know he's right.

But that doesn't change the aching. The burning. The inside-out charring that's devouring me alive, because all I've ever wanted is to be near her. Even if everything's changed, the world would be right again if I could only see her. Just for a moment.

I nod, letting my glare fade.

The moment King slides his gun into his pocket, I run.

I sprint out of the alleyway and race up the hill. This time, they don't follow me.

My dress shoes shred through the damp mud and grass. They pinch the skin of my callused feet, but I can barely feel it. I stumble to a stop when I see the greenhouse, tripping over my own legs. Every drop of blood in my body freezes.

For a moment, everything goes quiet. Like the wind has whistled the world to sleep, but I have been left awake to watch it stop spinning.

The glass dome of the greenhouse shatters. Glowing flames lick the empty space the breaking leaves behind, painting over every constellation in the sky with dark gray clouds. The embers floating into the air look like stars against the smoke.

It takes everything I have not to fall to my knees and sob.

This is all my fault.

Kingfisher and Heron walk by my side in silence as we head back to the cabin.

Night has fallen. The full moon is our only light and it watches us like an owl, knowing and silver. Damp debris crunches beneath our shoes, twigs snapping with each step. The wind whistles, but there isn't much else to hear aside from my own breathing.

We set up shop at the cabin when we arrived this morning, before we headed to the compound. We technically should be staying back at the Cut with the other Chasers stationed there, but the thought of bunking with so many Corps loyalists made me uneasy. Knowing of the cabin's existence, I suggested we stay there instead; as hauntingly familiar as it may be, at least it has the luxury of privacy. As my supervising Third, King has the privilege of leniency from his own superiors—and Heron and I get to reap those benefits under his wing.

I don't even have a ranking yet, I remind myself. I'm still just a prisoner. *A cageless, willing prisoner.* Like a bird who's clipped its own wings.

Now we're heading back for the night. We're still a good walk away when Heron stops dead in his tracks. "I need to take a piss."

King gives him a look, then shrugs as he continues walking. "Enjoy."

"Come on guys, it's creepy as hell tonight. Can't you just wait for me?"

"No."

"Who knows what's hiding out here? I can barely see shit."

"Then put on your Eyes."

"You know they give me a headache."

"I thought you said they make your head look small."

"That too."

"I'm not waiting for you. I'm tired," King says, already a few yards away. "You're a big kid now. You can handle yourself."

"We passed an old shed back that way." I point in its direction, then follow King. "Have fun."

"I hate both of you." With that, Heron walks away to find his privacy.

King and I hike in silence for a while until I clear my throat, smelling the smoke in the air. "You think they'll be able to get that fire under control?"

"There's gotta be at least a hundred Officers on site. They can handle a little fire in the greenhouse."

"So if it's cleared up by tomorrow..."

"Then Canary will still want his tour." He hesitates. "And any other information he requests."

I nod, staring at my feet. Beneath the moon, I can see my own reflection gazing back at me in the mirror of my shoes, until a cloud rolls over and the silver glow slips away.

"Man, this wind is really something else." King glances over his shoulder. "Haven't seen anything like this in years. Not since the last wildfire."

"I remember seeing that on the news." For a place as damp and rainy as the Northwest, we're still known to get a few fires, even with the supposed advantages the Nightjade order provides for our climate. Especially in forests like these.

I see a faint amber glow in the distance and know we must be close to the cabin; we'd left the light on this morning to make it easier to find our way back, and the fire going in the hearth so it'd be warm.

King fidgets with his lighter as we walk, flicking it open and closed until he slams it shut, looking over his shoulder again with a frown. "Where did Heron run off to?"

"Beats me."

King rolls his eyes, and we keep walking. He plays with his lighter again, and I try to ignore its ghost-like familiarity, but it's hard to pretend I can't hear its clicking. We're a few yards away when King snaps it closed and shoves it into his pockets. "You hear that?"

"What?"

He hushes me and draws his Nightjade gun. "Something's moving up ahead, in front of the cabin."

I squint, but I can't make out much from this far away with such little light. I remember King's shades, and while I still know little about the way they work, I know he's equipped with night vision.

King jogs forward. I follow his lead, and we hide behind a thick pine trunk close to the cabin. He presses a finger to his mouth and peeks his head around to assess the scene. I do the same. Although I don't have the sight he has, my lips part when I realize what's going on.

In the dirt clearing ahead of the porch, someone is fighting a Chaser.

The Officer's armor glistens in the faint moonlight, barely visible. I can't see the face of the figure who fights him over control of a knife.

"There's a Yesterday gun on the ground," King whispers, pointing a few feet away from the altercation. "Grab it while I step in."

I nod, waiting as King steps forward, Nightjade gun in both hands. "Nobody move."

Crouching low to the ground, I hurry toward the Yesterday gun and grab it as quickly as I can, then rise to my feet.

The Officer and the unidentifiable Unseen man freeze, but only for a second. The stranger takes the knife while the Officer is distracted, then reaches into his boot to retrieve a second blade that he throws at King.

King drops the Nightjade gun as the knife hits him in his side, just barely below the cutoff of the bulletproof vest that all Agents wear underneath their suits. My brows crease. *How did he know about the vest?*

This rebel is either highly educated, or extremely lucky.

"*Shoot*, Steller," King orders from the ground, wincing as he clutches his side.

I aim the gun right as the Unseen man steps behind the Officer, holding the knife to his throat, using him as a human shield.

"Go ahead and shoot, pal. That bullet's gonna bounce right back at you. Or better yet, hit your little friend here right between the eyes—if your aim's shitty enough."

My heart plummets. The color drains from my face.

With the faint glow seeping through the cabin windows behind him, he is only a silhouette; there's not enough light for me to see his features, or for him to see mine.

But I'd recognize that voice anywhere.

"Steller," King warns, breathing heavily. *You know what you have to do,* he says in silence. I can barely pay attention.

If Aaron is here, then Eddie is too.

I glance around, pulse thudding in my ears, trying to spot her between the trees. But she is nowhere to be seen. *Could she be in some sort of danger?*

"Steller," King repeats through gritted teeth. "Do it."

My hands shake. With or without our agreement, King is still an Agent—a Third Rank at that. He isn't in this to benefit anyone or anything but his own motivations. The cost of one rebel's life isn't as heavy to him as it is to me.

I swallow the lump in my throat, hands convulsing as I point the gun. If I don't shoot, Aaron will kill that Officer, and it'll be my fault. Even then, if I can't play my part—if I don't follow King's every command—there's no telling how long he'll be willing to honor our agreement.

If the Corps thinks I'm sparing a traitor's life on purpose, I may as well be sending myself to Extraction. And if I'm killed, then what has all of this been for? If I'm dead, who's going to protect the people I love? *Dying would be losing.*

If I hurt Aaron, Eddie will never forgive me.

But look at what you've already done. The Ren she knew is already dead.

You have to be willing to make the right sacrifices.

Stay alive. Keep her safe.

My hands stop shaking.

I steady my aim—and I shoot.

EDDIE

Sunday, April 7
70 Beds Made

♪ SEARCH AND DESTROY - SANDERS BOHLKE ♪

A scream pulls me out of my slumber.

I fold forward, heart racing as something cold leaps from my forehead and onto my lap. I kick my legs and scramble back until I'm pressed against the wall.

The frog hops away, still croaking on its way out.

Aaron snaps upright, immediately clutching his leg with a wince. "What the hell?"

My breathing slows, heart rate dropping as the dust in my head finally settles.

The fire. The Agent. *The bullet.*

My lips part. "You're awake."

"Yeah, no thanks to you." Aaron blinks painfully, rubbing his head with his palms.

I hurry back to his side and give him a sip of water. I press the back of my hand against his forehead. "How are you feeling?"

He lies back down.

He doesn't protest when I open his bandages to check the raw seam of his wound, relieved to find no apparent signs of infection. But I still grimace at the sight, remembering how awful it felt to dig those forceps into his flesh. *Another scar for him to bear.*

I glance through the mouth of the cave. Beyond the curtain of ivy, rain continues to fall in sheets, letting in only the smallest glow of soft gray morning light. I can barely see, but it's better than no light at all. My left hand cramps, still shaking.

Aaron's already asleep again when I dress his wound with fresh bandages, wishing I had more antiseptic salve to apply. If we had a fire, then I could get a tea going at the very least. I shiver, my arms still exposed from giving up my sweater.

Thunder rolls outside of the cave. It's far past sunrise. The van is long gone by now, and Aaron's in no condition to go anywhere—especially in this weather. Chasers will be looking for us too, swarming the area around the cabins. These whole woods, probably.

We'll be stuck here for a while.

I stop the panic before it has a chance to spread, swallowing it down to be saved for later. *Crescent moons.*

Fire. That's one thing I can get done.

When my eyes adjust to the light—or lack thereof—I decide it might be a good idea to take inventory of everything we have while the day is on my side. *We have to have something I can use, right?*

I begin with my immediate person. Margot's necklace and my dad's bracelet are the first items I check for. My three throwing knives are still attached to my empty holster, since I lost my Yesterday gun in the greenhouse. I've moved my walkie-talkie from my back pocket and into my traveling backpack, but it's still accounted for. The photo I stole from Aaron's cabin. Aaron's two carvings and Carmody's now-useless lighter reside in the front pockets of my jeans, as always, along with the piece of broken mirror. That would be a great fire starter if I only had direct sunlight and dry kindling.

The phone I took from M. Heron.

I release an exhausted sigh and move onto my traveling pack, the one Aaron prepared for me before we left. I still have that first aid kit, four more packs of instant oatmeal, the cinnamon, a few sips of fresh water—and that's pretty much it. The other backpack contains the Catnap clippings.

Now I tackle Aaron's satchel.

I open the bag and spread out all of its contents before me. A round water canteen. Three more packs of instant oatmeal. His hand-carved wooden glasses case, which I'm assuming either he or his father made. A roll-up travel-sized leather pouch with eight small carving tools. A few sterilized surgical scalpels, capped for safety. The jar of thimbleberry clippings we collected. Three tiny jars of tea, none of them labeled. A travel-sized leather notebook engraved with the title *How to Not Die*.

A CD case with a fading masking tape and permanent marker label titled *For Aaron*. The handwriting looks so similar to his. I pause to stare at it, wondering if it could be from his father.

A thin silver portable CD player with black wired earbuds. Or at least that's what I think it is. Milo was obsessed with them back at home.

A black switchblade. A stainless steel Leatherman. A mint tin first aid kit identical to mine. A pocket-sized copy of one of Simon's encyclopedias, which I recognize as the one he took from the lab. A metal cup that looks like it could double as a cooking pot. A cloth pouch filled with dropper bottles of miscellaneous tinctures. And the carving he's been working on —which I still can't make out yet.

The last item in his satchel looks like it's made of fabric. It's dark green and scrunched up in a ball at the bottom of his bag. I pull it out and unfold it, holding it up in front of me to see what it could be.

It falls out of my hands.

I can smell it. Beneath the scent of wood and dust, there is still the faintest hint of lavender and tea tree laundry soap.

The moment I realize what it is, I scramble to pick it up and hold it out again, arms trembling.

This is Ren's green crewneck sweatshirt.

The one he gave me on that playground so long ago—and the one he cleaned back in that cabin when I was sick. The one I was so sure I'd never see again. My last piece of Ren and the life I once knew so well, lost for good.

When I hold it closer to my chest, the dark inside this cave is not as cold as I once thought.

My throat burns, eyes fogging over as I scrunch the collar up to my face to breathe it in. It smells like Margot. *It smells like him.* It smells like all the things I used to know and thought I'd forgotten, bundled up into one damp, wrinkled piece of clothing.

"I tried to get your shoes too." I whip my head around to see Aaron grimacing as he pulls himself up to an almost-seated position, leaning against his elbows. "But they wouldn't fit in the bag."

I stare at him, vision cloudy, lips parting as I take in his words. *This is why he went to the cabin*, I realize. Not to go after the Chasers who were residing within it. *This is why he's hurt.*

I swallow the lump in my throat and wipe my nose, then kneel by his side. "How are you feeling? Do you need anything?"

He shakes his head.

"Are you cold?"

"No."

"What about food? Are you hungry?"

"I'm fine."

His voice is dry, his throat probably scratched from last night. *And dehydration.* I think back to the canteen I pulled from his bag.

I clench my fists to hide the trembling in my hands, turning away to conceal the gloss sheen of my eyes. *You need to stay put together*, I remind myself. *You need to stay strong, because no one else is here to do that for either of you.* "You need water."

"Voclain."

I try to stand up, but he grabs my wrist before I can move.

"*Eddie.*"

My eyes meet his, and his expression softens.

"Would you stop trying to take care of me for just one second?" He lowers his voice. "You've done enough."

His hand is still holding my wrist. And I'm still trying so hard not to cry, not to think about the sweatshirt I'm wearing or its laundry soap smell, or the fact that once it fades away for good, I will never get it back. Just like everything else I've lost. No matter how hard I try, the memories still grow hazier with each passing day, and I don't think there's anything I can do to stop it.

What will I be left with once it all finally fades?

I'm not sure how long I sit like that, cold and tired and shaking, before Aaron pulls me closer. Slowly, gently, until his arm is draped over my still-bare shoulder and my head is turned toward his chest.

"I meant what I said, Voclain. You won't forget him." His pinky wraps around mine. "We'll get him back."

And for the first time since any of this has happened, I bury my face in his neck—and I let myself cry. Because every part of me hurts, and there is only so much I can take, and so much I need to remember. Because if I don't remember every piece of the life I lost, they will fall between the cracks like lost change, and there is no one else to keep that from happening.

If I don't remember every part of Ren, how will I get him back before we both forget?

I'm not sure how long we lie like that, but when I open my eyes, I realize we must have fallen asleep. Aaron still looks so pale. Despite the downpour outside, his face plastered in sweat.

He's hurt because of me. Because he wanted so badly to bring me back a piece of my old life that it made him careless. I still don't know what happened back at the Cut, but I have a feeling he would have been a lot more careful if he wasn't worrying about me. *Irrational mistakes.*

How many more people will get hurt trying to bring Ren back to me?

M. Heron's words play over and over again in my head. If what he said was true... I can't even imagine the pain he must be going through, the torment he must have already endured. If he really is being held captive somewhere after all, there's no telling how much of the Ren I knew is still in there. I have to remember enough to bring him back.

Ren saved me, time and time again. I need to save him too.

Not Aaron. Not my brother. Me. Because it's my fault that he's in this mess to begin with. *This is my mistake to fix.*

I double-check to make sure Aaron is asleep. I pull out Carmody's empty lighter, toying with it as I open the burner phone. I dial the only number in its contact list, and it rings.

A tired voice plays on the other end. "Hello?"

My hands shake. My tongue is locked in place.

"I can hear you breathing, Lavender."

What am I doing? No matter what he's offering me, contacting an Agent under a vague, unsolidified agreement to provide him with the information he's asking for—information only someone Unseen can give him—is a risk I should know better than to take. If anyone knew what I was doing, what would they think?

You're not betraying anyone, I tell myself. *You'll only give him what he asks for, nothing more. Nothing about the Unseen, only his brother. You're not putting anyone in danger.*

I stare at Aaron, who still sleeps. *Then why am I hiding it?*

"I assume this means you're accepting my proposal. Otherwise you wouldn't be calling now, would you?"

I still can't open my mouth.

Heron chuckles on the other end. "So quick to betray everything she stands for to save the boy she cares about from himself. How romantic."

My brows furrow into a glare. I want to shout, but I keep my voice a whisper, careful not to wake Aaron. "I'm not betraying anyone."

"As far as you know. There are many costs to truths uncovered, aren't there?"

"I'll hang up."

"You do want to save him, right? The self is a hard cause to fight for once lost. Who knows how much time he has left?"

I listen to everything but Heron's voice. The whispering rain. Drops of water in the back of the cave. Wind whistling, rustling trees in the distance. The cry of a desperate crow. But the sound of his words keep ringing in my head like a bell, and no matter how hard I try to ignore it, the echo won't leave.

"I want to save him."

I can't see the Agent, but I know he must be grinning—I can hear it in his voice. "I knew you'd make the right choice."

I slam the phone shut. The sound bounces across the walls of the cave as I shove it back inside my bag.

I return to Aaron's side and drift to sleep once again, lighter still in hand.

REN

Monday, January 29

"It's about damn time."

My gaze locks on the pair of unused shades hanging from his collar, and the wrinkled suit he wears like it means nothing to him.

This man—no, this *kid*—is an Agent.

He's young. Too young, with a face that should belong to a freshly chewed-and-spat training cadet. An Officer, at most. *Not this.*

But I think back to my own training and remember just how possible it is for young cadets to be pulled into the Agency sector. Judging by his age and assuming we were in the same regional boundaries, we should have gone through the program together. I take the stranger's face and scan my memories for something recognizable without any luck. *He couldn't have been a part of my training.*

I take a second look. *Could he?*

I pause, finding something familiar not in the defining features of his face, but in his eyes. I can't help but wonder if I've seen them before.

He wasn't a part of my training, I realize. But my spine tingles when I understand why I recognize him. When I understand what we both have in common, because I've seen it in my own reflection.

They say the eyes are the window to the soul—and the glass is always cleaner when there's blood on your hands.

We observe each other like specimens in a jar, but he's on the other side while I'm trapped beneath an airtight lid. In spite of his youth, he studies me like he's ten years my senior. Like he's proud to know a thousand things I may never learn.

When the shock and contemplation melt away—when I remember just the kind of entity I'm dealing with—I suddenly want nothing more than to lunge at him.

He's an Agent. Maybe even the one who shot me.

Or at her.

Still seated, something snaps within me. I lurch forward in spite of the pain, forgetting about the handcuff until it digs into my skin and jerks me back. I squeeze my eyes shut and bite my bottom lip so hard that I taste iron, using my left hand to clutch the wound.

Breathe, the rational inch of my brain tells me. *You can't get out of this bind. Not yet.* My only way out of these cuffs is either with a key or a self-inflicted fracture I can't afford.

My eyes twitch open again, glaring so sharply it hones the pounding ache in my skull. I spit onto the sheets and it stains them red.

My words bleed out as an unrecognizable snarl, slow and thorny. "Where is she?"

The Agent chuckles.

I yank my arm against the handcuff. "Tell me where she is or I'm going to break my own hand and then every goddamn bone in your body until you do."

"That won't be necessary." He picks up a to-go cup from the ground near his chair, taking a slow sip. "Quite the firecracker, aren't you?"

I clench my jaw, imagining how satisfying the snap will be when I finally get my hands on his neck.

But then my attention fixates on the drink. I side-glance out the window, studying the water. It's unfamiliar—definitely oceanic, but maybe not right on the coast. An inlet, perhaps. While I can't see any nearby buildings through my limited view, I know we can't be too far from some sort of town if he visited a cafe recently enough for his coffee to still be warm. Or at all.

Where the hell am I?

"Relax, Sparks. You're safe here—for now." He takes another sip of his beverage before offering it to me like I have the ability to take it. "Coffee?"

Relax? *Relax?* I want to scream.

How can he expect me to relax when I am here and Eddie is not? When I have no idea where she is or who she's with, or if she's even—

I force the sentence to end. *Don't go there.*

My breathing is shaky, but it slows. *She has to be okay*, I reassure myself. Though I don't know where she is.

I don't know where *I* am.

I repeat the question through gritted teeth, this time slower. "Where is she?"

"That's neither here nor there." He shrugs, then finishes his coffee and tosses it in a waste bin. He walks to the right side of my bed and extends a hand. "Agent M. Heron, at your service."

I glare at his hand. He laughs when he realizes his mistake.

"Can't exactly shake my hand like this, can you?" He pulls a key from his pocket before unlocking the handcuffs. My arm falls to my side, numb and tingling.

I don't have time to think about the numbness or how long I've been out. When he extends his hand a second time, I take it with my right.

I was planning to pull him into a headlock—to wrap the crook of my arm around his throat until he stopped breathing, to watch the light fade from his eyes until it diminished to nothing. I want to end him for who he is and what he's done.

I want to leave. I *need* to leave, because I have people to find.

But I'm too weak. My right arm is nearly lifeless, my left sore from no movement. My wound hasn't even closed yet. And there doesn't seem to be enough light behind his eyes to fade, anyway.

The Agent shakes my hand.

I yank it away the second the handshake ends, every inch of my skin itching with the urge to take him on. *I could*, I tell myself, *if I was desperate enough.*

But I can't kill him yet. There is something else I'm desperate for, and he might just be the only one who can give me the answers I need.

"You hungry?" Heron leans against the wall near the window, folding his arms with one leg crooked like an aquatic bird. "Thirsty?"

The words draw my focus to the hollowness in my gut. The scorching dryness of my tongue and throat.

"What's wrong, Sparks?" He gestures at me with his chin. "Where'd that raging little temper go?"

I curl my fingers into fists, nails tearing into the flesh of my palms. He knows exactly what he's doing.

He unlocked my restraints. That means he knows I won't touch him. Maybe he thinks I'm weak. Maybe he thinks I don't have it in me. He offered me coffee, food, and water. In a matter of minutes, he's clearly displayed that he has a use for me—enough to keep me alive.

Whatever this is, we both have something to gain. Maybe that's what's feeding his crooked smirk.

What game is he playing?

The smirk fades when Heron clears his throat. "I think all parties would benefit if we cut to the chase here. Agreed?"

All? We? I keep my lips sewn shut and my fists tightly wound.

"Fish," Heron calls, turning his head toward the door. "Our prince is awake."

I wait in silence, heart pounding against my ribcage as a set of footsteps grow closer and closer—until the bedroom door opens.

I see his feet first—a pair of dress shoes so perfectly polished they could be made of glass. I smell his hair gel next, a pungent chemical fragrance I swear I've inhaled before. His legs are long and he wears a suit so free of wrinkles that I blink twice, just to make sure I didn't miss one. Only when my eyes land upon his do I finally realize who I must be staring at.

These are the cold gray eyes of Duke Carmody.

I recoil until my back is pressed against the headboard, ignoring the searing pain in my abdomen. Because there is nothing in this room but the eyes that are the same color as the sea that swallowed Duke whole.

I saw Eddie's bullet hit his chest that day. I saw the sea foam turn pink, and I saw what happened to his body once I deactivated the suit. No human can be sewn back together after breaking into so many parts.

If Duke is dead, then who am I staring at?

I blink rapidly, trying to make sense of it all. His eyes are more saturated than Duke's were, more spruce than gray. His hair is a darker shade of brown, and gelled far more neatly than Duke could ever manage. His face looks older and slender, maybe kinder. But he is an Agent; there can't be kindness.

My breathing slows. *I know who this is.*

"Ian."

He pulls up a chair and sits beside me. "It's a pleasure to finally meet you, Ren."

I always knew Duke had an older brother, but with him being five years our senior, I was never around him at school. This is my first time seeing his face in years.

Unlike Heron, he doesn't shake my hand. He studies me so closely I avert my gaze and stare at the wall, fists clenched. *He's here to kill me, isn't he?* Once he finds out what really happened to his brother, he'll exterminate me for what I did.

A brother's vengeance is matched by none. My own mistakes prove that true.

"You're awake," Ian says, leaning back in his chair with his arms crossed. "That's a relief."

A relief?

"I have to apologize for shooting you with that Yesterday gun," he says. "Well, both bullets were my fault."

My eyes dart to meet his. "You shot me?"

He nods. *So it wasn't Heron after all.* "I was making split-second decisions. I didn't think through them until after they were made, and for that, again, I apologize."

I keep my mouth cemented shut.

"They were right about you," he says. "You are pretty quiet."

"You should've heard him earlier," Heron says. "He's got quite the attitude."

Ian shoots Heron a look, then shifts his gaze back to me. "I'm sure you're wondering where you are. Why you're here. Why we decided to keep you alive. The works."

He's right, but I don't let him know it.

"And I'm sure you've already guessed what I am."

"An Agent," I say, only because I have to be sure. His shades are put away, and I can't help but wonder why.

"Agent I. Kingfisher. My ranking name, if you were wondering." He nods toward Heron. "And you two have met?"

Ranking name? I glance at Heron.

"The real name's Mallory, though I'm not supposed to tell you that," Heron says. "You're not really supposed to be alive either, yet here we are."

My stomach churns. *If I'm not supposed to be alive, then why am I?*

"I was assigned to my brother's case the moment his tracker went off," Ian explains. "It made sense; hunting down traitors is a specialty of mine, and I had unique insight regarding his behavior patterns, being his relative and all.

"When we got that call from the broadcasting center describing a pair of kids who sounded a *little* too much like his missing partner and runaway target to be a coincidence, I knew something wasn't right. That's when I found you."

And shot me, I think to myself, jaw twitching. *He was going to shoot Eddie first.*

"My priority was de-escalating the situation; I have higher-ups to please and I hadn't yet confirmed who you were." He leans forward in his seat. "And then I saw the bandage over your eye."

I touch my face; the bandage is gone. I remember the debugging surgery out in the woods and blink.

Now, my eyesight is perfectly clear—not a single scar or imperfection in sight. *They must have healed me while I was out.*

"I usually know a traitor when I see one. I realized there was a chance that you were only incapacitated by the Nightjade, not dead, with the tracker out of your system and all that." His eyes darken, only for a second. "But then that scarred friend of yours took out my partner, and I realized my opening for escape was brief. So I took you back to Headquarters."

"Is that what this is? Your Headquarters?"

"No. This is my safe house." Ian chuckles, pointing at the window. "That there? You're looking at Puget Sound. Nice view, isn't it?"

The wound in my side throbs. I dig my nails into my palms, trying so hard to stay calm. "If you were going to end up shooting me with a Yesterday bullet, why didn't you just take me out then? Why bring me here?"

"This was all very time sensitive," Ian says. "That little broadcasting stunt you pulled? No one's ever done anything like that before. Hesitating to immediately respond with our own counteracting message would risk the unfolding of a full-scale crisis. People riot when they feel like they've been lied to. We needed a quick and highly believable way to paint the Underground in a worse light."

Heron smirks. "And what better way to do that than with a fallen Chaser?"

"To the more... patriotic half of the population, a Chaser is a hero," Ian says. "Seeing authentic footage of an Officer's alleged death by the hand of a traitor was the perfect way to take away the broadcast's credibility. And it worked. We're still dealing with a few riots here and there, as expected. But most of them are in retaliation to what Voclain did to her family. To *you*."

My stomach twists into knots. *So it was all for nothing?*

I swallow the burning lump in my throat. "If it worked, then why revive me?"

"Revival was always the plan. I never meant to kill you; a bullet wound is child's play for a Corps healer. And I was planning on putting you through Extraction, after all. You wouldn't be useful to us dead. Yet, at least."

"Extraction?"

"It's a pretty self-explanatory term. Wouldn't you agree?"

A shiver runs down my spine. *That's why I'm alive? So they can harvest information from me?*

"Extraction is usually below my rank; for lesser threats like you, at least. But I volunteered to take your case, and considering our... mutual connection, I was given clearance."

"Is that what this is?" I ignore the pounding in my chest and the way the room spins. "Extraction?"

"God, no." Ian laughs, but his humor fades quickly. "You'd know if you were going through Extraction."

"Then why are you telling me any of this?"

He straightens his posture, crossing one leg over the other before shoving his hands in his pockets. "Because while you were out, Heron and I had some time to think."

Heron winks.

"We'd like to offer you a deal," Ian says. "You could be of good use to us, and you'd benefit greatly, should you choose to agree."

"I don't make deals with Chasers."

"Says the Chaser himself." Heron grins. His empty stare makes the hairs on the back of my neck stand on end.

"I've been playing this game for a long time, kid. Third Rank Agents don't earn that title unless they have the full trust of the Chaser Corps, and I earn my keep. I've been investigating the Unseen for a long time. They value my opinion."

My heart skips a beat. *Only the Unseen call themselves Unseen.* Not even Chasers use that term.

I can't bring myself to ask how he could possibly know that.

"I'd like to weave a story for my superiors," Ian says. "I'm the only living witness in the Corps who was there at that broadcasting center; in fact, I'm the only living witness who knows the truth about you, save for what I've told Heron. My partner is gone. You and your friends managed to kill the entire rescue unit we initially sent once your tracker went off under *suspicious circumstances*." He swallows, averting his gaze for only a moment. "And you already know what happened to my brother."

I stare at my trembling hands.

"In other words, there is no one who can argue against what I decide to present to the Corps regarding this case," he says.

"I'm guessing you want something in return."

"Let me tell you a story." Ian leans closer. "Ren McLellan—the honorable Officer who was working closely with my brother—was taken hostage by the Underground, who thought they could use him for information. The Corps, not knowing the full story, mistook him for a traitor. When they finally captured him, they publicized his false death to quickly counteract the broadcast before rioting began, to further villainize the Underground, and to keep the traitors from even thinking about retrieving him. But his loyalty was to the Corps all along, and Ren is still the hero he became the moment he put on that uniform."

"In other words..." Heron peels himself away from the wall, standing next to Ian's chair. "No Extraction."

"You get to keep your life and earn their favor."

I harden my stare. "You're mad to think I'd ever go back."

Heron scoffs. "You give them information as a rebel? They'll take it—*very* painfully—and dispose of you the moment you're no longer useful. You somehow manage to become the first person to ever keep their mouth shut during Extraction? Same end result." He crosses his arms, leaning in closer. "But prove yourself useful as a Corps loyalist, and they might just let you live. Hell, they might even reward you."

Ian's voice is calm. "If we don't spin this story, they'll kill you."

"And why do you care?"

"We need someone we can trust," Ian says. "Someone who's willing to get over themselves and whatever egotistical moral compass they think they have to do what has to be done. Someone willing to get their hands dirty to get what they want. You know what it's like to be on both sides. That's more valuable than you'd think.

"And..." Ian pauses, then clears his throat. "You knew my brother."

My throat tightens. "Why does that matter?"

"Because you saw him for what he was." He lowers his voice. "You know how to lie to people like him."

"And what is it that you want?" I ask. "You still haven't answered that question."

Ian and Heron exchange glances.

"We have answers to find," Heron says.

"People to protect," Ian adds.

"And I'm assuming you have a similar motivation," Heron says.

My eyes widen. "You're both..."

"We don't fall on either side of the split," Heron corrects quickly. "The rebels you associate yourself with are idiots, but targeting them serves us no benefit."

"We all know the Corps is... flawed," Ian says. "But it's not going anywhere, and it needs to be worked carefully. You know more than you think you do, Ren. You help us..."

"We help you," Heron finishes.

"And why would I trust you two?" I ask.

These are Agents. There's no telling what their true motivations are; this could easily be their method of Extraction—a way for them to win my trust and ease information out of me.

But what if there is an ounce of truth to what they're saying?

If going back is my only way to stay alive—my only way to protect the people I care about, as they're saying—is that a choice I'm willing to make? *Do I even deserve to be saved?*

I don't have the answer to that question, but I know one thing—my parents do. Eddie does. *All of them do.*

I already gave up on being human a long time ago. Who else can make this sacrifice but me?

I can protect them from the other side, can't I?

"Because at the end of the day, we both want the same thing." For a moment, Ian stares right through me. His eyes are so unbelievably human it almost stings.

So human I almost believe him.

"Evangeline." He studies his hands, drawing slow circles across the back of them with his thumbs. "She's my Lavender."

My breath hitches. I look away.

"This is our final offer," Heron says. "We'll help you get back into the Chasing game. Your life will be saved. You'll likely be promoted to an Agent under Ian's supervision if you play your cards right at the hearing. And hopefully, we'll get a cut of the cake in return. Jump a rank or two."

"Hearing?"

Heron nods. "It's already been scheduled."

"This is your only option," Ian says. "Unless you'd rather us turn you over to the Extraction Department after all."

"We'd get a little less credit if that ends up being the case, but brownie points are brownie points." Heron shrugs. "No one makes it out of Extraction okay enough to be useful, and they don't give Tomb sentences to ex-Chasers. No matter how you're exiting, the only way to truly leave the Corps is with a Nightjade injection. And you can't protect the people you love if you're dead now, can you?"

"So we bring your story to our higher-ups," Ian says. "We sell it damn good."

I swallow dryly. "Then what?"

"We get you promoted, of course."

Promoted? I study their suits and think back to my time at the training center, remembering everything Price once said about becoming an Agent. I think back to my time in the woods with Carmody, about the promises of rewards and promotions I spun to keep him in check. *Surviving rebel imprisonment isn't enough to earn my keep if I have nothing to offer.* "They wouldn't trust me enough to do that."

"Unless you give them a reason to," Ian says.

"What do you mean?"

Heron grins. "You'll show up to that hearing bearing gifts."

The color drains from my face. "No."

"Ren..."

"I'm not telling them anything."

So this is why they want me, I realize. If they bring me to that hearing and I give their higher-ups what they're asking for, they'll get credit for whatever it is I provide. And judging by their persuasion, they clearly see a use for me beyond that point.

If they can turn me into an Agent—if they can carve me into a chess piece for the Corps to use at their disposal—that's far more valuable than a single piece of information extracted through interrogation would be. *A gift that keeps on giving until it finally breaks.*

They'd earn the Corps' favor... and they'd get to keep me and my information on their side.

"That's the only way this will work, alright?" Ian says, frowning. "Look. You don't have to give away anything that will take down the whole operation. You don't have to initiate a massacre. Just give them something small. Something to secure your position and prove your value. Something only you would know."

I draw lines against my palms with the nails of my thumbs. Everything would be so much more simple if I chose death. Even with Extraction, it'd be the easy way out.

But no matter how desperately I'd like it to be any other way, I know they're right. *Maybe this is the only option.*

"So what's it gonna be, Sparks?" Heron leans against Ian's chair. "You really wanna flirt with the Grim Reaper?"

"Death," Ian asks, "or life?"

The question stirs something familiar within me. I think back to those woods, about everything I've already given up for the Unseen. I've sacrificed my eyes, my heart—my very *soul* to do what I thought was right for the side I thought was just. *And look where I've ended up in return.*

Maybe I'm not cut out to be like them.

Aaron was wrong when he said we always have choices. Because from the way I see it, I only have one. *There are people I need to protect.*

I turn my head, staring directly into those cold, human, uncovered eyes, blue as the Puget Sound itself. "Life."

When I look away, there are exactly seven words playing through my mind. Seven words, whispered to me out in those woods as Pittman took her last breath.

"There is no real leaving, Ren McLellan."

I don't think I've ever believed anything more.

EDDIE

Monday, April 8
71 Beds Made

♪ CRAWL BACK IN - HALF MOON RUN ♪

The rain is unending.

Beyond the curtain of vines shielding us from the woods outside, it falls in thick, heavy sheets, drumming against the roof of the cave. I can feel every drop's echo like a tap against my skin. It's maddening.

I lean against the wall, shivering as I hug my knees. Ren's sweatshirt is better than nothing, but it's still so damp in here and it doesn't do much to ward off the cold. I don't think we ever fully dried off from Saturday night. That was over forty-eight hours ago.

At least I think it's night right now. With the rain, there's no real way of telling. *And we still don't have a fire.*

It's easy to make my bed in the cave, a habit I've been keeping up with to preserve my sanity. All I have is a backpack to use as a pillow; to make my bed is to set it on top of a rock I've been using as a table, like a trophy on display.

I glance at Aaron, who picks at his bowl of oatmeal in silence, uninterested.

My stomach growls and I clutch my abdomen. *There are only two servings left in Aaron's bag*, I remind myself. *He needs them more than you do.*

"You should eat," I tell him. "Your body needs food to heal."

He looks at the oatmeal like it's a bowl of mud and worms. "I'm not in the mood."

I glare. "Would you rather be force-fed?"

He returns the expression and takes a bite, swallowing dryly. I offer him his water canteen, and he shakes his head.

"Take it," I demand.

"You first."

I scoff. "What, am I trying to poison you or something?"

"I wouldn't put it past you, but we're not exactly well-stocked on supplies here." His voice is raspy. "When's the last time *you* took a sip?"

Still glaring, I take a small gulp before shoving the canteen into his hands. "Now you."

Reluctantly, he chases his bite with a small sip of water, then returns the canteen to me. He plays with his food again, scooping up spoonfuls of oatmeal and letting them drip back into the bowl. He frowns at it, then sighs, leaning his head back to stare at the ceiling. "Is it possible to kill the rain?"

"I think we could manage."

"What are we thinking here? The classic blade-to-jugular?"

"Poison would be easier." I turn to look at him. "You know, since I already have some on hand."

He points a weak finger in my direction. "I like where your mind's at."

I can't help but chuckle, shaking my head. My grin falls quickly, and I glance at the rain falling beyond the vines. "We'll have to wait it out. There's no way you can travel in this weather."

He studies me for a moment, then stirs his oatmeal. "You can."

I snap my head back around to glare at him. "What the hell is that supposed to mean?"

"Just hear me out." He keeps his voice calm. "If we run out of food, or water—"

"Then I'll find more."

"That's not exactly a sustainable solution here, alright? We're still not very far from the Cut; Chasers will be looking for the traitors who *destroyed it*. You can't just wander around looking for shit." He sighs, swallowing a grimace as he clutches his stomach. "If something happens and you're putting yourself in danger by staying here…"

My eyes widen. "*No.*"

"Voclain…"

"You're being stupid again."

"I could get sick, alright?" He closes his eyes, taking a deep, strained breath before opening them again. "If that happens, I'm not letting you *starve* here with me."

"What are you gonna do, chase me out?"

"Maybe."

"You can barely keep your head up."

"Voclain, please. Just listen to me. I don't want…" He sighs. I look him in the eye, but I can't read him. "You don't have to stay here with me, alright? I can take care of myself."

"You think I'd leave you alone like this?"

"That'd be the wise thing to do."

I stare at him for a moment, inhaling deeply, trying to swallow my frustration. I avert my gaze and stare at the wall. "I'm so tired of having this conversation with you."

"What conversation?"

"*This.*" I face him again, vaguely gesturing in his direction. "You keep trying to convince me to leave you behind, and I'm sick of it."

He glares. "I'm *trying* to convince you to be smart about this. To be *safe.*"

"What about you? If you push me away, who's gonna keep *you* safe?" My throat tightens, and I try not to think about all the reasons why we're even in this mess to begin with. "If you're so worried about protecting everyone around you, how are you gonna protect yourself?"

"I can handle myself."

"So can I."

"Snakebite."

"Gunshot."

"You're impossible."

"And so are you." I fold my arms and stare at the wall again.

"You don't have to keep trying to prove yourself, Voclain." He picks at the scabs on his knuckles. "It's not weak to want to save your own skin, you know."

"You think that's what this is? You think I'm trying to prove a point by staying here with you?"

"I think you're stubborn."

"There's another variable to this equation you keep forgetting about."

"What?"

"*You*." I meet his gaze, jaw clenched, hands shaking. "This isn't about me, or proving a point, or being stubborn. I *chose* to be here, and I'm not abandoning you, whether you like it or not."

"Voclain."

"I would leave if I wanted to."

"And why don't you?"

"Because you're important to me, alright?" My voice echoes and I lower it to a near-whisper. "Because I..." I sigh, staring at the ceiling. In the dark, it looks like a starless sky. "I need you."

His lips part like he wants to say something, but he closes them without a word.

"Sometimes it feels like you're the only friend I have." I swallow dryly. "The only person who hasn't given up on me."

"So you understand."

"Understand what?"

"Why I want you to think about yourself every now and then." He stares at his hands again. "I think you need to realize that some people don't deserve to be saved."

For a moment I think back to what Milo said to me back at End Harbor. My shoulders tighten. *Is he talking about Ren?*

But when I realize who he's really referring to, my muscles relax—and my heart sinks.

"I don't want you putting yourself in danger," he says. "Especially not for my sake."

Now I'm the one who's stuck without anything to say. All I can do is stare at him, lips parted, trying to comprehend how someone I value so much could value himself so little. *Why doesn't he think he deserves to be saved?*

"If it ever comes down to it... if you ever need to choose between my sake and yours, or your safety, or your happiness or whatever..." He swallows. "I want you to choose yours."

"Aaron..."

"Can you promise me that?"

I study him. His face is pale and sticky with sweat. *He needs to hear me say it,* I realize.

"Yes."

He nods, something like relief spreading through him. "Thank you."

I don't realize my fingers are crossed until they begin to ache.

The vomiting begins sometime after we fall asleep.

I wake to find Aaron kneeling at the mouth of the cave, hair soaked, purging every last drop of sustenance from his body. For the first hour, it seems as unending as the rain that washes it away.

The hour that follows is harder to watch. The dry heaving that yields no results. The incessant trembling. The weakness that gradually curls its talons tighter around his throat until all of the strength has been choked out of him. He can't even hold his head up.

I don't know what happened. I've been monitoring his wound and regularly changing the dressing. I've been trying to keep it dry, in spite of the relentless rain and the moisture in this cave. But when he's too weak to keep up the heaving and he's on his back again, I grab my flashlight and peel away the bandages to take another look—and I cover my mouth with my hands.

The scabbing is soft and tinted green, the skin around it swollen and red.

I clean and redress the wound carefully, then press a shaking hand against his forehead. His face is sticky and drenched in sweat. *He's burning up.*

"It's cold," he mutters, eyes barely open.

Chills.

"I know. Let's get you away from the rain."

I'm not strong enough to carry him and I don't want to drag him, so I use the sled to bring him to the back wall, as far away from the mouth as possible. I arrange my jacket as his pillow again and glance around the cave. With the rain and our lack of fire, we've been freezing in here. *It must be weakening his immune system.*

He needs to get warm before the infection gets worse. With a fire, I could dry our clothes, boil fresh water, make some tea, and have a better source of light. With a fire, we'd be warm. *With a fire, we'd be okay.*

But there is so much rain. Only a wildfire could survive it, and I can't even light a spark.

Thunder cracks, and the drumming of the downpour grows louder. Somewhere outside, a flash of light blinks and dies out. *Lightning.*

This rain isn't letting up any time soon.

I try to keep my breathing under control and form a list of actionable steps. I've done all I can with the wound site, for now. I need to maintain his body temperature and keep that fever down. His skin is hot to the touch, but he still shivers from both his sickness and the cold. We are our only sources of warmth.

Aaron's teeth chatter. He rubs his forehead with little strength. "My head is killing me."

I charge up the pig flashlight with a few cranks and flip the switch that keeps it on, hoping the light will last long enough before I have to crank it again. I prop it up against our bags, then help Aaron sip some water.

I grab one of the already-used rags and hurry to the mouth of the cave, shivering as I wring the rag clean and soak it with cold rainwater. I return to Aaron's side and gently drape the cold cloth across his forehead. *Maybe this will soothe the ache.*

"Does this help?"

He shakes his head, eyes still closed. "Not that."

Maybe it's too cold. I pull away to remove the cloth, but he grabs my wrist, grip weak as he guides my hand back to where it was on his face. "This."

His hand falls away, and mine stays in place.

I pause for a moment, observing him as he drifts out of consciousness. I blink a few extra times before using the cloth to pat away the beads of sweat forming on his forehead. Loose strands of hair stick to his face, so I brush them out of the way, sweeping some behind his ears, combing others back through the rest of his waves.

Before getting stuck here, I don't think I've ever seen Aaron sleep. He's always keeping watch or on the other side of a wall.

I notice a few things now that I'm seeing it. In slumber, his ever-furrowed brows soften. His muscles relax, and his mouth curls slightly upward. He doesn't look angry. He doesn't look like a rebel with scars on his skin and blood on his hands. He looks like the child in those photographs. The lost one that he buried within himself, free of whatever it is that fuels those carving sweeps, those hollow stares. *He looks so peaceful.*

I don't realize my hand is lingering until his eyes open again, just barely. For a moment, he stares at me through his half-closed gaze—and then he chuckles. "Hi."

I pull my hand away with a frown. *He's getting delirious.*

I take the rag and head back over to the mouth of the cave to get it cold again, wring it out, then return to his side. He watches my every move, still grinning crookedly as I pat his forehead, until his smile fades. "God, Ed."

I stop wiping his forehead to glare, though I'm not sure he can tell. "What?"

"You're so nice to look at." He frowns, but it diminishes as his eyes flutter closed again. His voice is barely a breath. "Of your many maddening qualities, that one is by far the worst."

I blink, brows creased until I realize what he said. My face warms.

"That's the fever talking." I continue wiping away the sweat with the rag and then let it rest on his forehead. *His infection must be getting worse.*

"No, *I'm* talking," he mutters. He reaches out a hand, barely touching my cheek with his finger before lowering his arm. His brows furrow, like he can't decide whether to be relieved or disappointed. "You're still here."

"I am."

"I thought you could've been a ghost."

I shake my head.

He closes his eyes. He doesn't say anything for a moment, and I'm convinced he's finally fallen back asleep until he mutters something under his breath, so quietly I can barely hear it over the downpour. "You promised me."

My breath catches on his words. I try to avert my gaze, but it's drawn back to him. Somehow, it doesn't feel like I'm breaking my promise at all.

"Some people do deserve saving," I say.

But the flashlight finally flickers out, and I can't tell if he's still awake to hear it.

I open my eyes to the flat edge of a blade pressed against my throat.

I blink a few times before my mind wraps itself around the frigid metal sting, and the empty eyes that stare back at my own, only a few inches away and still so distant.

My eyes widen. "Aaron..."

He doesn't react to the sound of my voice. In fact, I'm not even sure he can hear me at all, or see me for that matter. Strands of hair fall in front of his gaze, and even in the dark I can tell his stare is unseeing.

"Aaron, put the knife away."

He still doesn't move. I hold my breath, waiting for something to happen. The rain continues to fall, and Aaron is frozen in the amber of his own time. I exhale when I realize he's asleep.

Slowly, I reach my hand up to meet his, gently prying the knife out of his hands. I set the weapon aside. He's still stuck in place, one hand planted against my shoulder.

I pull myself to a seated position, slipping out of his grip, trying not to wake him. Unless I want to leave him shocked and disoriented, which would only make it worse.

He leans back, sitting on his knees, his posture slumped. I sit there for a moment, watching him—and then his shoulders begin to convulse. He hangs his head low, and he sobs.

"Aaron?"

He still doesn't hear me. *He's still stuck.*

I've never seen him like this before—with his guard fully down, nothing there to hide behind but his own clammy skin.

My eyes widen. *This is why I've never seen him sleep.*

This is why he couldn't stay with me after he gave up his room. Why he's always insistent on keeping watch. Why he would stay up so late at End Harbor, busying himself with him and Milo's investigation in the lighthouse. Why he would go on those early morning swims in the sea, no matter how cold it was. *Better sleep*, he'd said.

Aaron has nightmares.

He buries his face in his hands. The notes of his sobs are high and light, like a child's laugh. I sit cross-legged in front of him, so close our knees almost touch. I reach out a hand, but then stop myself. *I can't wake him.*

His head falls forward, pressing against my shoulder. "It hurts, Eddie."

My heart lurches at the sound of my name. *He's already woken up.*

He keeps sobbing, forehead against my shoulder, hands resting on his knees in limp defeat. Something tells me he's not talking about the wound in his leg.

I wrap my arms around him. He feels small within my embrace, and he shrinks into it. My hands clutch his hair and back.

"I know," I whisper. "But I'm here, okay? I've got you."

He cries louder, still shrinking, collapsing into himself and my arms until I'm the only force holding him upright. I let my left hand meet his, and he grabs it, squeezing my unbroken fingers with his fractured ones. Like if he lets go, he'll never come back. My other hand combs through his hair in slow, soothing strokes.

"Why haven't I left yet?" he chokes out, voice cracking. "I thought I came back home."

My throat constricts. I have no idea what he's talking about, but I hold him tighter, closer.

"You are home," I say. "They can't hurt you anymore."

His sobs decrescendo, fading into the soft rhythm of the rain, the whistling of the wind. We remain like that for a long time until the storm finally lulls him back to sleep. *His fever's getting worse.*

He's shivering. I take the puffer jacket and guide his arms through it, zipping it closed. I lean my back against the wall, letting him sleep in my arms, still afraid to wake him again.

But no matter how many times I close my eyes, I can't keep them shut. I pull out Carmody's lighter without thinking, tracing the engravings on the side as I think back to Aaron.

What was he talking about? I stare at the starless blanket of dark above my head. *What place is he stuck in?*

I continue to draw circles around the lighter with my thumb, until it pauses over one of the etchings. Something feels different.

My brows furrow. I hover over the letters. I always thought it bore Carmody's initials, but as I focus my touch, that first letter begins to feel more like an *I* than a *D*. But it's too dark to tell. *Maybe I'm remembering it wrong*, I wonder. My memory is strong, but not perfect.

My mind wanders back to Aaron, and I open the lighter out of habit, lost in thought, ready to snap it shut again—and then I freeze.

Like a dancer in a music box, a delicate flame flickers to life.

R. STELLER

Saturday, April 6

♪ THEM SHOES - PATRICK SWEANY ♪

The bullet hits Aaron in the leg.

He calls out in pain and shouts an intricate string of swears as he clutches his thigh, knife still in hand. Instead of fleeing, the Chaser reaches for the weapon—and his throat is slit in an instant. Aaron falls down with him.

While Aaron's distracted, I run to King's side, helping him to his feet. "You alright?"

King grimaces. "I will be."

I let him wrap his arm around my shoulder for support as we hurry away from the cabin and back toward the Cut. *A Corps healer will be able to fix him in no time.*

We run into Heron on our way back, who immediately rushes to King's side to take his other arm. "I heard a gunshot. What happened?"

"Steller killed a traitor," King mutters.

"Nice going."

"I didn't," I snap, a little too defensively. "I only hit his leg."

"Yeah—right by his femoral artery," King says. "Even if you did manage to miss it, he'll die of blood loss without anyone there to help him. Or infection, if he does somehow escape—which he won't be able to do if his leg is compromised."

"He can survive a leg wound if I survived a shot to the *chest*," I point out. "The one *you* gave me, might I add."

King grimaces through the pain. "Yeah, well, I'm also the one who helped you survive it, aren't I?"

"And you had a Corps healer to tend to your wounds," Heron adds. "They can fix anything. *That's* how you survived."

"Don't worry about it, Steller. You did well," King says, swallowing through a painful cringe. "Canary will be pleased."

"You did what?"

Canary stands behind his makeshift desk with his palms flattened against the surface. It's a small wooden card table, square like his jaw and shoulders, where a mess of papers and a small black laptop reside.

He's a short, broad-built man with a head so closely shaven it shines in the dim light of the commander's portable, which he's already seemed to have made his own in less than twenty-four hours. Sleek black luggage is sprawled out across the floor near the bed, and exactly seven suits hang in garment bags in an open wardrobe, with a pair of polished shoes to match each one. Two Officers are in the back corner, removing art from the walls and knickknacks from the shelves as they clear the room of every last reminder that my mother ever existed at all.

I keep my eyes glued to Canary's, which are dark brown, almost black. He's not wearing his shades—his Eyes. *It's late*, I think to myself. *We must have interrupted his down time.*

I clench my jaw and curl my hands into fists, trying so hard not to let my gaze wander to the pair of Chasers. I want so badly to stop them, to find at least something of my mother's to keep.

Eyes all around, I remind myself. *Nobody knows about your connection to her—not even Heron and King. Keep it that way.*

I remain perfectly still as Canary's glare digs into me. Two Fourth Rank Agents flank either side of him, and he turns to one of them. "Both of you, leave the room." He snaps at the Officers, who pause, arms full of my mother's old belongings. "You too."

The Chasers nod, leaving us to face his wrath alone.

"He shot a traitor," King replies, clutching his freshly bandaged side. The Corps healers were able to remove the knife, clean his wounds, and dose him with pain medicine. Now he's back in his suit like nothing happened.

"I asked *him*," Canary says, furrowing his bushy eyebrows as he nods in my direction. He straightens his posture, folding his arms across his chest. I stand at least a foot above him. He frowns, as though noticing this fact for himself. "Have a seat."

Heron drags over two wooden chairs for King and me, then pulls one over for himself. We do as he says.

Even as he stands, now that I'm sitting, Canary is only at my eye level. He bores into me with his glare, his empty eyes fueled as he tries to keep his nostrils from flaring. He takes a deep breath, grounding himself, clearing his expression of all readability.

"So let me get this straight." He taps his fingers against his sleeve in slow, calculating rolls. "An Officer followed one of the fleeing traitors to the cabin. And this traitor killed him? With only a knife?"

"Yes," I say, holding his stare with my own.

"You shot him in retaliation."

"I did."

"And you didn't even think to preserve him for Extraction?"

I suppress a flinch, stomach churning. "Agent Kingfisher was compromised. My priority was his safe return to the compound for timely treatment. I couldn't reasonably manage helping my superior Agent back to safety and keeping a combative hostage under control."

"Where was Agent Heron in all of this?"

"Taking a piss." Heron leans back in his seat with crossed arms, unintimidated by the man in front of us.

"Of course." Canary sighs, rubbing his forehead. "Your poor father must be rolling in his grave."

Heron sharpens his glare.

Canary shifts his focus to me again. "So you shot the traitor to keep him from getting away?"

"That is correct, sir," I say.

"You haven't been equipped with your Eyes yet, let alone a Nightjade gun."

"I used the traitor's Yesterday gun, sir." I set the pistol on the table.

Canary picks up the weapon with both hands, inspecting it carefully. "So he's dead, I presume—not merely incapacitated? And if so..." He walks over to a shelf, where a framed photo of my mother and father as teenagers used to reside. He sets the gun in its empty space and returns to his desk. "Where is the body?"

I swallow dryly as Heron and King exchange unsure glances. I could say he got away. *That might buy Aaron a bit of time.* They wouldn't justify the resources it would take to locate a single missing traitor who already has a fatal wound, would they?

But if I tell Canary that and they find him—still bleeding in front of that cabin—my loyalty will be questioned in an instant. They know my background; even with the story King and Heron have helped me spin, the Corps would accuse me of trying to protect a traitor.

But what if Aaron did somehow manage to escape? If I tell Canary I killed him and the body is missing, I'll be penalized for not making sure he was really dead.

I've backed myself into a corner.

"Right where we left it," King says before I get the chance to reply. "I told Steller our priority was reporting back to you, not interfering with a crime scene. The threat has been neutralized. The scene should be investigated for any additional evidence."

Canary pauses, analyzing King's emotionless expression. His shoulders relax, only slightly. "Well done, Agent."

"Thank you, sir."

"So if I were to visit this cabin you speak of, I would find the body. Right where you left it, you say?"

King hesitates for only a fraction of a second. "You would, sir."

"Good." Canary strokes his chin, a cruel grin spreading across his face. "I'd like to see this dead traitor for myself."

Aaron is gone.

The only trace he has left behind is blood—a fresh coat of glistening crimson paint, blanketing the cabin's wooden porch.

Two Officers zip the dead one inside a black plastic bag before carrying him back toward the compound. We stand in silence, listening to the wind whistle as we wait for Canary to speak.

He stands in front of the blood with folded arms. He studies it carefully, as though he expects it to move. Or maybe he's watching it dry.

This is it, I tell myself, heart racing. *He knows something isn't right here. He'll have me sent to Extraction.*

"The other traitors must have taken his body back to wherever they ran off to," King says, face straight. If he's nervous, he doesn't show it.

Canary keeps his eyes glued to the blood, unmoving. We stand still like that for ages until he holds up a finger, beckoning me to stand by his side. Heron and I exchange glances, and I do as he says.

"You see these marks?" He points to a pattern in the dirt. I can barely make it out with the faint window glow, but I can see a trail breaking into the woods beyond the cabin. My eyes dart to the porch. *Didn't there used to be a sled there?*

My heart plummets, every organ in my body on pause. *She came back for him, didn't she?*

I clear my throat. "I see them, sir."

He nods, stroking his chin. "He must have gotten away."

The color drains from my face. "I suppose so."

Canary turns his head to look up at me. I can't break my eyes away from the tracks. "I assume you already know your mistake, Steller."

I force myself to glance at him, then stare straight ahead again. "I didn't check to see that he was really dead."

"If you are already aware of your error, then I must ask…" His voice lowers. "Was it intentional?"

Chills crawl against the back of my neck, like a thousand tiny spider legs are pricking every pore. "It was not, sir. I realized what I did wrong after the fact."

"So it's merely a coincidence that he was only shot in the leg—and managed to get away?"

My heartbeat slams against my ribcage as I shrug. I face Canary, Aaron's words replaying in my mind. "I think I just have shitty aim."

Canary stares at me in silence for a moment, my skin burning as he tries to read the stoicism I can only hope I'm upholding.

To my surprise, he chuckles. "I suppose Agent Kingfisher will have to fix that during your training."

Training? My pulse quickens. *Does this mean he wants me to complete initiation after all? Have I somehow earned his favor?*

The ounce of humor in Canary's expression falls away quickly. Even with his lips drawn into a straight line, his eyes somehow manage to grin. He wears a cruel, calculating, owl-like stare, and I can't shake the feeling that he knows more than he's letting on. "You have forty-eight hours to bring me his head, or you'll all pay for this mistake."

And with that, Canary walks away, following the distant Officers back to the Cut without another word.

Heron stands by my side, and we watch him disappear between the trees. "Surely he didn't mean that."

"It's Canary." Ian stands to my left. "When has he ever asked for something he doesn't want?"

My stomach twists into knots. *I wish I knew what game he's playing.*

Is he trying to prove that I'm on the wrong side? Or that I'm on the right one, after all?

How the hell am I supposed to find my way out of this one?

Thunder rolls above me, and I tilt my head to watch the sky. Before I have the chance to answer the question, it starts to rain.

EDDIE

Thursday, April 11
74 Beds Made

For a while, the fire is enough.

The sled is my only source of somewhat-dry lumber, and I've been snapping off pieces of it to serve as kindling. It's still functional, but smaller; I'm burning the last plank I can reasonably use. I wash our clothes in the rain and dry them out over rocks. I boil fresh water, I fill up both of our canteens, and I drink my fill. I wash Aaron's hair and clean the sweat from his skin. I cook the last oatmeal rations in Aaron's pot, but he's not awake to eat it, and I don't want him to choke. I force myself to take the bites instead. *I can't take care of him if I'm weak.*

He hasn't woken up since his nightmare. His breathing is slow and shallow, his pulse is weak—but it's still there, and the rhythm fuels me to keep going. Even as his wound gets worse, no matter how consistently and carefully I clean and redress it. Even as he grows weaker, no matter how many gulps of thimbleberry tea I help him down in slumber.

It's Thursday morning when the rain finally stops. The last plank burns until the flame flickers out.

Our food is gone, our fire is gone, and Aaron is slipping away. There's no telling when the storm will pick up again.

Every part of me aches. My leg feels worse somehow. My muscles are sore and unsteady, and even as I sit by the fire, I can't stop shaking. The cold makes my joints throb. The sprain in my left wrist has healed itself, but it still hurts, and the fingers in my right hand are still fractured. *And I'm just so tired.*

But I know what I have to do.

I pack up our things, slinging my two backpacks and Aaron's satchel over my shoulders. The one with the Catnap clippings is light, and my travel pack isn't too bad either, but the weight of Aaron's satchel already digs into my shoulder.

I secure him to the sled and reattach his old black sweater to it. Parting the curtain of vines, I pull him out of the cave.

After spending so much time in the dark, I squint in the faint gray morning light, shielding my eyes with my hand as I take in our surroundings. Although the clouds above my head cast a shadow, everything glistens with droplets of water, each pine needle a twinkling set of sharpened emeralds. The forest floor is damp and layered in a thick blanket of dead leaves, twigs, and other debris that blend in with the mud. Moss-covered rocks and fallen logs sprout mushrooms I know Aaron would love to investigate. I turn around to glance at his limp body. *There's no time for that.*

The air is thick with moisture, and a slight wind carries with it the earthy aroma of dirt and evergreen. I breathe it all in, filling my lungs with something other than the reek of damp rocks for the first time in days.

I pause, assessing the scent a second time. I smell a campfire.

I rotate where I stand, unable to peer over the towering pines, so I stare at the sky instead, trying to notice a stream of smoke. But even without the rain, the clouds are too dark to tell. *Maybe I'm just imagining it.*

I shove the thoughts down, take a deep breath, and move forward.

I am strong enough to push through the first half-hour without getting much worse, fueled by the adrenaline that masks my hunger and exhaustion and makes my heart drum loudly in my ears. I use Margot's compass and the memory of Cecil's maps as a vague guide. Maybe I can get a better sense of where we are once we reach one of the landmarks in my head, like a lake or a river.

At first, it's easy to keep myself occupied by my surroundings. I focus on everything but the noise inside my head, which isn't too difficult, considering that my only view has been slimy rocks and complete darkness for who knows how long.

It's eerie to me how alive everything feels. Leftover raindrops drip from the canopy, occasionally landing upon my forehead or the back of my neck. Squirrels scurry along branches like highways, their fur slightly damp. Deer graze on fresh foliage, scampering away as I approach. Birds preen their shimmering feathers, but I scare those away too.

A twig snaps above me. I pause, snapping my head upward, heart rate spiking. It dies down the moment I realize it's only a bird.

For a moment, I mistake it for a bluebird. But instead of boasting a warm red belly and light periwinkle cloak, this bird is a deep royal sapphire, with a navy crest and a penetrating stare. *A Steller's jay.*

But the bird doesn't go anywhere. It tilts its head, studying me carefully, like it can see right through me. A shiver crawls up my spine. *Why haven't I scared it off?*

I stand there for a while, watching it watch me until it flies to a nearby branch. I squint to make out the shapes, realizing it's flown to a nest. I hold my breath to listen to a delicate melody of faint chirps.

I almost smile until another bird erupts from the nest—a true bluebird, much smaller than the jay. The jay chases the bluebird, diving and pecking until its beak meets the smaller bird's eye. She cries out in pain, but she doesn't stop fending off the jay until she falls to the ground, motionless. The jay too goes perfectly still, studying the nest like a prize.

It turns its head to look at me one more time, seeing me wholly, until it flies away with a hatchling in its beak.

I cover my mouth with a trembling hand, eyes wide and watering. Bile burns in my throat.

It's already gone, I tell myself. *There's nothing you can do to save it.*

And I keep going, because that's all I can do.

The exhaustion catches up to me somewhere within the second hour.

I take a break on a moss-ridden rock, resting my back against the soggy tree trunk behind it. I lean my head back and stare at the endless canopy of pine needles above me, remembering how small I really am.

My gaze falls back to Aaron, who rests peacefully against the sled. I think he's too weak to have any more nightmares, but this stillness is somehow worse.

While we're stopped, I clean and redress his wounds, hiding the old bandages in a shrub. I prick my finger as my hand slides out, and I grimace, sucking the drop of blood as I take a closer look. It has no thorns. I must have snagged my finger on a broken twig. *It looks awfully familiar.*

My eyes widen when I spot a nearly hidden handful of red, fuzzy berries, like raspberries covered in a thin layer of frost. Little white flowers with round petals and yellow centers sprout from the plant, and I grin. *Thimbleberries.*

I gather as many as I can, eating some and storing the rest in Aaron's cooking canister. I replenish our jar of leaves and flowers to use as tea later. *Aaron will need this.*

As I'm putting everything away, something chirps inside my bag.

I drop the backpack like it's made of hot coals. I pause, waiting for something to happen. Another chirp chimes, identical to the first.

All the color drains from my face.

Slowly, I reach inside the bag and retrieve the phone.

I forgot it was in there. I've been so focused on healing Aaron and getting him back to safety that I've barely had the chance to think about what I've agreed to, let alone all the things that Agent informed me about Ren. I still haven't decided whether or not to believe him—and I still don't have a plan for helping him find the answers he's looking for. Because the moment I start thinking about it all, I know I'll spiral, and I can't afford that right now.

But I can't exactly ignore the phone either.

I swallow the lump in my throat and flip it open to find two text messages from the only contact. *M. Heron.*

M. HERON

> hey detective. rain's not covering your tracks anymore.

My eyes dart to the sled—and the obvious trail we've been leaving in the mud, which extends as far as I can see. The color drains from my face. *How could I have been so stupid?*

And how does he know about it?

I study my surroundings again. As far as I know, Aaron and I are the only human beings around for miles.

M. HERON

> don't worry. it's been taken care of. my secret weapon is still secret.

He's covering my tracks for me? A shiver runs down my back. I wonder what he could have done to hide my trail back at the cave. *Kick leaves over the marks? Drag a log or two around to mimic the lines I've been leaving with this sled?*

And wouldn't that mean he's been watching me?

I should probably be relieved, but instead, my stomach twists into knots. There is nothing a soldier in the Corps values more than return on investment. If he's putting this much effort to make sure that no one else uncovers his *secret*, I must be of more value to him than I thought.

The realization blankets my skin in goosebumps. *Is this really about finding answers to what happened to his brother? Or is there more to his story than it seems?*

I'm about to type a response when another message appears.

M. HERON

> but I have to say… you've left behind quite the inconvenient mess.

My brows knit together.

EDDIE

?

M. HERON

come on. you know what I'm talking about. use those detective skills of yours.

A pause.

M. HERON

you feel it in the air, don't you?

I peel my eyes away from the phone and stare at the sky. The wind runs cold fingers through my hair. Dark clouds still loom above me, with only a few pockets of sunlight peeking through. Everything seems hazy, and I can't help but hold my breath, wondering if the storm will return soon.

But then I smell it again—that deep, earthy campfire scent I told myself to ignore. Now that I'm paying attention to it, I realize it hasn't really gone away; it's gotten stronger.

Still holding my breath, I turn around, staring in the direction of the trail I've left behind. The woods are too dense for me to see anything but tree trunks, no matter how far I squint.

Only when I tilt my head upward do I see the amber glow in the distance.

Far away there is the faintest light, shrouded by the same dark gray clouds that lurk above my head. And as I let myself exhale to take a deeper breath, I start to wonder if they really are clouds at all.

He's not talking about the tracks in the mud, I realize, eyes wide. He's talking about the fire. *The one* I *started.*

It's still burning.

My heart lodges in the back of my throat. I shift my gaze back to the phone.

EDDIE

you're talking about the fire?

M. HERON

> what else would I be talking about?

Only a fraction of my worry subsides. *So he doesn't know where I am right now, or about the sled marks.*

M. HERON

> well, just a heads up, no one here knows you're the arsonist. no one that matters, at least. so you won't have to worry about any nearby bounty-hunting quests. for now.

Another pause.

M. HERON

> you're welcome.

I bite my lip in thought. How could he possibly know this is my fault?

EDDIE

> who says I'm the one who started it?

M. HERON

> the other traitors got away. that friend of yours was occupied. lucky guess.

My gut churns. *He knows about Aaron too?*

M. HERON

> well, I'd get moving if I were you. before all your little fires catch up to you.
>
> oh, and one more thing.

EDDIE

> ...

M. HERON

> from now on, be careful about the breadcrumbs you
> leave behind, detective.

> unless you want to be seen.

All I can do is stand there, staring, until an image pops up on the screen. I frown. He's sent me an invitation to start a game of checkers.

I slam the phone shut.

Maybe I should be relieved that the Corps still has no idea where I am, but I can't shake the feeling that it's not the good news it seems to be. Heron wants to keep me alive for his own sake. I just haven't figured out what he really wants yet.

You're doing what you have to do. I shove the phone into my backpack and zip it closed. *This is your only lead, and Ren is waiting for you to find him.*

I gather our bags and take one last look at the flames in the distance before I continue.

At nightfall, I take shelter beneath the canopy of a towering cedar. I use Carmody's now-functioning lighter to make a campfire. Aaron needs tea and warmth, and if the Corps is busy trying to put out the fire at the Cut, they won't notice our smoke in a sky that's already crowded with it.

I have no sleeping bag, so I prop myself upright against the tree, legs stretched out in front of me. Aaron sleeps on the sled by my side, too weak to even shiver. I've already cleaned and redressed his wound, helped him unconsciously down a few gulps of tea, and replenished our canteens with fresh water. It took me a while, but I was able to get him to eat a few berries in his state of half-slumber.

Sleep is waiting for me, and I'm exhausted enough to crave it desperately, but I still can't seem to reach it. I keep glancing over my shoulder to study the faint glow in the distance. I know the fire is too far to be a threat, and the Corps has the means to put it out—but there is still so much smoke, following me all this way like a looming cloud of bad luck.

I pull out the broken shard of mirror glass, fidgeting with it to the crackling light of the campfire. A jagged fraction of my reflection stares back at me, a single eye blinking to the beat of my own. And it still doesn't feel like mine.

The scars on my left arm itch. I reach a hand underneath my sweatshirt to trace each letter, and the cold from my own fingers sends chills throughout my body.

UNLUCKY

Since that day on the beach, the letters have healed to a cruel perfection. Each one is prominent and clear, bold enough to be read from a mile away. Like my own personal warning label.

I stare at the mirror shard again, my own eye blinking back. I know it's ridiculous, but part of me wonders if there is some truth to the word I've been called all my life. The word that I can never seem to shake, no matter how far I go to try and outrun it.

I turn the glass over in my hands, thinking back to the superstition. *Cloud it with smoke, bury it in a year.*

I reach out, holding it above the fire until the surface turns completely black. My reflection is gone.

I put it back inside my pocket and fall asleep beneath the cedar.

Saturday, April 13
76 Beds Made

It's past noon when I stumble across the road.

I crouch low in a ditch, keeping Aaron close as I observe my surroundings through the gaps in the trees. The road stretches and curves as far as I can see in either direction, with cracked pavement so sun-faded I almost wonder if it's still in use—until I spot the gas station across from me. A real, operational one with a clean market. No spiderwebs. No rats. *No skeletons.*

There are only two cars in the lot. One is an old pickup truck parked off to the side, probably belonging to whoever's working the station. The other is a dark blue sedan parked next to a gas pump, glistening in the bits of light that manage to seep through the gray sky and smoky haze. A middle-aged man stands by the vehicle, filling it up with fuel. I watch silently from my ditch. He finishes and walks inside the market.

When I watch him disappear behind the automatic glass door, I can see the rows and rows of food that line the shop's interior. My stomach growls. I'm all out of thimbleberries, and they don't do much to soothe the hunger anyway. It aches deeply.

I rub my neck, my burning lower back—the toll of dragging Aaron with this sled and sleeping in beds made of upright tree trunks and leaf litter. Every muscle within me feels like a string pulled taut. *How much longer can I keep doing this?*

Through the front door's glass, I see the man disappear to browse the rows of food. He doesn't have a good view of me, and when I squint, I see that the cashier is busy watching something on her phone.

My legs move on their own accord. I haul Aaron up from the ditch and across the road. My movements are swift but subtle as I hide behind the parked sedan, thinking back to everything Asa taught me about hot-wiring as a kid.

I open the front door, and I pause.

He left his keys in the car.

Before I have the chance to do so much as blink, I'm opening the back door. I maneuver Aaron off the sled and lift him into the seat, laying him across it and throwing our bags inside before slamming the door shut. I climb into the driver's seat, my life from before flooding back to me in an instant. *Do I even remember how to do this?*

And what about the risks? This car is new, equipped with a GPS system that could lead the authorities straight to End Harbor. *Not if I ditch it far enough,* I note. *I'll be able to carry him one last stretch, won't I?*

I think back to what Heron said about breadcrumbs and know this will leave many. *But what other choice do I have?*

I turn to stare at Aaron. His skin has lost all of its warmth. His cheekbones and nose are sharper, pronounced by hunger. Breath seeps out of his mouth in slow, shallow pulses, and the stray strands of hair that fall in front of his eyes don't even flinch—like he's barely even breathing at all. *He's running out of time.*

From the corner of my eye, I spot the man walking out of the store, a plastic bag of snacks in hand. He doesn't notice me yet.

It's now or never.

I turn the key and slam my foot on the gas.

The man shouts something as I drive away, but I don't hear it.

Sunday, April 14
77 Beds Made

I lose track of time on the road, fueled by my own adrenaline, trying not to think too much about what I'm doing. In my head, someone else is driving. Someone else is checking the compass chained around my neck. Someone else is going through the images of Cecil's maps that I store in my mind. Someone else is bearing my pain.

The radio is nice to focus on. The sounds are mostly static all the way out here, but I get bits and pieces of obscure commentary and odd instrumentals every now and then. It's not very cohesive, but filling in the gaps with my imagination is a good distraction.

I stare out the sky through the window. It must be mid-day. I drove as much as I could throughout the night, then pulled over to get a few hours of rest before continuing just before sunrise. I *made my bed* this morning by pulling my seat forward, comforted to know the habit still remains.

I eye the fuel gauge and bite my lip. It's an efficient car, but I've been driving it for a while now and I don't have much gas left. But if my calculations are correct and my map memories are clear enough, we should be approaching End Harbor soon, since I didn't take the careful zig-zag route Cecil did on our way to the Cut. Aaron doesn't have that kind of time. *In fact, I should probably change his dressing again.*

I pull over and retrieve a roll of bandages from my pocket, where I've been keeping it for efficient access. I walk to the backseat and open the door, peeling off his old bandages to check the wound. The visible inflammation has gone down since we've left the cave, but it's still a bit swollen and green. I clean the wound with fresh water and a cloth and bandage him up again. I shove the roll into my pocket, climb back inside the car, and keep driving.

I'm going over the maps in my head when a sound interrupts the static. For a moment I wonder if the radio is finally coming through. But when I listen carefully, I can still hear the scraps of noise in the background and know that can't be the case. *And what kind of radio plays a siren?*

I check the rear-view mirror. A sleek white car is trailing me, flashing red and blue lights.

My lungs stop. My heart feels like I've swallowed it and it's drowning in my stomach, flailing for a breath as its pulsing quickens.

I pull over, because that is all I can do.

I feel the weight of my knife in my boot as the car parks behind me. Time drips like honey as two Chasers climb out of their vehicle, white suits blinding.

They walk to the driver's seat window and tap on it. I roll the glass down and stare at a female Officer with short brown hair, squinting in the gray light.

"Were you aware of how fast you were going?"

Saying yes *is a sure way to get an injection.* I swallow, though it feels more like scraping the walls of my throat with sandpaper. "I was not."

"Is your speedometer functioning properly?"

Another injection opportunity. "As far as I know, yes."

"So your speeding was the result of simple negligence."

If they wanted to, they could kill me for whichever way I choose to answer the question. "Yes."

The woman nods, typing a note into the screen on her wrist.

The second Officer squints through the backseat window, crinkling his nose at Aaron. "What's wrong with him?"

My hands shake. "He's sleeping."

The Chasers exchange glances. "Step out of the car."

Every breath slips away as I do what she says. I can feel my heart thudding in my ears. I don't close the door behind me.

They look me up and down, taking in the dirt smudging my cheeks and the mud staining my clothes. The male Officer reaches out to pluck a leaf from my hair, observing it suspiciously before letting it fall away in disgust. He walks away to the back of the car to check the license plate, then whispers into his partner's ear. She nods, still pinning me with her gaze.

"Cards, license, and registration, please."

My arms shake when I roll up my sleeves, exposing the Jokers painted on my wrists in black ink. The Officer's brows crease together, almost like she can't believe what she's seeing.

While she's distracted, I draw my right arm back—and I punch her in the face.

I bite my tongue to ignore the searing pain in my already injured fingers. She folds forward and clutches her nose. Blood drips down her glistening white uniform.

I don't have the chance to move before the other Officer grabs me from behind, holding me close against his chest. I kick and try to pry his arms away, but I'm no match against anyone in Chaser armor.

Still clutching her nose with one hand, the other Officer brings her free arm to her mouth, speaking into her wrist. "Call off the search; we found the girl who stole the missing vehicle. She's combative. We're proceeding with extermination."

I flail, trying to wriggle my way out of the Chaser's grip, but he only retaliates by pulling my arms so far back I cry out. He cranes his neck to face me, studying my face. His brows knit together. "Hey, does she look familiar to you?"

His partner looks up, studying me for a moment until her eyes widen. "It's—"

I bite the man's ear.

He drops me in an instant, grabbing the side of his head as I spit out his blood. I take the chance to pull my knife from my boot and pin the female Officer against the side of the car, pressing the edge of my blade against her throat. She's dressed in armor and must be at least a foot taller than I am, but still, she looks at me in a way that makes me pause.

Of all the things to find within a Chaser's gaze, there is fear in this woman's eyes.

Suddenly, I can't smell anything but the smoke in the air. I see that dead Officer's face in the greenhouse, melting beneath flames.

I glance to the side. The other Officer is on the ground, holding his ear. Soon he'll stand, and I won't be able to take two of them. *I'm running out of options.*

I look in her eyes again, wondering how someone so seemingly human could wear a uniform like hers. There is no way to count how many lives she's taken in her stare. Without the white boots, she looks a little like me.

But I am not her.

I don't want to be a killer.

I keep one hand on my knife and use the other to take the bandages out of my pocket. I wrap it around her eyes to make a blindfold, tying it tightly.

"I'll be quick, I promise," I whisper, because she needs to fear me. "Hold still."

She bites her quivering lip, waiting. Blood still drips from her nose.

She doesn't see me sprint over to their car and slash a tire.

Two tires.

Three.

The other Chaser rises to his feet, his ear a bloody mess. He tries to grab me again, but this time I jam my finger into his eye. His cry echoes throughout the pines as I slash the last tire.

I'm back in the stolen car before he has the chance to pull out his Night-jade gun, speeding faster than I was before they pulled me over. I drive as far as I can go until the car runs out of gas. The sun is setting when I ditch it in the woods.

I pull out the sled and gently maneuver Aaron onto it, staying close to the road but hidden behind the trees as I haul him across the forest floor. This time, I cover the sled tracks as I go, kicking up leaves to hide it every few yards.

It's a slow, draining process, and I begin to play a game with myself. *When am I going to collapse?*

I ask the question over and over again in my head, placing imaginary bets.

After I pass this rock? After that bird flies away? Once the rain returns?

Night falls. The farther I go, the more cracks I notice in the road, spreading out like spiderwebs until it's more broken than put together. The trees around me seem to grow taller with every step.

When I see the Gate in the distance, I place my final bet. *I will collapse when I reach it. I can reach it, right?*

My knees buckle beneath me and I crumple to the ground.

I curl up next to Aaron, and as a dark curtain draws over everything I see, I pretend that I am warm.

REN

Friday, February 2

The knock on the door is what finally pulls me out of bed.

I've been awake for hours now, or at least that's what it feels like. I don't have any way to tell the time other than the sunlight seeping into my room through the curtains.

Ian's room, I correct myself. This is not my house. *I am a prisoner, not a guest.*

I roll out from under the covers and grab a white shirt from the dresser, pulling it over my head. It matches the other three I've been cycling through, along with the pair of dark jeans I climb into. They're not long enough to cover my ankles, so they can't be Ian's, who is just barely my height. Heron is too short for these to possibly be his.

I try not to think about whose clothes I've been living in and exit my lace-curtained prison cell. I close the door behind me and walk down the corridor until I reach the living room.

Ian's safe house is unlike anything I've seen in my life. Immaculate oak floors stretch throughout the room, spanning beneath a massive white couch and an open-concept kitchen with glistening quartz countertops. To my left, the wall is made entirely out of glass, with a sliding door that leads to a deck overlooking Puget Sound. There is only water and evergreen as far as the eye can see.

When Ian left with Heron a few days ago, he gave me strict instructions not to answer the door for anyone, so I stand still in the mouth of the hallway, waiting for something to happen. Another knock cuts through the silence, this one more aggressive than the last.

A voice calls from behind the door. "A little help, here?"

Heron.

I open the door. He stumbles inside, carrying two overstuffed grocery bags in his arms. He sets them on the kitchen island. "I come bearing gifts."

I close the front door and walk to the kitchen, watching Heron as he begins to restock the fridge with food.

"You don't have to stare at me like that." He puts away a gallon of milk. "It's creepy."

I keep my mouth shut.

"You like these?" He turns around to face me, holding a box of cookies.

"I don't eat sugar."

Heron looks as though I've just admitted to eating glue. "What the hell? Why not?"

"It's unhealthy."

"Well, yeah. But isn't that part of the allure? Knowing it's bad for you and eating it anyway? Craving something you know you shouldn't have?"

I don't say anything. Heron rolls his eyes. "More for me, I guess." He places the cookies in the cupboard and closes the door.

"Where's Ian?"

"So you're not happy to see me?" *Not in the slightest,* I want to say, but I think my face does the talking for me because Heron frowns. "He's waiting for us at HQ."

"Waiting for what?"

He pauses, brow raised. "You really don't know what day it is?"

I don't have any way of knowing that. I shake my head, and he sighs. "It's Friday."

My eyes widen. "What?"

He nods.

So that's why he's here.

Heron averts his gaze, pretending to scan the fridge for a place to store a bag of celery. "You know what you're gonna say at the hearing and all that?"

I nod. Ian must have gone over my script with me a dozen times before he left.

"Just a heads up—be careful what you say to Canary. He's a Fifth Rank."

"I don't know what that means."

Heron closes the door with a frustrated sigh. He sets the celery down on the counter and fishes something out of his back pocket before tossing it in my direction.

I catch it with a scoff. It's a red poker chip engraved with *M. Heron* on one side and *2* on the other. "What is this?"

Heron snatches it from my hands, shoving it back into his pocket. "I lose that, and I'm dead."

I furrow my brows.

"It's like an ID. White through black for all ranks."

"Ranks?"

"The Agency Division's hierarchy is split into five ranks. Determines responsibilities. Clearance. What you can get away with."

"Five?" I ask. "That's it?"

"There are higher-ups too. People the Fifth Rank Agents report to. But that's classified stuff. Even I don't know anything about them."

"And you're Second Rank?"

He turns around again, opening the fridge and shoving the celery in a drawer. "Very glad you know your numbers."

I glare. "How'd a guy like you get bumped up to Second so quickly? You're like, what, nineteen?"

Now he's the one glaring. "*You're like, what,* twelve?"

"Eighteen."

"Twenty-one."

"Still."

He stares at me in thought for a moment before shrugging and busying himself with a bag of spinach. "I started at this rank."

That only plants more questions, but I don't have time to ask them before he changes the subject. "Hungry?"

I shake my head.

"Oh, come on. You've been living on instant oatmeal for days."

"I'm not hungry."

Heron looks me up and down. "Sure you aren't." He puts away the last item, then grabs a carton of eggs and a bag of shredded cheese. "You've gotta feed yourself, McLellan. You're useless to the Corps if you can't pull your weight."

"I don't eat dairy."

He gives me a look, then sighs, replacing the cheese for spinach with a frown. "Of course you don't."

I take a seat at one of the wooden barstools lining the island, watching as he begins to scramble a few eggs on a frying pan. "You mentioned Canary."

He crinkles his nose. "Yeah. Just... be careful with what you say around him. He's not exactly easy to please." Heron pauses. "He'll be in charge of your hearing."

"What rank is he?"

"Fifth."

"Fifth Rank is the highest?" I conclude, thinking of standard poker chip colors.

"Yep. He's the leading Agent at Seattle's HQ. Head of House, they like to call it. He reigns over the entire Pacific Region."

So we're near Seattle? I glance at the view of the Sound through the glass wall. We must be pretty far out if this is the only house in sight for miles. *At least from my limited view.*

"And Ian is Third Rank?"

Heron nods. "He's been blue since he was my age."

"How come?"

"He led the Corps right to an entire encampment of Undergrounders. Or Unseen, as you guys like to call yourselves." Heron turns off the stove and scrapes the eggs into a white ceramic bowl. He retrieves a fork from a drawer and slides the dish in my direction. "There had to be at least fifty of them. It was the biggest traitor haul this region has ever seen."

My stomach cartwheels. "What happened to them?"

"Exterminated. Some were sent to the Tombs, but... it's death either way."

I swallow the urge to vomit, manually forcing my lungs to maintain their rhythm. "How'd he manage to swing that?"

Heron walks to the coffee maker to get a pot brewing. "It's all about who you know, I guess. He came across the right person by chance, back when he was still an Officer. That was his connection. The whole thing was pure luck, really. Or bad luck, depending on how you wanna look at it."

He returns to the island, pulling out a fork to steal a bite from my plate. I glare, taking another one myself. "Did he turn them in on purpose?"

Heron shrugs. "I dunno. He never told me."

"What do you think?"

Heron meets my gaze for a second, then lets it fall away. He steals another bite. "I think it was an accident."

I stare at my plate.

"Either way, it earned him a promotion. Officer to Second-Rank Agent is quite the leap, but he adapted. He's good at that, you know. Doing what needs to be done. Now he's Third."

I don't say anything.

Heron clears his throat, walking back to the coffee pot, which is now filled to the brim with a fresh brew. He pulls two mugs from the cabinet and pours the steaming liquid inside, handing one to me. "Drink up."

I slide the mug back in his direction.

He swallows a generous gulp of his own serving before frowning at me. "Oh, come on. Don't tell me you don't do coffee either."

I shake my head.

"Blasphemous." He slides it back toward me.

"I don't—"

"Ren." Heron looks me dead in the eye. "In this line of work, you'll need it."

I peer inside the mug and stare at my reflection. I've never had coffee before. Once Aaron's father figured out what was going on with Margot and suggested her strict diet to my dad, I committed to it right by her side. I cut out processed sugar, meat, dairy, gluten, corn, and coffee—all because I didn't want her to feel alone.

Now, I'm the one left in solitude.

I glance up at Heron, who waits in silence. There is a somberness to his expression that I can't ignore. I study him closer, noticing the bags that shadow his eyes, the tensity of his shoulders. I stare at the coffee again.

If the hearing is today, there's no guarantee I'll live long enough for the effects of this coffee to matter. This could be my last opportunity to drink anything at all. I stare at the plate of scrambled eggs Heron whipped up in minutes and wonder if this will be my last meal.

I stand without a word and walk to the fridge. I retrieve the bag of shredded cheese, sprinkling a handful on top of the eggs in my bowl. Heron watches me eat. I savor every crumb.

I take the mug in my hands and blow away some of the steam, watching my reflection distort. I take a small sip, and pause.

I down the entire mug in seconds.

Heron chuckles before chugging his own coffee. He sets the empty mug down with a grin. "Now there's a suit hanging in your closet—and I think it'll fit you perfectly."

The Seattle Agency Headquarters looks exactly like the training center.

Nestled between a tightly woven sea of pines is a sleek white building shaped like a cube, with tinted windows so pristine they glisten, even beneath the clouds. Sprinkles of rain freckle my face as I study it like a mirage, or maybe a ghost. Like it'll dissipate into the mist if I reach out to touch it.

This building is much larger than the one I attended last summer; there must be at least two dozen stories. Its parking lot is crowded with white, black, and gray sedans.

Heron climbs out of the driver's seat, slams the door shut, and locks his car. He stands by my side, watching me gape at the building with trembling hands. We remain like that for a moment until he reaches up to ruffle my hair.

"The hell?" I swat his hand away, trying to smooth it back down.

Before he left me alone at the safe house, Ian had insisted that I comb my hair carefully in preparation for the hearing. *"You need to look the part,"* he said. *"Make them believe you're already playing the role, and they might just cast you for it."*

Heron shrugs, taking a sip from the to-go cup he holds in one hand, the other shoved in the pocket of his wrinkled trousers. "You looked a bit uptight."

"Yeah, I'm supposed to look like one of *you*, aren't I?"

He ignores my jab and stares at the building. "Don't let them think you're trying too hard."

"Why not?"

He takes another sip, then adjusts my tie so it's slightly crooked. "There is no better safety net than underestimation."

"How wise." I slap his hand away again, trying my best to correct the tie without a mirror.

"Exactly." He winks and puts on his shades.

When we step inside, I pause in the doorway with my next breath jammed in my throat. Seamless white floors and walls. Round sensors guarding the lobby. Elevators carved into the back wall. All I can do is stand there, blinking, digging my own fingernails into my skin to make sure I'm not dreaming. Even the smell is the same—the harsh stench of chemical cleaners and plastic. It gives me a headache.

"There is no real leaving, Ren McLellan."

Heron glances over his shoulder. "You coming?"

I nod and follow close behind.

He passes right through the sensor in front of him without a second thought. I realize he's still holding his coffee and think back to the kid at training whose phone was destroyed, but the sensor doesn't seem to care about the drink. *Agent privilege?* A green light flashes to indicate his clearance, and he doesn't wait for me.

I take a deep breath and step through.

There is a buzz in my left eye, followed by a flashing green light. I swallow the lump in my throat and try to blink away the sensation. *You are here, not there*, I tell myself.

You are not there.

I jog to catch up to Heron, who's already waiting for me in an open elevator. The doors close behind me after I step inside, and when he touches something on the side of his sunglasses, the elevator shoots up.

"Eyes all around," he whispers. My brows knit together, but before I can question it, he places a single finger on his lips, then points to his ears and eyes.

I nod. *Mics.*

Ian's safe house is free of them, too off the grid to be under the Presidency's audible radar. Even if it weren't, privacy is a privilege that comes with Chasing. Household mics are shut down for active members of the Corps. I've spent so much time away from them that I'll need to get used to watching what I say again.

When the elevator doors open, I expect to step into a corridor, or maybe a lobby of sorts. Instead, we are spat out directly into a room so bright I shield my eyes. I blink, letting my eyes adjust, then drop my hand.

Like the first floor, this room is blindingly white. Every surface is covered in seamless tile that reflects the light glaring down from long LED strips embedded in the ceiling. A long conference table stretches from both ends of the room, with one chair at the front end and two on the sides. I notice Ian occupying one of them, but he keeps his shaded stare fixed straight ahead, pretending not to notice us. Three Officers guard both side walls, Nightjade guns at the ready.

The back wall appears to be a screen displaying the Corps' logo—a black poker chip spinning in circles against a dark blue background. In front of the screen is a raised platform, where an Agent with a black tie sits behind a blocky desk, staring at us through a pair of shades. He's a broad-built man with a closely shaven head and pudgy fingers that knit themselves together in patient, predatory waiting.

"Have a seat." The man's voice echoes throughout the room, bouncing off the walls in a way that makes it seem much louder than it really is.

Heron walks toward the chair on the left side of the table across from

Ian, leaving me with only one option. I take a seat at the end of the table, directly facing the man on the platform.

The elevator dings, and I turn to see a young woman walk in, wearing a suit and shades to match the other Agents in the room. She's tall, with warm olive skin and a curtain of black hair that flows behind her as she quickly makes her way up to the platform. Half of it is pinned back in a blue velvet ribbon. She can't be much older than Heron.

The new Agent takes a seat next to the man in the center, pulling out a tablet before folding her hands as he does.

"You're late, Agent Sparrow," he mutters to her through gritted teeth, keeping his stare fixed straight ahead.

"My apologies." Her face is expressionless.

"I would like to inform all participants that this meeting is being recorded and will be archived in the Chaser Corps database. Anything you do or say will be seen, heard, and remembered by the Chaser Corps," the man announces. "Speaking is Agent O. Canary, Fifth Rank, Head of House. I will be presiding over this hearing on the date of Friday, February 2nd, along with advisory Agent J. Sparrow, Third Rank. Presenting his case is defendant Officer Ren McLellan, supported by Agent I. Kingfisher, Third Rank, and Agent M. Heron, Second Rank. Will the presenting individuals announce themselves as present?"

"Agent I. Kingfisher," Ian says.

Heron takes a sip from his drink, crossing one leg over the other. "Agent M. Heron."

Sparrow's nose twitches.

Although I can't see a single gaze behind the Agents' shades, I can feel all eyes boring into me. I clear my throat. "Officer Ren Calder McLellan."

Canary nods, and Sparrow scribbles something onto the tablet with a white stylus.

"Our current record charges Officer McLellan with the following felonies: conspiracy and association with traitors; the murder of Officer Duke Orion Carmody, the previous Second Officer in a partnership to Officer McLellan; and the willing preservation of his assignment, civilian Lavender Adele Voclain, LAV-J-J, Runner status.

"The purpose of today's hearing is to evaluate the request of Agent Kingfisher to reinstate Officer McLellan as an active Chaser, upon the removal of the felonies previously reported by Agent Kingfisher, who wishes to revise his statement regarding the case of his deceased brother, Officer Carmody. Will the Agent bearing the request confirm this purpose?"

"Confirmed," Ian says. Sparrow takes note.

"As Head of House, it is my duty to judge this hearing to the standards of my rank and professional ability. It is also my responsibility to clarify the two potential outcomes of this hearing.

"If there is truth to what is being presented, Outcome A will entail the approval of Agent Kingfisher's request, as well as additional adjustments to database records and status as needed.

"If there is as much as a single falsity present, Outcome B will preserve the defendant's status as a traitor, and I will have no choice but to approve his Extraction and extermination, as well as a one-rank demotion of both Agents Kingfisher and Heron for negligence. Will the defendant and his supporters confirm their understanding of these outcomes?"

"Understanding confirmed," Ian says, his voice monotone.

Heron takes another sip. "Confirmed."

All eyes carve into me again, and I take a deep breath. "Confirmed."

"We will begin by going over the context Agent Kingfisher has provided prior to this meeting, from his revised perspective," Canary says, bringing a finger to the side of his shades.

"Officers McLellan and Carmody were assigned to exterminate Voclain to comply with the regulations established by the Nightjade Order, which requires the extermination of Picked individuals, as well as their immediate family in the event of attempted evasion. As honorable and law-abiding citizens, Voclain's family tried to detain her, and she retaliated violently to preserve her own life, resulting in the death of her father, mother, and younger brother, as well as the two Officers assigned to her extermination."

I clench my hands into fists, trying to maintain a calm composure.

"Voclain evaded extermination and fled, earning her the status of Runner. Her case was then transferred to Officers McLellan and Carmody. As a system that runs on the fairness of chance, the odds created this circumstance, despite the fact that Officer McLellan had been romantically involved with Voclain prior to his assignment."

The lie makes my leg shake. *Trust in Ian's story,* I remind myself. *This is your only chance to make it out of here alive.*

"Officer McLellan had extinguished this romantic involvement when he realized Voclain had treacherous ideals, although he did not have enough evidence at the time to properly report her for Slander. Upon receiving the assignment, Officer McLellan had no emotional ties to Voclain and was willing to follow through with the extermination in order to abide by the laws of the Nightjade Order, and bring justice for her fallen family."

I stare at my reflection in the surface of the table, trying to convince myself that I am here, and not there again, staring into the white boots I once wore. Or a lake of blood.

"Officers McLellan and Carmody were able to successfully track down Voclain. However, as a routinely combative individual, she murdered Officer Carmody with a stolen Yesterday gun, which she obtained as a member of the Underground, a name the public likes to assign to organized groups of traitors, often including Runners like Voclain."

Ian doesn't flinch. Heron sips his coffee.

"Voclain, still maintaining her romantic feelings for Officer McLellan, decided to spare his life and forcefully attempt to convert him to her treacherous ways by removing his tracker and holding him captive at the Underground base she'd been seeking refuge within. At this base, Officer McLellan was a hostage to the traitors, who wanted to use him to gather vital information about the Corps, which he refused to give.

"The Undergrounders had a plan to break into their nearest Broadcasting Center to spread false information about the Presidency and the Chaser Corps in an attempt to increase their ranks by converting civilians to their cult-like beliefs. Voclain and her associates took Officer McLellan with them in hopes that having an Officer as hostage would give them an advantage in the event of potential conflict with the authorities. However, at this Broadcasting Center, McLellan was able to borrow a phone and request backup. Agent Kingfisher and his previous partner, Agent B. Peregrine, were dispatched to the scene.

"The traitors fought back, killing Agent Peregrine. In order to neutralize the situation as quickly as possible, Agent Kingfisher shot Officer McLellan with a Nightjade gun, since his identity hadn't yet been confirmed. Upon realizing who he had shot, Agent Kingfisher managed to evacuate to safety with Officer McLellan.

"Once he arrived with McLellan to Headquarters, Agent Kingfisher, being the only surviving Agent left on the case, made the split-second decision to create a carefully crafted broadcast in response to the stunt Voclain and her associates pulled. A Corps healer was able to effectively revive Officer McLellan from the events staged during this response, as well as replace the tracker he'd lost, and heal his eye from the forceful surgery he faced as a hostage. Agent Kingfisher volunteered to mandate his Extraction.

"Now, after an initial interrogation, Agent Kingfisher understands that Officer McLellan is not the traitor the Corps believes him to be, and requests his reinstatement, and that all charges be dropped. Agent Heron, who was assigned as Kingfisher's partner after the death of Agent Peregrine, vouches for the provided context."

Everything goes quiet. No one moves to do so much as glance around the room, not even Heron, who holds his coffee cup like it's still full. But something tells me Canary's stare is glued to me. The others can't bring themselves to look. Like closing your eyes when you see the shark begin to circle its prey, because you know exactly what's going to happen next.

Canary reaches up to touch his shades again. He then folds his hands neatly, resting them upon the desk like this is a casual dinner with business associates, not the evaluation of my right to live.

"Ren Calder McLellan," Canary says, breaking the silence. "Born to an unknown mother on December 31st, eighteen years ago. Black hair. Brown eyes. 5'11. 181 pounds. Raised by Asa McLellan, twin to Margot McLellan —who both tragically ended their lives on the night of the Pick. A devastating but not uncommon occurrence."

My throat tightens, and I keep staring at my reflection, holding onto the few recognizable pieces of it.

"I know everything about who you are, Ren... except for one thing."

I can't see Canary's eyes, but I can see his expression. He looks at me like he knows there's more to the story, but he decides to move past it, carving into me. Like if he stares at me for long enough I'll be cut open and all my secrets will spill right out.

"Why should I believe this story?"

My face pales. It feels like my lungs are melting into my stomach. *Why should he?*

I blink rapidly to keep the room from spinning, clearing my throat. "Agent Kingfisher is an honorable man, sir. I would trust his word if my life depended on it."

"Are you?"

"Am I what, sir?"

"An honorable man?"

I pause. "I try to lead an honorable life."

"But are *you* honorable?"

He stares at me like he already knows the answer.

I lock my gaze to his. "Yes."

He nods in a way that makes me wonder if he really does know the truth behind that question after all.

Sparrow takes a note.

"You've told me why I should trust Agent Kingfisher's word, but you still have yet to explain why I should trust yours," Canary says. "This is your story, after all. He may be the one telling it, but it is your truth. Is it not?"

"It is my truth, sir."

"The evidence we have gathered for your case speaks volumes. While this story of yours provides context, it would be much easier to believe the theory that you are, in fact, a traitor. So tell me..." Canary leans forward in his seat. "Why are you worth the investment?"

"The... investment?"

"I think you know what I mean, Ren."

My eyes widen.

He's asking why I deserve to live.

I swallow dryly, remembering everything Heron and Ian said about bearing gifts. "My time as an Underground hostage has given me valuable insight. I believe I can use my experience to support the efforts of the Corps."

"And that is where your loyalty lies, correct?" Canary asks.

"I was kidnapped by the Undergrounders," I explain, keeping my voice calm and emotionless as I stare at the table. "They mutilated my eye. Forced me to watch as they killed my partner—my close companion."

Ian's hands twitch.

I squeeze my hands into fists. "Why would my loyalty ever belong to them?"

"You still haven't answered my question." Canary's voice is smooth, and I can't read it. "Where is it that you belong, Ren?"

Slowly, I lift my gaze away from my reflection. From my distance, I meet Canary's shaded stare, holding it as firmly as I can. "There is nowhere else for me but here."

There is a thick, cruel silence lingering in the air. I hold my breath, waiting for something to happen. Heron's legs shake. Ian is so still that I can't tell if he's really breathing at all.

A grin spreads across Canary's face. "How right you are."

I feel sick.

"There is one thing I must draw attention to, however." The grin falls away. "Anyone with the ability to speak has the ability to lie. Without value, words are only words." He leans back. "So tell me, Ren. What value do your words provide? Or are they truly hollow after all?"

My knees tremble beneath the table, Heron's warning ringing loudly in my mind. *Be careful with what you say around him.* "I'm not sure I understand the question, sir."

"Agent Kingfisher briefed me on a bit of this... insight you speak of." My stomach churns when his grin returns. "You, Ren McLellan, are the only person in this entire building who knows the exact location of what may be the largest encampment of traitors this region has ever seen."

In a moment, I'm no longer strong enough to keep the room from spinning or my head from pounding or my pulse from slamming against my chest. Every part of me trembles, but I know I can't show weakness.

Any sign of hesitation will get me killed, or worse. I force myself to remain still, swallowing the growing lump in my throat.

"I do."

Canary grins so widely I can see his blinding white teeth. "Now that is a value the Corps is willing to invest in."

I stare at my reflection in the table again, and it takes every ounce of strength within me to keep my eyes fixed there. It feels like my skin is on fire. All I can think about is Ian—and how there is nothing I want more than to hit him in the face.

You said I would only have to give up something small, I want to scream. But this? This is the opposite of small. This would be a blow to the Unseen that I'm not sure I have the power to repair.

If I tell Canary what he wants to hear, the Corps won't hesitate to act with violence.

I could lie and give them the wrong coordinates, but that's as good as signing my own extermination order—and they'll surely put me through Extraction before I get the injection.

When I first arrived at the Cut, my mother told me everything. And if Extraction really is as unbearable as Ian and Heron claim it to be, there's no telling how much information I'll give up. What they harvest from me during an interrogation like that could be far worse than what Canary is asking for. Maybe I can't recall the exact locations of her allies off the top of my head, but Extraction will pull them out of me. *You know more than you think you do.*

If I tell Canary now, there will be time to warn them, and I will be alive to do it.

This is my only option.

"So, Ren." Canary's shark smile falls away. "Tell me about this base."

I abandon my reflection, lifting my eyes to stare into his soulless gaze of tinted glass. "They call it the Cut."

EDDIE

Monday, April 15
78 Beds Made

"You need to eat something."

Lori sits in a chair at the side of my bed, placing a gentle hand on my shoulder as I stare into a bowl of soup. It mirrors my face, though my reflection is distorted by carrots, potatoes, and herbs so aromatic my mouth waters. But every time I lift a spoonful up to my lips, I can't bring myself to open them.

"I'm not hungry."

As if on cue, my stomach growls.

Lori sighs, pulling her hand away. "He'll be fine, Ed. But *you* won't be if you refuse to eat."

I stare at the wall that divides my hospital room from Aaron's, trying to imagine what Simon could be doing. *Checking his vitals, probably*, I think to myself. *Cleaning his wound. Cutting his stitches. Dressing it with proper ointment and bandages.*

Fixing everything I did and couldn't do.

I stare out the window to my left. From the second story of End Harbor's old hospital, I can see the docks, and all the old abandoned houseboats that rock slowly back and forth each time the tide breathes. Everything is drenched in cold gray afternoon light. No rain. *No smoke.*

The hospital room is small, with white floors and powder blue walls. An old TV from the Yesterdays sits on a cart by the wall across from my bed, playing an old cartoon about a woodpecker. After spending so much time in that cave, the lights in here hurt my eyes, so we've been keeping them off. The window is our only source of brightness. Everything feels like it's covered in a shadow. Like I'm still walking through smoke.

"Eddie." Lori's voice pulls my attention back. She folds her arms. "I'll feed you if I have to."

I sigh, pursing my lips as I stare into my reflection in the bowl again. I stir it with my spoon, watching my features shift even more. I scoop up a potato defeatedly, but the doors open before I can take my bite.

Mayor Wagner storms into the room, followed by Cecil, Noriko, and a frustrated Alice, who mouths *sorry* in our direction, hugging her abdomen.

"Come on, Wagner. Let's be reasonable here," Cecil says. "She needs rest."

Wagner stops in front of the TV with his arms crossed. He picks up the remote and changes the channel to the news.

A woman with a microphone stands in front of a screen showing drone footage of what looks like a wildfire. Deep amber flames crawl through an endless sea of evergreen, fanned by heavy winds. The sky is filled with embers and ash.

"Some call them Undergrounders, some call them Opticultists. No matter what name they go by, we know one thing about traitors: if left unchecked, they will become a danger to everything we hold dear.

"This was proved true last Saturday when a small group of traitors initiated a violent attack against an important base belonging to the Chaser Corps, ruthlessly slaughtering almost two-dozen Officers."

The footage switches to what appears to be a bonfire. When I squint to get a closer look, my blood runs cold. I've seen it before.

There are human bones within those flames.

Noriko clings to Cecil with one arm, and his shoulders grow rigid. Lori brings a hand to her mouth, eyes watering as Alice rubs her back in slow, comforting circles. I hold my spoon so tightly I can feel its edge cutting into my palm.

Wagner changes the channel, landing on another news station featuring the same drone footage.

"After decades of hiding as nothing more than an urban legend, the Undergrounders have finally emerged from the shadows to act upon their radical beliefs—starting by burning down a Corps research base."

Wagner switches the channel again. This time, the drone footage shows an entire neighborhood engulfed in flames.

"What officials are calling the Traitor's Fire has been spreading through-out the Olympic all week, climbing up the peninsula and into—"

Another switch. My face pales when I realize what the video is showing.

Through pixelated security camera footage, I see myself in front of that gas station, hauling Aaron into the car I stole before driving away. The video transitions back to the drone view of the wildfire, and an overlay of my senior school photo appears on the screen like a mug shot, with my name in bold white letters below it.

"Witnesses claim that Lavender Voclain—the young woman behind the malicious broadcast incident—was among the traitors who attacked the base. Reports say she stole a car to flee the scene, and authorities encourage the public to be on the lookout for Voclain, as well as this young man."

A screenshot of Aaron from the gas station security footage appears on the screen, and then transitions to another security camera screenshot of a figure that looks a lot like him, wearing shades and breaking into a building. Two more images of similar situations from his previous smuggling trips pop up on the screen.

"His identity remains unknown, but multiple witness accounts across the state lead authorities to believe he is in fact an Undergrounder, likely an associate of Voclain. Reports claim he has a scar running through his left eye."

My heart plummets. Now my mistakes are putting him in danger too.

"We also have evidence that Voclain attacked the two Chasers who were assigned to track her down for her theft."

A video appears, showing the male Officer I escaped from with a bandage over his eye and ear.

"She's ruthless," he says, pointing to his covered eye. "These Opticultists will stop at nothing to get what they want."

"And what is that?" a reporter asks, holding out a microphone.

The Chaser looks into the camera. "Our downfall."

The camera then focuses on the other Chaser from the scene, who averts her gaze, even when the reporter holds out a camera. "Do you have anything to say regarding Voclain's most recent crime?"

The Chaser shakes her head, and Wagner changes the channel once again.

"As a result of her involvement in the Traitor's Fire and the events that followed, the Chaser Corps would like to announce that the bounty has been increased to twenty lifetimes of Immunity. I repeat, twenty lifetimes of Immunity for you and your loved ones."

Another switch.

"With strong winds between forty to sixty miles per hour in certain areas, this is the first firestorm our region has seen in decades. Was it planned, or just plain bad luck?"

"Okay, that's enough." Cecil snatches the remote from Wagner, turning down the volume before tossing it back onto the cart.

"You're most certainly correct, Mr. Logan." Wagner purses his lips. "Enough is enough. We've quite literally opened the door for all of you— *even* miss Voclain here—and this is how you repay us? You may as well have taken red paint and drawn a target around all of End Harbor."

"I assure you, this was not intentional," Cecil says. "Accidents happen, alright? We're just having a run of bad luck."

"*Arson* is not an accident. *Motor vehicle theft* is not an accident. *Attacking two Chasers* in broad daylight is not an accident."

Cecil scoffs. "You think she set the fire on purpose?"

"That's what the authorities seem to think."

"If anything, this is my fault," Cecil says. "The smoke grenades were my idea. They catch fire easily. The kid saved Viv and Hugo's life by lighting up that church. And mine by creating that diversion in the greenhouse."

Noriko nods in my direction, offering me a sad smile. Like she knows the guilt I'm bearing.

"Accident or not, Voclain has proven herself to be just as reckless as I expected. She doesn't know how to think through the consequences of her actions or remain unobserved." Wagner glares in my direction. "She doesn't know how to be Unseen."

I don't even have it in me to disagree.

"That was unnecessary." Noriko's tone is somber.

"It is correct," Wagner argues. "She isn't meant for a quiet life like the one we choose to live in End Harbor."

"She's meant for whatever life she chooses," Cecil snaps.

"It wasn't an accident."

I don't realize I've spoken until everyone turns to look at me. I clear my throat, staring at my spoon.

"Aaron was in trouble. He needed a diversion to escape and I was out of smoke grenades." I meet Cecil's eye. "I set the portables on fire."

"How many?" Noriko asks, voice quiet.

I stare at my hands. "Half the Block."

She nods.

"First her carelessness with the broadcast, and now *this*?" Wagner gestures in my direction. He opens his mouth to continue, but he doesn't get the chance.

"Why aren't we seeing this as a good thing?" Alice asks, drawing the room's attention. "We've just dealt a serious blow to the Corps. They can't control that fire, even if they claim they can. We've shown that we bite back." She glances at me, then at her father. "Isn't that a good thing?"

Wagner shakes his head. "The Corps will not separate her youthful irrationality from the intentions of the Unseen. They will see this as an attack against the system, and they will retaliate."

No one says a word.

"After so many years of hiding, Voclain is the first and only face the public can attach to the Unseen. Every Chip across the nation wants that bounty. Now that she has everyone's attention, I firmly believe the Corps will use that to their advantage. Her mistakes taken out of context can easily stir a substantial amount of rage. They already have." Wagner snatches the remote again, flipping through the channels until he finds another one of interest. He turns up the volume.

This station shows footage of a group of people crowding the parking lot of a white building. It startles me at first, so closely resembling the training center Ren attended. But when I look closely, I realize this building is much larger.

There must be at least fifty people holding signs made of cardboard, painted with blocky letters. I squint to read some of the messages.

BURN THE UNDERGROUND
PROTECT US
EXTERMINATE LAVENDER VOCLAIN
NO MORE TRAITORS, NO MORE SNAKES

Four Agents stand in front of the entrance, flanked by about half a dozen Officers with their Nightjade guns at the ready. A female Agent with long brown hair shouts over the noise, trying to reason with the protestors, though it's hard to see much of her face with so many signs and people in the way.

A reporter speaks over the footage. "For the first time since the Nightjade Era began, protests are spreading through major cities like wildfire, demanding protection from the rebels during this new season of uncertainty."

The voiceover pauses, making room for the female Agent's shouts to carry through. "We are doing everything in our power to put out the fire and track down the individuals who started it before they can strike again. The Agency assures you that everything is under our complete control."

Her reasoning only seems to make the crowd angrier. They retaliate with shouts.

"You aren't doing shit!"

"The fire's only spreading, no one's putting it out!"

"Liars!"

This time, a male Agent with neatly gelled hair shouts to the protestors, gesturing with his hands. "Your safety is our top priority. Their numbers are small. The traitors are nothing to worry about."

More shouts ensue, and this time, someone throws a rock.

It hits an Agent with light brown hair in the face, knocking his shades off. Even through the noise, I can hear him swearing as he bends over, hands covering the place he was struck. A tall Agent with black hair steps in front of him, observing the damage with his back to the camera, shielding his colleague's identity.

Wagner switches the channel.

This news station is national, showing a similar group of protestors in a downtown setting.

NO MORE TRAITORS, NO MORE SNAKES
NO MORE LAVENDER VOCLAIN

This time, a wall of Chasers are corralling them, Nightjade guns in hand.

"A handful of protests from the recent spike in rallies against the Underground have turned violent, resulting in the extermination of thirty—"

Wagner changes the channel, landing back on the woodpecker cartoon. He turns down the volume and stares at Cecil.

But my eyes are still glued to the screen. My chest tightens, my lungs on pause. *This is all my fault.*

The bowl of soup falls out of my hands, rolling onto the floor with a loud clatter. Lori rushes to clean it.

"Her name is now synonymous with acts of violence against the Corps," Wagner says. "They are already using her as a scapegoat and they will continue to do so to control the public and remove blame from their own shoulders."

"That's not *her* fault, Earnest," Cecil says. "It's just—"

"It's just what? Chance?" Wagner chuckles bitterly. "Bad luck?"

The scars on my arm itch. Cecil doesn't say a word.

"Now that is something Lavender Voclain seems to carry a lot of, don't you think?" Wagner says. He glances at me in disgust before turning back to Cecil and Noriko. "She does more harm than good. As long as she is here, we are the target of not just the Corps, but chipped civilians as well.

If the public believes the Corps is doing nothing to solve the rebel problem, they will not hesitate to take matters into their own hands.

"And do you really think the other half of the Unseen will be happy with this new bout of attention and public anger? If we upset them, that is a conflict we can't afford."

"You're worried about the Gamblers?" Cecil lets out a laugh, but it fades quickly. "Now that's ridiculous."

"And what about the Syndicate?" Wagner says. "Neither the Cut nor End Harbor has solidified a true alliance with them. Just because we aren't on their bad side at the moment doesn't mean we couldn't get there quickly."

Cecil scoffs. "The Syndicate is too self-centered to give a damn about what we do out here."

What are they talking about?

"You saw the protests," Wagner says. "If Voclain's actions are causing unrest, the Corps will tighten their reins. Civilians will be watched closely. If her actions disrupt the Syndicate's operations in any way, they will be displeased, and you know it."

Cecil doesn't say anything to that.

"What is your point, Earnest?" Noriko asks, arms crossed.

"My point?" Wagner chuckles. "I will not let your little bad luck charm compromise everything I've built here."

"What are you saying?"

"We aren't opening our Gate for her again, unless we're opening them for the last time. She's proven that she can't handle being out in the real world without putting the Unseen in danger. If she leaves again, she will not be allowed back. She can choose to stay here and live under the radar with us..." He looks at me again, his gaze cold and empty. "Or burn out there with them."

My eyes widen.

"She's only nineteen, Earnest," Cecil says, voice grim. "Cut her some slack."

"Then she is old enough to think for herself."

Cecil's jaw twitches. "She's a kid."

"She's a *wanted criminal*."

"We all are."

"And she's the only one with a bounty on her head."

"What if your daughter were in this position?" Cecil gestures toward Alice. "They're the same exact age."

Alice waves.

"My daughter?" Wagner scoffs. "Alice would never be in this position, because I have raised her with discipline. Because I know how to keep her under control."

Her shoulders stiffen. I fidget with the bracelet on my wrist.

"I thought nineteen was old enough to think for yourself," Lori says, tilting her head in faux confusion.

I stare at the hospital blanket that covers me, unable to keep myself from suppressing a smirk.

"She's right, you know," Noriko says, glancing at Alice with a grin before turning back to Wagner. "This could be a good thing."

"It is a good thing," Cecil argues. "We do know how to bite back."

"For years, we've been doing *nothing* to help the Unseen. If we don't support our allies, how can we even call ourselves one?" Alice says. "And maybe it's time to make noise. Maybe we really do need to be seen, after all."

Cecil nods slightly.

Wagner laughs. "If there is one thing the Unseen will never be, that is united. There is no cause, no common goal. There is only survival. That has always been the sole purpose of our alliance with the Cut."

Alice scoffs. "You're pathetic."

"This fire will only burn for so long," Wagner says, ignoring Alice to glare at Cecil, Noriko, and finally, me. "The only change it will bring is destruction."

With that, he exits, slamming the door behind him. Alice follows, giving me one last apologetic look before she leaves. I can hear them arguing on their way down the corridor and out of the hospital.

"I'll try reasoning with him." Noriko leaves quickly, and Lori tags along.

Cecil stands in silence, arms folded as he pretends to watch the soundless cartoon. After a while he turns to face me, letting out a sigh. "I'm sorry, kid.

Earnest is—"

"It's alright," I say.

He forces a smile. "He's just scared."

"I know."

I stare out the window, watching the abandoned houseboats rock upon the water. Cecil takes a seat in the chair Lori was using, and we sit in silence for a long time as I soak in everything that was said. I have more questions than I know how to answer on my own, but all I can focus on is that fire.

I face Cecil, thinking back to the groups mentioned in his argument with Wagner. "There are other camps like us in the woods, right?"

"There are camps like us everywhere."

"But... are there a lot around here? In the Olympic?"

"There are all kinds of Unseen hideouts in our neck of the woods. We were the biggest, but there are others. Families in old Wandering cabins, encampments of a few dozen Runners. I'd say the largest actual base aside from End Harbor is Silver Fir—an abandoned ski resort from the Yester-days, about an hour's drive out of Seattle. But... we're not exactly on good terms with them."

I nod, staring out the window again.

"Hey." Cecil says. "They'll be okay."

I look at him, throat tight, trying my best to stay put together. "You don't know that."

"Wagner's a shithead, but he's right about one thing," Cecil says. "We Unseen know how to survive."

I force a smile, but it feels hollow.

"I mean, look at you." He gestures toward me. "You burned down an entire occupied camp of Chasers. That's pretty impressive."

I stare at my hands.

"Now we don't have to worry about the Corps extracting valuable in-formation from the Cut. Whatever evidence they gathered was likely still on site. And aside from that, you saved Aaron's life." His grin is small but genuine. "You do more than survive. You take care of others too. And that's what's important. That's why we're in this, right? To take care of people?"

I nod.

"I view what happened as a success," Cecil says. "And you're only one person, Ed. Just imagine what we can accomplish once we prove Wagner wrong about unity."

"Is that something we want?" I ask. "Unity?"

"Noriko and Simon and I built the Cut with the dream of bringing people together. The Blurt was our first attempt at making that a reality, but..." He clears his throat, unable to finish the sentence. "We'll try again someday."

"You mentioned something called the Syndicate," I say, changing the subject. "What is that?"

"Nothing you need to worry about."

"Wagner would argue otherwise."

Cecil sighs. "Crime isn't exclusive to being Unseen, you know. Even civilians have their own methods of smuggling goods and generating profit in... less-than-ethical ways. It's only illegal if you get caught, I suppose. And the Syndicate is pretty damn good at not getting caught."

I think back to what Milo told me in front of the church, the night the Cut arrived. *People will do anything for their vices.* "So they're like a crime ring or something?"

"I suppose you could call it that." He leans back in his chair. "They have roots in essentially every city across the nation. They've got different groups of course, just like we do. But Seattle's is one particular branch you should avoid crossing paths with. At all costs, if possible."

"And what about Silver Fir?" I ask. "Why aren't we on good terms with them?"

"Remember what Hugo said about one of the camps in California? About their... questionable philosophy?" I nod. "Silver Fir is part of an Unseen offshoot that likes to call themselves the Gamblers."

I furrow my brows. "The Gamblers?"

"It's stupid, I know. But their whole thing is... well, let's just say they're not exactly as quiet as End Harbor has been. Even *we* are flies on the wall compared to the Gamblers. They're a weird lot too. Real strange folk, fond of odd masks and flashy stunts. It's almost like they get a thrill from doing what they do. Like they *want* to be seen."

"What do they do?"

"They prefer more... violent ways of bringing change." He sighs. "A lot of them are mostly Runners and young Chip strays. Lots of kids and fresh adults—and anyone else who doesn't have much to lose. It makes them impulsive. They haven't made any significant strikes yet, but they've been stirring the pot quite a bit, and they have plans to keep cooking."

"Plans?"

"Forced Debugs. Targeting big Corps pain points like NOT research centers and Sitter offices, even if others get caught in the crossfire. Assassinating Officers and Agents. There's even talk that a few of them were responsible for a revolt that took place at a Tombs facility a couple years back."

"A revolt at the Tombs?" My lips part. "I didn't even know that was possible."

Cecil nods.

"Why don't they talk about this on the news? Wouldn't they want to highlight Agent assassinations? Paint us in a bad light?"

"The Corps is strategic with what they present to the public. They only show what they have under control—never anything they're actually worried about."

"So they're worried about the Gamblers, then?"

"Oh yeah." Cecil nods. "They may not have the numbers or the means to make highly organized strikes like what we pulled with the Blurt, but the Corps is definitely afraid of them. As far as we know, they still assume all Unseen are the same, which is probably why they've been so afraid of you lately too."

"They've really assassinated Agents?"

Cecil nods. "That I know for certain."

He looks at the wall as though he's somehow looking through it, when he gestures toward it with his chin, I know he's talking about Aaron. "Did he ever tell you how he got that scar on his arm?"

I shake my head, thinking back to the jagged line of flesh that I've only seen in the daylight a couple of times. The one he keeps hidden. "No."

Cecil hesitates. "You met Henry and Abigail, right?"

I nod.

"Abigail's father used to be one of our own." He lets out an exhausted sigh, staring out the window at the boats. "Greer would go on smuggling trips with Aaron every now and then, but mostly alone.

"Aaron had his suspicions about where Greer was really going on those trips and decided to spy on him. He learned that Greer had started out hunting Chasers, then eventually worked his way up to Agents. Managed to make quite the name for himself in the Agency. They called him the Suit Killer. Had a pretty recognizable signature."

"What do you mean?"

"He'd skin the Cards right off his victim's bodies. A souvenir of sorts."

Chills run down my spine.

"He'd been keeping it a secret from the rest of us because he knew we wouldn't approve of his methods. When Aaron confronted him about it, Greer offered to let him in on his little operation."

"Why?"

"The kid's... more knowledgeable about that sort of thing than most. Skilled, as you know. He's highly educated on Corps matters, and he does what he's told, as long as it's for the benefit of the Unseen. Greer thought Aaron would be interested in helping him out."

"How did Aaron react?"

"He dug a little deeper and found that Greer was actually working with a contact in the Agency to get leads. If this contact wanted to make a particular power play—take out competition to rise up in the ranks, that sort of thing—he'd contact Abigail's father. And no one would be able to suspect this contact if they think the Suit Killer's motivation is to take out key players in the Corps. Understandably, Aaron found this disloyal to the Unseen and threatened to let me and Noriko know what was really going on, unless he agreed to stop."

I nod.

"The man snapped. Started getting real defensive, accusing Aaron of all kinds of incompetence. And we all know how he gets. It turned physical real quick." He nods at the wall, where Aaron would be. "But Greer was the one who pulled out a knife."

My eyes widen. "On a kid?"

"Oh yeah. He was convinced Aaron would ruin his operation or somehow out him to the Corps for a reward. There was a bounty on the Suit Killer, you know. Much less spoken of than yours. But... no one beats Aaron in a knife fight."

I nod, staring at my blanket.

"He wasn't dead, but Aaron did leave him there. Regretted it like hell later." Cecil shakes his head. "The poor kid was only seventeen."

I stare at the wall again, knowing Aaron resides behind it. *That's why he feels so obligated to take care of Henry and Abigail.*

"Greer went missing after that. We thought he might have been dead for a while, but the Suit Killer was still making hits. We eventually found out that he'd sought refuge with the Gamblers at Silver Fir. But the Suit Killings have been dormant for a few months now. We're guessing he finally got caught."

"Is that why you don't associate yourselves with them?"

"We've all done bad things in the name of the Unseen." Cecil stares at the wall. "But a lot of what the Gamblers do is flat-out unnecessary. They take things to the extreme."

The door opens. Simon pops his head in, nodding toward Cecil. "Lori just radio'd me. You're wanted at the church. Wagner's throwing another tantrum."

Cecil gives me a small grin, saluting as he takes his exit. "Take care, kid."

I salute back.

"Hey." Simon gestures toward me with his hands. "Can you walk?"

"I think so."

He pauses. "Come here."

I climb out of the bed, holding onto the chair for support as the blood rushes to my head. Although I'm still sore, finally getting a good night's sleep has soothed some of the aching. I look down at my clothes. While I was out, Lori changed me into a black sweater and soft, flowy cotton pants. I turn my head and stare at the dresser where my old outfit sits, just to make sure Ren's green sweatshirt is still there, cleaned and neatly folded. When my head clears, I follow Simon into Aaron's room.

He rests in bed with his head lolled over to the side, sleeping soundly. Puffs of air flow from his nose, moving the hair that falls in front of his eyes. I reach over and place two fingers against his neck to feel his heartbeat. *It's stronger*, I note. *That's a good sign.*

I pull back and stand next to Simon, who studies his son with his hands in his pockets. We remain in silence for a long time, watching the rise and fall of Aaron's chest, as if it'll get easier to believe he's really breathing if we see it for long enough.

My stomach ties itself into knots. *This is all my fault.*

If I had been more skilled, more careful, maybe I could've prevented the infection.

If I had stayed behind when he asked me to, maybe he would've been more careful too. Maybe none of this would have happened. The Cut would still be there, and there would be no wildfire, no protests. Our faces wouldn't have been made public.

But he was so busy worrying about me—my safety, my comfort—that he forgot about watching his own back.

I turn to Simon. "I'm s—"

"You saved his life," he says at the same time. I blink for a moment, realizing what he said. He clears his throat. "So... thank you."

I shrug, eyes glued to the boy in the bed. "I did what I could."

"For being trapped in a cave in the middle of a storm—out in the woods with such limited resources—you did an excellent job. You stayed on top of cleaning his wounds. You made sure he was hydrated. You used the little antiseptic that you did have. Anything else I'm missing?"

"Thimbleberry," I say. "I made him tea."

Simon glances at me, his lips curling into a slight grin. "Resourceful."

He stares at Aaron again, swallowing. "I can confidently say that under anyone else's care, he would no longer be with us."

The silence returns, and I watch Simon study his son, brows curved downward in what I can only read as concern. "Does he..." He pauses, unsure of how to pose the question. "He knows, right?"

I take a moment to understand what he's saying, but when I do, I smile. "He loves you too."

Simon nods.

I walk to the nightstand next to Aaron's hospital bed, which his satchel and my bags sit on top of. I open the satchel and pull out the CD Aaron took. I take the book too, turning it over in my hands. Now that I'm in the light, I see that it's clearly one of his father's old encyclopedias. I hand the objects to Simon. "Out of everything at the Cut, this is what he kept."

Simon takes them, rolling his eyes at the CD. "This is Cecil's mix. Can't believe he didn't think to grab any of my jazz."

So that's who made it.

"This..." Simon smiles at the encyclopedia, leafing through the pages. "This was the first edition I made."

He hands them back to me, and I hold up the book. "Big fan, by the way." I return both items to Aaron's satchel. "Asa had tons of these. I ate them up as a kid."

"So you've been my apprentice this entire time, and neither of us had any idea?"

I hold back a grin, shrugging. "I guess so."

Simon chuckles, staring at Aaron, then the wall, then back at me. "I heard what happened in there."

I stare at my shoes.

"In case anyone hasn't told you yet... you've always got a place here, kid. You're Unseen, through and through."

I try to smile, but I don't think I manage.

"My son carries too much on his shoulders. I try to bear my own weight, but this job isn't easy. Especially with this." He points to his foot, and I remember what Aaron told me so long ago about his injury. "He has learned to love his art and will take on whatever burden he can in the name of someone else, but he can only do so much. Now with the bullet wound... it might take his leg a while to fully heal. He should be able to walk, but it will cause him discomfort."

I nod.

"We need another healer around here, and I think you've got it in you."

"Me?" I shake my head, staring at Aaron. "I don't think I'm skilled enough for that."

"You are more skilled than you think you are, Lavender. And should you choose to accept my offer, I could teach you a thing or two."

I suppress a grin. "That would be nice."

"So if you ever do decide to stay, remember what I said about your place. Places, I should say, because I'm sure we all have many." He offers a smile. "Wherever they are, you've got one here."

"Thank you."

"Look after him for me, will you?" He starts to walk out, then pauses, looking over his shoulder. "He could use someone like you to keep him grounded."

Simon leaves.

I pull a chair over to Aaron's bedside and take a seat. I watch him for a long time, so focused on every sign of subtle movement that I miss the sun setting beyond the window behind my back. Like maybe if I stare at him long enough, waiting for him to wake up, he really will.

A chirp rings through the room, and I jump to my feet. I glance at Aaron, making sure he's still asleep before fishing the device out of my backpack.

M. HERON

> nice going with the breadcrumbs. I had you covered.

> now everyone knows. and they're saying the fire's your fault.

I close my eyes, exhaling shakily before typing my response.

EDDIE

> what do you want

A few moments pass before the Agent responds.

M. HERON

> you've got friends in the woods, right?

My eyelids flatten. *Is this the real reason why he offered the deal?* It would be the perfect ruse—distracting me with one seemingly harmless task like investigating his dead brother's case while he works to gain my trust and gather other information from me instead. Information he could easily use against the Unseen.

EDDIE

> I'm not telling you that

M. HERON

> fine. let them burn.

My brows furrow. I slam the phone shut and shove it in the bag. *I can't deal with this right now.* I still haven't opened that file about his brother.

I return my focus to Aaron. He sleeps in a plain black t-shirt, the scar on his arm exposed. My gut churns when I think about Cecil's story. I stare at my backpack, knowing the phone hides inside of it.

Aaron hates Chasers—that much I know. I think back to his empty stares, the anger he's overcome with whenever the topic is mentioned. His carving.

If he knew I was in contact with an Agent—even if I have a good reason for it—would he react the same way? Would he see it as disloyalty?

But Ren is depending on me, and as of right now, M. Heron is the only solid clue I have. I'm not doing anything disloyal. *Am I?*

I go over my messages with Heron in my head, scanning over every response, checking for any sign of something he could use against me. So far, I haven't given him anything worth noting, although his question about the fire was suspicious. *But what did he mean about letting them burn?*

I think back to the news, and everything Cecil said. *They only show what they have under control—never anything they're actually worried about.*

I stand up so quickly the chair falls back, cracking against the floor.

Heron is warning me.

My face pales. It feels like every ounce of oxygen has been drained from the room, and I'm left with no way to breathe or keep my head from spinning as the realization hits.

The Corps is letting the fire burn. That is how they are in control. *They're smoking us out.*

R. STELLER

Saturday, April 6

I thought I was over hunting down Lavender Voclain.

Yet here I am again, holding a hand against my brow to shield my eyes from the rain as I scan my surroundings for any sign that she has passed through. Whatever trail she'd left behind her near the cabin is now gone, washed away from the rain. But before the grooves in the forest floor melted into mud and gooey piles of rotting foliage, her tracks led us far enough into the woods to get us lost.

Heron and Kingfisher fare surprisingly well in this weather, their faces shielded by their Eyes to utilize the infrared feature. Heron wears his now that he has to.

My suit is sopping wet and my dress shoes have no traction, but no matter how badly I shiver or how much mud I trudge through, all I can think about is Eddie. I still have no idea if she is really the one who took Aaron after all. Whether or not she is close, finding Aaron will lead me back to her, in one way or another.

I just need to make sure she's okay, I tell myself. *And I need to see that*

Aaron is alive too.

Ever since the cabin, my stomach has been doing cartwheels. With every step I reconfirm what happened in my head, the realization sinking deeper and deeper the farther I walk.

I shot Aaron.

I don't care much for the guy, but I don't hate him, and I certainly don't want him dead—for both his sake and Eddie's.

Even if he makes it out of this mess alive, if she finds out what I did, she won't forgive me.

I go over every detail in my mind, scraping each part of the memory for some sort of sign that Aaron recognized me. But it was too dark, and I am not supposed to be wearing the suit of an Agent. *I don't think he knows who hurt him.* For now, at least.

Heron slips on a pile of leaves for the second time this evening, but King catches his arm before he can fall. "Watch your step."

"*Aww*, my knight in shining armor."

King lets go and Heron slips, landing on his back.

"Just leave me here. This is disgusting. If I take another step, I'll implode."

I step over him.

Heron rises to his feet with a loud groan, covered from head to toe in filth. "Seriously, guys. Where the hell could they have gone?"

"They couldn't have gone very far," King says, shouting over the downpour. He is soaking and his shoes are coated in mud, but the rest of his suit still manages to avoid as much as a single crease. He carries a black backpack over one shoulder. "We'll catch up to them eventually."

"Unless they're hiding," I say.

King looks at me over his shoulder, then nods. "Smart thinking." He steps forward. "You really think Voclain is with our target?"

"I do," I say.

"What makes you say that?" Heron asks.

"They're close."

Heron raises a brow in my direction. "You know the guy?"

"Not very well."

"And you shot him?"

I nod. Heron gives me a puzzled look behind his shades, then shrugs.

"If he's here, then she is," I say. *If not with him at this very moment, then somewhere within the vicinity of the Cut, at least.*

"We don't really have a better lead, so I'm trusting your intuition on this one, Steller," King says as we walk. "You're the only one who's actually met her. What do you think she's doing? Leaving or hiding?"

Heron slips again, and this time I catch his arm out of instinct. He yanks free and averts my gaze.

I pause, thinking about King's question. Eddie is smart enough to know she can't get far in this weather—and if she felt like she had to, she's stubborn enough to try. From what I saw after first arriving at the Cut, I know that she values her friendship with Aaron. He's important to her, and if he's injured, his safety is going to be her priority.

"She'll likely try to get him somewhere safe to tend to his wound before moving on," I say. "Maybe try to wait out the rain too."

"Are there any other cabins out here?" King asks.

"Not that I know of."

"I'm not sure how much farther *we* can go in this weather," he says. "I think you're right, Steller. She couldn't have gone far. I think we should set up camp and regroup. Waiting out the rain sounds like a good idea. We'll find her in the morning once the storm clears a bit."

King removes a bundled-up square of black tarp from his backpack. Heron helps him spread it across the ground underneath a towering cedar tree. King then retrieves a black cube from his bag, resembling an Officer's uniform when compacted, only smaller. He sets it on a corner of the tarp, then takes out three more to do the same for the remaining corners.

He presses a button on the side of his Eyes, and immediately, the cubes open like a cardboard box, a folded tent pole sprouting from each one. Each pole rises and unfolds until all corners are connected with thin black metal bars. A sheet of waterproof fabric drapes from each bar to form walls, then a roof. Before I know it, I'm staring at a comfortably sized black tent.

This would have been useful as an Officer, I think to myself, though I'm not surprised that Agents have the privilege of better tech.

We set up camp inside the tent, removing our sopping wet suit jackets.

King places a lantern in the center and we sit around it, trying to ignore the dampness and the cold until we fall asleep.

When I close my eyes, all I can see is her face meeting mine, submerged together in the darkness of water, hair reaching above her like arms of kelp. She is still there when the rest of the world fades away.

Sunday, April 7

The rain persists.

I wake to the smell of fresh coffee. It cuts through the smell of noble fir and mud like a hot blade through butter. Droplets of water crackle against the tent's roof as I take in my surroundings. No one is here. Our jackets are gone.

I follow the smell outside, unzipping my way through a person-sized flap in the tent. I find Heron sitting on a log underneath the shelter of the cedar's canopy, poking at a campfire with a stick. An extra tarp has been spread over some of the branches to create a makeshift roof that protects the flames. Our suit jackets hang to dry.

"He's awake."

Heron takes a sip from a black metal mug. A pot of water boils over the fire. A second mug sits next to him on his log, steaming as he points the stick toward it.

"Made you a cup. Instant, but it's better than nothing."

I nod in thanks, grabbing the mug and taking a seat next to him. He pokes the stick around in the fire a bit more, then points it in my direction, the tip glowing red. "Don't let Fish see your hair. It's a mess."

"Would you cut that out? Once you put something in the fire you don't take it out." I swat the stick away. "Your parents never taught you basic fire safety?"

Heron laughs. "Fire *was* my babysitter." His smile fizzles out. "But it's cute of you to assume they were around to care."

I roll my eyes, and he continues to play with the stick, poking at the flames and using it to set damp pine needles ablaze before stomping them out.

I take a sip of my coffee, taking in its bitterness, feeling it scald my throat and stomach. A calming sensation spreads through me in an instant, embedding itself into my skin. But even the coffee and its warmth can't make me feel less than unsettled. *I wonder if she is warm.*

"Speaking of King, where is he?" I ask.

"Went off to get a head start on today's search," Heron says. "Left me here to spill the game plan to you once you woke up.

"Which is?"

"Split up. Search for an hour. Meet back here and regroup."

"Why split up?"

He pauses, then shrugs. "Efficiency."

I study our surroundings, observing the rippling mud and downpour beyond the protection of our fragile shelter. Whatever tracks Eddie and Aaron left behind last night will be completely washed away by now. Finding her will be a game of pure chance.

"I don't have Eyes yet," I point out. "How am I supposed to track my coordinates?"

"Instinct. Reasoning. All else fails and you get lost, we'll track you." He points the stick at my left eye, and I swat it away again.

"Do I really need to keep reminding you to be careful with that? You know how easy it is for fire to spread?"

Heron draws a crude smiley face in the dirt and takes a sip from his mug. "I'm always careful."

"And I'm ten feet tall." I down the rest of my coffee before setting the mug down and rising to my feet. "I'm getting a head start."

Heron reaches into King's backpack and throws a tightly bundled black windbreaker in my direction. "Bundle up, Sparks. It's chilly out there."

I'm too tired to say another word as I zip it on and start walking.

I step over rocks and part through clusters of vibrant green sword fern, weaving between trees, deep in thought. Guilt sours my stomach, and though the jacket I wear is light, it weighs down on me like it's made of gold.

While Eddie is out there going through God knows what, I will sleep comfortably in a tent tonight, filled with half-decent coffee and sheltered from the storm. Something about it feels sickeningly familiar.

I need to find her.

Although the guilt is corrosive, I can't say my pulse races without the smallest hint of anticipation. After everything, the thought of seeing her again is what grounds me, centering me in a world where there never seems to be enough balance to stand upright. I think of her eyes, her smile, her hair. And selfishly, her lips. The way her breath hitched when I met them with my own, the solidity of holding her and tasting her and—

"Steller?"

Focus.

I turn to my left to see King approaching me, lifting up his shades to make sure it's really me, then letting them fall back over his eyes with a frown. "Where's Heron?"

"He told me you wanted to split up the search."

"Yeah, in half. He's supposed to be watching you."

My brows furrow. "Watching me?"

"After that stunt you pulled running off like that yesterday? Yeah. You get stupid when your Runner's a part of the equation." He sighs. "It's mostly Heron I'm concerned about leaving alone anyway. *You* should be watching *him*. He just might be more irrational than you are on a Voclain high."

"Any leads?" I ask, ignoring the jabs.

"No." King eyes the tightly knit canopy above us. "I don't think this rain will let up any time soon."

"She has to be around here somewhere." I glance over my right shoulder. "Have you checked this way yet?"

"No." He steps forward. "Let's scope it out."

We spend about half an hour searching in aimless and uncomfortable silence. The rain does all the speaking for us, filling the air with a sound like crackling flames as we snap twigs and rustle through damp foliage. Everything is shadowed in a deep, all-encompassing kind of blue. Like we are navigating a world underwater, not above ground.

After a while, King pauses, letting out a sigh. "I don't think they're over here. We should get back before Heron does anything stupid."

"I'd like to keep looking," I say. "If you don't mind."

He exhales again, exhausted. "Look, kid. I know you're desperate to find Voclain, but... I'm not sure how much good an aimless search will do."

"Ian," I plead, meeting his gaze through his shades. He flinches at the sound of his true name. "I just need to know she's okay."

He stares at me, almost calculating, contemplating whether he should trust me. For a moment I worry I've overstepped, until his posture relaxes, and something about the way he holds himself tells me he understands. "Okay."

I nod. "Thank you."

He retrieves a black case from his pocket and opens it to reveal a pair of sleek sunglasses, resembling the pair he wears himself.

"I've been holding onto these for you, just in case." He hands me the shades. "You're not technically supposed to wear Eyes until after initiation, but you'll need these to see. Our little secret. You know how they work, right?"

"Somewhat."

"Remember your uniform? The screen on your wrist?"

I nod.

"Works like that. Touch controls are on the temples. Voice commands work too. Enable infrared and toggle coordinate tracking."

He removes his thick black raincoat and offers that to me too. "I'll trade you for the windbreaker. You'll need this if you're gonna be out here for a while."

I stare at the jacket he holds out, brows creased. "What about you?"

"I've been doing this for a long time. I'll be fine."

I pause for a moment, then accept his offer, trading him for the better jacket.

"And Steller?" King lowers his voice, removing his shades to lock his gaze with mine. "If your intuition is right... if you do find Voclain with that traitor... you call me right away. Not Heron—*me*. Don't say her name over the phone. Tell me you've had a stroke of good luck and I'll know what you mean."

"Call?"

He points to the glasses. "Just give the command."

"Okay."

"If that ends up being the case, I'll come find you. We'll make sure nothing bad happens to her, alright?"

I hesitate, then nod.

"I'll look around a bit more, and then track down Heron." He pauses. "Promise you'll let me know."

"I promise."

I zip on the raincoat as he starts to walk back toward camp, slipping the hood over my head.

"You have one hour, Steller," he shouts over his shoulder. "Then we're brainstorming another way to get us out of this whole mess."

He disappears between the trees.

When he's gone, I turn the Eyes over in my hands, studying them. Curiously, I uncross the temples and slide them over my head.

Immediately, a chirp rings in my ears. I snap my head around to locate the source of the noise, then realize it came from one of the temples. *They must contain speakers.*

I nearly jump back when the lenses shift, automatically adjusting to the level of light until I can see my surroundings clearly, as though there is no rain or darkness at all. I lift up the shades, then drop them back down again, studying the differences.

I reach up a finger to touch the temple, searching for some sort of button. The moment my skin comes into contact with the plastic, a menu pops up, like I'm staring at a screen. I slide my finger along the sides, selecting a button labeled *MODES*. I follow King's command, enabling infrared and coordinate tracking.

A string of numbers appears in the upper right corner of my vision, but aside from that, nothing changes; the clarity remains the same, as though I'm viewing the forest around me in the clearest, brightest daylight. But when I hold a hand in front of my face, it glows a bright red. *It detects heat,* I realize. A twig snaps above me, and I see a bluebird hop across it, though it doesn't glow the way my hand did. *Only human levels are detected.*

These glasses are meant for hunting people.

I push the thoughts aside, recentering my focus as I spend the first twenty minutes of my solitude in silence, navigating the woods with newfound clarity. I scan every rock, every tree trunk, every leaf for any sign of human life, but there is nothing that gives me any sort of lead. No broken branches, no faded sled tracks in the mud. All I sense is the cold.

I shove my hands into the pockets of King's raincoat as I walk, then pause, feeling something cold. I reach inside and pull out the object, then freeze.

For a moment, I mistake it for Carmody's lighter. It's identical to the one I took from him, except this one is carved with Ian's initials, not Duke's.

I.C.

I put it back in the pocket and keep going.

The clock ticks. Each minute of my given hour slips through the cracks slower than the last. Time inches on, and I barely notice it pass me by at all. The only indicator that I haven't been out here for days is the timer I've set for myself, which hovers in the top left corner of my vision.

Every next step feels like torture. Instead of growing closer to the one moment I've spent all this time waiting for, it's as though I am walking farther and farther away.

Just as I'm starting to believe I will find nothing out here, something in my peripheral sight snags my attention.

I stare at what appears to be a moss-covered stone wall, and when I squint, I realize it's the side of a large rock formation, topped with trees and dripping with vines.

Through the gaps between the ivy, I spot something red.

From my distance and with the barrier of vines, I can't tell if the heat is coming from one source or two. There is no separation, only one mass of glowing crimson. My heart sinks. *What if it really is only Aaron after all? Could those tracks we saw be from dragging a bad leg?* I blink to make sure I'm really seeing a heat signal, and when a sentence typed in blue blinks in the direction of the red, there is no mistaking it.

HUMAN: NO TRACKER IDENTIFIED

I stand in stillness for a long time, because I know what I have to do.

With every step I take toward the cave's opening, my heart pounds decibels louder, slamming against my ribs and skull and throat. I taste salt and iron on my tongue, which is dry and hot. Every bone in my body feels like it's shaking and I don't think it's because of the cold.

I stand a yard away, watching the wind sway the vines. Through the Eyes, I can see clearly in the dark, as though the rain isn't here at all and there are no clouds to block the sun.

I keep each step soundless. I press my back against the wall, feeling damp moss tickle the back of my neck.

If it really is only Aaron, and Eddie isn't here after all, it would be so easy to take what I need.

If I don't deliver what Canary requested, everything I've already done while wearing this suit would have been for nothing. *All of those deaths at the Cut, and for what?*

I've already come to terms with the fact that what sliver of humanity I'd preserved after my time as an Officer has slipped away. That once they gave me this new name, this brand new life, Ren McLellan slipped away with it.

There is no real leaving.

Do I have it in me to exterminate someone I know? Someone Eddie cares about? Her friend? Lori's brother?

What if she never found out it was me?

It would all be so simple. I could kill him quickly, and we'd be able to take his body back to Canary before our time runs out. I could give up a piece of information and pretend we interrogated him beforehand. Canary would have his head, and we could keep ours. He might even be pleased.

My hands twitch, every finger itching with the urge to move. Instinctively, I reach into my pocket for a Nightjade gun, then pause, remembering I have none. I scan the area for something I could use instead.

I notice a rock the size of a fist, with a sharp edge. My arm trembles when I pick it up.

The edges of my inhalations are jagged. I take in as much oxygen as I can, letting some of it go in a slow, shaky stream of air. *No right moments.*

I turn my head, and I peer through the vines.

Even with my enhanced vision, it takes me a moment to realize what I'm staring at. I blink behind the glasses, heart stilled as the scene beyond the ivy melts into something coherent.

Aaron leans against the back wall with his legs outstretched, barely upright as he holds something in his arms. *Alive*, I note, an unexpected wave of relief throwing through me. But the relief is quickly overshadowed with guilt. Even though he's clearly awake and breathing, his eyes look sunken in, his skin sticky with sweat, his wavy hair tossed this way and that. He isn't doing well.

I take a closer look, and my blood freezes.

Tangled beneath his arms, holding onto his torso with her face buried into his neck, is Eddie.

Her shoulders convulse as he gently rubs her back, whispering something to her that is carried away by the wind and rain so that I cannot hear it.

I can't even see her face.

Time stills as I stand in the rain, watching him hold her just as she held me so long ago. My chest aches with a burning so deeply rooted I wonder how my heart manages to pound at all, let alone this fast. I can't stop staring at her hands, which clutch the fabric of his shirt, holding it so tightly her knuckles turn pale. The storm carries her sobs away too.

Now that she is near, I can see the distance clearly. We are as separate as we have always been, so far out of our element that the space feels more familiar than whatever closeness we once called ours. I can barely see her, but she looks so different now. Her skin has lost its vibrancy. Her hair is longer, but dull, like she hasn't seen the sun in a long time. She wears a white camisole that reveals her arms and shoulders, which are bonier than I remember them being, sharp at the joints. I know what it looks like to watch a person wither away. *Eddie isn't eating enough.*

My heart plunges to my stomach.

She has no idea that I'm alive, does she?

I watch the way she sobs, thinking back to what I saw in the woods so long ago, when she buried that rabbit and grieved the brother she thought she lost. I remember her crying in the snow and know these are sobs of mourning too.

I don't know why I'm surprised. She watched me die. I wonder if my parents think I'm gone too. Sometimes *I* think I am.

My eyes drift to Aaron's callused hand, curled around the bare skin of her shoulder. I study the way he watches her, as though her wounds are deeper than the one I put in his leg. Like he would give just about anything to make her hurt go away.

I know what it's like to stare at a person like that. To look at what you desire above all else and know it could never be yours.

We watch her in harmony, and he has no idea.

Time goes on, but I don't even notice. All I can do is watch, until the sobs grow more sparse, and Eddie falls asleep in Aaron's arms.

My fingers wrap so tightly around the rock in my hand that I feel it leave indentations in my skin. I would trade places with him in a heartbeat if I could. There is nothing more I would rather do than approach, to ignore King's warning and finally reach her.

I thought I was done hiding behind boulders.

But I know the Agent is right. Eddie can be irrational, but she isn't stupid. If she saw me standing here in this suit, right here at the Cut of all places, she would know in an instant that I'm the one who gave up its location. That it was occupied because of me. That I have once again be-trayed every belief I was raised up believing to run back to the safety of the wrong side, because I'm afraid of what I could lose if I stand against it.

I'm choosing this life. It wasn't forced on me. I could have taken the injection I was offered.

I watch Eddie, her head pressed against Aaron's chest. His hands remain where they were, one on her shoulder and the other on her back, and she sleeps so soundly within the solidity of his embrace. And when my gaze flickers back to Aaron's and I see the way he looks at her, I know that in this moment, she is just as safe as she must feel. He will make sure of it.

I take off my Eyes, seeing only darkness. They have no light in their cave, no fire. I put the shades back on, and see that even as she sleeps, Eddie trembles. They are their only sources of warmth. *They're not stupid*, I think to myself. *They would have started a fire if they could.*

But even as she shivers in the cold and the rain, there is a truth I cannot deny.

She's better off like this, isn't she?

My grip on the rock loosens, and it tumbles to the dirt.

Aaron snaps his head up, but I'm gone before he can see me.

I'm not sure how long I stand there with my back pressed against the wall, unmoving, but I snap out of it when the timer chirps in my ear, warning me that I have ten minutes left.

I stare through the vines, giving them one last look. Aaron is asleep now too, and I notice something in Eddie's hands. *Carmody's lighter.*

It must not work, I realize, thinking back to the fires at the Cut. *She probably used all of the fluid.*

I study Eddie and Aaron carefully, making sure they're really asleep. When I'm certain, I inhale deeply, and I step inside the cave.

I keep every step silent, holding my breath as I walk closer and closer until I'm standing above them. I kneel down and gently pry the lighter out of her fingers, replacing it with King's.

I'm about to stand up again when I notice something bundled up in her arms, pressed between her and Aaron.

That's my old sweatshirt.

My heart pounds. My hand lingers on hers and I can't stop staring, taking in every detail of her face, committing all of her to memory. Like I've been wandering a desert for weeks and have finally stumbled across a drop of water.

I nearly jump back when one of her fingers curls around mine.

My eyes dart to hers, but they're still closed. *She's still asleep.*

I pull away, and I leave before I can convince myself to stay.

When I make it back to our tent, Heron and King sit shadeless around the fire, eating hot rice with canned tuna. They offer me a bowl, and I shake my head.

"Any luck?" King asks. I know what he means.

"No."

"None on our end either. A real shame. Would've been great to find Voclain with that traitor." Heron shakes his head. "Man. Imagine the bonus we'd get if we turned her in. We'd definitely rise a rank, that's for sure."

I ignore his remark and remove my Eyes and the sopping wet raincoat, handing them both back to King. "Thanks for the jacket."

He takes it with a nod, rising to his feet to hang it up to dry with our other coats. He reaches into the pocket, taking the lighter before he sits down.

My pulse races as I watch him fidget with the object. He pauses, studying it with creased brows.

Before he can notice the changed initials, I take a seat on one of the logs and nod toward the object. "Duke had one of those."

"My grandfather gave them to us when we were younger," King says, shoving it in the pocket of his pants, then studying the fire instead, like the lighter is harder to look at. "He was the closest thing to a decent parent we had. Still pretty hard on us, though."

Heron plays with his food.

"Are you still in contact?" I ask.

"He was Picked fourteen years ago."

"I thought your family was Immune."

King shakes his head. "He was my mother's father. Our dad was only paying for Immunity for his immediate family, not hers." He stares at his hands. "My parents were taking me out to dinner when it happened. Duke was the only one home. I was ten. He was five."

I avert my gaze, staring at the fire instead, swallowing the lump in my throat.

"A high-ranking Agent at twenty-four." Heron changes the subject, shaking his head. He takes his last bite of food before setting the bowl aside, crossing his arms over his chest, almost teasingly. "Impressive."

"You're the prodigy here. You're what, twenty-one?" King says, matching the Agent's dry tone. "Though I'm sure you have at least a bit of nepotism on your side.

Heron squares his shoulders.

I raise a brow. "Nepotism?"

They both glance at me, but Heron averts his gaze quickly.

"You don't know?" King gestures toward Heron with his chin. "His dad was the *great Agent H. Finch.*"

"That's why they forced me to enlist," Heron mutters, glaring at the fire.

"Forced?"

"Cornered is more like it." Heron scoffs. "My brother was a traitor. Putting on a suit was the only option that didn't put me on the receiving end of a Nightjade syringe."

"The Agency is fond of legacies," King says. "The talented bloodlines have a greater chance for higher return."

"I'm gonna take a walk." Heron stands up so quickly he hits his head on a branch, but he doesn't seem to care. He grabs his jacket, shoves his hands into his pockets, and leaves.

After he's gone, I glance at King. "What was that about?"

He shrugs. "He doesn't like talking about his dad."

I nod. We sit in silence for a moment, the fire crackling at our feet, until I clear my throat. "Can I... ask you something? About your brother?"

King flinches. A muscle in his neck twitches, and he nods.

"Back when we were... you know." I swallow. "He said something about you."

He nods again. "What did he say?"

"He told me you opted out of sharing your Immunity."

He scoffs. "Is that really what they told him?"

King notices my confusion and shakes his head, staring at the fire. "I offered. My parents declined. For him, at least."

My brows crease. "Why would they do something like that?"

He sighs. "My parents... they were hard on Duke. Much harder than they ever were on me. They didn't like it when I stuck up for him at school, or at home. Or when I'd help him with his chores. His homework. With anything, really. I was the *perfect son*. I wasn't supposed to compromise my success for his. They were always pushing him to be better. To be more like me." He stares at his hands. "Eventually, I started to push him too."

I'm not sure what to say, so we watch the fire until he speaks up again. "What made you ask?"

"No reason."

"You want to know why I'm in this, don't you?"

I glance at him, then look away with a nod.

"Can I be honest with you?"

I nod again.

"I can't remember."

After a while, I head inside the tent to rest until Heron gets back. I lie on a bedroll and stare at the ceiling, listening to the pattering of the rain. Thunder rolls somewhere distant.

I can't stop thinking about Eddie. About what it felt like to kiss her. The laugh I would give my own heartbeat to hear again. I try to remember the last time I heard the sound, wondering if I knew it would be the last at all. Wondering if I will ever be free of the ache that is burning for someone who doesn't burn back. But I only wonder for so long, because the questions are easy to answer.

I will spend years of my life caught in the minute that I was briefly yours.

EDDIE

Monday, April 15
78 Beds Made

♪ HUSH, I'M ON TV - ALL THEM WITCHES ♪

No one sees me sneak out of the hospital.

It's dark out as I zip up my freshly cleaned orange jacket, then shove my hands into my pockets. I walk as quickly as I can without drawing attention to myself, forcing a grin toward the few Harbor folk I pass by on the sidewalk.

When I pass the church, I hear the echoes of a loud argument between Wagner and Cecil, and Noriko—who attempts to calm them down. I try to ignore the mentions of fire and my name. I almost don't see Alice standing out front until she waves at me. I study her as she leans against the wall by the front door, then wave back before moving on.

No bell above the door greets me when I hurry inside the Vermillion's front lobby. I make my way upstairs, glancing back to ensure I'm not being followed.

I knock when I reach Cecil's room, wait a few moments, then step inside, closing the door behind me.

His room isn't laid out like mine and Aaron's. It's larger, more like a one-bedroom apartment than a studio.

I take in my surroundings in the dark. It's a lot neater than I thought it'd be. From the volumes lining an old mahogany bookcase to the dishes neatly stacked upon floating shelves in the kitchen, everything seems to have a place. It smells like old wood, yellowing paper, and cinnamon.

I walk into the bedroom, which contains not much more than a simple bed and a desk in the corner that displays the only visible mess in the apartment. Papers upon papers cover the entirety of its surface, leaving no inch untouched. I notice open books and letters, but it's the maps that catch my attention.

There must be a dozen of them sprawled across his desk—maybe more. I lift one up and study it, identifying it as a topographical map with a red dot in the center, and a name attached to it. *Noble Ridge.*

I commit the map to memory, and I snap a photo with my phone.

I find two more similar maps—one for a location labeled Pine Point, another for a place called Glasmack Falls. I memorize them, then take photos of those too.

I take a deep breath, and I send them to Heron.

I accept his checkers invite, and I make my first move.

EDDIE

don't let them burn.

The fourth map I find has a name I recognize. *Silver Fir.* I scan over it, absorbing every detail, pulling out the flip phone to take a photo. But before I get the chance, it chirps.

M. HERON

I'll try my best, detective.

you did the right thing.

I get notified that he's taken his turn. He moved his pawn.

M. HERON

> friendly reminder—clock's still ticking. your prince is
> still waiting.

My stomach churns and I bite my lower lip. He's right. Heron is evasive at best; I have no solid idea of how much time Ren has left, or if that particular countdown can even be quantified. I need to check the file. *I need to give him what he wants.*

I exit out of my messages with Heron. My finger hovers over the folder icon on the home screen, shaking.

Before I can press it, the door opens.

I slam the phone shut and shove it in my pocket, snapping my head up, an apology already forming in my mouth—but pause when I realize I'm staring at Alice, not Cecil.

We stand there in silence for a long time until she speaks. "I won't tell."

"Thank you."

"Don't worry about it. We've all got secrets." She shrugs, then creases her brows. "You aren't the rat, are you?"

My eyes widen, face pale—and then I remember she's talking about the person who gave up the location of the Cut. "No."

"I was kidding, but good to know." She looks at the maps on the desk, shaking her head. "You and your brother. Both obsessed with maps."

My brows pinch together, but then I remember his investigation with Aaron and force a chuckle. "Yeah."

"Looking for someone?"

I turn around, arranging the maps so they're exactly how Cecil had them, down to the inch. "No."

"Right." Alice chuckles, unconvinced. "That's what your brother said when I caught him doing exactly what you are."

I force a fleeting grin, trying not to think about the room he and Aaron hid from me in the lighthouse.

"You're trying to find him, aren't you?" Alice says, her voice soft. "The one you lost."

My throat constricts. "Something like that."

She's better off believing that, I think to myself. If anyone discovers that I'm in contact with an Agent, they'll think I'm giving up End Harbor in exchange for Ren—or that I'm the one who handed over the Cut.

And her guess isn't too far off, anyway. *I'm always trying to find Ren.*

"Speaking of Milo, have you seen him around?" Alice asks. "I have something for him. Well, I did. It's missing. But still."

"I haven't seen him since I got back."

Alice furrows her brows, arms crossed. "Now that you mention it, I don't think I've seen him since you *left*."

We exchange a single wide-eyed glance before running out of Cecil's room and down the hall, bursting into Lori's. She stands in the kitchenette, packing food into a basket that must be for Aaron.

"Lor?" Alice jogs up to her. "Have you seen Milo?"

She shakes her head. "No."

"And you don't think that's weird?" Alice says. "That he hasn't tried to bother you at least four times today or collapsed onto your couch because he's *dying of boredom* and needs a cure or possibly a snack, otherwise his death will be on your hands and you won't be invited to his funeral unless you're providing the after-party refreshments?"

"I assumed he was busy." Lori raises a brow. "He called a wake an *after party?*"

Alice crinkles her nose. "Busy with what?"

"That's what he told me." Lori shrugs. "He said he was working on a project and not to bother him for a few days."

"And how long ago was that?"

Lori's face pales.

We hurry down the hall to Milo's room, and when I open the door, my heart plummets.

He's not all that's missing—his stuff is too.

I feel like I'm going to be sick.

Alice and Lori call after me as I sprint out of the room and down the stairs, running as fast as I can through the lobby door and down the road to the lighthouse. Milo's words ring in my ears with every pounding footstep.

"Don't do anything stupid, okay? That's my job, not yours."

"I'm just trying to look out for you, Ed."

"Some people just can't be saved."

All this time, he's been pushing me away on purpose. Convincing me that Ren doesn't care. Telling me how stupid it would be to go after him because he's my brother, and he wants to keep me safe.

I hear Alice and Lori chasing after me as I run up the hill and storm into the lighthouse, stopping only when I stand in that closet, out of breath. They stumble in right as I pull the light's chain.

Everything that once covered the walls—the notes, the documents, the articles—all of it has been cleared, except for a single map, with a bright red pin in Seattle. A set of coordinates are scribbled next to it in thin handwriting I recognize but can't place. I think back to the list I once saw on the wall—and the circle around the Seattle Agency Headquarters.

All of the breath drains from my lungs when I turn around, hands shaking. "Milo's gone after Ren."

Saturday, April 20
83 Beds Made

I shiver as Aaron and I walk around the hospital's perimeter for the second time this afternoon.

I shove my hands into my jacket pockets, walking slowly enough to match his pace as he limps by my side. He wears a black sweatshirt with the hood up, hugging his abdomen as his breath materializes in front of him, curling and unfurling like rolled ferns. Droplets prickle my exposed skin, but there isn't enough to call it rain. Just End Harbor's usual coat of mist.

"How's the pain?" I ask, keeping my eyes glued to the damp sidewalk.

"Not bad. My leg's just a little stiff."

"The antibiotics your dad's been giving you are helping?"

He nods. "No more infection."

"That's good." I nod too, glancing up at him. "How are you feeling?"

"Tired."

We continue our walk in silence.

Ever since he woke up on Thursday, we haven't talked much. He knows about Milo's disappearance, but aside from that, our conversations have been small talk, brittle and bland. There's an elephant in the room that neither of us can really see, but we both know it's there. We still haven't talked about what happened in the cave, but I'm not sure what there is to talk about.

I glance at Aaron, watching him walk. His limp has gradually improved over the last few days, but it's reached a bit of a plateau now. Simon says he'll most likely be walking like this for a while.

I study his face, observing the bags under his eyes. I've spent every night in the hospital with him and have yet to witness another nightmare. He seems to be getting enough sleep, as far as I can tell. But his shoulders are weighed down by something. *I wonder what's wearing him out.*

He does look a lot better, though. The vibrancy has returned to his skin, which is no longer green and sickly. His cheeks don't look so hollowed out. He's not at his best, but he's certainly not at his worst either.

We finish our lap and walk back inside the hospital. I help him up the stairs, and we head back into his room, closing the door behind us. He takes off his hood. I turn on the TV and take off my jacket, hanging it on the coat rack.

"Voclain?"

"Yeah?" I walk over to the kitchenette in the corner and start boiling a kettle of water for tea.

"Can I talk to you for a sec?"

"Sure." I walk back to where he stands. "What's up?"

He opens his mouth to say something, then purses his lips with a sigh. "I've been meaning to—"

"Hold on."

My brows crease as I walk over to the TV, turning up the volume. I hadn't realized I'd put on the news, but a reporter stands in the frame, holding a microphone as more drone footage of the fire plays in the corner.

"Three smaller *sub-fires* have appeared in these separate locations. We have reason to believe the traitors associated with Lavender Voclain may be starting smaller fires in hopes that her destruction will spread, as these specific locations once belonged to classified Corps research sites, like the one she initially burned. It is clear that these rebels, who once lived among the shadows, will stop at nothing to witness our downfall."

The reporter points behind her, where the screen has transitioned to a map of the forest. A red *X* symbol marks the location of each new fire.

"Voclain, I really need to—"

I hold up a hand, and he stops talking. He could be glaring, but I'm too busy staring at the map to notice, brows creased. *Where do I know these locations from?*

My blood freezes.

These are the exact points that I sent to Heron.

Aaron says something, but I don't hear it. The world starts to spin. The tea kettle whistles, ringing in my ears as I run to the sink and vomit.

"Whoa, whoa..." Aaron turns off the television, running up to my side. He holds my hair back, and I vomit again.

My arms quake as I grip the sides of the sink, unable to do anything but stare at the wall while Aaron pours me a cup of tea. I wipe my mouth and wash my hands, unblinking, even when he guides me toward the bed to take a seat at the edge of it. He sits next to me. I'm still shaking.

His hand lifts like he's going to place it on my shoulder, but he stops himself, setting it in his lap instead. He stares at his hand, then at me. All I can see are the patterns in the floor tile.

"Is this about the fire?"

I don't say anything. I *can't* say anything, because if he finds out what I've done, I don't think he'll look at me the same way again.

"It's not..." He stops himself. *He can't say the fire isn't my fault.* He swallows, staring at his hands. "You did what you had to do."

I glance at him, recognizing the guilt in an instant.

"I still haven't thanked you for that, by the way." He can't bring himself to look at me. "I don't think I'd be alive right now if it weren't for you, so... thank you."

"You don't have to thank me." I avert my gaze. "I did what I had to do, remember?"

I glance at the TV, watching the flames. I swallow the growing lump in my throat. *Milo's out there somewhere.* "I have to go after him."

"He'll come back," Aaron says. "He's smart like you, alright? He'll realize he's made a mistake and turn around, I'm sure of it."

"You don't know Milo like I do." I shake my head, lip quivering. "If he's trying to get Ren back for my sake, his rationality will go out the window."

"How do you know that?"

"Because he's like me," I snap, then lower my voice. "We grew up looking out for each other. Even if it made us do stupid shit. He was getting made fun of in elementary school? I was the one throwing punches. My dad was screaming at me for something I didn't do? Milo stuck up for me. Even if it ended up getting twisted around on him."

My throat tightens and my eyes burn as my parents' faces resurface against my will. "I loved my parents—I still do. But it wasn't easy to grow up like that." My voice cracks. "Milo always made sure everything was okay."

Aaron's hand twitches.

I look up at him. "He's not coming back without Ren."

He stares at me, his expression soft, brows curved downward. "Okay."

"I need to follow him." I study my reflection in the mug of tea, seeing it clearly. "Tonight."

"With all the fires out there?"

"I have no other choice." I look back Aaron, trying to keep my voice from wavering. "I need to catch up to him before he does something crazy."

"Then let me find him for you."

I laugh bitterly. "You're not going out there alone."

"Neither are you."

I rise to my feet. "You can't stop me."

He stands too. "You don't know that."

"I made it back here all on my own, alright? I can do it again."

In an instant, Aaron steps forward. I step back, not realizing I've walked into the wall until his palms are flattened against it. I glare up at him, arms crossed.

"I don't need you to remind me of how capable you are, Voclain. Because that's exactly what I'm worried about. You're stubborn and smart and you'll think of something wild and I..." He exhales sharply, darkening his gaze, speaking lower. "Just because I'm weaker than I usually am doesn't mean I can't stop you from walking out that Gate."

I pull my knife from my boot. "Don't think I won't stop you from doing the exact same thing."

He leans closer. "Stab me."

"Gladly."

We glare at each other for a long time, his face inches away from mine. His nostrils flare, and then his gaze softens. I find mine doing the same.

"If I can't stop you..." He swallows. "Take me with you."

When I stare at him, I find the same guilt that I recognized before—and a pleading so desperate and familiar that it would be both hypocritical and cruel of me to do anything but nod.

So I do. "Okay."

The Gate looks larger beneath the cover of night.

It towers above us as we stand in front of it, bags slung over our shoulders. I wear my jacket, warm within my sweater and jeans. This time, Aaron doesn't make the mistake of forgetting his own jacket and wears a black waterproof one over his brown sweater. *We'll be ready for the rain.*

"You ready?" he asks, unable to take his eyes away from the Gate.

"Not really."

He nods. "Me neither."

Before we can step forward, a twig snaps.

We whip our heads around, exchanging puzzled glances.

"Hello?" we ask.

Silence.

Aaron pulls out a knife, listening, waiting, until another twig snaps. He turns toward the sound, throwing the weapon just as someone stands from behind a bush. The blade pins their sleeve to the tree trunk behind them. "What the *hell*, man?"

I frown.

Aaron walks over to where Beau stands, plucking the knife from the tree.

"You missed."

"I never miss." Aaron sheaths his knife, then folds his arms across his chest. "What are you doing here?"

"We're following you."

I raise a brow. "We?"

Aaron rolls his eyes. "Come out, you two."

Alice and Lori step out from behind a tree, bags slung over their shoulders as they scowl at Aaron and me.

"We're going with you," Lori says.

"No."

"Aaron, you're being stupid."

"I said no, Lor."

"You can't exactly tell me what to do, alright?" Lori crosses her arms. "We can help."

"Lor—"

"I've already let you convince me to stay behind once and I'm not letting that happen again," she snaps.

"And what are *you* doing here?" Aaron frowns at Alice. "You couldn't talk her out of this?"

"Nope." Alice flashes a faux grin at Aaron, chewing at the end of a honey stick. She lowers it when she turns to me with a sigh. "Look. We care about your brother, okay? He's a good friend of Lori's and he's been a good friend to me."

"And I'm pissed that you didn't ask me to come with you." Beau glares daggers at Aaron. "I used to be your partner in crime for things like this, remember?"

"This isn't a trip to the city to sneak into movie theaters and fairs, alright? We're not stealing a goat here."

I raise a brow, and Aaron glances at me briefly. "Long story. Look. My point is, this is serious. Everything's going to shit out there and if we're not careful, there's no telling what might happen."

"You think I don't know that?" Beau steps forward. "I know exactly how dangerous this is. Why else do you think we're going with you guys?"

Aaron clenches his jaw, neck twitching.

"If you don't let us go, we'll stop you," Lori says.

"How?"

"We'll tell on you," Alice says, chewing on the stick of honey.

Aaron flattens his eyelids. "Really?"

"Yup," Alice confirms.

He runs a hand through his hair, laughing cynically. "This is crazy, isn't it?"

"Yup."

Aaron takes a deep, strained breath, then sighs, kicking a rock as he slings his bag over his shoulder, walking toward the Gate. "So are you all coming, or not?"

I'm about to walk after him, but I stop myself, remembering what Wagner said. If I leave again, I can't come back.

I think about everyone I'd be leaving behind. About Asa and Noriko, the man who practically raised me, and the mother of my two closest friends, who I've grown to deeply care for. They're the closest thing I have to parents.

And Simon, who offered me a job, who means so much to Aaron. And Esmerelda, his mother, who I got to know and love all those months ago back in Port Keys. Cecil, who always tries so hard to protect everyone, who is always there to make sure I'm okay. Hugo and his genius, his witty remarks, the chess games he tried to get me to play when I wouldn't come out of my room after first arriving at End Harbor. Viv, and the moments of spoken and unspoken understanding we share, and the late-night visits with ice cream and regency romance films she'd watch with me until I fell asleep—or until Aaron pounded on the wall, threatening to commit all sorts of atrocities if he heard us scream about an averted gaze or hand flex one more time. I even think about the End Harbor man who makes bread every morning, or the woman who walks her dog past the Vermillion every other evening as the street lamps light themselves.

Everyone I've known—who has looked out for me in one way or another —will be in End Harbor. There have been days where it's felt more like a cage, but it's the only home I've got left, and it's safe. And I'm about to leave it all behind for what could very well be for good. *Where else is there for me to go?*

I could live a quiet life in hiding, as Wagner offered, watching the world get worse from within the safety of End Harbor's walls. I could wait out the rest of my life here, until my bounty is forgotten, and the places outside the walls tear themselves apart. It would be bland, but I'd be safe. Scared— yet safe.

But what life is there to live without my brother in it? Without Ren?

I will save my quiet for a better place.

I take a deep breath and follow Aaron through the Gate.

R. STELLER

Sunday, April 7

♪ BURNING EFFIGIES - TIGERCUB ♪

Heron returns from his walk, and we still don't have a head.

The three of us sit around the fire in silence, legs shaking, deep in thought. The rain falls in sheets beyond our makeshift shelter.

Somewhere far, a flash of lightning strikes, followed by a roll of thunder.

"Our best option is our original plan," Heron says. "Find the guy, take his head, serve it to Canary."

"We're running out of time," King says. "We've looked everywhere. Our chances of finding him in this weather are slim. We're better off spending what little time we have left coming up with another solution."

"I don't think finding him is worth the trouble either," I say. "And I'm not exactly keen on the idea of decapitating someone."

"Why so protective all of a sudden?" Heron folds his arms, suppressing a smirk. "You're the one who shot him."

I stare at the fire, trying to ignore the question I already know the answer to. *For her.*

Heron chuckles, letting out a low whistle. "Okay, now I get it."

I frown. "Get what?"

"Why you've been so reluctant about this whole ordeal."

"I'm not reluctant."

"King said you didn't want to shoot him."

"I didn't," I snap. "Unlike you, I'm not fond of mindless killing."

"I'm not fond of it either, but I'll do what I have to do." Heron grins. "Kind of like protecting another guy for the girl you love."

I shoot him a glare, rising to my feet, but King yanks me back down. "Knock it off, you two."

"I'm not protecting him," I say, staring at the fire again. "King's right. We can't find him, so we need to come up with another plan."

"We can't exactly come back empty-handed." King places a palm over his mouth in thought.

Heron sighs. "Where the hell are we gonna find a human head?"

The three of us go quiet.

I keep my eyes glued to the flames, watching them dance to the rhythm of the downpour, inhaling the smoke the wind blows in my direction. The burning logs are white with heat, coated in so much ash they look like bones.

I lift my head up. "I think I have an idea."

It's late in the evening by the time we make it back to the Cut.

The compound is in near ruins. Every once-flammable structure is now a pile of rubble, still smoldering, even in the rain. A few brick buildings remain, but aside from that, all the detrimental evidence the Corps was trying to extract is gone.

I stand in the square again, Heron and King by my side. We stare off into the distance, where an orange glow festers. It must be miles away, but we can still smell the smoke.

"Ironic, isn't it?" Heron says over the howling wind. "This fire stops, another one starts all the way over there."

"Could be from carried embers," King suggests. "The wind is certainly strong enough for it."

"Or lightning." Heron shoves his hands into his pockets. "That's probably what they'll end up pinning it on if that fire spreads. Especially with the recent spike in public rage."

King nods. "The Corps will blame anything but themselves."

We walk out of the square and toward the clearing west of the Block in silence.

"You two do what you gotta do," Heron says when we arrive. "I'll keep watch over here."

King and I don't protest when he walks behind a large pile of rubble.

We grip our shovels tightly, staring at the scorch marks where the bonfire used to be, and the freshly filled trench that was once empty. I try to ignore the rain and the churning in my stomach, swallowing the urge to vomit. It doesn't go away.

I glance over my shoulder, confirming that we really are alone. Most of the Officers that were stationed at the Cut have been dispatched elsewhere, now that there isn't much work left for them here. The remaining Agents are staying in the library, which is one of the brick buildings that somehow managed to evade the flames. Its collection of Yesterday books are the only pieces of the Cut left to comb through. With the Agents busy with that and the rain keeping them trapped indoors, we're completely alone out here.

"Ready?" King says, staring straight ahead.

"No," I say, but we get started anyway.

Digging mud in the rain is more impossible than I thought it would be. Though the grave is relatively shallow, it takes us almost an hour to make a mere foot's dent. The shovels are slippery and difficult to grip, and my hands blister, not used to labor like this. What we do manage to dig is quickly filled with rainwater, and we slip easily.

"Isn't it bad luck to dig a grave?" I shout over the rain.

"Probably," King shouts back. "But we don't have much of a choice here, do we?"

Every part of me is shaking by the time we're two feet deep. Even King is exhausted, and we have no other option but to take a break beneath the shelter of a nearby tree. We're too muddy to care about the dirt as we slump against the trunk, out of breath.

"Didn't realize I was signing up for Tomb labor when I took my entrance exam," King says.

"Me neither."

We sit there, watching the rain fall around us. It's quieter here underneath the branches.

I turn to face him. "That's where you're headed, right?"

King nods, unable to meet my gaze. "That's where Evangeline is."

"How do you know?"

"I watched them take her away."

It's quiet for a moment before King sighs, leaning his head back against the trunk. "Doing all of this is my only way in."

"What do you mean by that?"

King glances at me, then stares at the half-dug trench. "What do you know about the Tombs?"

"They're corpse-management facilities. For the bodies who don't get a tombstone, if their families can't pay for one." I stare at the mud too. "Where they send criminals and traitors. People the Corps can't afford to exterminate yet because they still have weight to pull." I swallow. "The sick ones."

King nods. "It's all burning and burying there. Makes this job feel like child's play."

I study the blisters on my hands.

"They're impossible to break into. The only way you're getting in is as a Guard or a high-ranking Agent. Or a traitor shackled to a shovel."

I raise a brow. "A Guard?"

"That's what they call the Chasers who get stationed there. It's not a real division, technically—just a role for them to assign to the cadets who aren't good enough to be an Officer but won't do well at a desk job either. Or the ones who do something stupid and need a demotion." He stares at something in the distance. "The ones who like their job a little too much."

"So it's punishment for us too?"

"Once you're a Chaser, being sent to the Tombs as a prisoner is no longer an option. The only way to leave the Corps is with a Nightjade injection. Retirement is death, as you know." He sighs. "I thought about doing something stupid before. To get myself demoted to a Guard on purpose. But once you're an Agent, you can't get demoted to anything lower than that. You know too much. And by the time Evangeline was sent away, I was already being offered this suit."

"So your only way out is up?"

King nods. "If I can get promoted to a Fourth Rank, I'd have control over where I'm stationed. The assignments I'm handling. I'd be working directly under Canary with minimal supervision. I'd still have to report back with what I'm doing, but I wouldn't always require permission or clearance for anything."

"So you could transfer to the Tombs, no questions asked?"

"Exactly," he says, drawing circles in the damp earth. "I could say I'm conducting an Underground investigation and station myself there to collect information from the rebels. And... I don't know. Maybe I'd find her too."

"How would you get her out?"

"I'll figure it out when I get there." He shrugs half-heartedly. "Agents are the only ones who can come and go as they please. No one else has an exit ticket. Guards are heavily monitored by supervising Agents and traitors are never left unattended by Guards. The alarm systems are crazy good too, after the revolt and all that."

I give him a puzzled look. "Revolt?"

He creases his brows. "You don't know?"

I shake my head.

He suppresses a smirk. "Sometimes I forget you're not already an Agent."

For a moment, I almost take it as a compliment.

"The only revolt in Tombs history took place almost two years ago. Security has been impenetrable ever since."

"What happened?"

"I don't know the full story, but apparently a few prisoners started a fire. A big one too. They put some sort of accelerant in the water tower and knocked it down."

"How did they manage to swing that?"

"Rumors claim they teamed up with a Guard or two. Five prisoners were in on it. One didn't make it out. A few Guards and prisoners were killed in the fire too. No one knows where the ones who started it all ran off to." King stares at the rain-filled trench again. "They were the first and only people to escape."

"I had no idea." I watch the rain send ripples through the mud at my feet. "I'm assuming the Guard got caught."

"They tortured him until they got the story out. He was an Unseen sympathizer. They were going to execute him, but he managed to escape before they got the chance."

"How?"

"Another Guard helped him out." King glances at me. "But the Corps thinks an Agent may have helped him disappear."

"Shit."

King nods.

"How come they never mentioned it on the news?"

"The Corps is the news," he says. "You think they want people fantasizing about the possibility of a revolt? Or so scared of a rebel uprising they try to hunt down the Unseen themselves?" He shakes his head. "It'd be asking for madness either way."

We sit like that for a while longer, watching the rain rinse our shovels clean, until King rises to his feet, offering me a hand. "Ready to make your hands bleed?"

I take it with a nod. "Yeah."

I set the bag on the desk with a thud. "Your head, sir."

Canary sits behind it, mouth and nose pinched in disgust as Heron, King and I stand in his library office, caked in mud, rainwater dripping off our soaked suits and staining the carpet. Dried blood paints my palms red. I shove them into my pockets, waiting for Canary to move, until he takes the mud-stained cloth bag into his hands. He unties the knot and peers inside.

He stares for a long time, unfazed by the gift. He wears his Eyes, so I can't read him when he finally looks up at me. "This is a skull."

"It is, sir."

He nods, glancing into the bag again, then back at me. "There are scorch marks on the bone."

"There are."

"Why is that?"

"The man who robbed the armory was hiding in a cave with the traitor I shot." I keep my expression blank. "I smoked them out."

"With fire?"

"I thought they deserved a taste of their own medicine, sir."

"So they're both dead, then?"

I nod.

Canary carves me with his shaded gaze, scouring me for any visible indication that I'm not telling the truth. "Where's the other skull?"

My blood freezes. I hold my breath. "This was the only one I could salvage."

"If there is no face, no eyes, how can I be sure this really belongs to the rebel?"

A painful piece of silence stretches on for what feels like an eternity. Heron and King remain perfectly still, unflinching beneath the flickering orange glow of the library's lamplight. I'm not even sure they're breathing.

"You asked me for a head," I say. "I've brought you exactly that."

Canary doesn't say a word. My heart races and I try to keep my breaths steady, so sure I've made my final mistake.

And then, Canary laughs.

He leans his head back, face turning purple as the sound erupts from his throat. Heron and I exchange unsure glances.

When his laughter dies out, he removes his shades to wipe a tear. The smile fades and he puts the sunglasses back on. I'm not sure he believes the head is Aaron's, but his face is certain as he turns to face King.

"I think he's ready for initiation."

EDDIE

Saturday, April 20
83 Beds Made

When the Gate closes behind us, I take a piece of paper from my pocket and pass it around for everyone to read.

"These are the coordinates I found on the wall," I explain. "It's somewhere near Seattle."

When the paper reaches Aaron, his brows crease. "Milo and I never talked about these before."

"I remember seeing a note about the Seattle Agency Headquarters," I say.

"That was a dropped theory. And those coordinates don't match these ones." He hands the paper back to me, which I put back in my pocket. "I explained to Milo that HQ doesn't exactly store prisoners on-site, so I don't think he'd go there."

I open my mouth, then close it. *They can't know I know the Agents have Ren.* "Well, wherever these coordinates lead, Milo's headed right to them."

"Or maybe he's throwing you off his trail," Aaron says.

"Maybe he found new information while you were gone," Lori suggests.

Aaron shakes his head. "It's just a little weird, that's all."

"This whole thing is weird," Alice says, chewing on her stick of honey.

"I think we should go where Eddie decides," Beau says. "It's her brother, after all."

Aaron glares for a moment, then glances at me, eyes softening with a sigh. "Okay."

We walk for a few hours, and my whole body is sore by the time we decide to set up camp in a small clearing next to a running stream of water. This time, we thought of packing a tent, which Aaron and Alice set up while Lori helps me get a fire started. We won't have to worry about the smoke giving us away, since there is already so much of it lingering in the air.

Once the campfire is going and the tent is all set, Lori and I sit on logs around it with tea while Aaron takes watch a few yards away. Beau is already asleep inside the tent, and Alice is croaking at a kitten-sized bullfrog that sits upon a rock in the stream.

Lori and I rest in silence for a while, sipping our drinks. A gray fleece blanket is draped over her shoulders. The fire casts shadows across her face when she looks up at me. "I never got the chance to thank you for bringing Aaron back."

"You don't have to thank me."

"But I *am* thankful." Lori watches the flames as they crackle like rain. "He means the world to me."

I smile, observing the fire too. "I know what you mean."

"It's really hard when he's not around." She stares at her hands. "Not knowing when he'll come back."

"I can imagine."

"Growing up without my best friend was... God, it was unbearable." She shakes her head. "Asa and my father did the best they could to take him to visit me in secret, but it's a long trip to Port Keys, as you know. And they could only safely stay for so long."

"That must have been really lonely."

"It was." She nods. "Now that we've been around each other more... now that I'm really Unseen... I don't know. It almost feels harder."

"What do you mean?"

Lori glances at her brother as he leans against a tree. "I've gotten used to having him around. So when you two went missing..." She bites her lip and shakes her head, returning her gaze to the fire. "I can't believe I let him talk me out of going with him."

"It meant a lot to him." I give her a sad, fleeting smile. "He cares about you very much."

She returns the expression, then looks at me. "He cares about you too, you know."

I stare into my tea, then back at Aaron, unable to stop thinking back to what happened in the cave. About the ways we kept each other close and warm. About the things he said. *It was only the fever*, I remind myself.

But in spite of my own reason, I can't help but wonder if there could have been some truth to what he told me. *What if the fever was only stripping his guard away?*

I observe my reflection again, thinking about what it would mean if that were the case.

It's not like I haven't thought similar things about him before. He's not unpleasant to look at. There have been moments where I've found my gaze lingering a bit too long on his hair, or his eyes, or his arms. But not on purpose.

And it's Aaron. *My* Aaron—the closest friend I have, and the only thing in my life that is solid and sure. When I look at him, I know with confidence that I would take a bullet for him. Several, if I had to. And something tells me he'd do the same.

But if we were both bound by fever—if our guards were both stripped down—would it be truth, or madness?

Madness, I tell myself, forcing the thoughts away. *Definitely madness.*

I glance at Aaron again. I can see the weight on his shoulders from here. Even after everything, there is still so much he hides. So much I don't know.

"Lori?"

"Yeah?"

I open my mouth, then close it, unsure of how to pose the question. "Did something happen to him?"

Lori averts her gaze. "You'll need to be more specific than that."

"At the cave. He..." I stare at my hands, unable to finish the sentence.

"The nightmares?"

I nod.

"He's had them ever since we were little. After he left Port Keys." Lori sighs. "But they've gotten worse over the years. I guess there's just more and more to be afraid of."

I nod again, staring at him, then back at Lori, who watches her brother, shaking her head. "Sometimes it feels like I don't even know him."

I look at my drink. *I know exactly what she's talking about.*

"It's like he's always pretending to be someone else." She takes a sip of her tea. "I just wish I knew how to help him."

"Me too."

There is a comfort in knowing that I'm not the only one who notices. But the comfort only reaches so far, because that means my worries are valid enough to encompass a real, tangible problem. A problem I may not have the ability to fix.

After a while, the bullfrog hops away, and Alice walks over. She takes a seat next to Lori, leaning her head against her shoulder. "Hold me. I'm cold."

Lori rolls her eyes, but she's grinning from ear to ear. Alice is much taller than she is, but Lori wraps her blanket and arms around her. I can't help but smile, though there is an ache I feel too. The lack of a closeness like theirs.

I glance over my shoulder again, facing Aaron, who watches them with a weak but genuine grin. It fades, and his gaze shifts to settle on me.

He leans against the tree with one leg crossed over the other, still carving as he watches me study him.

I want to say something. I want to tell him that he's cold, and the fire is warm, and the seat next to me isn't taken. But I've said those things before, and I know how this goes. He will keep watch as he always does, observing from afar while the rest of us talk and laugh, and we will all fall asleep to the rhythm of his blade scraping against wood.

I turn around to stare at the fire again, following the path of the rising embers that flutter like moths, dissipating into the night. I think about how strange it is that something so destructive can still be so beautiful, offering warmth and light in return for taking so much.

My head is still tilted upward when I feel someone take a seat to my left.

"Nice night," Aaron says, watching the embers. Watching me.

Watching him, I say, "It is."

And when the others finally fall asleep, I lean my head against his shoulder, and I drift off to a rhythm that is near.

Sunday, April 21
84 Beds Made

I smell something burning.

My eyes pry open. My back is leaning against a log, and my head is against Aaron's shoulder, whose arm is around me. *We must have fallen asleep like that.* Lori's blanket is draped around us.

I blink my view into place, squinting through what must be morning fog. But there is a strange tint, almost yellow. It's still thin enough to see through—more of a haze than anything, like a humid summer day.

But my throat burns, and when I cough, I can feel it deeply within my lungs, scraping the sides like something is clawing to get out. It still smells like a campfire, even though ours has gone out.

My eyes widen when I realize there is smoke all around us.

I tap Aaron's shoulder. "Wake up."

He groans, unmoving.

"Wake up," I repeat. Still asleep, he pulls me closer to him.

I tap his shoulder again, repetitively, making sure to use the tip of my nail.

"No."

I reach into his satchel and pull out the pig flashlight. It whirs loudly when I crank it, shining brightly in his eyes.

He folds forward, covering his eyes. "God, Voclain. You're lucky I fell asleep without my knife."

He notices that his arm is around me and pulls it away.

I shove the flashlight into my pocket, make my bed by rolling up Lori's blanket, and stand on a log to shout. "Everybody, wake the hell up!"

Aaron begins to cough much worse than I did as Beau, Lori, and Alice stick their heads out of the tent.

"What?" Beau asks, eyelids droopy. I gesture around me with my hands, and his eyes widen. "*Shit.*"

"The fire's spread," Aaron says between coughs. "We can't walk through this."

"What are you saying?" Lori asks as we all begin to pack our things. She and Alice take down the tent.

"We shouldn't be traveling through the woods."

I zip up my bag. "They're smoking us out on purpose."

Lori stares at me with creased brows. "What makes you say that?"

I freeze, then shrug. "It's the only answer that makes sense."

"She's right," Aaron says. "The Corps wouldn't waste time putting out a fire this big to save a few rebels."

Lori stares at a tree. "It's doing their job for them."

"So what do we do?" Alice asks.

Aaron slings his bag over his shoulder. "We'll have to travel like Chips."

We skip breakfast and locate the road, hiking alongside it. We still walk between the cover of trees, but we stay close to the pavement, watching it closely so we know where we're going. Aaron wears his sunglasses now, hiding his scarred face and eye.

After about an hour's worth of walking, we take a break on the roadside. Aaron winces, rubbing his leg with his eyes squeezed shut as he takes a seat on a boulder.

"You okay?" I ask.

He nods. "Yeah. I'm fine."

"I don't believe you."

"What do you want me to say, Voclain? No? That my leg's on fire? That I'm miserable?" He keeps rubbing the wound site, massaging it with his knuckles, then sighs. "Sorry. I'll be fine."

I open my mouth to ask if there's anything I can do to help, but I close it when I realize that's a stupid question. There isn't anything I can do about his pain. "At least let me carry your bags."

He coughs. "No."

I take his satchel anyway, slinging it over my shoulder.

Before he has the chance to threaten me, a silver minivan starts to approach.

Quickly, he takes off his sunglasses, putting them on me instead. "What—"

"Shut up." He fixes my hair, then untucks his so that parts of it cover his eye and scar. "My face is less noticeable than yours."

He takes out his regular glasses and wears them, and although they draw attention away from his identifying features, they're not invisible. I blink, adjusting to the dark lenses, but the world still looks blurry through the haze of his prescription.

The minivan comes to a halt, then shifts into reverse, rolling back until it comes to a final stop in front of us.

We rise to our feet quickly, putting away our things and hiding anything that might look suspicious. Aaron stands in front of me to cover my face.

We stand there in a painful, smiling silence, waiting for something to happen. My heart races as the window rolls down.

An older man with graying hair and a mustache sticks his head out. He wears a faded brown cap with a fish on it. "You kids need a ride?"

"Yes," Aaron says quickly. I shoot him a look, but he stands in front of me, so he can't see it. I hit his arm instead.

"What?" he whispers under his breath. "You really think I can walk another hour like this?"

"Don't you know *anything*? *Never. Hitchhike.* That's like, the first thing my parents taught me."

"If he pulls a knife on us, I've got seven. Worst case scenario, we've just gained a car."

"You wanna *steal his car*?"

"It's better than getting murdered."

We file into the car with fake grins. Beau takes shotgun, and I climb in first, sitting against the left window. Aaron gets in after me, followed by Lori and Alice, who share a buckle. It's cramped, but I know Aaron is right. We need to be efficient here, and with his leg and the smoke, we shouldn't be hiking through the woods. *This is our current best option.*

The first stretch of the ride is silent, save for Aaron's coughs. The man hums to himself, tapping his fingers on the wheel cheerfully to a country song playing over the radio. The song makes Aaron's shoulders tense.

"I can hardly remember the last time I picked up hitch-hikers," the man says. "Sure ain't as common as it used to be. Especially around these parts."

"You've picked up hitch-hikers before?" Beau asks.

"Oh yeah." He nods. "I used to be a truck driver. Traveled a lot for work. Now I mostly do it for hunting."

Aaron's nose crinkles.

"So what brings you young folks to this neck of the woods?"

"We're students conducting a research project on the migratory habits of lesser scaups," Lori says.

Aaron gives her a look.

"Alright." The man shrugs. "The name's Herman, by the way."

Beau offers him a handshake, his expression serious. "I'm Hubert."

The man shakes his hand, then returns his attention to the road. "So tell me about these migratory patterns."

No one says a word. From the corner of my eye, I can see Lori squeeze Alice's hand, their faces pale.

"Lesser scaups are migratory waterfowl that can be found in the Olympic National Forest during their annual migration," I say.

Aaron raises a brow in my direction.

I take a deep breath, going over what I've read about them in my mind, scanning every page of the book I'd found as a kid in the McLellan's library as though I'm seeing them clearly. "They typically arrive here in the fall, seeking refuge in the wetlands and freshwater bodies within the forest. As winter approaches, many of them will continue their journey southward to warmer regions, making these woods an important stopover point in their migratory route."

The car goes quiet, and we all hold our breath.

The man laughs, and I suppress a sigh of relief. "You're like a walking textbook."

"She sure is." Beau forces a grin, then glances back at me briefly, worry in his gaze. *He's trying to take the man's attention away from me.* "So, Herman.

Tell me about your uh... hunting trips."

Herman studies me through the rear-view mirror. His brow furrows, and he squints, as though he's realizing he might have seen my face before. Aaron notices—and he puts his arm around me. He leans over slowly, casually bringing his mouth to my left ear, blocking my view of the driver in the mirror. I'm about to ask him what he's doing, but he whispers before I get the chance, his breath tickling my neck. "Play along. He's watching."

He's hiding my face.

Something about his arm around me and the closeness of his mouth reminds me of last summer—of breaking into my dad's office, and the act we played when we got caught.

"What are you doing?"

"Pretending to whisper," he says. "How's the weather down there?"

"I'll stab you."

"You keep saying that." He looks down at me. Adrenaline salts my tongue and jumpstarts my pulse. I can feel the driver looking. "Can I kiss you?"

What?

My face warms, and I can feel it turning red. *This is just an act,* I remind myself. We want to make the driver look away.

It's only Aaron.

"Alright."

He brings his face closer—and he kisses the top of my forehead.

We remain like that for a moment, staring until Aaron pulls his face away from mine with a faux smirk, but he still keeps it close, looking down at me as I look up at him.

I steal a glance of the driver's expression in the rear-view mirror. He rolls his eyes at us and shifts his focus back to the road.

Aaron pulls away, removing his arm. He shifts slightly to the right, so there is an inch of space between our shoulders and knees, which don't touch. While the driver's attention is gone, I put my hood on, bring my collar up to my face, and rest my head against the window, pretending to sleep.

But behind my borrowed shades, I watch the driver closely with open eyes. If he recognizes me, he doesn't act like it. He chats with Beau about trucks and hunting and other things I tune out.

After a while, I can't help but shift my focus to Aaron. He assumes I'm asleep, and he can't see me staring behind the sunglasses. But I study him anyway, trying to understand.

It's just Aaron. It was just an act.

Then why was I so...

Herman pulls over to the roadside, putting the van in park.

Lori and Alice exchange unsure glances, and I peel my head from the window.

"Why are we stopping?" Beau asks.

Herman doesn't say anything. Instead, he opens the door and climbs out. We exchange puzzled glances and do the same, stepping out of the vehicle. We stand there in a dirt clearing, wind whipping our hair. No one speaks.

Herman stares at Aaron, and he pulls out a Yesterday gun.

Every drop of blood in my body turns to ice.

He's a hunter. Of course he has a gun on him. But hunting isn't a thing anymore. Even with Immunity, no Chip is allowed to participate in a sport involving the use of weapons. And this man is definitely not Immune—or Unseen.

My stomach twists when I realize exactly what kind of prey he must hunt out here.

"It's April," Herman says. "You're gonna have a hard time finding a lesser scaup around here this time of year. They're late migrants; they're moving north."

Aaron blinks. "Uh... sorry?"

Herman aims the gun at him.

"Whoa, whoa." Aaron raises his palms. "Let's put the gun down."

"I know who you are," Herman says. "You're the guy on the news. The traitor with the scar."

"I don't know what you're talking about."

My gut lurches when the man steps toward me. He takes off my shades, then yanks down my hood, gripping my collar. "And I think I know exactly who this is."

"*Back off.*" Aaron steps in front of me and shoves the man's arm away. "You're right. It's me. Great job. What do you want, an award?"

"Watch it," Herman warns.

Aaron points to his scar. "I'm the one you want here, alright? This girl isn't who you think she is. Lavender Voclain ran off. That's why we're out here—to try and find her before she does something stupid."

Herman doesn't say a word.

"Just take me and let them go. I'm sure I have a bounty too. That's what you want, right?" Aaron steps closer. "Better yet—I'll lead you right to her. Then you can get the bounty for the both of us."

The man looks at Aaron, then at the rest of us, as though he's really considering it. The wind blows.

"I couldn't give a damn about that bounty." Herman lifts the gun and presses it against Aaron's forehead. "What I want is for you traitors to leave my country the hell alone."

From the corner of my eye, something moves. I glance at the car to see Alice sneaking into it from the other side, climbing into the driver's seat. She notices me staring and gives me a look. *We need to stall him.*

Herman places his finger over the trigger.

"Wanna hear a fun fact about scaups?"

The man turns around to face me. Aaron's eyes widen, searing into me in warning, but I ignore him.

"They primarily feed on mollusks and aquatic invertebrates, which they find by diving underwater. What's interesting is that in Western Washington, particularly in areas like Puget Sound, they've adapted to consume a significant amount of saltwater prey like clams and mussels. Which is quite unusual for freshwater ducks."

Herman clenches his jaw.

"In my professional opinion, this adaptability showcases their *remarkable* ability to thrive in various habitats and make the most of available food sources during their winter stays in the region."

Herman points the gun at me now. "I'd stop talking if I were you."

"Or what?" I laugh. "You're not gonna shoot me. If you kill me, you'll piss off the Corps. They want me alive, remember?"

I walk forward, right into the end of the gun, pressing my own forehead against it. Aaron looks like he's going to vomit. "But I don't think you have the guts to shoot me anyway."

We all stand completely still, holding our breath as the wind whistles on, tangling my hair, brushing it back so that I can see the man clearly. His face contorts with anger. His finger traces the trigger. I squeeze my eyes shut.

The sound of the bullet cracks through the sky like thunder.

I wait for something to happen. For a light to appear, or a tunnel, or whatever it is you see when you're dead. But when I open my eyes again, I'm still standing.

In the center of Herman's forehead is a red circle from which a thick red liquid spouts like syrup from a tap. He falls forward like a plank of wood, and I dodge his corpse just in time.

Beau stands behind him, a smoking gun in his hand.

We are frozen until Aaron hurries to my side. He places both hands on my shoulders, gripping me like I might dissolve into thin air if he doesn't hold on tight enough. "You alright?"

"I'm fine." I nod, suddenly out of breath. "You?"

His arms move, and I almost expect him to pull me into a hug. He gives my shoulder a squeeze instead, plucks his sunglasses from Herman's dead hands, and stares at him. His gaze hardens at the sight of the blood.

"What the hell, Beau?" Lori shouts, running to the fallen man's side. She reaches out to check his pulse, but decides against it when she sees the bullet hole in his brain. She whips her head around, standing up and marching toward him with a glare. "You *killed* him?"

Alice climbs out of the car, staring at the man, then at Beau, gaze sharp. "I had it handled. We could have taken his car and left him here."

"He recognized Eddie," Beau says, not even mentioning Aaron. "Can't have him reporting a sighting to the Corps."

"He didn't have to die," I say.

"I was saving your life, alright? A bit of thanks would be nice." Beau scoffs. "And who knows how many Unseen he's *hunted* out here?"

Aaron's jaw tightens, neck muscles twitching.

"They'll see that this man's tracker went off and send Cleaners here," Lori says. "Maybe even Officers if they find it suspicious enough. Or *Agents*."

Beau tucks the gun into a holster I didn't notice he'd been wearing, hidden under his brown sherpa-lined jacket. He climbs into the driver's seat, face grim as he starts the car. "Then we'd better get moving."

321

R. STELLER

Saturday, April 6

♪ YOURS TO STEAL - GREYHOUNDS ♪

Living in King's safe house isn't as horrible as I thought it'd be.

He's nice enough, though he isn't around much. Heron comes by —with groceries and movies I don't watch—more often than Ian does.

Kingfisher, I correct myself. *That's what they want you to start calling him.*

I appreciate the solitude for the most part. Some days it feels unbearable, and it takes a lot of pacing and several cups of coffee to keep my mind from spiraling.

But what usually pulls me out of that is the fact that out here, I don't have to worry about pretending. Out here, I am safe from the suit they want me to wear. I can just be *me* for as long as I know how to be, for whatever time I have left to be Ren, and not R. Steller.

I suppose Ren is already gone. Thanks to Kingfisher's broadcast, the public already thinks I'm dead, so it made more sense to mark me as so in their database. R. Steller is more than my potential ranking name, should I get promoted to an Agent after all; it's my legal name too.

R. Steller. The name Canary assigned to me after my hearing doesn't quite feel like it belongs to me yet. I still don't understand the point of these ranking names beyond the purpose of secrecy, and it's hard to get used to a new name when no one is around much to call you by it. Although technically, I have yet to earn the right to be called R. Steller.

"We will give you your ranking name, and you will shadow Agent Kingfisher, who will be your supervising Agent, should your initiation be successful," Canary said. *"If all goes well and the occupation is fruitful, you will be rewarded with a First Rank in the Agency Division of the American Chaser Corps. I will decide when you are ready for initiation, a right you will have to earn with my complete trust, given your unique situation."*

Every now and then, when it's morning and I'm staring out the window wall in the living room, breathing in the Puget Sound, I stare at my reflection too, and I view it with the new name on my tongue.

"R. Steller," I whisper to myself, cup of coffee in my hands as I study my reflection in the glass. The name tastes sour and I frown, returning my focus to the Sound instead.

I sip from my mug, feeling the coffee's warmth travel down my throat. I think about the person I used to be, back when I could recognize my own reflection. When my hair was an uncut mess, and not parted neatly down the middle. Not once did the Ren of before ever consider the possibility of drinking coffee.

Now, I need it every morning.

And every night, when I'm too frightened of what I'll have to face in my sleep, and would rather wait out the hours in front of this same window, pretending I can see the Sound in the dark.

A knock grabs my attention.

I furrow my brows at the door. *Heron doesn't knock like that.* His knocks have an obnoxious swing to them, like a song. This knock consists of exactly three perfectly timed intervals, emitting from a higher section of the wood than Heron could reasonably reach.

I wait for too long and hear a series of beeps as someone enters the passcode.

Kingfisher and Heron walk in together, their faces unreadable. Today, they are fully decked out in Agent attire, Eyes and all.

"The occupation was successful," King says. "Get ready to go."

Friday, April 12

Heron and King haven't said anything all morning.

Even as we travel up the elevator—even when their white doors slide open with a hiss—they don't utter as much as a single word. They simply watch with shaded eyes, waiting for me to move.

I take a deep breath, and I step out of the elevator.

When I turn around to give them one last look—one silent plea for any unspoken indication of what to expect—they are already gone. There is nothing but an empty wall, white to match the floors.

I stare at the wall for a long time until a voice calls my name.

"R. Steller?"

I spin around.

I'm at the end of a white corridor so long I can't see the end of it. A few yards away from me, Agent Sparrow stands there waiting with her arms crossed.

"Come with me." She turns to walk down the corridor, and there is nothing I can do but follow her.

I remain a few feet behind her as she leads the way, heels clicking against the hallway's spotless floors. The walls are an endless blank canvas. The ceiling is too, save for a few circular lights that are so white they almost appear blue. They burn my eyes.

I'm not sure how much time has passed when I finally see the corridor's end, where there is only a narrow door without a knob. Agent Sparrow pauses in front of it. A faint buzz in my left eye tells me we're being scanned, and the door slides open.

But Sparrow doesn't walk through. Instead, she stands next to it, waiting for me to enter first. It's unlit, so I can't see what awaits me.

I hold my breath when I walk through.

"Eyes all around."

That is the very last thing I hear before the door slides closed, taking the last bit of light with it.

For a moment, I stand in total darkness. I trace my thumb along my left index finger, where my father's ring usually resides. But I left it at the safe house, and I can't say why.

Don't go there. Something tells me that if I do, I won't have the chance to put that ring on again.

A light turns on.

There is only one—a round spotlight embedded into the ceiling that is not strong enough to illuminate the whole room, leaving every corner and edge shadowed. A ring of light shines down on a single white chair.

I walk forward slowly, inspecting it before taking a seat. It's stiff and cold. I feel another twitch in my left eye, and a robotic voice fills the room.

Welcome, Ren McLellan.

The sound of my real name makes me flinch.

I hear another sound and glance at the ceiling to see a single tile slide open. From it extends a long white pole with what appears to be a pair of white goggles attached to the end. The goggles stop when they are perfectly aligned with my eyes.

When I stare into them, I'm immediately shown a display of an empty white room so realistic I could be standing in it.

A portion of the virtual room's back wall slides open, and in walks a woman with long red hair and bags beneath her eyes. Her lips look chapped, her skin pale. She trembles as she walks inside, and I notice a metallic collar locked around her neck. The door closes behind her, and she stands in the center of the room.

A voice comes from the goggle's speakers.

Welcome to the first phase of your initiation. Should you complete all three phases perfectly, the ranking name R. Steller will be yours to keep as an Agent of the Chaser Corps.

Phase One requires you to judge a series of scenarios designed to test your knowledge on the Nightjade Order, your decision-making skills, and your compatibility with the unique responsibilities of the Agency Division.

Proceed wisely, and you will be rewarded.

The voice ceases, and words appear in the bottom left corner of the screen.

SUBJECT: KRJ-QD-3C

I take a closer look at the woman, who appears to be in her thirties. I squint to get a clearer view of her face, and when I do, I realize she's crying.

"My name is Karina." Her voice is raspy and quiet. "I have been found guilty of treason."

The text on the screen shifts, replaced with two different options.

A – Seek more information
B – Exterminate subject

My breath catches in my throat when I read the second option.

Please indicate your decision.

I swallow. "Option A."

There is a pause, and the woman speaks again.

"I failed to report my father for smuggling weapons to Underground traitors," she says. "In my failing, I myself was committing an act of treason against the Presidency and the laws of the Nightjade Order, which are in place to protect us."

I think back to the Yesterday guns we used at the Cut—the very same kind I used to send a bullet into Aaron's leg. The kind Eddie used to stain the sea red with Carmody's blood.

"I have..." Tears well in her eyes, and she can't finish the sentence. She gasps, squeezing her eyes shut, grabbing at the collar around her neck as she folds forward.

My eyes widen. *She's wearing a shock collar.*

My pulse quickens, stomach churning. *It's only a simulation*, I remind myself. *You're not in the room. You're only watching it happen. It isn't real. They're just testing you.*

"I have four members in my immediate family. A husband, a son, and two daughters. Ages thirty-nine, sixteen, fourteen, and"—she chokes on the last word—"eleven."

More choices appear on the screen.

> *A – Exterminate subject and immediate family*
> *B – Exterminate subject only*
> *C – Sentence subject to a lifetime of tomb service*
> *D – Subject is not guilty and should be spared*

Every bone in my body screams the fourth option, but choosing it will take down my score—or disqualify me completely.

I know the answer they want to hear.

It's not real.

"Option A."

The text disappears. Within the virtual room, a table rises from the ground, displaying a black Nightjade gun, a dagger, a rope, and a Nightjade syringe.

The voice speaks again.

Choose a weapon.

I swallow, hands shaking. *It's only a simulation.*

"Nightjade syringe."

I expect a mechanical arm like the one holding these goggles to appear —for it to take the syringe and bring an end to this character's life. But instead, the sound of another door opening hisses through the goggles' speakers, and a man walks in from the other side of the room. The woman stares across at him in horror.

A mechanical arm does appear after all—but it is not her neck the syringe plunges into.

The man crumples to the ground.

The woman shrieks, then gasps, grabbing at her throat. Her eyes remain open. Silent tears stream down her cheeks.

Someone in a white suit of armor removes the corpse.

This isn't real.

The weapons remain. I wait for the table to disappear, but it doesn't.

Choose a weapon.

My arms tremble. "Nightjade gun."

This one must be for her.

The woman's eyes peel even wider as someone else walks in. This time, I see the back of a young boy. My stomach lurches. *This is her son.*

A bullet hits the boy's arm, and he crumples too.

The sound of her screaming shreds at the inside of my skull. I want to close my eyes and cover my ears and throw the goggles to the ground, but I know that isn't an option.

This is just a game.

I know her daughter will be walking in next when the voice asks me to make another choice. If they're sending them in by age as they have been, it will be the older one.

The knife would be quicker, right? A clean swipe to the throat—no suffering. No pain.

I save the knife for last, and I choose the rope.

But when the door opens, it is not a fifteen year old girl whose back I see. This girl is only eleven.

I bring a hand to my mouth to keep myself from vomiting. When the mechanical arm begins to prepare the noose, I close my eyes. *I can't watch.*

The voice blares through the speakers.

Open your eyes, Ren. This is your only warning.

I open my eyes.

I carve my nails into my own skin, and I watch the extermination unfold.

The last death is as quick as I expected it to be.

The mother has screamed herself to death. The collar did its job well.

The scene changes, shifting the camera to show a separate room with a new character. This one is a young man with messy brown hair. He can't be any older than I am. He glares straight ahead, jaw clenched. His arms are bound by white handcuffs, but he wears no shock collar.

SUBJECT: TPB-KC-45

The presented subject will not be able to speak freely. Before detainment, he cut out his own tongue.

He opens his mouth, and my gut cartwheels.

The subject was once an honorable member of the Chaser Corps, serving the Officer Division. In addition to failing to exterminate his assignment, he was also found guilty of hiding her within his own home for six months—a feat only made possible because her tracker had been removed. He is guilty of treason. What should his fate be?

A – Sentence subject to a lifetime of Tomb service
B – Exterminate subject
C – Pardon subject, then promote to the Agency Division

A chill weaves between every disc in my spine. I scan over the third option again and again, just to make sure I read it correctly.

I blink, then read the last option.

D – Request more information

"Option D."

The subject's assignment managed to Run before his detainment. However, since his tongue has been removed, he cannot go through Extraction. He is no longer able to provide information. He is no longer useful to the Corps. His purpose has been served.

What will be his fate?

My hands shake. The message is clear, and I know my only choice. *He's not even eligible for Tomb service.*

"Option B."

The man doesn't flinch when a Nightjade gun is inserted into his neck. His body is disposed of quickly.

The goggles shut off, and the metal pole rises back up into the ceiling. I wait in bone-chilling silence until the voice comes back.

Congratulations. You have successfully completed Phase One.

Relief floods through me as one of the floor tiles next to my chair opens. A mechanical arm rises through it, with a needle attached to the end. My heart thuds against my ribcage as it grows nearer.

Please place your left arm against its rest.

I do as it says.

I force myself to hold still, keeping my eyes pried open as the needle begins to draw something on me. After what feels like hours, the machine pulls away, disappearing into the floor again.

I study my wrist. Beneath my left Card—my Ace of Spades—is an outline of three hearts in a row, each no bigger than a dime.

They've given me a tattoo.

The light shuts off, and I wait in a dark, devitalizing silence, trying everything in my power not to think of the simulations, or what I witnessed.

There is nowhere for me to run—no bathroom sink for me to heave into. There is only me and a cold, empty room.

The outline of a door lights up. I stand and approach it, and it opens automatically, leading me into a separate room. This one is well-lit, and I walk into the light.

The door shuts behind me as I take in my surroundings. This room is circular, with the same seamless white floors, walls, and ceiling the rest of the building is composed of—save for a black circle embedded in the floor.

Please step into the ring.

Slowly, I do as the voice says. I stand in the middle of the circle, waiting, until a mechanical arm sprouts from the floor, offering me a pair of sleek sunglasses.

Here is where you will shed your old name and earn your Eyes. You have already proven to the Corps that you can exterminate a stranger.

I shudder, trying not to think about training. The man in that white room. The syringe I stuck in his neck.

But can you exterminate a face you recognize?

A door opens on the other side. Someone walks in, escorted by two Officers. There is a cloth sack over the person's head.

Please put on your Eyes, and do not remove them.

I hesitate before putting on the glasses.

The Officers remove the sack before exiting the doors, leaving me alone with a face I know better than any other.

My own.

I blink, every breath caught in my lungs. The person standing in front of me has my exact face. My black hair, my brown eyes, my height, my build —every physical attribute is identical to mine.

But his lips are sewn shut, and there is a metal collar around his neck.

The ground shakes. My knees buckle and I steady myself as the circle we stand on begins to rise out of the ground, growing taller and taller until it stops, creating a platform that must be ten feet in the air. I glance around me, looking for stairs or a ladder. There is no way down.

Phase Two will now begin.

The person with my face lunges at me, knocking me onto my back. My head cracks into the floor, and the room spins as he throws a punch directly into my stomach—right where my still-healing scar is. I see stars and I turn over, swallowing the urge to vomit as he punches me again.

Why aren't they doing anything? He's wearing a shock collar—why isn't it going off?

My eyes widen. This is supposed to happen.

I writhe out of his grip, crawling back so far I'm only a foot away from the platform's edge when I finally manage to scramble to my feet. He swings at me again, but this time, I manage to dodge it.

I don't want to fight him. I don't want to hurt him. But I don't seem to have another choice.

I punch him in the face—my face. I hit him square in the nose that looks alarmingly close to my own. He calls out in pain through his sewn lips, bringing a hand up to his face to catch the blood that trickles down. Drops of it fall from his hands, splattering onto the floor.

This only seems to make him more angry. His fist slams into the side of my face, nearly knocking off my Eyes. I swing my own punch. This one lands. I swing another, and another, and he falls onto his back.

I pin him to the ground, my palms flattened against his chest as he writhes beneath me. I punch him again, once in the face and once in the stomach until I am kneeling on his knees, and he is under my control.

I've done what I'm supposed to do. I've overpowered him. There is nothing else for me to do but wait for an arm to appear with a Nightjade syringe, so I can carry out the extermination they clearly want me to complete.

But nothing happens.

A minute passes by, and the man gathers enough strength to throw me off him, pinning me on my back instead. He punches me in the gut, knocking the wind out of me. Before I have the chance to blink or even breathe, both of his hands are gripped around my neck, squeezing as hard as he can.

The room spins as the air slowly seeps out of me. My throat burns and I can already feel bruises forming. Spots appear in my vision, which blurs beneath the tint of my shades. I claw at his hands until there is blood underneath my fingernails, trying to pry his grip. But nothing works.

My face is all I can see. Mine, but not mine. *How is this even possible?* My eyes widen. *The Eyes.*

I've already used a pair before; I know they function like a computer. There must be something programmed into them to make this man's face appear as my own—some sort of computer-generated imagery. I stare closer at his face, and I notice that one thing is off.

I have a freckle on the lower left side of my neck. This man does not.

I have minutes. Seconds, maybe. And if I don't act, they will be my last.

I stop trying to pry his hands off me. I think of Eddie, and that night at the playground.

I jam two fingers into his eyes. I can feel the tissue stretch around my nails, gelatinous and sticky. I push them farther until something bursts.

He screams behind his stitched lips, pulling away. I feel bile rise in my throat and swallow it down, coughing and gasping for air, inhaling every painful breath I can.

I overpower him again. This time, when he is pinned to the ground, hands covering his eyes—my eyes—I wrap my hands around his neck. Every ounce of rage and desperation pours into my fingers, and I squeeze his throat so tightly my nails carve into his skin. I feel something snap beneath my grip.

He stops struggling.

I sit back on my knees. His lifeless hands fall away from his face, revealing his mangled eyes.

I lean over, flatten my hands against the floor, and vomit.

My shoulders convulse, and I sob.

I didn't know this man. I don't know his name, or his face. And I grieve him like I have lost myself.

I'm not sure how long I remain like that until the platform lowers back into the ground. I wait for someone to come and remove the body, but no one does. Instead, the voice comes back again through invisible speakers.

Congratulations. You have successfully completed Phase Two.

A mechanical arm appears, offering me a glistening knife coated in blood. Reluctantly, I take the weapon and watch the arm disappear.

I turn the blade over in my hands, inspecting it. Something about it seems familiar, and I think about where I could have seen it.

The knife falls out of my hands, spinning across the floor.

I crawl back, desperate to get away from the body, away from the dagger I wish I didn't recognize. I bump into the wall, then go still. My breath catches in my sore throat. Slowly, I pull my knees to my chest.

The first phase was never a simulation.

Those were real people, and I decided their fate.

They would have died anyway, a desperate voice inside my head tells me. *The Corps would have used them to initiate another Agent exactly like you. There was nothing you could do to save them.*

I press my forehead against my knees, sobbing, squeezing my eyes closed. I lean my head back, clutching my hair in fistfuls, ready to scream, but my throat is bruised and scratched, and no sound comes out. I punch the wall and feel my knuckles crack. My blood stains it red. I punch it again, and again, and again, and—

Retrieve the knife.

I pause.

My arms shake. I press my lips into a thin line, eyes unblinking, so wide I wonder if they might pop out of my skull. I rise to my feet, clenching both hands into fists, no matter how badly my broken fingers burn. I turn around and stare at the ceiling.

What was the point? I want to scream. But I still can't force a single sound. *What game are you playing?*

The voice speaks again.

This is your last chance to retrieve the knife.

Every breath is shaky as I walk toward the weapon and pause in front of it.

Phase Three will now begin.

I bend over and take the knife. The metal handle is cold to the touch, like ice, or lifeless flesh.

The truth lies within yourself, Ren McLellan. Do you have what it takes to retrieve it?

I stand there, every inch of me trembling, swallowing the urge to vomit for a second time.

I kneel next to the body. The body with my face, my shredded eyes, my stitched lips. For some reason, I am no longer crying.

I cut it open.

Time stands still. I'm not sure how much of it has passed when I finish sawing open his torso. I hold my breath and reach inside with my bare hands, until I find what they want me to discover.

I pull out a bright red poker chip, its surface and my hands stained with blood. I wipe the liquid off onto the dead man's shirt, and realize the chip isn't red after all, but white, with a *1* engraved into it.

I hold it in my palm and stare, unable to believe it's really there at all.

Congratulations, Agent R. Steller. Welcome to the Agency Division.

Canary's office is a cold, empty room, containing nothing but a mahogany desk with perfectly sharp corners and edges. The entire back wall is made of glass. Beyond it I can see evergreens, and farther than that, the Sound.

But I am trapped here. He may have been the one to invite me in, but I am locked within a cage I created with my own two hands.

The room is dimly lit. The only source of light comes from outside of the glass, soft and gray. I stand in front of the desk and place the poker chip on its surface. It's still stained red.

This is what you wanted, right? I try to speak, but I still can't manage to get a sound out.

Behind his shades, Canary stares at the chip with his nose crinkled, like I'm offering him a dead animal I found on the side of the road. He studies the bruises on my neck, then meets my gaze. We both wear our Eyes.

"Keep it. You earned it." He flashes a fake, fleeting grin. "It has your name on it after all."

Reluctantly, I pick up the chip and flip it over. Sure enough, *R. Steller* is engraved in bold letters on the other side.

"That is your badge. You are required to have it on you at all times, or risk extermination in the event that you are caught without it. We take imposters very seriously."

I swallow painfully and place it in my pocket.

"So, Agent Steller." Canary rises to his feet, placing his hands behind his back as he paces the room slowly. "How does it feel, now that you have earned your name?"

I can't speak, and he glances at my bruised neck again with a chuckle. He walks to the window and stares through it. "It's a lovely day, isn't it?"

I study the view. The screen of my Eyes automatically corrects my vision so that I am not affected by their tint, and still, everything is coated in a dark blue haze. Like it's about to rain, but the sky isn't ready for it yet.

Canary looks back at me, and I realize he wants me to join him, so I do. We stand there in silence for a while. He places his hands in his pockets, but I keep mine stiff at my sides.

He turns to glance at me. "Do you know why we have ranking names?"

I shake my head, and he studies the view again. "Secrecy is the obvious reason, which I'm sure you've already realized. Signature is another. Every region has their own. We are the Pacific Region." He glances at me. "You know what ours is, correct?"

I turn to face him and manage to choke out the word. My voice hoarse. "Birds."

He chuckles. "Birds."

It's quiet for a moment until he speaks again.

"Why birds, you might be wondering?" He shrugs. "Why Cards? Why anything?"

He looks at me, waiting for an answer. I don't have one.

"Because it is simply the way it has been done." He stares at the sea of evergreens beneath us. "As long as a system works, we keep it, until it no longer suits us."

I nod.

"Have you ever seen a Steller's jay, Agent?"

I pause, then nod. *Once, on a trip to the river with my father and Margot.*

"They're resourceful little birds. Many folklore systems view them as a symbol of adaptability. They embody hope amid ruin and a strong instinct for survival. They possess a great amount of talent for resolve, but a talent that needs to be developed and used wisely.

"They are incredibly cunning. They raid nests. They are opportunistic feeders known to steal food from other animals. They can be rather bold when provoked, defending their territory with aggression and tenacity."

He pauses. "They are also known to be deceitful."

My stomach lurches. Canary observes me as a birdwatcher might, his face riddled with curiosity.

"They have been observed using mimicry to deceive other species. They can copy the calls of birds of prey to scare other creatures away from food sources." Canary chuckles, and his grin quickly fades. "While their boldness can be useful when it comes to scavenging and territory defense, it can also put them at greater risk of predation. Do you know why?"

I stare at him, then force the word out. "No."

"Because they are less cautious, they often find themselves facing dangerous encounters with predators from whom more timid birds might have stayed hidden."

I nod, studying the view again.

"Some view the Steller's jay as a warning; others see them as a sign of good luck, or fortune to come. They are ruthless survivalists who will stop at nothing to keep themselves from going hungry, and they are fueled by a motivation that just so happens to be their primary flaw." He glances at me. "Do you know what that is?"

I shake my head.

He grins. "Greed."

My face pales. He notices, chuckling again, before his gaze drifts back to the sea of fir and pine.

"Welcome to the Agency, R. Steller."

EDDIE

Sunday, April 21
84 Beds Made

♪ CARNIVAL - KEVIN DEVINE ♪

The drive is almost a silent one.

None of us say a word while Beau steers the minivan, his shoulders tense. Wind reaches through the open driver's seat window, tousling his auburn hair. He keeps his knuckles tight and his eyes fixed straight ahead.

The minivan must be decades old. The radio seems to be stuck on the same static-corrupted country station the vehicle's owner had been humming along to only an hour before. It crackles so much I can hardly make out what it's saying. We haven't figured out how to turn it down.

Aside from the radio and the roll of wheels against pavement, there is no sound.

It's past noon by the time we approach the outskirts of a small city. We abandon the stolen car in the woods nearby and walk our way into town.

Eerily enough, it reminds me of End Harbor, minus the ghosts. Townsfolk weave in and out of rustic brick buildings, carrying cups of coffee and shopping bags so full of books and trinkets my chest aches. I didn't realize

I'd miss the little things so much.

No one pays us too much attention. A carnival of sorts seems to be operating in a grassy park downtown, where couples and families wander about, carrying spools of cotton candy and oversized stuffed bears. We stand in the middle of the sidewalk as people walk around us, too busy talking and laughing to find anything wrong with our appearances.

"Looks like there's an event going on or something," Beau says.

"Is that a bad thing?" Alice asks.

"I think we've lucked out," Aaron says. "The Chasers will be concentrated over there on crowd duty."

"It'll be easier to blend in too," Lori adds.

My forehead wrinkles. "What do you think they're celebrating?"

Aaron shrugs. "Beats me."

Alice pokes Lori's arm. "Can we go check it out?"

Aaron laughs, then looks her dead in the eye. "Absolutely not."

We walk through town with our heads low. I have my hood on and give Aaron back his shades, since that man recognized his scar, and let him hold onto my arm for support to conceal his limp.

The clouds that once loomed above our heads have dissolved now, letting buttery pools of sunlight coat the town. Everything in sight glistens with remnants of downpour, and the smell of damp pavement and fried food lingers in the air. We find an empty automated train station and head over to the map to analyze the routes.

Aaron stands in front of it, arms folded. "We need to get out of here as quickly as possible."

"To go visit Grandma," Lori adds, eyes wide. *We're in Chip territory now.*

"Yes. Grandma is in dire need of assistance. So we need to find the quickest way to get as far from here as possible. Before Grandma thinks we're not coming and starts looking for us."

"The next train to Seattle doesn't leave until tomorrow," I say.

"We can't wait that long. And we shouldn't put ourselves directly in the middle of a city that populated, anyway." Aaron studies the map, tilting his head to try and make sense of the routes, rubbing his thumb over his lip. "What's the soonest we can get out of here?"

"Two hours."

"Where?"

"Brim Creek."

"Never heard of it."

I study the map, realizing how close the destination is to Silver Fir. *But Aaron can't know I know about that.* "It's near Snoqualmie."

Aaron flinches, glancing at me, then back at the map. "Really?"

I nod.

"And that's our only option?"

"If we wanna get out of here before sunrise, then yeah."

He purses his lips, inhaling and exhaling sharply. "Brim Creek it is."

Beau walks up to the nearest kiosk, pulling out a thick wad of cash to pay for all of our tickets.

Lori frowns. "Where'd you get so much money?"

"Had some lying around." He shrugs, and she gives him a look. "What? It's useless where we're from."

He hands each of us our tickets, and we exit the station.

We find a diner downtown and step inside. Less than a dozen people are scattered about, sitting at dark orange leather booths, chatting and filling the air with the scraping of forks against ceramic. The diner's wood panel walls are covered in old clocks and license plates from the Yesterdays, and faded photographs of the same forest we see through the windows.

We take a seat at one of the booths. Aaron makes sure I slide onto the bench first so my face is the most hidden, covering his own by opening a menu. Beau slides in next to him, and they elbow each other for more room as Lori and Alice sit across from us.

Alice tilts her head upward, eyes wide, studying everything from the ceiling tiles to the cat-shaped clock whose tail and eyes flick back and forth with every ticking second. She reaches out to touch it, and Lori gently nurtures her hand away as a young waitress wearing jeans and a blue button-up shirt approaches.

"What can I get started for you all?"

I lean my head against the wall, hood still on, pretending to sleep.

Beau clears his throat, drawing the attention to him, over-pronouncing things as he speaks. "I will have the... Big Bear Breakfast, please."

Aaron manages to keep a straight face.

"And what side would you like with that? We've got gravy, biscuits, and we've got whole wheat toast."

"Biscuits."

She takes note of his order, then nods toward Aaron. "What's with the sunglasses?"

He lifts up his head to face her. "Hmm?"

"You shouldn't wear those inside, you know." She grins. "It's rude."

"I'm just protecting myself, sweetheart." Aaron smirks, resting an arm on the back of the booth. "You're trying to blind me with that smile, aren't you?"

Beyond all odds, I resist the urge to vomit. Lori appears to be overcoming the same challenge.

The waitress clicks her pen. "What are you having?"

Aaron tilts his head, studying the menu before setting it down. "I'll take a green tea and a salad. No bacon, please."

She raises a brow. "No bacon?"

"I'm vegetarian."

She nods toward his arm. "You don't look like one."

Now Aaron's face is the one turning red. He laughs nervously. "Is that a bad thing?"

"Not at all."

"He works out," Beau adds. Aaron kicks him under the table, and Alice has to cover her face to avoid laughing.

"I can tell." The waitress winks, then turns to face me. "And what can I get for you?"

I sink lower in my seat. "Nothing, thank you."

"You sure?" She raises a brow, then squints. "Have I seen you some-where?"

My heart races, and Aaron intervenes before I can say anything. "You know what, I was actually thinking the same thing about you. We must have met before. I swear, you look *so* familiar."

"No, I don't think so." She laughs. "I'd definitely remember you."

"Excuse me?" Alice interrupts. "I have a question about the menu."

Thank God.

"Sure."

"Would you recommend the uh..." She scans the menu. "Waffle Tower?"

"Oh, absolutely. We've got the best waffles in town, you know."

"Oh excellent. I'm a *huge* fan of waffles."

"It comes with five, is that alright with you?"

"Five waffles?" Alice raises a brow. "And how big are they?"

"Um, waffle-sized?"

Alice forces a grin. "Great. I'll have that."

Lori orders pancakes, and the waitress takes our menus before walking away.

Alice lets out her laugh now, and I glare at Aaron. "Was all that really necessary?"

"What? I was distracting her."

"You were drawing more attention to yourself."

"If someone was flirting with *you*, wouldn't you be less inclined to report them to the authorities for being suspicious?"

"Depends on how bad their flirting is."

He leans closer. "Would you report me?"

"Absolutely."

Lori snorts. "Admit it. Your ego is soaring right now."

Beau rubs Aaron's arms, raising the pitch of his voice. "*I can tell.*"

Aaron elbows him off and slouches in his seat. I roll my eyes and stare out the window, jaw clenched.

The waitress brings our food and drinks, and Beau slides me his biscuits. I nibble on pieces of it, taking sips of water from a root beer-colored plastic cup.

Alice stares at her Waffle Tower with wide eyes, jaw dropped. The waffles are much bigger than I thought they'd be, smothered in a mountain of whipped cream and sprinkled with enough blueberries to fill a pie. "What the hell is this?"

"That's what you ordered," Lori says between bites.

"You think I know what a waffle is?" Alice whispers frantically.

Aaron almost chokes on a bite of his food. "You don't know what a waffle is?"

"Dude, I grew up in..." She stops herself. "You really think my dad is the kinda guy who would make me waffles for breakfast?"

"I bet you can't eat all five of them," Beau says.

"Oh really?" Alice folds her hands across the table. "What's the wager?"

"You'll have to run around the diner a hundred times."

"Fifty."

"Deal."

"And if I *do* eat them all, you'll have to take us to the carnival and pay for an ungodly amount of tickets so I can win a teddy bear."

Aaron frowns. "No."

"Oh, come on. We'll be stuck here for at least another hour. Might as well do something while we wait."

"I don't think that's a good idea—" Aaron interrupts his own sentence with a series of coughs, this round worse than the last. He gulps a cup of water, but the coughing continues.

I glance out the window. The air isn't as bad over here, but everything is still covered in a soupy yellow haze. It's hard to believe how far the reach of smoke can extend. *It must be affecting Aaron more than the rest of us.*

"I'll be back." He stands up and coughs his way to the bathroom.

We pick at our food in silence, too hungry and nervous to say much. I eat slowly, pushing through the ever-growing knots in my gut. There is so much I want to avoid thinking about that it makes my head ache.

I hear laughter and glance over my shoulder to see Aaron leaning against the back corridor's door frame, arms crossed. The waitress talks with him, playfully hitting his shoulders.

I can tell Aaron catches me staring, even with his shades. He looks away, focusing on the waitress again. She stands on her toes to whisper something in his ear, and he blushes for a moment before laughing nervously with a nod. The real kind that shows his teeth and dimples.

The knots in my gut tighten. I look away and down the rest of my water.

Aaron returns to the booth a few minutes later, glaring at my half-eaten biscuit. "You didn't finish your food."

"I'm not hungry."

We continue to eat in quietude, and by the time we're finished, Alice is still sawing away at her waffles, unfazed by the challenge.

Aaron crinkles his nose at her. "I don't understand how you can eat whipped cream from a can."

"I don't understand how I've lived my life *without* it," she says with a mouth full of food.

To our surprise, she manages to eat the entire thing, even licking the plate clean. Beau, a man of his word, reluctantly agrees to hold up his end of the bargain.

While we wait for the check, I stare up at the TV in the corner, watching the same woodpecker cartoon from the Yesterdays that I had on in the hospital back in End Harbor. There's something alluring about the colors, though I can't hear much of the sound.

Someone switches the channel to the news, and the television shifts from animated animals to a forest being devoured by flames.

"The wildfire continues to spread, consuming both trees and abandoned structures from the Wandering. Authorities are still trying to locate the perpetrator of this disaster and urge you to stay vigilant..."

I stand, shoving past Aaron and Beau to make my way to the bathroom.

There are only two stalls, and both of them are empty. I shoulder my way through the door, fall to my knees, and vomit.

I squeeze my eyes shut, trying not to see the color orange or smell the smoke lingering in my hair, but it's no use. All I can think about is what I've done.

All of those camps, annihilated.

All of those innocent Unseen reduced to nothing but bones—and it's all my fault.

The room spins. It reeks so badly of air freshener and bright pink hand soap, every chemical scent burying its way into my skull. I vomit again, arms shaking, hot beads of saltwater blurring my eyesight and streaming down my cheeks.

I reach under my jacket, under my shirt, and I trace my left arm up and down, feeling the bumps of the scar Carmody carved into my once-smooth skin. I reach into my pocket and hold the shard of burnt mirror glass so tightly it cuts my palm.

I am as unlucky as they come.

The bathroom door swings open and shut. "You okay?"

I don't say a word as Alice walks over to the stall, knocking on the door. "Eddie?"

I heave again.

"If you don't say anything, I'm coming in. Get decent."

Alice climbs onto one of the sinks and over the top of the stall. She sees me and hops down, kneeling by my side.

We sit there in silence for a long time until she speaks, shaking her head. "God, this feels familiar."

I wipe my mouth, pulling the handle. "What do you mean?"

"You know who my dad is." She stares into the bowl, which is now filled with clean, reflective water. "After a while, living with people like that makes you sick."

I nod, feeling the bracelet on my wrist. "My dad wasn't exactly easy to be around either."

Alice looks at me. "I'm sorry."

"It's fine, I think." I sniffle, wiping my eyes with my sleeve. "I mean, I know he loved me. But it was like he was two different people, you know?"

"One minute they're laughing and joking with you at the dinner table, the next they're screaming at you for spilling the salt." Alice laughs emptily. "Then your crying is somehow insulting to them and suddenly they do *so* much for you."

I turn to look at Alice. "Yeah."

It's quiet again. We listen to the commotion outside, the scraping of forks, the laughter and chatter. It sounds muffled from here. Like we're so far away from the noise, even though the only thing separating us from it is a single door.

"Do you want to talk about it?" She asks, her voice soft. "Or whatever it is that's making you sick?"

I shake my head.

"Okay." We sit there, staring at our reflections in the toilet bowl. "I think

I'm gonna be sick too."

"Beau's bet?"

"Yep."

Somehow, I manage to laugh.

But the feeling is fleeting, and the knots remain.

The carnival is a collection of vendors and games with bright yellow stalls, filled with the echoes of loud music and laughing children. The scent of fried batter and sugar melt together with the smoke in the air, making my stomach churn. I swallow down the nausea, hugging my abdomen as Beau hands us all tickets.

"I think we should split up," he says. "Traveling in a big group would draw more attention."

"Absolutely not," Aaron says. "Unless you're trying to make us miss our train."

"Actually, splitting up might be a good idea," Lori says.

Aaron frowns. "You just wanna go off with Alice."

"Yep." Alice beams, taking Lori's arm as they waltz away with their tickets. "See ya."

"I'm gonna get some food," Beau says.

Aaron frowns. "We just ate."

"Yeah, well, I'm hungry again." He gives us a wave before disappearing into the crowd, leaving Aaron and I alone.

We stand there in silence for a moment.

Aaron shoves his tickets into his pockets. "You wanna do something?"

I shrug.

"We have tickets," he says. "We might as well use them."

We wander around with our arms crossed, glowering. Now that the sun has come out, I feel hot and cramped in my jacket, and the crowd feels like it's closing in on me. I almost wish for more rain.

"God, I hate this place," Aaron says, scrunching up his nose at the sight of someone taking a bite from a turkey leg as big as their head.

"Me too."

We stumble across what appears to be a dart-throwing booth in a quieter corner of the carnival, and Aaron and I exchange glances, coming to a silent agreement. We walk over, handing an attendant in a white shirt our tickets. He smiles at us and gives us both a set of darts, mine red and Aaron's black.

Aaron stares at the board, tossing a dart back and forth in his hands. "Wanna make a bet?"

"You sound like Beau."

"What can I say? I'm inspired."

I frown. "Fine."

Aaron pauses, cupping his chin with his hands before turning to me. "I win—you gotta tell me a really dark secret. Something you've never told me before. We're talking about body-burying type stuff here."

The attendant gives him a questioning look, and Aaron waves at him. "I'm kidding."

I look up at Aaron, then roll my eyes. "Alright."

We throw for a while, but our practice with knives gives us a bit of an edge, so we tone it down to avoid suspicion. Too many thoughts crowd my mind to make room for enthusiasm, and I let Aaron win.

"Okay." He leans against a post. "Now pay up."

"I plagiarized an essay in high school." I fold my arms, unamused. "I memorized the whole thing ahead of time."

"Not as evil as I'd hoped, but resourceful."

"I cheated."

Aaron shrugs. "We all get desperate." He gives the attendant more tickets, and we start another round.

He studies me as we throw in silence, head tilted as though he's trying to read me like a book, or a map of bus routes, or a menu.

"Your shoulders are tense," he says.

I ignore him.

"If you keep clenching your eyebrows like that you're gonna get a headache."

I throw a dart. "Okay."

He gives me a questioning side glance before shifting his focus to the board, throwing a dart. "I know you saw me."

"I don't know what you're talking about." I pull my arm back and throw a dart.

"With the waitress."

I throw again.

"You really didn't think to rescue me?"

"Rescue you? You looked like you were enjoying yourself." I throw another dart. "Quite a bit, actually."

"Well, I wasn't." He throws. "We're trying to blend in here, remember?"

"That's one way to do it."

We throw in silence, and this time, I win. I turn to face him. "What did she say to you?"

Aaron trades more tickets for darts. "When?"

I throw. "When you were laughing."

He throws. "I don't understand why it matters."

"I'm just trying to have a conversation." I throw again. "And I won, remember?"

"Does it have to be about this?" He throws.

I glance at him, then back at the board. "Fine. Forget I asked."

I throw again. Aaron presses his lips together, then sighs. "It was about you, alright?"

I pause. "Me?"

"Yes."

My pulse quickens, every inch of my mouth suddenly dry. "Did she recognize me? From the news?"

"No." He throws again, averting his gaze.

"I'm lost." I reach back to throw another dart.

"She said you were cute." He throws. "Her words, not mine."

My arm suspends in midair, and I lower it with a snort. "She did not."

Aaron frowns. "She did, okay?"

"Why would she say that?"

"I told her I wasn't interested in... her offer. And that's what she responded with." He shrugs. "Look, can we please just drop it?"

"Alright, alright. I'll drop it." I conceal a grin and throw my last dart.

"I have one more question, though."

"What?"

I walk over to him, standing on the tip of my toes to whisper in his ear. "Do you work out?"

He's glaring, but I can't stop laughing. And for the briefest of moments, when he's scowling and droning on about everything he has to put up with, I forget the taste of smoke.

Apparently, I get a prize, so I choose a tiny stuffed frog the size of an apple and hand it to Aaron. "Here."

He holds it close to his chest. "I'll protect him with my life."

We're all out of tickets, so we walk away from the booth, wandering through the crowd, hoping to stumble across one of the others.

"I can't believe they let us use darts," I say. "I think that's the first time I've seen them in a public Chip setting."

"Yeah, it is a bit weird," Aaron says, glancing around with his hands in his pockets. "But if they have Officers stationed at events like this, then I guess it makes a bit of sense. Some local Chasers are more forgiving with the rules, depending on where you'd go. I wouldn't be surprised if a town like this had—"

"Aaron?" I stop walking, eyes wide, stomach churning.

He pauses, turning around to look at me. "Yeah?"

"What color shirt was the man at the dart booth wearing?"

"White," he says. "Why?"

It takes him a moment to realize what I'm saying, and his face pales when it does. I glance around, scanning our surroundings, trying and failing to act natural as my breathing grows shallow.

Every single game attendant is dressed from head to toe in white clothes. *Every single one of them is a Chaser.*

The crowd begins to spin, blurring into a pinwheel of shapes and colors. I grab Aaron's arm. "We need to get out of here."

We start walking quickly to locate the others—just as a chirp rings from my bag.

Shit.

Aaron stops walking, looking around. "Did you hear that?"

"I didn't hear anything."

"Sounded like a bird."

"It's probably one of the games." I tug at his sleeve. "Now let's go."

The phone goes off a second time. "There it is again."

My heart thuds against my chest like a hammer. *I need to distract him.*

"Aaron?" I look up at him. "Can I tell you something?"

"Yeah?"

I open my mouth, and from the corner of my eye, I can see Beau walking our way. *He's a better distraction.* "I... gotta go to the bathroom."

I hurry away, whispering in Beau's ears as I walk past. "Whiteboots. We gotta go. Aaron's over there. I'll find Lori and Alice."

Beau doesn't have a chance to respond before I'm too far away to hear.

I weave through the crowd, dodging crying, sticky-fingered children and exhausted parents as I reach the edge of the carnival. I sneak behind one of the game tents, take a deep breath, and flip open the phone.

I have two unread messages from Heron, but my blood boils and my vision is blurred and I can barely see a thing. Every part of me trembles, and I grip the phone so tightly I worry it might snap. *I am going to demolish him.*

I open the messages, and I pause.

M. HERON

you still haven't thanked me, yet.

Thanked him?

I trusted him.

I was stupid, and I believed the things he told me—an *Agent*—and I sent him the locations of those camps. I was blinded by my desperation, by my longing for Ren's safety, by my guilt about the fire—and now they're gone. Because of me. Because of *him.* And he says this?

I want to scream and cry and pull my hair out, but all I can do is stand here, shaking.

Unless...

My body stills as I think back to our earlier messages.

He made it seem like he was going to warn them of the approaching fire —to let them know that the Corps was not going to do a thing to put it out. After seeing the locations go up in flames, I realized it was probably a ruse to get me to hand over information. To take down a few more rebels because the Cut just wasn't enough.

I know he's responsible for burning the camps. But what if he really did warn the Unseen residing within them after all?

My eyes widen as I think back to what Noriko said, when she and the rest of the Cut arrived in End Harbor. They were tipped off. That's how they made it out alive. *Could that have been Heron's doing?*

But what would motivate him to take a risk like that?

I read the next message.

M. HERON

> if you want me to keep playing so nicely, I'd hurry up with that job of yours.

My stomach lurches. I've been so distracted with the fire and Milo and everything else that I still haven't had the chance to browse through that file.

It's time, I tell myself. *Who knows when you'll get the chance to be alone like this again?*

I exit our messages and stare at the home screen. I take a deep breath, tap on the folder, and take a look.

I scan over the file, taking in every piece of information. I learn all I can about Heron's older brother, committing each detail to memory. I study his name, his physical traits, his history. I read everything over exactly three times before I pause, glancing back to the top.

I recognize his last name.

My eyes widen, breath hitching as I call Heron. The phone rings, and right when I think he isn't going to answer, he does.

"I know who your brother is," I say.
A gentle wind blows through my hair before he replies.

Go on, Detective.

"Have you ever heard of the Suit Killer?"
The Agent goes quiet.
"Hello?"

I've heard of him.

I hesitate. "They have the same last name."

It's not an uncommon name.

Another pause.

What makes you so sure it's him?

"His signature. That's not public knowledge, is it?"

That's a high-clearance piece of information. Mine is the
only division in the Corps who even knows the Suit Killer
exists for certain.

"He confessed to one of my... associates a few years back. About the
stolen Cards."
Heron goes quiet again.
"Does this help?"

Well, I now have a good reason to reopen his case. I can
get clearance to access his record if it's under the guise of
an investigation. If I can get a good look at that, I might
just find what I'm looking for.

There's another pause, and the wind continues to blow.

Good work, Detective.

I swallow dryly, guilt stirring my stomach. "Does this mean I'm done?"

Oh, you're not off the hook quite yet.

My skin grows hot. "I gave you what you wanted."

You gave me a lead. I still don't know who killed my brother.
Not to mention the fact that I have yet to confirm the
validity of said lead.

I clench my hands into fists. I've given him enough information to work with. *He wants to keep me in his back pocket, just in case he needs me again.*

It's not easy to find a contact on my side of the Unseen who is willing to do so much as speak to an Agent without wanting to put a bullet in their head. But I'm desperate, and Heron may as well have struck gold.

I'm his insurance policy.

And I almost laugh, because if it means I can get Ren back, I'd choose to be exactly that a thousand times over.

I want nothing more than to yell at the Agent—to give him a piece of my mind and detail all the ways in which I would like to skin the flesh from his bones for being what he is. But he has more leverage than I do. He knows something that I don't. And if all else fails, he could easily track me down and trade me in for a reward. *If I could only get the upper hand.*

My eyes widen. *If Greer is Heron's brother, that could only mean...*

"There's something else I haven't told you yet," I blurt. "About your brother."

Heron pauses.

Tell me.

"Not until I see Ren."

That's not how this works, Detective.

"It has nothing to do with who killed him, so I'm not obligated to tell it to you."

And I'm not obligated to play so nicely, Lavender.

His shift in tone sends shivers down my spine.

No one knew you started the fire, until you messed that up. We were ready to blame it on a lightning strike. The camps were all warned, thanks to me. And Ren?

He chuckles cruelly.

I'm helping him stay afloat in this goddamn hell hole when I could easily let him sink, if I had a good reason to. Would you like to be that reason?

I grind my teeth together.

I didn't think so.

He laughs again.

So tell me, Lavender. What is it that I need to know?

I don't say anything.

I'm starting to think you don't have a secret to keep at all.

"Your brother had a daughter," I blurt out.

Silence.

"And I don't think I feel like telling you where to find her."

Detective, wait—

I snap the phone shut.

If Heron really needs me as much as he claims he does, he'll keep Ren safe.

Right?

I swallow every worry that tries to resurface, plastering on a straight face as I head back into the crowd to search for Lori and Alice. When I finally stumble across them, they've already reunited with Aaron and Beau.

"Where were you?" Beau asks, giving me a questioning look.

"I got lost," I say.

Aaron raises a brow, then shrugs.

We walk through the commotion, approaching the opposite end of the carnival. A dense audience crowds around what appears to be a stage in the distance, cheering as a man dressed in white stands on top of it, shouting things at the onlookers. People whistle and cheer, and children hold helium balloons on top of parent's shoulders.

We stick close together, trying to avoid catching the Chaser's attention as we weave through the crowd, chins tucked to our chest. I pause when I see something strange.

"Do you smell that?" Aaron sniffs, stopping next to me as he brings a sleeve to his nose.

Lori, Alice, and Beau all do the same. "What is that?"

I extend a shaking arm and point at the stage.

At once, the color drains from our faces as we realize it isn't a stage at all.

Behind the Chaser, a horizontal wooden beam stretches across the platform, supported by posts spiraled with colorful streamers.

Five bodies, blued by the dye of time.

Five bodies, swaying in the wind, and the creaking sounds like ships.

And the flies hum, and I imagine their eyes, like a shattered red mirror.

A bright yellow banner hangs with them, hand-painted with blocky green letters.

TRAITOR'S DAY

From my feet to my lungs, every part of my body is frozen. The sounds melt together until there is only one collective hum, the buzzing of an insect.

Somewhere distant, Beau leans over and asks a woman a question that I can barely hear.

"Excuse me, ma'am. We're from out of town. Mind filling me in?"

"Oh, this is just an annual event we like to hold," the woman says. "There seem to be a lot of Runners around these parts, so a few of our hunters take a trip every spring."

"And the Chasers allow it?"

"Why, of course! They usually join in."

From the corner of my eye, something glints in the sunlight. Amidst the crowd, Aaron stares at the Chaser on the gallows. His stare is hollowed of all things recognizable, and he's pulling a knife from his sleeve.

I grab his arm. "Put that away before someone sees you."

He doesn't move.

"*Aaron.*"

The knife slides out further.

I stand in front of him, pulling his head down so he's looking at me and not the blue bodies. My hands cup the sides of his face. "Aaron, look at me."

He does, and slowly, the hollowness fills in.

"We need to leave. *Now.*"

Aaron nods, taking one last look at the man dressed in white before we hurry away—away from the crowd, away from the sounds, away from the blue. I spare one final glance.

One of the children lets go of their balloon. It floats away, rising higher and higher until it finally pops.

R. STELLER

Monday, April 15

On my first day on the job, Agent Canary summons me to his office.

The moment I pass through the scanners, Agent Sparrow escorts me away from Heron and King and into the elevator. Her guidance ends when we reach the top floor, and I step through the open doors. She doesn't enter the room with me.

Canary is sitting in a tall black swivel chair, gesturing toward a simpler wooden chair across from him, where I take a reluctant seat. He folds his hands on his desk, lacing his thick fingers together like a student eager to learn.

"Good morning, Agent Steller." He grins, and it makes me shudder. "Can I get you anything? Water? Coffee?"

I would give just about anything for another cup of coffee and something to do with my hands, but I shake my head.

"How does it feel to be officially on duty? Invigorating?"

"Something like that." There is a pause, and I clear my throat. "Sir."

"Ah. I remember my first day as a First Rank." He chuckles, and his grin falls away, replaced by a disgusted contortion. "I was paired with that idiotic Agent Finch."

My brows crease. *Isn't that Heron's father?*

"You were partners with Agent Finch?"

"He was the only partner I ever had. Even after he became a Fifth Rank and surpassed me as well as the need for an official partnership, we still enjoyed working together. That man was like a brother to me. I took his place as Head of House upon his unfortunate passing." He shakes his head with a sigh, then returns his shaded gaze to me. "But, there is nothing to do about death but let it happen."

He forces another grin, and shivers crawl down my spine.

"I wanted to be the one to inform you of your first assignment." Canary rises to his feet, walking over to stare at the pines, which are laced with smoke from the distant fire. He stares at the view for a long time, then sighs. "It's a shame what a little bit of lightning can do, isn't it?"

I realize he's talking about the wildfire, and I nod.

Corps specialists were able to determine the cause of the wildfire; it really was lightning after all. Eddie had nothing to do with it, but I doubt that information will be publicized.

"How ironic that something born of nature could also be the very thing to bring its destruction." Canary chuckles, turning over his shoulder to face me. "There is a beauty to it, don't you think?"

"I do, sir."

"The duality of destruction and rebirth is an odd one at that." He stares out the window again. "Although they are often seen as solely destructive forces, once they've finished burning, a wildfire can bring wondrous benefits to the environment. Isn't that peculiar?"

"It is, sir."

"A wildfire enriches the soil. The ash left behind is a good source of potassium and phosphorus, and other nutrients, making it fertile. Promoting new plant growth," he explains. "But... you know what I find to be the most interesting benefit?"

"What would that be, sir?"

"A wildfire removes diseased plants and harmful insects from an ecosystem. It reduces the spread of sickness and pest infestations, leading to a healthier forest overall. It is the perfect example of sacrifice for the greater good, reminding us that from destruction can come growth, and from the ashes, new life can emerge." He walks away from the window, taking a seat at his desk again. "You are aware of the wildfire, yes?"

I nod. "I am, sir."

He leans forward. "I assume you are also aware that the majority of this region's Underground population resides within our extensive forests."

I swallow, stomach churning. "I am aware, sir."

"This wildfire—this... peculiar gift from nature itself—provides us with the perfect opportunity."

My blood freezes. "How so?"

"You see, I've been thinking, Agent Steller." He leans back again, stroking his chin. "At first, I was organizing a press conference to discuss the fire with the public. To explain to them that although this disaster is unfortunate, we will be handling it to the best of our ability and providing support to all those who may need it. You get the picture."

I nod.

"However, I decided to go in a different direction with the press." He leans forward, folding his hands again. "Because I realized that the cards we have been dealt are indeed opportunistic."

Every part of me urges to tremble, but I force myself to remain still.

Canary grins. "We're going to smoke out the Underground."

My eyes peel open behind my shades, unblinking as my breaths grow shallow. I can feel bile inching its way up my still-bruised throat and swallow it back down. It burns.

"You were the one who inspired me to make this decision, actually," he says, still smiling cruelly. "If they want to go around setting fires, let them burn. In fact, we just might fan their flames."

I think back to our conversation at the Cut, and the lie I told him about how I obtained the skull. Goosebumps prick at my skin and I clear my throat. "I thought this wildfire was caused by lightning, sir."

"That is what our experts are saying, yes. But a recent event has inspired us to tell a different story to the public." He presses a button on the side of his shades, and the wall of windows transforms into a black screen. He presses another button, and a video plays over every panel.

I study it carefully, realizing it's security footage of a gas station. A girl drags a young man and a plank of wood inside a car, then drives away. Canary presses a button, rewinding the footage, playing it over and over again until my eyes widen. My heart catches in my throat.

That's Eddie and Aaron.

My pulse pounds a mile a minute, every inch of my skin suddenly burning hot as I feel Canary's gaze bore into me. *He knows Aaron is alive after all.*

"We're pinning the fire on the rebels." He shuts off the video, and the windows return to normal. "Lavender Voclain's most recent crime motivated us to make her the disaster's primary scapegoat."

I swallow the lump in my throat. "That's a clever move, sir."

"It is, isn't it?" He flashes his pearly white teeth, and the faux smile drops. "Don't act foolish, Agent Steller. I know that young man is the rebel you shot."

He leans forward, so close I can smell the coffee on his breath. "I find it rather peculiar that Lavender Voclain is the one who managed to save him."

I no longer have the strength to keep myself from trembling. I don't know what to say, so I say nothing at all.

He leans back again. "This security footage confirms that Voclain was one of the rebels who attacked the Cut. In fact, we believe she's the one who burned it down on her way back out. It's purely an event of good luck that her fires didn't spread to the scale of the one that's currently ravaging our forests."

My mouth is dry. "That does seem rather lucky, sir."

Canary studies me, and it feels like he's peeling my skin right off, carving right to the bone. "I know she is the reason why you spared that rebel."

I stop breathing.

"However, you were not an official Agent of the Chaser Corps when you shot him, and then spared his life, for whatever reason. And I am aware that you did have the pressing matter of Agent Kingfisher's safety. Even with this information, a decent Head of House should exterminate you for your mistake. There is only one thing preserving you from that fate."

My voice is quiet. "What would that be?"

"I like you, Agent Steller. You intrigue me, and I see great potential within you. In fact, in you, I see glimpses of my younger self. We are fueled by the same hunger. The same greed."

I clench my hands into fists beneath the desk, keeping my expression emotionless.

"And because I am Head of House... because I have sacrificed more than you could ever imagine to earn the title of Fifth Rank... I have the privilege of looking the other way."

He leans back. Relief floods through me, only for just a moment.

"But I would like to inform you that one more mistake on your part will result in consequences. In fact, although I am keeping you alive, you will still face consequences for this particular mistake."

He presses a button. One of the tiles opens up, and a mechanical arm sprouts from it, with a needle on the end.

I think back to initiation and rest a shaking arm on Canary's desk. He studies me in silence as we both wait for the machine to finish its job. Minutes pass, and when it finally pulls away, disappearing within the floor once again, I see that one of the hearts has been filled in with black ink.

"Are you aware of the Tally of Hearts?"

I shake my head, pulling my arm away.

"It is the primary accountability system we use within the Agency," Canary says. "Every time you make a mistake worthy of a tally, one of your hearts will get filled in, until there are no more mistakes left to be made."

I blink. "Is that it?"

"Ask Agent Kingfisher about it if you'd like to know more." Canary smirks. "I'm sure he'll explain it to you perfectly."

I don't know what to say.

"Well, now that your little slip up has been handled, I'd like to briefly explain what your first assignment will entail." He folds his arms. "I mentioned that I would like to let this fire burn, correct?"

"You did, sir."

"I want the public to believe that this fire was no accident. That the

Underground is organizing attacks. That they deserve to burn. I also would like to avoid leaving as many components to chance as possible. While this fire is rather destructive and did survive a bit of rain, there's no telling how long it will burn. Who knows? It could rain again tomorrow and the whole thing could die out. Or maybe—because luck really is a fickle thing—it will miss certain pockets of traitor populations entirely.

"My hope is that this fire will force them to flee. That they will have no choice but to come out of hiding and seek refuge in more populated areas. Or, if luck really is in our favor, perhaps the fire will exterminate them for us." His lips flatten. "But we do not always get what we want in this world, do we?"

"Not always, sir."

"You made it known during your hearing that you had access to sensitive information during your time as an Underground hostage, and that you would be able to use your knowledge and experience to serve the Agency."

"I did, sir."

"I am feeling inspired by the flames, and I like the idea of using fire as a weapon." He straightens his posture. "I would like you to locate a few Underground encampments that are still standing and organize their coordinates for an attack unit, which will consist of aircrafts equipped with firebombs, arranged by our weapons department.

"We will burn these camps, and in addition to ridding ourselves of a few traitors, we will also promote them as targeted attacks by the rebels—the Undergrounders, the Opticultists, whatever name will stir the most anger —against important Corps... research sites, if you will.

"The public is upset with us because of the fire and our country's growing pest problem. We want to retarget their anger toward the infestation, not the house that is infested. Are my intentions clear?"

"Crystal."

"Good." He rises to his feet, flashing a fleeting grin. "Agent Sparrow will debrief you on logistics shortly."

I stand as well, turning around to take my exit.

"One more thing, Steller."

I pause.

"We invested a lot into your future here in the Agency, just by allowing you to live. Bringing you back was a great risk." The air in the room goes cold. "Don't make me regret my decision."

"I won't."

His words echo in my mind on my way to the elevator. *Not one more mistake.*

Agent Sparrow leads me to a conference room where Heron and King await.

The room is cramped, filled with only a rectangular table and a glass dry-erase board on the back wall. I take a seat between Heron and King as Sparrow walks in front of the board.

"I would like to start with a small order of business," Sparrow says.

"You can drop the formality, Jade." Heron folds his arms. "We all know each other here."

She ignores him and continues with a clenched jaw. "Now that Agent Steller is officially ranked, Agent Canary has requested a partnership change. He believes these changes will allow the affected parties to better serve the Agency."

Heron laughs, leaning back in his seat and crossing his legs on top of the table. "Looks like someone isn't happy with dear old Dad's request."

My brows crease, and I look at King. He nods, and my eyes widen. *Canary is her father?*

"Agent Heron." She flashes a faux grin. "You and I will be partners from this day forward. You are now under my official supervision."

His smile fades.

"Agent Steller, Agent Kingfisher is now your supervising partner."

King and I nod.

"For the sake of efficiency, I'm cutting to the chase." Sparrow uncaps a black dry-erase marker, then turns around to write on the glass panel behind her. "The four of us will be working on this assignment together. We don't have a Syndicate mole at the moment, so we'll need to generate a few solid leads regarding the Underground encampment locations on our own." She turns back around.

Slowly, I raise a hand.

"Yes, Agent Steller?"

"I'm not sure I understand what the Syndicate is," I say.

Her brows furrow. "You've never heard of them before?"

"No."

"Even during your time at the Cut?"

I shake my head.

"Then it's likely for a reason," King interjects. "They don't like strangers meddling with their business."

Sparrow glares at him. "That was a necessary assignment, Agent Kingfisher. Agency moles provide invaluable insight regarding their operations and the relationships they hold with not only other Underground settlements, but our own civilians and leadership too. Their power is deeply rooted in both sides—"

"I don't doubt their influence. That would be a death wish," King says. "All I'm saying is that they aren't exactly *fond* of Agents, and if we go around putting our noses where they don't belong, *again*, it'll only cause more trouble for us."

Sparrow glares. "Relax, alright? I'm not suggesting another infiltration job."

"Yeah, Fish," Heron says. "Relax a little, will you?"

King ignores him and turns to face me. "The Syndicate is a... neutral party, of sorts. An organized crime ring of chipped citizens operating in densely populated areas. They're everywhere, really—in most major cities throughout the country."

"Most key players live ordinary lives and maintain separate Syndicate identities to protect their real ones," Sparrow says. "They run on alliances with both smaller Underground camps and wealthy Immunity holders. Most of these relationships are pretty hush-hush and unofficial. The Corps doesn't classify Syndicate activity as treasonous unless it's directly connected to the Underground, so... a lot of people can get away with certain things if they have the Immunity for it."

"Privilege and loopholes," King mutters.

"Like bootlegging," Heron adds. "They've got underground speakeasies and secret tunnels and everything. And they do it all right under our noses. *Literally*. Hell, I could list about a dozen Agents who visit these *fine establishments* themselves. Allegedly, of course."

Sparrow frowns, "Let me guess: you're on that list? *Allegedly?*"

Heron shrugs, raising his palms. "I'm a law-abiding citizen, okay?"

"And they don't get exterminated for their crimes?" I ask.

"Sometimes," King says. "But again, these are established civilians we're talking about. Immunity plays a pretty significant role here. Not to mention connections."

"It's all about who you know in the Syndicate," Sparrow adds. King nods in agreement.

"And a crime is only a crime if you get caught," Heron says. "We're not invincible. The Corps can only do so much, and our higher-ups usually prefer keeping the peace with the Syndicate over starting an all-out war with them."

"They're very different from the Undergrounders you're used to," King says. "They're not even Unseen at all, technically. They still have trackers. They don't have a cause, aside from financial gain. They don't care about treason or change or anything like that. Actually, they'd prefer it if things stayed the same, since they already know how to work the system so well."

Sparrow lets out an exhausted sigh, folding her arms across her chest. "Every now and then the Corps will send Agents on short-term or long-term infiltration jobs. The three of us were on the same team for an assignment, and our operation went a little... sour."

Heron picks at his nails in boredom. "Jade crashed a Syndicate wedding and blew our cover."

"That's because the groom was an asshole, and the bride wanted a way out, alright?" She shakes her head. "Look, it doesn't matter. The point is, our region is a little behind on fresh insider information at the moment. That's why Steller is here, right?"

My breath catches in my throat.

Sparrow turns back to the dry-erase board. "Agent Steller will provide us with the locations we need. From there, we'll head out to investigate those locations and confirm their coordinates to send back to HQ so an aerial attack unit can be dispatched. And that's it." She caps the pen and turns around, arms crossed. "Any questions?"

Slowly, I raise a hand.

"Agent Steller?"

"While I was a... hostage, I never did come across any information regarding the location of other traitor camps," I say, mouth suddenly dry. "The Cut was the only location I knew about."

"We were able to salvage a bit of evidence from the Cut that didn't burn," Sparrow says. "Would you be able to help us sort through it? See if anything leads back to other bases?"

"I..."

Heron glances at me, meeting my gaze. His brows crease when he notices my hesitation.

He knows, I realize. *I can't give her anything useful without causing more damage to the Unseen than I already have.*

As if to change the subject, Heron looks at Sparrow and raises a hand.

She presses her lips into a thin line. "Yes, Agent Heron?"

"Over the past few weeks, I've experienced my fair share of extremely confusing events. I've dealt with arsonists. Traitors. The emotional toll of realizing that the Underground is *much* more complex and a far greater threat than the Agency initially believed. On an assignment, I even saw a man rob a grocery store specifically for the purpose of stealing their entire supply of canned cat food, and only their cat food. I thought he could have been a rebel smuggler, but he really did have *twelve* feline companions to care for. And still, above all else, there is one thing I understand the least."

"And what is that, Agent Heron?"

His hand falls. "Why haven't you called me back?"

Sparrow's face turns beet red. King suppresses a snicker as she clears her throat. "I'm afraid I don't know what you're referring to, Agent Heron."

"What? I thought we had a nice time at dinner last week and I really would like to know—"

"We'll discuss it later."

"It's a simple question."

Sparrow inhales deeply, nostrils flaring. "Fine." She walks to the door and holds it open, gesturing for Heron to go through.

He rises to his feet, hands in his pockets as he follows her instructions.

"The four of us will meet in the lobby in half an hour," Sparrow says before taking her leave.

Heron pokes his head through the doorframe to give us one last look. He stares at me, mouthing two words in my direction. *You're welcome.*

He leaves, and I realize what he's doing.

He's stalling.

But for what? Could he be giving me time to come up with a good lie? To plan some way out of this with King?

I know Heron and King aren't exactly allied with the Unseen, but they both have connections that make them partial to it, and neither Agent is interested in taking them down. *Would they really be willing to take active steps to help them?*

I think about Heron, whose brother was Unseen before getting exterminated. I think of King, who fell in love with a traitor before dooming her family's encampment. And I think of myself, and everything I would do to save the people I care about.

"We can't let this happen," I mutter between clenched teeth, trying to stay as vague as possible.

Maybe I could lie, I think to myself. *Create a few red herrings by giving false coordinates.*

But if Canary sends attack units to false camps, he'll know I'm protecting the rebels and he'll exterminate me. And all of this—everything I've sacrificed to reach the footing I have—would have been for nothing. *No more mistakes.*

"I know," King mutters back.

I look up at him, and he removes his Eyes. I remove mine too.

He sits there with his arms folded, staring at the table, unable to meet my gaze. Something tells me I know what memory he's thinking back to.

"Playing this game is a dangerous dance, Steller," he says. "You want to keep people safe. But there is always crossfire."

I nod.

He opens his mouth, trying to figure out how to word his next sentence in a way that won't trigger the mics. He glances at me, then looks away. "I always think back to what she would want me to do."

Evangeline.

"She would want them safe," I whisper.

He nods. "Alarm clock."

I face him and blink. "What?"

"I forgot to set my alarm last night," King says.

"Okay?"

"When I set it again, it'll go off the next morning."

"Yeah..." My brows crease.

"I need to remember to set my alarm."

I pause.

"Because I have to go to work." He stares straight ahead. "And there is no getting around it."

I sit in silence, retracing his words in my head until it clicks.

He wants to warn them.

Maybe we can't get out of our assignment. Maybe there is no getting around it. If Canary wants fire, that is what he will get. Giving him false information is not an option.

And if we fail to give him what he wants, he'll assign this task to another team, who likely won't be as forgiving as we are. A team of genuine Agents who want the rebels dead. *We are the best people for the job.*

If we can track down real Unseen camps and get to them first, we can warn them of the fire and please our higher-ups with true information at the same time. It'd be killing two birds with one stone.

"Hey King," I say, turning to face him. "Remember to set your alarm."

He pauses for a moment, then suppresses a grin. "I will."

We sit there in silence for a while, waiting for the minutes to pass. My leg shakes up and down as I stare at my hands, studying the hearts inked into my wrist. *Didn't Canary want me to ask him about these?*

"King?"

"Yeah?"

I pause. "Do you know what happens when a heart gets filled in?"

His eyes dart to the side, meeting mine. "What?"

"Canary told me to ask."

He purses his lips, then nods solemnly, sighing through his nose. "One tally, one civilian." He stares at his hands. "Two tallies, two civilians."

My stomach lurches. I can feel bile rising up into my throat, threatening to come out. I swallow it back down, every part of me shaking. My wrist feels like it's on fire.

One innocent civilian. That is the cost of my mistake.

My voice comes out quiet and dry. "How many for three?"

King can't look at me. "Thirteen."

I feel like I'm going to be sick.

I can see his tattoos peeking out behind the sleeves of his suit. Beneath his left wrist, a Seven of Clubs, there are three hearts just like mine. Three of his are already filled.

"I started out with two," he says when he notices me staring.

"Why's that?" I whisper.

"I turned in the camp, but upon investigating my case, Canary had a feeling that she was... special to me," King says, avoiding the use of her name. "That I didn't mean for her to get caught in the crossfire."

I nod, staring at the table.

"On paper, I technically did report her to the Corps. But even after she was sent away, they knew I never stopped loving her." He swallows, staring at his hands. "I think that's what they were punishing me for."

"And the third?"

He can't look at me. "I tried looking for her file in the Corps database without clearance."

The realization settles in quickly, and I think I understand why he can't afford to wrinkle his suit.

If he makes one more mistake, he's gone.

King and I step out of the elevator, meeting Heron and Sparrow in the lobby as planned.

"The Cut evidence is being processed at one of our NOT research sites," Sparrow says as we walk toward the entrance. "From what I'm hearing, they weren't able to scrap anything of high interest, but I think it would still be worthwhile to take a visit, just to see what we can—"

The moment we step through the front doors, the air erupts with sound.

A sea of at least fifty civilians swarm the front of the building, shouting and raising handmade signs in the air.

We freeze in our tracks, watching the scene unfold in stillness until Sparrow places a finger on her Eyes. "We need Officer backup out front. Now."

The crowd presses closer, our presence only fueling their rage. I take a look at the signs and my blood curdles.

BURN THE UNDERGROUND
END THE OPTICULTISTS
NO MORE TRAITORS, NO MORE SNAKES

My stomach lurches when I spot Eddie's name in the commotion.

The Officers arrive quickly, Nightjade guns at the ready. I can feel the one I was given pressed against my leg, hidden in its small black holster. I wear my bulletproof vest too.

Sparrow signals for the Officers to hold off on firing and steps forward.

"We are doing everything in our power to put out the fire and take down the individuals who started it before they can strike again. The situation is under our complete control."

The mob screams louder. Every angry cry melts together in a nauseating flurry of noise.

King steps forward. "Your safety is our top priority. Their numbers are small. The traitors are nothing to worry about."

The noise escalates—and something flies through the air.

A rock cracks into Heron's face, sending his Eyes flying. I retrieve the sunglasses as he bends over with his face in his hands, swearing loudly. Blood trickles from his fingers.

I step in front of him. "You alright?"

"Damn dandy," he groans, peeling his hands away from his face. His nose is bleeding, but it doesn't appear to be broken. Not from the rock, at least. He pinches it while I hand him his Eyes, and he continues to curse under his breath while putting them back on, massaging his forehead.

"We need to warn them," I whisper in his ear. The commotion is too loud for anyone or anything other than him to hear. "King thinks so too. We'll give Canary what he wants, but we can't let all those people burn."

"You think I don't know that?" Heron's pinched nose makes his voice stuffy. "Obviously we're warning them. I'm not *that* big of an asshole."

For a moment, with the crowd shouting behind us, all I can do is stare at him. How can a person wearing a suit like his say a thing like that?

I give him a nod. "Thank you."

He blinks, taken aback, then forces a quick smile. "Don't mention it."

"What about..." I glance at Sparrow, who's still trying to calm the protestors with King, then look back to Heron.

"Jade?" He smirks through his pain. "Oh believe me, I can keep her distracted if the need arises."

I roll my eyes. "What makes you so sure of that?"

"I've known her all my life, Sparks." He pats my shoulder. "I know how she thinks."

All his life? I think back to what Canary said about being close with Heron's father, and it makes sense.

I stare at my shoes, brows creased, my stomach weaving itself into knots. *Why are they being so quick to dismiss the idea of killing traitors? Isn't that the whole point of wearing this suit to begin with?*

And if it isn't, then what is?

Everyone has a reason to be a Chaser, I remind myself. *Everyone has something to gain.*

I'm pulled out of my thoughts when Sparrow steps back, standing next to us with her finger pressed against the side of her shades.

"Yes, Agent Canary?" A pause. Her face pales. "All of them?"

More silence. Heron and I exchange glances.

"Are you sure this is the wisest decision?" Another pause. "Sir, If I could just—" She sighs. "Dad, please."

I can't hear the other end of her call, but her gaze hollows out. She nods, jaw clenched. "My apologies. Yes, sir."

She drops her hand and walks up to one of the Officers, whispering something into his ear. She shoves Heron and I back inside, King following close behind.

The crowd's shouts fade when we shut the doors behind us.

"What was that about?" King asks.

Sparrow clears her throat, her face expressionless. "The Tombs will be receiving fifty-four new workers."

My eyes widen. King looks like he might be sick. Heron doesn't flinch.

"Take the rest of the day off. We'll start tomorrow."

And with that, she disappears into the elevator, unable to spare a single glance behind her.

R. STELLER

Tuesday, April 16

When we meet in the lobby the next day, there is no sea of people. No screams. The absence of the crowd somehow manages to ring loudly in my ears.

"Change of plans." Sparrow walks toward us with folded arms, nodding toward me. "Heron thinks he has a few solid leads."

I exchange glances with King. "What do you mean?"

Heron shrugs, hands in his pockets. "Sometimes there are rumors of camps that the Agency doesn't pay much attention to. Either because the rumors are from unreliable sources and not much more than a ghost story, or because the camps don't seem significant enough to investigate. Not every traitor base is Cut-sized and sometimes investigating is deemed a waste of resources. I thought we'd have more luck checking out the smaller rumored sites than we would digging through scraps of likely incoherent Cut evidence."

"I've followed leads like that before," King says. "They're usually dead ends. Nothing but an empty clearing or an unoccupied abandoned house."

"Yeah, well, we don't exactly have a better option here, do we?" Heron shoots King a look, warning him not to question it.

King purses his lips, and he doesn't.

Why does Heron have so much faith in these leads?

I shove my thoughts aside and follow Heron and Sparrow as they lead us into the elevator and up to the top floor.

"Last time I was in one of these, you were holding Agent Steller like a baby!" Sparrow points at King from the cockpit as she pilots the helicopter, yelling over the machine's roar.

My eyes widen. *So that's how he managed to get me away from the Blurt so quickly.*

"I didn't know you were our getaway driver!" I yell back.

"King has a bad habit of inconveniently getting himself into situations that require prompt escapes!" Sparrow shouts. "It's annoying."

King frowns. "I didn't exactly want it to be you, alright?"

"That's kind of what happens when you request backup. You get backup." She turns to flash him a fake grin. "I just happen to be our most competent pilot."

"Would you rather have me die?"

"Don't make me answer that question, King."

I stare out the window at the stretch of woods beneath us, trying not to think about how it would feel to fall from such a great height. From up here, I clearly see a thick blanket of smoke curling around the pines, even though the fire is still distant. But if I squint far enough in its direction, I can see a faint orange glow in the horizon. *It's getting closer.*

It takes us about an hour to reach what Heron calls Noble Ridge. I can see it from above, first. There is a dirt clearing filled with about a dozen rusting RVs from the Yesterdays, each more run down than the last. There are a few tents too, and a handful of minuscule hand-built log cabins. *This must be an abandoned campsite.*

Sparrow lands the helicopter in the clearing, and we step outside.

A flock of about thirty unarmed Unseen surround us in equal parts curiosity and fear, trembling as they take in our black suits and Eyes, and the shape of the guns in our holsters. I swallow dryly when I realize how thin they are, and the dirt staining their cheeks, and the ragged clothes they wear. *This isn't a camp like the Cut*, I realize. The sky is hazy with smoke.

"Please do not be alarmed!" Sparrow shouts. To my surprise, she removes her Eyes, unfolding the sunglasses and letting them hang on her collar. Heron does the same, and King and I exchange glances before following their lead. "My name is Agent Sparrow, and I'm here to inform you all that you need to evacuate immediately."

A wave of whispers rolls over the crowd as soon as the word *Agent* escapes her lips.

My eyes widen. *What is she talking about?* I exchange glances with Heron, who looks just as surprised as I am.

"Sparrow..." King whispers in her ear. "What are you doing?"

"Do you really think I'm going to let my father get away with this?" she hisses to him.

"But they're—"

"Traitors, I know," she snaps quietly. "But a massacre is not what the Agency needs right now. How do you think the other Undergrounders are going to retaliate once word gets out? With more Agent killings? Mass tracker removals? Something worse?"

King opens his mouth, but Sparrow interrupts him again. "If you want me to honor your secret, you won't say a word about this to my father."

His secret?

King frowns. "I was going to tell you we were planning the same course of action."

She creases a brow in his direction, then clears her throat, turning back to the crowd.

"As I'm sure you can already tell due to the smoke, a wildfire is coming your way. If you want to make it out of this alive, then I suggest you pack up your things and relocate."

For a moment, the group is silent.

"We've been out here for a long time!" an elderly man shouts, his body shaking. "There's always a fire somewhere. We know what we're doing."

"That isn't the only threat you and your people are facing here, alright?" Sparrow releases a drawn-out sigh. "The Corps is planning an attack."

The crowd shifts in a panicked murmur.

"What do you want from us?" A man yells. "Can't you see we have nothing? We aren't doing anyone any harm. We have no weapons. We only wish to live peacefully."

"We don't want anything from you," King says. "We only ask that you leave."

"Liars!"

"Dirty rats!"

"He's telling the truth," Sparrow says. "We're not even supposed to be doing this, alright? We don't have much time here. If you don't evacuate by the end of the day, your camp will be annihilated. The Corps wants to spread the fire and take people like you down with it."

"Why should we trust you?" a young woman yells. "We know what you are."

All of them shout in agreement.

"They aren't listening," Heron whispers to her.

"*I know*," she snaps.

The shouts escalate. Every person yells something as the crowd presses closer, surrounding us and the helicopter, until Sparrow calls out.

"Because my sister is one of you!"

The crowd freezes.

I give King a look, who nods at me. *She's telling the truth.*

"Now whether you believe me or not, if you care about your lives, you'll evacuate immediately. We don't have time to waste on convincing you to believe us."

Sparrow climbs into the helicopter. We follow, and the crowd backs away as we lift up into the air.

Our next ride is quiet. Sparrow doesn't say a word as she pilots the helicopter with tightly wound knuckles, grinding her teeth.

The second location Heron points us to is another abandoned campsite, but the only place for us to safely land is in a meadow of wild grass and dark purple wildflowers.

"The camp is two miles away," Heron says as we climb out of the helicopter and onto the grass. "We'll have to make the rest of the trip on foot."

We walk in more silence, still soaking in the events of the last hour. None of us expected Agent Sparrow to be on board with our plan, let alone to come up with the same idea on her own.

I study her as she walks. Since the protest, her shoulders have been tenser than usual. I think back to the phone call she had with Agent Canary, and how upset she was about his command.

I jog up to walk by her side. Heron and King hike a few yards ahead of us. She gives me a confused glance, then averts her gaze.

"I never knew about your sister," I say.

"And if I had it my way, it'd still be a secret."

"I won't tell." It's quiet for a brief moment. "Heron and King didn't seem too shocked to hear it, though."

"I made the unfortunate mistake of trusting Mal—*Heron*—with it a while back." She sighs. "His older brother always had his suspicions about her. He told Heron, who then confronted me about it."

"His older brother?"

She glances at me, then looks away. "Randy and my sister were close."

"You all grew up together, right?"

She nods. "Yeah."

"What happened to Heron's brother?" I ask quietly.

Sparrow flinches. For a moment she stops walking, then continues. "He's dead."

I don't question it further.

It's silent again, save for the crunching of dirt beneath our feet and the distant chatter of Heron and King ahead of us. I continue watching Sparrow, but she can't meet my gaze.

I shove my hands into my pockets. "I'm assuming King knows about your sister too."

She rolls her eyes. "Heron got drunk and blabbed on about it to him once they were made partners. So I found dirt on King to make sure he never told." She gives me a look. "Don't think I don't have dirt on you too."

"On me?"

"Oh, please. I was in that hearing." Sparrow scoffs. "Your story is bullshit, and we both know it."

My stomach churns. I stop walking. "What makes you say that?"

"I'm not stupid, Steller." She stops too. "You're not over that girl, are you?"

I swallow and stare straight ahead. "I meant it when I said I won't tell a soul."

She nods. "Good."

We continue our trek through the woods, stepping over rocks and fallen trees.

"What was she like?" I ask, cutting through the uncomfortable silence. "Your sister."

If she's suspicious, I need her to trust me. To believe I'm not a threat.

Sparrow studies me for a moment, as though scanning me for some ulterior motive. She looks away. "She was my best friend."

I nod, watching a bee land on a nearby dandelion. The flower sways beneath the insect's weight, still dancing even after it flies away. "Mine was too."

Sparrow looks up at me. Something like understanding glosses over her eyes for just a moment before she averts her gaze again. "What happened to her?"

My throat constricts. "She was sick."

Sparrow nods, and there's another long, quiet pause before she speaks up again. "Raven always had a rebellious streak in her."

"Raven?"

"My sister," she says.

"Margot." I say, then purse my lips, unsure of how to approach the topic. "What... happened?"

"Randy's suspicions were right." Sparrow sighs. "One day, Raven's rebellious streak turned into meeting the wrong people. People close to the Underground. I always thought Randy was being paranoid when he confronted me about the people she started hanging out with. He was so overprotective when it came to us and Heron." She shakes her head. "She went missing a while back."

I nod.

"Canary's so worried about losing his position that he refuses to investigate."

"That's why you became an Agent." I pose the question like an answer.

She hugs her abdomen. "If I can rank high enough, he might just let me handle her case."

There is another long stretch of silence. She purses her lips, shifting her gaze ahead to stare at King instead. "I know what he's doing, you know."

I furrow my brows. "King?"

"That's the dirt." She looks up at me. "He and I are competing for the same thing."

They're both trying to climb to the same rank.

"If you two share a goal, wouldn't it be easier to work together?"

"Oh, please." She laughs emptily. "You think I would ever trust him?"

"You seem to trust me, somewhat," I point out.

She glares. "The offer to blackmail you still stands."

"King's not that bad, you know." I nearly stop dead in my tracks. *What did I just say?*

I study him and Heron, then Sparrow, then my own body. We are all dressed in the same suits.

He's an Agent, I remind myself. We all are. *Bad Agents are the only kind.*

Sparrow laughs again. "Not that bad, huh? How do you think he got this far?"

I part my lips, then close them, unsure of what to say.

She answers the question for me. "By using other people. Betraying them to rise up, because that's what a good Agent does. The girl he loved? He turned in her family."

"I thought that was an accident."

"*She* was the accident. He never meant for her to get turned in too. He thought that if he used the information she trusted him with—the location of the camp she had connections to—he could get a decent-enough promotion to pardon her. You know, do the whole marriage thing, pretend he had nothing to do with the turn-in. If your rank is high enough, the Agency will bend the rules for you. He was stupid enough to believe he could warn the camp in time."

She stares ahead, studying the Agent's back. "He has a greedy streak to him. He'll do anything to get what he wants."

Another wrinkle in his suit.

I stare at King too. "And he wants to get her back?"

"That's probably part of it," she says. "I think most of him just wants to feel competent."

Sparrow stops in her tracks, bringing a finger to the side of her Eyes.

I stop too. "What?"

She swallows. "The attack unit hit Noble Ridge."

She walks ahead of me, and I don't get the chance to ask her if our plan worked.

The rest of the hike is silent until we reach another abandoned campsite that Heron calls Pine Point.

This one is nestled into a thicker part of the woods, with taller trees and a canopy of evergreen that casts a deep shadow over everything. I can hear a waterfall churning somewhere in the distance, and the forest is thick with mist.

This campsite consists entirely of small cabins. They appear less comfortable than the one back at the Cut, but large enough to house at least three people per building. There are about a dozen of them built in a circle around a large stone fire pit that's still burning.

The four of us stand near the fire pit, studying our surroundings.

"Hello?" Sparrow shouts. There isn't a single person in sight.

From the corner of my eye, I see a tattered curtain draw shut in one of the cabins. I lean over to Sparrow and whisper, "I think they're hiding."

"We've come to warn you!" Sparrow shouts, cupping her mouth with her hands. "You all need to evacuate immediately."

Nothing stirs. A soft breeze blows, toying with a strand of her hair, and the tails of the dark blue ribbon pinned to it.

"The Corps is attacking Unseen encampments like yours," King yells. His voice echoes throughout the woods, bouncing between the trees. "We're here to make sure you all have the chance to leave before that happens."

Still, nothing.

"Come on, you guys!" Heron yells. "We mean no harm. We're only trying to help."

This time, when no one responds, Sparrow marches to the nearest cabin and slams her hand against the door. "Please, open up."

Silence.

"I know you're in there." She hugs her abdomen. "Please, come out."

We stand still for a full two minutes before she walks over to the next cabin, pounding on the door. Their curtain draws shut too. "We don't want anything from you. We just want you to leave."

She tries the next cabin, and the cabin after that, until she's knocked on every single door in the camp. Not a single traitor steps out of their home.

Defeated, we walk back to the helicopter, but Sparrow is still standing in the center of the camp by the fire pit. I pause, studying the way Heron places a gentle hand on her shoulder, urging her to get back into the vehicle.

"We really are trying to warn you!" she shouts. "We're leaving in peace, but please. Evacuate."

"We tried," Heron says. Sparrow ignores him, and we climb back inside the helicopter.

Glasmack Falls is unlike anything I've ever seen before.

As with Pine Point, we hike to the coordinates from a small clearing. This part of the forest is thicker than the rest we've visited, with trees that have trunks so big my arms wouldn't be able to fully wrap around a single one of them.

At first, we wonder if Heron could have gotten the location wrong, or that this particular rumor really was a dead end after all. We spin around, trying to find any sign of life until Heron pauses, pointing up at the canopy.

Above our heads is an intricate web of wooden structures and platforms, built directly into the trees themselves. Round cabins with railed balconies are scattered throughout the canopy, each one connected to another by suspension bridges, rope ladders, and twisting spiral staircases made of wooden planks. Everything is so high up I'm amazed we managed to notice it at all.

They notice us too.

About a dozen Unseen stand above us holding wooden bows, arrows drawn.

"We mean no harm," King says, palms up. "We just want to—"

An arrow whips through the branches, landing in the dirt right next to his foot.

"We didn't say you could speak!" a woman shouts.

None of us say a word.

"We know what you are!" a man yells. "You have sixty seconds to convince us not to kill you where you stand."

"We come in peace, and in warning," Sparrow begins. "The Corps is organizing an attack, and all of you need to evacuate immediately if you want to keep your lives."

"Now why should we trust a single word from the mouth of a filthy Chaser?" a bearded man spits.

"My sister is one of you."

"One of us?" The same man questions, brow raised. "As in here?"

"I'm... not sure."

An arrow whistles down next to her shoe. "That sounds like a lie to me."

"I don't know where she is right now, but I promise I'm telling the truth."

"My brother was one of you too!" Heron shouts, but the bearded man is still focused on Sparrow.

The man's expression shifts. He squints at Sparrow, as though he's seen her before.

"Your sister," he shouts. "What's her name?"

Sparrow hesitates. "Raven Silva."

Every bow creaks as their arrows are drawn back further, each one pointed directly at her. The man looks like he might shoot her on the spot. "You're working with Raven?"

Sparrow doesn't know what to say.

"The Gamblers are crazy," a woman shouts. "We want nothing to do with them!"

"Did she send you here?" another woman yells.

"She didn't. We're only here to warn you." Sparrow swallows. "Do you know where she is?"

Another arrow lands near her feet.

"Look, I haven't seen her in years, alright? We just want to—"

"Your sixty seconds are up," the bearded man says.

In an instant, at least five arrows fly at our feet, corralling us backward —until one of us takes a wrong step.

A rope tightens around Heron's ankle, pulling him off the ground until he's dangling upside-down from a tree branch.

"We're on your side, assholes!" Frantically, Heron stretches his arms upward to try and grab his feet, but he can't reach, and it only makes him spin.

More arrows fly, and another trap catches King next, then Sparrow— leaving me the last one standing.

Instead of backing away, I stand in place, alternating between feet as I dodge their shots. But I lose my balance, and I fall flat on my back.

I close my eyes and wait to be impaled.

But nothing happens. They open again, and I bring myself to a seated position in the leaves. For a moment I wonder if they've run out of arrows, but then I realize that someone is standing right in front of me. I can only see his legs, but he holds a bow, and I know he must be one of them.

"I know you."

I lift my head up, and when I do, my face pales.

"I had to wash your vomit off my lawn."

Slowly, I rise to my feet, unblinking, taking in the image just to make sure it's really him.

This man—this boy—is Todd Birch's son.

My eyes widen as I bring myself back to the day of my first assignment with Carmody. Our first kill on the job, and I didn't even have the strength to do it myself. And I still couldn't handle the guilt.

I still can't.

What could he possibly be doing here?

The brown-haired boy turns his head up, shouting to the people in the trees. "He's not a killer!"

Nobody moves, and I wonder if they really will shoot me after all. But slowly, each one of them lowers their weapon. *They must trust him.*

"You." He nods toward me. "Come with me."

The boy leads me up a thin rope ladder, and I struggle to keep up with his pace as he crosses a round platform, then steps onto a thin suspension bridge so high it makes me nauseous. But he travels across it with ease, unfazed by the way it swings or the gaps between the planks.

Eventually, we reach what appears to be the tallest and widest treehouse. He pauses at the door, and his gaze carves into me.

I can't meet his eye. I want to tell him I'm sorry—that I didn't mean for any of it to happen—but they've shown how they treat liars here.

"My dad…" the son begins, then trails off. He can't finish the sentence. "He didn't know how to be a good father."

My throat constricts.

"I'm not saying he deserved it. No one deserves a fate like that," he says, voice stern. "But I'm not like you. I don't think you deserve to die either."

Not like you.

He releases a long, drawn-out sigh. "My sister and I would've never left our home if it weren't for you. We would have never stumbled across Brick over there, and he never would've taken us here." He gestures toward the bearded man, who studies us from a faraway platform, disarmed, but still gripping his bow, like he could shoot me in an instant if he wanted to.

"Your sister's here?" I ask, my throat dry.

"She is." There's a silent pause. "You were supposed to exterminate us, weren't you?"

I glance at him, then avert my gaze with a nod, shoving my hands into my pockets. "Policy isn't fond of protestors."

"But you didn't."

"No."

He hesitates. "Why?"

I study him, swallowing the growing lump in my throat. "Because I'm not like me either."

He nods, as though in some twisted, impossible way, he understands. "You made sure we didn't see it happen. So..." He stares at his shoes, then at me. "Thank you."

A nod is all I can give, and I swallow the urge to vomit.

You're wrong, I want to say. *I am a killer, remember? I don't deserve to be thanked.*

The boy knocks on the door, and we enter the treehouse.

The interior is hauntingly similar to the cabin back at the Cut, which I know must be ashes by now. There are eight walls made of warm wood logs, creating an octagon shape. An intricate red rug blooms in the center of the room, and an iron lantern hangs from the ceiling, casting everything in a deep amber glow. The only pieces of furniture are a mattress covered in white blankets and a square table, where an elderly woman with silver hair and a dark green dress sits with a cup of tea.

"Hello, Seth." She takes a sip, then sets her mug down. "Who is this?"

"We found him and his friends down below," the boy—Seth—explains. "He says he has a message for us."

She takes a long sip of her tea, studying me carefully, as though she knows exactly what I am. "You're awfully overdressed for the occasion, aren't you?"

My stomach churns, and she chuckles.

"Don't worry, my dear. I do bite, but only when provoked." She looks up to the boy. "Seth, make him a cup of tea, would you?"

He nods, exiting the room.

She stares at me for a long time, taking another slow, knowing sip that makes me shudder.

"My name is R. St..." I stop myself, forcing the right words out, as wrong as they feel. "Ren McLellan."

A brow raises. "McLellan, you say?"

I nod.

"You aren't related to a man named Asa, by any chance, are you? Tall, thin, gray eyes?"

"He's my father."

"The son of Asa McLellan is a Chaser?" I feel like I'm going to be sick, but then she laughs. "How peculiar indeed."

I force a fleeting grin.

"How is Asa these days? I heard he's retiring in End Harbor." She takes a sip. "We've missed trading with him and his associates, although I could do without the boy with the scar he often brought with him. His tongue is much too sharp."

My brows crease. *End Harbor?* "I'm not sure."

Her lips part, and she nods. "End Harbor is a very safe place to settle for us Unseen."

A sigh of relief floods through me, and then my brows furrow. *Us?*

I glance up at her, and I know she can see right through me.

"My name is Flora," she says, gesturing to a wooden chair across from her. "Come, join me."

Reluctantly, I take a seat.

"You are the spitting image of your parents," Flora says. "You hold them both within you."

"You knew my mother?"

"Oh, yes. Before she got busy with greater things, she would visit me on occasion. Back when her encampment was only just getting started, we were good trading partners. And that man—he had an eyepatch like hers. What was his name?"

"Cecil?" I ask.

She nods. "A kind man."

There is a long stretch of quiet, and I clear my throat. "My associates and I have come to warn you about an attack."

"An attack, you say?" She raises a thin, gray brow.

"You and your Unseen need to evacuate. Immediately, if possible."

She takes a thoughtful sip from her cup, then sets it down. "I'm afraid we have nowhere to go."

"What about that place you mentioned?" I ask. "End Harbor?"

"I suppose that could be a reasonable solution. We're not a large group, as you can see. Barely a threat. Being acquainted with your parents may give us a way in."

She pauses, and the way she looks at me makes me wonder if she knows exactly what I'm doing here. That in warning Glasmack Falls, I am selfishly soothing my own conscience before everything they've known and built is destroyed. That I am actively playing a part in the very destruction I'm warning them about.

"Should I tell End Harbor who sent me?"

I swallow dryly. Grains of guilt spin in my stomach like sugar until I'm filled with cotton. Suffocating in it.

Warning the Unseen residents of these camps and giving them time to evacuate doesn't change the fact that we are still the ones bearing the torches. Maybe we ourselves aren't a part of the attack units, but we're the ones providing the leads, confirming the locations.

This is the option that is best for everyone, I remind myself. *Any other team Canary could have assigned this case to would have just let the Unseen burn. We are milder villains than them.*

From the beginning, that's what this whole thing has been about. If I can't avoid being a villain, I will be the better kind.

But that still means I'm a villain. And I don't want my parents to know what I've become.

Eddie can never know.

"No," I say.

Flora nods, and again, I get the feeling that despite my suit, she understands. That in some strange way, she knows something I don't. Like she can see the human parts of me that I no longer know how to recognize in the mirror.

Seth comes in with a kettle and two cups. The three of us drink our tea in silence. It's lavender, I think. It should be soothing, but it only upsets my stomach, and I begin to list all the things I'd trade to be sipping a good cup of coffee instead.

"I really should be going," I say, rising to my feet. "Thank you for the tea."

I start to walk toward the door, but pause when Flora speaks. "You can come back any time, you know."

I glance at her over my shoulder.

What are you talking about? I want to ask. *There won't be a place to come back to. Your home will burn, and it will be my fault.*

I quickly realize she isn't talking about Glasmack Falls.

I think back to the man I exterminated at training, because he is still alive in my head. I fall asleep every night hearing his name over and over again, and the names of every assignment I ever witnessed Carmody execute under my command. I see the faces of the people whose fates I decided like a strategy game. I feel the burning of a heart-shaped tattoo.

And I see my own face, attached to a dead stranger's body, and I remember how it felt to saw him open with that bloody knife.

Sometimes I wonder if I crawled inside his skin and walked out of initiation wearing it, like a wolf in sheep's hide. *Because I'm not like me either.*

"Thanks again for the tea."

I exit the treehouse. I climb down the ladder. Seth helps me cut the others down. King and Sparrow land swiftly on their feet. I catch Heron bridal style, and he complains the entire hike back to the helicopter as we leave Glasmack Falls behind. But when we are in the air, and Sparrow is confirming the coordinates with her father, it feels like I'm leaving something else behind too.

EDDIE

Sunday, April 21
84 Beds Made

♪ STRAY - YELLOW HOUSE ♪

The wait at the station is a game of pretend.

We sit on a bench and pretend that we are elsewhere. We pretend that everything is okay, that we are in a place where we can have small talk about waffles and the people passing by, that we breathe easily. We pretend that we aren't all thinking of how nice it would be to disappear and cry while no one else is looking. We pretend the flies never hummed at all.

The train arrives on time, slowing to a stop at the platform. It's silver and perfectly smooth, and it glistens in the now blinding sunlight. We walk up to the doors, scan our tickets, and head inside to find our seats.

The train is filled with gray tables accompanied by dark blue leather benches. We find an isolated booth, and I take a spot by the window. Alice sits next to me, and Lori and Beau climb into the seat across from us.

We wait in silence until the train starts moving. Aaron runs over and grabs a seat next to Beau, just in time.

"The hell was that little stunt you pulled?" He glares at Beau. "I almost missed the train, genius."

"Why's that Beau's fault?" I ask.

"Because he…" Aaron glances at Beau, then at me, then at Lori and Alice, who study him with puzzled expressions. He frowns, crossing his arms and staring out the window instead. "Forget it."

"Where were you?"

"Nowhere."

"Actually, I think Aaron's onto something," Lori says. "I overheard Beau telling him that Eddie wanted to meet him in the bathroom."

Alice snorts. Beau grins.

Aaron leans his head back. "Oh my God."

Alice raises a brow. "Did she?"

"No," Aaron and I snap in tandem.

Alice conceals a grin. "Now why would she wanna meet you in the bathroom, Aaron?"

"I thought she wanted to talk to me or something, alright?" Aaron shakes his head. "You're all idiots."

The first half-hour or so is silent as we pass through towns and stretches of forest. Sunlight blinks in through the window and seeps into the glass from beyond gaps in the trees, casting glowing yellow shapes on everything inside. It would be beautiful if we weren't all sick to our stomachs.

Alice is the only one who seems to be enjoying herself. She leans over me to point out something new every minute, pressing her palms against the window like a puppy in a car for the first time.

"How are none of you freaking out right now?" she says, pointing at the cows outside.

At the moment, we're traveling through what appears to be an endless expanse of green dairy fields. Once, I would have joined Alice in her enthusiasm. Now the view makes my stomach churn.

"You're acting like you've never seen a cow before," Beau says.

"I haven't."

Beau laughs. "What do you mean, you haven't?"

"We don't have them back home."

My eyes widen. "This is your first time outside of…"

Alice nods.

Beau's jaw drops. "No way."

I can't help but think back to what Wagner said back in the hospital—about the lengths he would go to keep her within End Harbor's walls.

Alice eventually removes herself from the window and pulls out a stick of honey from her bag to chew on.

I wonder how her father feels about her going missing. Given what I've seen and what she's told me about their relationship, I know she didn't leave a note.

I zip up my jacket and hide under the hood again, but I'm not sure it's doing enough to conceal my face. A man gives me a strange look on his way to the bathroom, then again on his way back.

"You're getting weird looks," Aaron says.

"Yeah, I wonder why."

"It's the jacket, not your face," Beau says. "You're acting like it's snowing in here when it's actually kind of warm. It's weird."

"What else am I supposed to do?"

"Here." Aaron pulls out his glasses case, giving me his clear ones while he keeps wearing his shades.

I put them on. The train blurs behind Aaron's prescription as I remove my orange jacket.

We're quiet for a while until Aaron rises to his feet. "Motion sick. I'll be right back."

"I think she needs a better disguise." Beau observes me carefully, stroking his chin. "We could dye her hair."

"I could help with that," Alice says.

"I can cut it," Lori adds.

I shake my head. "No."

Beau furrows his brows. "Why not?"

I lean over the table, whispering. "Won't they expect me to do something drastic like that?"

"At least let us do *something* to it," Alice says. "It looks exactly like it does on the news."

"Here." Beau climbs over the table to trade seats with Alice. He sits next to me, combing through my hair with his hands before braiding it. Only this time, he weaves it into a loose crown. Alice reaches over to tug out a few strands, letting them frame my face.

Lori reaches inside her bag, tossing me a wadded up bundle of clothes. "Here. Go put this on."

Alice smiles at Lori. "You brought a dress?"

Lori shrugs. "You never know when you might need one."

I stare at the ball of fabric in my hands. "I can't wear this."

"Oh, come on," Alice says. "Don't be afraid of dresses, that's dumb."

"I'm not." I glare. "I actually enjoy a good dress."

"Okay, then what's the holdup?"

My scars itch when I think about them, and how they show so prominently against my skin. As far as I'm aware, Ren and Noriko are the only people who know of their existence. A dress like this would expose them, and I can't afford to be noticed. *I could still hide them with my jacket.*

"Fine." I frown and rise to my feet with the dress crumpled under my arm. "You guys are ridiculous."

I walk to the back of the car, inside the alcove where the restrooms are. I step into one of the two bathrooms, which feels more like a closet than anything. It's only about three feet wide. I barely have room to change, but I manage to slip out of my own clothes and into the dress, shoving my old outfit into my backpack. I rotate to stare in the mirror above the sink.

It's a dark green collared dress with rust florals and a pinched waist. It falls to the middle of my calves. Although it's a casual item of clothing, it feels strange to wear it after spending so many months in nothing more than End Harbor's hand-me-down jeans and sweaters. With my hair up and Aaron's glasses covering my face, I look like an entirely different person. It sends shivers down my spine.

I study my scars in the mirror. The last thing Duke Carmody ever wrote, etched into my skin forever.

I put my jacket back on and step out into the alcove.

Someone walks out of the other bathroom at the same time as me, and we bump into each other. A polite hand flies to my shoulder. "Sorry. You okay?"

I readjust the glasses and look up to find Aaron. His hand remains, and he uses the other one to slowly lift up his sunglasses, squinting at me before letting them fall back down. "Didn't recognize you."

"That's kind of the point."

He's still staring, and his hand is still there. I glance at it. He pulls it away and rubs the back of his neck, then clears his throat, gesturing toward me. "You look... different."

I frown. "Different?"

He shrugs and shoves his hands in his pockets. "I don't know. You look nice, alright?"

Oh. "Thank you."

We turn to exit at the same time and bump into each other again. He holds out a hand for me to go, and I walk in front of him.

Not a second passes by before he pulls me back into the alcove.

I glare. "What the hell?"

He shushes me and points to his shades.

I shake my head. "I don't get it."

"*Suits.*"

I poke my head out. At the other end of the train, still so distant I can barely see it, a man and a woman wearing neat black suits and sunglasses speak to a table of passengers, pointing to something displayed on their phone.

Agents.

Before I have time to panic, Aaron pulls me into the bathroom and locks the door behind us. There's barely any space for one of us, let alone both. It's so narrow our knees press against each other, even if we lean as far back as we can.

I pat the walls. "Where's the light?"

"Don't turn them on. We're hiding, remember?" We stand like that for a few more moments until Aaron frowns. "I can't see shit."

He pockets his sunglasses and takes his clear ones back from me. I blink, adjusting to the dark. I rub my arms. *It's too cramped in here.*

"Move over that way," I say.

"I can't."

"Fine."

I step to the side and try to get closer to the sink, only to accidentally knee his injured leg.

He winces. "*Dammit*, Voclain."

"Shit. Sorry."

He rubs his upper leg. "It's fine."

"God, I'm getting claustrophobic." I take off the puffer jacket and set it on the ground. "Feels like my skin's on fire."

Aaron tries to move his leg to give me room, and I try to move the other way—but the train is still traveling, and I lose my balance.

He steadies me, hands gripping my waist. He holds me like that for a moment before clearing his throat. "I think we should stop trying to move."

I nod.

We finally manage to adjust ourselves so our backs are pressed against the wall. We lean against it, legs outstretched, but crossed together, so my knee isn't digging into his wound.

"Well now we're finally meeting in the bathroom," I say. "Happy?"

"I *will* stab you."

"So *that's* why you actually believed Beau. You wanted to get me alone because you've been plotting my murder this entire time."

"I see you're an espionage pro now."

"Oh absolutely." I cross my arms, dropping the act. "But really. This is Beau we're talking about here. Why did you believe him?"

Aaron shrugs. "I thought you wanted to talk."

"About what?"

He looks at the door, then back at me. "Is it just me, or has Beau been acting weird lately?"

"Beau is always acting weird."

"Weirder than usual."

"How so?"

"He's been... off... since we got back."

"Are you talking about the..." I pause for a moment, then realize there must be no mics in the bathroom. "The gun?"

"Partially."

"He saved my life," I say. "I wouldn't have chosen that particular method, but... he still did."

"Okay, well there's that. But I also nearly *missed the train.*"

"It couldn't have been intentional. He was probably just trying to mess with you."

"I didn't find it funny."

I suppress a grin. "It was pretty funny."

He narrows his eyes at me.

"Look. Beau's going through a lot," I say. "The Cut was his home too."

"You're right." Aaron sighs. "I'm just... worried about him. That's all."

We stand in silence for a while, trying to remain steady, although the movement of the train makes it difficult to do so. My eyes have adjusted a bit to the darkness now, but it's still hard to see.

"How long do we need to stay in here?" I ask. "And what about the others?"

"They'll be fine. We're the ones who make them look suspicious, anyway."

"So..."

"Unless you have a death wish, you're stuck with me until the end of the train ride, Voclain." He flashes a fake grin in my direction. "Get cozy."

"Ugh." I roll my head back.

Aaron shifts slightly, leaning closer to me and propping his head up with his arm. "So what's new with you?"

"Arson. Wanted posters. The usual."

"All good things."

"What about you?"

"Well, I'm trapped in a bathroom with said arsonist and wanted criminal." He nods. "So I'd say things are going very well for me."

"Think you'll make it out alive?"

"I don't know. We'll see." He leans back again, shoving his hands into his pockets. "If I piss her off she might set me on fire."

"That does sound like a probable outcome."

"I'll just have to keep her entertained."

Something about the way he says that sentence makes my breath catch in my throat. "Like her own personal jester?"

"Something like that." He pulls up his sleeve, showing the Joker Card on his left wrist, crossed out with the *X* he tattooed himself. "Think we look alike?"

"Let me check." I hold my left wrist up to his face. "I'd say there's some resemblance."

Aaron studies me for a moment, holding my gaze like it's a challenge. But his eyes drift to my wrist, tracing down the skin of my arm—until they stop moving, and his brows furrow.

I frown. "What?"

His eyes darken, all humor drained from them. "What is that?"

He reaches out to touch my upper arm, then pauses. His hand lingers in midair before his fingers curl inward, and he lets his hand fall to his side, clutching it into a fist.

My scars.

I glance down at my arm, then back up at him. The hollowness has returned to his stare, so empty that the hairs on the back of my neck stand on end.

"Who did this to you?"

Never have five words felt so cold against my skin. Shivers crawl up my spine as I try not to think about the answer to that question.

His voice deepens. "I'm not playing around here."

"Just drop it, alright? It's nothing."

He presses his lips into a thin seam, nostrils flaring. "Eddie, tell me who did this or I swear to God I'm gonna—"

"He's already dead." I glare, then avert my gaze. "I killed him, okay?"

Aaron looks at me, then nods. He knows.

I reach down to grab the jacket, ready to put it back on again, but he stops me.

"I know what it's like to hide scars, Voclain." His eyes are soft and full again, and I look away. "You don't have to hide them from me."

I glance at his arm. "You hide yours."

He lowers his voice. "No one's seen them all, Voclain."

"Then you understand."

His lips part, then purse with a sigh.

"And I *have* to hide them." I point down to my dress. "Disguise, remember?"

Aaron pauses before nodding. He can't look at me, and neither can I, because the more I think about it, the more I realize he's right. I'm tired of hiding my scars, tired of pretending they're not there, tired of pretending that day never happened at all.

Tired of being unlucky.

"Aaron?" My voice falls to a whisper. I bite my lip. "Can you fix it for me?"

He looks down at me for a moment, letting the words sink in until he understands what I'm asking. "Are you sure?"

"I'm sure."

He nods, eyes glossy. "Okay."

Aaron reaches into his satchel, pulling out a blade. He cleans it, and I lift up my sleeve, exposing each and every letter.

He studies the entirety of the scar, neck muscles twitching. He inhales through his nose and out through it too, placing one hand on my shoulder while the other readies the blade. He pauses, eyes still glued to the letters. "Tell me to stop."

"I don't want you to stop."

He gives me one last look, almost pleading, until his gaze falls away.

The blade burns as it cuts through my skin. I squeeze my eyes shut and curl my free hand into a fist, digging my nails into my palm. But his other hand finds it, weaving his fingers through mine so I can hold it until he's finished.

When I look down at my arm, a bright red *X* crosses through the first two letters, dripping blood.

I let go of Aaron's hand. He cleans the knife and puts it back inside his bag before retrieving a cloth, which he soaks in fresh water from the sink. He wrings it out and wipes the blood away from my skin, then takes out a jar of ointment. His fingers are cold when he carefully applies it and bandages my arm. I let the sleeve of the dress fall back down.

"Thank you," I say.

He nods.

I stare at the wall, throat suddenly tight as I hug my stomach.

"Hey," he mutters. "Look at me."

I do.

"You have never been, nor will you ever be, unlucky." He pauses. "You know that, right?"

I turn away.

"You know that, right?" he repeats, voice firm.

I look at him again, barely able to take a breath. *Why do I feel like crying?*

"Knowing you has been one of *the* best things that's ever happened to me. When you're around..." He swallows. "God, Ed. You make me feel like..."

He can't finish the sentence. The train continues to roll against the tracks, and a horn sounds, so distant beyond our seclusion.

When he can finally speak again, his voice is quiet. "You make me the luckiest person."

I stare up at him, eyes watering. *How can he say that after everything I've done? Everything I've burned?*

When he looks at me like that, for a moment, I almost believe him.

Something roars outside the door. My breath hitches, and I grab Aaron's arm, snapping my head to the left. My eyes bulge, hands shaking as the realization sinks in. *That was a Yesterday gun.*

Another gunshot erupts, followed by screams, and a loud *hiss*. The train lurches to a stop, and we hold onto each other for balance. We exchange glances, a gun in my mind with one name attached to it. *Beau.*

Aaron steps in front of me and opens the door.

I peek out from behind him, trying to make out what's happening beyond the alcove, but there's white smoke everywhere, and I can't see a thing. *A smoke bomb?*

Aaron covers my mouth and nose with his hand, then lifts his shirt up to cover his face. "Whatever that is, don't breathe it in."

I nod, lifting the collars of my dress too.

The train fills with screams and coughs as civilians scramble to cut through the smoke, desperate for an exit. But the smoke is too thick and opaque.

It's almost impossible to navigate through.

Aaron coughs, and I look up at him. "You okay?"

He nods.

We hurry out of the alcove, weaving through the commotion to try and locate the others. Aaron holds onto my wrist, and I stay close behind him. We make it to a window and peer through. We're no longer in a dairy field, but in a stretch of tracks surrounded by trees. There is no town in sight.

We peel away from the window and keep moving until I almost trip over something. I look down to see what it is, and my breath catches.

Both of the Agents are dead. A thick pool of blood seeps from their heads and into the carpet.

I dig my nails into Aaron's skin, every part of me shaking, unable to tear my gaze away from the horrific sight. I feel like I'm back in front of that cabin, Aaron's blood sticky between my fingers. I blink, and I'm farther back, staring at my parents as Milo kills an Officer in blind rage.

"We gotta go, Voclain. Come on," Aaron says between coughs.

I step over the bodies, trying not to lace my footprints with their blood.

We continue to weave through the smoke for a few moments, but then I stop in my tracks. "Do you hear that?"

Aaron pauses too. "Hear what?"

I look at him, eyes wide. "Exactly."

We spin around. There are no screams, no hurried civilians rushing to find a way out. Every one of them is on the ground, eyes closed, completely still.

Aaron kneels by a man's side and checks his pulse. "He's alive."

He checks a fallen woman's pulse and her child's with the same results.

He lets his shirt fall back down, breathing in the air. Nothing happens. I do the same, and I'm still standing.

My brows draw together. "Why is the smoke affecting *them*, and not us?"

Before he can answer, something hisses, like a set of doors opening. Slowly, the smoke begins to drift outside. A quick flash of black cuts through the fog. The haze clears away just enough for me to see four hooded figures, standing perfectly still as they watch us in what must be disbelief.

I can't see their faces, but they all wear masks. Plague masks, I think, with black beaks—a relic from a time long before the Yesterdays. Each one of them holds a Yesterday gun.

They stare at us. Shivers crawl across every inch of my skin. I grip Aaron's hand tighter. To my surprise, he's shaking as well.

Two of the masked figures leap through the door. One turns to leave, their hood falling, revealing a head of black hair and a red velvet ribbon pinned to it. The last remains there, staring. The one with the ribbon has to pull them away, and they are all gone before I can blink.

We stand in silence for a long time until I look at Aaron. He stares straight ahead, eyes so wide I wonder if he could be sick. "Aaron?"

Slowly, he turns his head, sniffs the air, and waits, almost like he's hoping for something to happen. I do the same, trying to catch something familiar in the scent. His face pales as we both come to the same conclusion.

"Catnap," I mutter. He nods.

"Out of everyone who's had access to it, who's the only other person aside from Beau who'd know how to make a bomb like that?"

My stomach churns. I stare at Aaron, head spinning.

"I know who killed those Agents," he mutters. "And I think they might have Milo."

R. STELLER

Tuesday, April 16

Heron orders pizza to celebrate our destruction.

After filing our individual reports back at HQ regarding the assignment, which conveniently left out our evacuation warnings, Sparrow let us know that all three attack units were successfully dispatched. Our job is done. A public relations team is already crafting a news feature that will hopefully scare both traitors and civilians into a period of relative quiet. No more daring Undergrounder moves; no more protests.

Sparrow said Canary was thoroughly pleased. We were shocked to hear that he offered to take her out to an expensive dinner, which she politely declined. She was too tired. We all headed to King's safe house, also tired.

It's well past midnight. The four of us huddle around the kitchen island in a silence that feels far from celebratory. King leans against the fridge, arms crossed, drinking a bottle of cider. Heron rests his elbows on the counter, eating a slice as he stares at the wall. He drops a cube of tomato. Against King's spotless countertops, it looks like blood.

Sparrow stands next to him without pizza. Their shoulders almost touch.

She folds her hands together and stares at them, picking at her nails, which are already bitten to the quick. When she tires of that, she readjusts her hair ribbon instead.

I sit on a barstool across from the three of them, resting my head in the crook of my arm, face down against the counter next to a depleted mug of coffee.

I'm not sure how long we remain like this, but Heron seems to be the only one eating the pizza. I spot him between the gaps in the hair that covers my eyes. He takes his third slice and lowers half of it into his mouth.

He sees me staring and pauses, offering me the half-eaten slice. "Want some?"

"No."

"Oh, come on. Don't tell me I got this whole pizza for nothing." He turns to Sparrow. "Here."

"I don't want your used slice of pizza."

Heron scoffs, genuinely baffled. "Used?"

"You've literally slobbered all over it."

"And your logic is flawed."

She hits him in the arm.

"What?" He laughs. "I'm not wrong, am I?"

"I'm going for a walk." Sparrow heads for the door, grinding her teeth. She grabs her coat and puts it on. "You're all getting on my nerves."

King glares. "What did *I* do?"

"Jade. Baby." Heron watches her walk away, lifting his hands up in confusion. She slams the door on her way out. He shrugs, then drops the rest of the slice into his mouth. "More for me."

He takes another slice from the box, ready to subject it to the same fate, but pauses before it touches his mouth. He offers it to me again. "This one doesn't have my germs on it."

I ignore him.

"You need to eat, Steller."

"I don't do dairy."

"I'll wipe the cheese off."

"Or gluten. Or the sugar that's definitely composing seventy percent of that crust."

He plucks off a basil leaf, dangling it in front of me. "Does this strike your fancy?"

"No."

"You didn't do coffee either, and now look at you." He gestures toward the empty mug. "You're almost as hooked as I am."

Something about that idea leaves a bitter aftertaste in my mouth. I lift my head up, too tired to glare at him. I study the pizza.

"Is it an allergy?"

I shake my head.

He extends the pizza so far it brushes against my mouth. I'm about to swat it away, but I pause, smelling it up close.

As a child, wanting the foods Margot wasn't allowed to eat never even occurred to me. I remember how other children would try to share with me at school, worried that I felt left out because my lunches were boring or healthy. But I never did.

No one was forcing me to follow her diet with her, but to me, there was no other choice. Her sickness was isolating enough, in more ways than having to hide it from the world. She couldn't have friends beyond Eddie. She missed out on social events and important life experiences and the simple freedom of being able to exist without some form of taxation. She was the only person who knew what it felt like to be her.

When people don't understand what you're going through—when you play pretend and put on a mask so the world doesn't see you at your worst, to the point that they believe you're okay, and expect you to be just that, and penalize you for being anything less—that is the loneliest existence. And all I wanted was for her to feel less alone.

Now I am the one left behind.

Heron is right. I need to eat, and I can't remember the last time I did.

For the first time in my life, I wonder what it's like to want this thing I shouldn't have. Something I spent so many years believing was wrong. In this moment of hunger and greed, there is nothing I desire more than to take a bite—and it feels like betrayal.

I take the pizza. I study it.

And I betray.

I hate that it's the best thing I've ever tasted. That I want more of it. That I am sitting here with King and Heron, sharing a meal with the exact kind of people I should despise more than anyone. That for the briefest of moments, I believe I am enjoying myself.

We eat the entire box.

After a while, Heron goes off to track down Sparrow, leaving King and I alone in the kitchen. He offers me a bottle of cider. The pizza made me nauseous, so I decline. He fidgets with his poker chip in silence, rolling it over his knuckles like a coin.

"Your chip is still blue," I say. "Heron's is still red."

He freezes, then shoves it in his pocket. "I'm aware."

"I thought you two were supposed to get a promotion." I clear my throat. "After my initiation."

"So did I." He chuckles bitterly, studying the windows. "But Canary seems to have a greater interest in you, at the moment."

The thought makes me shiver.

"I know I'm close. I can feel it." He takes another sip. "I'm just an assignment away."

"Do you really believe that?"

He glances at me, then nods. "I do." He leans his head back against the fridge. "God. I could really use a stroke of good luck right now."

I nod. *Me too.*

It's quiet for a while until he clears his throat, shifting his body to face me. "How did it go?"

My stomach lurches when I realize he's talking about initiation. I shrug, staring at my hands.

"Do you... want to talk about it?"

I look up at him, confused by the peace offering. I look away again. "I just don't get it."

"Me neither."

I pause. "What was the point of the first phase?"

He glances at me. "What do you mean?"

"They wasted more time and resources putting on that performance than they would have by simply injecting them with Nightjade. I don't understand what the Corps had to gain. What return they're getting for that investment."

"The performance is the point, Steller. *You* are what they want to gain."

Don't they already have me? "That doesn't make any sense."

"There is a purpose they want you to serve. They would have killed you off a long time ago if they believed otherwise. They clearly see potential in you—enough to invest in."

I scoff. "Potential?"

"The Corps is well aware that even their top Chasers still possess fundamental human weakness. Even the ones who choose this life on purpose for no reason aside from greed still have pain points to be exploited. They're shaping you into exactly what they want you to be."

"And what is that?"

He hesitates, eyes flickering to meet mine briefly before he returns to staring ahead, trying to find the view of the Sound through a night too dark to see anything at all. He grips his bottle tighter. "Perfect."

Sparrow comes back from her walk without Heron or a word to say, eyes puffy. She storms down the hallway and closes herself in an empty guest room.

King is too busy staring at his poker chip to notice. I glance at him, then back at the closed corridor.

I'm not sure why I rise to my feet, or why I walk down the hallway and knock on the door. I'm not sure why Sparrow answers either, but I can hear her muffled voice. "Come in."

I open the door and peek inside. The lights are off. The door lets in just enough of an orange glow from the hallway for me to see Sparrow curled on top of a neatly made bed, back facing me. "If you're going to tell me everything's okay too, then I don't wanna hear it."

"I'm not."

She turns around, brows furrowed. "I thought you were Ian."

I shake my head.

She brings herself to a seated position and wipes her nose with the back of her hand. "Sorry."

"For what?"

Thin black streaks of eye makeup paint her cheeks. She stares at her hands and shrugs.

I walk over to the bed. "Mind if I sit?"

She shakes her head, and I take a seat next to her. We stare at the floor in silence, studying the amber rectangle of light the door casts on the hardwood. I'm not sure how much time has passed when I finally speak. "This sucks."

"Yeah." She sniffles and wipes her nose again. Her hands drop into her lap and she stares at her palms, tracing the lines with her fingers. "Nothing's okay."

I nod in agreement.

She sighs, patting away some of the makeup running beneath her eyes with a finger. "He means well, you know." She observes the new black marks beneath her nail. "He never means to make me cry."

Heron, I realize.

"An argument?" I ask.

"He was trying to calm me down," she says. "But I don't think we deserve to feel calm right now."

I nod.

"He's just so oblivious sometimes." She shakes her head. "I know he's a good person, but..."

"He doesn't always take things seriously," I say.

"Yeah." It's quiet again. Sparrow purses her lips, then sighs. "Sometimes it feels like he's too used to the fact that the world is a terrible place." She swallows. "He ignores the bad things instead of really feeling them. Like some sort of survival mechanism or something."

I nod. *I know what that's like.*

She sniffles. I watch her pick at her nails.

"You two seem close," I say.

"That's one way to put it."

"Were you ever..."

She nods. "Once."

"And what are you now?" I ask.

She shrugs. My throat tightens. I'm not sure why I think of Eddie, but I do.

"Why's it so easy to love people you shouldn't?" she mutters.

I glance at her, then back at the light on the floor. "I don't know."

Sparrow and I sit like that for a while, until I give her a friendly pat on the shoulder and rise to my feet. She nods in thanks. I close the door behind me when I leave.

I'm standing outside on the deck when Heron comes back. He walks over to the railing with a mug of coffee and nearly jumps back when he notices that I'm out here too. "Didn't see you there."

I turn back to face the view. A gentle breeze carries salt, seaweed, and pine on its breath, and something like damp rocks after rain. But there is no rain; there hasn't been any since the storm. Somewhere far, I smell a hint of smoke too. Or maybe it's just lingering in my hair.

"Want me to go?" Heron asks.

I shrug. He stays.

We stand like that for a long time, leaning over the railing, trying to make out our little piece of Puget Sound in the dark. But I can hardly see a thing, and none of us are in the mood to wear our Eyes.

"It's beautiful out here," Heron says, surprising me. He lets out a fleeting one-note chuckle. "Almost makes me tear up."

"It is."

"Not that I would know what that feels like."

I almost believe he's joking, but something about the way he says it makes the sentence ring sincere. My brows draw together. "Crying?"

"I've never cried before." He looks at me with a half-hearted smile. "Weird, huh?"

"Do you... want to?"

"Do I *want* to cry?" He repeats the question, and I nod. He takes a sip from his coffee, staring at the emptiness outstretched before us. "I don't know. Maybe."

He offers me the mug. The need for what it contains is too strong to refuse. I don't even care about the germs anymore.

"Wanting to is a good sign, I hope." Heron chuckles. I hand the mug back to him. He sets it on top of the railing. "Maybe I'm not completely heartless at all."

I study him. "Are you worried?"

"About what?"

"That you're heartless."

He holds my gaze, then discards it. "All the time."

"How come?"

He sighs. "If I say it, you'll think I'm stupid."

"I don't think you're stupid."

Heron chuckles, leaning his head back before lowering it again with a long, exhausted sigh. "I don't wanna end up like my dad."

I furrow my brows. From what I've gathered, Agent Finch was one of the greatest Agents this region has ever known. Wouldn't Heron *want* to take advantage of that legacy and follow in his father's footsteps? Considering Finch's connection to Canary and Heron's closeness with Sparrow, he's been handed a one-way ticket to rise to the top, a feat someone like King would do just about anything to achieve.

But when I study him closer, when I notice the mess his hair is in or the crookedness of his tie or the wrinkles in his loosely fitted suit, I can't help but wonder if he even wants this life at all.

"Why did you do it?" he asks, pulling me out of my thoughts.

"What do you mean?" I say.

"I can see it in your eyes, Sparks. *You* are not like *me*." He traces circles in the thin layer of dirt coating the railing. "You're not heartless."

"You don't know that."

"You weren't cornered into this like I was. And if your parents are like you, then you wouldn't have dealt with the pressure Fish was raised with." He looks at me. "Why did you choose this life?"

"Why did you?"

"I told you, I was cornered. I didn't start with a reason." He downs a generous gulp of coffee, then walks away from the railing to sit on a cushioned chair in front of a sleek stone fire pit. He turns it on, and flames sprout from a bowl of crushed glass. "I found one because I had no other choice."

I walk over and take a seat across from him. "You wanted to find out what happened to your brother."

He nods, then glances at me. "You still haven't answered my question."

I'm not sure why, but when I look at Heron, beneath the cover of darkness that makes it so difficult to tell he's even wearing a suit at all, I believe he's human.

"Same reason you did." I turn back to the Sound. "I was cornered."

Heron observes the fire. "For Lavender?"

"For my sister."

It's quiet for a moment, and I swear I can hear the waves whispering, even from our distance. "What's her name?"

"Margot."

He nods. "You were... protecting her?"

"She needed the Immunity." I take a long sip of the coffee. It's gone cold. "She was sick."

"Shit."

"Yeah."

It's silent again. "Where is she now?"

"She's gone."

We watch the fire pit in stillness.

"Your dad was an Agent too," I say, changing the subject. Heron nods. "What happened to him?"

He picks up a pine leaf from the ground and pinches it between his fingers. "Ever heard of the Suit Killer?"

I shake my head.

"A few years ago, a traitor started assassinating high-ranking Agents." He spins the leaf. "My dad was one of them."

"I'm sorry."

"Don't be."

I give him a questioning look.

Heron takes the last sip from the mug, then sets it down. "The man was a piece of shit."

"Did they ever catch the guy who did it?"

Heron shrugs, slouching back in his seat. "Not sure. There's been a bit of radio silence for some time now." He keeps twisting the leaf around in his fingers until he grows tired of it. He tosses it into the fire pit, and it shrivels up in an instant, nothing more than a curl of smoke in the air. "My dad was the last person he killed."

"What was he like?"

"Can I be honest with you, Steller?"

I nod.

He chuckles. "I don't think he was human."

"What makes you say that?"

He goes quiet, like he's trying to form the words but can't, so he picks up another leaf instead, spinning it and spinning it until the needles begin to fall off.

"My brother's biological mom left when he was young—smart move on her part. By the time mine was in the picture, she took my brother in as her own. Raised both of us." He throws the leaf into the fire. His eyes glisten, and he watches it dance, and burn. "She was perfect."

I nod.

"Until she left too."

It goes silent for a while. He leans his head back, staring at the sky. I do the same. There are a few stars out here, but not many, and the clouds make them hard to see. I can't make out any constellations.

"When I was five, my brother brought home a stray dog. Can't even remember what we named him. We kept it a secret from our dad, of course." He swallows. "Every time we'd bring home a pet, they'd disappear."

I shudder. "How'd you manage to swing that?"

"My father wasn't exactly... attentive. He didn't notice we were keeping the dog in our room until we decided to let him run around in the backyard one day when Dad wasn't home. He started digging near a rosebush. And my brother and I got so excited. We were in our treasure-hunting phase. Always going on walks to the park, trying to find something magical, something better than what we had. Something that could bring us someplace better. We thought the dog was onto something. Dinosaur bones, buried treasure, whatever."

"What'd you do?"

"My brother got a shovel from the tool shed. I was too small to hold it, so he dug it up himself." Heron smiles, but it fades. His eyes gloss over. "That's when he learned our mothers never left at all."

A chill crawls over every inch of my skin. I lower my head and study him, brows pinched together. He's still staring at the sky. He looks so unfazed, like he's told this story to himself a thousand times, turning it over and over so that its ridges have corroded, and it is no longer sharp. In this moment, I know there isn't a single untruthful molecule of his being.

He straightens his posture, then slouches forward, closer to the fire. He stares at his hand. "My brother recognized our mom's wedding ring. It was a really distinctive one—a gold band with jade and diamonds. Real flashy. So he took it. Distracted me while he buried them all over again, so I wouldn't see. So I wouldn't know." He swallows. "But I did."

There is nothing for me to say that feels right, but the silence feels worse. "Did your dad find out?"

"He realized that my brother had been messing with the rose garden. Locked him in the shed for three days."

My eyes widen. Heron can't look at me, and I can't help but ache for my own father and mother, who love me. The ones I chose to leave behind. *The ones I betrayed.*

"No one ever talked about where the dog went after that." Heron stares at the fire. "Or why there was a new rosebush in the backyard."

My throat constricts. I pick up the empty mug, trying to find one last drop of coffee, but it's all gone.

I listen to the crackling of the flames. An owl speaks in the distance. I try to stare at the fire too, seeing my reflection in the broken shards of glass. But I study it for so long that the brightness and the heat begin to burn my eyes. I look at Heron instead.

There is a hollowness to him that I try to understand. It's not the bitter lack of a man who had everything taken away, but the patient emptiness you'd find in a person who had nothing to begin with—not even the desire to be any different. He is a soul stripped bare.

"Heron?" I say. He looks up at me. "I don't think you've ever told me your brother's name."

"Horace Randall Greer." Heron smiles painfully at the fire. "I always called him Randy."

I drop the mug.

The ceramic shatters. The sound echoes between the trees, so loudly it startles a handful of crows out of roosting, and they flee with ringing cries. Bats flutter like moths. I fall to my knees to pick up the pieces with trembling hands.

Heron joins me, gathering shards. "You alright there, Steller?"

I don't blink. "I'm fine."

I can't look at Heron again, or his hollowness. We sit there in silence, picking up the broken pieces until there are none. Until the deck is clean, and there is no sign that there ever was a mess at all. Only when every shard is cupped in our hands do I finally spare him another glance.

He has every reason to hate me, and he doesn't even know it.

EDDIE

Sunday, April 21
84 Beds Made

♪ HEADACHE - FRANK BLACK ♪

The five of us stand outside of the train, surrounded by a thick forest that seems to stretch as far as the eye can see in either direction. Cold mist clings to my skin, prickling every pore. Everything is slick with moisture and coated with moss, tainted orange by the distant wildfire's haze. But the cold and the dark are not the only things bringing me chills.

"The Gamblers?" Lori repeats, hugging her abdomen as she stares at a tree, brows drawn together. She looks at Aaron again, face pale. "You mean from Silver Fir?"

"We're right in their backyard, Lor," Aaron mutters, arms folded across his chest. His voice is low and grim. "Who else could it be?"

Silver Fir. My breath catches in my throat, and I swallow it down as I remember everything Cecil told me about them, and the map I memorized from his office. I may not know as much as they do, but Aaron's theory makes enough sense to leave me unsettled.

I turn to face him. "How do you know?"

"I just know, okay?" he snaps.

I glare. "I was only asking."

He sighs, parting his lips, then closing them. "The masks gave it away. It's a signature of theirs. They like to be remembered."

Cecil's words echo in my mind, and I nod.

"If they have Milo, we need to get him out of there," Alice says, swallowing dryly.

Lori turns to Aaron. "Do you know where Silver Fir is?"

He shakes his head.

"I do." Everyone looks at me. I clear my throat. "Cecil told me."

I take out the piece of paper with the coordinates from my pocket, turning it over. I hold a hand out to Aaron, who reluctantly gives me a pen from his satchel, brows furrowed. I scrawl down the coordinates from the map I saw. I hand them to Lori, and she and Alice look them over.

"I think we should stay on track here," Beau says. "Stick to the plan. Locate the original coordinates."

We all blink. Somewhere far, a waterfall churns.

"We don't know for sure that Milo's at Silver Fir," he continues, crossing his arms. "I mean, Aaron and Simon developed Catnap all on their own. Who's to say the Gamblers didn't come up with something similar?"

"But what are the odds of them managing to find or create a substance that works with the trigger?" Aaron argues. "The chemical the trackers release is complex; it took Dad and I *years* to understand it, let alone to get a decent sample of it. Or steal the right equipment. You really think the Gamblers have the capacity for that kind of experimentation? They're reckless. They aren't organized like we were at the Cut."

"He has a good point, Beau," Lori says.

"But how did Milo even get his hands on a good-enough sample of Catnap?" Beau points out. "Whatever he could have stolen from our initial supply back from the Blurt would be no good by now. It just doesn't make sense."

"This Catnap you're talking about..." Alice says. "What does it look like?"

Aaron reaches into his satchel, pulling out his *How to Not Die* notebook. He flips through pages of chicken scratch and sketches, then pauses when he finds what he's looking for. He shows it to Alice and her eyes widen. "I've seen this plant before."

Aaron puts the notebook away. "What do you mean?"

"When you guys first arrived at End Harbor, Milo came to the nursery and gave me a bag of clippings for this plant I'd never seen before," she says.

Of course. When we arrived, Milo was the one holding the bag of Catnap. No one thought anything of it; we were all too occupied with what had happened to pay attention, and it took me weeks to even leave my room at the Vermillion.

"He asked me if I could propagate them," Alice explains. "And I did. A lot of the samples died out, but I experimented and managed to get a few healthy plants growing. That's actually why I was looking for him. They went missing."

"You think he took them?" Aaron asks.

Alice nods. "He was the only one who knew where they were."

"Still, none of this is adding up," Beau says. "I don't think we should risk going off course based on some weak speculation. The coordinates he left on the wall? That's clearly where he was headed."

"What if he changed plans? Or ran into the wrong people?" Aaron says.

"What if, what if, what if..." Beau crosses his arms. "This is serious shit here, Aaron. If Milo takes one wrong step, makes one wrong move, it could affect more than just him. There's a lot at stake here. Are you really willing to risk the safety of everyone at End Harbor for your *intuition*?" He steps forward. "An impulse?"

Aaron flinches. His nostrils twitch, and I can tell there's more to Beau's comment than I have the capacity to understand.

"Look." Aaron steps forward too, speaking through gritted teeth. "If there's even the smallest chance that these people have Milo, we *have* to find him. They don't work like we do. They're ruthless and greedy and they don't care about who gets caught in their crossfire."

"You're being ridiculous."

"They're dangerous, Beau," Aaron snaps. "Milo's safety is our priority here, alright?"

"We had a solid plan. We *need* to stay on track."

"What is your problem, man? Why are you so obsessed with those co-ordinates?"

"Because I'm the only one being rational here, and your little grudge against the Gamblers is getting in the way of your better judgment."

Aaron's eyes hollow out. "Grudge?"

The temperature lowers. Lori and Alice exchange worried looks.

Slowly, Aaron steps forward until his face is inches away from Beau's. He looks down at him, every muscle in his body drawn taut. "I know how they work. Better than anyone else here. I'm not holding a grudge." He leans forward. "I despise them."

What is he talking about?

Lori bites her lip. "Aaron—"

He holds up a hand, and she doesn't continue.

"We're standing in their territory. Hell, we probably shouldn't even be here right now. They'd kill us just for setting foot where we aren't supposed to," Aaron says. "I saw them on that train. The only reason why they let us go is because we were passing through, and they probably had better shit to do. They're using Catnap in those smoke bombs, they probably have Milo, and we're getting him out of there."

Beau stares up at Aaron, his jaw glued so tightly shut the muscles in his neck twitch—and he chuckles, stepping closer. "I think you're stupid for being so afraid of them."

There's a pause. Aaron places his hands on his hips, staring at the ground, nodding slowly.

He draws his arm back and punches Beau in the face.

A hand flies to my mouth as Beau holds the side of his chin, eyes wide. Lori and Alice don't say a word.

Beau's fist slams into Aaron's cheek, knocking his glasses off. Somehow, they land in the leaves without shattering. He bends over, cursing under his breath—and Beau tackles him to the ground.

Aaron's back slams into the dirt, and Beau pummels him, hitting him over and over and over again. But Aaron is quick to overpower him and pins Beau to the ground to do the exact same thing.

"What the hell, you two?" Lori yells.

They wrestle for the upper hand as the rest of us stand back and watch, unable to intervene without getting hit ourselves. My stomach lurches when Beau kneels on Aaron's bad leg, and he calls out in pain.

Beau continues to kneel on the leg, pinning Aaron down.

Then he pulls out a knife.

My pulse hammers in my chest, fear rooting me in place. Lori and Alice look like they might be sick. Aaron stares up at Beau, eyes wide, brows pinched together in confusion.

But the shock only lasts for a minute before Aaron's eyes flare with rage. He pins Beau down, pulling out a blade of his own and pressing it against his throat.

"Aaron—" Alice begins, but he holds up a hand again.

"What is with you, man? First the gun, and trying to get me to miss that damn train, and now *this*? A *knife*? You're being a real piece of shit and you need to get a hold of yourself."

Beau stares up at Aaron, glancing at the blade, and then back up at him. He laughs, every note bouncing between the trees. A bluebird scatters at the sound. "You're not fooling anyone, Aaron."

Aaron glowers. "What are you talking about?"

"You're not gonna hurt me and you know it." Beau's cruel smile falls away. "We all know the real reason why you hide behind a knife."

Aaron presses the blade deeper, seething between gritted teeth. "You're on real thin ice, pal."

"Because you're scared." Beau extends his neck, leaning forward to get a better hold of Aaron's glare. "You're a coward."

Aaron's gaze empties again. He stares at Beau in a screaming, cutting silence, tosses the knife aside, and cracks his fist into Beau's face.

He doesn't stop hitting him.

"Aaron, that's enough!" Lori shouts.

He doesn't listen. He hits Beau like he doesn't even recognize him. There is a smoke screen between his eyes and the body he strikes, like he's forgotten how he loves him as a brother, that he's worried about him, like he said on that train. But in Aaron's hollow stare, the only thing I can find is anger.

Lori and I rush over to him. We each grab an arm and drag him away from Beau and up to his feet. Alice kneels at Beau's side, helping him up into a seated position. His face is covered in crimson. He spits out a tooth and feels the bloody gap in his lower row with a finger.

Aaron yanks himself free, every hair out of place. His glare is still pinned to Beau, and all of us stare at him, unable to find a single word to stay.

Slowly, his edges begin to smooth, and his expression softens. He sees the way we look at him. His breathing slows. When his eyes meet mine, the emptiness is filled in. He turns to Beau, face paling when he realizes what he's done to his friend. *His brother.*

He grabs his glasses and knife. He looks at me one last time, and he storms off, disappearing through the trees.

Lori catches my sleeve. "Don't."

"But I—"

"Let him go," she warns. "He'll come back."

"We need to get going, *now.*" Beau says, rising to his feet with a wince. "They'll send someone after those dead Agents any second now, if they haven't already."

I don't say anything.

"We have to go, Ed," Beau urges. "If he's smart, he'll follow."

For a moment, I stare at Beau. And I don't listen.

I run after Aaron until I'm a few yards behind him and slow my jog to a walk. His legs are longer than mine, and he navigates the forest with ease while I struggle to keep up the pace, climbing over fallen logs and dodging mossy stones.

"Aaron."

"Stop following me."

"No."

"I mean it."

"Where are you going?"

"Away."

"Can't you just talk to me?"

"*God*, Voclain. Would you cut that out?" He spins around, arms trembling. "Stop pretending like you understand, alright? Because you don't. And I don't think you ever will."

I stop walking.

He runs a hand through his hair, exhaling shakily, then glares at me. "I've been Unseen for a *really* long time. This life is all I've ever known, and you've only seen a glimpse. What you know about us—about the Cut—is only a fraction of what it's really like out there. And you have... *no idea* what I've done to play my part."

"Then tell me."

"Has it ever occurred to you that maybe I don't want to?"

The sentence takes me aback. I study him, brows drawn together, blinking as the weight of it buries itself into my chest. I feel like I'm back in the woods by that boulder, convincing the stranger with the hidden eyes to let me in. How is it that after all this time, I'm still convincing him?

"I'm getting real tired of you pretending like you know a single goddamn thing about me." He turns away.

"I do know you."

He starts walking again, and I follow after him, trying to keep up with his pace.

"I know you're hurting." I climb over a fallen log that he steps over with ease. "You're stubborn, and angry, and selfless and gentle and *ridiculously* loyal, and it's taking everything you have not to stop and imagine what you could carve from that Pacific yew or think about the tea you could brew with its needles—and your shoulders are tensing, and your fingers are twitching, and I know that means you want me to shut up, but I'm not going to."

"You're spot on about that last part, Voclain."

"But you wanna hear what I know above all else?" He ignores me. "You hate that you're wrong. You hate that I can see the parts of yourself you bury so far beneath the surface—and you hate that I don't despise what I see. Not like you do."

He stops walking, and I do too.

"I know you, Aaron."

He turns around, his chest rising and falling in slow, wavering breaths. For a moment I expect him to yell, but what he says manages to be so much worse.

"If you really did, you would've left me in that cave like you promised."

He isn't glaring anymore. When he can't look at me a second longer, he walks off again, and all I can do is stand there, watching him go.

There is nothing I want more than to understand.

But how can I if he doesn't talk to me? How can I help him if he doesn't let me? I don't know what's going on with him—and so far, no one has given me a single straight answer about the parts of himself that he hides away.

I want to be mad. I want to scream at him, to tell him to stop being an idiot, that what he did to Beau was irrational and stupid and out of line, and what he's doing to himself is even worse. But I can see how badly he's hurting. I can see the remorse, and I'm not angry. Not even a little bit.

I'm just tired.

He doesn't want me here.

I turn around to walk the other way, then stop myself, Cecil's words ringing in my head. I think back to everything he said about when Aaron was a child. About the struggles he faced, and how Simon was always trying to understand *why* instead of simply being there to help him through it.

He just needed someone to read to him every now and then. Someone to hold his hand and guide him through it until he figured out how to guide himself. Someone to simply enjoy the story with.

I turn back around, watching his figure shrink in the distance.

Maybe Aaron is right. Maybe I can't understand, and maybe I never will.

But I can be here.

He pauses and leans against a tree. I stop following him when I'm yards away and lean against my own, watching him from across a clearing.

He gives me a fleeting glare before reaching into his satchel, pretending to ignore me. He takes out a Yesterday device no bigger than a playing card and I recognize it instantly. Milo had something similar back home. He retrieves a pair of wired earbuds too, and he plugs them into the device before placing them in his ears. He slides it into his pocket and folds his arms across his chest.

We stand there like that for a long time, acting like we aren't watching each other, until he grabs my gaze again.

In something like surrender, he extends an earbud. I walk over to stand by his side.

He hands it to me without a word, and I place it in my ear. I wait a moment, breath hitching when I hear the drums begin. I don't remember the last time I heard a song play. The vocals join, and slowly, I piece the lyrics together.

"This is the one you were muttering to yourself," I say. "After my snakebite."

Aaron looks down at me, squinting through a swollen eye. His lip is split. "You remember that?"

I nod, suppressing a grin. "God, I love this feeling. I couldn't remember the words, and it was driving me crazy."

"You sang it too," he says, voice soft. "In the rain."

Now, I'm the one looking up at him. "You remember that?"

He nods.

It's quiet for a moment. We let the song continue until he speaks up.

"I've seen horrible things, Voclain. Things I should have been more afraid of." He shoves his hands into his pockets and stares at the ground. "But I think carrying you like that was the most scared I've ever been."

It's silent again. He takes out his earbud and turns it over in his hands. I take mine out too.

"Cecil used to play this song for me a lot growing up," he says. "This one... it's medicine. No matter what I was crying about as a kid, this was the instant cure." He looks me in the eye, then down at his hands. "Now it reminds me of you."

I take the earbud he holds, placing it back inside his ear. "Is it helping?'

He keeps his eye on me. "Still the best remedy I know."

He puts the other earbud back in my ear, and he restarts the song.

We lean against the tree, listening, staring at the canopy above our heads. After a while, it starts to look like the pines are dancing, spinning together in a pinwheel of deep green.

When it's over and I've heard the whole thing, it feels solidified in my memory. I can hear every line, recite every word as though it's playing in my mind.

Aaron plays the song again. Halfway through, he starts tapping his foot. Instinctively, I tap mine.

He restarts it again, and this time, I start muttering along to the words. He looks down at me, trying not to smile as he does the same thing.

I start reciting the words louder.

He does too.

We don't know how to sing or dance, but we do both as though we've spent our whole lives doing nothing else. Like for all of time, there has only been us, and this space we think about, and the trees we count, and our pounding hearts, and the ache in our heads.

Before I know it, we're spinning around and laughing like idiots to a song only we can hear, screaming the words so ridiculously off key I swear I see a bird flee its nest. But I can't be sure, because I'm so dizzy I can't see anything properly at all. He twirls me clumsily, dipping me in his arms. The music is intoxicating and all I can smell is cedarwood. I can feel the track in my soul, and I think it's the most human song I've ever heard.

Until it ends.

The laughing stops. We stand completely still, panting, and the only movement is the rise and fall of our lungs.

Breathless, our foreheads touch.

I don't remember when my hands found their way to his chest, or his to my waist, but he holds on like once he lets go, he won't be able to find his way back. Like the song will end all over again, and our space will melt into all the others, and we'll pretend our heads were never aching at all.

He traces the curve of my waist with his thumbs. Slowly, my hands glide up his chest, reaching his shoulders. His neck, which I cling to.

His face inches closer. I realize mine is moving too.

My bottom lip twitches, and we freeze. In this moment, in our amber, there is nothing else. In an endless sea of pine, he is all I can see, all I can smell, all I can touch, all I can feel. And he is so close.

My hands tremble. *What are we doing?*

Don't be an idiot, I warn myself. *Don't be an idiot don't be an idiot—*

When I look him in the eye, my shield of reason shatters like glass.

I don't think I've ever wanted anything more. *Needed* anything more. Not to an ache like this. Like I've swallowed fire and there is only one way to put it out.

I have never felt so angry at a centimeter of space in all my life.

He stares at my mouth, breathing shakily, like it's taking every ounce of strength he has to remain still. "I can't do that to you, Voclain."

And in silence, the song ends again.

Reason returns. I pull away, clearing my throat. I avert my gaze and remove the earbud. Aaron does the same, staring at it, like he wants the music to start playing again.

It's better this way, I tell myself. He can't want me like that. I *shouldn't* want him like that. We are just two hurting, angry people who happen to be hurting and angry together, and that's all it is. That's all it can be. In a moment we will walk back to the others, and whatever this is will be quickly forgotten.

He doesn't want me like that.

Something whistles through the air.

When I snap my head up, there is a dart in Aaron's neck.

We freeze, unable to do anything but stare at it until he finally plucks it out. He holds it between his fingers, turning it over and over. He looks at me.

He crumples to the ground.

Something pinches my arm, and the world goes dark.

R. STELLER

Monday, April 22

♪ DON'T YOU FIND - JAMIE T ♪

I have never felt so incorrect inside my own skin.

King left sometime after we all fell asleep last night, leaving nothing but a note on the fridge stating that he needs time off. I don't think twice about it, given what our assignment must have reminded him of. Sparrow woke before sunrise and departed without a word. Heron slept on the couch.

Heron and I take his car to work in nauseating silence. He taps his thumbs nervously against the steering wheel, lips pressed together in thought. His incessant need to fill in gaps of quiet with his own noise seems to have subdued, telling me his mind is elsewhere.

I am quiet too, not because I'm distracted, but because there is nothing to say. I am quiet because I have no strength; I spent all night squeezing my eyes shut, praying for sleep to come, curled in a ball on my side, no matter how badly the wound in my abdomen ached because of it. I am quiet because my tongue is so dry it burns. I am quiet because if I open my mouth, I might just say the name.

Horace Randall Greer.

My hands shake. I hold my disposable to-go cup so tightly I worry I'll crush it beneath my grip, but that would only leave me with another mess to clean.

I study Heron again and regret it when my stomach churns. Bile threatens to rise up in my throat. I stare out the window instead.

"Sparrow and I have shit to do today, so you'll have to keep yourself occupied and refrain from doing anything particularly stupid," Heron says when we walk inside the lobby and through the scanners.

I nod, still unable to open my mouth.

"Oh, and Canary wants to see you."

My stomach lurches as we step inside the elevator. *What could he possibly want from me this time?* "In his office?"

"Actually, the roof." The elevator doors shut. Heron taps the side of his Eyes, telling it where he wants it to go. "He wants to take you on a hike."

I meet Canary on the roof. He is already there waiting for me by the time I arrive. Neither of us says a word as he opens the door to a helicopter and gestures for me to take a seat inside.

He flies us deeper into the woods, gliding over a blanket of evergreen until he lands in the middle of a meadow. Wild grass bends around the machine as it slows to a stop. He turns off the engine, and we step outside.

It's a hauntingly beautiful day, the kind where beams of sunlight somehow manage to find a way to shine through the sky's perpetual shield of deep gray clouds, but only just enough. Like white hot liquid gold seeping into fabric. It makes everything that isn't already shrouded in patches of darkness cast a dramatic shadow.

Canary stands in the middle of the field, hands held behind his back. He stares straight ahead at nothing in particular. I walk over to join him, standing a few feet behind him with my posture as perfect as I know how to keep it. *No mistakes.*

There is an endless stretch of silence until Canary speaks, loud enough to conquer the wind rustling through the grass. "You and your team did an excellent job with those camps. All three of them have been completely annihilated. The press campaign was successful."

My stomach feels like it's folding in on itself. "Thank you, sir."

"Heron said you gave up those leads without hesitation."

My brows knit together. He was the one who provided them, not me. *Why is he giving me the credit? Doesn't he know what I did?*

"However, when our Cleaners investigated the burn sites, we found something peculiar. Actually, the peculiarity lies in what we did not find." He turns around to face me, shades glinting. "There was not a single human corpse within the rubble."

I blink, listening to the wind blow. His words register, curing something within me so intensely I have to look away to conceal my relief.

For a moment, I feel so happy I just might cry.

Not a single human corpse.

If what he's saying is true, that means our efforts weren't for nothing. The Unseen made it out okay. *They really did listen after all.*

For the briefest glimpse, time stands still. I am the only one in the meadow, and the wildflowers bend with the wind that undoes my hair and whispers into my ear.

I really am making a difference from the other side, I realize. Because I am here, seeing the plays unfold, I can prevent tragedies from happening. *Isn't this what I wanted all along?*

Have I finally done something good?

"Do you know where we are, Agent Steller?" Canary asks.

"I do not, sir."

The breeze continues to trace everything in sight. "Have you ever heard of a place called Harebell Hill?"

"I don't think I have, sir."

"Good." He glances at me, then continues to study the clearing, like he sees something I cannot. "That's because we burned it to the ground."

I force myself to stare at my feet. Beneath my shoes, between the blades of grass and vibrant bell-shaped flowers, there is a broken shard of glass. I pick it up, turning it over in my hands. It's still clouded gray from smoke.

I drop it quickly.

Canary turns around to look at me. "Agent Kingfisher is the one responsible for our victory."

My blood freezes, shoulders tense as the hairs on the back of my neck stand on end. *This was Evangeline's camp.*

"Did he ever end up telling you about his tallies, Agent Steller?"

I swallow dryly. "Somewhat."

"He made many mistakes, but we were willing to pardon them, given the significance of his contribution." Canary stares at his perfectly trimmed fingernails. "We sent about a dozen traitors through Extraction and pulled helpful information from each one of them. Some we had to exterminate on the spot for combativeness, but most of the Undergrounders were sent to the Tombs without protest. It was the first large-scale rebel encampment to be fully occupied in this region. But mistakes are mistakes, and there is no room for them here."

Goosebumps spread over my skin. I clench my fists, staring at the swaying grass, studying how every blade bends together in the same whispering strokes.

"His first mistake was the girl," Canary says. "He fell for her in a way that could not be erased by the discovery of her true origins. She was a traitor living out here with her family, and others. She would visit the city scarcely with her associates for supplies, reminiscence, whatever it is she needed at the time—until he became what she needed. The pull between the two of them was an unfortunate gravity. He was a Chaser, you see. And there is no place for treason in the Corps.

"His next mistake was thinking he was clever. It was dangerous for them both to keep seeing each other in secret. And when his father found out and discovered the young lady was with child, he threatened to turn in Ian if he didn't end things. The man was afraid that his son would fall victim to treason and ruin the life he'd built for them."

My eyes widen. *With child?*

This is why King is so desperate to find Evangeline—why he wanted so badly to secure a future for them both, even if it came at a cost.

I think back to what Sparrow said about dirt, and I realize that Canary has shoveled his own. Over King, he has complete control.

"Knowing his time was running out, Ian needed to come up with a plan. So he came to me, reporting their location, hoping it would earn him my favor. That I would pardon him for his sins and spare the girl's life." Canary chuckles. "The poor young man really believed he could warn the traitors in time to help them evacuate. He believed he could get away with it.

"But I saw the drive in him, you see. I saw the desperation. I saw the greed, and I wanted it in my ranks. So I let him live, I let him atone—and he's served me well. I'd say he's become one of this region's finest.

"And yet the grit I once admired in him is fading. He's losing his edge. It's an unappealing decline, and I have my doubts regarding his future here." He lets out a long sigh. "It's a disappointment, really. I just don't think he has what it takes to become what I thought he could be."

It's silent again. I try to keep my arms from shaking. The wind whispers. Somewhere far, I hear birds chirping.

"I would like to say that I am extremely intrigued by you, Ren McLellan." Canary glances at me briefly. My skin prickles at the sound of my name. "I must admit, I've had my suspicions about you at times, but... I'm curiously invested in your loyalty and resolve, the distance you place between yourself and your humanity, duty and doubt. I believe that with the right encouragement, you have the potential to become something very special."

"Thank you, sir."

Canary turns his whole body to face me. "I must also admit that a certain question has been eating away at me for quite some time now, and I believe the day to ask it has finally arrived." He takes off his Eyes, folding the shades and placing them in his pocket. "What is your relationship to Lavender Voclain?"

Every part of me turns frigid. My face pales and I clear my throat. "She was an acquaintance of mine growing up, sir. I believe it was explained during my—"

"Don't play the fool, Agent Steller," Canary interrupts, his voice stern and cold. "That is not the role you were cast for."

I can't keep myself from averting my gaze, and even though I hide behind my shades, I can't shake the feeling that he knows.

"Now let me ask again." He takes a step closer. "What is your relationship to Lavender Voclain?"

"Like I said"—I swallow the lump in my throat—"we grew up together."

"I sense some soreness around this subject. Are my senses wrong?"

I stiffen. "She's a traitor, sir. She selfishly chose her own desires over the good of the people. She is exactly the kind of flaw the system seeks to eradicate."

"Is that how you've made it this far? Fluency in Corps language? Telling people what they want to hear?"

"I'm only being honest, sir." I keep my voice calm. "I've made it this far because I know which side will keep me alive the longest."

"Honest indeed." Canary's face is stoic—and then, he laughs. "You're rational. I can see that."

"I like to think I am."

"So tell me, Agent." He leans forward. "For a boy who boasts such rationality, why didn't you kill her?"

I almost ask him which time, but I can't without giving myself away.

"When you were an Officer, Lavender Voclain was your assignment, and you failed to exterminate her," he says. "Unless there are special instructions in place to lift the order, you understand that she must be dead by January, correct? Otherwise, you'll have an order on your head to match."

"I remember the rules, sir."

"And you understand that I could easily have you exterminated for warning those traitors?"

I nod. "I understand."

"And yet, there is still that *unless*." He chuckles. "You prolonged her extermination on purpose, didn't you?"

I freeze.

"Why is that?"

I squeeze my fists tighter to control my tremors, every inch of my skin clammy and cold. "Because I thought she would make a valuable resource."

"Because you love her."

I flinch. I urge my mouth to open, to deny it, but my jaw is screwed shut. I don't have the skill to spin that kind of lie and get away with it.

"It's because I decided to follow her that we were able to disable an entire Underground base." I keep my voice steady. "The largest one that we know of on this coast, in fact."

"That may be true, but I don't hear you denying my claim."

"What I may have felt before she became a traitor doesn't matter, nor does it change what she is now."

"So you bent the rules because you thought it would serve the greater good?"

I hesitate before nodding. I wait for his face to contort with anger, for his uncannily calm composure to morph into something raw and exposed —but instead, he grins a shark smile. "You see, that is exactly why the Agency exists."

Somehow, that response is worse.

Canary steps forward, pacing through the grass. He stops in front of a tall, narrow plant sprouting violet blooms that hang like bells. He plucks a flower from it to inspect. "The harebell is a beautiful thing, is it not?"

"It is, sir."

"People once believed witches used these flowers to transform into hares." Canary spins it between his fingers. "Today, we are much more boring than that. Now it is a symbol of lost youth. A symbol of humility, of grief. A symbol of submission."

He crushes the flower in his fist, then drops the petals. The wind carries them out of sight. He folds his hands behind his back and starts through the grass. "I would like to offer you a deal."

I clear my throat. "A deal, sir?"

"Lavender Voclain is a... unique phenomenon, to say the least. She herself isn't very special, when you think about it. She's young, she's foolish. There is nothing to set her apart from the rest of the Underground except for pure good fortune."

"Good fortune?"

"That broadcast was the first stunt of its kind. People haven't had a face to hate—a name to rage against—in years. *Decades*, even. That is exactly why we keep all seven members of the Presidency anonymous; so people have no solid place to direct their frustrations." He keeps pacing, lifting his chin up to study the molten-gold clouds. "But there is no pleasing everyone. Even in a system as successful as ours, we are all human, and there will always be the illusion of injustice. The collective truth of the public is cyclical in nature, and we are approaching the turn of a new tide. There is a stir; the sediment is unsettling.

"The public is afraid of this turn, whether they are aware of it or not. They fear change; there is a sway, and they do not know in which direction the tree that is being cut will end up falling.

"They have always feared the Underground as a fabled possibility, but now, they are waking up. There is truth behind every ghost story, and as they arrive at this conclusion, they target *us* for not having a proper handle on the rebellion they fear will begin, rather than the traitors who are causing the stir in the first place. But I believe there is a way to fix that." Canary stops walking, and he turns to face me. "Because Lavender Voclain just happened to be in the right place at the right time."

"How so?"

"She has presented us with the perfect opportunity to let the Underground orchestrate its own downfall." He laughs, like he's genuinely pleased. "As she scrambles to fix her mistakes, she will make more. She is under a spotlight she didn't sign up for and her desperation will snowball. She will feel the burden of being known and feel obligated to bring whatever foolish idea of change she possesses to light. But if she goes too far in the direction she thinks will bring peace, she will only bring less of it to us all."

It feels like my chest is caving in on itself. "I'm afraid I don't understand what you're getting at, sir."

"People always need a villain, Agent Steller. Without one, there is no order. There is no justice." Canary's grin wraps cold, invisible hands around my throat. "And I want her to be mine."

My breathing grows shallow. What little light reaches through the gaps in the clouds burns my eyes, even with my shades. My gut churns, and I swallow the urge to heave as my lungs take in less and less air. There is nothing to steady myself with; nothing I can grab onto to maintain my balance. My knees lock, and I stand perfectly still.

Everything Canary is saying makes sense.

Eddie didn't choose this path. She didn't want to leave her old life behind. She didn't want to be put in the spotlight; she didn't know that broadcast was going to have the effect that it did. She didn't know how the Corps would choose to spin it.

She has always been reckless. She thinks more with her emotions than she does with her head, and if her anger is fueled just right, she will act on it. Her rage against the system that took away everything will collide with her desire to bring the change she is so desperate for, and she will get in over her head.

I think about the Cut, and the chaos she was able to incite. A few sparks, and the whole place went up in flames. I think about how the Corps retaliated, blaming the wildfire on her instead of the lightning that caused it.

Eddie has never looked at a problem without wanting to fix it herself. What will happen when she starts to believe she can solve something bigger? When this game she's playing becomes something more than just survival?

One more injustice—one final straw—and Eddie just might think she can do something greater.

What will happen when this path finally becomes one she chooses herself?

She is only one person. She won't be able to do anything to change the way our world runs; no one can. Playing along is the only option that ensures survival. But she is on the path to believing she can rewrite the game, and that will only bring destruction.

If I agree to what Canary is suggesting... if I can somehow prevent the downfall he predicts... then maybe I can save the cause I was raised to believe.

And maybe I can save her too.

"You mentioned a deal," I say. "What exactly are you offering?"

"We'll keep Voclain alive, as long as she's useful." He smirks, and I shudder. "I would like to sit back and watch. See how this plays out. Let her sway the rebels to their own destruction. But... with a few strings attached."

"Strings?"

"You see, while I would love to let her do all the work for me, total improvisation would be leaving too many factors to chance. I would like to maintain some control over this performance." Canary displays every one of his pearly white teeth. "And I want you to be her puppeteer."

I swallow. "And what would that entail, sir?"

"No matter what cards you two are dealt, it seems as though you always find a way back to each other. I can't say for certain that you will ever lack a soft spot for her, and her for you."

My jaw tightens, and I nod.

Canary picks at his nails. "Under my command, you will inspire her to make certain choices that will end up playing out in our favor. You will monitor her every move. You will help her become the villain our country so desperately needs. In exchange, she can live for as long as I see fit. That will be your reward. However, this arrangement needs to remain between us. No one can know—not Agent Kingfisher, and especially not Agent Heron. Not even my daughter."

I nod.

"And your loyalty?" Canary looks me dead in the eye. "It belongs to me."

"I understand, sir."

"Voclain can't know either. The strings need to be invisible. She needs to think she's doing this all on her own."

The muscles in my neck twitch, and I nod again.

"So, Agent Steller. Have we come to an agreement?"

"I believe we have, sir."

"I knew you would make the right choice." He pats me on the back, then stares at the field of harebells spread out before us. "There is one condition this whole arrangement depends on."

"What condition?"

"There is a book from the Yesterdays about a wolf called *White Fang*. Have you heard of it?"

"I have, sir."

"Then you know that sometimes we must force the people we love away for a greater good."

My pulse slows to a stop.

"Here we have an opportunity to kill two birds with one stone. If you were to meet with Voclain... to stage a betrayal... it would sever the connection that makes you vulnerable, and it would fuel her rage. I believe this could be the tipping point we want her to reach."

When he looks at me, every inch of my skin sprouts goosebumps.

"Would you give up your love for her if it meant saving her life?"

Answering the question feels like swallowing fire. "Without a doubt."

"I have a special job for you, Agent Steller, and I think you are perfectly suited for it. But maintaining this bargain, as well as your life and place in the Agency, will require you to undergo the proper... training."

"Training?"

Canary grins. "Have you heard of the Correction department?"

M. HERON

Monday, April 22

I stand on the roof, watching the helicopter fade into a speck against the horizon.

And when they're finally gone, I don't waste another second.

I hurry inside and enter the elevator again. I program it to stop at the library floor. I tap my foot, hands in my pockets, staring at the ceiling until the elevator opens, and I walk out.

I manage to reduce my panicked hurry to a casual stroll, nodding polite greetings toward the other Agents I pass by on my way to a free desk.

The library is a towering room with high ceilings and five levels, all of which I can see from the first floor. The walls seem to be entirely made of books. Above my head, railed walkways wrap around each level, and blinding panels of light embedded within the ceiling cast a nauseating glow, leaving every inch of the room completely visible. I can't shake the feeling that like the books, I too am being studied.

I hate this place.

A dozen rectangular white tables occupy the first floor, each one set with three monitors on either side. I locate an empty one in the farthest corner and take a seat at one of the computers. I glance over my shoulder, then quickly log in.

Using Agency computers for research has always felt like swimming in a fishbowl to me. As an Agent, the entire Corps database is just a search away. I have access to any piece of information I could ever dream of knowing, but at a cost. There really are eyes all around. One wrong inquiry —one question that flies dangerously close to some unspoken sun—and I'll get scorched.

If I do what I came here to do and I look into something I shouldn't, there's a good chance my higher-ups will crack down on me for it.

I stare at my wrist. Each heart carved beneath my Four of Clubs is hollow. *If I do this, will it stay that way?*

I have my excuse—I have my justification for digging into my brother's file. But what if my little detective ends up being right about this whole thing after all? Best case scenario, she's wrong, and Randy wasn't who she says he was. Maybe I'll find the comforting reassurance that my brother really was just as good as I remember him being. That he didn't possess a single one of my father's ill-intended, unfeeling bones in his body. That would mean the Suit Killer is still out there somewhere—and I could be setting myself up to be their next victim by looking into this whole thing.

Worst case scenario, there is truth, and I become an even greater target. *But either way, I'll get an answer. Isn't that better than not knowing?*

I close my eyes. I take a deep breath. And I search.

Randy's file pops up in an instant. I scan through it. It tells me things I already know—that he is my blood, that he has dark brown hair and earthy eyes, that he was caught and exterminated for treason.

As with any of us, there are thousands upon thousands of hours of public surveillance footage and mic recordings tagged with his voice. It's all categorized by year, and then month, down to the hours of each day. I click on the last one ever recorded, which was a video of him at a grocery store, strolling through the aisles with a cart, pausing to study a gallon of milk.

My heart crawls up into my throat.

That was years ago. There is no piece of data available from beyond the moment his tracker was disabled, aside from the date of his extermination.

Saturday, July 29th.

It's as though his time spent as a traitor never happened at all.

My brows knit together. That's pretty strange, even for an Unseen man. If he stepped foot in public areas, surveillance cameras still would have processed and recognized his face, with or without the presence of his tracker. It can take a few days for the system to fully process that footage and sort it into the right files, but there has been more than enough time for that to happen.

There is the possibility that once he turned, he never did come into contact with public surveillance. Or, he concealed his identifying features, maybe with a mask. Maybe he really did spend every single one of his days hiding out in the woods as most of the Unseen do.

But Randy was my brother, and like me, he was never fond of sitting still.

I rub my forehead and press my face into my hands. This is giving me a headache. *I wish the answers were simpler than this.*

I drop my hands. There is still one question I can answer simply.

My heartbeat quickens as I scroll through the file, scanning every section for the information I'm looking for. But to my dismay, there's not a single name attached to his cause of death, aside from his own.

This is getting weird.

I bring a finger up to the temple of my shades, tapping through the controls of my Eyes until I'm ringing up Jade.

What do you want?

"Is it possible to delete something from the Corps database?"

I'm not helping you clear your search history, Mal.

I can practically see her frown.

"No, no," I say. "This is for an assignment."

She pauses.

We're not assigned to a case right now.

"This is for an ongoing one I was assigned to with King a while back. It's more of an interest than anything, nothing high priority. All for the good of the Corps, of course."

Fine. Whatever.

She sighs.

Short answer? No.

"Long answer?" I ask. "If I'm the one searching, not hiding."

As you know, the Chaser Corps database stores everything. Mic recordings, security footage, case files—any piece of information or evidence you could possibly think of is kept within its cloud. It can be hard to find exactly what you're looking for without the right search parameters or organizational programs, but nothing can be fully erased. Ever. Encrypted, yes, but never completely deleted.

Only the Presidency has the ability to access all of it without any sort of block. Higher ranking Agents encrypt things all the time to keep critical data as classified as possible.

I lean back in my seat, grinning like an idiot. "You are *so* smart."

This is basic stuff, Mal.

I fold one arm across my chest. "So it would be hidden from lower ranks, correct?"

If a high rank is encrypting something, they clearly don't want other eyes in the Agency stumbling across it.

"Thanks." I blow her a kiss. "I owe you one."

Ugh.

She hangs up.

I log out, and I return to the elevator before I can talk myself out of it.

My leg shakes as I wait for the doors to open on Canary's floor. I use my Eyes to check the time. *There's no way they're back by now*, I tell myself. I open the map feature just to make sure that Sparks and his tracker are still where they were when I last checked—careful not to check on Canary's, because as Head of House, he gets pinged for unwarranted checks on his location. *They're still gone.* The elevator lets me out, and I hurry my way down the short hallway leading to Canary's Office.

I stop dead in my tracks when I see two armed Officers, guarding the frosted-glass door that separates me from what I'm looking for.

I straighten my tie and posture, clearing my throat and rubbing my hands together as I approach. "Good evening, gentlemen. I'm here to retrieve something for Agent Canary. Would you mind stepping aside for a quick second?"

They exchange glances. "What is it that you're looking for, exactly?"

"I'm afraid that's confidential."

They raise a brow, not sold quite yet.

"You shouldn't be asking questions like that, but fine. I'll tell you." I force an annoyed sigh. "He forgot his jacket. You don't want him to be cold, do you?"

"What does it look like?"

"Again with the nosiness?"

"My apologies, sir. We're only trying to help."

I rub my forehead. "It's a black windbreaker. Very high quality, of course."

One of the Officers turns to walk through the door.

"*Whoa whoa whoa.*" I slide on my shoes a bit as I hurry to step between the Officer and the door. "You don't want to do that."

The Officer glares. "Why not?"

I look at him, pretending to be baffled, then laugh. "You really think Canary wants a low-ranking Officer like yourself rummaging through his things? Especially when he's not around?"

The man clenches his jaw, and I get a feeling I know exactly what he thinks about Agents like me. He closes the door, stepping between me and the glass again.

"If you would please step aside so I can get the kind man his jacket—thank you very much."

They don't move.

"You don't want to leave him waiting now, do you?"

Not even a flinch.

"Look, Canary's an impatient man with important places to be. If he finds out that you two are the reason he's running late to his arrangement, he won't hesitate to punish those responsible. Who knows what he'll do?"

That seems to do it, and they swap unsure glances.

"This is between you and me, alright?" I lean in, looking over my shoulder before lowering my voice to a whisper. "I heard he demoted an Officer to a Guard just for looking at him funny."

They don't say anything, and I assume I've hit a sore spot. I pull away, nodding. "Yeah. Talk about a wild card. Am I right?"

The Officers look at each other again, and then one of them rolls his eyes, bringing his wrist to his face to speak into it. "Agent Sparrow, we have a situation here."

"*Whoa*, put that thing away." My face pales as I swat at the Officer's arm. "What are you thinking, calling her up here?"

"We know what you're doing, Agent. We were given strict orders to guard Canary's room while he's gone. No one is allowed in. No exceptions."

"Please." I step closer. "I have... *so* much money. Let me spoil you. What do you want? A car? I can get you a car if you let me in for one minute. *One minute*—that's all I need."

"No exceptions."

I press my lips into a thin line, exhaling through my nose. "You're really getting on my nerves. You know that?"

The Officers don't say a word.

Well, shit.

I squeeze my eyes shut. If any other higher-up Agent were summoned instead, I'd be exterminated on the spot for trying to break into Canary's office.

Jade's wrath will be so much worse. Just the thought of how she might react makes me shudder, like someone's scraping their nails against a chalkboard. She'll probably get angry and mean and worry that she'll get blamed for my bad behavior—which is probably my fault anyway, given all the trouble I've gotten her into before. Regardless, I can't help but feel a bit screwed.

"You know what? On second thought, he just messaged me. The jacket was in his car all along! Can you believe that?" I chuckle nervously, walking back toward the elevator. "Thanks for your help. Have an *excellent*—"

The elevator door opens, and I don't need to turn around to know whose angry footsteps I hear behind me.

"Is there a problem?"

I spin around slowly, offering Jade my best grin and a wave.

"This guy's trying to break into Agent Canary's office," one of the men behind me states. "We thought it'd be wise to notify you."

"Thank you, Officers. You did the right thing. I can handle it from here."

"We were given—"

"Strict orders not to let anyone into *my father's* office. I know," she finishes for them. "Please give Agent Heron and I some privacy. I'd like to have a discussion with him about his behavior."

The Officers hesitate but eventually walk down the hall and into the elevator, leaving Jade and I alone.

"What the hell are you doing up here?" She folds her arms. "This could warrant *extermination*, Mal. What's wrong with you?"

I clench my jaw, averting my gaze.

"Mal?"

I sigh, leaning closer and lowering my voice. "Look. I just wanna check something in Randy's file real quick. That's all."

Her gaze sharpens. "I knew you were up to something."

"Jade, please. I only need a second. Just one quick little search."

"You don't even have his login information."

"But you do," I beg. "What if you do it for me? He wouldn't exterminate his own daughter, would he?"

"*No.* I don't care what it is you're looking for, but you need to drop it, alright? Whatever it is can't be something you don't already—"

"It's about the Suit Killer."

Her eyes peel open, brows drawing together. "What?"

"I think he's..." I sigh, taking off my Eyes and running a hand through my hair. I can't look at her for a second, but when I do, I'm pleading. "I think Randy did something bad, Jade. And I've been driving myself mad trying to convince myself he didn't. And if I'm right, the information missing from his file could be encrypted if it's a part of a big investigative case like that. I need to access those parts." I swallow. "I just need to know."

"What makes you think he—"

"Just trust me on this one, alright?"

Jade takes off her Eyes too, folding them and letting them hang on her collar. She places her hands on her hips, staring at the ground, then back up at me, her gaze sincere but stern. "I can't help you. I wish I could, but I can't."

"Jade. Please."

"What are you going to do when you have your answer? What if you find something you don't want to find? Something you shouldn't?"

I grit my teeth.

"You need to think beyond the moment you're in. Beyond what your impulsivity wants you to do this very second." She lowers her voice. "Do you realize what you could be getting yourself into?"

"I do."

"Do you know what happened to the last Agent who was assigned to this case? Or the one before that?"

I look away. "Yeah."

"He became a victim himself. And that's why it went cold. Canary was too afraid of losing more Agents, and there hasn't been a new lead since."

"You're right. There hasn't been a hit since *July*," I say. I sigh. "If I'm right, the killer's gone."

She doesn't say anything.

"I know what I'm getting myself into, Jade." I swallow dryly. "The whole reason why I'm even in this at all is to figure out what happened to my brother and who's responsible. *You're* the one who suggested it when you knocked on my door all those months ago."

"Because I didn't want you to die," she snaps. "I *begged* my dad to consider having you enlist instead of charging you for what Randy did. And I knew you wouldn't agree to it unless you had a good reason to, so I gave you one. I didn't think you'd actually follow through with it. I need to stay on his good side, Mal. For my sake, and yours."

We can't look each other in the eye. I glance over my shoulder at the door to Canary's office. *We're running out of time.*

"We only have a brief window to get in there, Jade. He and Steller will be back soon, and then who knows how long it'll be before we have another opportunity like this?" I lower my voice and look Jade in the eye. "You could find her."

She pales.

"Raven's probably got a file just like my brother's. We can go inside, do a quick search, and be out of there in under a minute."

"There's a reason why I follow the rules, Agent Heron." Her voice is cold.

I pull my head back, brow furrowed at the formality.

"I've spent my whole life trying to be perfect. *Especially* after Raven went missing. Because if I want to be given his permission to look into her case, I need to be exactly that." Her voice wavers. "Perfect."

I break just a little, but I swallow it down. "Can't you just look into it on your own? Without him knowing?"

"If that were the case, she wouldn't be missing anymore."

I shake my head. "I just don't understand why you need his permission."

"Because he knows everything, Mal." She looks at the wall, then me. "It's taken me *years* to earn my place here. Hell, I've spent my whole life convincing him that I deserved to be born. That I was worth the investment."

My fists clench at my sides.

"He watches my every move, and if he notices me putting my nose where it doesn't belong, *behind his back*, he'll take away *everything* I've worked for. My relation to him is nothing if I'm jeopardizing his position."

"Jade—"

"What you're suggesting is too big of a risk for the slight chance that we *might* stumble across a lead. If I weren't his daughter, he'd have me exterminated for doing something like this." She trembles, wrapping her arms tightly around her abdomen while mine itch to take their place. "But I could be wrong about that."

I look at her with inverted brows, and my shoulders slump. I can feel my throat tighten, and I want nothing more than to hold her, or maybe dig my fist right into Canary's face.

"But what if you do find something?" I step forward. "What if you take that risk, and instead of worrying about meeting his expectations, or being a good daughter—being *perfect*—you do something for yourself for a change?"

She stays quiet.

"Nothing you ever do will be good enough for him." My voice cracks a little. "I wish it were different, Jade. *God*, how I wish it were. But no one has the ability to change a man like that." I pause. "Not even you."

Her eyes are watering, and I bite my lip. *Shit. I didn't mean to make her cry.*

But when I study her closer, I realize that nestled among the hurt and the defeat is an anger that overshadows everything else, and I have absolutely nothing to do with it. She stares at my collar. "I miss her."

I bring her into my chest, and she presses her head against it. "Me too."

We stay like that for a while until she speaks. "I'm done."

I pull away, keeping my hands on her shoulders. "What do you mean?"

"I'm exhausted, Mal. I don't know how much more of this I can take." Jade looks down at her suit, then up again, averting her gaze. "This job was *his* dream, not mine. And I'm tired of doing things I don't want to do to get on his good side when I should already be there."

I want to kiss her, but I probably shouldn't.

"Then let's find her," I say.

We sit at Canary's desk, watching a large monitor rise out of the floor in front of it. It's a little much in my opinion, but it's all we've got, and Jade is able to log into his account.

I eye the keys her fingers press. She spells out *RAVEN*.

I wear my Eyes so I can keep track of Canary and Ren's location on the map. They're flying back now, so we don't have much time, but they're still far enough away to give us an opening.

"You ready?" Jade looks back at me as I stand behind her chair. The mouse hovers over Randy's file.

I don't have time to be anything less. "Yeah."

She opens the file. Everything looks like the one I saw—except for one extra folder of security footage, labeled with a name, not a timestamp.

BARN CAT

"What the hell?" I squint, trying to make sure I'm reading it right.

"Does that mean anything to you?"

"No."

Jade's brows crease, then soften, her face paling. She turns to look at me. "What do barn cats do?"

I clutch the back of her chair so tightly my knuckles blanch, keeping my eyes pinned to the folder. "They handle the rat problem."

Her hands shake, and she opens it.

The entire thing is filled with hours of security footage, photos, and audio files, each one labeled with a timestamp. There are no thumbnails, so we can't tell what they contain.

"What is all of this?" Jade's lips part as she scrolls through. There must be hundreds of files, if not thousands—and none past summer.

Every part of me trembles. "Open the most recent one."

Reluctantly, Jade clicks on the file. This one is from July.

A video appears, taking over the entire monitor. I squint as the scene sets in front of me. It's security footage outside of what appears to be an empty parking lot. My brother stands with his arms crossed, wearing a sherpa-lined jacket and holding a plastic grocery bag that's been knotted shut. His dark hair has grown out, and he wears it tucked behind his ears. A beard obscures half his face. I almost don't recognize him, but when he's illuminated by the eerie glow of a street lamp, I see him clearly. My attention shifts as someone else steps into the frame.

Canary stands across from him with his hands folded behind his back.

Jade and I freeze, but the video continues.

"Is it done?" Canary asks.

Randy doesn't say anything. He tosses the plastic bag, which Canary catches eagerly. The Agent unties the knot and peers inside, observing the contents without expression. He ties it closed. "Well done, Randy."

My brother's face is completely blank.

"I have your next assignment in mind," Canary says. "Are you interested?"

"When have I ever refused an opportunity for pest control?"

My stomach churns. I feel like I'm going to be sick.

Canary chuckles. "Now that your father is out of the picture, with my competition already handled, I'm very close to getting what I want. In fact, this might be your last job before I decide to set you free. But... there is still one final obstacle standing in my way."

Randy glares. "And who would that be?"

"The Presidency is fond of legacies. There is an unspoken rule that surviving heirs get priority. It's the reasonable investment; if a parent is successful, the odds of any offspring contributing to similar results are higher. You yourself are quite a good example of this. You've turned out to be the same heartless killer your father was—and I wouldn't be surprised if your brother turns out the exact same way."

Randy's neck twitches. "Get to the point, Canary."

Canary uses his free hand to pick at his nails. "They will want to test the waters with Mallory and see if he's a good fit for taking your father's place in the Sixth Ring. Chances are, he will be." He lowers his hand and stares at Randy. "I want you to take care of him for me."

My lungs pinch shut.

"What?" Randy's face pales. He takes a moment to register what Canary is suggesting before scowling. "Are you crazy? This is *Mallory* we're talking about here."

"You're forgetting your place."

"I won't do it."

"Oh really?" Canary chuckles, but the sound diminishes quickly. "Don't think I won't expose your dirty little secret, Randy. The Agency is hungry for this case to be closed. In fact, I could benefit greatly from turning you in. The Corps will be pleased if I solve this little whodunit."

"And don't think I won't expose yours," Randy snaps. "If you turn me in and claim I'm the Suit Killer, they'll know you're the one I've been in contact with. Especially when they realize how convenient it is that every eligible candidate for Sixth in this region has been taken out—and now there's finally an opening for you to step in."

Canary grits his teeth. "This is your last chance, Randy."

"He's my brother."

"And I sent my own daughter to the tombs to protect my position here. You really think I won't do everything in my power to track down yours?"

Jade covers her mouth with her hands.

"And what about that lovely, lovely Henrietta?" Canary adds.

Randy clenches his jaw. "I'm not doing it."

Canary stares at him for a long time. "Alright then. I'll turn you in for your Underground association—nothing more. I'd rather let the system take care of you for me than get my hands dirty at the moment." He swats a bug off his shoulder and wipes it on his suit. "There are enough desperate people in the world. I can find another Suit Killer."

Randy steps even closer. "You so much as *touch* a single hair on Mallory's head, and I'll tell them everything."

"You really think they'd believe you? A traitor?" Canary laughs, reaching into his pocket. "I'd cut off your tongue, but it'd be a waste of my time." He pulls out a Nightjade syringe, plunging it into my brother's neck before he has the chance to react.

Randy falls unconscious, and Canary drags him out of frame. I hear the sound of a car driving away.

The footage ends, and Jade and I can't move. I'm not sure how long we remain frozen until she stands, clutching her stomach. She storms through the glass door and makes it to the elevator. It doesn't close before she falls to her knees, vomiting onto the floor.

I itch to run after her, but a quiet rage roots me in place. There is still one question left unanswered. One other desperate itch I have that will make all of this okay—and I need a name to be able to fulfill it.

I close out of the security footage, scroll to the bottom of Randy's file, and stop breathing.

I know who killed my brother.

EDDIE

Sunday, April 21
84 Beds Made

♪ HONEST - BAND OF SKULLS ♪

"Anvil."

The word pries my eyes open.

I fold forward, instantly regretting the sudden movement when my vision darkens, blood rushing to my head. I squeeze my eyes shut, reaching to rub my forehead—but my hands rest in my lap, bound by rope.

"Pool cue."

I blink my surroundings into place. I'm in a room with metal walls. No —a van. I look left and see a driver and another figure in the passenger's seat, but I can only view the back of their heads. They wear hoods that hide their faces.

"Incentivized monitor lizard."

Just enough light bleeds through the van's tinted windows to illuminate Aaron's bruised face as he slumps against the wall across from me, hands tied together. His legs are stretched out in front of him, and his feet nearly touch my wall. Even with the restraints, he tosses what appears to be a pinecone back and forth each time he speaks. If he notices I'm awake, he doesn't show it.

"Lead dinner plates."

I lean forward, glancing at the people at the front, and then back at him, whispering. "Did you hit your head?"

"Not yet, but I've been thinking about it." He flashes a fake grin before returning to tossing his pinecone. "I've been playing a fun little game with our friends over there. I'm calling it my Homicidal Bucket List."

Our captors seem unfazed by the subtle threat and ignore him. I wonder how long they've been subjected to his list of ways to kill them. They're either unbothered, or don't see him as a real threat.

Aaron tosses the pinecone into the air and catches it. "Care to join in?"

I glare, unamused, then look outside again. Beyond the windshield, all I see is pine and glimpses of a desaturated setting sun. "Where are we?"

"Why would I know that?"

"How long have you been awake?"

"An hour. Maybe less." He sneezes, likely from all the dust. The whole van is covered in it.

"Have we made any turns?"

He pauses to think. "Not since I woke up."

"Has the road been windy at all?"

"No."

"So we've been going in the same direction for a while."

"Probably."

I stare at my dress, knowing Margot's locket is tucked inside. I try to reach for it, but I can't turn my hands inward when they're bound together at the wrist like this.

"Hey," I whisper. Aaron looks at me, and I use my chin to quietly gesture for him to come over. He glances at the driver and passenger, then slides over to sit at my left side.

"Check my compass," I whisper.

Hands still tied, he opens my locket and reads it, then closes it. "Northeast."

If we've been going directly northeast for this long...

"Silver Fir," I mutter.

His eyes dart to mine. "What?"

"That's where we're going. It has to be."

Aaron looks like he might vomit, and I don't think it's from motion sickness. "What makes you so sure?"

I don't get the chance to answer, because the van takes a sharp turn. We aren't buckled in, and the bend nearly makes me slide in the other direction, but Aaron holds onto my arm. Just as the turn mellows, the van takes another one.

"Road's getting windy," he mutters.

"Yeah, no shit."

"We gotta get out of here. If that's really where they're taking us, we're screwed." He glances over his shoulder. "Especially if they recognize me."

I furrow my brows. "What do you mean?"

He looks over his shoulder again and leans in closer, letting out a strained sigh. "I had a... run-in with some Gamblers a couple years back. It wasn't exactly pretty—I'll tell you that."

So that explains the grudge Beau was referring to. "How bad was it?"

He picks at the pinecone. "They probably want me dead."

I look around the van, trying to find something we could use to cut our ties. It's a stolen vehicle, from the looks of it. There are plastic bins filled with painting supplies, a tarp, and a few mostly empty cans. Aside from the painting gear, a few stray pinecones, some leaves, and blankets of dust, we are the only cargo.

My eyes widen, then flicker down to my boot. *My knife is still in there.*

I shift so I'm sitting cross-legged and bring my foot close enough to reach inside. It takes me a moment with my restraints, but I eventually unsheathe it. I'm about to reach over and cut Aaron's bonds but pause when I realize he's holding back a grin. "What?"

"Nothing." He sees my glare and sighs. "I like it when you use knives. There. Happy?"

I roll my eyes. He turns so his back is facing the front of the van, covering me as I saw away at the rope. The van makes another sharp turn, but we keep ourselves steady, and I cut through the ties. He cuts mine when his hands are free.

I realize his satchel is still slung over his shoulder. "You have your bag. Why couldn't you have used one of your knives while I was out?"

"I couldn't reach into it. And it's not like I would've been able to cut through mine myself."

I crease my brows at the bag. "They let you keep your stuff on you?"

"I guess."

"That's kind of weird, isn't it?"

"This *whole thing* is weird." He lets out another sneeze, then looks at our captors again. "Look. We need to do something about *them*."

"Like what? Hijack the van?"

"Something like that."

I glance over him, staring through the windshield. The road is windier now, and through breaks in the trees, I catch glimpses of smaller trees blanketing the horizon, like we're high up.

He yawns, grabbing the side of his jaw. "My ears are popping."

"I think we're going up a mountain." I look through the windshield again; there are no railings on the exposed side of the road. The driver's steadiness is the only thing keeping us from falling a thousand feet over the edge. "There's no way we're hijacking this van all the way up here."

"Then what do you suggest we do?"

"We'll figure it out when we get there."

"That's a shit plan."

"Well it's the only one we have, alright?"

Aaron leans his head back against the wall and stares at the ceiling.

"What about the others?" I whisper. "Do you think they'll be able to track us down?"

"We've traveled pretty far. I wouldn't count on it."

"They have the coordinates to Silver Fir," I say, remembering I left them with Lori.

"Yeah, but those won't mean anything unless they know who took us. They might not even realize we were taken right away. Whatever tracks we left behind could be gone by the time they come to that conclusion."

I study our surroundings again. There's nothing useful in this van. I'm about to give up on trying to find a solution when my eyes linger on the paint cans. I glance at the taillights in the back.

The driver is focused on the turns, and the captor in the passenger's seat appears to be asleep. They don't notice me as I make my way toward the back of the van with my knife.

I use my hand to stir up some of the dust, sending clouds of it flying in Aaron's direction. He scowls, but before he can ask what I'm doing, he lets out another loud sneeze.

At the same time, I jam my knife into one of the taillights.

It doesn't shatter completely, but the crack I created is large enough for me to take one of the nearly empty paint cans and pour a trail outside. White paint leaks through the break, and hopefully onto the road behind us.

"Are you sure that's the wisest idea?" Aaron hisses. "What if the wrong person finds your breadcrumbs?"

"You really think a Chaser would be all the way up here?" I whisper back.

"It's unlikely, but not impossible."

"We want the others to track us down, don't we?" I argue. "Lori has Chaser training. She should be able to follow our tracks. It might take them a while, but it's better than no plan at all."

The paint can empties. I start to pour another one through it until that one is empty too. The other ones have no more paint left to give, so I return to Aaron's side.

After a few more turns, we're no longer on the side of the mountain but winding deeper into the woods. When I study the view from the windshield again, I notice patches of snow on the roadside. The patches turn into full blankets as we drive higher, until everything is coated in white. The sight of the snow makes my stomach churn.

Aaron looks even sicker. *Maybe he is motion sick after all*, I wonder, remembering him on the train. I know he hates riding in cars, but that can't be it. He almost looks afraid.

I try not to think about what the Gamblers could have done to create an impossibility like that.

The van comes to a stop. Aaron and I exchange glances as our captors climb out.

Unsteadily, we rise to our feet. Aaron bends to whisper in my ear. "Keep your knife close."

I hide it behind my back, and the doors swing open. Our captors are wearing plague masks like the ones we saw on the train. They both hold Yesterday guns. *There's no way I'm overpowering them with a knife.*

Aaron freezes at the sight of them, speechless.

The two figures stare at us, not uttering a single command. We snap out of our shock, and Aaron steps in front of me to walk out of the vehicle. While I'm covered, I quickly lift my foot up behind me and slide my knife back into its sheath.

The van doors slam shut. The sun has dipped below the horizon just enough so that everything is shadowed in a cool, dark blue, but there is still enough light left for me to take in our surroundings.

We've reached an expansive clearing in the middle of the woods, entirely blanketed with snow. A few wooden buildings are scattered around the edges of the clearing, maybe tool sheds or cabins. But what catches my eye is the towering A-frame lodge that rests at the top of a hill, with log walls, glowing amber windows, and railed balconies at every level.

It sure as hell looks like an abandoned ski resort to me.

"So this is Silver Fir," I mutter to Aaron. He nods.

I can see something moving in the corner of my view, drawing my eyes upward. A ski lift carries swinging seats up and down the hill in both directions. I start to wonder how they're still running, but then I notice that solar panels are fixed atop every post.

Our captors press their guns to our backs, corralling us toward one of the oncoming seats.

"Guys, guys. Let's talk about this," Aaron says, turning his head over his shoulder. "Is this really necessary? I mean, I don't mind walking up the hill, if that's where we're headed."

One of them pushes him onto the lift, and I'm next.

Aaron keeps his gaze fixed straight ahead, trying not to look down as the lift carries us farther up the hill, rising higher and higher. I glance behind us and see the masked figures sitting in a seat behind us, watching in silence.

"What if we don't jump off?" Aaron whispers in my ear. "This thing runs in circles, right? We could just stay put forever and never come down."

"That's stupid."

"I'd rather starve to death up here than face what might be down there."

"They could shoot at us."

"What if we jumped and made a run for it?"

"You really think they'll let that happen? Just by being here, we've seen too much, haven't we? I've heard enough about the Gamblers to know they'll kill us before they let us escape. And I don't think we can make it very far in the snow."

Aaron doesn't say a word.

It's quiet for a moment as the lift carries us higher, and I shake my head. "I don't understand why they didn't just kill us for trespassing on the spot. I mean, why go through all the trouble of knocking us out and driving us up here?"

"They probably want information," Aaron mutters. "They'll want to know why we were trespassing. Maybe even more."

"About the other Unseen?"

"Like I said, they're disorganized. They don't have any sort of sustainable structure like we did at the Cut. They'll want to use us for whatever they can before killing us."

I stare at my hands, which are a little red from the bonds, but otherwise fine. "Don't you think it's weird they didn't tie us up again?"

"Maybe they think we won't escape. Or can't."

The thought makes me shudder.

We approach the top of the hill, and I glance over my shoulder. Behind us, our captors casually aim their guns.

"We have to jump," I whisper.

"*What?*"

"Aaron."

"I'm not jumping."

"Aaron."

"You can't make me."

I push him, and we land on our feet in the snow.

The masked figures land swiftly behind us, then return to our backs to guide us up the remaining stretch of hill to the front of the lodge. We walk up the porch steps, and they open one of the glass double doors before shoving us through.

We step inside what appears to be a lobby of sorts. It's not as terrifying as I thought it would be. The room has high ceilings crossed with wooden beams, and in the center is a red rug filled with black and brown geometric patterns. A coffee table rests on top of it, circled by three plump brown sofas, each one adorned with cross-stitched throw pillows that say things like *HOME SWEET HOME* and *ALL I NEED IS COFFEE AND A GOOD BOOK*. I crinkle my nose.

A fire flickers in a massive stone fireplace that extends up to the ceiling. Faded paintings decorate the mantle, along with old clocks from the Yesterdays and painted wooden sculptures of bears. Nothing is coated in dust, but I have a feeling that everything has been in its place for a long time.

Someone stands in front of the fireplace, arms crossed.

Like the captors who guard the door behind us, this person's face is covered with a mask. They're dressed in an oversized maroon knit sweater, and worn jeans patched with miscellaneous scraps of green and brown fabric.

For an entire minute, no one moves a muscle—until the figure takes off their mask.

She's young, close to our age. Her wavy black hair is choppy and falls just below her chin. Half of it is loosely tied back in a red velvet ribbon I recognize from the train. I can tell she cut her bangs herself, and they look like feathers strewn across her forehead.

She stares at Aaron like she wants to set him on fire.

He stares at her, unblinking. "Raven."

She steps forward, pausing in front of him. Her face is expressionless. "Take off your glasses."

A slight crease forms in Aaron's brow. "What?"

She clenches her teeth. "Just do it."

Slowly, he removes his glasses. They stare at each other for a moment—and she punches him in the face.

Her fist cracks into Aaron's jaw. "You greasy rat bastard!"

He squeezes his eyes shut, folding forward and grabbing the side of his face. "What the hell is wrong with you?"

"I thought I told you I'd skin you alive if I ever saw your face again."

"You mentioned it." Aaron seethes through a grimace, straightening his posture. "But I'm not exactly here by choice, remember?"

"You were trespassing." She steps even closer, and he glares down at her, fuming. She's taller than I am, and she almost meets him at eye level. I can practically see the raging static flickering between their glares. She's the one to speak first. "Sit down."

Aaron presses his lips together, exhaling heavily through his nose before doing as she says. We both take a seat on the sofa behind us. The fireplace crackles in the hearth, and Aaron studies it with his arms folded across his chest, leg shaking incessantly.

"You two." Raven nods toward the figures guarding the door. "Come over here."

They walk over and stand by her side.

"Why don't you take off your masks?"

The one to her right obeys, removing the mask and tossing it to the ground. He's a tall, narrow-framed boy with bony features and a long face. He has board-straight black hair that falls well below his shoulders, and his skin is so pale it almost looks sickly. Dark circles shadow his green eyes, and I notice he wears a set of silver rings in his ears. He coughs into a handkerchief before shoving it into his pocket and staring at Aaron, whose eyes widen in recognition.

The boy sharpens his gaze, and he doesn't say a word.

My attention shifts to the figure on Raven's left. They remove their mask next, tossing it onto one of the couches before facing us. He shoves his hands into the pockets of his black hoodie, and my breath catches in my throat.

"Hey."

I stare at Milo, unmoving, eyes peeled so wide I can feel the heat from the fireplace burning into them. But all I can do is study him, rooted in place.

The stillness only lasts for so long before I jump to my feet and wrap my arms around him.

I hold him like that for a long time, squeezing him so tightly I'm surprised I don't break something. I close my eyes and bury my face into his chest. "You're an idiot."

The relief only lasts for so long, and I open my eyes.

"You're an *idiot*." I pull away from him, folding my arms with a scowl. "Darts? Really?"

"Hey, don't give him all the credit." The other boy pulls out what appears to be a homemade dart flute, then shoves it back into his pocket. His voice is gravelly and deep, like he has a cold. "He was waiting in the car."

Aaron clenches his jaw. "Was that really necessary, Lockley?"

"Thought you were trespassers. Spies for the other half." He glares at Aaron, nostrils flaring. "Wasn't until I got up close that I realized it was *you*. And that Raven would wanna know what you're doing in our neck of the woods."

Aaron rises to his feet. "Oh, you little piece of *shit*."

Lockley crosses his arms. "Hey, I'm not the one who—"

Aaron pulls a hand back, but Raven catches it, fuming. "You two. Out. Now."

They freeze. Lockley nods before pushing Aaron toward the entrance of a hallway at the other end of the lobby.

Aaron shrugs Lockley off him. "Don't touch me." He looks over his shoulder, sparing me one last glance before they disappear down the hall.

I sit in silence, my glare flickering between Raven and Milo, unsure of who to be angrier at. Raven takes a seat on the sofa across from me, crossing one leg over the other. "Let's clear the air, shall we?"

I don't say a word.

"I'm assuming you're the *Eddie* your brother's been going on about."

"I am."

Raven nods. It's quiet for a long time. "Your brother's been... helping us out, as of late."

I look at Milo, who is still standing, but he can't meet my gaze. "It was you on that train?"

"So those Agents were right after all." Raven points a finger at me. "Someone *did* spot the infamous Lavender Voclain at the Traitor's Day festival."

My face pales.

"You're welcome, by the way." She leans back. "They would have found you if we hadn't taken them out."

"You killed them?"

"They're Agents," she spits. "They're the lowest breed of Chaser. Each and every one of them deserves to be exterminated."

I clench my jaw. "Isn't that exactly what they say about us?"

Raven stares at me for a moment, then chuckles. "We'd been trailing that pair of Agents for a while; they'd been getting a little too close for comfort. Investigating our territory for traitors and whatnot. We saw them get on the train and realized it was the perfect opportunity to strike—and test out your brother's little gift, which made the job *very* easy."

My eyes widen. *Aaron was right about the Catnap.*

Raven studies me for a while. "I'm sure you're thinking of all the ways to break your brother out of here and escape with that waste of skin you brought with you, correct?"

I don't say anything.

"Well, before you do anything stupid, I just wanted to let you know— your brother's with *us* now. No one's holding him against his will."

My jaw tightens, and I stare at Milo, eyes glossy. "What is she talking about?"

It goes quiet. I can hear a familiar voice shouting in another room.

Raven turns up to Milo, who still can't look at me. "I think Lockley might need a little help."

Milo nods, sparing me one fleeting glance before taking his exit, leaving Raven and I alone.

She stares at the fire, studying the way it dances in its hearth. I watch it too, until I feel her stare return to me.

"The kid came to us, you see," Raven says. "He wanted our help with a little operation he's been planning, so we struck a deal."

"A deal?"

"He helps us, we help him. That train ride was the first of the four agreed-upon strikes."

"What exactly is he bargaining for?"

"The kid's smart—I'll give you that. Managed to come across coordinates for what he believes to be an Agency safe house. He thinks a friend of yours is located there."

My heart plummets.

"We're going to help him break in." She picks at her nails. "After he helps us, of course."

I keep my mouth glued shut, grinding my teeth as my stomach churns. My fingers curl into fists. *I'm supposed to be handling this,* I think to myself, remembering the phone that's still in my jacket pocket. *I'm supposed to be the one fixing this mess—not Milo.*

"I've been watching you for a long time, Lavender," Raven says. "Don't think I don't know who you are. We all saw that broadcast. We do keep up with the news here, you know."

I dig my nails into my palms. "You don't know a single thing about me."

"Let me make something clear." Raven leans forward. "I could kill you right now, if I wanted to. I probably *should,* given the fact that you and that friend of yours were trespassing on *our* land. Just by being here, you've already seen enough to give us a good reason to silence you. And I've dreamt of slitting that backstabbing rat's throat for a very, very long time."

"Then why don't you?"

"You see, I've grown to enjoy your brother's company. I like him, and I find his particular set of skills quite useful. The kid can build anything. I'll spare your life because I need Milo's cooperation, and I think he'll make a valuable asset to my team." She pauses. "But mostly, I'd like to strike a bargain with you too."

"What do you want?"

"I think you're on the wrong side."

I blink, listening to the fireplace. Wind whistles outside. "What are you saying?"

"I'm not talking about the fact that you're a traitor." She shrugs. "I just think you're the wrong kind of traitor."

"That doesn't make any sense."

"Like I said, I've been keeping a close eye on you. And the thing you pulled with the fire? That was genius. The Corps is raging. They're slowly realizing we're capable of more than what they originally thought, and they're scrambling to get back on the public's good side."

"That fire wasn't planned." I clench my jaw. "I didn't mean for it to get so out of hand."

Raven laughs. "You expect me to believe that?"

A shiver runs down my back.

"Admit it, Eddie." She leans closer, folding her hands across her knees. "You want to see the world burn."

A muscle in my neck twitches. "That's not true."

"I can see it in your eyes. You're angry, and you don't know what to do about it." Her expression turns grim. "I know that feeling well."

"You still haven't told me what you want."

Raven shifts, sitting cross-legged on the couch. "Your little broadcast backfired, and now your people want to keep you hidden. But I think they're missing out on a big opportunity here." She smirks. "I want to make you seen."

My brows draw together. "What do you mean?"

She picks at the stitching on one of the throw pillows. "I hate my father, but there was something he always said that resonates with me to this day." Her gaze flickers to meet mine. "People need a villain."

The look in her eyes sends a chill coursing through my veins, turning every drop of blood cold. Goosebumps prick at my skin.

"You're lucky, Eddie. Do you realize that?"

My scars itch. "How so?"

"You're in the perfect position to manipulate the tide to turn in your favor. The Corps is slowly understanding how useful you could be for their agenda. Everyone knows who you are—everyone saw what you did to your family, to those Chasers."

"Those are lies," I snap.

"But does it matter?" Raven chuckles. "People hate you. For years, they haven't had a solid place to put their anger. But your name? Your face? That's where they're attaching their rage. For us, for the Corps—for everything. I mean, you've seen the protests, right?"

I hesitate, then nod.

"There have been a few riots across the country supporting the Unseen, but most of them are angry at the Corps for allowing the Underground to grow. They can smell the change in the air and they're scared of what might happen. Scared we might disrupt the order they think they need."

Raven picks at the pillow again, the one that reads *HOME SWEET HOME*. It displays a log cabin made of stitched thread with smoke curling out of the chimney and a blue bird flying above it.

"At first, I thought you might be the symbol of hope this rebellion needs. That you could use your spotlight to villainize the Corps and show the public that we can fight back. To sway them to our side. But now, I think your situation—your luck—will be more beneficial to our cause if it's used in... other ways."

I swallow. "What do you mean?"

Raven grins, and it makes me shiver. "If they hate us enough, they'll take down the Corps themselves."

"Unless they target us instead," I say, trying to keep my voice steady. "Start following the Corps' footsteps. Smoking us out. Or worse."

"Then we'll make sure they fear us more than them."

I stare at the fire.

"Either way, no matter who they target, if we cause enough of a stir, we can make the other side self-destruct. Don't you understand how powerful this could be? How angry people get when they feel like they've been betrayed? I want them to fear us so much they tear themselves apart. Brick, by brick, by brick."

I scoff. "And what makes you believe you're capable of something like that?"

Raven pauses. She stares at the pillow for a moment, then tosses it aside. "When there's a wildfire, foxes will use it to their advantage."

My brow creases.

"When prey is fleeing the flames—insects, rabbits, whatever—they take the opportunity to strike."

"I don't know what you mean."

"I think the primary flaw of the Unseen is their hesitation. Their fear," she says. "Groups like your lovely little Cut, for example, believe that in order to make the changes we desire more than anything, we need numbers. That we're simply not strong enough to do anything yet. So they sit, and they wait, and they hope that if they attract enough people to their side, in a decade or two, the numbers will be there. That they can overpower the system in one bold go. But I don't think that someday will ever come."

"They're only trying to go about this safely," I argue. "They want to build up to a downfall, slowly and carefully."

"But that isn't enough." Raven clenches her hands into fists before relaxing them. "People die every day. And eventually, there won't be enough of us left to do anything about it."

I stay silent, unsure of what to say.

"I think the way of the Unseen needs to change. People need to restructure their way of thinking. We can make a greater impact than we realize with smaller, strategic plays. If we can send the state into utter chaos, that'll make room for more capable and organized groups like your Cut to make bigger strikes. We can find their vulnerabilities and prey on them, because a thousand little fires are still a pain in the ass." She looks up at me. "A thousand little fires will draw out the rabbits."

I swallow. "*We'd* be the rabbits."

"No, Eddie. We're the foxes." Raven smirks. "And I want you to be the worst."

"You think I'd make a good scapegoat."

"That's a simpler way of putting it."

"That doesn't sound like something anyone in their right mind would agree to."

"But you aren't in your right mind anymore, are you?" Raven says. "Or maybe, you *are* angry, and your mind is righter than it's ever been."

I meet Raven's stare, glaring. We study each other in silence as the fire continues to crackle in its hearth. But the longer I look into her eyes, the more they begin to feel like a mirror. And for some reason beyond me, I can't deny that there is something like understanding inside of them.

"Maybe," I finally say.

"Can I ask you something?"

I nod.

"Why are you in this?"

"I'm in this because I have to be. I had no other choice."

"I don't think that's true." She narrows her eyes. "What is it that you want?"

I look at Raven, then back at the fire. I think of every burning Unseen camp, of trees reduced to twigs, of the bones that hide beneath melting flesh. My mother's cries. My father's blood. My Margot. My Ren. My everything.

"I want them to burn."

"That's exactly what I'm offering you."

I can't peel my eyes away from the fire.

"Help us with a few jobs. I *won't* kill your pet rat. We'll help get your friend back. You and your brother can stay here, if you like; we know how unbearable End Harbor folk can be. Consider it a trial run of sorts. Then you can make your decision." She picks at her nails. "But if you decline, or try anything stupid like an escape, I won't have a good enough reason to spare *his* life," she says, gesturing toward the hallway.

Aaron.

My throat constricts. Even if I wanted to, I don't think I could escape. Aaron and I can't overpower an entire camp of angry rebels—especially ones with their reputation.

I stare at the hallway, knowing Milo is somewhere beyond it. If Raven is right and he's found what he believes to be a place here—if their cause resonates with him and he is set in his ways—he's not going to back down. We both share the same stubborn blood, and I won't be able to sway him.

I am here because I want to keep my brother safe. That's why I left End Harbor. And right now, my best bet isn't to stop him, but to help him. To agree to Raven's trial run and help Milo fulfill his end of their bargain so I can make sure nothing happens to him.

And maybe—if Milo's right about those coordinates—we might be able to find Ren all on our own. No Agents. No betrayals.

I look at Raven, and I nod. "Okay."

Raven, Lockley, and Milo sit on the couch across from Aaron and me.

I'm not sure how long we've sat in our silence, but it feels like it's been years. Aaron's leg won't stop shaking. When the quiet is too much to bear, he clears his throat. "You cut your hair."

"Really? I hadn't noticed." Raven rolls her eyes. "Small talk doesn't suit you."

"I was just gonna say it looks nice," Aaron snaps. "You're not exactly cut out for it either."

She shakes her head. "I'm in absolute awe, Aaron, that the first substantial thing you have to say to me is a painfully obvious observation about the length of my hair." Her face contorts in disgust. "I should fulfill my promise right here, right now."

It's quiet again, and Aaron looks up at her. "I'm—"

"It would be daring of you to finish that sentence." Raven's voice is cold.

Milo and I exchange confused glances.

It goes quiet again. Aaron's legs keep shaking. He fidgets with his thumbs, and when that's no longer enough, he reaches into his pocket.

"Don't even think about pulling that knife out," Raven snaps. "You're a big kid now. You can sit still for one minute without leaving wood shavings all over my floor."

Aaron doesn't say anything.

I study the way Raven glares at him, and the way he can't bring himself to look at her. *How does she know he carves when he's nervous?*

If she has this much control over him, Aaron either did something wrong, or he's afraid of her—maybe even both.

"Okay, what did he do to you?" Milo turns to Raven. "I mean, his ego could use a good blow every now and then, but... I feel like there's a very good story behind this."

"He betrayed us—that's what." Raven folds her arms, skinning Aaron to ribbons with her stare. "But I guess that's what I deserve for trusting a Chaser."

I laugh, and everyone stares at me in silence.

Raven blinks. "I don't get the joke."

"Guard," Aaron mutters with his teeth clenched, like he's correcting her.

My smile fades. "What?"

Raven exchanges confused glances with Lockley, then studies me. "You really don't know?"

The way she looks at me makes my heart drop to my stomach. Like all the air in the room is slowly depleting. "Know what?"

Aaron's eyes darken, and he glares at her. "Raven..."

She scoffs. "Of course he kept it from you."

"Aaron?" I turn to him. "What is she talking about?"

He can't seem to meet my gaze.

"*Aaron.*"

It feels like the floor is shattering beneath me. The room spins, every edge blurring.

"You know what a Double is," he mutters.

My heart pounds. I can't breathe.

Finally, Aaron looks at me like it's the hardest thing he's ever done. "I was our first."

PART THREE
CAP
SIZE

EDDIE

Sunday, April 21
84 Beds Made

It feels like someone is deflating my lungs with a needle.

All the oxygen drains from my body as I watch the fire dance in its hearth. The room spins. It's caving in, and I can't do anything but let it devour me whole.

Aaron was a Double.

Aaron was a Double.

"You were a Chaser."

I feel sculpted, like I'm made of marble and I can't move. And if I do—if I turn my neck to look at him—I will crumble.

"I was never a *real* Chaser, alright?" Aaron stares at the fire. His throat twitches. "I was a Guard."

"A Guard?" Milo asks.

"Who do you think runs the Tombs?" Raven says.

It feels like my stomach is turning inside out. My lungs fill with cold, empty air, like I'm out in the snow again. My chin quivers. "You were at the Tombs?"

"That's where they send cadets who didn't perform well enough to be an Officer and aren't tame enough to be put behind a desk." Aaron looks at his hands. "The ones who either need to be discarded efficiently, or taught a lesson."

My throat burns like I've swallowed hot coals. I force myself to speak unsteadily. "When was this?"

He glides his thumb across the back of his hands. "The summer before last."

One year before I met him.

My lips tremble. "You were seventeen."

He still can't look at me. "At first."

I can feel my heart constrict. "You turned eighteen in there?"

He doesn't say anything.

Every muscle in my body stiffens. My hands curl into fists in my lap. It feels like I'm not even here. Like the words coming out of Aaron's mouth are only figments of my imagination, and I'm trapped in a nightmare with a scream congesting my throat.

Only one whispered word manages to fall out. "Why?"

"Command's had an interest in establishing Doubles for as long as the Cut's been standing. They sent a few candidates out for training, but... there was an issue regarding success rates."

A pallor spreads over my face. "They didn't make it."

He barely nods, still unable to meet my stare.

"By the time they were ready to move forward with their next operation, I was the only person my age they could trust with an operation like that." He keeps his eyes glued to his hands. "My dad was also in the middle of conducting his Nightjade experiments, and since I was the only one with training from him, they thought I'd be able to bring back some samples. Not to mention the fact that my eye was already blinded from my first debug. I could handle being given a tracker with a false identity. My dad made special contacts to cover the scarring and everything.

"It was supposed to be a simple job. Complete basic training, fake my false identity's death, bring back information and samples of Nightjade serum."

He leans forward, resting his arms on his lap. He studies the fire, watching the embers dance before disappearing into thin air. "But it didn't work out that way."

I swallow. "What happened?"

"I couldn't complete the final test."

"Test?" Milo asks.

"Your first extermination," Aaron mutters.

Chills weave up my spine.

"I was stupid back then. I didn't know how to think with my head or get my priorities straight, and I couldn't do it."

Milo's voice is quiet. "What'd you do?"

"I tried to help him escape."

My brother's eyes widen.

"Used the syringe to take out one of the Officers who came into the room when I refused to exterminate the prisoner. Took the other one hostage with his own gun. Had him program the elevator to take us to the main floor. And I told the prisoner to run." He chuckles, but the sound is empty and bitter. "I didn't realize the scanners stationed by the entrance could be turned into electric fences."

My stomach churns as I try not to paint the image in my head.

"The Agent they dispatched to neutralize the situation was supposed to kill me for what I did. But he was impressed. Said I completed the extermination in record time." He stares at his hands. "My target was wrong, but no one had ever killed that quickly before."

Raven stares at him with something like pity, or maybe understanding. She notices me watching her and looks away.

"The Agent was forgiving. They were initially going to assign me to the Agency Division if I followed through with the final exam, and he thought it would be a waste to exterminate someone with..." He pauses and swallows. "*A darkness so raw and untamed.*"

Aaron shakes his head. I notice his leg has begun to twitch, like he's trying to keep it from shaking. "He didn't want to kill me, but I wasn't suitable for the Officer Division. So he made me a Guard."

He goes quiet for a long time. We all watch him in silence until he speaks up again. "I didn't believe in hell until I met the Tombs."

I want to reach out to him, to give him my hand. But every part of my body is frozen, and I'm not even sure I'm blinking or breathing at all.

"That's where we met," Raven intervenes. "We were planning to escape together, but... he had other plans."

My eyes widen as Cecil's words flood back to me. *They were responsible for the revolt? And Cecil didn't mention Aaron?*

Aaron snaps his head up. "I was trying to protect all of you."

"By ratting us out to the Guards for a promotion?"

"I turned myself in so *you* could escape." His eyes darken as he lowers his voice. "*Without* the damage you still ended up causing."

"At least we tried to fight back," Raven snaps. "At least we didn't give up like you did."

Aaron flinches, neck muscles twitching. Like he's trying with everything he has to stay calm. He breathes in shakily and forces himself to continue.

"I managed to escape on my own." He traces the *X* that cuts through his 2 of Spades. "Removed the false tracker. Somehow managed to make it back to the Cut in one piece. And that was that."

No one says a word. My eyes gloss over, still unblinking as the words slowly seep in.

Aaron was a Guard. A *Chaser*. And he never told me.

No one did.

In my mind, I stretch as far back as I can, retracing every single memory from the moment I first stumbled across him in those woods, desperate for any missed sign, any indication that he was keeping something like this swallowed down, buried where I couldn't find it.

This is why he knows so much about what it means to be a Chaser. This is why his hatred for them is so strong—why his gaze carves out at the thought of them until there is nothing but emptiness. Because he was once the very thing he despises more than anything else.

This is why he hates the Gamblers too.

Maybe I don't know the full story, but I see the way he interacts with Raven. He trusted her once—and he was betrayed.

But he never told me about any of it.

All this time, I thought I knew Aaron better than I knew myself. And throughout every moment, he was hiding this side of himself as though it didn't exist at all.

I thought he trusted me too. And I was wrong.

"Voclain."

I can't breathe.

"Say something, Eddie." His voice cracks a little. "Please."

Raven clears her throat. "I'll leave you two alone."

She and Milo walk toward the room's exit. My brother turns his head to give me one last glance before leaving.

I'm shaking by the time I gather enough strength to turn my head and look at Aaron. When I see his face, the pain behind his eyes, all I can think about is that night in the cave. The way he cried over wounds I didn't yet understand. His nightmares.

What did they do to him?

"You should have told me." I think of everyone back at the Cut who wouldn't give me a solid answer about Aaron, or his anger, or his hurt. Every word takes strength to say. "They all knew, didn't they?"

Aaron doesn't look at me. "I told them not to say anything."

"Why?"

He stares at the fire. "I didn't think you'd understand."

"How could you even say a thing like that?" I rise to my feet, trembling. I try to keep my voice steady. "You went through hell in there, and you thought I'd be angry at you?"

"You *are* angry."

My voice cracks. "Because you don't trust me."

Silence.

My throat tightens, like a snake is tied around it and it won't stop constricting. Like I'm suffocating. Because I do understand. He was doing what he thought was right. *He was trying to help the Unseen.*

Of course I hate Chasers. I hate the world we live in and Raven was right when she said I'm angry, and I was telling the truth when I said I'd love to see it burn.

But I could never hate Aaron, and he should know that.

"Don't you see how unfair it is to just assume I don't care? To assume I can't understand? You've never trusted me as much as I trust you, and you won't even tell me *why*." My eyes are watering. "Every scar you have—physical or not—you keep from me. And I don't know what I did wrong."

He creases his brow, jaw twitching. His lips part, like he wants to say something he believes he shouldn't. They close. *He still won't talk to me.*

I stare at him, exhausted and hurt and tired of poking the same snake. Maybe he was right when he said I don't know him. When he said I could never understand.

The room is a pinwheel, and I can't stop shaking. It feels like every frustration I've had with Aaron and his distance is snowballing, compacting into one giant, inescapable block of ice, and I'm trapped within it. I hug my stomach and turn around.

"Voclain—"

"Don't."

"*Eddie.*"

My blood freezes. I spin around to find Aaron standing behind me. He is so close I can smell him. The familiar sharpness of evergreen and cedarwood, herbs and earth. He's looking at me like he wants to say something, but he still has so much to guard—and it makes me want to scream.

"I trust you." His words are soft. "More than anyone."

"Then why do you—"

"Because I can't lose you."

I blink, letting the world around me dull to a pause.

"There are parts of me that I don't want you to see. That I *can't* let you see. Because if you did, you'd turn away. And I'm not sure you'd ever want to look back." He meets my gaze, which wrangles my stomach into knots. His voice wavers. "I don't think it's possible to heal a wound like that, Voclain."

My words are snared in my throat.

"You have—*no idea* how angry I am. All the time." He laughs cynically. "And I—I don't want you to see me angry. Because there is *nothing* I hate more than the person I become when I'm like that." He swallows. "I don't want you to hate me too."

It feels like he's twisting a knife into my chest. My voice falls to a whisper. "What's making you so angry?"

His eyes are red. His lips press together. "You're really gonna make me say it?"

"Aaron." My voice falters. "Please."

"*Me*, alright?" He closes his eyes and runs both hands through his hair, clutching it in fistfuls. "*God*. It's always been me."

All I can do is stare at him, unable to move or speak or blink. Like he's in another nightmare that I can't pull him out of, no matter how badly I want to.

Every bone in my entire body would break to put him back together again. But I've tried, and I've failed every time.

He shakes his head, and he walks out of the room.

I want to go after him, but I can't move. My legs are made of lead, and I'm trapped underwater.

I sit in front of the fire, bring my knees to my chest, and watch it burn.

I'm not sure how much time has passed when Milo sits next to me, or why I start to cry. But he hugs me, and we sit like that for a long time, and the fire is warm.

EDDIE

Sunday, April 21
84 Beds Made

♪ CHAMELEON SKIN - THE FLATLINERS ♪

Lockley, Milo, and I sit on the bench of a long wooden dining table, which is covered with all kinds of dishes I can't bring myself to eat.

The other two seem to have no problem with the food, and they converse like friends about some Yesterday album between mouthfuls of chicken and mashed potatoes. Lockley coughs a lot, I notice—the way Aaron did when we were around the smoke—likely due to his time spent at the Tombs. If Aaron was a Guard there, even for a little bit, the furnaces would have damaged his lungs.

I wonder how much time Lockley spent as a prisoner for him to have to carry a bloody handkerchief in his pocket.

The dining hall is on the second floor, decorated to match the lobby. The deer head mounted to the wall across from me is supposed to be charming, but I can't shake the feeling that it's watching me. I avoid making eye contact with it like the plague.

Across from me is a wall of floor-to-ceiling windows showcasing a small balcony outside, where Aaron and Raven converse. They lean against the railing with their backs turned to me. They don't notice me staring.

But Milo does, and he leans over to whisper into my ear. "They were totally a thing."

I glance at him, then back out the window. "What makes you say that?"

"The bickering. The touching." He studies Raven, who elbows Aaron's ribs in annoyance. Then he glances at me again. "Kind of reminds me of you two."

I give him a glare, and he goes back to his conversation with Lockley. After a while, I'm surprised to see Aaron and Raven hug. They pull apart and shake their hands in mild reconciliation.

The two of them look at me, and I avert my gaze quickly. From the corner of my eye, I see Raven nod in my direction. Aaron frowns. She frowns. He glares, rubbing the back of his neck. She smirks.

I stare at my plate and force myself to take a bite of a stale dinner roll.

After a while, they come back inside and join us at the dinner table. Raven sits next to me, and Aaron sits across from her, still unable to look me in the eye. Lockley and Milo drop their conversation, and I focus my attention on the awkward scraping of knives and forks against ceramic.

I nearly jump out of my seat when the door flies open. In walks a young girl with a long braid of auburn hair, carrying a crying toddler on her hip. The toddler has a head of curly brown hair and can't be any older than two.

The girl approaches Raven with an exhausted sigh. "She wouldn't stop asking for you."

Aaron chokes on his food, face pale.

Raven takes the child, who buries her head into her neck, and the crying subsides. "Thanks, Fern. I can watch her for a bit."

Fern studies Aaron with a blank expression, then exits without another word.

Aaron lifts a glass of water, downing a gulp with a shaky hand. He sets the cup down and clears his throat, nodding casually toward the toddler. "Is that—uh—*yours*?"

Milo gives me a look, eyes wide. *I told you*, he mouths, and I kick him under the table.

"*She* is all of ours." Raven glares, but the look melts into something sadder, maybe even guilty. She studies the child in her arms. "This is Jelly."

Aaron's face shifts. He nods, understanding something I don't. "She looks just like her."

"She does, doesn't she?" Raven smiles. "I just wonder where she got those eyes. Her mom's were green."

Jelly finally peels her face away from Raven and stares at me. Her eyes are so wide and icy gray it almost startles me. They're not unsettling, just... knowing. Like she can see right through me. Like she knows something I don't.

"Okay, I'm lost," Milo says. "Do we need a paternity test or what?"

Aaron's face heats up, and I kick Milo again. "*Shut up.*"

"Jelly was our friend. Back at the Tombs," Raven says. "She's named after her mother."

Was.

Milo nods, giving Raven a sympathetic look. "What was she like?"

Raven's smile is sad and brief. "The kindest person I've met."

"She could read you like a book," Lockley says. "It was like she could see straight into your core with a single look and immediately know how to reach it."

I smile, unable to stop picturing Margot. "I've known people like that."

Raven hugs the child, and I can hear her humming what must be a lullaby. It soothes something in me. I sit there, listening, and for the briefest of moments, I forget where I am. *It's beautiful.*

It ends when Lockley starts coughing into his handkerchief. This fit seems worse than the others I've seen. Milo pats him on the back and slides him a glass of water. Lockley takes a grateful gulp, and my brother helps him to his feet. "Come on. Let's get you upstairs."

Lockley keeps coughing, wrapping an arm around Milo's shoulder as the two of them take their exit.

"How is he?" Aaron asks.

Raven's voice is somber. "You saw him."

"Leaving the smoke didn't help?"

She shakes her head. "It's slowed the progression, but nothing's reversed."

There's a pause, and Aaron folds his arms across his chest. "Elecampane. Tea or tincture. You can use it as a stimulant expectorant. That'll soothe the bronchial spasms."

Raven glances at him, suppressing a smirk. "You really know your stuff."

He shrugs, picking at his plate. "We've all changed."

It goes quiet.

"You can use thyme too. That'll help with spasmodic coughs," I add. "Licorice root, elderberry. As much green tea as he can stand."

Raven's smirk finally comes to light. "You too."

Aaron stands. "I need a shower."

"Milo's room is on the third floor," Raven says. "Fourth door to the left. Room 307. He's with Lockley right now, so you'll have it all to yourself."

Aaron leaves without another word.

It takes me a while to finish my dinner. Raven stays with me the entire time, watching my every bite. For some strange reason, the silence isn't uncomfortable. I think I prefer her company to being left here alone with the buck.

"It's getting late," she says once I'm done, rising to her feet. "I should put Jelly to bed."

I nod. She turns around to walk away.

"Raven?"

She pauses, glancing over her shoulder.

"Thank you."

I'm not entirely sure why I said it, but she seems to understand. She gives me a small smile before taking her leave.

Now I'm alone with that deer.

I can't stand the way it looks at me, so I get up and walk through an open doorway, entering what appears to be the kitchen. It's tight, with dark wood cabinets and speckled blue laminate countertops. There's a textured white fridge from the Yesterdays covered in magnets shaped like deer and bears, and a window overlooking the mountain, dressed with green gingham curtains.

I start carrying dirty dishes from the table to the sink, scrubbing each one clean. I place the last plate on the drying rack, wash my hands, then lean against the counter with my hands in my pockets. *I really don't want to go upstairs.*

I glance at an old clock hanging on the wall, which appears to be stuck in time, so I peer over my shoulder to look out the window instead. It's dark. It's getting late, and I'm exhausted. *I can't stay down here forever.*

I'm about to walk out of the kitchen when someone else enters, and I recognize her as the girl from earlier.

Fern stops when she sees me. "You startled me."

Close up, I notice a splash of freckles dusted across her nose. Her eyes are the same vibrant green as her sweater, and she wears a patched pair of denim shorts, like she's not even fazed by the cold.

"Sorry," I say.

"It's alright." Fern walks to the counter and opens a wooden bread box, retrieving two slices. She hands one to me. "Want one?"

I eye the slice of bread with suspicion. "Just... bread?"

She takes a bite of her slice. "Yeah. What about it?"

I hide a smile and accept her offering, taking a bite. Then another, and another, until I've eaten the whole thing, and I'm convinced it's the best bread I've ever tasted.

"Good, huh?" She grabs another slice from the box, and hands me another one too. "Made it fresh yesterday."

"You made this?"

She shrugs. "Someone has to."

We eat our second slices in silence.

She hops onto the counter and takes a seat. "You're that girl on TV."

I nod.

"Did you really... you know... kill all those people?"

"No."

"Good." She nods. "I didn't think so."

It's quiet, and I stare at the ground, unsure of what to say.

"You're Milo's sister, right?"

"I am."

"I'm Fern." She reaches out a hand to shake mine, and I take it. "Jelly's aunt." She kicks her legs as they dangle over the counter's edge, and I realize just how young she is. She can't be any older than fourteen.

My stomach twists. *She was only a kid when she was sent to the Tombs.*

"How's he doing?" Fern asks, pulling me out of my thoughts.

"Aaron?"

She nods.

I instinctively prepare the polite answer but decide against it. "I'm... not sure."

Fern stares at her hands. "I don't think he's as bad as Raven and the others think."

I give her a sad smile. "He really isn't too bad, is he?"

Something about that sentence makes my chest ache. I stare through the kitchen's open doorway, seeing beyond the dining room, studying the distant stairwell's polished wood steps. I turn back to Fern, who's still fidgeting with her hands.

"He helped us a lot." She pauses. "At the Tombs."

"How so?"

"He was a Guard, but... not really. So he could sneak us food, better water. He's really smart too. Knew a lot about healing. He wasn't very good at it yet, but he was the best we had." She sighs. "I don't think Jelly would be here today if it weren't for him."

"Really?"

Fern nods. "He made sure my sister was fed and healthy. We all worked to cover her shifts for her, but he did too. Picked up a shovel himself and everything. The other Guards thought he was crazy and gave him a lot of trouble for it." She pauses. "He's the one who helped deliver Jelly. Before we got out."

My throat tightens. "Sounds a lot like Aaron."

It's quiet for a moment, and she looks up at me, eyes glossy. "I never got to tell him thank you."

I give her another small smile. "I'm sure he knows."

"Take care of him for me, will you?"

I nod. "Alright."

She grabs another slice of bread, hops off the counter, and leaves.

I continue to stand in the kitchen in solitude until my legs ache and my eyelids feel heavy. I take a deep breath, and I walk upstairs.

I find Milo's room and knock. No one answers, so I step inside and close the door. It's a lot smaller than my room at End Harbor, with dark wood floors, log cabin walls, and one-too-many decorative plaques displaying taxidermied fish for my liking. There's one bed with a dark green quilt and more cross-stitched throw pillows. I crinkle my nose at one that says *ALL ARE WELCOME HERE.* Everything smells like the leftovers of some cheap floral candle burned long ago, and the earthy aroma of wood.

I glance at the cracked-open door to what must be the bathroom. I smell tea tree soap and feel humid remnants of hot steam drifting through, but the lights are off and no one is inside. Aaron must have showered and then left, maybe on a walk to clear his head.

I turn off the room's main overhead light, leaving only the dim glow of a bedside lamp. I reach inside an ornate mahogany dresser and find an old oversized tee twice my size. It's black with a bear on it, who appears to be wearing some sort of park ranger's hat and is telling me something about fire safety that I don't bother reading. I find a baggy pair of gray sweats too, and I change before climbing into bed. I set my knife on the nightstand, and I'm about to turn off the lamp when the door opens.

I fold forward and whip my head to the left, pausing when I realize it's Aaron.

He closes the door behind him. His hair is damp and glossy in the dim lamplight. As always, a few wayward strands hang in front of his eyes, refusing to stay in place. He wears a similar pair of sweats, likely stolen from the same dresser, and a loose olive green tee that says *WOMEN WANT ME, FISH FEAR ME* in dark letters, circling around an illustration of a fish who doesn't look too happy to be at the receiving end of a hook. It's short-sleeved, so I can see the scar on his arm.

I climb out of bed and hug my torso. I'm still unable to hold his gaze for very long, let alone open my mouth to speak.

There's a long pause. I wait for him to tell me why he's here, but instead, he limps his way to where I stand, pausing only inches in front of me. I look up at him, trying to read his stoic expression. I fail miserably.

We stare at each other for a long time. His voice is low when he finally speaks.

"I jumped off a roof when I was four years old."

I blink.

"I was trying to make it to a tree I'd never been able to climb. The one across from my bedroom window, back when I still lived above the shop." He studies his palm, tracing a thin line with his finger, so faint I'd never noticed it before. "And I did. I caught the closest branch and pulled myself up."

My voice comes out as a whisper. "Then what?"

"I climbed it."

I want to nod—to say something—but I can only stare.

"I almost made it to the top too." The corner of his lip twitches. "Until I saw Lori. Barely even three years old, wandering the beach across from the shop, all on her own. So damn close to the shore."

He lifts his eyes to study mine. We hold each other like that for a moment, caught in each other's gazes, trying to decipher what stares back.

"So I jumped down. And I got there just in time." He looks at his palm again. "A branch gave my back a good gash on the way down. Sprained my ankle too."

Another long pause fills the air. I divert my stare to the scar, eyeing the way the line cuts through his callused skin.

And then, he reaches out—and he takes my right hand in his. Gently, so that my fingers can trace the scar. So I can feel it for myself.

"Is this it?" My words are barely more than a breath.

"No. This was my first carving mistake."

"First?"

"*Only*," he corrects, lips curled with the hint of a smirk. But it falls away, and so does my hand when he lets go.

Before I realize what's happening, he's removing his shirt, and he turns around.

A jagged ghost of a gash warps a diagonal line through his back, the flesh raised and bumpy. I reach out, like he's guiding my touch again. But he isn't. There is only my hand, moving on its own accord, suspended by invisible puppet strings beyond my control. I trace the gash so lightly my fingers barely touch his skin at all. But now that I'm up close, I notice more than just the mark from the tree.

Dozens of thin cuts crosshatch across his back, each one clearly a blade's footprint. I try to count them, but I give up when I reach twenty. My lips part. My touch lingers.

What happened to him?

"You didn't have to show me," I mutter. My hand shakes.

He stands like that for a while, every inch of him tense. It's his rigidity that pulls me back down to earth, grounding me as the reality of what we're doing settles in. I remove my hand, but his fingers catch mine.

"Eddie." His posture softens. He turns his head to the side to look back at me, but it's not enough for me to see his expression.

I'm not sure why my pulse quickens, or why I suddenly feel so uncertain. Like in a blink, I could start crying, or throw up, or laugh, or maybe all three at once. But there is one thing I am sure of.

He is standing here, and I can't seem to think of anything else but the fact that I want him to be.

Aaron's next words are whispers. "I wanted to."

His fingers twitch, like he wants to hold mine tighter. But his grip loosens instead. My hand falls away.

He takes a seat on the edge of the bed. I sit next to him. He brings a hand to his left shoulder and traces a faint line. "This one's Beau's fault."

"How so?"

"Car crash." He lets out a one-note chuckle. "He flipped the damn thing over in the woods. Hurt his leg real bad. I had to drag him home."

No wonder he doesn't trust cars. *He's been hurt by them before.*

He lifts his leg and crosses it over his lap so I can see the bottom of his foot. The skin is callused and thick, like it's been burned. He stares down at it. "They make you run over hot coals when you step out of line."

"In training?"

Aaron nods, slowly adjusting his posture, lowering his leg and turning so he's facing me. He rests his hands in his lap and studies them.

In this moment, I realize I've never seen Aaron like this before. When I saw him swimming back in End Harbor, he was too far away for me to make out his scars. But now, he is vulnerable up close, unguarded next to me.

My stare drifts to his jaw. His neck. His shoulders. All the way down to his chest—where I pause.

He is crosshatched there too.

He still can't meet my gaze. "Now you've seen them all."

I look up at him, eyes glossy as his stare finally nestles into mine. I think about what he said to me on the train. *"No one's seen them all."*

Only when I feel his breath reach my skin do I realize how close we are. And how much I would like it to stay that way, just for a while.

The door flies open and we jump to our feet. Milo pauses in the doorway, watching Aaron put his shirt back on.

"Oh." He raises a brow. "Am I—uh—interrupting something?"

"No." We both say it a little too quickly.

"He was just..."

Aaron rubs the back of his neck. "I was—"

We exchange glances.

"I was checking his bullet wound." I clear my throat. "To see if it's scarring okay."

Milo leans against the doorway, folding his arms with a smirk. "Shouldn't you be taking off his pants for that?"

Aaron's face turns red and I glare. "What do you want?"

"Well, this is my room, after all." He suppresses his grin. "I was just gonna bunk with you two, but... if you need the space..."

My fists clench at my sides. "Oh my God."

Milo raises his hands in false innocence. "I'm just being cordial, alright?"

"You're being delusional."

"That would be you." He winks at me, then looks at Aaron. "I assume you're not sharing a room with any of your old pals tonight, are you?"

"I can't confidently say they won't slit my throat while I'm asleep."

"Alright. Well, I'm just gonna bunk with Lockley, then." Milo turns around to close the door, peeking his head through on his way out. "Goodnight, you two. Don't have too much fun."

I make a mental note to kill him later.

"Milo," Aaron says, but my brother ignores him and shuts the door. "Milo, come back."

He doesn't.

We stand still for a while until we both speak at the same time. "I'll take the floor."

I frown at him. "But—"

"My leg will be fine," he says.

"I wasn't talking about your leg."

He pauses and looks away, like he's surprised I remember the nightmares. "I don't think sleeping comfortably will do anything to help with that, Voclain."

It's quiet again. I hug my abdomen. His hands are in his pockets, and he stares at the floor.

We were trapped in a cave together for a week. How is this any different? Why can't I look him in the eye? *It's only Aaron.*

I wonder if that's the problem.

I think back to what he said in that cave. About the train. About what he meant when he said he *couldn't.*

I don't protest when he takes the *ALL ARE WELCOME HERE* pillow and tosses it on the floor. Reluctantly, I climb into bed, and I turn off the lamp.

I close my eyes, but they don't stay shut. There is nothing I can do to keep them from staring at the ceiling, trying not to think about every worry swarming my head. About what I now know. Guilt knots my stomach.

"I'm sorry," I whisper, because it's easier to say it in the dark.

It's quiet, and when Aaron doesn't say anything, I wonder if he heard me at all. I turn over on my right side. I almost wish he were here. Not there.

I hear something shift. Footsteps. The soft rustling of the quilt as he climbs into the other side of the bed. "You have nothing to be sorry for."

I turn around to face him. He's facing me too.

"I was being stupid," I say, throat tight. I close my eyes. I can't stop picturing the scars on his skin. "You have every right to keep things from me, and I push you to open up, and I shouldn't do that."

I open my eyes, and he looks right into them.

"I just… I see you, Aaron. I see you, and I see that you hurt, and I hate knowing there's nothing I can do to fix it."

His voice is soft. "I know."

Mine cracks. "I just want to make it go away."

He stares at me, and I can't stand it, so I turn around again, back facing him.

"When I'm with you, it does go away."

My breathing stops. He whispers his next words so quietly I can barely hear them at all. "You heal me, Eddie."

My pulse quickens. I can feel it ringing in my ears.

"I've spent my whole life building the same walls. It's… safer that way, you know?"

Turn around, something tells me. But I force myself to stay perfectly still.

"But you…" I can hear him swallow. "You're burning them down, and it scares me."

I curl my knees, making myself smaller.

"I shouldn't have kept things from you. Because… things are different with you, Ed. They always have been. And I was wrong to say you don't know me, because you do. Better than anyone. And I didn't realize that by guarding myself, I was hurting you and your trust. And I just… I didn't know I could lose you by pushing you away too. Even if I thought it was for your own good." It's quiet again. "I don't want to push you away."

I whisper. "Then be closer."

There is a pause. I wonder if he heard me. I shut my eyes.

Slowly, I can feel him reach me.

He pulls me into his chest and wraps his arms around me. My hand moves, and it finds his, and he holds it. We are still for so long my breaths tune into his, in time with the rise and fall of his chest.

"Voclain?" he mutters.

"Yeah?"

"I've been meaning to ask you something."

My chest tightens. "Alright."

A pause. "What do you think of my shirt?"

I pull away to turn around and frown at him. He sets his elbow on a pillow and props his head up with his hand. His expression is completely solemn.

I don't think I've seen an uglier shirt in my life.

But my eyes drift to his face. The sharpness of his jaw. The dampness of his messy hair. The tendons in his arm. I force myself to stare at the fish instead.

He speaks before I get the chance to tell him how much I hate it. "I think it's superlative."

I suppress a grin. "Oh really?"

He nods, holding my gaze. "But I think it'd look better on you."

My face flushes with heat. I part my lips, unsure of what to say.

He sees my expression and laughs, grin crooked and cheeks dimpled. "I'm kidding. It's ugly as shit."

I roll my eyes and turn around. His laughter dies down, and it's silent again.

"Aaron?" I whisper.

"Yeah?"

I pause. "You can come back."

He hesitates, but slowly, he returns. I feel his heartbeat against my back. For a long time, all we are is perfectly still.

His pinky finger curls around mine. "No more secrets."

I think about the phone in my jacket pocket. About the things that I have kept from him in return. *Maybe I don't deserve the trust I ask for.*

I tighten my pinky around his. "No more secrets."

We fall asleep like that, and for the first time since I started making my bed, I rest well.

I don't think Aaron has a single nightmare.

R. STELLER

Monday, April 22

The room is a white box.

There are no windows. No visible doors. When I wake up, all I know is that I'm sitting in an angular chair made of cold white plastic, and my wrists are cuffed to the arms. My neck is cuffed to the back of the chair too. Everything is spinning, but eventually it slows to a stop. I blink, memories slowly seeping back into my mind.

I remember the meadow. I remember the silent ride back. I remember stepping out of the helicopter—and feeling someone inject something into my neck.

I remember one word spoken on Canary's tongue. *Correction.*

My heartbeat quickens as I try to take in more of my surroundings. I glance down. I'm still wearing my suit, but my bulletproof vest is not present beneath it. My Nightjade gun and Eyes are nowhere to be seen. The only piece of furniture in the room aside from my chair is a white table a few feet in front of me.

I can't move my neck much, but I can move my eyes enough to stare at the ceiling. There is only one square of white light so bright it's searing. Even when I close my eyes, little green patches take the form of its shape. My mouth is dry, my throat parched.

I count my heartbeats to try to keep myself grounded, but I lose track of them quickly. I can't stop looking over my shoulder or shaking the feeling that I'm being watched.

The wall across from me opens, letting in two strangers dressed in white. It then closes, becoming as seamless as before. One of the figures is carrying a briefcase that matches their clothes. They're not wearing an armored suit, so I know they can't be Officers.

They come to a stop behind the table. I squint to study their coats, noticing a black cross embroidered into their front pockets. *These are healers from the First Aid Division*, I realize, thinking back to the people who stitched King back together after our run-in with Aaron.

My brows crease. I'm not injured or sick. I look down at my restrained body just to be sure. *If I'm not hurt, then why are they here?*

"Good day, Agent Steller." One of the healers grins at me, but her eyes are empty, and it sends a shiver down my spine. Her black curls are tied in a low ponytail. "How are you feeling?"

The other healer hoists the briefcase onto the table, and I watch him open it as I respond, "Fine."

"That's wonderful news," the first healer says. "My name is Dr. Mullins. I've been sent from FAD to facilitate your Correction this evening, along with my assistant, Dr. Bishop."

Dr. Bishop rummages through the contents of his briefcase with gloved hands, pulling out what appears to be a metallic pill. He hands it to Dr. Mullins, who holds it up in front of me.

"We want to be as transparent as possible to help you understand the goals this procedure is designed to accomplish," she says. "Do you know why you're here, Agent Steller?"

I don't say anything.

"You made a mistake, Agent. A mistake Agent Canary has deemed worthy of Correction to ensure that you are able to continue serving the Corps to the best of your ability."

They're protecting their investment.

"The goal of the Correction procedure is to rewire the thought process of candidates who meet specific requirements," Dr. Mullins continues. "In the Officer Division, most mistakes result in a Nightjade injection. Luckily for you, things operate differently for the Agency. Agents are valuable, cutting-edge machines. Unfortunately, as with any piece of machinery, repairs are often expected."

She steps closer. "It is usually far more efficient to attempt a repair before replacing the machinery entirely. Wouldn't you agree?"

I clench my jaw.

"You, Agent Steller, have been deemed worthy of repair."

Her smile is nauseatingly sweet.

"The Corps only Corrects Agents who have the mental fortitude to be able to withstand the process—candidates they believe will come out of it stronger, more capable. However, since we are being transparent, positive results are not always guaranteed, even for the most promising candidates.

"Before we follow through with the procedure, we will need to run a few tests to make sure that you are really as compatible as the Agency believes."

She studies the pill, pinching it between her gloved index finger and thumb. "This capsule is what we like to call a digital pill. It uses artificial intelligence to detect and analyze the chemicals in your brain, allowing for an accurate and complex breakdown of who you are. Your personality, your weaknesses, your flaws... all of it can be quantified. This pill will tell us exactly what must be fixed and monitor our efforts to make such corrections."

Dr. Mullins steps forward, extending her hand. I study the pill hesitantly, stomach turning inside out.

"However, there is a reason why the Corps doesn't simply give one of these to every Agent as a standard precautionary measure. They are incredibly complicated to manufacture, and it would be quite the waste of resources to distribute one to every Agent. In addition to that, there is a small amount of radiation emitted from these capsules that would be detrimental to your health if you were exposed to it constantly. If you do prove yourself a worthy candidate, we will induce vomiting and retrieve the device as soon as the procedure is complete."

She hands the pill back to Dr. Bishop, who watches us patiently.

"Now, you will show us, Agent Steller?" She leans forward. "Are you really worth being Corrected?"

I swallow the lump in my throat as Dr. Bishop rummages through the briefcase again, retrieving what appears to be a handheld remote. He gives it to Dr. Mullins, then pulls out two cords, each one attached to what appears to be a circular sticker. He walks behind me, plugging the cords somewhere into the chair before sticking either of the circles to the sides of my head.

"There's no need to be afraid," he whispers into my ear. "A Corps healer can fix anything."

A shiver courses through my veins.

He steps away, and the two healers stand behind the table. Dr. Bishop takes out a tablet, studying it as Dr. Mullins presses a button on her remote.

In an instant, my wrists and neck are set on fire.

I bite my lip as the rings that cuff me to my chair emit a scalding heat. My eyes squeeze shut and I writhe in my seat, trying to free myself. But the cuffs won't budge.

The heat stops. My entire body trembles as I force my eyes to open. Dr. Bishop makes note of something on his tablet.

The button is pressed again.

This time, the heat is more intense, and I can't keep myself from calling out in pain as the burns already present in my skin are deepened. The seconds stretch on like hours, and the burning stops.

I open my eyes to glare at the healers, breathing heavily. They aren't fazed by my pain in the slightest.

With every burst of heat, the temperature is higher, the duration longer, with exactly ten seconds of rest between each one. By the time I reach the sixth wave, I'm drawing blood from biting my tongue and curling my nails into my skin. The seventh one finally makes me scream.

By the fifteenth wave, I am so numb that I don't flinch at all. I don't even blink as my entire body trembles, head hanging low, hair falling over my eyes and sticking to the sides of my head with sweat.

The burning ends. When the ten seconds are up, I twitch, expecting another burst of heat.

"Phenomenal," Dr. Mullins mutters. She steps forward, studying me with a grin. "Most candidates lose consciousness by the seventh round."

Slowly, shaking, I lift my head an inch, just so I can see her. I spit. Drops of my blood stain her shirt crimson.

She frowns, pulling out a white handkerchief to wipe my blood from her face, but it doesn't do anything to remove the stains in her clothes. "He's certainly maintained his resolve."

Dr. Bishop makes a note.

"I think he's ready for the first phase," Dr. Mullins says to her associate. *First?* My heart plummets. *It hasn't even started yet.*

I twitch every ten seconds. Dr. Bishop takes out a bottle of water and pours some into a paper cup, which Dr. Mullins lifts to my lips. I drink the water greedily, feeling the liquid wash away the blood, cooling the scrapes and dryness in my throat. She places the capsule on my tongue, and when she forces another cup to my lips, there is nothing I can do but swallow.

The pill is so large I can feel it traveling down my esophagus, stopping somewhere in my chest. The weight of it burns a little, and I fold forward, letting it settle. She gives me one last sip of water before putting the bottle away.

The healers study the tablet, pointing to charts on the screen, whispering among themselves. I keep twitching.

After what feels like years, they remove the electrodes sticking to my head, pack up the briefcase, and turn to leave. The doorway in the wall opens up again, and the table lowers into the floor. Dr. Mullins pauses to look over her shoulder. "Farewell, Agent Steller. You are exactly where you are supposed to be."

The wall swallows her whole, and I am left alone.

I wiggle my wrists, making another desperate attempt to slip out of my restraints. But even an inch of movement is enough to make me bite my tongue. The cuffs dig against my burns, which are already stiffening. I give up on escape quickly.

The lights shut off.

My pulse quickens. Everything is pitch black. I can't even make out my arms or legs. There is only darkness, and it sucks the air right from my lungs.

The wall in front of me lights up like a screen, at first flashing only the Chaser Corps logo—a black poker chip spinning in place. The image fades, replaced by another one that nearly makes me choke on my own saliva.

It's a photo of Eddie.

It's a school photo, I think. I recognize it from the yearbook. It looks like her senior portrait. She's wearing a black sweater and a brown plaid skirt, her long curls billowing like curtains in the wind. I recognize the blossoming Callery pear tree and the wood fence behind her, and know she's standing in my backyard.

I remember now.

Margot took that for her. She was always skilled at photography. She had an artist's eye; she knew how to make anything look good.

She knew how to make Eddie look ethereal.

Margot wouldn't stop talking about Eddie's senior photos. She was so proud of them. She had one in a frame on her desk. It bothered me to hear my sister go on and on about the girl who got on my nerves more than anyone else. But deep down, I always thought Eddie looked nice.

I study the photo of her like it's a painting. Like it's not real. Something someone made up in their head and created with oil and a brush.

I miss her.

The moment the thought runs through my head, the cuffs around my wrists and neck reignite. I squeeze my eyes shut, Eddie's face still clear in my mind. I try to hold onto it, grasping the fix of dopamine like I'm drowning and her relief is the only solid thing I can find. But the burning doesn't stop. I can tell the heat is on the lowest setting, but it lasts far longer than any of the previous bursts did. My teeth clamp down on my tongue so hard it fills my mouth with blood again.

Blood. That's what I focus on. I focus on its metallic sting, its penny taste. I think of crimson.

And the burning stops.

Shaking, I let my eyes open.

Ten seconds pass, and another photo fills the screen.

It's Eddie again, standing in a field with her family. She looks no older than fourteen. She's taller than Milo, whose face is rounder than I remember, his black curls nowhere near as grown out as they were the last time I saw him. Eddie's mother stands behind both of her children, wrapping her arms around them affectionately. Their father towers over them all, grinning as widely as I've ever seen him grin. My eyes glide back over to Eddie. *She looks so happy.*

The burning begins again. I call out in pain, leaning my head back. I try to hold onto the image of Eddie in my head, but the longer I keep it close, the hotter the burning feels. I let my eyes flutter open, studying the family photo. My attention falls back to the taste of iron in my mouth, and when I close my eyes again, the image shifts.

I can't stop picturing the Voclains, lifeless on the floor, soaking in a pool of thick red blood.

The burning stops.

I'm breathless when I peel my eyes open again. My head hangs low, and all I can think about is how badly I want to sleep, or just close my eyes and keep them shut until this whole thing is over.

But I remember what Dr. Mullins said about losing consciousness. If I'm not awake throughout Correction, the procedure won't be successful —and something tells me they'd kill me for failing.

I have to stay awake. *I have to make it to the end.*

The photo shifts. It's Eddie again, and she's standing behind a podium, dressed in a maroon cap and gown. *Her valedictorian speech.*

Immediately, I'm brought back to graduation. I think of the fence, and the night, and seeing her on top of that slide. And I didn't join her. *I should have joined her.*

Like clockwork, the moment the longing returns, so does the heat.

My throat is sore from calling out. I bite my tongue, keeping my eyes glued to the photo. The gown looks a lot like blood.

And the burning ends again.

I blink, trying to steady my breathing. *That's what this is about, isn't it?*

I think of the pill in my body, of everything Dr. Mullins said about the way it functions. Whoever is monitoring this test will have access to everything. My thoughts, my feelings, my pain.

They're punishing me for missing her.

When the ten seconds of stillness are over, what appears next is not a photo, but a video. It's a little blurry, possibly even security footage.

I'm seven, and I'm standing in front of the playground at school. Eddie runs and jumps into my arms, hugging me for a reason I can't even remember. I lift her off the ground and spin her.

I burn.

The pain is so intense I scream again. I can feel the cuffs melting my skin, worsening the burns I already bear. I wonder if these scars will ever heal. But I'm desperate, and I open my eyes.

The video plays on repeat. I watch it replay over and over and over again until I'm sure I'll finally lose consciousness, but I don't.

I know I'm not supposed to miss her. I know I'm not supposed to feel this longing, but for a moment, I don't care about the burning. I just want to see her. I want to hold onto the memory I'd lost for a bit longer. *I don't want to forget her.*

The temperature rises. I squeeze my eyes shut and try to force myself to stop thinking about her, but no matter how hard I try, the video is still playing in my head. I can't rid her from my mind, and I chew on the inside of my lip, tasting iron once again.

Blood, I tell myself. *That's what gets it to stop.*

I hate blood; I always have. I hate it so much it overrides the fading images of Eddie in my head, replacing them with flashes of her dead parents. Of Carmody, lifeless in the sand. All I see is red.

It stops.

Ten seconds.

We're fourteen, and we're lab partners. We're arguing over how to approach the assignment until Eddie has had enough of me. She pours a beaker of water over my head, expressionless. I blink, and I pour one over hers.

The burning returns. The pain is unlike anything I've ever felt before. It makes me miss the coals I once ran over, the training that I thought would break me. But none of it holds a candle to forcing Eddie out of my head.

I focus on the blood in my mouth, in my memories, in the sea. And she leaves me, and the burning does too.

Ten seconds.

I'm sixteen. I find Eddie crying by herself in the library, face planted in an open textbook, notes sprawled over the table. She is worked to near-exhaustion, probably upset about something her father said. I don't say a word as I sit across from her, pull out a book, and read in silence until she stops. I stay with her, and when she picks up her pencil again, we both pretend I'm not there.

I remember the way we still pretended, even when I gave her a ride home. Even when I stopped for coffee and ordered one for myself so she wouldn't think I was doing it for her. I never drank it.

I cry out again when the fire starts, unable to keep a tear from sliding down my cheek. I kick my feet against the chair, so tired of the burning, so tired of being stuck. So tired of not being able to do a single goddamn thing about it.

Blood. Think of the blood. You hate blood, remember? You hate it.

When the burning stops, it feels like a reward. I take a deep breath, soaking in the ten seconds of silence, feeling what I felt the moment I first let myself take that sip of coffee with Heron. The moment I took a bite of pizza. The moments I gave in.

I'm seventeen, and we're asleep beneath a playground. We have sand dotting our hair like stars.

I'm seventeen, and we're in a grocery store, arguing as we look for a candle.

I'm seventeen, and we're in a cow field.

There are cameras on telephone poles, I remind myself. *Eyes all around.*

The camera reaches far. I see how close we were, and I remember how badly I wanted to be closer.

The burning is unbearable, but I'm getting better at making it stop. The intervals are shorter every time. The ten seconds are sweet, like sugar on my tongue.

I'm eighteen, and we're in the control room at the Blurt, and I'm kissing her like she is my last breath.

That fire is the worst. It lasts longer than the others, hotter than anything I've ever felt before. The pain courses through my entire body, numbing my entirety, tugging at the corners of my vision. I see stars. I wait for everything to go dark, but it doesn't.

I think back to the blood, but it doesn't work. It's not enough to cleanse my head.

I think of the man in training, who begged me to spare him before I filled his neck with Nightjade. I think of my first assignment, of the man I watched Carmody exterminate, of the kids whose father we took away. I think of burning rebel camps. I think of the bonfire of bodies smoldering at the Cut and the burnt bones I dug up like they were nothing. I think of the bullet I put in Aaron's leg, of how ill he looked when he held Eddie in that cave. He was completely unconscious by the time she hauled him out of there.

I've done horrible things. Selfish things. Vile things.

I think of them all, and I am rewarded with ten seconds of bliss.

The next video plays, and I am on the ground in the Blurt. Aaron is holding Eddie back.

Ten seconds.

I'm in that white room, blood blooming in my chest. This time, nothing burns.

Ten seconds.

Now, the footage they play is nothing I recognize, and I am nowhere to be seen. I see Eddie in an apron at Port Keys Coffee Co., wiping down tables with Aaron's mother.

I burn again.

I see Eddie and Aaron in what appears to be her father's office, which I've only been to once. He's teaching her how to throw the knife. He's so close to her. They hide under a desk.

Eddie and Milo sitting in her car in the parking lot of a fast food restaurant, drinking milkshakes, listening to music and laughing.

Eddie and Aaron leaning against the front wall of Port Keys Coffee Co., sipping drinks as wind whips her hair, the sea behind them.

Eddie and her father at a grocery store, arguing loudly about a frozen fish.

Eddie's bedroom window, filmed from the street lamp, and Aaron climbing into it.

Eddie in her apron inside the coffee shop again, spinning and dancing to a song I can't hear as Esmerelda twirls her, dish rags in hand.

Eddie and Aaron laughing hysterically outside the shop. He buries his head in his hands. She collapses against the wall, wiping tears from her eyes.

Eddie and her mother, getting towering cones of ice cream from a parlor with pink walls.

Eddie and Aaron, sitting on her roof.

Slowly, I feel myself fading further and further out of the picture.

The content shifts again, plucking me from the past and dropping me in the present, where I am still absent.

I see security footage of Eddie stealing the car.

Ten seconds.

From another telephone pole, I see her standing on the side of the road. Beau, Aaron, and Lori are there too, with a girl I don't recognize. There is a man with a gun, and Beau shoots him.

It burns less that time.

Eddie and Aaron sitting next to each other inside a diner. He steals glances at her while she eats.

Eddie and Aaron throwing darts at a carnival.

Eddie and Aaron in what looks like a train. She's wearing a dress, and he studies her. He pulls her into the bathroom and closes the door.

Eddie, eighteen, lying on my front lawn with Margot. They point at the clouds.

Eddie, leaning against a tree, reading a book by herself.

Eddie.

Eddie.

Eddie.

I want to scream, but the burns are growing deeper, and I feel the searing against my throat. I want to claw my own eyes out, but I can't even move my own hands.

The screen turns black.

Next, they show me everything I've already been drowning in.

I see a photo of Eddie's parents, and the dead Chasers, and the blood lake. I see myself complete my training perfectly. I see myself vomiting on Todd Birch's perfectly mowed lawn, and the bluebird that flies away.

Not a single moment of it is set on fire.

I do not blink when the healers return.

The cuffs around my neck and wrists unlock. I'm elsewhere when they apply a stinging ointment to my wounds and wrap them in clean white bandages. The doctor now wears a shirt that is not stained with drops of my blood. I twitch every ten seconds.

But I don't even flinch when a needle sprouts from the floor, and my second tally is filled in, right below my burns.

I am perfect.

EDDIE

Monday, April 22
85 Beds Made

The other side of the bed is cold.

I blink slowly, taking in its emptiness. The unfamiliarity of the room around me. A sickening knot forms in my gut when I remember where I am.

I make the bed quickly. I wash up, change into my clothes from yesterday, lace up my boots, and slip my knife into its sheath before heading toward the door. I pause with my hand wrapped around the doorknob. I turn my head around, giving the bed one last glance before exiting the room and heading downstairs.

To my surprise, the second floor is filled with strangers. Children and adults alike hurry past me, grabbing food from the kitchen or making their way downstairs and out of the lodge toward other parts of the resort. Everyone looks busy, and I try not to think about what tasks are keeping them occupied.

I walk into the dining room, searching for familiar faces. Milo and Raven sit at the table, chatting over plates filled with pancakes while Fern feeds Jelly pieces of toast. A few people I don't recognize sit at the table as well, reading or talking amongst themselves. The air is thick with chatter and the smell of sugar and smoky bacon, but I still pick out notes of pine and wood-burning fireplaces. I take a seat across from Milo.

"How'd you sleep?" Raven asks.

"Fine."

Milo gives me a look that I ignore. I scan the room for Aaron, but he's nowhere to be seen.

I remember watching him wake up early with my eyes half-closed. He told me to go back to sleep. I did.

"He's in the kitchen," Raven says. "Earning his keep."

I pause, not realizing my thoughts had been so obvious, then nod.

Lockley walks in from the kitchen with a rag over his shoulder, carrying a clean stack of plates and a handful of utensils. He sets them on the table before gathering up dirty dishes and offering me a silent but polite nod. I offer one back. He exits right as Aaron limps in with his sleeves rolled up, holding a platter piled with a fresh batch of pancakes.

I'm not convinced he notices me at first, as he reaches over my shoulder to set the pancakes down without a word. But then I know he *has* to see me, because he's piling pancakes onto my plate. More than I have the appetite for. When he walks away, I swear I feel his hand brush against my back.

I turn my head and watch him disappear into the kitchen again. I wonder if I imagined it.

I pick at my pancakes in silence, taking small, uninterested bites. Milo and Raven keep talking and laughing, but I don't pay attention.

The buzz of breakfast dies down after a while, until the five of us are the only ones left at the table. I haven't eaten much of my food, and I'm not sure I have the stomach for it. Fern hands Jelly to Raven and walks into the kitchen, returning with a piece of bread. She sets it on my plate, then sits down next to me to nibble at a slice of her own.

I smile at the gesture and eat the bread. It really is delicious. Feeling the food in my stomach makes me realize just how hungry I really am, and I eat the rest of my pancakes too.

I glance at Fern, then at Raven and the giggling child in her lap. Milo makes faces at her, and Lockley walks in and sits down next to them to do the same thing.

If I didn't know any better, I'd believe this was nothing more than a camp of odd, young Unseen misfits with no other place to go—not the violent group of rebels everyone else paints them as. *Are they really what Cecil and Aaron have made them out to be? What if Silver Fir isn't that different from the Cut after all?*

I'm pulled out of my thoughts when Aaron takes a seat to my left. Before he digs into his own breakfast, he looks at me and my empty plate. "You finished your food."

"What can I say? The chef really outdid himself."

He leans in and speaks in my ear. "I'll let him know."

Something about his voice pricks the back of my neck. My lips manage to curl upward, just a bit.

I sit and wait for Aaron to eat. It's quiet for a while, until someone else comes downstairs and enters the dining room.

A boy our age freezes in his tracks when he notices Aaron, eyes wide. He has buzzed hair and deep brown skin, and he wears a gray fleece quarter-zip jacket with a pair of cargo pants and snow boots. Aaron reacts similarly, setting his fork down and rising to his feet. *They must know each other.* I think of Lockley's and Raven's reactions to seeing Aaron and wonder if he might get punched again.

The boy walks up to Aaron and leans over to wrap him in a hug.

"I never thought I'd see you again," he mutters.

To my surprise, Aaron holds him right back. "It's good to see you too, man."

The two of them stand like that for a long time, eyes squeezed shut, clutching the back of each other's shirts. When they pull away, they're both suppressing wide grins.

The boy looks at me, then at Milo. "This is your sister, right?"

Milo nods.

I'm surprised when the boy walks over to give me a hug too.

"Nice to meet you." He pulls away and offers me a hand. "Marty."

I can't help but give him a smile when I shake it. "Eddie."

Marty then looks at Aaron, eyes darting back and forth between the two of us. He folds his arms, rubbing his chin in thought, narrowing his eyes mischievously. "How do you two know each other?"

Aaron glances down at me, then at Marty. "Partners in crime."

Marty nods. "I see."

"It's true," Fern chimes in. "I saw them on TV. They stole a car."

Marty takes a seat, helping himself to a serving of pancakes. "I'm guessing there's a good story behind that."

"If you'd call getting shot by an Agent a good story, then sure."

Raven's head lifts up, brows pinched with a surprising hint of concern. "You were shot by an Agent?"

"That's what I said."

"Shit," Marty mutters.

Aaron shrugs, elbows on the table as he takes a sip of water. "It is what it is."

"Screw that," Raven snaps. "Agents are a problem, and you know it."

The phone in my jacket pocket suddenly feels a lot heavier.

Aaron looks at Raven like he wants to say more, but he doesn't.

While the others return to their food and conversation, Aaron leans closer to whisper into my ear. "I need to talk to you."

Before I have time to question it, he's rising to his feet, and I follow him into the kitchen.

My stomach cartwheels when I think about what he could possibly want to talk about. *Is this about what happened in the woods yesterday?* The thought makes me nauseous. *Or maybe my phone went off while I was still asleep, and he found it.*

Somehow, talking about last night sounds worse than both.

We enter the empty kitchen, and he leans against the counter, glancing around the room to make sure we're really alone before whispering to me. "We need to get out of here."

I relax my shoulders, relief spreading through me. "We already agreed to help them out."

"*You* did," he corrects. "Not me."

I hug my stomach. "What are you suggesting?"

"I'm obviously not leaving you here." He glares, then sighs. "I just... I don't think this is a good idea."

"Neither do I, but it's not like we have any better ones."

"I have lots of good ideas. You know how easy it would be to steal that van we came here in? We can just take Milo and leave. I've stolen cars before. *You've* stolen cars before. We'd be out of here like that." He snaps his fingers.

"It's not that simple."

"Why not?"

"Milo's ten times more stubborn than I am. If he's made up his mind about something, he's the only one who can change it." I sigh. "Raven said he wants to stay here."

Aaron furrows his brows. "You mean for good?"

I nod.

"You have to talk him out of it, Voclain."

"Did you not hear what I just said?"

"Well have you at least *tried* to knock some sense into him?"

"No, not yet. But he already made that deal with Raven. I don't think he's going anywhere until that's over with."

"Why not?"

"He thinks Ren's at that safe house, and he thinks they can help get him back."I stare at my feet. "That's why he left in the first place. To find him for me."

Aaron's face softens. "You really think he's connected to those coordinates somehow?"

"He could be." I shrug. "Look. Whether he's there or not, we can't exactly do anything about it on our own. We already came all the way out here, and I think it's worth a shot."

Aaron sighs, looking at me with something like understanding. "Okay."

"We'll help Milo out with the last two jobs he agreed to, they'll help us figure out what's going on with that safe house, and then we're out of here. We'll deal with Milo after."

"He can't stay here, Voclain," Aaron mutters. "You know that, right?"

I think back to what Wagner said about me not being welcome back at End Harbor. If he really meant it, where else is there for Milo and I to go?

Milo could stay in End Harbor; it's safe there, and I could find somewhere else to stay. Somewhere like this place.

But would he really want to be separated from me, for who knows how long? Could *I* handle that?

I look at Aaron. *And what about him?*

Don't worry about it right now, I tell myself. *You'll figure it out later.*

"I know."

"They've been treating you nicely so far, but I promise you, the Gambler mindset is dangerous. I've seen people go down that path and never come back."

Greer, I think to myself, remembering the scar on Aaron's arm.

"You can't be Unseen without being angry, but they don't know how to control themselves," he continues. "In the end, we all want the same thing, but they're willing to do horrible things to get it. They're trying to start the war the rest of the Unseen want to avoid. And they don't care who gets hurt along the way."

"What about Marty? Fern? They don't seem like bloodthirsty monsters." *Even Raven and Lockley don't seem all that bad.*

"They're here because they have nowhere else to be. And I'm not saying they're *all* bad." Aaron sighs. "I'm just saying they're not as careful as we are."

"Is that really such a bad thing? Aren't we supposed to be taking risks?"

"Not at whatever cost."

My lips part, but I close them when I realize I don't have much else to say. *He's right.*

"I just don't want to see Milo getting hurt," Aaron says. His voice gets softer. "For both of your sakes."

"Me neither."

It's quiet. I hear the others out in the dining room finishing up what's left of breakfast as they talk and laugh. Aaron slides his hands into his pockets and stares at the floor for a while, then looks at me. "How'd you sleep?"

There it is.

"Fine." I nod. He nods. "What about you?"

"Fine," he says.

Aaron holds my gaze, and for the briefest of moments, I don't mind it.

He averts his stare first with a grin. "You talk in your sleep."

My face warms. "No I don't."

"Yeah you do."

"What did I say?"

He pulls away from the counter and walks out of the kitchen backwards. "That's between me and sleeping you."

I watch him return to the dining table and take a seat.

The song about time and space and headaches won't stop playing in my head.

Fern cleans up breakfast while the rest of us move to the couches in the lobby. A new fire burns in the hearth today, crackling softly and filling the room with the smell of charcoal.

"I want to go over our plans for the day," Raven says, bringing her legs up so she's sitting cross-legged on her couch. Jelly sits in her lap, playing with a stuffed rabbit. "For those who haven't already heard it."

Her eyes dart to Aaron and me. We exchange glances before Aaron crosses his arms, jaw slightly clenched. "Alright."

I look at him, noticing the hesitation in his features. He's already made it clear he doesn't agree with the Gamblers' way of doing things, and I get the feeling he isn't too happy about being dragged into this.

"There's a Corps-run library in Brim Creek," Raven explains. "It's mostly used by Officers and Agents as a research center. It's small, but just big enough that some people come from out of town to visit it too. In other words, it's the perfect target."

"Small enough to be easy to infiltrate, big enough to make a dent," Marty confirms.

"We've been eyeing this particular target for a few weeks now, but the recent arrival of the Voclain siblings inspired me." Raven looks at Milo, then at me. "We're burning it down."

My eyes widen. "What?"

"You heard me."

"Should be easy enough with Catnap bombs," Milo says.

Aaron's teeth grind together.

"Actually, I'm thinking of saving the last of your stock for another project I have in mind," Raven says to Milo. "We're approaching this the old-fashioned way."

"And what would that be?" I ask quietly.

"A group of angry kids with guns and masks is a pretty good scare tactic, if you ask me," Lockley says.

My brows draw together. "What about the people inside?"

"We'll evacuate any civilians."

"And if they're Chasers?"

She pauses, noticing my hesitation. "We won't kill anyone unless we have to."

"I'm having a hard time understanding the point of all this," Aaron says. "You said it yourself—the library's small. All their vital data is stored in the Corps database anyway. Its only likely value is a place for Chasers to use computers while passing through."

Raven narrows her eyes. "I don't remember asking for your opinion."

"It just seems like a waste of energy to me."

"It's the principle of the matter," Raven says. "The point is to be seen. To show the Corps that a new era is beginning, and we're the ones turning the tide."

"One burnt library isn't going to do shit," Aaron argues. "All that'll do is piss people off and put a bigger target on your back. On the entire Unseen's back, probably."

"A thousand little fires, Aaron," Raven says quietly. "Remember?"

I find Aaron's gaze. *Just this one job*, I tell him in silence. He presses his lips together, exhaling through his nose. "Fine."

The library is not what I expected it to be.

It's set on a corner in Brim Creek's eerily charming downtown. The roads are dark and damp, and the thick clouds above us tease a downpour that doesn't come. Unlike what I remember the training center looking like, the exterior of the Brim Creek Public Library still resembles the Yesterdays, with charcoal-painted wood siding, vintage street lamps, and metal signage set into the wall above the front double doors. It's late enough that the windows emit a soft amber glow.

I sit in a cramped van with Aaron, Milo, and Raven's team—minus Fern, who's staying behind to look after Jelly. We're all sitting so close together it makes my skin itch, and with the plague masks Raven insisted we use sitting in our laps, I feel even more claustrophobic. All I can think about is getting this over with.

The van is parked in the back lot of the library. It's a quiet day; I haven't spotted a single pedestrian. Although today's weather predictions say there will be no rain, there are still clouds and a soft breeze. People are likely staying inside, just in case.

We've been given the perfect opportunity.

"In, then out." Raven turns around from the passenger's seat, lifting her mask to speak. "Lockley and I will run in and pull the alarm to initiate the evacuation. The second it goes off, the rest of you will follow. Once we pull the alarm, we only have twenty minutes to light the place up before authorities arrive. We'll need to make sure there's nothing left for them to recover after we're done, so be generous with the gasoline. Every room, every closet. Got it?"

We nod.

"Good." She lowers her plague mask again. "A thousand little fires."

"A thousand little fires," Milo and Marty repeat.

Aaron's leg is shaking up and down. He stares at the floor with his arms crossed. He hasn't spoken a word since we've left.

Raven and Lockley climb out of the van, and the rest of us sit in what feels like an endless silence—until screams ensue from inside the building, followed by a series of thunderous Yesterday gunshots.

Aaron snaps his head up. "What the hell was that?"

"Relax, they're not shooting anyone," Milo says. "Just startling them."

Aaron grinds his teeth together, staring out the window until the fire alarm cracks through the quiet.

"It's time," Milo says, pulling his mask over his head. Marty follows suit.

I look at Aaron. "Ready?"

He doesn't say a word. He just puts his mask on and climbs out of the car with the other two, and I follow close behind.

Marty opens the back doors of the van, retrieving four red jugs of gasoline and distributing them to each of us. "Every room, remember?"

Milo and I nod.

"We should split up. Milo and I will take the left wing, you two will take the right."

We sprint up the steps, dodging fleeing civilians and Corps researchers as they flood out of the building. No one gives us a second glance; everyone is too desperate to escape, and by the time we make our way inside, the whole library is empty.

Except for the three lifeless bodies resting in the center of the first floor, their chests stained with red.

Aaron and I stop dead in our tracks. The bodies are dressed in white clothes, but not Officer armor; they weren't field Chasers.

"What the hell?" Aaron mutters through his mask. His fists clench at his sides.

"We don't have much time," I say, pulling him away.

While Lockley and Raven tackle the upper floors and Milo and Marty handle the lower-left wing, Aaron and I cover everything in our assigned section with gasoline. The smell makes my head and stomach spin, and Aaron starts to cough.

The first floor is filled with dark wooden desks, each one set with sleek white computer monitors. Every wall is lined with leather-bound books, and I recognize some titles from the Yesterdays, which takes me by surprise. The library is a combination of old and new, and something about it makes me shudder.

Once we're done with the main room, Aaron and I make our way down a narrow hallway lit with soft orange lamps. We leave a trail of gasoline behind us, making sure to be strategic while using it sparingly. When we reach the end of the hall, we open the door and enter what looks like a storage room. It's filled with old desks and chairs, crates of books, and dusty file boxes that look like they've been here since the Yesterdays. The door is heavy and slams shut behind us, and the perpetual screaming of the fire alarm makes my ears ring as we pour out the last of our gasoline.

We drop the jugs and hurry back to the door—but it won't open.

Aaron tries the doorknob again, jiggling it in case it's jammed. It doesn't budge. "It's locked."

My eyes widen. "Let me try."

No luck.

Aaron slams his palms against the door. "Hey dipshits! We're locked in here!"

His shouts may as well be whispers with the sound of the alarm. We wait one minute, two—but no one hears us.

I pound my fists against it. "Hello?"

No matter how hard we knock our fists against the wood or how loudly we scream, no one comes to help.

We're stuck.

My pulse races, every muscle in my body tensing painfully. My throat tightens, and my lungs constrict, and all I smell is gasoline.

Shit shit shit SHIT. I take off my mask and toss it onto the ground, running my hands through my hair, pacing away from the door. "We're literally trapped in a tinder box right now." I gesture toward the file boxes, the books, and the empty jugs.

Aaron takes off his mask too. "They won't start the fire without us." I can barely hear his shouts over the alarm.

"What if they do?"

"They won't."

The alarm stops.

Aaron and I exchange glances, then pound on the door again. "*Hello?*"

Still, no one hears us.

"God, it's cramped in here." I continue pacing, rubbing my arms up and down. "Do you feel cramped? I feel cramped."

The alarm is gone, but I can still hear it echoing in my head. The ringing in my ears intensifies. I feel like I'm drowning in the smell of gasoline, and my skin burns. *I can't breathe.*

"I'm fine, Voclain."

"How are you fine?" I snap.

"They'll notice we're missing, and they'll come find us. Milo's with them, remember? You really think he'd leave without you?"

"That doesn't change the fact that we're stuck, alright?" I hug my abdomen tightly, still pacing. My heartbeat quickens and my breathing grows shallow, and I swear the distance between the walls is decreasing with every second. "God, there's barely any room to breathe in here."

"Just sit down, Voclain."

"There's not even a place to sit!"

Aaron walks to one of the old wooden chairs and removes a crate of books from the seat. He pulls it away from the mountain of junk in the center of the room, distancing it from the clutter, then frees another chair from the mess.

"Here." He places a hand on my shoulders and shepherds me toward one of the chairs.

After he helps me take a seat, I keep rubbing my arms with my hands, staring at the floor, legs trembling. A hard knot forms in my chest, and I can't swallow or breathe or see straight and I—

Aaron brings his chair in front of mine. Our feet touch. He pulls an amber bottle from his satchel, opens it, and sprinkles a few drops of what look like oil onto his wrist. He rubs it in, then slowly holds his wrist up in front of my nose. "Take a deep breath."

Reluctantly, I inhale shakily. Beneath the reek of gasoline, I notice the hint of something earthy and sweet, something familiar. My breathing slows, and my pulse falls back into its regular tempo. "Cedarwood."

Aaron nods softly. "I wear this all the time. It's calming."

I inhale it again and swallow the lump in my throat, the result of both my panic and the stench lodged in my lungs. "I think cedarwood is my favorite."

Gently, he takes my hand in his. He applies a few drops of the oil to my wrist and uses his thumbs to rub it into my skin. The drops are cold, and his touch is grounding. He does the same for my other wrist.

He brushes my hair to one side of my shoulder. He pours some of the oil onto his fingertips, and he rubs it into my neck. His hand lingers. Slowly, I glance up at him. He looks away and lowers his hand.

We sit quietly for a while. Aaron walks over to bang on the door again, and still, no one comes. He scans the room for another exit, but there is none. He eventually gives up with a sigh, dragging his chair so he can sit next to me. We soak in more silence.

"Sometimes I forget there's a point to all of this," he mutters after a while. He places his elbow on the arm rest, leaning his head in his palm.

"What do you mean?"

"That there's a reason. A goal beyond broadcasts and smoke and setting things on fire."

It's quiet again for a moment. "What's your reason?"

"To protect people." He says it with a fleeting and empty grin, like he thinks it's stupid. I watch him stare at the tattoos on his wrists, tracing the *X*s he drew through them. "To make this world less shitty to grow up in."

I think about what he's saying for a moment. He's right; it can be easy to forget. To lose sight of what it feels like to hope for something better. To forget about the people who can't always fight for themselves. My chest tightens when I think of Margot.

"Do you ever think about what that would be like?" I look up at him. "An after?"

"I just did."

"No. I mean... *your* after."

He pauses, thinking about the question before sitting up and leaning back in his chair. "Can I be honest with you?"

I nod. He averts his gaze with a chuckle, staring at the wall behind me. "I hardly even think about an after. For myself, anyway."

"Why not?"

"Feels like a waste of time."

"I don't think it's a waste of time."

He shrugs. "There's no guarantee I'll live long enough to see it."

"There's no guarantee you'll live long enough to see tomorrow either."

"Okay, *grim*, Voclain."

I frown. "Says you."

"I'm being practical, not existential."

"Really though." I soften my voice. "Isn't that part of it? Believing in something better than today? Even if you can't see it?" I pause. "Even if it's not guaranteed?"

He opens his mouth, then closes it, brows knit together in thought.

I look at the wall. "You have to know what you're fighting for to fight for it all the way, don't you?"

"I never thought of it like that."

"So?" I suppress a grin. "What's your After?"

He stares at me for a moment, lips parted, before closing them and looking away. "I'll have to get back to you on that." It's silent again, then he glances at me. "What about you?"

I bite my lip. I haven't given much thought to it either. Not the specifics, at least. I'm not entirely sure how to answer the question.

"Quiet," I say.

He leans his head against his knuckles again, studying me. "Like hermit-in-the-woods kinda quiet?"

"No. Not the lonely kind of quiet. The peaceful kind."

He points to my head. "Quiet up here?"

I nod.

"What else is there?"

"Leaves."

"Quiet leaves." He nods. "I never knew leaves could talk."

I roll my eyes and grin. "I'm serious."

"Okay. Quiet *and* serious leaves."

I kick his foot.

"Don't let me stop you. I wanna hear more about these leaves."

"I wanna be somewhere with lots of them." I pause. "I want a cow-field kind of quiet. The kind where you can step outside and listen to how little there is to hear. Just... wind. And grass."

"A cow field. Noted."

"A lake kind of quiet." I lean my head back and stare at the ceiling.

"Still water. Like a mirror. And a dock with a lantern at the end. One that creaks when you walk across it."

He nods. I can feel him holding back a smile as he studies me closely.

"And a library kind of quiet. Rows and rows and rows of books on fancy wooden shelves with a rolling ladder."

"What kind of books?"

"Novels. Nature encyclopedias."

"Mine?"

"Can you make really cool leather-bound editions?"

"Do you even have to ask?"

"Then yes."

He grins. "I didn't realize I was in your After."

I soften my voice. "Are you?"

His smile fades. "Am I?"

We stare at each other for a long time.

"You're not quiet." I whisper it like a statement, but it feels like a question.

The humor drains from his voice. Not in a cold way; just serious. Certain. "I could be."

Something about the way he says that makes my breath hitch. "I've gotta have *some* noise, don't I?"

"I have to say, Voclain. I know you like to yell at me, but..." He studies his hands, then meets my gaze again. His voice is gentle. "You are the quietest person I know."

I chuckle. "What does that even mean?"

Aaron shrugs, leaning back in his chair. He folds his arms and stretches his lips into a thin, crooked grin. "Let me know when you figure it out."

I shake my head—and nearly jump out of my chair when someone pounds on the door.

"Eddie? Aaron?" Marty shouts, his voice muffled. "You in there?"

We hurry to the door.

"We're locked in!" I yell back.

Marty opens the door, ushering us out of the room. "We gotta get out of here. Chasers should already be on the way."

We put on our masks and run out of the library into the parking lot.

We stare at the building—and it engulfs in flames.

The fire grows, swallowing the library from the inside out. Lockley and Raven jog into the parking lot, out of breath, still wearing their plague masks.

"Where's Milo?" Marty asks.

"I thought he was with you," Raven says.

Marty nods toward Aaron and me. "We split up to look for those two when they got stuck."

My heart plummets into my stomach. "Where is he?"

No one says anything.

My breathing grows shallow. Every part of me shakes as I stare at the burning building in front of us. The flames grow taller with every passing second, and the air is already thick with smoke. My face pales.

I don't wait another second before running.

Aaron calls after me as I sprint toward the entrance, coughing as I breathe in smoke. I make my way up the front steps, and I'm about to go back inside when Aaron catches up to me.

"Don't even think about it, Voclain."

I turn around. I give him one last look before running through the double doors—and straight into Milo. He steadies me. "Eddie?"

Aaron grabs us both and shoves us back through the door. By the time we reach the parking lot, the entire building is glowing orange. Every window is shattered.

I take off my mask and wrap my arms around my brother. "You scared the shit out of me."

"I'm here." Milo takes off his mask and hugs me back. "I'm here."

When we finally pull apart, I whip around and glare at Raven. "You set the fire before verifying that we were all accounted for?"

"I told you all to be quick," Raven says plainly. "None of you are idiots. I trusted you'd find your way out."

I knit my teeth together and step closer. "He could have been *killed*."

"But he wasn't."

My hands curl into fists. "The library's on fire. You got what you wanted. We're going."

"Eddie—"

"Whatever it is you're planning—whatever fight you're trying to start between us and them—we can't be a part of it."

"Why not?"

"It's dangerous."

"Not any more dangerous than simply existing," Raven argues. "Seen or Unseen, in this world, tomorrow is never a guarantee. One wrong word, one wrong move, and you're dead. There's no point in playing it safe when safe isn't even a real option to begin with."

"We're leaving."

I grab Milo's arm and push Aaron forward, corralling both of them toward the abandoned cars in the lot. I scan them for Yesterday models I might be able to hot-wire.

Aaron was right. The Gamblers aren't careful; they don't care who gets hurt. We need to leave, and once we track down the others, get as far away from Silver Fir as possible.

"One more job, Eddie," Raven calls after me. "One more job, and Milo's deal is done."

I keep walking.

"One more job, and we'll help you find your friend."

I freeze in my tracks, then turn back around. Wind toys with my hair. "Why should I trust you?"

"Because you're desperate." She pauses. "Because you know we're your only way of getting him back."

My mind flashes to Heron—to the flip phone in my pocket.

I purse my lips, letting out a frustrated sigh. *Maybe Raven's right.* If we can get Ren back without a bargain with an Agent—even if it means doing things their way, just one more time—isn't it worth it?

But I've already paid my price. I already helped Heron find what he was looking for. What if he *does* follow through with his end of the bargain after all? *There's no guarantee*, I remind myself. *He's an Agent.*

And I'm desperate.

"Fine." I clench my teeth. "One more job, and that's it."

It's dark by the time we make it back to Silver Fir. We're all exhausted. The smell of smoke still lingers in our hair, and all I can think about is getting in the shower and scrubbing myself clean of this whole nightmare. But smoke is hard to wash out.

When we walk inside the lodge and into the lobby, Fern is standing next to the fireplace waiting for us. Her eyes light up when we arrive.

"You guys can come down now!" Fern shouts over her shoulder. "It's them."

We wait in silence as a collection of footsteps thud downstairs. Aaron and I exchange glances as three familiar faces enter the room.

I don't have the chance to blink before Lori and Alice run up to us. Lori pulls Aaron into an embrace that she wrangles me into. Alice hugs Milo so tightly I think he might burst, and Beau watches, a smile spread across his face. For a moment he observes Aaron with something like guilt before looking away quickly.

"I'm so glad we found you idiots," Lori says. She pulls away, looking us up and down. "Are you hurt?"

"We're fine." Aaron hugs her again. "God, I was so worried about you."

They hold each other for a long time, and when they finally break apart, Lori's attention shifts. Her gaze carves into Raven's.

I don't think I've ever seen her eyes fill with so much rage.

"This is her?" Lori asks, not even looking at Aaron. He creases his brow. His silence answers her question. She walks to Raven and pauses a foot away.

Lori slaps her in the face.

Alice and I exchange glances, jaws dropping in unison as we study Lori in shock. Beau and Milo snicker.

"She's flipping her shit," Alice whispers under her breath.

We stand in bone-chilling quiet, waiting for Raven to say or do something. Anything. But to my surprise, she just stands there, expressionless.

Aaron's eyes widen. "What the *hell*, Lor?"

"Shut it," Lori snaps, whipping her head around to glare at him before facing Raven again. "I think you know exactly what that was for."

Raven doesn't speak. Milo and Beau stop laughing.

"Do you have *any* idea what he went through in that cell?" Lori's voice cracks. "What they did to him when they found out one of their Guards was helping all of you?"

Silence.

"Well, *I* do. And it took him an entire *year* to tell me just the half of it. An entire *year* for him to say anything at all."

My throat constricts.

"It took my dad *months* to get him out of bed. Hell, everyone had to take turns watching him. Making sure he ate. Making sure he didn't try anything stupid when no one was looking." She wipes a tear. "He was on your side, and you left him there."

"He turned us in." Raven's voice is calm and steady. "He betrayed us."

"He turned *himself* in," Lori shouts. "He was trying to help you escape."

Raven clamps her mouth shut.

"I still have no idea how he managed to get out alive, but it certainly wasn't thanks to you." Lori's lip quivers, like she's trying so hard not to cry. "After all he did to help you guys, you just left without him."

Raven stares at her, shaking. For a moment, I worry she might hit Lori back. But instead, she storms out of the room without another word. I hear her footsteps clumping upstairs. Lockley follows after her.

Aaron is completely still. He stares at the flames flickering in the fireplace, unmoving. Wind sings outside.

"We know he helped us," Marty says quietly, placing a kind hand on Lori's shoulder. "We owe our lives to him."

"He saved us," Fern adds.

Lori trembles. Marty gives her a friendly pat before he and Fern walk out of the room to follow Raven and Lockley.

"Raven just... has a hard time coming back around," Milo says. "But she will eventually. Deep down, she knows the truth." He nods toward the stairs. "Come on. You guys must be tired. I'll catch you up and get you something to eat."

Lori wipes another tear from her eye. Alice walks up to her, placing a hand on her shoulder. "Let's get you to bed."

Lori doesn't argue when Alice walks her to the stairwell and out of the room. Beau leaves too. Milo looks over his shoulder one last time before following them, giving me a sad smile.

Aaron and I stand alone in the lobby for a long time.

He eventually takes a seat on the couch. His leg shakes, and I watch him pull out a knife and his most recent carving—the shape is still undefined. Unlike usual, he lets the knife and carving rest in his lap.

I walk over and take the knife and wood, setting them on the coffee table. I sit down next to Aaron, observing him carefully, trying to find something in his gaze, but he can't even look at me.

My heart sinks as I connect what Lori said to the scars covering his back and chest.

"You didn't talk for a whole year?" I whisper.

He shakes his head.

"What made you start again?"

He looks at me, then his hands.

"I found a girl in the woods." He swallows, still unable to meet my gaze. "She didn't look at me like I was broken."

My eyes water. My breath catches in my throat, and the realization feels like shattering glass.

This is why he kept his secret for so long.

"You're not broken, Aaron."

I wrap my arm around him and bring his head to my shoulder.

He keeps it there.

R. STELLER

Monday, April 29

I blink every ten seconds.

For the past week, I've been breathing in similar intervals. My inhalations are monotonous, my exhalations unsatisfying. Like I can never really take a full breath, or let go of one either.

I recover in the safe house, but it doesn't feel like *recovery*. Heron applies ointment to my wounds every morning and night. The burns fade away in a matter of days. *A Corps healer can fix anything.*

But even after the blistering red marks have been completely erased from my skin, I still see them. I still feel them. I still scratch the places they used to be, like they are still scarring and not invisible. Now the scratches are all that scab me.

I still blink in waves of ten.

I haven't spoken a word. King is still gone, and Heron is the only one around who cares enough to keep me from rotting away. He's been nauseatingly attentive lately. Save for food runs, I don't think he's left me alone once. The gesture is supposed to be sweet, but it feels poisonous. It's a cruel reminder that I have a reason to be trapped here at all.

But I won't be trapped for much longer. I'm supposed to return to work today.

Although, maybe that fate isn't different. *I'm just moving to a new cage.*

Heron walks into my room carrying a to-go cup filled with coffee. I assume the coffee is for him, but he sets it on my nightstand and takes a seat in the chair by my bedside. I grab the cup and down it quickly, hoping it'll do something to soothe the pounding ache in my head.

Heron watches me drink, leaning forward in his seat, foot tapping the floor. Like he's waiting for something to happen.

Just as I'm about to take the last sip, he snatches it out of my hands.

"What does this one say? Sweetened?" He glares at the label that was scrawled onto the side of the cup with a permanent marker. "Screw this. Can't believe they got my order wrong."

I squint to make out the label. It doesn't say it's sweetened at all. It didn't taste that way either. It was more bitter than usual, actually.

I don't have the energy to question his odd behavior before he exits the room with the nearly empty cup in his hand. He throws it into the kitchen trash, then returns to the chair and clears his throat. "How are you feeling?"

I don't say anything.

"I got you donuts." He pauses. "They're in the kitchen, if you wanna go out there and indulge."

I can't meet his gaze. *Why is he being so nice to me?* I'm the last person in the world who deserves his kindness.

"I'm fine," I say.

"It's way too dark in here. I can't see shit." Heron walks to the window and opens the curtains. "There we go." He sits back down. "Sunlight feels nice, doesn't it?"

I nod, staring at the wall.

"When's the last time you went outside?"

I shrug.

"I think you need some fresh air."

I shake my head.

"Come on." He walks over, picking me up by the arms. I glare as he drags me out of bed. "Up you go."

I shove him off me. He grabs my jacket and shoes before guiding me toward the front door.

King's safe house is in the middle of the woods. I know by now that it's about a half-hour or so from Seattle, and there aren't any other structures around for miles. There's a large pond on the property, surrounded by towering pines. Heron and I walk around it with our hands in our pockets.

Neither of us say anything, and Heron whistles cheerfully. I can't bring myself to be annoyed, though I want to be. My mind is entangled in thorns. The guilt is pricking.

We're quiet for a long time, letting the distant cawing of seagulls and the wind that rustles through evergreen needles do the talking for us. The air feels clean out here, but no matter how hard I try, I can't seem to take a full breath of it. It's so peaceful it doesn't feel real.

A chirp draws my attention upward. I stop walking, lifting my chin to inspect the source of the sound. Heron stops too.

I notice a vibrant blue bird with a dark navy crest, perched on a branch and staring down at us with beady black eyes.

"A Steller's jay." Heron steps back, hands in his pockets, staring up at the bird as he grins from ear to ear. "They're striking, aren't they?"

I nod.

"It's a shame. They're such deceptive little birds." He glances at me. "Insidious, really."

I can't stop staring at the jay. It looks me in the eye like it knows what I've done, and for a moment, I swear I see its head twitch. Like it's giving me a nod of approval.

It flies away, and I observe Heron closely as we continue our lap around the pond. A breath of wind runs through his wavy hair. He studies the trees, but I'm not sure he's paying attention to them. It's like he's trying to avoid eye contact. He keeps looking at me when he thinks I don't notice, and I find myself doing the same.

We're so alone out here. So far away from the rest of the world. It's just him and me, for miles and miles.

We stop by a towering oak with gnarled limbs. I can't tell if it's dead, or just really old. Heron looks up at it before turning to me.

"Hey Steller," he says. "Come here."

I pause. *He never calls me Steller.* "What do you want?"

"Just do it."

I step closer until we're only a foot away.

Heron stares at me for a moment—and he punches me in the gut. *Hard.* I fold forward and heave until every drop of coffee I had resurfaces.

I wipe my mouth with the back of my sleeve and glare at him. I barely have the strength to stand straight as I shake and clutch my gut. "What the hell was *that* for?"

"You'll thank me later," Heron mutters. He slides his hands into his pockets again and heads back toward the house, but I'm rooted in place. I watch him disappear between the trees with my lips parted. My stomach churns—this time, all on its own. *Surely he can't know what I've done.*

A shiver traces my back. *Does he?*

I follow him back, and I don't question it further.

I sit at a conference table with King, Heron, and Sparrow, awaiting Canary's instruction.

He stands in front of a screen, which displays a map with four red dots indicating different locations outside of HQ. I don't recognize any of them.

"Now that you're all here, I'd like to inform you of your next assignment. You four seem to work well together, so I'm assigning both of your teams to this case."

Behind my shades, I crease my brow. *We're the ones who warned the camps. Shouldn't he be hesitant about pairing us together again?*

"Recently, there has been a series of Underground attacks near Brim Creek that I would like you all to investigate."

Unseen attacks? My breath catches in my throat. I scratch at the skin of my wrists and neck.

Don't think of her.

"The most recent of these attacks involved one of our libraries," Canary explains. "As you know, we value research and intelligence in the Corps, especially in our division of work. Our libraries are vital parts of who we are, how we operate, and what we stand for. Unfortunately, we lost three Sitters."

A chill spreads through me.

"The Brim Creek Chaser Corps Library was not our most notable or sophisticated, and we're suspecting that the purpose of this attack was not to make any major blows to our intelligence system, but to send a message. I firmly believe there is significance to their choice of damage."

Canary brings a finger to his Eyes, pressing a button that fills the screen with a photograph of a smoldering pile of rubble.

"The day before they burned the library down, another attack took place on a train set to stop in Brim Creek, where two Agents were assassinated. These Agents had been investigating the area for Underground presence until a local sighting report marked Lavender Voclain nearby. They think she could have escaped on the train and were inquiring passengers about the matter when the attack took place. Upon analyzing the security footage, we can confirm that she was in fact on this train, leading us to believe she has a connection to this recent string of attacks."

The photo shifts to a screenshot of Eddie in her disguise.

I blink every ten seconds.

"It's clear that Voclain and her rebel associates are becoming a bigger problem than we anticipated. However, she has been rather elusive thus far, and I want to make it clear that your focus for this assignment is not finding her, but rather getting to the root of these attacks and preventing another one from taking place.

"We have reason to believe there is a significant Underground base somewhere outside of Brim Creek, and I have a feeling this base is responsible for these acts of terrorism. Please keep this in mind during your investigation. Any questions?"

The four of us are silent.

"Good." He shuts off the screen. "You leave tomorrow."

We rise to our feet and make our way to the door. Canary stops me before

I can exit. "Agent Steller?"

I freeze.

"A word, please."

King and Sparrow leave. Heron glances back at me before walking out too.

I stand by the door with my hands behind my back, staring at Canary through my shades in a long stretch of silence.

"How was Correction?" he finally asks.

The question makes me flinch. I don't know how to answer it, so I keep my mouth shut.

Canary chuckles. "Effective, I presume."

I don't say anything.

"During our last conversation, I mentioned having a job in mind for you."

"You did, sir," I say. "Should I retrieve Agent Kingfisher?"

"No." He shakes his head. "This assignment is just for you, Agent Steller."

I shudder.

"I want you to complete an extermination for me." He strolls to where I stand. "Let's keep this one between you and me, shall we?"

I keep my mouth glued shut as he pulls a folded paper out of his pocket and holds it out. I take it.

"This will be an ongoing assignment." Canary walks around me to reach the door, looking over his shoulder with his hand wrapped around the knob. "Strike opportunistically, little jay."

And with that, he opens and closes the door, leaving me completely alone.

My heart thuds, echoing in my ears as I slowly unfold the paper.

When I see the name of my new assignment, the page slips out of my hands, fluttering to the ground like a moth that tried to find the moon in lamplight.

> *MALLORY PERRY GREER*
> *AGENT M. HERON*

I know what I have to do.

EDDIE

Tuesday, April 30
93 Beds Made

Thirty minutes outside of Brim Creek, there is a warehouse nestled within the woods.

This is where the Pacific Region's Agency Headquarters stores its Nightjade.

It looks like a gray box dotted with flickering white lights that are so weak the moonlight overpowers them. It's a full moon, to our luck, so we can see everything clearly as Lockley puts the van in park between the trees, a short walk away from the parking lot.

Raven sits in the passenger's seat, already wearing her mask. Aaron sits next to me in the back, along with Milo, Marty, and Beau. Lori refused to help, and Alice stayed behind with her.

"Remember the plan?" Raven asks.

We all nod.

"Lockley and Marty will help me take care of the workers. Then we'll light up the inside." She nods toward the bag of Catnap bombs in the back.

"You four will be on gasoline duty outside."

Milo salutes.

"Remember, this is a brick-and-steel building. We probably won't be able to burn it to the ground, so we'll focus on lighting up what's inside, not the warehouse itself. We'll also burn some of the landscaping around it to keep any dispatched authorities from putting out the fire and saving their stock. *We'll* gas the Nightjade—you four will gas the perimeter."

We nod again. Lockley puts on his mask, and so does Milo.

"Ready?" Raven asks.

Beau and I put on our masks in silence. Aaron hesitates before putting his on too.

"Count to 300." Raven and Lockley hop out of the car with Marty. "Five minutes, then you're up."

With that, they head toward the warehouse, Yesterday guns and Catnap in hand.

Like we did when we burned down the Brim Creek Public Library last week, those of us on gasoline duty wait in the van. Since they're using the Catnap bombs this time around, we don't hear any gunshots or frightened screams as the three Gamblers knock out the workers inside.

At least they'll be saved, I tell myself. *Raven and the other two will drag them out.*

According to Raven—and confirmed by Aaron and Lori—the workers in the warehouse won't be field Chasers like Officers and Agents. They're likely from NOT, the Nightjade Operations and Tech Division—or WALS, the Weaponry Application and Launching Sites Division. In other words, they're researchers, not fighters.

They're still Chasers, Raven had pointed out. *So we'll treat them like Chasers.*

She and Aaron got into an argument about it—the shouting kind of argument that makes other people leave the room. I've seen how Aaron gets around Officers and Agents; he hates them almost as much as Raven does. But Lori was a Double in tech, so Aaron seems to have a soft spot for the Chasers that aren't direct killers. Raven doesn't seem to have the ability to differentiate between the divisions.

The five minutes we count in our heads seem to stretch on like hours. But eventually, we reach 300—and file out of the car.

Milo and Beau open the back of the van and grab two jugs of gasoline each, handing two to Aaron and I as well before shutting the doors. The *slam* echoes between the trees, sending crows scattering in all directions.

We haul the gasoline to the warehouse. It's surrounded by a dirt clearing, which seems to serve as the parking lot. A handful of sleek black and white cars reside throughout it.

Raven, Lockley, and Marty are still inside, so we split up to tackle the perimeter of the building first, pouring thin trails of gasoline around tree trunks. We're down the mountain, so without the elevation, there is no snow, but the dead leaves and other litter that blankets the forest floor are damp. Sprinkles of mist prickle at the exposed skin of my neck and hands, and a few clouds obscure the sky, but there still hasn't been any rainfall.

A breeze rustles through the evergreen needles, carrying with it the sweetness of pine and the stench of gasoline. A chill runs through me.

I'm still leaving my trail when I spot Beau a few yards away, one jug in hand while the other rests by his feet. I pause and squint to make out what he's doing, creasing my brow when I realize he's checking a phone.

It's a black flip phone, and it chirps exactly like mine.

That looks exactly like the one in my pocket... same ringtone and everything.

Beau flips the phone shut, then puts it in his pocket. He continues leaving his trail, not realizing I'd seen him.

What is he doing with a phone like that?

I don't have the chance to approach him before a twig snaps behind me, and I turn around to see Milo approaching. He connects his trail to mine, then tosses the now-empty jug, still holding a full one in his other hand.

We stand in silence for a moment, waiting for Aaron and Beau to finish their trails. The wind continues to run its fingers through our hair and the branches above us.

I turn my head to look at Milo. *This is my chance*, I realize.

"Why are you choosing this?"

The question startles him. He's quiet for a moment. "You know why I left."

"I mean *this*." I gesture toward the jug of gasoline in his hand, then the warehouse. "Are you sure this is the kind of life you want?"

He looks me in the eye. "I've never been more certain about anything in my life."

When I see his gaze, all I can see is Milo stabbing those Chasers to death. Because he has the same look in his eye. The same cold, empty hatred that frightened me back then. That still scares me now.

I know the anger he feels because I feel it myself. But he's my little brother, and I need to protect him. *He can't go down this road.*

"End Harbor is safe," I say. "Once this is all over, I think you should go home."

"Home?" Milo laughs bitterly. "Don't you get it, Ed? We don't have one of those anymore."

"What about Asa? Noriko?"

"She's the one who wanted me to leave in the first place."

A twig snaps. Aaron approaches, then stops dead in his tracks.

"What are you talking about?" I mutter.

"I thought you knew," Milo says.

Aaron and I exchange glances.

"How do you think I got the coordinates to that safe house?" Milo asks.

"What do you mean by that?" Aaron says.

"Noriko found me looking through Cecil's room. I was trying to find maps, and she realized what I was doing and gave me the coordinates. She believed I could get him back, alright? She wouldn't have trusted me with that if she thought it was too dangerous for me to handle."

Aaron looks at me, puzzled. "Why didn't she tell us?"

"Look, I don't know, alright? She probably thought you two would get like this and try to stop me."

"That doesn't make any sense," Aaron says. "No offense, but why would she send a kid with no experience on a jailbreak job without backup? That's like feeding you to sharks."

"I'm not breaking into their headquarters or anything. I'm not stupid." Milo glares. "This is a safe house we're talking about here. It's in the middle of the woods. The backup we're buying from Raven will be more than enough."

"How do you know that?" Aaron asks quietly.

"Know what?"

"About the safe house."

"Noriko."

My forehead wrinkles. "Where did she get that information?"

Milo shrugs. "She has connections."

"None in the Agency," Aaron says. "Or the entire Corps, for that matter. Lori and I were the Cut's only Doubles."

"That you know of," Milo says.

I turn to Aaron. "You think she has a contact in the Corps?"

"I know just as much about this as you do, Voclain."

"None of this is making any sense."

"Look, I don't know what you two are freaking out about." Milo frowns. "We have the coordinates. We know that safe house has some connection to Ren. Don't you want to get him back? Isn't that what you've wanted this entire time?"

"Of course I do," I say. "It's just... something about this isn't sitting right with me."

"What are you suggesting?" Aaron mutters.

"I don't know."

We're interrupted when Beau returns, connecting the last section of our trails. Raven, Lockley, and Marty run out of one of the warehouse doors. I catch a glimpse of smoke and fire before they slam the doors shut behind them. They jog over to where we stand, breathless.

"There was so much shit in there," Lockley pants.

"Thousands of vials of serum," Marty confirms.

"Ammunition. Guns. Probably a year's supply of Nightjade weaponry," Raven says. "Did you guys handle the perimeter?"

We nod, then walk outside of the circle.

Raven turns to me. "Would you like to do the honors?"

My face pales. "Me?"

"You have a lighter, don't you?"

Reluctantly, I pull it out of my pocket.

"Anyone have something flammable?" Raven asks.

I reach into my pocket again. The note Aaron gave me weeks ago is still in there, crumpled into a ball. I retrieve it, take a deep breath, and flip my lighter open. The paper lights up in my hands. Everyone takes a step back.

I toss the paper onto the trail, then step back too. It ignites immediately.

The circle of gasoline burns quickly, wrapping all the way around the warehouse. The line itself is made of flames, but the trees it's connected to slowly begin to catch fire.

We don't waste another second standing around. We jog back to the van, climb inside, and take off.

Lockley drives over a narrow and winding dirt path that leads to the main road back to Silver Fir. We remove our masks.

"Are you sure everyone got out okay?" Aaron asks.

Raven looks at him over her shoulder. "What do you mean?"

"The workers."

She doesn't say anything.

Aaron's face pales. "You said you were taking care of them, remember?"

"And what did you think we meant by that?" she snaps.

My heartbeat slows to a stop. The back of my throat burns as my lungs pinch shut, making it impossible to release a single breath. "You were taking them out?"

"We couldn't risk them calling anybody or reporting anything about us once they woke up," Lockley argues.

Aaron clenches his teeth. "What was the point of the Catnap then?"

Raven turns back around in her seat. "To make it easier."

Aaron's hands curl into fists. He folds his arms across his chest, gaze hollow as he stares at the back of Raven's head, then out the window once that becomes unbearable. His arms tremble with anger.

I feel like I'm going to be sick.

My breathing grows shallow, and the world around me spins as my head turns light and my vision hazy. *All of those workers, gone.*

And it's all our fault.

"Guys?" Milo says, cutting through the silence.

We all turn to look at him.
"Where's Beau?"

R. STELLER

Tuesday, April 30

The Brim Creek Public Library is a pile of rubble.

It's been this way for a week. What was once a violent concoction of gasoline and flame is now a yellowed, quiet gray. Everything is blanketed in a thick coat of dust and ash. Cars that were once brand new lie warped and degraded in the lot, nothing more than piles of scraps that look as though they've been here since the Yesterdays. A bluebird hops around in the dirt, plucking plump worms from the damp soil beneath the ruins.

"This is..." King begins.

"Creepy as hell?" Heron finishes.

King glances at Heron from behind his shades, then back at the debris. "Yeah."

"I'm bringing up security footage from the day of the attack," Sparrow says, bringing a finger to her Eyes. She presses the button a few times. "I suggest you all do the same."

I follow her lead, pressing the buttons on the side of my Eyes. The screen built into the lenses displays a selection of hours, each one displaying a thumbnail of something the computer analyzed as notable. I find a clip from the afternoon with a worn-down white van and click on it.

A group of six people file into the van, all of them wearing what appear to be replicas of plague masks from the Yesterdays, with pointed black beaks and round holes where the eyes should be. The sight makes shivers claw at my back and neck. They slam the doors shut, and they drive off sloppily and quickly, leaving tire tracks in their wake.

"Ew," Heron mutters, likely viewing the same footage that I am. "Where do you even find masks like that?"

"Unless you're an Undergrounder, you don't," Sparrow says. "They've shown they like hiding in abandoned places. I can only imagine all the weird shit they stumble across."

"So we're certain they're traitors?" Heron asks.

"What else could they be?" King says.

Sparrow turns to me. "Do you recognize those masks, Steller?"

I shake my head. "No."

"Does this behavior... speak to you in any way?" she asks. "Do you know of anyone who would do something like this?"

"No one I knew at the Cut would act this rashly," I say. "That broadcast took them months—if not years—to plan. They're extremely cautious. This looks like it was planned in a matter of weeks. Days, even."

"So you think a different group is responsible?" King asks.

I nod.

"You saw how Glasmack Falls reacted when you mentioned Raven," Heron says to Sparrow. He turns to me next. "You think it's possible that the Underground is split into factions? Groups with bad blood or conflicting interests?"

"The Uns—the Underground is not an organized entity," I explain. "It's mostly pockets of people trying to survive outside of the system's reach. They have alliances, but they're not unified. They wouldn't have official factions, but... I'd say conflicting priorities is a possibility."

"So you don't know these people, or what they're trying to accomplish," Sparrow says.

I shake my head.

"They clearly didn't think about taking out security cameras before-hand," King says. He holds up a finger to the side of his shades, studying what's playing on his screen. "I can trace the van's path to the edge of town."

"Should we follow it?" Heron asks.

Sparrow is already walking back toward our car. "Definitely."

We follow the security footage as far as it goes, with Sparrow driving under King's instruction as he monitors the route the van took with his Eyes. The surveillance stops at the border between Brim Creek and a thick forest of evergreens.

We reach an old dirt road packed down by tire tracks. Sparrow drives our sedan over it while Heron and I sit in the back.

It's uncomfortably quiet in here. Heron is staring out the window, humming something to himself as he studies the pines beyond the glass. The faintest whisper of guilt sparks a fleeting pang in my chest. The blood on my hands and the scrap of paper in my pocket weigh heavier than ever.

But the guilt is quickly overpowered by desperation—necessity. Canary's words echo in my head like a stuck record. *"Strike opportunistically, little jay."*

Heron catches me staring. He winks. Something about it makes me shudder, and I study the trees through the window instead.

The dirt road snakes through the woods, then cuts through an expanse of emerald green farmland. My wrists and neck itch when we pass by dairy fields speckled with grazing cows. It eventually turns into a real road, with cracked, sun-faded pavement, sparsely lined with leaning telephone poles that look like they haven't seen maintenance in decades. They definitely aren't equipped with security cameras. *We're reaching Wandering territory.*

We continue down the road through another stretch of woods, this one thicker than the last. There is nothing out here but evergreen.

Sparrow parks the car at a fork in the road, and the four of us climb out to investigate. One path bends to the right, going farther into the forest. The other prong stretches farther until it curves around the base of a tree-covered mountain to our left, which I can't see the top of through the thickness of the woods surrounding us.

I take a closer look at the road to the left, noticing a trail of something white dried against the pavement.

"Is that paint?" Heron asks, folding up his shades and hanging them on his collar.

We walk towards it. King crouches down, tracing it with his hands before rising up to his feet again. "Looks like it."

Heron's brows pinch together. "That's... odd."

"It can't be that old," King says. "I doubt it's meant for the road. It should've washed away at least a little bit with the last downpour we had. It's not very faded either."

"So you think it was made after that storm?" Sparrow asks. King nods.

We climb back into the car, following the trail of paint, rising higher in elevation until the trail stops, and we step out again.

"Why would there be a trail of paint all the way out here?" Sparrow asks.

"Maybe someone wanted to leave breadcrumbs," Heron says.

King checks the security footage again on his Eyes. "Looks like the van has a cracked taillight."

Sparrow raises a brow. "You think the rebels kidnapped someone?"

"If they did, it would've been sometime before they burned the library."

"Between the storm and the attack," I say. King nods again.

"There's literally nothing out here, so it has to be them. And they *have* been assassinating Chasers recently." Heron shrugs. "Maybe they decided to take one back for questioning."

"Chasers still have trackers. They wouldn't have taken anyone back to their base unless they were debugged at another location first," I say. "Have there been any recent Officer deaths in the area?"

"Aside from those two Agents on the train and the Sitters from the Library, none," King says. "No recent civilian deaths in the vicinity either."

"Only someone who wants to be found would leave a trail like that on purpose," Sparrow adds. "So who was being taken against their will?"

"Probably another traitor," King says.

"That would confirm our theory from earlier," Sparrow says.

"Heron was right about Glasmack. How they acted when you mentioned your sister," King says. "They clearly have some sort of bad blood with her, or whoever she's associated herself with."

"So whoever left this paint trail wanted to be found by other Underground associates," Sparrow says.

Heron crinkles his nose. "This is weird."

King squints, stepping forward to take a closer look at the tire tracks on the pavement. He picks up a thin plastic tube that looks like a straw. "What is this?"

"Looks like a honey stick," I say. "I used to eat those all the time."

"It's not degraded at all. There's barely any dirt on it." King studies the empty tube. "It was right on the tire tracks but not run over. I'm guessing it was dropped after the van passed through. After they made their way back from the library."

"You think whoever's following the person who was taken could've left it?" Sparrow asks.

"Maybe."

"Either way, these tire tracks will definitely lead us somewhere," I say.

King nods. "Let's keep going."

Wherever we are, I've never seen anything like it before in my life.

The road led us up the side of a mountain, so high up we spotted patches of snow and frost lacing the trees, until everything eventually morphed into white. We stopped the car at the edge of the woods, where the road seemed to lead to a clearing.

We stand hidden between the trees and beneath the cover of darkness, observing the sight before us with wide eyes. Dozens of cabins dot the landscape, each one glowing with soft orange light. At the top of a hill, a lodge made of logs towers above everything else. A functioning ski lift circles around the clearing, carrying passengers up and down.

This must be the base Canary was talking about.

"This is almost as big as the Cut," King mutters in awe, eyes glued to the scene.

I nod.

"Did you know anything about this?" Sparrow asks me.

I shake my head. "I had no idea this place even existed."

"Should we... do something?" Sparrow asks. "Confront them about the attacks?"

"That's the assignment," King says.

"I didn't realize whatever base my father suspected would be this heavily populated," Sparrow says. "We can't just walk up there and ask to talk. We're Agents. They'll kill us on the spot. Especially if they're the kind of people who commit arson and kidnap other rebels."

"They're clearly aggressive," King adds, rubbing his chin. "We need to come up with a better plan. A different way to approach this."

"You think we can go in with disguises or something?" Sparrow suggests.

"We have Steller on our side," King argues. "If they haven't heard of his name, he knows things about the Underground we don't. He might be able to convince them we're on their side. Then we can get to the bottom of the attacks."

"And what happens after that?" I ask quietly.

"You saw what my father did to those camps," Sparrow mutters, averting her gaze. "If we tell him this place exists, he'll send an attack unit. It'll get firebombed like the others." She observes the lodge, and the cabins, and the people walking around in the snow. She swallows. "There's simply too many people to evacuate."

"How many do you suspect there are?" Heron asks.

"From the looks of it? I'd say over a hundred. If not more," King says.

"I don't know about you guys, but I don't want a hundred exterminations on my track record," Heron mutters. "I don't care if they're traitors. It just doesn't feel right."

Sparrow nods softly, still staring at the camp. "Me neither."

"So we get to the bottom of it," King says. "We find a way to convince the rebels to stop the attacks. We tell Canary we caught and Extracted a few traitors, then exterminated them. If we have to, we'll bring a couple back to HQ to make our story believable. Please Canary." He lowers his voice. "Then we pretend we never saw this place."

Even though he's wearing his shades, I can see the stiffness of King's shoulders, and I know the look that must be in his eyes. I stare at the tallies on his wrist, the two filled-in hearts that exist to remind him of his mistakes. *He's thinking about Harebell Hill.*

Heron shoves his hands into his pockets and walks away, pulling me out of my thoughts. "I've gotta take a piss."

King frowns. "Again?"

"What can I say?" Heron walks backwards. "I'm over-caffeinated and slightly hydrated."

Sparrow shakes her head, and I watch Heron disappear between the trees.

We continue hiding, observing the camp in silence, until a chirp sounds from the speaker built into my Eyes. King and Sparrow bring a finger to the sides of their glasses, so I'm guessing we've all received the same notification.

It's a message from Canary.

"Guys?" Jade lifts up her shades, resting them on her forehead, eyes wide. "The traitors just burned a Nightjade plant."

My face pales.

"Where's Heron?" I ask.

Sparrow puts her shades back on to radio him. "Get back here." She drops her hand, facing King and me. "We'll scope this place out later."

The smoke burns my eyes.

The warehouse spits it out through shattered windows. A soft breeze carries the familiar reek of scorched flesh, and all I can think about is the bonfire at the Cut. The white room. My neck and wrists itch.

"Ten trackers went off," Sparrow mutters as we watch the scene from afar. Flames devour nearby trees, and I see them reflected in her gaze. Ash and embers fall all around us like fireflies.

None of us can pry our eyes away from the fire.

King speaks into his glasses. "It's Kingfisher. We need a team dispatched immediately to handle a fire. Once it's put out, send Cleaners to the same address."

He waits for a response, then folds up his Eyes.

"The fire hasn't spread far," Sparrow says. "The perpetrators could still be nearby."

"We should split up," Heron suggests. "Try to find them before they get away."

"I agree," I say, keeping my eyes pinned to Heron. "We should split up."

Sparrow and King nod, and we spread out into four different directions to search the woods.

The moon is full tonight, and it casts an eerie glow over everything I see, lighting the way so I don't need the assistance of night vision. My shades are giving me a headache, so I keep them folded over my collar, until I've walked far enough away from everyone else. Now that I'm completely alone, I put them on again, and I check Heron's tracker.

He's not too far from where I am. King and Sparrow went to the right of the warehouse; we took the left.

I fold up my Eyes again and pull out the piece of paper in my pocket. I unfold it, staring at the handwriting scrawled across its blankness, making sure for the thousandth time that I'm reading it correctly. The creases are worn thin, so delicate they could tear the next time I unfold it.

My hands shake. I read the name over and over again, until it's all I hear in my head.

I know what I have to do. But I don't know if I have it in me.

I know Eddie has something to do with these attacks; Canary confirmed that suspicion, and he told the others not to focus on her. *Strike opportunistically, little jay.*

I realize now why he paired us together, and my gut twists with nausea. This assignment is about more than the attacks alone. He wants me to follow through with my agreements.

Kill Heron.

Betray Eddie.

I think back to the location of Heron's tracker. Of our distance from the other two. Of the Nightjade gun tucked away in my holster, hidden by my suit jacket. There will be no better opportunity than this.

If I want Canary to hold up his end of the deal—if I want to keep Eddie alive and safe—I have to make it worth the investment. I already went through Correction. All that's left is the extermination.

Then I'll find her.

Every part of me trembles. I fold the paper for the last time and shove it back into my pocket. I never want to unfold it again.

I lift my head up and stare at the moon—the same moon that must be shining down on Heron. On Eddie. On the wildfire that will surely catch up to us.

I need to do this.

Something clicks behind me.

Slowly, I turn around.

Agent M. Heron stands ten feet away with a Nightjade gun in his hands. And he's pointing it right at me. His arm shakes as he grips the gun with pale knuckles.

When I lift up my own gun, we are the same.

There is a fire behind his eyes that burns into mine, and it stings more than any breath of smoke ever could. His jaw is clenched so tightly I wonder how his teeth don't shatter.

I feel empty when my gaze meets his glare.

Time is suspended, and we are too, hanging somewhere between the seconds.

My face is stoic, but Heron's is contorted, twisted with an anger I've never seen him display. His entire body convulses like the ground is quaking beneath us, and I am perfectly still. We are both rigid.

His glare is unmoving as I bury my gaze within it, reading him. I find something in his eyes I wish I hadn't, and my shoulders soften. I know that pain. I know that rage.

It will devour him alive, as it has already done to me.

It feels like there is nothing left of me. Like all the parts belonging to the name I used to bear are broken, and the pieces are scattered, and I will never find them again.

What is left for me?

I keep studying Heron, who still hasn't brought himself to pull the trigger his finger traces. *He needs this more than I do.* Maybe it will put out the fire within him before it burns him to nothing but dust.

My grip on my gun loosens. Slowly, my hand falls to my side. "Shoot me."

Silence.

"Just shoot me." My shout echoes between the trees. "You know what I did."

Heron continues to clench the gun with shaking hands, mouth glued shut.

I step forward until there is only a foot of space between us.

"You know I deserve it." My voice cracks. "*I* know it."

Heron raises the gun to my forehead. It feels cold against my skin.

My throat tightens. *This is peaceful enough, isn't it? It'll be a quiet, painless death. That's more than I deserve.* I close my eyes, waiting for the bullet. It will end quickly.

My neck and wrists itch. I think of the moon.

The bullet never comes.

I open my eyes.

Heron looks into them, lowers his arm, and drops the gun.

He falls to his knees, eyes glistening, body trembling. His hands rest limply in his lap. He stares at the ground, unblinking.

Slowly, I meet him there.

His shoulders convulse. He hangs his head low, and he starts to sob.

The wail carves into me, like all the pain he's felt in a life without crying is coming out all at once. He leans forward, and to my surprise, he's holding me. I freeze, muscles stiffening, until slowly, I wrap my arms around him.

He clutches my shirt and cries into my chest like a child. "Why couldn't you have been heartless?"

I can't tell if he means his brother, his father, or me. Maybe even himself.

"It would've been so much easier if it had been you." He closes his eyes. "*God*, how I wanted it to be you."

"What do you mean?"

"Randy was a traitor, Steller. You only knocked him unconscious with that Nightjade. A damn Cleaner finished the job." He pulls his face away, wiping his nose. "I tried, Ren. I tried, but I can't blame you."

My eyes widen. I stop breathing.

I never killed him.

I never killed him.

Horace Randall Greer. That's the name I've spent months trying to forget. The name I thought I'd wiped from existence. The name I thought I tossed into that fountain of dead, along with every other person exterminated by the Corps.

All this time, I thought I was a monster. A murderer. Inhuman. *Perfect.*

And I never even killed him.

"I'm sorry, Ren."

My brows crease. "For what?"

Heron looks up at me with guilt behind his eyes. "I've been playing checkers with your girlfriend."

My neck burns. My heart pounds, and my voice lowers to a whisper. "What are you talking about?"

He lifts up a sleek black flip phone. "Do you want to see her?"

All the air depletes from my lungs.

The thought of her makes my skin itch. I blink every ten seconds.

I try not to want her. I try not to cry. I try to breathe.

He's been in contact with her?

There is a fog draped over the parts of me that used to burn for her, but I remember enough to understand how little I want her to know what I've become. *If she finds out that I've been an Agent all this time, she'll hate me.*

But isn't that the point?

Canary wants me to betray her. He wants to give her a reason to become the villain he believes we need. He wants to make her angrier than she already is. He wants her to bring the Unseen's downfall. *He will only keep her alive if he gets what he wants.*

I study Heron, who has red eyes and tear-stained skin and something broken behind his gaze. *I can't kill him now. He knows where Eddie is.*

I ignore the phantom burn in my wrists and neck, and I look Heron in the eye. "Take me to her."

EDDIE

Tuesday, April 30
93 Beds Made

♪ IN CIRCLES - SUNNY DAY REAL ESTATE ♪

Lockley stops the car.

Through the rear-view windshield, I can see the fire glowing behind us.

"Why are we stopped?" Raven says. "We have to get out of here. Once they see how many trackers went off, they'll dispatch a team of Agents to scope out the damage. Not Officers. *Agents.*"

"We're not leaving Beau behind," I seethe.

"He found his way to Silver Fir once. He can do it again."

Aaron grits his teeth. "Raven."

She looks at him for a moment, then sighs. "You have ten minutes. If you're not back before then, this van is gone."

"Ten minutes?"

"The clock's already ticking."

Aaron and I climb out of the van, slamming the doors behind us. He can't run very well with his leg, but we jog as fast as we're able to the warehouse.

Cold air fills my lungs, scraping against my throat. We're breathless by the time we reach the site, coughing from the smoke.

"Beau!" I shout.

Nothing.

We scan the perimeter for him. There are still gaps between the circle of flames we created, but most of the trees are burning, creating a sparse but towering barrier of fire. We jog around it, searching for any sign of Beau, shouting his name.

We don't see anything.

The smoke is already filling my lungs, and Aaron is coughing almost uncontrollably. There's no way we can go inside the warehouse to look for him, but we step over the circle of fire and study the parking lot.

"Let's split up," Aaron says. "We don't have much time."

I nod, and we jog in opposite directions.

My throat is sore from shouting, and I cough from the smoke. No matter where I turn or how loudly I call, there's still no sign of Beau. I cross over the barrier and away from the flames, searching through the surrounding woods instead. The violent cracking of the fire becomes nothing more than a soft rustling behind me.

I nearly jump when a chirp emits from my pocket, echoing between the trees. Frantically, I pull out the phone, flipping it open.

M. HERON

> brim creek's an odd vacation spot.

My eyes widen. *How does he know I'm here?*

I think back to the train, and the Agents that were asking about me. *I was spotted. Of course he heard about that.*

EDDIE

> what do you want?

M. HERON

> to be a man of my word.

My breath hitches.

EDDIE

> go on

A pause.

M. HERON

> you fulfilled your end of the bargain.

My heart is racing, and I can barely breathe. *What is he saying?* He's typing.

M. HERON

> do you want to see him?

Everything around me melts into one quiet, muddied mess of nothing. I can't smell the smoke. I can't hear the warehouse burning behind me. I can't feel the cold, or the fire in my lungs, or anything at all.

Could this be a trap? I wonder before I get ahead of myself. I pause, biting my lip. *If he was really interested in turning me in, he would've done so by now. Unless he's finally done with me.*

But do I care?

I look behind me, studying the fire in the distance.

I want to see him, but we've already held up our end of the bargain with Raven. If she really meant it, we have her backup.

But what if something bad happens, even *with* her backup? *What if someone gets hurt?* Breaking into an Agent's safe house would be incredibly risky. *One Agent can do more than enough damage.*

If I can get Ren back myself, no one has to get hurt. Not Milo, not the Gamblers, not Aaron.

EDDIE

> yes

The seconds I wait for him to respond last years.

EDDIE

> hello?

M. HERON

> gotta go, detective. I'm in the middle of something.

EDDIE

> you said I could see him.

Nothing.

EDDIE

> heron???

My throat constricts. I close out of our messages and dial his number, but it goes straight to voicemail.

I call him again, and again. Still, no response.

A twig snaps, and I shove my phone away when I hear Aaron jog up to me, breathless. "I don't see him anywhere."

I turn around.

"But one of the cars is missing."

My brows crease. "What?"

"He must have realized we left without him and started driving back by himself."

We hurry to the road as fast as we can, trying to locate the van. But just as Raven promised, it's nowhere to be seen.

"Shit." Aaron hits a tree, nostrils flaring.

My eyes widen. "They really left us."

"You can hot-wire cars, right?"

"Only Yesterday models. Anything newer will have an immobilizer, and that lot was full of Chaser cars."

"So no?"

"No."

Aaron swears under his breath, putting his hands on his hips. He looks at the fire in the distance before his gaze drifts to me. "Then how did Beau take one?"

I pause. "I... don't know, actually."

"If none of the cars can be hot-wired, he must have stolen keys from one of the workers, right?"

"That's the only explanation." I bite my cheek. "But that would only be possible if he'd done it before the fire started. Not after we left."

"We split up, remember?" Aaron sighs. "He might've snuck in when we weren't looking."

"But why would he? It's not like he knew he was gonna get left behind."

He pauses. "Unless he stayed behind on purpose."

My brows draw together. "You think he ran off?"

"You heard how obsessed he was with those coordinates," Aaron mutters. "You saw the fight. He never wanted us to stray from our original plan."

We both go quiet. I smell smoke drifting toward us from the fire in the distance. Somewhere far, a crow calls, its cry echoing throughout the trees.

"He's clearly up to something," I say, thinking back to the phone. I glance up at Aaron, then avert my gaze. *I can't tell him how suspicious Beau was without giving up my secret too. And he can't know about the deal I made.* So instead, I add, "I just don't know *what*."

Aaron nods. "We can continue that conversation with Milo once we're back." He looks over his shoulder, then steps forward. "We need to get the hell out of here."

We walk along the road so we don't get lost. I have my compass; we know we're going in the right direction, and I saw the route we took to get here. It should be easy enough to retrace our steps back to Silver Fir, but it will definitely take a long time.

We hike for about half an hour, until Aaron can't take another step. He squeezes his eyes shut, wincing as he sits against a fallen log, rubbing the scar tissue in his thigh. He leans his head against the bark. I take a seat across from him, resting against the trunk of a tree.

It's not snowing since we're not at the same elevation of Silver Fir, but it's still really cold, and the light breeze drifting between the trees doesn't make it any better.

Everything smells like smoke, but the warehouse fire hasn't traveled this far yet and the air doesn't have that soupy haze to cover us. And while we're far enough from the warehouse to be safe for now, we're still close enough so that any Agents on site would be able to see a campfire if we started one. So we shiver, even with our jackets.

I glance over my shoulder. In the distance, I see the warehouse glowing. We're only a short hike away; we weren't able to get far with Aaron's limp.

But we should be safe, I assure myself. *For now, at least.*

I lean my head against my tree, staring at the night sky between the gaps in the pine branches above our heads. The full moon is beautiful tonight, so bright it casts a silver glow over everything around us. It's haunting.

"I never thought I'd say this, but I'm so over being in the woods," Aaron grumbles. He's shaking from the cold.

"Me too."

"At least we'll be done with all of this soon." He pauses. "Hopefully."

I nod. It goes quiet again, and we listen to the wind's gentle hum.

"If he is at that safe house..." Aaron says. "What happens when we find him?"

I glance at him briefly, then stare back at the sky. "We go back to End Harbor."

He still doesn't know I can't return.

But if I tell him, he'll do something stupid. He'll try to fight it somehow and end up getting banished too. Then he'll be just as stuck as I am. *I want him safe.*

I can't tell him. He'll find out eventually. *I'll just have to leave once I see him walk through that Gate.*

I shove the thoughts aside, saving them for later.

Aaron nods, not really looking at me. But then his brows crease. He stares at something behind me, eyes wide. "Voclain?"

"Yeah?"

He lowers his voice to a whisper. "Don't move."

My pulse quickens. "What?"

"Don't move," he repeats, carefully rising to his feet. "Turn around slowly."

I stand up and turn around, stifling a gasp when I meet the amber eyes of a fox.

It stands a few yards away like it's frozen in time, observing us while we study it right back. My gut churns when I see the dead rabbit hanging limply from its mouth, its white fur soaked in blood.

The fox blinks, and it runs off.

Aaron walks over to where I stand, watching the fox weave between the foliage. "They're beautiful, aren't they?"

"Yeah."

"Predators... but beautiful."

I nod, watching the fox disappear. We stand there for a long time, eyes glued to the empty space.

I look up at him. It's still dark, but I can see just enough with the glow of the moon to know that he is looking at me too. He holds my gaze the way the fox did.

We let ourselves remain in this stillness, and I notice how beautiful his eyes are. The one that isn't scarred is a deep, earthy brown, and the faint gray light seeping through the trees illuminates pathways within it, grains of red and gold and amber. His left one is just as striking, a soft green specter I can't pull away from. Like the light around us, I'd call it haunting, but it's the kind of haunting you want to be possessed by. I hardly even blink.

It startles me when he brings his hand up to the side of my head. He pulls a leaf out of my hair, pinches it between his fingers to study it, then lets it fall to the ground. He brings his hand back to my hair like he's found another one, but it lingers there, long enough for me to realize he hasn't.

And I still can't pull my eyes away.

My heart thuds in my chest, so loudly that it rings in my ears, resonating in my jaw. All I can think about is that song, and what happened when we were alone in those woods. What *didn't* happen.

"You said you couldn't," I whisper.

Aaron stares at me for a while, his touch still lingering. Like he's trying to pretend I didn't say anything at all. His hand falls; he knows exactly what I'm talking about.

"It would've been unfair to you," he mutters. "And you know it."

"I don't."

He presses his lips into a thin line, then relaxes them.

"I know what happened, Voclain." He says it softly—not bitterly, but tired, like he's worn thin. "I see the way you hurt. The way you miss him." He swallows, lowering his voice so I can barely hear it at all. "You want him."

My breath catches in my throat. I study him, the words tangled around my tongue until I finally manage to whisper. "I thought I was going to die."

His brows draw together.

"What happened in that control room... was survival. It was something I didn't understand, and in that moment all I wanted was to know that we would be alright. That I could remember the happy feelings and the innocence and every good part of the life I had when he and I were still kids." My voice cracks. "I just wanted her back."

"Who?"

"*Me*. The parts I buried." I'm not sure why my eyes are watering, but they do. "And I couldn't find them in him."

I feel for Ren what I felt for Margot. An endless, timeless love for someone whose blood may as well be mine. We were barely five years old when we met, and I don't remember a life before knowing him. I've spent every moment since then wanting him near, even when I pretended I didn't.

But not in the way he learned to want me.

"Is that horrible of me?"

Aaron averts his gaze. "Just because you love someone differently doesn't mean you love them any less."

"But he took that bullet for me," I whisper.

He pauses. "Would you take one for him?"

"I'd take them all."

He nods, and he holds my gaze firmer than he ever has. "Then it's real, isn't it?"

I look at him. I notice the way he stands, shifted to one side, putting no weight on the leg that took a bullet just to bring me the comfort of a sweater that wasn't even his. And I know what he's saying.

"Did you want to?" I ask.

There's a long, drawn-out pause. When Aaron finally speaks, his voice lowers. "What do you mean?"

"You said you couldn't," I whisper. "But did you want to?"

"Did I *want* to?" He laughs cynically, running a hand through his hair. "*God*, Voclain. It doesn't matter what I want."

"That's not true."

"What I want and what you deserve—what you *need*—are completely separate things. And I am... *so much less* than what you deserve."

My throat constricts. I stare at him, eyes glossy, tongue tied in knots.

"You need to be happy. *I* need you to be happy." Aaron lowers his voice. "It would be selfish of me to ask you to be anything less than that."

My heart sinks like it's made of lead. "You know what's selfish?"

He doesn't say anything.

"What's selfish is the way you believe you're not good enough. That you don't deserve safety, or protection, or happiness, or whatever it is you want." I hug my stomach. "Have you ever even asked me what I want without assuming you already know the answer?"

He raises and drops his arms in defeat. "What do you want, Eddie?"

The fog lifts. For the first time in a long time, it finally feels like I'm thinking clearly. "*You*, you idiot."

For a moment, I swear he stops breathing.

"So stop being selfish and tell me." I step closer. "What do you want?"

When he looks down at me, I assume he's angry. His shoulders stiffen. His jaw tenses. We are so close that I smell herbs in his unsteady breath, salt and cedarwood on his skin.

He tilts his head, dropping it lower so he can read all of me. My hair. My neck. My mouth. The waist his hands trace, then hold onto. He swallows, and I can see the muscles in his neck twitch as his eyes carve into mine.

There is only one person I want like this. One person that every part of me aches to be nearer to in all the ways only he could be.

"You."

His lips collide with mine.

Aaron kisses me like he can't breathe. Like I am oxygen, and my sigh is the only air his lungs know how to take. He pulls me closer. There is not an inch of space between us, and he still doesn't feel near enough.

He draws his mouth back and presses his forehead against mine, breathing heavily into my neck. "Tell me to stop."

"I don't want you to stop."

"Me neither."

I grab his sweater and pull him in again. He tastes like cinnamon and fennel, ginger and yarrow. My head spins, and all I know is the give and take of hunger, the tidal pull of wanting as my hands snake up his chest and around his neck.

His lips are still on mine when I pace backwards in slow, intoxicated stumbles. He presses my back against a tree. His satchel falls to the ground. We take off our jackets. I remove his glasses. His mouth drifts to my jawline, tracing its way down to my neck.

I shudder when he exhales against it. "You're killing me, Voclain."

"Apparently I do that a lot."

"This time..." He breathes into my ear. "You're killing me right."

He lifts me up to his eye level and kisses me more, until I'm certain we'll run out of air. But we never do. There is more of it here than there ever has been anywhere else. Beneath my shirt, his palm glides up my waist, my ribs. His touch is cold, and the shivers it sends are static, prickling currents. I cling to his neck, clutching his hair. I bite his bottom lip. He grins with a low chuckle.

"Hey there, Detective."

We freeze.

Somewhere, there is the fleeting of wings, the echo of a cawing crow.

Slowly, Aaron sets me down. He turns his head around.

Agent M. Heron steps out from behind a tree with his hands in his pockets.

And when I see who's with him, the world spins slower and slower until there is only stillness, and I forget how to breathe entirely.

I whisper, "Ren."

"Is something wrong?" Heron asks, taking in my stillness. "You gave me what I wanted. Now I'm giving you what we agreed upon. I am a man of my word, after all."

I don't ask how he found me; I can barely even hear him. His voice sounds muffled, like I'm frozen in amber and he's on the outside of my resin cage, unable to reach me.

My eyes are glued to Ren, and there is nothing else I can do but stare.

I've thought about this moment a thousand times—about all the things I'd say to him when I finally saw him again. I imagined running up and wrapping my arms around him, holding on as tight as I can to make sure that he is solid, and not the ghost I've been haunted by for so long.

Every part of me trembles with the urge to do just that. I want to cry, to tell him how much I missed him—how glad I am that he's okay. But as the image settles deeper into my mind, I realize how little I recognize the person standing in front of me.

His hair is neater than I remember—not perfect, and still long enough to run his hands through, but parted down the middle like it's been combed that way. He's looking at me, but there is no light behind his eyes anymore. I can hardly recall what they used to be like when they were full of it. Like me, he doesn't blink, but when he finally does, it's slow and monotonous, almost programmed. Ten seconds pass, and he blinks again.

He wears a suit as black as night.

My gaze shifts to Heron. In the moonlight, I realize they wear the same clothes, and the same folded shades hang from their white collars.

Why is Ren dressed like an Agent?

"Voclain?"

I turn around slowly.

Aaron's hands shake, clenched into fists. His shoulders are stiff, brows furrowed in confusion. "What is he talking about?"

I look at Heron, then Ren, then back at Aaron. I open my mouth to speak, but I don't have the words.

Heron walks over to us, placing a hand on Aaron's shoulder. "Let's give them a minute."

"Don't touch me." Aaron tries to shrug his hand off, but Heron grips his sleeve tighter.

"Look, I'm on your side here," Heron says. "Just ask your little fire-starter over there."

Aaron looks at me, eyes glossy. He exhales through his nose and frees himself from Heron's grip, grabbing his jacket and bag before walking away without another word. The Agent gives me one last glance before following in his footsteps.

Ren and I stand completely still.

We stare at each other, only yards away and still so far. I can hardly believe I'm looking at him at all. My feet are rooted in place. I wait for him to move, to say something. To smile.

He doesn't look like the kind of person who smiles anymore.

My hands tremble, and my knees feel like they're melting. I swallow the growing lump in my throat, and when I finally manage to speak, my voice is barely a whisper. "You're not..."

"An Agent?" The sound of his voice fills me with so much relief my eyes water. But it's bitter, like plain coffee. He doesn't even look happy to see me. "You really think I'd wear something like this for any other reason?"

I feel like I've been set on fire.

There is nothing for me to hold onto to steady myself, nothing to see but his cold, empty stare. My lungs fill with air so frigid it burns, until they can't take any more of it. But they don't let go of it either, and I am stuck here, suffocating, and from somewhere far, I smell smoke.

All this time, I thought Ren was being held captive. That the Agency was torturing him for information, or brainwashing him, or keeping him locked away in a place where I'd never be able to find him. I had nightmares about all the ways they could break him.

I wondered if he could have been exterminated.

I was so desperate to save him. Desperate enough to rely on an Agent. I gave Heron the location of those camps, and even if they evacuated, their homes are still gone. The Corps is realizing the Unseen is larger and more of a threat than we pretend to be, and I contributed to that. I was sick with guilt and grief. I stopped eating, stopped exhaling, stopped caring.

I wanted nothing more than to get him back, and all this time, he was choosing to be with them. He *chose* to go back to their side.

He chose to be far away.

Ren still doesn't move. He stands there with his hands in his pockets like nothing is wrong at all.

I don't know the full story yet, I remind myself. *This is Ren. He had a good reason for becoming a Chaser; he must have a good reason for going back.*

Right?

"I need to talk to whoever's in charge of your recent attack operation," he says.

I blink, pausing to let the question settle in as a gust of wind passes through. It pricks my skin and gives me goosebumps.

I've made my bed ninety-three times.

For ninety-three days, I've been trying to keep myself from unraveling completely, and I'm still a mess of tangled threads.

Ninety-three days, and he isn't happy to see me at all.

Ren doesn't move. His blinks are so inhuman, so perfectly timed. *What's wrong with him?*

"Why?" I ask.

"That's confidential."

Frustration knots in my gut. "That's a shit answer."

"It's important."

"You're with *them*." My voice wavers. "They've been burning down camps." I swallow dryly. "They took the Cut."

The mention makes him flinch.

I crease my brows—and my breath catches in my throat. "You're the rat."

Ren hesitates. "What are you talking about?"

"You're the one who gave us up."

He has no words to give me.

I feel sick. I think of the bonfire of bodies, of little Abigail getting hurt and witnessing her mother kill a Chaser to protect her. I think of the Cut burning in my wake, and the wildfire that followed.

"Just tell me where—"

"You gave us up." My eyes well with water. "And now you're here."

He's quiet again.

I can barely hear my own words. The breeze picks up again, whistling softly through the trees. "How am I supposed to trust that another attack won't happen?"

"Because I'll make sure of it." His words come out needle-sharp. "All these little fires you're setting? The Corps is catching up to you, and they *will* if you don't take me to whoever it is you're working with. If you don't let me work this out."

I pause. "Are you going to hurt them?"

"I'm here to stop the attacks. Not to turn you in."

"You didn't answer my question."

He tightens his jaw.

"I need you to promise me you won't turn them in either."

It's silent for a long time. The wind continues to blow, toying with my hair. When he speaks, his voice is low and soothing. "You trust me, don't you?"

I freeze. *Do I?*

I take a step back.

"Come on, Eddie." Slowly, Ren steps forward until he's standing right in front of me. I can't stop shaking. He reaches out a hand, placing it on my cheek. "It's me."

His touch is ice, and it sends shivers down my spine.

But it's what I've wanted for so long, and it's finally here.

It takes him ten seconds to blink. He's touching me, but his eyes are still empty. Like it doesn't make him feel anything at all.

My blood runs cold. Every instinct in my body tells me to run, like I'm a rabbit staring down a fox who would love nothing more than to lure me into its jaws. But the predator is so beautiful, and the rabbit has been alone in these woods for far too long.

"Okay."

Ren nods. He lowers his hand and walks past me to find Heron. I grab his arm before I realize what I'm doing. He freezes, looking down at me.

I'm barely breathing when I pull him into a hug.

He goes rigid for a moment, then softens, hugging me back loosely. I press my head against his chest, and I am certain he is not a ghost. We close our eyes, and we hold each other for a long time. But when I pull away, his stare hasn't changed. *Something is missing.*

I'm still studying his gaze when I see it shift away from mine, fixating on something behind me. Before I get the chance to turn around, something presses against the back of my head.

"Hello, Lavender."

My breath hitches.

I believe in ghosts again.

M. HERON

Tuesday, April 30

The guy with the scar won't stop looking at me.

He leans against a tree with his arms crossed over his chest, and he's glaring at me like I've just admitted to kissing his mom. You'd think I kicked a puppy or something.

"Sorry for... you know." I clear my throat, breaking the silence. "Interrupting."

His stare hardens. He doesn't say anything.

"You've got a little..." I gesture toward my neck.

His face turns red. He pops up the collar of his jacket and turns the other way with a frown.

It's quiet again. His leg shakes up and down. He glances over his shoulder, then continues glaring at me.

He looks a bit familiar, now that I think about it. I squint to get a better look at him, and I realize he's the guy on TV. The one Sparks shot... then protected.

"You got a name?" I ask.

He doesn't say anything. I let out a bored sigh, leaning against a tree of my own—just as someone shouts.

I snap forward and straighten my posture. Scar and I exchange glances. We wait for more sounds to pierce the quiet, but there is only silence.

We don't waste another second before running.

We hurry to where Sparks and Detective were having their talk, only to find them gone.

"Where the hell did they go?" I mutter.

Scar's face pales.

I fish my burner phone from my pocket and flip it open, pulling up a map to track the matching one I gave to Detective weeks ago. I then unfold my Eyes just to check Sparks' tracker. His location matches the location of Detective's phone exactly.

This is weird.

Scar clenches his hands into fists. "Did he take her somewhere?"

I fold up my shades again and hang them back on my collar, just as my attention snags on something in the corner of my eye. I squint, noticing a disrupted patch of dirt. I walk over to investigate.

There are two tracks in the dirt, like something was dragged.

My stomach lurches. *Not Sparks too.*

I turn to Scar. "I think someone took both of them."

He looks like he's about to throw up. "What do you mean?"

I frown. "I know as much as you do right now."

He starts pacing and runs a hand through his hair. "We have to find them."

"No shit."

He grits his teeth. "I'm not playing around."

"Neither am I."

"Then why the hell are we just standing here?"

I pause. He stops pacing.

I walk up to him, and I slap him in the face.

He holds a hand to the side of his cheek, nostrils flaring. Now it *really* feels like I've kicked a puppy—but a really scary one who might maul me to death if I don't calm him down, and quickly.

"You need to pull yourself together, alright? You can't help her by acting like a complete mess. Compartmentalize."

Scar exhales shakily through his nose, like it's taking everything he has to keep himself from hitting me back—or dismembering me, from the looks of it. He's taller than I am. He could definitely overpower me without a problem.

"If you want her back, we've gotta work together," I say. "I know you don't give a damn about Ren, but I kind of do. So if you can't bring yourself to trust me, then trust that we're both looking for the same person here."

He decides against chopping me to bits and leans against a tree again.

"Hang on a sec." I pull out my Eyes again, wearing them so I can ring up Fish. I bring a finger to one of the temples and radio him. "Fish. We have a problem."

Nothing.

"Fish?"

He still doesn't respond. I crease my brow, checking his tracker on the map. And when I do, my stomach churns.

Shit.

"Hey, Scar?" I say as calmly as possible. I don't want him freaking out on me.

"What?"

I pause. "I know who took them."

Scar and I hike over to the warehouse. I park him behind a bush and tell him to stay. He'll listen, if he's smart.

I hurry to the scene. Cleaners and Officers are picking through the mess, dragging burnt debris from out of the warehouse. Most of the fires around the building have been put out, but everything still smolders. I spot Jade talking to two Officers and run up to whisper into her ear.

"Clear the scene."

"What?" she asks.

"I'll explain later. Just do it."

Jade creases her brow, then sighs, turning back to the Officers. "Alright team. We've got it from here. Leave us a car."

The Officers and Cleaners load the last of the burnt corpses into the back of a truck. Everyone drives away—leaving behind one black sedan, keys included.

When the scene is finally cleared, Jade stares at the warehouse. "Whoever did this is a monster."

"Yeah, well..." I stare at the building, then back at the bush where Scar is hiding. "We have a little situation here."

"What situation?"

I sigh. "Steller found Voclain."

Her eyes widen. "Where is she?"

"King's taken them both."

"What do you mean, taken?"

"Like, knocking-them-out-and-dragging-them-in-the-dirt taken."

"What the hell?" Her brows knit together. "Why would he do that? It doesn't make any sense."

"I think he's finally snapped, Jade." I swallow the lump I hadn't realized was growing in my throat. "This isn't like him."

"You think he's the one who stole our car?" she asks.

"It's missing?"

"He must've taken it while everyone was busy handling the fire."

"Wonderful."

She shakes her head. "What is he doing?"

"You think I know?"

"We should follow him."

"Yeah, no shit. We can't leave Ren with him." I sigh again. "But... we have another problem."

"What?"

I glance behind me, studying the distant trees and foliage. "Hey. Scar. Get over here."

There's a pause. For a moment I wonder if he ran off, but then I see him rise up from behind a bush, still glaring—knife in hand. He walks over cautiously, looking over his shoulder. He pauses when he sees Jade up close and squints at her.

"This is the guy." I point at him. "The one that was shot."

His eyes darken when they dart over to me. "I swear to God, if you were the one who—"

"Not important right now." I hold out a hand. "I'm Mallory, by the way."

He doesn't take it.

"Jade Silva." She extends a hand too.

He freezes. "What did you just say?"

She and I exchange puzzled glances. "Jade Silva."

Scar looks like he's just seen a ghost. He can't take his eyes off the ribbon in her hair, which billows in the breeze.

I pinch my brows together. "What's wrong?"

He exhales through his nose, putting his hands on his hips and averting his gaze, like he's contemplating something. He lets out a frustrated sigh and turns back to Jade. "Is there any chance you might have a sister?"

It took us a while to convince Scar—whose name turns out to be Aaron— that we weren't going to kill him or burn his current hideout to the ground, and that although we wear these suits, we're not idiots, and we've realized by now how greatly we prefer treacherous company. But he seems to trust Jade, at least a little bit, and he's desperate to find Detective. He was also stuck without a car, so we were his only option for getting back to what he calls Silver Fir to collect the backup he needs.

He told us that's where we'd find Raven.

The three of us now stand in the lobby of what appears to be an abandoned ski lodge. A flame flickers in the fireplace. It's the only sound I hear as Jade and Raven stare at each other from across the room, unblinking.

We seem to be stuck in time. Scar and I don't move a muscle. All we can do is watch in silence, waiting for one of the statues in front of us to move.

"You're an Agent," Raven finally mutters.

She looks smaller than I remember her being, and I realize I've probably grown since the last time I've seen her. She and Jade always had the advantage of height growing up. Now, the three of us are equals.

"And you're..." Jade doesn't know how to finish the sentence. "You."

Raven, who has made herself queen of the organization that burned the warehouse to the ground, doesn't seem to see the suit her sister wears.

Jade, who has a Nightjade gun in her holster and a poker chip in her pocket, doesn't see the violent rebel she's been assigned to hunt down.

There is only one sister and another, and they both wear ribbons in their hair.

The run across the room is quick, and the embrace is strangling, and they rock back and forth like a ship at sea, clutching each other so tightly you'd think they were drowning. They fall to their knees, and they cry, and they hold each other for a very long time.

"I've been looking for you," Raven mutters.

Jade is sobbing. "Me too."

I stand in the corner with Scar, and we let them have their moment until Raven peels her face away from her sister to glare at me. "Get in here, asshole."

I walk over to where they kneel, and before I know it, I'm on the ground, and the girl I once knew like a little sister is wrapping her arm around me. Jade is smiling for the first time in so long, and I kiss her forehead because there's nothing else I'd rather see.

We are all the same crying, snotty mess.

I can feel something beating in my chest, and for the first time in my life, I am certain I am not heartless.

EDDIE

Tuesday, April 30
93 Beds Made

♪ KINGFISHER - WOLF PEOPLE ♪

It's Duke Carmody. It has to be.

It's the voice I hear every time I go to sleep. It's his words I hear when I look in the mirror, when I see what he carved into my skin like a cattle brand.

It can't be him. You killed him, remember?

"I can't believe I found you," the voice says. He grips onto my upper arm tightly. "Looks like I've finally had that stroke of luck after all."

"Get the hell off me!" My shout bounces between the trees, sending crows flying. I try to free myself, but his grip only tightens. I can already feel it bruising. Whatever he's holding against my head digs further into my skull.

"King," Ren seethes, eyes wide. "Put the gun down."

The stranger Ren calls King pulls me into his chest, locking his left arm around my neck. "What? It's just a little bit of Nightjade. It'll only knock her unconscious."

I shudder.

"But you?" I can see King's right arm move to point the gun at Ren instead. "You'll drop dead."

My eyes widen. *Ren has another tracker in him?*

My heart pounds, and I can't peel my eyes away from Ren. I only just got him back, and it still doesn't feel like he's here all the way. Whoever this is, he's not taking him away from me again.

I try to elbow him, but his instincts are sharp and he catches my arm with his free one. "Not so fast, Lavender."

The Nightjade gun is still pressed against my head, but I don't care. I writhe in his arms, trying to free myself from his grip, but he overpowers me easily. He uses the arm with the gun to tighten his lock around my neck, and the other to bind my wrists behind my back with what feels like a zip tie. He clutches the back of my shirt and steps closer to Ren, pointing the gun at him again. He touches it to his chin. "But I can still knock you out the old-fashioned way."

Ren's brow creases, and before he can do anything, King hits him on the side of the head with his gun.

It cracks against his skull, and Ren crumples to the ground.

I don't have time to scream, because a Nightjade syringe is plunged into my neck.

The world is blurry when my eyes flutter open.

I don't know where I am, but I can tell I'm on the ground, propped up against a smooth wall. My head is against someone's shoulder, and when I lift it up, it feels heavy. I blink, trying to make out the face of the person I'm slumped against. I see black hair and empty brown eyes.

Ren.

My attention narrows to the scabbed gash on his forehead, and the trail of dried blood snaking down the side of his cheek. His hands are tied too. There is something like relief in his gaze, but it's still so cold.

I sit upright. My arms are tied behind my back with something plastic.

I know my knife is still in my boot, but I can't reach it.

I blink, taking in my surroundings. I expected to be in a warehouse of sorts, but I smell the woody aroma of a clean house, and as my eyes adjust to the dark, I realize that's where we must be. We're in a hallway, and when I look up, I see a man in a black suit sitting in a chair with his legs crossed, Nightjade gun in hand. A folded pair of shades hang from his collar, and I know he must be an Agent.

"Good." His voice makes me flinch, and I squint to make out his face. *Why does he look so familiar?* "You're all awake."

All?

I glance to my right, realizing there's a third person sitting next to Ren. And when I see who it is, my lips part in shock.

"Noriko?"

Ren's mother doesn't look at me. Instead, she glares at the Agent in a way that sends shivers down my spine. "We had a deal, Kingfisher."

"A deal I no longer need," the Agent says. "You see, I managed to find her all on my own, without our little setup."

My eyes widen, brows creased in confusion. I turn to Noriko, who still won't meet my gaze. "What is he talking about?"

"I'm sorry, Eddie." She finally looks at me, her eyes glossy. "You have to understand. I needed him back."

"What are you saying?" Ren mutters.

Noriko looks at Ren, seeing the way his son studies her, confused and maybe even hurt. She closes her eyes and lets out a wavering sigh. "I was caught."

No one speaks.

"When I went back to that gas station to get fuel for the van, I... ran into Agent Kingfisher." She looks at the Agent, then at me.

Ren stares at the wall. "The wrinkle..."

"I thought he was going to kill me," Noriko continues, "but he saw my eyepatch and quickly realized my affiliation. Asked me if I knew anything about Lavender Voclain." She swallows. "I asked if he knew anything about my son."

I feel like I'm going to be sick.

She turns to Ren again. "I didn't know of her exact whereabouts, since they were all on their way to the Cut, and Kingfisher had an obligation to attend to. So... we arranged for a meeting."

I don't think I've ever heard her voice sound so unsteady.

"What do you mean?" Ren still blinks every ten seconds, but his neck muscles twitch.

"He gave me the location of his safe house. I agreed to deliver her here." Her eye snaps up to Kingfisher, who simply watches, not fazed in the slightest. Then she stares at the wall. "But I knew I couldn't take Eddie here on my own without upsetting those under my Command. Eddie has sympathizers in my ranks, and I have a position to maintain."

"So you used Milo as bait." It feels like I'm screaming, but when I speak, the sounds barely come out at all. I think of Beau's strange behavior. All that cash he had on him. The gun. The phone that looked too much like mine. "And you sent Beau to make sure I bit."

Noriko doesn't say a word.

The room starts to spin again. I realize how narrow the hallway is, how trapped I feel as the walls seem to grow closer together. I still can't move my hands. My breathing grows shallow, and my skin turns hot. Bile rises up my throat and I swallow it down, trying to keep my lungs steady.

She was trading me for Ren.

"As entertaining as this is, I'm afraid this conversation needs to be cut short." Kingfisher chuckles, but his smile fades quickly. "I've waited long enough."

We all glare at him in unison.

"You see, I'm looking for something. *Someone*, to be exact. And I've been looking for a very, *very* long time. And while I have you here, you're going to tell me what you know. But I would first like to remind you all of the position you're in."

I curl my hands into fists behind my back.

"I'm turning you in to my higher-ups alive, but I can certainly make your world a living hell before that happens. I've been doing this for a long time; I have quite the history in Extraction."

The word spreads goosebumps over my skin.

"So tell me." Kingfisher leans forward. "What do you know about Evangeline Goodwin?"

"I've already told you, I know nothing about her," Noriko spits.

"What about you?" He looks at me, pointing the gun at me casually. I glue my eyes to it, beads of sweat forming on my brow. If he knocks me unconscious again, there's no telling where I'll wake up—or what he'll do with me when that happens. "Does that name mean anything to you?"

I try to swallow the lump in my throat, but my mouth is too dry. "I've never heard of anyone named Evangeline."

"Think harder, Lavender." He rises to his feet and steps closer before crouching in front of Ren. He presses the Nightjade gun to his forehead. "You two are going in alive, but he doesn't have to."

"I'm telling the truth," I seethe, trying to hide the racing of my heart and the trembling of my limbs.

"She has red hair. Green eyes." Kingfisher swallows, almost emotionally. "Really beautiful green eyes."

My glare softens a bit. I look into his own gaze, and when I do, I almost flinch again. His eyes remind me so much of Duke's, but they're not cold and empty like his were. They're so... human.

My breath hitches when I realize who I'm staring at. "You're Ian."

I've only seen him a few times in my life, but I grew up with Duke. I've heard all about his brother, the prodigy Agent.

He hesitates, and I wonder if I got it wrong. But the hostility returns, and his stare darkens. "And you killed my brother."

"I didn't know Evangeline," I mutter. "I'm sorry."

Ian nods slowly, then rises to his feet. He starts to pace with one hand in his pocket, the other holding his gun. His hair is neatly styled, but one strand is out of place, falling in front of his eyes.

His suit is full of wrinkles.

"What about Alvin? Ellen? Her parents?"

I shake my head.

"I thought she was at the Tombs," Ren says.

The Tombs?

"She isn't." Ian shakes his head, still pacing. I realize his hands are trembling like mine. "Not anymore."

"How do you know?"

"I just *know*, alright?" he snaps.

"I'm trying to work with you here, Ian," Ren says. The Agent flinches at the sound of his real name. "I'm trying to help."

The way Ren speaks almost makes it sound like they know each other. Like they're friends. Like he's Ian, not Agent Kingfisher. *He isn't threatened by him.* "Just tell me what's going on."

Ian stops pacing. His arms tremble. "Canary let me go."

"To the Tombs?" Ren's brows furrow, and Ian nods. "That's where you went?"

"Yes." His leg shakes up and down impatiently.

"But that doesn't make any—"

"I checked the records, Steller." He swallows. "She was marked dead."

Ren's eyes sadden.

"But the Guards think she had something to do with the revolt," Ian says, almost desperately. "She could've escaped."

The revolt?

"But that's a high-clearance case," Ian continues. "Canary said if I get Fourth... if I can earn that promotion... he'll put me in charge of it." He chuckles, eyes glossy. "I could find her."

"Ian..." Ren looks up at him. "If she was marked dead—"

"Don't you dare say it, McLellan." Ian holds the gun to Ren's head, gripping the weapon with tight, convulsing muscles. "I swear to God, I'll shoot you."

My heart races, and when I see the look in Ian's eye, I realize just how much he means it.

We need to find a way to calm him down. A way to get that gun out of his hands, before he does something we'll all regret.

If this Evangeline had something to do with the revolt, she would've known Aaron and the others, I realize. My eyes widen. "Ian."

He turns to look at me.

"Did Evangeline have a—"

The door flies open.

I hear footsteps—lots of them, until they come to a halt at the mouth of the hallway.

Raven, Aaron, Lockley, Marty, and Beau all point Yesterday guns at the Agent. The others follow close behind, including Fern—and Heron, who's standing next to a female Agent I don't recognize.

"Gun down, dipshit," Aaron seethes. "*Now.*"

Ian doesn't remove the gun from Ren's forehead. "You first."

Raven and Aaron exchange glances. There are eleven of us—four Gamblers, four Cuts, two Agents, and only one Ian.

The Unseen guns lower. Ian lowers his, but it's still in his hands.

"What are you doing, Fish?" Heron steps forward, and I assume he must be talking to Ian.

Ian clenches his teeth. "Stay back."

"We have you outnumbered," Raven says. "Drop the gun."

He doesn't.

"We're not here to hurt you, man," Heron says. "Come on. This isn't what you want."

"You know *nothing* about what I want," Ian snaps. He lifts the gun, this time pointing it in Heron's direction.

"Lower the gun, Fish."

Ian's finger traces the trigger.

Before he has the chance to make another move, the Agent I don't recognize takes the Yesterday gun from Raven and shoots at Ian's feet. I yelp, startled by the noise. *It's so loud.* I fold forward and squeeze my eyes shut.

No bullets hit Ian, but he drops the Nightjade gun, just as shocked as I am. The shooting stops. My ears ring. There are holes in the now-splintered floorboards in front of me.

Raven is quick to run up and take the Nightjade gun, handing it to the Agent, which makes me crease my brow. *Raven would never trust an Agent, would she?*

Ian stands there, breathing heavily, glaring at the crowd in front of him. To my surprise, he lets out a chuckle, which escalates into a full laugh.

"Numbers, numbers." He takes the shades hanging from his collar and unfolds them, then slides the arms behind his ears. He lets the sunglasses rest on his forehead. "Do you know where you stand?"

Heron and the other Agent exchange unsure glances.

"This is my safe house," Ian says. "And do you know what I am?"

No one says a word.

"A Chaser. An *Agent*." He chuckles again. "Do you really think I'd hesitate to install a security system?"

"What are you saying?" Heron mutters.

"You've outnumbered me. You've taken my gun." His grin is so cold it sends shivers down my spine, and all I can picture is Duke on that beach.

He brings a finger to his sunglasses, pressing one of the temples like a button.

Beyond the hallway, behind where the others stand, I see a living room with a wall of glass. In an instant, it's replaced with a wall of metal. The room darkens. Throughout the house, I hear a series of clicks, like the locking of a dozen doors.

"But you're trapped inside a house that was built to self-destruct in a moment's notice, and I'm the only one who knows the escape route."

My heart lurches.

My vision adjusts to the lack of moonlight, and I see Ian lower his shades to cover his eyes. He keeps his finger against the temples, showing us how ready he is to initiate another command. And how quickly he'd be able to do just that.

"I'm calling backup of my own," Ian says. "I'd much rather turn in a handful of traitors alive, but if you so much as *think* about moving a single inch, don't think I won't hesitate to blow you all to pieces."

"Fish, think about what you're doing here," Heron says, trembling. "You really don't wanna call backup."

"Stop talking."

"I know you, Fish," Heron says.

"I'm warning you."

"You're better than this." Heron's voice softens. "This isn't you."

"Stop talking, Heron!"

"Ian!"

He freezes.

"My name isn't Heron." Slowly, the Agent steps forward. The room is so silent you could hear a pin drop. He stops three feet away from Ian and places a hand on his own chest. "It's Mallory."

No one says a word. I hear branches creaking in the wind outside. The rustling of leaves.

"I never wanted to be M. Heron. And I don't think you ever really wanted to be I. Kingfisher." Mallory pauses. "Did you?"

"I need this, Mal." Ian's voice cracks, like he wanted the words to come out angry, but they shatter against a weight I can't see. His entire body trembles. "If I hand them over to Canary—"

"You're not handing anyone over to my father." The female Agent steps forward, shoving past Heron.

Canary must be who they report to, I realize. *And she's his daughter?*

Heron's face pales. "Jade—"

The Agent, Jade, holds a palm to Heron's face and steps closer. He tries to hold her back, but she shoves him off. She stops only a foot away from Ian. "This isn't what you want."

"You know nothing."

"Canary is a piece of shit," Jade hisses. "He's using you, Ian. Can't you see?"

He flinches once again at the sound of his real name. "You don't know what you're talking about."

"You've been loyal to him for *years*. You work harder than any other Agent in the entire Pacific Region, and for what? Talk of a promotion you'll never receive? How many lives are you willing to sacrifice for a *maybe*?"

Ian's shaking violently, skin sticky with sweat.

"Do you really want to trust a man who sent his own daughter to the Tombs?"

Ian's eyes widen. He stares at Raven, who she's pointing to. *They're sisters?*

"You're never getting that promotion, Ian. Trust me. I've been there. But nothing you do will ever be good enough for him. No one can be perfect." She swallows, lowering her arm. "Aren't you tired of trying so hard to be an impossibility?"

Ian stands there, frozen in place. He doesn't even shake anymore. The finger pressed against his sunglasses twitches, like he's fighting the urge to press the button.

"Be good enough for her." In the dark, I can tell Jade's eyes are watering. "Not him."

The seconds that follow last for years. No one breathes.

I hear the sound of unlocking doors. The metal wall slides back into the floor, and the glass is clear again. Ian removes his shades, and they fall to the ground.

Jade picks them up quickly, and Lori and Milo run over to remove our zip ties with wire cutters. Lori squeezes me so tightly I nearly choke and kisses my forehead. I bring my hands to her arms, exhaling in her embrace, throat tight as relief floods through me. When she pulls away, she hugs Ren too. The corner of his lip twitches.

I rise to my feet, rubbing my wrists. Ren and Heron urge Ian out of the hallway, and the others flood into the living room. I nearly jump when I realize Beau is standing right in front of me, eyes red.

"I didn't want to, Eddie." He puts his gun into his holster.

I pause.

"My sisters are gone. My dad's been missing for years." Beau's chin quivers. "I thought he was all I had left, and Noriko said if I helped her, the Agent would find him."

All I can do is stand here, rooted in place.

"But I know he's not coming back." His voice cracks, and it tugs at something in my chest.

"Beau..."

"I couldn't do it, Eddie. I couldn't do it, and I knew Noriko was already waiting here to get Ren because I was keeping her updated, and I drove here to tell her I wouldn't do it, but I chickened out." His eyes are watering. "I went back to Silver Fir, and Aaron and... that guy were there, and they said you were taken by Kingfisher. And I knew where."

A single tear runs down his cheek. His voice is a whisper. "I didn't want to."

I step closer, and I wrap my arms around him. "I know, Beau. I know."

He hugs me, sobbing. "I'm sorry."

"It's okay." My throat tightens, and suddenly I feel like crying too. "You just saved me, remember?"

He holds me tighter.

When I pull away from him, he wipes his nose and gives me a sad smile.

"Here." I retrieve the pig flashlight from my pocket and hand it to him. "I think this belongs to you."

He takes the flashlight and studies it, then looks at me like I've given him a bar of gold. His eyes are still watering. "Thank you."

We walk out of the hall and into the living room where the others stand. My eyes snag on Aaron's. He stares at me with a tightened jaw, and my heart sinks. *He's still angry.*

Aaron doesn't wait another second before running up to me. He holds me tighter than he ever has, burying his chin in my hair, and when he finally speaks, his voice falters. "I thought I lost you."

Something slams into us, and I feel my brother's arms wrap around me too. "You're both idiots."

We pull away. For a moment, Aaron's hand lingers on my waist, but it falls to his side. I look up at him, trying to read his face, but he can't look at me.

I see Raven and her sister talking in low volumes with Heron next to the couch, where Ian sits, staring at the floor while Ren sits next to him.

Fern stands next to Raven, studying Ian with her brows creased. He doesn't notice her looking, and I realize her arms are shaking. "It's you."

Everyone freezes. Ian peels his eyes away from the floor, staring at the girl with furrowed brows until his face pales. He rises to his feet. "Fern?"

They stare at each other for a long time. Nobody moves—until Fern lunges at him.

She tackles him to the ground and punches him. "You *monster*!"

"I never meant for anyone to get hurt!" Ian holds up his hands to shield his face.

"She's gone!" Fern claws at his face and neck like a feral cat. "She's gone, and it's all your fault!"

"Whoa, whoa, whoa!" Raven runs to the scene, grabbing Fern and lifting her off Ian. She's still kicking and shouting and biting, but Raven falls to her knees with her, hugging her gently from behind like she's done this a thousand times. "Shh. It'll be okay."

Fern sobs, curling into Raven's chest. Gentle Fern, the child who shares her bread and loves her niece to death. Raven closes her eyes, resting her chin on the girl's head. I hear her humming softly. It sounds like a lullaby, and I recognize it as the one I heard her singing to Jelly when we first got to Silver Fir.

Ren helps Ian to his feet. The Agent's legs buckle, and he wipes blood from his nose, staring at Raven. "Where did you hear that song?"

Raven looks up at him, brows creased in confusion. She squints, and then her expression softens. "I know those eyes."

"Where did you hear that song?" Ian repeats, every part of him trembling.

Raven hesitates. "I think you know where, Agent."

He looks defeated, like he already knows the answer to the question we all know is screaming in his head.

"Fern," Raven whispers to the crying girl in her arms. "Do you know who this is?"

The sobs slow to a stop. Fern looks up at Ian again, and for the second time this evening, she says, "It's you."

Everyone is perfectly still. Somewhere outside the window, the wind hums.

Fern rises to her feet, face wet with tears, eyes wide. "You're her father."

"Her?" Ian chokes.

Fern nods. She's crying again, but this time, the anger has melted away.

"Evangeline," she says with a smile. "We call her Jelly."

A tear streams down Ian's cheek. "Can I see her?"

EDDIE

Tuesday, April 30
93 Beds Made

Aaron debugged Ian at his safe house. He wears an eye patch made of cotton and tape.

We're all at Silver Fir now, and apparently we're celebrating the reunions this evening offered us. Lockley and Fern make more food than we can reasonably eat, filling the table with dishes of herbed chicken, salad with goat cheese, and mountains of glistening rolls drenched in so much butter you could swim in it.

Raven and Jade are almost as inseparable as Ian and Jelly. It was strange, really, how quickly she realized who Ian was. Like there was something connecting them that didn't require words to be understood. She just held onto his shirt with her head pressed against his chest, and she hasn't let go since. It's strange to think that she is just as much Duke's niece as she is Fern's.

Amidst the commotion in the dining room, I think about him. I relive that day on the beach every time I see my own scars, and I regret not being able to do more. I wonder if I could've done something to save him before he turned to the Corps. Maybe I could've cracked through his abrasive exterior and reached him somehow. Maybe if I had been his friend a long time ago, he would be standing here with his brother, and the niece he never knew he had.

But wondering what could've been done differently doesn't bring people back. And although Ian is laughing, I know he misses the laughs that aren't here.

There are laughs that I miss too. I watch the way Ian looks at his daughter, and I can't stop spinning the bracelet on my wrist.

Aaron must notice, because he's staring at me—but when I catch him, he averts his gaze, and neither of us can look at each other. He's been avoiding me all evening. We still haven't talked about the lie, and the thought alone churns my stomach.

I glance around the room. Ren is standing by himself, sipping a mug of coffee and staring at the dining table from a distance. He's watching Raven and Jade with watery eyes. *Since when did he drink coffee?*

Noriko isn't here. She slipped away to return to End Harbor in her own car without saying goodbye, leaving Ren alone. I saw her departure; her car was packed. I think she was planning on running away with him once the deal was done. Once she traded me for him. *She was willing to leave Asa? Cecil? The others?*

All this time, I trusted her. I trusted her, and she was willing to use me as currency. To hand me over to the very side I thought we were supposed to be fighting against. We all know how they treat traitors like me. In my head, I hear Ian's voice saying the word *Extraction,* and my skin pricks with goosebumps.

I look at Ren again, and in spite of everything, I can't find it in myself to blame her.

Thousands of thoughts and questions flood my mind. The room is loud, but I feel still within it, unable to ignore an uneasy feeling in my stomach. I'm glad Ian and Raven had their reunions, of course. Milo is safe—and Ren is back.

Shouldn't I be happy? Overjoyed? Relieved? *Why do I feel like we shouldn't be celebrating?*

Memories of this evening course through me. Raven and the Gamblers are treating the burning of the Nightjade plant as a victory, but we've done a terrible thing. Guilt sends a gulp of bile to my throat. If I knew we were going to take the lives of all those people—even if they were working for the Corps—I never would have signed up for this.

Everything is right. But everything is wrong too.

I don't realize I'm still staring at Ren until he meets my gaze, pulling me out of my thoughts. He looks away, and it tugs at something in my chest.

Why does it feel like he's avoiding me? Like he's hiding something?

I'm about to walk over to him when Ian beats me to it, still holding Jelly in his arms. They converse in hushed voices, faces grim. It looks too important to interrupt.

Raven calls Aaron over to talk to her and Jade. He still won't look at me. Now I'm the one who's left alone.

I scan the room again and spot Heron standing on the balcony. He leans over the railing, drinking a cup of coffee. *I guess I'm not the only one standing by myself.*

I walk over to the sliding glass door and open it, shutting it quietly behind me. My footsteps thud against the deck's old wood as I join him, leaning my elbows against the railing too.

"Are you done holding Ren for ransom?" I ask.

"I think so."

It's quiet. "I'm sorry about your brother."

He nods. "Thank you."

We stare over the balcony's edge, and his shoulders relax a bit. "Man, this place is cool."

I frown. "Have you seen the decor?"

"I think it's tasteful."

"I don't think I'd call a wooden sculpture of a salmon smoking a pipe *tasteful.*"

"It's a pretty funny joke though. You've gotta admit."

"Can't argue there."

It's quiet again. I study the snow-dusted pines, then him again. "Are you going back to End Harbor with Ian?"

Heron turns around to glance at Jade, who's laughing with Raven. He looks back over the edge. "I have a feeling I'm not done with the Agency just yet."

I nod.

We're silent for a long time, listening to the distant commotion drifting out from inside the lodge. The soft wind lacing through the trees.

"You're uneasy," he says.

"What makes you say that?"

Heron shrugs. "I feel that way all the time. It's easy to recognize."

I hesitate for a moment, then glance over my shoulder. "Ren is..."

"Different?" he asks. I nod. "The Agency does that to you."

"You said you're not done with it yet."

He nods.

"What about Abigail?"

Heron looks at me, confused for a moment until the realization settles in. He smiles and takes a sip from his coffee, staring at the pines below. "I have a niece named Abigail."

"You have a niece named Abigail." I nod.

"I'll meet her someday. After all of this is over." He looks back at Jade again with a sigh. "Knowing what their father did, I don't think Jade's gonna let that piece of shit keep his position for much longer. Her sister is giving her ideas."

"You think she wants to clean the Agency?"

"Something like that."

I pause. "You really think that's possible?"

"Probably not." Heron shrugs, then smirks at me. He's not much taller than I am. "If we have a few good traitors on our side, then maybe."

I almost smirk back.

"How will you explain Ian's tracker going off?"

He shrugs. "We'll think of something."

I nod. "Heron?"

"Detective?"

"I don't think I wanna kill you anymore."

He chuckles. "I'm glad to hear that." I reach out a hand, and he shakes it. "Nice to meet you, Lavender."

"Call me Eddie."

He smiles. "Call me Mallory."

We stare over the railing again until I hear the sliding glass door open behind us. I turn around to see Milo walk onto the deck with his hands in his pockets. Heron—or Mallory—takes his sign to leave. He heads back inside, joining the conversation with Ren and Ian.

Milo joins me. We let the wind toy with our hair in silence for a moment until he speaks. "We got him back."

I force a smile. "We did."

Why does that feel like a lie?

We look out across Silver Fir. Smaller buildings are scattered around the clearing at the bottom of the snow-covered hill, their windows lit with soft orange glows, like embers in a night sky.

"He's different, isn't he?" Milo says. "Like something's missing."

I nod, swallowing the lump in my throat.

Milo shakes his head. "I can't believe he's an Agent."

"Me neither."

It's quiet again. "We did good today."

I glance at him. "You mean the warehouse?"

"We burned an entire year's supply of Nightjade," Milo says. "That's a huge setback for the whole Pacific Region."

"They'll replace it in a day. They have more Nightjade farms than they know what to do with. As long as those exist, the Corps is untouchable."

"They're not untouchable, Ed. That broadcast made a bigger dent than we realize, and you've seen what this fire is doing to people. The panic it's causing. The Presidency is freaking out. The Unseen are freaking out. Chips are freaking out. It's made everyone realize just how fragile our structure really is. We're standing on a house of cards and it's only a matter of time before it topples."

I study Milo, lips parted. I had no idea he cared about fighting back. All this time, I thought my mistakes had roped him into something he didn't want to have any part in. But when I think back to the acts of rebellion he committed before—his homeschooling, his Yesterday music, his typewriting and the stories he wanted to tell—I begin to wonder if he's always been this way.

And as much as I want to deny it, even with the guilt of what we've done, I can't argue that the burning of the warehouse won't have any impact. Part of me knows he's right; things are changing. We're doing what the Unseen have been afraid to do for so long.

We're saying the wrong thing. Doing the wrong thing. *Being* the wrong thing. And it warms something inside of me, just as it sends shivers down my spine.

"Stay in Silver Fir with me."

Milo's request pulls me back to earth. I study his eyes, searching for some sign of confusion. I don't see anything but crystal-clear certainty.

And then I remember the burning bodies. The scars covering Aaron's back and chest. The look of betrayal I saw in his eyes when he realized I'd made a deal with an Agent behind his back.

Aaron never wanted to be here, and he's made it clear that he wants no part in the Gambler motive. Although he and Raven appear to be acting docile, I know the hurt he feels after whatever betrayal happened in the Tombs will never fully fade

If I choose to stay here—after everything he's trusted me with, knowing everything he does and doesn't believe in—wouldn't that be another form of betrayal?

My heart plummets. It's either Silver Fir, or Aaron. *I can't have both.*

"I can't," I mutter.

"It's not like you can go back to End Harbor," Milo says. "Beau said Wagner flipped his shit when you guys left. Noriko was keeping him updated about the whole thing. The old man said you broke some deal, and he blames you for Alice running away too. He'll do a lot more than just refuse to open the Gate if you go back." He stares back over the railing. "He said you're a danger to the Unseen. That you should turn yourself in so people stop looking for you. So other Unseen don't get hurt. And if he ever sees you in End Harbor again, he'll do it himself."

I stare at my hands.

"That man's scum, but you shouldn't have left, Ed," he says. "You would've been safe there."

"I had no other choice," I snap, then lower my voice. "I had to make sure you were okay."

"I told you being an idiot was *my* job, remember?"

When Milo looks at me, I realize he's not angry. *He's scared.*

He sighs. "Look. Ren isn't the only reason why I came here."

"What do you mean?"

"I obviously left to bring him back for you. That's always been what I've wanted. To make you happy." Milo pauses. "But I can't see you happy in a place like End Harbor. Either of us, actually."

"You were trying to find somewhere else to go?"

Milo nods. "I thought this place sounded pretty cool. So I wanted to scope it out. Form some kind of alliance or something."

My throat tightens. "You like it here, don't you?"

"I do."

I think back to everything Cecil and Aaron said about their methods, about what I've witnessed during the mere week we've spent with them. *Is this really what's best for Milo?*

I know this is what he believes he wants. But Aaron was right when he said this is a dangerous path for him to go down. If he feeds into his anger —if he makes his desire to see the world burn the only thing that fuels him —who will get hurt along the way?

"He can stay too, if he wants," Milo says, pulling me out of my thoughts. "Raven isn't as mean as she pretends to be."

"Aaron?"

He nods.

"His whole family's in End Harbor," I say.

"Where they'll be protected."

I shake my head. Aaron doesn't want the war Raven is trying to start. He wants to fight back too... but differently. Not as violently as the Gamblers do. "He'd never choose to stay here."

"Not even for you?"

I look at Milo, then stare back at the houses below us. They look so tiny from up here.

"I think he's pretty hurt," Milo says. "About the deal you made."

"I know."

"You should talk to him." There's a pause. "He cares about you a lot, Ed. More than I think you realize."

My breath catches in my throat. My brows pinch together, but Milo continues before I can say anything.

"Look. You don't need to give me an answer about any of this right away. You can think about it. But... I don't think you're meant to live quietly." He pulls himself away from the railing and walks toward the sliding glass door. He holds onto it, pausing to look over his shoulder. "Eddie?"

"Yeah?"

"I love you."

I don't know why I feel like crying. "I love you too."

He goes back inside.

I stay out here where it's quiet, trying to keep my breathing steady as talk and laughter emits from the room behind me. Trying to navigate the buzzing swarm of thoughts racing through my head. But I can't do either. *Everything feels like too much.*

Ren's an Agent. He's alive, but he still feels gone, and he doesn't want to see me, and I don't know what's wrong with him.

Aaron's mad at me because I broke his trust by making that deal with Heron in secret to get Ren back. The deal I didn't even need to make in the first place, because Ren didn't need saving. He *chose* to become a Chaser again, and now neither of them will even talk to me.

Milo wants me to stay here in Silver Fir and join the Gamblers, but I want him to go back to End Harbor where it's safe.

Raven wants to turn me into a villain so I can help her start a war—whatever that means.

And me...

When I stare down at my hands, at the burn scar on my palm, all I see is every fire I've ever set. Every lie, every mistake, every wrongdoing. *When will they catch up to me?*

What do I want?

I lean forward against the railing and bury my face in my hands.

I stay on the deck for a long time before sneaking back inside and heading upstairs. I head to the room Aaron and I have been staying in, and I shut the door behind me.

I nearly jump back when I see that he's here too.

He's sitting on the edge of the bed, carving something. He glances up at me, then looks back at the block of wood in his hands.

"Need something?" His jaw is still clenched.

I shake my head.

He nods, scraping his blade against the wood. It leaves shavings on the floor.

I stand by the door, one hand rubbing my arm while the other holds my stomach. I want to walk back out. I tell myself it's to let him have his peace, not because I'm scared of the conversation I know we're about to have. But I stay.

I hug my stomach with both arms now, staring at the floor. "I wanted to tell you."

His knife sweeps over the wood in his hands.

"Aaron…"

"Did you talk to Milo?" he mutters, changing the subject.

I nod. "He's not coming back."

"You know how they are, Voclain." He still can't look at me. More shavings fall to the floor. "You were there."

I force myself not to think about the bodies burning in the warehouse. "I know."

"They weren't field Chasers. They weren't Officers and Agents; they were from research and tech divisions. Like Lori. They may as well have been civilians." Another scrape. "They didn't deserve to die."

I stare at the floor. The guilt makes it impossible to take a full breath.

I glance up at him, watching his hands as they continue to work. I think about the way they felt against my skin. I think about falling asleep next to him—about the promise he thought we made when he curled his pinky around mine. *"No more secrets."*

I know there is still more I need to tell him. Raven's proposal. My banishment from End Harbor. *He still doesn't know I can't go back.*

And I still can't tell him.

"I'm sorry," I whisper. "About Heron."

His knife glides across the wood.

"Did—"

"I heard you."

"Then say something."

He finally looks up at me, and sets the knife and wood down on the nightstand a little too roughly. "You want me to say something?"

I nod.

"You made a deal with an *Agent.* Behind all of our backs. He may be acting friendly right now, but that doesn't change what he is. You shouldn't have trusted him."

"I was desperate, Aaron." My words are worn thin, so drained of energy. "I thought it was the only way."

"Milo and I were handling it, and you knew that. We could've worked something out if you let us."

"I didn't want you two getting hurt, alright? It was my fault he was taken in the first place. It would've been unfair of me to let you clean up my mess."

"Don't you get it?" He chuckles cynically, rising to his feet, tightening his fingers into fists. "Working with an Agent put all of us in danger. All of End Harbor too. Hell, the entire Unseen could've been compromised."

I avert my gaze. *They* were *compromised.*

"He cornered me into it. I know I could've said no, but he said he'd protect Ren. And he threatened to hurt us both if I told anyone." I swallow. "You said it yourself; he's an Agent. Agents always have a way of finding things out."

"Then why didn't you come to me?" Aaron raises his voice. "If you were scared—if you thought he was going to hurt you—I would've taken care of it." He speaks softer. "I would've protected you."

When I see the look in his eyes, my heart plummets.

All this time, I thought he was angry. *He's hurt.*

"Whatever happened to trust?" His voice cracks.

I can't bring my lips to move.

"I trusted you. I..." He averts his gaze, then returns it to mine. "No one's seen them all, Voclain."

My throat tightens, eyes watering. "I know."

"I trusted you, and you know how hard it was for me to do that. You *knew*. And I did. From the very beginning." He swallows. "All this time, I thought you trusted me too."

"I do trust you."

He looks at me, shoulders tense. He's trembling. "How long were you in contact with him?"

The words won't come out.

"How long, Voclain?" he repeats, this time louder.

"Since we burned down the Cut."

His shoulders slump. "When we were in the cave..."

I nod.

He inhales shakily. "Was he the one who shot me?"

"No."

"How do you know?"

"He was with me when it happened."

He nods, shoving his hands into his pockets and staring at the floor. The wall. The bed. Anything but me. "You kept it from me this entire time?"

"You kept things from me too."

I regret the words the second they come out of my mouth.

His shoulders stiffen. His eyes darken. "That's different, and you know it."

I stare at the wall.

"I don't care why you did it." His voice is quieter now, almost defeated. "I'm not stupid. I know you were desperate. But this is an Agent we're talking about here. That's not the kind of secret you keep from..." He chokes up, unable to finish the sentence. He studies the ground, then me. "If you came to me for help, I would've understood."

When I meet his gaze again, his eyes are glistening, I know we're both thinking of what happened in the woods. Of what would have happened if Heron and Ren hadn't shown up. *"Things are different with you, Ed. They always have been."*

"I couldn't," I say.

"Why not?"

"Cecil told me about Greer."

He freezes.

"You were angry at him for working with an Agent." I hesitate, struggling to form the words. "I didn't want you to hate me like that too."

"This is *you* we're talking about here, okay?" He exhales through his nostrils. "I could never hate you."

"How was I supposed to know that?"

Aaron looks at me like I've just stabbed him in the chest. I hug my abdomen tighter, tears welling in my eyes. I stare at the nightstand, and the knife resting on top of it.

"He said you held up your end of the deal." He pauses in thought. "What did you give him?"

I bite my lip, still unable to look at him. I take a deep, pained breath, closing my eyes. "He wanted information about his brother." I pause. "The Suit Killer."

From the corner of my eye, I can see Aaron's widen, brows creased.

"I didn't give him anything I thought he would use against us, alright?"

"You were trading information with him?"

My shoulders draw up, elbows tucking further into my sides. I nod.

His muscles relax, eyes unblinking. His fists uncurl. "The camps that burned."

I don't say anything.

"You gave them up, didn't you?"

I lower my voice to a whisper. "I had to."

"Voclain..." His face pales. "You didn't..."

"He was warning them about the fire."

"Those were attacks," he mutters. "They were separate from the wild-fire."

My chest tightens. "No one was hurt."

"They lost their homes." Aaron's words are louder now. Sharper. When I see the way he looks at me, I know he's thinking about the Cut. About the home that was taken from him too.

"Did you trade the Cut for Ren?"

My head snaps up. My eyes widen, brows drawing together. "How could you even think that?"

"I don't know, Voclain." He raises his arms in the air, then drops them to his sides. His voice is colder now. "You made a deal with an Agent. A deal you were too afraid to tell anyone about. What else am I supposed to think?"

I glare, raising my volume. "I told you, it wasn't me."

"The way you were acting when everyone evacuated to End Harbor? How you thought it was all your fault?" He laughs bitterly. "That's starting to make a lot more sense, now."

I grind my teeth. "That happened before I made the deal."

"Do you really expect me to believe that?"

"I'm telling the *truth*."

"And I'm done trusting liars."

My pulse slows to a stop. Every muscle in me weakens as my lungs pinch shut, refusing to let any air in or out. I press my lips together to keep them from trembling, lifting my chin.

I shake my head, and I storm out of the room.

I shove my way through the dining room and out into the hall, and before I know it, I'm in the lobby. My backpack rests on one of the couches. I grab it before shouldering the back door open. I let it slam shut and wipe my nose before shoving my hands into the pockets of my jeans, boots crunching against the snow. I feel Aaron's carvings and the cold sting of the lighter and instantly switch to the pockets of my jacket instead.

It's dark outside, and I can't see where I'm going, but I walk far enough into the woods so that when I turn around, the lodge has shrunken. I see the back of it, glowing amber in the night. My throat burns.

I know I've messed up. I know I'm a liar. But I was only trying to do what I thought was best. To protect as many of the people I love as I can. I realize now that's just about as easy as juggling lit matches.

Aaron thinks losing the Cut was my fault.

I stop walking. Nausea blooms in my stomach, and I pin my arms to it.

I thought I knew him better than that. And I thought he knew me better too.

Once I locate a good tree, I reach into my backpack and retrieve my throwing knives from their case. I put two in my pocket and start to un-sheathe one of them, right as a twig snaps behind me.

I whip around, sharpening my tongue, ready to shred Aaron to ribbons with all the angry words lodged in my throat. But when I see who's really there, I freeze.

Standing three yards away, hands shoved in his pockets, is Ren.

R. STELLER

Tuesday, April 30

♪ MISS EVENING - MAÑANA ♪

I finish talking with Heron and King and walk out on the deck, leaning over the railing to study the trees below me.

Our conversation echoes in my mind, and I think about everything they said. Canary will notice Ian's disabled tracker soon; Heron and Sparrow and I will need to leave Silver Fir quickly. Heron will think of a good story —that Agent I. Kingfisher died protecting us from traitors or something heroic like that.

My stomach churns at the thought of what I still need to do before then.

My Eyes chirp. I unfold the shades and place them over my eyes to check the message, heart sinking when I realize it's from Canary.

CANARY

> Remember our deal. And remember what I said, little jay.
> Strike opportunistically—before your chances run out.

My gut flips inside out.

> I have high hopes for you, Agent Steller. I want to see you make the right choice. Do not disappoint me.

The Nightjade gun weighs heavily in my holster.

Do I really have it in me?

Am I really heartless after all?

I stare out over the pines, over all of Silver Fir, and I do something I shouldn't. I think of Eddie—and I regret it instantly.

Every time I look at her or even think of her, I burn. In spite of the pain —the phantom of my Correction—I close my eyes.

I ache for the feeling, for the fire that once flickered in my chest, always warming me when I was cold. The wind blows. The flame never comes.

I close my eyes and I think of her again, in all the ways I can.

I think of her in the cow field. I think of her in the control room. I think of her sitting on that slide, asking me to join her. I think of her hair caked in mud. I think of her underwater. I think of her pressed against that tree, with her arms and legs wrapped around Aaron. Dangerously, I think of what it would be like to be in his place instead. The softness of her skin. The sweetness of her tongue. The heaviness of her breath.

I think of her smiling, ten times over, until I can't take the hurt anymore.

I feel nothing.

The warmth she once ignited within me is gone.

I hear a twig snap and open my eyes, noticing something orange in the distance. I see a jacket the color of rust, and a head of dark brown curls trailing behind it.

Eddie walks into the woods with a bag over her shoulder, and she doesn't look back.

Before I lose her, I head back inside, slipping away from the dining room and down the stairs, hopefully unnoticed. I cut through the lobby and out the back door, entering the forest behind the lodge. I weave between the trees, following her farther and farther into the dark, catching her right as she pulls out what looks like a throwing knife. *She's angry about something.*

She hears me approach and whips around, then freezes. Her lips part as wind toys with her hair.

My skin feels like it's on fire.

I stand a few yards away with my hands in my pockets. And when I look at her, I don't think I care about the pain it brings. About the horrible images that flash through my mind against my will to try and replace it.

I just want to see her.

She stands in the snow, cheeks rosy from the cold. Her breaths form clouds in the moonlight. She looks just as she did when I found her all those months ago, eyes closed and freezing to death, surrounded by so much white.

She looks innocent.

If she feeds into what the press and picket signs are saying about the girl in the broadcast—the girl with the lighter in her pocket and rage behind her eyes—there will be no turning back. It would be so easy for her to turn into the target Canary wants her to become.

It will break her, and I don't think I can survive watching that happen.

I need to convince her to leave. To hide, where no one can find her. Because if she doesn't pull herself away from the Unseen, she'll get hurt. Or worse.

And if she won't... if I can't convince her... the only option I have to keep her safe is to rely on Canary's deal. *I have to try.*

"I'm leaving," I say, shattering the silence.

Her brows crease. "What?"

"Come with me, Eddie." My skin burns. I blink every ten seconds.

"Where?" Her voice is quiet.

"Anywhere but here." I swallow. "Your bag is packed. No one else is around. You can disappear."

Her gaze softens. "Ren..."

"It'd be so easy." My mouth is dry. "You see the suit I'm wearing. I can find somewhere for you to go. Somewhere you'll be safe. Where you won't have to fight anymore."

"But Milo—"

"Bring him. Bring Aaron. Bring whoever you want." My words quicken. "But you can't live this life anymore, Eddie."

Her eyes water. "I can't go."

I blink every ten seconds.

"Eddie." My voice cracks. "Please."

"This is what I've always wanted, Ren. Don't you remember?"

I try so hard to forget.

"Whatever we've gotten ourselves into is only the beginning. And if I abandon the Unseen now—I don't think I'd ever be able to live with myself." She bites her lip. "I need the Unseen. And I think they need me too."

"Eddie—"

"No, Ren." Her voice is stern. "I can't leave."

When I look in her eyes—when I see the way she tightens her shoulders and clenches her fist—I see the burning anger I remember. And I don't think there's anything I can do to put it out.

The realization feels like swallowing broken glass. *She will never abandon the Unseen.*

My throat constricts. *"Strike opportunistically, little jay."*

The sound of Eddie's voice pulls me back to earth.

"But you can stay." She steps closer, staring up at me with something like desperation. "You don't have to go back to them, Ren. We can debug you again. You can come back to the right side, and you can stay." Her words waver, and she whispers. "Stay with me."

I swallow the growing lump in my throat. *I have to leave.*

She's fighting for a lost cause. I've seen what she's up against firsthand. She's right; the broadcast was only the beginning. But the Unseen will fall if the Gamblers try to start a war. The only way to make a change—to keep her safe—is from the inside. *I can't leave the Agency yet.*

She's trying to save me from the system, but I'm trying to save her from its collapse.

I can't break her heart and pretend to hate her like I did when I Chased her. This time—I need her to hate *me*. She needs to feel betrayed, just as I promised Canary.

"I can't stay."

"What?" she mutters.

"Don't you get it, Ed?" I force a chuckle. "I don't want to stay."

She doesn't say a word.

"I went back to the Corps for a reason." I swallow, doing my best to get the next words out. "You and Raven and the Gamblers or whatever the hell they call themselves aren't doing anything good. You're hurting people. You're assassinating Agents. You're committing *arson*. And you expect me to join you?"

Her neck muscles twitch.

"I'm trying to put a stop to this rebellion before it begins." I sharpen my stare. "I thought you of all people would understand that we need to go about this peacefully."

"You're delusional if you think the Corps is peaceful," she snaps. "Treating killing like a business expense doesn't change what it really is."

"And what is that?"

"Wrong."

"What about the Unseen? What about the people they've killed?"

"I wanted no part in that," she seethes. "I'm in this so we can do it the right way. So we can do *something*. Because nothing about the way things are running is okay. *Nothing*, Ren."

"You're thinking recklessly."

"That's better than putting on a tie and turning into a doormat."

I pause, forcing myself to look angry. Forcing my teeth to clench, and then soften.

"You know what?" I step forward. I lower my voice and banish all warmth from it. "If anything, I should be thanking you."

Her brows draw together.

"If you weren't too pathetic to save yourself, I would've never taken that bullet. And let me tell you something, Eddie." I step even closer, so there's inches of space between us, lowering my head to meet her gaze. I make my grin as cruel as it can be. "I quite like being an Agent."

She trembles.

I take a step back, hands still in my pockets. "More money than I know what to do with. More freedom than a mere Officer could ever dream of. More *power* than any human being should be given. I'm a walking get-out-of-jail-free card, and I have you to thank."

Eddie looks like she can't decide whether to be angry or brokenhearted. "This isn't you, Ren."

"You know nothing about who I am anymore."

She flinches. I steady my breathing.

"I'm the one who gave up the Cut. I'm the one who gave them the idea to smoke out the Unseen. The Ren you knew is long gone, Eddie. And he's never coming back."

She steps closer, matching my rising volume. "You were also the one who warned the Cut to evacuate. The one who made sure all those camps got out alive."

"You know what else I did?" I step forward. "I shot Aaron."

Eddie freezes. Slowly, her brows meld together. "What?"

I lean closer. "I. Shot. Him."

Every part of her trembles. She stares straight ahead, unblinking, hands clenched into fists.

"Don't think I didn't see what happened. I saw the way he kissed you. The way he touched you." My voice lowers, and I lean closer to speak into her ear. "How much you liked it."

This is all pretend, I remind myself.

Then why doesn't it feel that way?

"I shot him, because when I saw him ready to kill that Chaser he was holding hostage back at the Cut—I couldn't stop imagining *exactly* what you two were doing against that tree tonight. Because I've seen the way he looks at you. I've spent the last fourteen years feeling what you learned to feel for him in less than one. Because it's always been you, and it's never been me."

I pause, breathless. My pulse thuds ruthlessly in my ears.

When she finally looks up at me, her eyes are red and wet with tears. She wears a bitter, empty anger, and it makes me shudder. "You almost killed him."

"I did what I had to do, and I would've done it with or without you in the picture." I straighten my posture and adjust my tie. "Because unlike you, I know what needs to happen to fix this country."

A pallor spreads over her face, like my words are making her sick.

"No more traitors." I lean in close again to whisper, "No more snakes."

Her jaw quivers as she steps back. "Everything we've done... it was all for nothing, then?"

"I wouldn't say all for *nothing*." I shrug. "It led us here, didn't it?"

"What about your parents?" She softens her voice, and it cracks. "What about Margot?"

"They would want me to stay alive. That's exactly what I'm doing." I swallow the lump in my throat and turn to walk away—then pause to glance over my shoulder. "You're better off running for the hills than rising with the Unseen. That's a sure way to get yourself killed."

"I'd rather die than turn my back on them like you did."

"You're being stupid."

"I'm not running anymore," she spits. "I'm not a coward."

Her words feel pointed—and it's tearing me apart.

"This isn't a fight you can win, Eddie. I'd hate to see you get caught in the middle."

"I don't think you really care where I end up anymore."

My head is on fire and my skin feels like it's ready to fall off in sheets.

Of course I care, I want to scream. No matter how hollow I feel—no matter how Corrected I may be—even with the pain that devours me from simply being around her. There is nothing I can do but care, and it's a butchering I couldn't escape if I tried.

"If I didn't care, I don't think I'd be giving you advice right now." I turn to face her fully, lowering my voice. "There are things going on in the world that you know nothing about. There are shifts in play you can't even see. Storms brew before they pour, Ed."

She doesn't say a single word.

"Get out while you still can. Because when it pours, he won't protect you. If it ever boiled down to a choice, he'd choose the Unseen over you in a heartbeat."

"You don't know what you're talking about."

I study her, and in her glare is a fire she never had around me.

She doesn't care about me like that, I realize. *I wonder if she ever did.*

"And what makes you so sure?" I ask.

"Because he..." Eddie stops herself, then scoffs. "You think this is about *him*?"

I go quiet.

"You think *he's* the reason why I'm not choosing to go with you?"

Still, I am silent.

"I'm not in this for safety, or refuge, or comradery. I'm not hiding. And I'm not in this for him." Her volume rises. "I'm in this for *me*. Because I want things to be different. A better kind of different that I'm not going to just sit back and watch unfold."

"Eddie..."

"No matter what happens, you can't seem to stop circling back to the idea that I don't know what I'm doing. That I'm stupid and impulsive and need protecting. Has it ever occurred to you that there are people *I'm* trying to protect?"

Her voice echoes between the trees.

"And you were one of them, once." Her words soften. "I thought you would remember that."

I wish I could forget.

I turn my back to her, arms shaking as I try to gather enough strength to walk away. But she moves before I get the chance, standing right behind me. "Ren."

Don't look at her.

"Ren, look at me."

Don't do it.

"I know you're still in there."

For the love of God, don't turn around.

"You're so afraid, aren't you?"

She steps in front of me. Slowly, she reaches out. Her fingers brush against my cheek, and it sends shivers down my spine. All my strength is spent holding still. Her hand lingers like she's waiting for me to grab it. I wait too long and it falls away.

When I see the look in her eyes, I don't see what Canary tried to smoke out of me.

I see pity.

She doesn't have the burning that I once had. Her fire is in another hearth, whether she knows it or not. We are two separate flames who will never share the same fuel.

I look away because I can't stand to be seared for a second longer. "I'm not afraid, Eddie."

"You're tired." Her voice is soft. "Come home."

God. If only things were as simple as that—a single choice, a single want. A *need.* But I can't have her. That's always been the issue, hasn't it? We're stupid enough to think we know how to hold our threads together, but when we're near, the truth is that we fall apart. Unraveling is the only sure thing in our cards.

If she is home, then I need to keep her safe. To do what I agreed to do and keep her alive. That's what this is all about.

Her.

I sterilize my gaze, hardening it so she will only see emptiness. "I already am."

She looks at me like I've plunged a knife into her neck.

I shove my hands into my pockets, and I walk away. "At least my place is on the right side of the split."

Even from my distance, I can feel her anger scald my back. "You're a monster."

I freeze in my tracks.

She can't see me squeeze my eyes shut. She doesn't know that I scream at my entire body not to tremble. She can't tell that my chest folds forward, just an inch, head dropping lower, hair falling in front of my face as the aching consumes me from the inside out, like I've been shot all over again. She can't see me shudder as I force myself to inhale and keep moving when all I want is to stay.

But if I turn around—if I see the way she looks at me—I will reroute my steps. I'd forget about the elsewhere flame and pretend that she holds me in her mind the way mine holds her.

If I look back, I'm not sure I'd ever be able to leave, and I am no good for her here.

We are no good for each other.

There is an ancient Greek myth from the Yesterdays that tells the story of Orpheus and his attempt to save a snakebitten Eurydice from the realm of death. He risked his life to venture into the underworld and secured his wife's return in exchange for beautiful music. Hades agreed to let Eurydice go, under one condition: Orpheus must not look back until they both reached the surface. He was supposed to trust that no matter what, she would follow. That they would both see the sun again.

And when Orpheus looked back, Eurydice faded away.

So I keep my eyes ahead and wipe my nose and pretend the pines aren't blurring together into one endless sea of dark nothing, wondering if the sun will ever come back to me.

And I almost make it too.

But when the roaring thunder of an engine rolls over my head and drifts off behind me, I look over my shoulder.

The aircraft's wings are seamless with the night.

And when the firebomb falls, the explosion is the loudest thing I've heard.

EDDIE

Tuesday, April 30
93 Beds Made

♪ PERFECT SPEED - 13 & GOD ♪

The lodge burns.

My body locks in place when the sound carries through the evergreen. I watch the glow with unblinking eyes, replaying the last ten seconds in a loop that never seems to end—until the pieces finally fall into place, and everything clicks.

A plane. A bomb.

A thunder that cracked the sky in half.

A fire reaching into the night, like it's trying to claw its way to heaven.

An empty, gnawing feeling dwells in the pit of my stomach, like I've been hollowed out. My lungs constrict as I am gripped by some invisible hand that keeps me from breathing or moving at all. Embers fall around me like flecks of gold. I feel like I am floating too.

Ren and I don't waste another second before sprinting.

I don't think I've ever moved so desperately in my entire life. I've traveled no greater distance than the yards between the woods and the back of the lodge that won't stop burning.

I stumble to a stop, staring up at the flames as smoke stings my eyes and throat. I hear screams as dozens of Gamblers I don't recognize flood out into the snow from the lower levels of the building, evacuating into the woods as another firebomb drops somewhere down the hill.

When the aircraft finally leaves, shrinking into nothing but a dot in the horizon, I mistake its wings for a bird's.

I weave through the crowd toward the fire, every breath quick and short. No part of me refuses to tremble. It's a battle just to remain upright as people shove past me.

The last of the crowd trickles out, gathering in the woods behind the lodge. I stand yards away from it, shielding my eyes with my hand, covering my mouth and nose with the collar of my shirt. I cough up smoke and listen to the sound of creaking beams. Whistling wind. Flames that crack and roar up close.

Why haven't they come out yet?

A post falls and barely misses me by an inch. Ren grabs the back of my shirt and pulls me away from the fire.

All I can do is stand there, rooted in place. It feels like I'm staring at the sun.

The seconds are hours, until something emerges from the flames. No— *someone.* Two figures, carrying the arms and legs of a person too limp to move themselves.

Raven and Mallory are covered in soot and scrapes. Parts of their clothes are singed. My breath hitches when I see the burns spanning across Mallory's arms and neck.

I bring a hand to cover my mouth. It's like his sleeves have melted into his skin.

The crowd parts as they haul a nearly unconscious Jade away from the fire, making room for them to lay her in the snow. Mallory drops to her side, propping her up so her torso leans against him. My gut twists at the angle of her broken leg. Her eyes are squeezed shut, her face pinched in pain. When he tells her that he has her—that she's safe—his voice sounds muffled and distant. Like we're all trapped underwater.

The healer in me itches to run toward her, but my attention is pulled away. Marty and Fern stumble out of the lodge, helping Lockley stand upright as he coughs. Fern's eyes are so wide and unblinking the smoke has turned them red. She's shaking violently. Beau runs out after them, along with Lori and Alice.

Marty helps Lockley to where the others are gathered. Raven holds Fern, who sits on the ground with her knees tucked into her chest, soothing the girl with the same lullaby she used before. It doesn't seem to be working.

I run up to Marty, my voice fractured and hoarse. "Where are they?"

He doesn't say anything. His eyes are glued to the fire.

"Marty, I swear to God—"

I'm interrupted by the voices behind me.

"He's losing a lot of blood."

"No shit!"

I whip around.

Milo and Aaron drag out an unconscious Gambler man I don't recognize. A jagged wooden stake is plunged into his abdomen, and his shirt is soaked red.

Two more Gamblers run from the crowd, taking the stranger into their arms and bringing him to safety. Aaron shouts brief instructions their way, and when he runs back into the building, Milo follows.

My heart lurches so violently I worry it'll tear straight through my chest. I scream at my legs to move. To take me after them. But I'm frozen in place. All I can do is watch as they disappear within the flames that grow taller with every passing second. I don't think I'm breathing at all.

Lifetimes pass in the minutes it takes for them to emerge again. There is some relief when I see Milo carrying Jelly in his arms—who is sobbing, but unharmed.

Aaron stumbles out with Ian leaning into him, barely conscious.

"The man's a goddamn idiot," Aaron grumbles, coughing violently as he hauls him toward the crowd. "But he saved Jelly's life."

"She's completely unharmed." Milo hands the child to Raven and Fern. "A beam fell when the bomb hit. Ian covered her. His right arm's broken pretty bad."

"He's falling in and out of consciousness." Breathless, Aaron sets Ian down next to Jade and Heron. He drops his satchel to the ground and takes off his jacket and glasses. "Keep him awake. He has a concussion"

Wind tangles my hair. My eyes glisten, and I watch him, lips parted. I want to call his name—but no words come out. He catches my eye, and he runs back in.

Milo hurries to follow, but I'm close enough to grab his arm and stop him. "*Don't.*"

"There are more people trapped inside." His eyes are wide, fists and jaw clenched so tightly they tremble.

"Milo." A tear streams down my cheek. "Please don't go."

He pulls himself free.

He gives me one last look, and he walks into the fire.

This time, I try to run after him. To stop him. But Ren wraps his arms around my torso and holds me back. "Let go of me!"

I writhe in his arms, using every ounce of strength I have to try to free myself from his grip. But no matter how hard I kick or scream, he only seems to hold me tighter. Seconds melt through my fingers. The fire sprouts higher, crackling so loudly I can barely hear the sound of my own sobbing.

With an injured Gambler on his back, Aaron emerges from the flames —and he walks right back into them. Milo drags out two before doing the same.

I start kicking again, desperate to run after them. But I'm still no match for Ren.

"Let me go, or I swear to God I'll kill you!" My voice is hoarse. I can taste blood in my throat.

"You can't go after them!" Ren shouts over the rising flames. "That building will collapse any second now."

"Then I need to find them."

I elbow him in the ribs, and he folds forward, calling out in pain. But he still doesn't let go.

Ren doesn't care about the flailing, the elbowing, the biting. He doesn't care how many times I tell him I hate him. He keeps me exactly where I am, and I fight him until I can't anymore—until the only thing I can do is sob.

I curl into him. He holds me like he was never gone, stroking my hair as I cry into his chest.

"I hate you," I mutter, still clutching his shirt. Each word scrapes and burns against my throat. It must be the hundredth time I've said it, and I say it again. "*I hate you.*"

He keeps stroking my hair.

Aaron comes back out, this time with two people. He coughs viciously. His sweater has turned into rags. His skin is covered in soot and burns. And still, he returns to the flames like a moth to lamplight.

He comes out weaker each time.

With every person he saves, he emerges bearing a new burn, a new cut, a new coat of soot. He stumbles out like a drunk man, coughing into his fist as Gamblers help take the injured to safety.

He limps toward the crowd of evacuees, placing a hand against a tree trunk for support. His voice is so hoarse I can hardly recognize it. "I think that's everyone."

"Where's Milo?" Raven asks. "He hasn't come out in a long time."

Aaron's shoulders rise and fall with his chest, every breath heavy. He lifts his head up, meeting my stare, reading my desperation. Hearing my silent pleas.

He turns around, and for what must be the thirteenth time, he walks into the fire.

The wind blows as we wait for him to return. Two minutes pass. Three. Five.

And when the seventh minute ends, I don't think I remember how to breathe anymore.

I stare at the flames like a child to an eclipse. I don't care how badly it burns my eyes. I just want to see them. *Please let me see them.*

Slowly, Ren loosens his grip around me. He hands me off to Beau. "Watch after her."

I don't even have the strength to protest when Beau gently wraps his arms around me. He holds me upright, and I watch Ren step toward the fire.

"Where are you going?" My voice cracks.

He doesn't say anything. He just keeps walking.

"Ren?"

He turns around, and when he looks at me, his eyes are still empty. But in spite of everything, he smiles.

He steps into the building—and it caves in.

No one moves a muscle.

Every Silver Fir evacuee watches the burning lodge from a safe distance, holding our breaths. The fire glows brighter. The wind whistles.

Beau stands next to me, dead silent. He's supposed to be holding me back, but he doesn't. Neither of us can move.

I want my legs to run. I tremble, trying to force them to work. They don't budge. I can't even blink.

Time feels warped, every second stretched into one infinite expanse of eternal amber as I wait for any sign of them. The throb of my heart in my throat is deafening. Every pulse is staccato against my ribcage. It's impossible to breathe or swallow or even think beyond the raw fear welling in my gut. The knot in my stomach is made of lead.

Slowly, Raven begins to order the evacuees away from the scene. She shouts something about not having much time—about the need to escape. But I can barely even hear her as the crowd slowly begins to dissipate, seeping into the woods.

So much time has passed. *Too* much time has passed. And I can't even think about what that means. I stand rooted in my spot, tears gliding down my cheeks as I dig my nails into the skin of my palms.

Please come back.

My nails draw blood with cuts the shape of crescent moons.

I need you.

There is nothing more suffocating than the silence.

My legs buckle. I'm about to fall to my knees when something moves.

Slowly, two figures emerge from the lodge with their arms around each other. They are limping silhouettes against the sun of the ruin, and as they inch closer, their features slowly define.

Ren and Aaron approach, covered from head to toe in ash and burns. Aaron can't hold his head up as he falls to his knees. Raven hurries to his side. I turn to meet Ren's gaze, pleading in silence.

He can't even shake his head.

I step backwards. The wind blows, and flames crack behind me. Saltwater blurs my sight. Aaron forces his chin up, meeting my stare behind the hair falling in front of his widened eyes.

There is fear within them.

I turn back toward the lodge, studying the fire that clouds the sky with so much smoke. It sounds like a creaking ship when it caves in a second time. The ashes look like stars.

I run toward it.

I can barely hear Lori calling after me. "Eddie, come back!"

Ren and Aaron catch up to me before I get very far. They both grab an arm.

"There's nothing left to run to!" Aaron's voice cuts through the roar of wind and fire.

"If you go in there, you'll die!" Ren shouts.

"I don't care!"

There is nothing I have fought for like this. I writhe with everything I have, kicking and elbowing and clawing with every sob. I bite Aaron's hand so hard I draw blood. When he loosens his grip, I punch Ren in the face. He stumbles back with a hand over his nose, blood dripping between his fingers. Aaron tries grabbing both of my arms, and I elbow him in the gut as hard as I can, wriggling one arm free, but he won't loosen his hold on my other one.

Never in my life have I felt so trapped. Helpless. *Desperate.*

There is only one thing left for me to do.

I don't feel like I'm in control of my own body when I reach inside my pocket. I unsheathe the throwing knife quickly—and I plunge it into Aaron's thigh.

He drops to his knees, squeezing his eyes shut and swearing under his breath as he brings his hands to the wound, chin pressed against his chest.

Slowly, he lifts his head.

And when his eyes open again, he looks up at me like I've stabbed him in the heart instead.

But I don't waste a second.

I sprint toward the lodge as fast as I can. Smoke scrapes my throat and fills my lungs, but I don't care. I don't care that it's all fire. I don't care that there's nothing left to run to. I don't care that I'll burn. Because I'm almost there. *I'm going to reach it.*

A different kind of thunder cracks through the air—and something digs into my left calf.

I scream in pain and stumble to a stop, biting down on my tongue. I taste iron. When I open my eyes and stare down at the wound, my jeans are soaked in blood.

Slowly, I turn around with wide eyes.

Aaron kneels in the melting snow with a knife in his thigh, and a Yesterday gun in his hands.

He never misses.

I crumple to my knees, flattening my palms against the ground. I curl my fingers, grabbing fistfuls of dirt and snow, rocks and ice. My calf is burning. I tell myself to get up, but my body doesn't listen. It won't let me move with a bullet in my leg.

I fold forward until my forehead meets frozen ground. I clutch my hair. And I scream.

I can't run anymore.

All my little fires have finally caught up to me.

I have never known pain like this. But somehow, I stop feeling it entirely. Every part of me goes numb, and I only watch the lodge as the last of it finally collapses.

And as I sob with the wind that carries ash like stars, there is nothing I can do but wish the fire would take me too.

R. STELLER

Tuesday, April 30

The lodge is a smoldering pile of rubble.

It didn't take long for the fire to devour it. Almost entirely made of wood, the lodge made excellent fuel.

We stare at the ruins in an infinite silence. There is no time anymore, no breathing. Embers fall around us, biting whenever a glowing red fragment lands on my skin and turns gray. But I can hardly feel it.

The hollowing out of my chest was a far more painful carving.

If I feel this empty, I can't imagine the pain she must be bearing.

Aaron's wound is bandaged, but Eddie won't let him treat hers. For the past half hour, all she has done is remain on the ground, holding her bleeding leg only yards away from the lodge, watching it reduce to charcoal in heartbreaking quiet. No face is unstained by tears. Their pathways clean soot from our skin.

Watching the energy drain from Eddie is the hardest thing I've ever done. She's losing blood, but she won't let anyone help her or pull her away. None of us have the heart to force her.

The smoke is making all of us sick. It fills my lungs and scrapes my throat, and I can't stop coughing. Being so close to the fire can't be good for her. *We all need to get out of here.*

Something chirps.

Everyone but Eddie glues their eyes to me as my shades go off a second time. Slowly, hands shaking, I unfold them, and I wear them.

Canary is calling.

I lift a finger to my sunglasses, and I answer. "Agent Canary."

A name has never felt more foul on my tongue.

Aren't you going to say thank you?

My hands clench into fists so firm I wonder how my fingers don't break.

Are you there, Agent Steller?

My arms tremble. "I'm here."

Everyone is listening. The wind blows.

I waited for your tracker to leave the building. I deserve at least an ounce of gratitude, wouldn't you agree?

My pulse drums against my ribcage. I can hear blood rushing through my ears. "Your daughters were in there."

Yes, but they both came out unscathed, didn't they?

Canary chuckles.

Lucky day, I suppose.

My heart plummets. No part of me is left unwavering. "How do you know that?"

I hear another chuckle—but the phone call has ended.

Slowly, I turn around.

Agent Canary emerges from between the trees, the glow from the fire illuminating his features and casting shadows across his face. He pauses only a few yards away from where we stand with his hands behind his back. "I had to see this little hideout for myself."

Everyone who can stand rises to their feet. Eddie turns around.

"It's a shame, really, that you failed to complete your assignment while you had the chance." Canary studies his hand, picking at a speck of grime beneath his perfectly manicured fingernails. "I had such high hopes for you, Agent Steller." He lowers his hand, eyeing me with a hollow grin. "I thought you would make a great replacement for the Suit Killer."

Mallory faces me, but before he can say anything, Canary continues.

"I truly believed Correction would repair your weaknesses. I didn't expect you to have a soft spot for one of your fellow Agents. I thought you would have the resolve to make the choice before the air strike, but..." He drops his hand and his grin. "Things don't usually go the way we expect them to."

Broken leg and all, Sparrow props herself upright, staring up at her father with glistening eyes. "You did this?"

"I think you already know the answer to that question, Agent Sparrow."

A pallor spreads across her face as her eyes widen, her chin trembling. "This is what you wanted all along."

Canary doesn't say a word.

"It was never about stopping their attacks." Her eyes well with tears. "You wanted to plan your own."

He shrugs half-heartedly. "I've been interested in finding this base for a while now. You four may be difficult to manage, but you are capable Agents. I knew that if I mentioned my plans for *destroying* the base after discovery, you would try to pull that evacuation stunt again and warn the traitors inside. So, I kept tabs on your progress myself. And when I realized your trackers were quite fond of this particular area, I knew you must have found it."

"So you sent an attack unit to firebomb it while we were inside?" Sparrow's teeth are clenched.

Raven can't stop staring at the man who won't even spare her a glance.

Everything around me seems to slow to a stop as my head spins instead. Nausea churns my stomach. The air depletes from my lungs. It takes everything I have to remain upright.

We were so absorbed in the situation and our own personal agendas that we completely forgot about the trackers.

How could we have been so stupid? *How could we have overlooked something so simple?*

I want to scream. I want to pull my hair out and close my eyes and curl up in a ball and forget any of this ever happened. I want to go back in time. I want to turn back the clock and retrace my steps and do everything right, but I'm stuck here in this moment instead, blinking every ten seconds.

Before I get the chance to blink again, Sparrow climbs to a stand, gripping onto Mallory for support. I see her muscles stiffen, jaw tightening as she glares through the pain. Her hair billows in the breeze, and so does her ribbon. She reaches behind her head and unclips the bow. The wind carries it away.

She pulls out her Nightjade gun, and aims.

Canary lets out a low, bitter chuckle. "You won't shoot me."

"You sent her away."

Canary doesn't reply.

Sparrow's grip on the gun tightens. "You could have killed her."

"We must all make sacrifices for the greater good. I was doing what I thought was best for her. For you."

Sparrow traces the trigger. "You sent her to the *Tombs*. How did that help anyone but yourself?"

"I have a position I need to protect," Canary seethes. "Your sister's treachery and foolishness compromised everything."

"You're a monster."

"You have *no idea* what I am working towards," he spits. "What I've dedicated my entire life to planning."

Sparrow doesn't say a word.

"Nothing is right anymore." The wind taints his words. "The Nightjade Order that once protected us is failing. Controlling the population seemed like the solution our country needed; it *worked*. But systems are easily out-grown. The plateau we've been surviving upon is now curving downward. Crops are dying. Water is growing scarce again. The illnesses we thought we eradicated by exterminating those who carried it are reappearing. People are getting restless again, and criminal executions are rising. We are in dire need of reformation. We need to start fresh—to build something better from the ground up."

Sparrow's grip weakens. Her arm drops an inch lower, and it shakes violently.

"I want you to join me, Jade."

Her eyes widen at the sound of her true name.

"When I rise above Head of House, you can take my place. We can work side by side to bring the change we so desperately need. Isn't that what you've always wanted?"

She swallows, gaze welling with tears.

Canary steps forward. "Work with me, not against me, and we will start over with a blank canvas. We can build something great."

"A blank canvas?" Her brows crease, then raise. "You don't want to fix things." The wind blows. "You want to replace it completely."

Canary is silent.

"You want destruction, don't you?" Sparrow's voice quiets. "You want to flatten what's already here. To make room for what you want to build."

His stare darkens. "There is no other way."

"You don't care who or what gets in the way, do you?" Her eyes glisten.

It's quiet for a long time until Canary speaks. "I have priorities you don't have the capacity to understand."

"What about Raven?" Sparrow raises the gun higher, gripping it so tightly her arms shake. Her voice fractures. "What about me?"

Canary's voice lowers. "I'm doing this for the both of you."

"You sent her away to *die*." She presses the barrel against his head. Her arm trembles. "That's not love, Agent Canary." She grits her teeth, tracing the trigger. "That's villainy."

Mallory steps closer. "Jade..."

"I need to do this, Mal," she hisses.

"Jade..." Raven can't peel her eyes away from Canary. "If you don't... I will."

Canary's chuckle makes my blood run cold. He stares at Sparrow with empty eyes. "You say you need to, and yet you can't."

No one says a word.

"Go on, then. Shoot me."

Silence. A shiver runs through me.

"Prove to me that you are the daughter I raised you to be." Canary grins cruelly. "Prove to me that you are perfect, and kill me."

She doesn't.

Her arm quivers when it falls to her side. Tears stream down her cheeks. Without her ribbon, the wind has turned her hair into a tangled mess.

"You are just as cowardly as your sister." He looks at Sparrow in disgust. "If only that fire had done its job. Maybe then I'd be spared the shame."

The wind blows, carrying embers with it.

A black throwing knife flies through the air and hits Canary in the eye.

The Agent shrieks in pain when he falls to his knees. He brings both hands up to where the blade protrudes. If he pulls it out, the eye will come with it. Slowly, I turn around.

Eddie stands behind me, expressionless. No one moves when she limps closer, wounded leg and all.

In one fluid motion, she takes the gun from Jade.

She kicks Canary to the ground.

She steps on his chest, digging her boot into his throat.

She aims the gun, ready to pull the trigger.

A Nightjade bullet hits him between the eyes—but it isn't hers.

All eyes turn to me, and the Nightjade gun in my hands.

Eddie trembles when she stares at me. Rage pries her eyes so wide that I can see the redness within them, the mark of the smoke that still tries to strangle us all. Sparrow looks at me with tears running down her face, and she doesn't say a word. Raven studies me in silence—and I swear she mouths the word *thank you.*

I stare at the dead man in the snow. The blood trickling from his forehead stains it red.

Agent Canary is the first person I kill by desire, and I can't say I feel a thing.

EDDIE

Tuesday, April 30
93 Beds Made

♪ ALMOST WAS GOOD ENOUGH - SONGS: OHIA ♪

The gun falls out of my hands.

I stare at the dead man in front of me, ignoring the impossible pain in my leg. That is the only thing I can do for what feels like years, until Mallory and Ren drag his body toward the burning lodge and let the fire do its job.

Raven says we need to go. His tracker went off, and they'll send an entire search team after him, and the Gambler evacuees need to go somewhere safe. She tells us we should go with her. Lori shakes her head. Alice doesn't say a word. Aaron doesn't need to speak for us all to know he will never join them.

They all turn toward the woods. The Gamblers go one way, the Agents go another, and the rest set their sights on End Harbor. But I turn toward the fire. I limp over to the rubble that smolders like it's breathing.

The fire has spread to the surrounding trees. With no rain to stop it and so much wind to feed it, there will be another wildfire. I'm certain of it.

The breeze cuts against my skin, tangling my hair and obscuring my vision. My face is wet, but I'm not crying anymore. I'm not sure I can feel anything—not even the bullet still lodged in my leg. The pain exists; I know it's there and I must be feeling it. But my brain doesn't seem to register it as real. It's convinced itself I'm imagining it.

Because the ache in my chest is far worse than any bullet could ever be.

Why can't I feel it?

Why can't I cry anymore?

"We need to go."

Slowly, I turn around.

Aaron stands a few yards behind me, shouting over the howling wind, the roar of remaining flames. "His tracker went off. It's not safe anymore."

I turn back around, and I don't say anything.

"We need to go back to End Harbor."

The whistling sounds like singing, and the rustling pines are whispers. "I'm not going anywhere with you."

He studies me, blinking as the sting of my words settle in, but he swallows it down. "We have to leave."

"You shot me."

The quiet is infinite until he brings himself to speak. "Let's go home, Eddie."

I spin around. "I don't have one."

"You have *me*."

I freeze.

"You'll always have me, Ed." He's still shouting over the wind, and his voice cracks. There are tears in his eyes. "Now and After."

I look him dead in the eye, and I know exactly what he's saying. Once, it would have done something to me. But I don't feel a thing. "I don't want to be quiet anymore."

I have never seen anything shatter the way he does now.

Even when he found out about my deal with Mallory—even when he thought I betrayed the Cut, or when I plunged that knife into his leg without a second thought—the look he gave me was nothing compared to this.

"Where will you go?"

I don't even tremble anymore. I study the flames again. I hate how beautiful they are. How much I love to look at them. "I'm going with the Gamblers."

His face pales. "What do you mean by that, Voclain?"

"It means I'm leaving, Aaron." I turn back around, facing him. "And I want you to leave too."

"Voclain..."

"I don't care where you go or what you do." I harden my voice. My eyes. "I never want to see you again."

The wind sings through the silence. "You don't mean that."

"I could have saved him, and you shot me."

"I was trying to save your life."

"And you destroyed it."

My words echo like the ringing of a bell. He doesn't say a word.

"Every fire has been my fault." My voice cracks. "The Cut burned because of me. Those other camps burned because of me. Silver Fir burned because of me. I lied to you. I broke your trust." I swallow through the dryness in my throat. "Hate me, Aaron. Because I deserve it. Because I can't run anymore, and I'm not choosing you."

"Is this really what you want?" he shouts. "You've seen what they've done. You know what they're trying to do. Do you really want to be a part of that?" A tear streams down his cheek. "Because I can't be."

We are both rooted in place, locked in the amber we have always shared. Beyond the wind and dying flames, there is so much quiet. Maybe yesterday I would have found it peaceful. But I can't stand it anymore.

"If you side with them, I won't be the only one you're going up against, Voclain. Others will try and stop you." His jaw tightens. "Don't you understand what that means?"

Silence.

His voice is desperate. "I can't protect you anymore."

When I look at him, my eyes water. The smoke stings, and I try so hard to feel it. But I can't.

"I understand perfectly."

He freezes. Wind tangles his hair.

"Leave, Aaron."

He gives me one last hollow look—and he does.

Thunder rolls above me. I turn my head to the sky. I close my eyes.

And when the rain finally pours, every fire I've left behind reduces to nothing but ash.

EPILOGUE

Monday, June 3

It's a disgustingly beautiful day.

When I threw on my suit and stepped outside this morning to find the sun glaring above my head, it made me pause. I backtracked, shut the door, and tried again, only to find the same results.

Gorgeous, golden sunlight. The pale kind that emerges just after the rain stops and makes everything glisten like shattered glass.

I soak it in as I walk down the sidewalk with one hand shoved inside my pocket, the other wrapped around a steaming latte too large to be wise. I'm only two blocks away from the shop, and I've already chugged half of it.

Jade likes to yell at me for the habit, but what she doesn't understand is that it's my secret to sleeping at night—staying awake for as long as humanly possible, so that when my body finally does crash, it doesn't even have the energy to dream.

Although I wouldn't call what usually keeps me up at night a dream.

I focus on the sun instead, taking it in while I have it. We don't get a lot of sun around here. It feels like a breath of fresh air.

My hand shakes violently as I take a generous swig. There are dark circles beneath my eyes that no one can see behind the shades as they pass me by with a polite wave. People usually avoid me like the plague, but ever since the Suit Killer was caught and the story was publicized, strangers notice me as the Agent on TV who helped put an end to the killings, once and for all. I tell Jade the attention is from my killer good looks, but she says the burn scars lacing my arms and neck are what make me recognizable.

It's a shame, really. About Agent Kingfisher. No one in the Agency ever suspected that he was the one behind the assassinations. Everyone always says the same thing. *He was so perfect. He never came to work with a single wrinkle in his suit.*

But we all have secrets, I suppose.

I take a sip of my coffee and turn the corner.

The real shame that's shaking up the city is the passing of Agent Canary —the Suit Killer's final victim. We all miss him dearly. Aside from my father, he was the greatest Head of House this region ever saw. Images of him flash everywhere, from television screens and billboards to flyers and the occasional picket sign.

Luckily, I was able to help Agents Sparrow and Steller solve the mystery and exterminate Kingfisher. He didn't go out easily; the fire he set to take us all down with him was painful, but we survived.

While the absence of Agent Canary has certainly taken its toll on the Agency, a few positive changes have been implemented. I finally got the promotion I'd been waiting to receive. Since the Suit Killer case was such a vital one, I was bumped up to Fourth, which just so happened to be the very same position Kingfisher was fighting for. Steller's poker chip is just as green as mine.

The pay is higher, the esteem is delicious—but unfortunately, I am now a glorified errand boy for the Pacific Region's new Head of House. Which gets annoying, especially when I do something to piss her off and she gives me that one look that never fails to drive me absolutely crazy, and I grin, and I forget how tired I am or how itchy my arms feel or what I did wrong, and she assigns me something boring and tedious, and the cycle continues.

I take another sip of my coffee.

Agent J. Sparrow will be better than her father was. I can feel it.

I turn another corner and locate my car, just a block away. As I walk, I lift my chin and stare at the sun through my shades. It's blindingly bright.

A black sedan with tinted windows rolls to a stop right next to me.

The glass slowly lowers, and I freeze when a man wearing sunglasses points a Nightjade gun at my stomach.

"Agent M. Heron."

I don't say a word.

"Get in the car."

My heart races. I tell myself the caffeine is what makes my hands shake. "What if I don't want to?"

His finger traces the trigger. "It would be in your best interest."

"Kiss my ass."

"We have an opportunity for you, Mallory Greer." The man grins, and it sends a shiver down my spine. "Have you ever heard of the Sixth Ring?"

The back door opens, and someone pulls me inside before I have the chance to answer.

"It's a beautiful day for a funeral."

— Aaron Kabir

ACKNOWLEDGMENTS

CUT DECK exists because of one-too-many late nights, a disturbing search history, my espresso machine, and some very supportive people.

First, I'd like to thank the Lost Island team for working so hard (again) to bring another one of my books to life. Mel, *Cut Deck* wouldn't be here today without your guidance, insight, and patience. I am beyond grateful for everything you've done for this trilogy.

I'd also like to thank my editors Manny and Rochelle for their creativity and attention to detail. You are both such a pleasure to work and chat with! I can't wait to read your stories someday. And thank you to our wonderful artists! Gonzalo, your illustrations are perfect. Aleksandra, you've done it again—I couldn't be happier with this cover.

Big thanks to All Them Witches, Wilco, The Wooden Birds, and Earl Greyhound, because I listened to them a whole lot while writing this book.

Raina—your support, humor, and *podcasts* get me through every Tuesday, no matter how many turkeys they might be overrun with. Thank you for threatening me—I mean, *encouraging* me to do things that scare me. I am gradually collecting vertebrae for my backbone, I promise. The you of this moment wants us to remember how beautiful it is that in life we choose our witnesses, and what we ourselves want to witness. May the Bagel Saga go on.

And thank you, Rachel. Our conversations make every day so much brighter, and I can't wait to see where your books take you. You are such a talented writer and an incredible friend. Here's to all the cozy cabin writing retreats in our future—and top-secret author shenanigans, of course.

Lastly, I thank my family. I adore you all so much. I would not be where I am right now without your endless love and support. Thank you for being there through everything, and shaping me into the person I have become.

ABOUT THE AUTHOR

JULIA ROSEMARY TURK is the author of the *Lone Player* series and winner of the 2021 Lost Island Writing Contest. Born and raised in Northern California's wine country, Julia currently lives with her family (and two adorable dogs) as a full-time content writer and avid indie music enthusiast. She also has chronic Lyme disease and co-infections and is passionate about raising awareness. When she's not working on her next novel, Julia enjoys spending time outside, going on long drives, and brainstorming book ideas with her brothers.

JULIAROSEMARYTURK.CARRD.CO

Learn more about Lyme and how you can make a difference

NIGHTSHADE ACADEMY
MEL TORREFRANCA

Twenty teenagers are selected for an elite military boarding school, but only five will emerge as guardians—destined for a life of glamour and brutality.

THE MEMORY JUMPER
AMANDA MICHELLE BROWN

Adelaide, an illegal Memory Jumper, lives in an underground safe house with a narcissistic mother who secretly exploits her mind-altering powers for money.

MY BROTHER'S SPARE
SHIRA BEHORE

Valeria's secret investigation to find her mother's murderer pulls her into an alliance with Alias Black, the most infamous hitman in the kingdom.

ABOUT THE PUBLISHER

LOST ISLAND PRESS publishes dystopian, sci-fi, and fantasy books. Unlike mainstream presses, we don't publish everything for everyone. We publish for *you*. Our catalog offers grounded, character-driven stories that linger long after the last page. The kind you get lost in, that keep you up at night. And because our books have the same vibe, if you enjoy one, you'll enjoy them all.

LOSTISLANDPRESS.COM

Join our newsletter to claim a free ebook